MONSIEUR FRANCISQUE'S TOURING TROUPE AND ANGLO-FRENCH THEATRICAL CULTURE, 1690–1770

MONSIEUR FRANCISQUE'S TOURING TROUPE AND ANGLO-FRENCH THEATRICAL CULTURE, 1690–1770

Robert V. Kenny

THE BOYDELL PRESS

© Robert V. Kenny 2025

All Rights Reserved. Except as permitted under current legislation
no part of this work may be photocopied, stored in a retrieval system,
published, performed in public, adapted, broadcast,
transmitted, recorded or reproduced in any form or by any means,
without the prior permission of the copyright owner

The right of Robert V. Kenny to be identified as
the author of this work has been asserted in accordance with
sections 77 and 78 of the Copyright, Designs and Patents Act 1988

First published 2025
The Boydell Press, Woodbridge

ISBN 978 1 83765 242 6

The Boydell Press is an imprint of Boydell & Brewer Ltd
PO Box 9, Woodbridge, Suffolk IP12 3DF, UK
and of Boydell & Brewer Inc.
668 Mt Hope Avenue, Rochester, NY 14620-2731, USA
website: www.boydellandbrewer.com

Our Authorised Representative for product safety in the EU is Easy Access
System Europe – Mustamäe tee 50, 10621 Tallinn, Estonia,
gpsr.requests@easproject.com

A CIP catalogue record for this book is available
from the British Library

The publisher has no responsibility for the continued existence or accuracy
of URLs for external or third-party internet websites referred to in this book,
and does not guarantee that any content on such websites is,
or will remain, accurate or appropriate

CONTENTS

List of Illustrations	vi
Preface	viii
Notes	x
List of Abbreviations	xi
Introduction	1
1 Moylin, Sallé, Cochois, the gathering of the clan: 1690–1714	5
2 Francisque at the Fairs: 1715–1718	22
3 The first London season: 1718–1719	41
4 The open road between London and the Paris Fairs: 1720–1721	66
5 Success and failure in London and Paris: 1721	86
6 The fight goes on: Francisque and the first plays of Alexis Piron: 1722–1723	107
7 A provincial interlude and a Paris triumph: 1724–1726	130
8 Farewell to the Fairs and return to the provinces: 1726–1734	146
9 Monsieur Francisque in Brussels and London: 1733–1734	170
10 The London season, 1734–1735: Part One	188
11 The London season, 1734–1735: Part Two	215
12 Brief scenes from the French provinces: 1736–1737	240
13 'A sharp and bloody battle': the Haymarket riot: October 1738	250
14 'Comédiens du Roi': last years and final curtain: 1739–1770	272
15 Francisque's legacy and family fortunes	297

APPENDICES

I Contract for the Théâtre de la Monnaie: Brussels 1733	316
II The repertoire of the London season 1734 to 1735	321
III Micault's manuscript list of performances in Dijon, 1739–40 and 1750–1	328
Bibliography	331
Index	352

ILLUSTRATIONS

1 John Rich's Theatre at Lincoln's Inn Fields (Alamy). 16
2 Frontispiece, *La Princesse de Carizme*, from Lesage and d'Orneval (Robert Bonnart, artist; François (II or possibly III) de Poilly, engraver) from *Le Théâtre de la Foire ou l'opéra-comique,* vol. 3 (1723) (photo: Françoise Rubellin). 27
3 *The Fair of Saint-Germain*, title-page of the bilingual edition of 1718. (Reproduced with the permission of Special Collections, University of Wales Trinity Saint David.) 44
4 Façade of the King's Theatre in the Haymarket (Alamy). 47
5 'Chaconne pour Arlequin', noted by F. le Roussau, *Collection of Ball and Stage Dances*, pp. 72–3. (Reproduced with the permission of the University of Edinburgh Library, La.III.673.) 79
6 Antoine Watteau's *Les Comédiens Italiens* (National Gallery of Art, Washington, D.C., open access). 80
7 Façade of the Little Theatre in the Haymarket (Alamy). 87
8 Frontispiece, *Les Comédiens Corsaires* from Lesage and d'Orneval, *Le Théâtre de la Foire ou l'opéra-comique,* vol. 6 (1726) (photo: Françoise Rubellin). 153
9 *L'Embarras des Richesses,* frontispiece of 1735 London edition. (Reproduced with the permission of Special Collections, Leeds University Library, Brotherton Collection [BC Lt d/EMB].) 172
10 Marie Sallé, detail from engraving of the painting by Nicolas Lancret (Alamy). 190
11 *The Gate at Calais, or, the Roast Beef of Old England* (1748), engraved by C. Mosley and William Hogarth from the painting by William Hogarth. Open Access Image from the Davison Art Center, Wesleyan University (photo: T. Rodriguez). 259

12 Babet Cochois and her brother Francis, by Antoine Pesne.
    (Alamy). 305

The author and publisher are grateful to all the institutions and individuals listed for permission to reproduce the materials in which they hold copyright. Every effort has been made to trace the copyright holders; apologies are offered for any omission, and the publisher will be pleased to add any necessary acknowledgement in subsequent editions.

PREFACE

My interest in the theatre of the Parisian fairgrounds was first aroused in the 1980s when Slatkine Reprints published a complete facsimile of Lesage and d'Orneval's *Le Théâtre de la Foire, ou l'opéra comique*, and a brief selection in paperback was edited by Dominique Lurcel. I was captivated by the comic vivacity of these little plays. As I was then teaching in the French department of the University of Leicester, and also the licensee of the Attenborough Theatre Workshop (now, alas, sadly disappeared), I mounted a student production of four of these plays, which I called *Arlequin à la Foire* [https://www.facebook.com/profile.php?id=100065120463816]. My musical director was former student Graham Campbell, who led a small band that included brother and sister Rosanna and Simon Keefe, both now distinguished academics. The cast were taught to sing by my friend, the late Moira Finch, a distinguished music teacher and voice coach. The success of this 1986 production further aroused my academic curiosity and I became intrigued by frequent references to an exceptionally talented performer known as Francisque. I was surprised to find that this famous man, whose career extended far beyond the fairs, is now known only through footnotes and casual mentions. He clearly merited a more thorough study. This is what I have tried to write.

In the very early stages of my research I was much helped and encouraged by the late Barry Russell of Oxford Brookes University, who founded *CÉSAR* (Calendrier électronique des Spectacles sous l'Ancien Régime et sous la Révolution), the important website devoted to the history of the Théâtre de la Foire; the website lives on after his death, hosted by the University of Grenoble-Alpes. Françoise Rubellin, director of the Centre d'Études des Théâtres de la Foire et de la Comédie Italienne at the University of Nantes, has given me friendly encouragement, advice, and assistance with the illustrations. The fact that I have been able to correct and amplify so much of the genealogical information about Francisque and the members of his family is due to the indefatigable archival researches of my friend Jean-Philippe van Aelbrouck of the University of Brussels, long before any of this material was available online.

In piecing together this complex account, I have benefitted from the help of librarians and archivists at the Bibliothèque Nationale de France, the Bibliothèque Royale de Belgique, the Archives du Royaume de Belgique, the Bibliothèque Municipale de Dijon, the Archives Municipales de Bordeaux, and the Bibliothèque Municipale de Nancy. In England, both the Library of the University of Leicester and the British Library have been extremely helpful. Several friends offered me the peace and quiet of their homes to continue my writing, especially Anne-Marie and Raymond Rushforth-Cervera in Lyon, Pauline and Terry Sketchley in Valencia, and Mme Wendy Guilbert in the forest of les Landes.

In the later stages of this project, when a sudden onset of advanced macular degeneration made editing of any kind impossible, The Society for Theatre Research awarded me several generous grants which enabled me to employ the admirable Dinah Bott (formerly Dinah Verman) for the standardisation of the manuscript and the creation of the bibliography. I owe a particular debt of gratitude to Professor Russell Goulbourne and to the late Professor Robert D. Hume, whose expressions of interest in my work were extremely helpful at crucial moments. Sincere thanks are also due to the excellent reader for Boydell & Brewer, Sarah McCleave, Reader in the School of Arts, English and Languages at Queen's University, Belfast, whose painstakingly detailed and positive report helped me to improve my manuscript.

At Boydell and Brewer my manuscript was warmly received and carefully analyzed by commissioning editor Elizabeth McDonald and also benefitted from the expert attentions of production editor Henry Lafferty, copy-editor Claire Ruben, and indexer Marie-Pierre Evans.

In 2024 some of my research appeared online: 'Mademoiselle Sallé and her Discontents' on Sarah McCleave's blogspot on *Dance Biography* (Queen's University, Belfast) and 'A French Première on the London Stage: *Arlequin Balourd,* 1719' in the series of occasional essays published by the Society for Theatre Research. I also gave a lecture to the Johnson Society of London on 'Dr Johnson, francophobia and the Haymarket Theatre riot of October 1738'.

Former Leicester students James Dolan and Edward Godfrey helped me to keep body and soul together at my home during the Covid lockdown. Thanks also to the ophthalmic department of Leicester Royal Infirmary and Specialist Nurse Mandy Babington, whose constant care and attention has helped preserve such sight as remains to me.

But this manuscript would never have been completed or submitted to a publisher without the tireless work of final editing and formatting generously undertaken by my friend and former Leicester colleague, Lois Potter, Professor Emerita of English Literature at the University of Delaware.

I am grateful for the kindness and help of all the above-named persons, but I acknowledge any remaining faults as my own.

NOTES

Francisque almost always signed documents with his full name, 'François Moÿlin', or 'François Moÿlin, dit Francisque', although he was usually referred to simply as Francisque. All the family members used a diaerisis or tréma, writing Moÿlin, but for the sake of simplicity I will use the form Moylin. The spelling 'Molin' (used by some scholars) does not appear in any of the surviving manuscript documents I have examined. His signature, with those of other family members and fellow actors, appears on letters, contracts and civil registers in Paris, the French provinces, in Brussels and in London. The earliest example I have discovered dates from 1715 and the latest from 1756. Max Fuchs speculated that there might even have been several Francisques but my comparison of many virtually identical signatures across the years confirms the fact that there was indeed only one.

It should be remembered that names were not stable in this period; without tiresome repetition each time, I shall give alternative forms only at the first use of a name.

Throughout this study I will use the French form, Arlequin, when referring to the character in the Comédie Italienne and the Théâtre de la Foire. The form 'Harlequin' will normally refer to the character (as exemplified by John Rich) in the dances and pantomimes on the London stage.

In quoting from plays published in the Lesage and d'Orneval collection, *Le Théâtre de la Foire*, I have omitted specific page or scene references; these are short works in any case and the quotations can easily be found. All the volumes of the original *Théâtre de la Foire* are now freely available online at Google Books.

I have made reference to dates in the Julian and Gregorian calendars (Old Style and New Style) only where movement between England and the continent makes the difference relevant and necessary. Otherwise, all dates in France are New Style, all dates in England are Old Style.

All translations, unless otherwise indicated, are my own.

ABBREVIATIONS

AD	Archives départementales
AM	Archives Municipales
Campardon, *SF*	Campardon, Émile, *Les Spectacles de la Foire* (Paris, 1877; Geneva: Slatkine reprint, 1970)
Dacier	Dacier, Emile, *Une Danseuse de l'Opéra sous Louis XV, Mlle Sallé (1707–1756)* (Paris, 1909)
Fuchs, *VT*	Fuchs, Max, *La Vie théâtrale en province au XVIIIe siècle et Lexique des troupes de comédiens* (Paris, 1944; Geneva, Slatkine reprint, 1976)
Fuchs, *Lexique*	Fuchs, Max, *Lexique des troupes de comédiens* (Paris, 1944; Geneva: Slatkine reprint, 1976)

[These are two separately numbered books published as a single volume.]

Lagrave, *TP*	Lagrave, Henri, *Le Théâtre et le public à Paris de 1715 à 1750* (Paris, 1972)
Lesage, *TF*	Lesage, Alain-René, and Jacques Philippe d'Orneval, *Le Théâtre de la Foire ou l'opéra-comique* (Paris, 1721–37; Geneva: Slatkine reprint, 2 vols, 1968)
Mercure	*Mercure de France*
Parfaict, *Dict.*	Parfaict, Claude and Quentin Godin d'Abguerbe, *Dictionnaire des théâtres de Paris* (7 vols, Paris, 1767; repr., Geneva, 1967)
Parfaict, *Mém*	Parfaict, Claude and François, *Mémoires pour servir à l'histoire des spectacles de la foire* (Paris, 1743)

Introduction

As long ago as 1944, the French theatre historian Max Fuchs wrote that the history of Francisque Moylin and his family was still far from fully known. From such information as he was able to gather for his *Lexique des troupes de Comédiens au XVIIIe siècle*, he felt able to affirm that the Moylins were an important and influential family in the theatre world of the French provinces and the Paris fairs, and that their extremely mobile companies were an example of wide-ranging and prosperous activity. In an earlier article Fuchs had declared that Francisque's troupe was 'une des plus célèbres et des mieux organisées parmi les troupes circulantes, une de celles dont il serait le plus intéressant de pouvoir reconstituer l'histoire en détail'[1] [one of the most famous and well-organised of the itinerant troupes, and one of those whose history it would be most interesting to reconstruct in detail]. Sadly, to this day, the detailed reconstruction for which Fuchs called has still not taken place. Francisque's name often appears in the theatre histories of the brothers Claude and François Parfaict – their *Mémoires pour servir à l'histoire des spectacles de la foire par un acteur forain* (1743), and their seven-volume *Dictionnaire des théâtres de Paris* (1767). A brief anonymous contemporary source – *Nouveaux Mémoires sur les spectacles de la Foire* – often corrects Parfaict in ways that have been confirmed by other documentary evidence.[2] Later sources of information include Émile Campardon's *Les Spectacles de la Foire* (1877) and Émile Dacier's biography of Francisque's niece Marie Sallé, *Une Danseuse de l'Opéra sous Louis XV* (1909). Many modern studies, even the important work of Max Fuchs – *La Vie théâtrale en province au XVIIIe siècle et Lexique des troupes de comédiens au XVIIIe siècle* (1944) – often seem content merely to repeat this earlier information, which is not always accurate. Sybil Rosenfeld's

---

[1] M. and P. Fuchs, 'Comédiens Français à Londres (1738–55)', *Revue de Littérature Comparée*, 13 (1933), 44.

[2] '*Nouveaux Mémoires sur les spectacles de la Foire, par un entrepreneur de Lazzis, dédiés à l'acteur forain* [New Memoirs on the Fair performances, by an impresario of Lazzis, dedicated to the fairgound actor], ms. Bibliothèque de l'Opéra, rés 611. Clearly a response, and supplement, to the Parfaict *Mémoires*, these fragmentary and garbled notes can be read online at https://cesar.humanum.fr/cesar2/people/people.php?fct=edit&person_UOID=309214.

pamphlet, *Foreign Theatrical Companies in Great Britain in the 17th and 18th Centuries* (1954–5), deals briefly with the groundbreaking visits of Francisque's company to London in the first half of the eighteenth century. On the other hand, Francisque is not mentioned even once in Martine de Rougemont's otherwise excellent study, *La Vie théâtrale en France au XVIIIe siècle* (2001), nor is he mentioned, despite his dealings with the London Harlequin and impresario John Rich, in *The Stage's Glory: John Rich (1692–1761),* edited by Berta Joncus and Jeremy Barlow (2011). Two substantial recent theses, Anastasia Sakhnovskaia-Pankeeva's 'La Naissance des théâtres de la Foire' [The birth of the fairground theatres] (2011), and Erica Pauline Levenson's 'Traveling Tunes: French Comic Opera and Theater in London, 1714–1745' (2017), are valuable additions to our knowledge of Francisque's early years.[3] None of the aforementioned studies, however, deals with Francisque's double career in both France and England.

François Moylin, known as Francisque, was an exceptionally gifted actor-manager, star of the Paris fairs during their most turbulent years, and leader of an extended family of actors, singers and dancers who performed in every corner of France and beyond its borders. They were the first company to bring the full range of French drama to London, where their audiences included George I and George II, and they later played before Louis XV, who gave them the title of *Comédiens du Roi*. Francisque's career spanned more than half of the eighteenth century and the next generation of his family included many gifted performers, notably his niece, the great dancer-choreographer Marie Sallé, whose contribution to the history of dance is generally agreed to have owed much to her fairground family. The children of his sister Marguerite (Babet, Marianne, and Francis Cochois) starred at the court of Frederick the Great in Berlin and Francis went on to perform in the Imperial Theatre of St Petersburg.

It may seem surprising, therefore, that no one has yet taken up Max Fuchs's plea for a detailed study of this exceptionally talented family. Yet there are reasons for this neglect. There is no known portrait of Francisque, and little has survived in his (apparently eccentric) handwriting apart from his signature.[4] With very few exceptions, his performances were reviewed only when he was in London or Paris, and reviews at this period were often rudimentary and uninformative. Though a few contemporary accounts give a sense of his

---

[3] Sakhnovskaia-Pankeeva draws extensively on the ground-breaking but sadly unpublished diploma thesis of Agnès Paul, 'Les Théâtres des Foires Saint-Germain et Saint-Laurent dans la première moitié du XVIIIe siècle (1697–1762)' (École nationale des chartes, 1983).

[4] John Ozell's note to his translation of *The Fair of St. Germain* (London, 1718), says that the Prologue for the London performance 'was sent me written out in Harlequin's own hand, which is as grotesque as his person'.

exuberant and theatrical persona, we know virtually nothing of his domestic life or private beliefs. His name constantly appears in footnotes to the history of French theatre (and particularly in accounts of the Paris fairs, which have recently become an important object of study), but the sheer range of his activities throughout the French provinces and in London has eluded those who know only one aspect of his career. Tracing that career is further complicated by the fact that, although it was clearly Francisque who was known and remembered as a personality, the mask of Arlequin could also be worn by his brother Simon, to whom he sometimes delegated his acting and organizing roles, especially in his later career, and who sometimes seems to have run his own company. There are also long periods in which it is impossible to locate the company at all: itinerant players did not bother to keep archives.

In the present study I hope to make amends for this long neglect and, among other things, to fill a gap in our knowledge of cross-channel cultural relations. My study begins where Francisque's story begins, shedding new light on his extended family and its relation to the theatrical traditions which it inherited and which it developed at the Paris fairs of Saint-Germain and Saint-Laurent. The first part of the book traces his career at these Paris fairs, where, for some two decades, both as performer and as *entrepreneur* [director], he took an important part in the struggles of the fairground performers against the established theatres, and in those between rival fairground companies. I analyse in detail the repertoire of new opéras-comiques in which he appeared, and those in which, even when absent from the fair, he is implicitly present.

Between the fair seasons, however, and sometimes in place of them, Francisque was also taking his company on tour, first to the French provinces and then abroad. Though dance historians know about the visits of Marie and Francis Sallé to London as children, beginning in 1716, almost no attention has been paid to Francisque's remarkable London season of 1718–19 or to his subsequent visits which, until 1721, alternated with the Paris fairs.

I then trace Francisque's movements after the end of the season of 1726, when he turned his back on the fairs for good. He can be found in 1733 playing a season in Brussels, while preparing to take his company to London. Francisque's London season of 1734–5 was so varied, and received so much press comment, that I have devoted considerable space to a full analysis of it. Far from the trivial harlequinades and farces which English critics of the time often associated with French drama, it included a number of serious plays, examined here for the first time, which were capable of dangerous interpretations in the political climate of the day. I also stress the importance of music and dance in all of Francisque's seasons. These Anglo-French cultural exchanges were brought to a catastrophic end by one of the worst riots in theatre history, the causes and consequences of which I examine in new detail. I go on to show how Louis XV made amends for this humiliation and trace the subsequent years of Francisque's touring life and retirement, on which new information has only recently become available.

Throughout the book, the career of the famous dancer/choreographer Marie Sallé has been closely intertwined with that of her uncle. I briefly discuss the rest of her career, and those of Francisque's other nephews and nieces, as well as the importance of his legacy in French cultural history. It is my contention that, if a single figure in that history deserves to emerge from the shadows, it is surely 'François Moylin, dit Francisque', or, as one London newspaper called him, 'the *inimitable* Monsieur Francisque.'

1

Moylin, Sallé, Cochois, the gathering of the clan: 1690–1714

François Moylin was the second of the five known children of Christophe Moylin and his wife Françoise de Plon (or Duplong): Marie-Alberte (born c. 1684), François (born c. 1689), Guillaume (born c. 1694), Simon (born 1697), and Marguerite (born c. 1699). Simon is the only sibling for whom we have a baptismal certificate. The other dates are extrapolated from death certificates, where the age given for the deceased may often be extremely inaccurate; an approximate age can also be inferred from marriage certificates, where the bride and groom are sometimes referred to as *mineur*, which in France meant under twenty-five.

The first fully documented mention of the Moylin family is in 1699, when Christophe Moylin signed a marriage register.[1] On another marriage register in 1715, Christophe Moylin, now deceased, was described as an army surgeon, 'chirurgien major des armées de sa majesté', and his son Guillaume as 'natif de Bruxelles en Flandres' [a native of Brussels in Flanders].[2] Although some of the Moylin children were described in eighteenth-century accounts as Flemish by birth, they were born in Flanders simply because their father was in the army of Louis XIV that invaded the Low Countries in the 1690s.[3] Christophe was in fact a native of Coucy-le-Château in Picardy,[4] but the family also had strong links with the south-west of France. Throughout their careers, all three brothers returned there frequently, particularly to Toulouse and Bordeaux.

---

[1] AM Ghent, registre 142 (St-Nicolas).
[2] AM Lyon, registre 413 (Ste-Croix).
[3] An edict of Louis XV in 1716 speaks of 'les quatre Chirurgiens-Majors de nos Camps et Armées de Terre; les Cinquante Chirurgiens-Majors pour nos Hospitaux établis dans nos Villes Frontières et Places de Guerre' [the four Surgeon-Majors of our land armies and camps; the fifty Surgeon-Majors for our hospitals established in our frontier villages and war zones] (Imprimerie Royale, 22 July 1716). For the role of the army surgeons, see the *Dictionnaire des sciences médicales,* ed. Charles-Louis-Fleury Panckoucke, 58 vols (Paris, 1812), vol. 5, p. 96.
[4] This information is given on Francisque's marriage certificate, AM Bordeaux, GG 151 (Saint-Christoly).

Francisque's entire family had theatrical connections. (Soldiers and travelling players in this period were often to be found in the same locations.) Marie-Alberte, the oldest sibling, married Étienne Sallé, leader of a troupe of rope dancers, on 11 April 1699 in the church of St Nicolas in Ghent.[5] Their children, Francis (b. 1705), and Marie (1709), were dancers from a very early age.[6] The *Nouveaux Mémoires* state that Francisque married 'la demoiselle Le Suisse [Marie-Catherine Lesuisse] première danseuse de l'Opéra de Bordeaux', and the entry in the parish register, discovered by Jean-Philippe van Aelbrouck, confirms this statement. Curiously, both bride and groom were the children of surgeons. The wedding took place in Bordeaux on 25 March 1710 and the marriage certificate states that both bride and groom were *mineurs*. All of Francisque's siblings were present, as was his brother-in-law, Étienne Sallé.[7] In July 1715, Guillaume married Jeanne Gaillardet at the church of Sainte-Croix in Lyon. (They had several children, only one of whom, Martin Simon, seems to have entered the family profession.)[8] All three Moylin brothers, Guillaume, François and Simon, were again present, with Étienne Sallé, now a widower.[9] Marie-Alberte had died in Rennes on 17 November 1712, aged twenty-eight; the *Nouveaux Mémoires* attribute her death to an accident while dancing;[10] her daughter, only three years old at this time, was to become one of the greatest dancers of the century.

The youngest of the Moylin siblings, Marguerite, was married in Dunkirk on 24 May 1714 to Michel Cochois, 'maître à danser.'[11] The register was signed by her brothers Francisque and Guillaume. The couple had five children, three of whom – Francis (c. 1720), Barbe ('Babet', 1723), and Marianne (1725) – went on to have highly successful careers of their own.[12] Francisque's youngest brother, Simon, married Jeanne-Marie Villeneuve in Bordeaux on 18 March

---

[5] AM Ghent, registre 142 (St-Nicolas).

[6] Several other siblings died in infancy. See J-P van Aelbrouck, *Les comédiens itinerants à Bruxelles au xviii siècle* (Brussels, 2022), p. 126.

[7] AM Bordeaux, GG 151 (Saint-Christoly).

[8] A daughter, Françoise, is known only from her presence at a baptism in 1730 and her death certificate from the following year.

[9] AM Lyon, registre 413 (Ste-Croix). Max Fuchs was unaware of all the details of the marriage certificate and did not realise that Guillaume was Francisque's brother. Fuchs, *Lexique*, p. 158.

[10] AM Rennes, GGTous77 (Toussaints). This is the only known reference to the company visiting Rennes.

[11] Michel Cochois, 'comédien italien', was licensed in Amiens on 1 October 1714, to perform 'des comédies et des sauts'. Cochois brought a troupe to the theatre in the rue du Chai-des-Farines in Bordeaux in 1717: Henri Lagrave, *La Vie théâtrale à Bordeaux, des origines à nos jours: Des origines à 1799* (Paris, 1985), p. 134. A 'Michel Lecochois' was licensed to perform at Nantes in 1724: Fuchs, *VT*, p. 30.

[12] The remaining two, as we shall see in Chapter 15, died young in Berlin.

1727 – unusually late compared to his brothers.[13] Their first known child (of at least seven children) was baptised in Besançon in October 1731. It seems that only Francisque and Marie-Catherine were childless.

Because members of the acting profession were still barred from the sacraments of the church, including marriage, none of this versatile family were officially known as actors. On his marriage register in 1710, Francisque is described as a musician, while his brothers, Guillaume and Simon, were called 'maîtres à danser'.[14]

Touring companies and the Paris Fairs

The story of Francisque's apprenticeship is also the story of itinerant troupes in the French provinces at the beginning of the eighteenth century. The growing puritanism at the close of the reign of Louis XIV had led to the expulsion from Paris in 1697 of the long-established Comédie-Italienne, now considered too irreverent.[15] However, as a concession, Giuseppe Tortoriti, known as Pascariel, obtained a royal *privilège* to perform anywhere in France more than thirty leagues from Paris. Max Fuchs found traces of his troupe in Toulouse, where he seems to have been based for a time around 1701, and in cities all across France.[16] On 11 March 1703 in Grenoble, Pascariel's daughter, Jeanne-Jacquette, married Pierre-François Biancolelli (b.1680), known as Dominique after his father, Dominique Biancolelli, the much-loved Arlequin of the old Italian troupe who had died in 1688. By the time the troupe reached Marseille and Toulon in 1705, Dominique was *chef de troupe* and writing new comedies of his own. In the first decade of the century his troupe performed in every corner of France, disseminating the Italian repertoire far more widely than when the old company had been based in Paris.[17] While the Moylin siblings

---

[13] AM Bordeaux, GG 573 (Saint-Pierre). Michel Cochois was apparently the only family member present on this occasion.

[14] An interesting exception was the baptism of a child in Lyon in 1722, where two 'comédiens' were allowed to be godparents. See, below, p. 117.

[15] For a full account of the old Comédie-Italienne, see Virginia P. Scott, *The Commedia dell'arte in Paris 1644–97* (Charlottesville, 1990).

[16] Fuchs, *Lexique*, p. 164. For Tortoriti and Dominique, see also Parfaict, *Mém.*, p. 79.

[17] For further discussion of Dominique's provincial activity see the introduction to *Les Plaisirs de la Tronche* (attributed to Pierre-François Biancolelli), ed. P. Monnier and J. Sgard (Grenoble, 2006). See also Margherita Orsino, 'Les Errances d'Arlequin. Pierre-François Biancolelli aux Théâtres de la Foire entre 1708 et 1717', in Irène Mamczarz, ed., *La Commedia dell'Arte, le Théâtre Forain et les Spectacles de plein air en Europe: XVIe-XVIIIe siècles* (Paris, 1998), pp. 115–27, and Charles Mazouer, *Le Théâtre d'Arlequin: comédies et comédiens italiens en Belgique au XVIIe siècle* (Paris, 2002), p. 311.

were taking their first steps in the acting profession, they may well have crossed paths with the Italian performers.

What is certain is that from 1708 to 1718 the Moylin-Sallé-Cochois family appeared alongside most of the major players at the two great Paris fairs. The Foire Saint-Germain, held near the Abbey of Saint Germain, began in February and ended before Easter, while the Foire Saint-Laurent was a summer event, beginning in July or August and taking place in the area near the present Gare de l'Est. Parfaict is certainly wrong in claiming that 'Francisque, célèbre sauteur' [famous tumbler], first came to Paris with his family in 1718.[18] The *Nouveaux Mémoires* claim, on the other hand, that Francisque, his brother (Guillaume), and the Sallé couple were hired as performers in February 1708 in the troupe of Charles Dolet and Antoine Delaplace, both of whom had worked with the Italians in the provinces and joined forces at the Foire Saint-Germain in 1707. This statement, however, must refer to 1709, as the writer also mentions a pregnant Marie-Alberte and 'Sallé le père'. The troupe of 'Le Sieur Sallé, sauteur', was licensed in Dijon in March 1708,[19] and did not appear in Paris; Sallé's troupe of rope dancers is indeed recorded as having performed at the Foire Saint-Germain in February 1709,[20] and Jean-Philippe van Aelbrouck's discovery in 2018 of the baptismal certificate of 'Marie Salé' [*sic*] finally clarifies the whole matter. Marie Sallé was baptised on 17 April 1709, in the church of Saint-Jean-du-Pérot in La Rochelle, with her uncle Guillaume Moylin as godfather.[21] The Foire Saint-Germain closed on the eve of Palm Sunday, which in 1709 fell on 23 March, thus giving the troupe ample time to reach La Rochelle.

The management and personnel of the Fair companies was constantly changing. At the Foire Saint-Germain in March 1710, the troupe of Dominique, Desgranges, Belloni and Paghetti included Michel Cochois, future husband of Marguerite Moylin, among the tumblers and rope dancers and in 1711 Francisque appeared at the Foire Saint-Laurent in a troupe led by Charles

---

[18] Parfaict, *Mém.*, pp. 207–8.

[19] Louis de Gouvenain, *Inventaire-sommaire des archives communales antérieures à 1790, ville de Dijon 3 vols* (Dijon and Paris, 1867–92), vol. 3, p. 47.

[20] Anastasia Sakhnovskaia-Pankeeva, *La Naissance des Théâtres de la Foire: influence des Italiens et constitution d'un répertoire* (doctoral thesis, 2 vols, University of Nantes, 2013) vol. 1, p. 221, n. 5.

[21] AM La Rochelle, GG 354 (Saint-Jean-du-Pérot). The sceptical priest first wrote 'fille naturelle' (illegitimate daughter) but then crossed out 'naturelle'. See also Françoise Rubellin, 'Marie Sallé: du nouveau sur sa naissance (1709)', *Annales de l'Association pour un Centre de recherche sur les Arts du Spectacle aux XVIIe et XVIIIe siècles* (ACRAS), n° 3, June 2008, pp. 21–5.

and Pierre Alard.[22] (It was at this fair that Charles Alard died as a result of a fall while performing a dangerous acrobatic leap.) At the Foire Saint-Germain of 1712, Dominique's company included many players with whom Francisque was later associated as well as a 'Mlle Francisque, danseuse' who may have been Francisque's wife, though Francisque and his siblings were in the troupe of Dolet and Delaplace. In February 1712, Catherine de Baune hired Michel Cochois at the same time as the English-born Arlequin, Richard Baxter, and his companion, Joseph Sorin.[23] The 'Dame de Baune' (née Vonderbeck, also known as 'Veuve Baron') was one of the leading impresarios of the Fairs. Her rivalry with the 'Saint-Edme couple' (Louis Gauthier de Saint-Edme and his wife Marie), was a crucial factor in these years.

After the Foire Saint-Germain of 1712, the Moylin family went with Dolet and Delaplace for a summer season in Lille,[24] and in August the *Nouveaux Mémoires* place Francisque and his wife at the Foire Saint-Laurent in a company that included, among others, Dolet, Delaplace, Pierre Alard, and Jean-Baptiste Hamoche (the Pierrot who was later to join forces with Francisque). All of these actors were skilled at the Italian *commedia all'improvviso*. Francisque may have learnt some of his acrobatic skills and mimicry directly from Dolet and Delaplace, who had been pupils of Pascariel in the provinces. Dominique and the whole Moylin family were in Lyon in the spring of 1715 and may even have worked together, since rival companies rarely competed in the same provincial town. Anastasia Sakhnovskaia-Pankeeva rightly stresses these affiliations between the Forains and the old Italian theatre, its players and its repertoire.[25] The first reference to Francisque himself as a 'comédien italien' occurs in a legal document of 1715.[26]

Francisque-Arlequin

Regular dramatic performances had begun at the Fairs with the father of Charles and Pierre Alard, whose creation of the comic entertainment *Les Forces de l'amour et de la magie*, given at the Foire Saint-Germain in 1678,

---

[22] Minutier central des notaires de Paris, XCVIII, 372bis, 21 March 1710.

[23] 18 February, 1712. Archives Nationales, Minutes et répertoires du notaire Nicolas Duport, MC/ET/XXVII/70, p. 203.

[24] Sakhnovskaia-Pankeeva, *La Naissance*, pp. 277–8. Sakhnovskaia-Pankeeva notes that Agnès Paul's thesis, 'Les Théâtres des Foires Saint-Germain et Saint-Laurent dans la première moitié du XVIIIe siècle (1697–1762)' (École nationale des chartes, 1983), adds Michel Cochois to this list; Cochois did not marry Marguerite Moylin, who was only about twelve years old at this time, until 1714.

[25] Sakhnovskaia-Pankeeva, *La Naissance*, vol. 1, p. 126; p. 133.

[26] 'Antoine Dumény, simphoniste dans la troupe du s[ieur] Francisque, comédien italien…': Campardon, *SF*, vol 1, p. 307.

had the express permission of Louis XIV.[27] At the end of the century, the departure of the Italian players created something of a theatrical vacuum which fairground performers were eager to fill. However, the Comédie-Française and the Opéra, which had been licensed by the King to perform spoken drama and musical drama respectively, frequently obtained legal bans designed to silence this unlicensed competition. The restraints placed on the fairground players by the hostility of the official theatres had served only to sharpen the wit and ingenuity of the underdogs and to attract greater public sympathy and patronage. Gustave Attinger summed up the situation perfectly: 'En donnant tant d'importance aux forains, la Comédie-Française les élevait à son niveau'[28] [By giving such importance to the Fair players, the Comédie-Française raised them to its level].

Since 1710 the fairs had been attracting the services of playwrights of real distinction, particularly Louis Fuzelier, Alain-René Lesage, and Jacques-Philippe d'Orneval. Lesage's bitingly satirical comedy *Turcaret* had been given at the Comédie-Française in 1709 and Fuzelier, who went on to become editor of the *Mercure de France,* had the distinction of writing for every major Paris theatre, including the Opéra. The evolution of the new genre can be traced in the published volumes of *Le Théâtre de la Foire* edited by Lesage and d'Orneval between 1721 and 1737. The first three pieces in Volume One are entirely mimed, the next seven are sung, and it is only with d'Orneval's *Arlequin traitant* in 1716 that dialogue begins to creep back, as the form that was to become opéra-comique (spoken dialogue interspersed with singing and dancing) was gradually taking shape. Often, three short plays were given, preceded by a prologue: this was not, as in the English theatre, a rhymed address to the audience, but a short play in its own right, often of topical interest or related to the plays which followed.

Opéra-comique was at first the name of the licence (*privilège*) granted by the Opéra, but the term was not initially used to describe the genre of works performed. If a troupe of players held the licence, they *were* the Opéra-Comique; if not, they were merely Les Forains.[29] From 1714, the fairs offered an increasingly sophisticated public a rich diet of comedy containing characters from both the *commedia* and traditional French farce, with satirical plots frequently lampooning the official theatres, their staid repertoire, their technical shortcomings and unwillingness to innovate or experiment. Music was provided by accomplished ensembles, in some seasons numbering fifteen

---

[27] For an account of the Alard family, see Parfaict, *Mém.*, vol. 1, p. 4.

[28] Gustave Attinger, *L'Esprit de la commedia dell'arte dans le théâtre français* (Neuchâtel, 1950) p. 293.

[29] See Maurice Barthélemy, 'L'opéra-comique des origines à la Querelle des Bouffons' in *L'Opéra-comique en France au XVIIIème siècle*, ed. Philippe Vendrix (Liège, 1992), especially pp. 9–29.

or more players, as many as at the official theatres. To circumvent the ban on dialogue imposed by the Comédie-Française, the players initially displayed scrolls (*écriteaux*) held in their hands. By 1711, larger scrolls with new lyrics set to popular airs would be lowered from above the stage by two small boys dressed as cupids.[30] Songs were set to the most popular tunes of the day or parodied versions of famous tunes from the Opéra; the audiences, by now extending from aristocrats to lackeys, joined in the well-known refrains. Attinger comments on the novelty of this audience participation which, although it began as a desperate remedy, continued for many years to be an essential ingredient in the irreverent atmosphere of performances at the fairs:

> On ne soulignera jamais assez l'importance, pour le succès de la Foire, de cette participation des spectateurs; ils deviennent de véritables collaborateurs [...] Ils sont ravis, en outre, de cette connivance qui tourne les règlements, brave les comédiens ennemis et assure en fin de compte l'existence du spectacle.[31]

> [One cannot overstress the importance, for the success of the Fairs, of this audience participation; they become genuine collaborators [...] Furthermore, they are delighted by this collusion which gets around the rules, outfaces the enemy actors and in the end guarantees the existence of the performance.]

The *Nouveau Mercure galant* reported that in July 1715 the Comédie and the Opéra were deserted as crowds of all ages and classes flocked to see Dominique and Baxter at the Foire Saint-Laurent.[32]

It is in the context of this constant battle with privilege and authority that the name of Francisque in the role of Arlequin is first mentioned in a legal document. One of the *procès-verbaux*, legal documents recording official complaints against the Forains, reveals the presence of 'le Sieur Francisque', at the Foire Saint-Germain of 1715, at the head of his own company. On 27 March 1715, two actors from the Comédie-Française appeared before the comissioner of police to lay a complaint against the manager Jacques Pellegrin, whose troupe included 'Francisque et ses autres camarades' [Francisque and his other associates]. The *procès-verbal* which followed this complaint constitutes the first account of a performance by members of the Moylin family. It not only describes the use of 'écriteaux' to which the players had been reduced, but

---

[30] See the preface to Lesage and d'Orneval, *Le Théâtre de la Foire*, and Ardelle Striker, 'A Curious form of Protest Theatre: The Pièce à Écriteaux', *Theatre Survey*, 14:1 (1973), 55–71.

[31] Attinger, *L'Esprit*, pp. 301–2.

[32] *Mercure*, July 1715.

also reveals how the actors contravened these restrictive regulations.[33] The comissioner declares that Francisque's infraction in 1715 was audacious, in that he (with the actors of Pierrot and Mezzetin) performed what amounted to a fully sung and spoken opéra-comique with the *écriteaux* merely serving as song sheets for the audience. As the report said, the result was indistinguishable from a performance at the official theatre.[34]

At the same fair 'Francisque et ses camarades' also played the principal roles in Fuzelier's *Arlequin Lustucru, grand Turc et Télémaque*.[35] The presence of the Moylin and Sallé families at the marriage of Guillaume Moylin several months later in Lyon suggests that the group was already made up largely of family members, and that Arlequin, Pierrot and Mezzetin were played by Francisque, Guillaume and Simon Moylin. Two further signatories at Guillaume Moylin's wedding confirm the fact that Francisque and his family were already part of an established company at Saint-Germain in March 1715. The first was Dartenay who, according to the Parfaict *Dictionnaire*, had made an unsuccessful debut at the Comédie-Française in 1712; he joined the Saint-Edme troupe at the Foire Saint-Germain in 1715, and then toured the provinces.[36] Another signatory was Nicholas Le Tellier, apparently the N. Le Tellier, 'auteur forain' whose opéras-comiques were performed at the Fairs between 1713 and March 1715.[37]

According to the *Nouveaux Memoires,* Francisque had begun his career playing young lovers. As the Arlequin in Pellegrin's troupe in the previous autumn had been an actor called Raguenet, the Foire Saint-Germain of spring 1715 may have been Francisque's Parisian debut in the role. At the Foire Saint-Laurent on 25 July 1716, the complaints of the Comédie-Française reveal the presence in the Saint-Edme company of 'Molin' (either Francisque or Guillaume). Once again, the complaint concerns the use of continuous dialogue and songs in a prologue and a three-act comedy: *La Précaution inutile, ou Arlequin gazetier de Hollande*, performed by 'Dominique, Paghetti et Molin' accompanied by an enormous orchestra of twenty players. Here at last is clear evidence of the Moylins working with Dominique and Paghetti and thus in direct contact with the traditions of the old Comédie-Italienne.[38] A further complaint from the Comédie-Française in September 1716 refers to a performance of *Arlequin peintre et la Fille muette*, with Dominique as

---

[33] BnF, Département des Manuscrits, Ms. fr 25480. This was a parody of *Télémaque* by l'abbé Pellegrin and Destouches. See the preface to Lesage, *TF*, and Striker, 'A Curious form'.

[34] Campardon, *SF*, vol. 2, p. 223.

[35] See Sakhnovskaia-Pankeeva, *La Naissance*, vol.1, p. 344 and pp. 618–24.

[36] Parfaict, *Dict.*, vol.1, p. 311.

[37] *Ibid*, vol.5, pp. 374–5.

[38] Campardon, *SF*, p. 355.

Arlequin; special mention is made of the particularly vocal contribution of 'ledit Molin dans un rôle de paysan qu'il joue' [the said Molin playing the rôle of a peasant].[39]

In May 1716, however, an event had taken place which was to have a profoundly negative effect on the fortunes of the fairground players. After an absence of 19 years, Italian performers had returned to the Paris stage.[40] Following the death of Louis XIV in 1715, the Regent, Philippe d'Orléans, invited an entirely new troupe, led by Luigi Riccoboni, to become, once again, the third officially licensed theatre in the capital. Riccoboni, whose goal was principally to perform high classical Italian tragedy in the original language, soon discovered that in the intervening decade much of the old company's comic repertoire and stock characters had been transformed into native French comedy by the players at the fairs, and it was something like this that the public expected from the newly arrived Italians.[41] The novelty of performance in Italian quickly paled and the company was obliged to interpolate scenes in French, thus becoming a rival to the Comédie-Française.

Measnwhile, the fairground rivalries had become self-destructive. Catherine de Beaune paid an enormous amount to obtain a fifteen-year-licence from the Opéra to present musical comedies under the title of l'Opéra-Comique. She and the Saint-Edme company, who were supposed to be in partnership, got into legal wrangles which made it impossible for either company to present plays at the Foire Saint-Laurent of 1717. Dominique's company, according to Parfaict, gave the only performances at that fair. At the end of the season, on the orders of the Regent, he joined the new Italian company (Paghetti did so as well in 1720) and, as a member of a legitimate theatre, became yet another enemy of the fairground performers with whom he had so recently acted.

The First London Visit, 1716–1717

In order to follow the fortunes of Francisque's extended family, I will now turn to the visit to London of Francisque's niece and nephew, Marie and Francis Sallé, in 1716. This new development is not altogether surprising. Dancers and acrobats had been going to London from the Paris fairs since before the beginning of the century, and newspaper announcements make it clear that these visits were much appreciated. Judith Milhous notes that 'On July 25, 1696, Joseph Sorin was hired at Lincoln's Inn Fields for 30s. a week, on a

---

[39] Campardon, *SF*. p. 356.

[40] For a brief history, see Robert V. Kenny, 'The Théâtre Italien in France', in *Italian culture in northern Europe in the eighteenth century*, ed. Shearer West (Cambridge, 1999), pp. 172–86.

[41] For a full account of Riccoboni, see Xavier de Courville, *Un Apôtre de l'art du théâtre au XVIIIe siècle, Luigi Riccoboni dit Lélio* (Paris, 1945).

contract to act and dance.'[42] In the 1701–2 season at Drury Lane, the Alard brothers gave a much acclaimed Night Scene. One of the oldest *commedia* routines, the Italian Night Scene (scène de nuit / scena di notte), is based on the convention that the performers cannot see each other, though they are clearly visible to the audience.[43] Though it is not recorded in the relevant season in *The London Stage*, their performance can be dated by an attack in *A Comparison between the Two Stages* (1702), which claims that they were 'Rogues that show at Paris for a groat apiece', but, in London, considered 'an entertainment for the Court and his late Majesty' (that is, William III, who died in March 1702).[44] Another Night Scene is recorded in August 1702, at Drury Lane, performed by 'Serene and another person lately arrived in England'. They were the already mentioned Joseph Sorin ('Serene'), performing as Scaramouche with his regular companion, Richard Baxter, as Harlequin. They returned to London in the 1705–6 season and gave what the *Daily Courant* called 'that celebrated Italian Scene by Sorin and Baxter, at the request of several persons of quality' at Lincoln's Inn Fields in October 1705. These are among the first London performances recorded in the eighteenth century in the style of the *commedia dell'arte* as it had evolved at the Paris Fairs. The Night Scene, 'dark scene', or 'Italian shadows' lived on in English Christmas pantomimes for over two centuries.

Over the next ten years the London theatres regularly offered interludes and afterpieces of dancing in the French or Franco-Italian manner, featuring dancers said to have lately come over from Paris. An entertainment at Drury Lane on 8 March 1716 included 'A Mimick Night Scene after the Italian Manner, between a Harlequin, Scaramouche, and Dame Ragonde', advertised as 'being the same that was perform'd with great applause by the Sieurs Allard 14 years ago'.[45] The word 'Mimick' is also a first indication of an element of pantomime in the sense in which it was later used by John Weaver and John Rich.

---

[42] Judith Milhous, 'The Economics of Theatrical Dance in Eighteenth-Century London', *Theatre Journal* 55:3 (Oct. 2003), 481–508, at 485.

[43] For a discussion of the Italian Night Scene, see Kenneth and Laura Richards, *The Commedia dell'Arte, a Documentary History* (Oxford, 1990), pp. 207–9; Allardyce Nicoll, *The World of Harlequin, A Critical Study of the Commedia dell'Arte* (Cambridge, 1963), pp. 137–40; Viola Papetti, *Arlecchino a Londra: la pantomima inglese, 1700–1728 (studi e testi)* (Naples, 1977), pp. 22–3; see also the illustrated discussion, 'Un Lazzo italien: la scène de nuit', on the website *Théâtre à la Source*, https://alexandrin.org/focus/scenesdenuit/.

[44] Anon [Charles Gildon?], *A Comparison Between the Two Stages: A Late Restoration Book of the Theatre*, ed. Staring B. Wells (New York, 1971), p. 28.

[45] See Milhous, 'Economics', pp. 485–6; *A Comparison Between the Two Stages*, p. 28.

John Loftis has noted the curious fact that the last visit to London of Baxter and Sorin was at the invitation of the arch enemy of pantomime, Sir Richard Steele, manager of Drury Lane. Steele, who protested that he was obliged to hire foreign mimics to compete with Rich at Lincoln's Inn,[46] had obtained the services of Baxter and Sorin through Lord Stair, British ambassador to the French court. The latter had written to Steele from Paris in November 1715 explaining that 'Mr Baxter and his companion' were already engaged 'for ye Fair of Saint-Germain which begins ye 2nd of February'.[47] In April and May 1716, after appearing at the Foire Saint-Germain, Baxter and Sorin returned to Drury Lane, giving several performances of a popular Night Scene entitled 'The Whimsical Death of Harlequin'.[48] John Weaver's *History of the Mimes and Pantomimes* (1728) claims that vestiges of the ancient art of pantomime were to be found in 'the Night Scene of the Sieur Alard and his two sons, performed on the stage in Drury Lane about seven or eight and twenty years ago. And such also was a Night Scene or two, the performance of Sorin and Baxter. Upon this old ruin, most of our present pantomimes have laid their foundation.'[49]

At his recently renovated theatre in Lincoln's Inn Fields, the impresario John Rich was eager to outdo the exotic visitors to Drury Lane. Francis and Marie Sallé were already pupils of Françoise Prévost and Claude Ballon, the leading dancers at the Opéra. Although it is not known how Rich came to hear of the Sallé children, what is certain is that Sorin and Baxter knew the Moylin-Sallé families. After a six-week season at Drury Lane, Baxter and Sorin were back at the Foire Saint-Laurent in July 1716, at the same time as Francisque and his family.

Whether or not Baxter and Sorin had a hand in arranging the visit, in October 1716 (after the closure of the Fair) the Sallé children came to London accompanied by their father – and possibly, as Otto Deutsch believed, by Francisque Moylin himself.[50] Francis was about eleven and Marie seven years old. Given Marie's youth, it is likely that at least one of the women of the family also came with them; there are in fact almost no records of any member

---

[46] John Loftis, 'Richard Steele and the Drury Lane Management', *Modern Language Notes* 66:1 (January 1951), 7–11.

[47] Richard Steele, *The Correspondence of Richard Steele*, ed. Rae Blanchard (Oxford, 1968), p. 109.

[48] Viola Papetti in *Arlecchino a Londra*, p. 20n, mistakenly attributes these performances not to Sorin and Baxter but to the Alard brothers.

[49] Viola Papetti reproduces Weaver's complete text in *Arlecchino a Londra*, pp. 197–8. The important contribution of these French artists and their Night Scenes to the English balletic pantomimes of Rich and Weaver is discussed at length in Virgina P. Scott, 'The Infancy of English Pantomime', *Educational Theatre Journal* 24:2 (May 1972), 125–34.

[50] Otto Deutsch, *Handel: A Documentary Biography* (London, 1955), p. 75.

Fig. 1　John Rich's Theatre at Lincoln's Inn Fields (Alamy).

of the family elsewhere during this period. Deutsch's claim is given more weight by the fact that, although the children's father is recorded as dancing with them in London, Parfaict says of Étienne Sallé that he had no stage talent,[51] whereas Francisque, who was much younger than his brother-in-law, was a handsome and graceful actor-dancer. Artur Michel is convinced that it was thanks to her uncle Francisque that Marie 'acquired the use of gesture-language in dancing and had, while still a mere youngster, learned to vivify her dancing through mimic expression.'[52] The same must also have been true of her brother Francis.

Francis and Marie were billed in the press as 'the two children, scholars of M. Ballon, lately arriv'd from the Opera at Paris. [...] Their stay will be short in England.'[53] They were contracted to dance on average three times a week, from 18 October to 15 December. On the opening night of their

---

[51] Dacier, p. 3.

[52] Artur Michel, 'The Ballet d'Action before Noverre', *Dance Index* VI:3 (April 1947), 64–6, at p. 64.

[53] *Daily Courant*, 16 and 18 Oct. 1716. The children are mentioned by name on 27 November. For the earliest brief account in English of their London visit, see Emmett L. Avery, 'Two French Children on the English Stage, 1716–19', *Philological Quarterly* 13 (1934), 78–82.

season, as well as 'serious' dances, the children danced in *Two Punchinellos, two Harlequins and a Dame Ragonde*, 'the Harlequins to be perform'd by the two Children'. This seems to be Rich's deliberate challenge to a dance just performed at the rival Drury Lane theatre in March and again on 22 October 1716, *Dame Ragundy and her Family, in the Characters of a Harlequin Man and Woman, Two Fools, a Punch, and Dame Ragundy*. Whether or not their uncle Francisque was in London with them, the children's version of a Harlequin dance would surely have been more impressively authentic than anything in the rival theatre.

Rich's gamble seems to have paid off; the children were immensely popular and box-office takings improved spectacularly. To drum up further enthusiasm, on 5 December Rich began to announce in the press the farewell performances of the children 'who stay but nine days longer', then eight days, then seven days, until 'the last time but one of their dancing on the stage during their stay in England.' At their farewell benefit performance on 11 December, the box-office takings were £162 7s. 0d, a sum only exceeded twice in the whole season, and this at a time when takings of around £50 were considered healthy. Rich's shaky finances were so restored that he determined to prolong this lucrative engagement, and on 18 December he announced in *The Daily Courant*, 'In consideration of the diversion the French children have given the town, Mr. Rich has engaged their stay in England for some time longer, and on Thursday next they will perform again.'

In fact, they stayed on in London until June 1717. The repertory of dances, which were given as afterpieces to the plays, was largely based on *commedia* themes, but the two youngsters, who had learned the art of mime from their uncles and aunts at the fairs, must have responded readily to the enthusiasm for 'mimic dancing' which John Weaver was pioneering at Drury Lane. Weaver's ground-breaking pantomime, *The Loves of Mars and Venus*, was first performed on Saturday 2 March 1717 with Louis Dupré (known as the 'London Dupré' to distinguish him from his more famous cousin at the Opéra) in the leading role. As Colley Cibber was later to write, 'to make [dancing] something more than Motion without Meaning, the Fable of Mars and Venus was form'd into a connected Presentation of Dances in Character, wherein the Passions were so happily expressed, and the whole Story so intelligibly told, by a mute Narration of Gesture only, that even thinking Spectators allow'd it both a pleasing and a rational Entertainment'.[54]

French dancers and choreographers in London, led by Anthony l'Abbé, contributed significantly to the development of dance away from a purely spectacular adjunct to opera or drama towards an independent narrative art

---

[54] Colley Cibber, *An Apology for the Life of Colley Cibber, Comedian*, ed. B.R.S. Fone (Ann Arbor, 1968), p. 279.

form.⁵⁵ An embryonic example of such a 'mute narration' at Lincoln's Inn was a 'burlesque' scene from 'the French Andromache' in which Francis danced Orestes, and Marie Hermione. They also gave a version of the ever-popular 'Night-scene'. Marie performed in four other serious pieces. The children's second benefit, on 11 May, was 'By His Majesty's Command'. In total they gave some 114 performances. Marie's association with the operas of Handel began at the King's theatre on 5 June 1717 when she and Francis danced in the entr'actes in *Rinaldo*, 'With Entertainments of Dancing by Mons. Sallé, and Mademoiselle Sallé, his Sister, the two Children, who never perform'd on this Stage before'. ⁵⁶

Marie Sallé's very first London season already contained music and dancing of real quality and sophistication. *The Daily Courant* announced the performance on 21 February as '*The Submission*, a new Dance compos'd by Kellom and perform'd by Sallé and Mlle Sallé, his Sister, The two French Children.' Kellom Tomlinson, a dancing master and author of *The Art of Dancing Explain'd by Reading and Figures*, created the choreography to music by the composer and virtuoso flautist Jean-Baptiste Loeillet. Jennifer Nevile stresses the sophistication of this dance which 'opens with an elegant section in triple time followed by a minuet section and ends with a lively rigaudon section.'⁵⁷ The children danced this suite of dance movements four times between 21 and 25 February – 'to very considerable audiences', according to Tomlinson.

The fact that an elegant dance was created especially for the French children by a gifted English choreographer is surely evidence that, far from being an exotic sideshow to rival Drury Lane, they were respected and fully integrated into the dance fraternity of the London theatres. The rivalry was between the managements, not between the dancers themselves. Moira Goff suggests that the children would have been taken to watch Hester Santlow, the leading female dancer at Drury Lane;⁵⁸ similarly, the London dancers would have been keen to see and learn from the talented young pupils of Claude Balon and Françoise Prévost. Indeed, it may be no coincidence that Weaver's *Loves*

---

55 See Moira Goff, 'The Loves of Mars and Venus in Context': https://danceinhistory.com/2017/01/09/the-loves-of-mars-and-venus-in-context/.

56 *The Daily Courant*, 5 June 1717. For Handel's relationship with the Francophile and theatre-loving John, second Duke of Montagu, see the pages on Opera and Ballet in 'Handel at Boughton' : https://boughtonhouse.co.uk/wp-content/uploads/sites/6/2022/03/Handel-A0-All-Panels_lower-res.pdf.

57 Jennifer Nevile. *Dance, spectacle, and the body politick, 1250–1750* (Bloomington, 2008), p. 143. Moira Goff notes that 'The Submission is the only dance performed by Marie Sallé to survive in notation, for it was published by Tomlinson that same year.' See her blog, 'Dance in Western Europe, from the 17th to the 19th century', https://danceinhistory.com/tag/francis-salle/.

58 Moira Goff, *ibid*.

of Mars and Venus, the first 'English ' Pantomime, was not premiered until the Sallés with their father and Francisque had been in England for some six months. The Harlequin dances at both theatres owed a common debt – as Weaver himself clearly admits – to the Alards, Baxter and Sorin, and I believe that there was in these seasons a rich cross-fertilisation between several dancing traditions: the *belle danse* of the Opéra, the *commedia* and peasant dancing of the Paris fairs, and a native British tradition of country and ethnic dance ('lasses and lads', 'A countryman and Woman', 'a Scotch dance', 'a Dutchman and his Frouw'). Given their long stays in England between 1716 and 1719, Francis and Marie Sallé were uniquely placed to take this rich amalgam back to France and then return to London to star in its further development over two decades of fruitful collaboration.

Francisque and 'Lun'

If C. A. C. Davis's intriguing hypothesis is correct, Francisque's first London performance took place at Easter 1717, while Francis and Marie were at the height of their popularity.[59] Davis suggests that Francisque came over after the Foire Saint-Germain to visit his brother-in-law and children, probably in the hope of securing a contract for himself and the rest of the family. In fact, as we have seen, there was so little activity at the Foire Saint-Germain of 1717 that Francisque could not only have come to London with the children in autumn 1716, as Deutsch suggested, but have remained there until Easter 1717. It is just possible that the children, with their father and Francisque, saw the first performances of Weaver's *The Loves of Mars and Venus*. On Easter Monday, April 22, perhaps as a response to Weaver's pantomime, Rich's theatre offered an afterpiece called *The Cheats or The Tavern Bilkers*, featuring an 'Italian Night Scene' and a mimed Harlequin. This was the first appearance of an actor called simply 'Lun'.

Lun was the name which Rich assumed when he became famous in the role of Harlequin. Speculating about this theatre manager's 'first foray into the emerging genre of pantomime', Moira Goff asks, 'When and where did [Rich] acquire his notable skills as a Harlequin? Was he perhaps a player at the Paris Fairs – where he could have learned Harlequin's idiosyncratic movement style at first hand...?'[60] While there is no evidence at all to support Rich's

---

[59] C. A. C. Davis, 'John Rich as Lun', *Notes and Queries* 192:11 (May 31, 1947), 222–4. Otto Deutsch had stated, without giving his source, that 'they were brought to England from France by their uncle Francisque Moylin' i.e., 'Moylin': Deutsch, etc. See Deutsch, *Handel*, p. 75.

[60] Moira Goff, 'John Rich, French Dancing and English Pantomime', *The Stage's Glory: John Rich, 1692–1761*, eds Berta Joncus and Jeremy Barlow (Newark, 2011), p. 89, p. 94.

presence at the Paris fairs, he clearly knew many of the performers there. Rich may not have gone to Paris, but the Paris fairs came to him, first in the performances of Sorin and Baxter at Drury Lane, and then, more decisively, through the presence in his own theatre of the young Francis and Marie Sallé, their father Étienne and their uncle Arlequin-Francisque, all fresh from Paris.

As Davis points out, eighteenth-century writers state that Rich had learned the role from someone else. William Cook in *Elements of Dramatic Criticism* (1775) referred to 'the celebrated Lun and his pupil Mr. Rich', while Tate Wilkinson, who had acted for Rich and was also a friend, wrote in 1790 that 'Lun had been the name of a famous man who represented Harlequin in Paris, therefore when Mr. Rich appeared as Harlequin the name of Lun was inserted in the bills'.[61] Davis argues that Lun was a misreading or corruption of Moylin (or possibly 'L'Un' [the One]) and that the first Lun on that Easter Monday was not Rich but Francisque. The main piece of the evening was Aphra Behn's *Harlequin Emperor of the Moon*, adapted from the French of Fatouville, with James Spiller in the title role as a speaking Harlequin in the French style. It would have been odd for the theatre manager to make a debut appearance as Harlequin in a mimed Night Scene, when such scenes had been the acknowledged speciality of the French Alard brothers, Baxter and Sorin. Rich's brother Christopher, in his list of plays at the theatre, makes no mention of the afterpiece that night, a surprising omission if it was his brother's debut in a new career. Francisque, however, may have persuaded Rich to allow him to give a sample of his skill in this genre in the hope of obtaining a contract for his entire company at some future date.

Most scholars, including Allardyce Nicoll and Laurence Senelick, have accepted Davis's hypothesis that Rich had learned to play Harlequin from Francisque Moylin.[62] However, Virginia Scott has argued that the original Lun was Richard Baxter, on the grounds that he was a famous Harlequin in 1717, whereas 'Francisque was still a hireling who could hardly have been arranging an engagement for a company which did not exist until 1718. [...] Rich and Baxter could have known each other from the early years of the century when Baxter played for Christopher Rich at Drury Lane.'[63] This argument is less plausible than it appears. Baxter, now approaching the end of his career, was still popular with London audiences and, on what proved to be his last visit to Drury Lane in 1716, he was, as usual, advertised in the playbills by name.

---

[61] William Cook, *Elements of Dramatic Criticism* (London, 1775), p. 168; Tate Wilkinson, *Memoirs of His Own Life* (London, 1790), vol. 4, p. 153.

[62] E.g,, Allardyce Nicoll, *History of English Drama 1660–1900* (Cambridge, 1959) 6 vols, vol. 2, p. 427; Lawrence Senelick, 'John Rich' in Selma Jeanne Cohen and Dance Perspectives Foundation, eds, *The International Encyclopedia of Dance* (Oxford, 1998), 6 vols, vol. 5, p. 350.

[63] Scott, 'The Infancy of English Pantomime', p. 131.

It would have been strange for him to re-appear a year later at Lincoln's Inn under some other name, without any press comment. Dancers rarely made headlines at this time, but Baxter and Sorin were a special case. They were star performers at Drury Lane, possibly even, as Moira Goff argues, inspiring the career of John Weaver and his groundbreaking 'Dramatick entertainment of Dancing'.[64] When William Cook and Tate Wilkinson wrote of these events more than half a century later, Baxter was completely forgotten; he had retired from the theatre in 1721. If anyone in London in later years remembered 'a famous man who represented Harlequin in Paris', they would almost certainly have been thinking of Francisque rather than Baxter. Indeed, had the allusion been to Baxter, Wilkinson would surely have added the unusual detail of Baxter's nationality. Most importantly, in 1717 Francisque Moylin was far from being a mere 'hireling'. We have already seen evidence of the existence of the 'troupe du sieur Francisque' in Paris and Lyon in April and July of 1715. It therefore seems perfectly possible that Francisque was in London in 1716–17 hoping to secure a contract for his company. Most of his later London seasons were preceded by such a visit, some six months ahead of the arrival of the full company.

After their highly successful and lucrative London season, the Moylin family returned to France, where they continued to tour the provinces. In autumn 1717 they were in La Rochelle where Guillaume Moylin's wife Jeanne Gaillardet gave birth to a son, baptised on 15 October in the church of Saint-Sauveur. The child was named François after his godfather Francisque.[65] The company then returned to Paris in readiness for the Foire Saint-Germain of 1718.

---

[64] See Moira Goff's online article, 'Season of Dancing: 1716–1717': https://danceinhistory.com/2021/06/19/season-of-dancing-1716-1717/.
[65] AM La Rochelle, GG 590 (Saint-Sauveur).

2

Francisque at the Fairs: 1715–1718

Catherine de Baune had paid such a high price for her opéra-comique licence that her company was almost bankrupt by the time of the 1718 Foire Saint-Germain,[1] while the unlicensed Saint-Edme troupe were reduced to advertising a flying donkey before their performances of Lesage's *Le Château des Lutins*. Crowds flocked to see a poor donkey sliding down a rope, and it was lampooned in a contemporary satirical song, 'L'Âne de la Foire':

> Autrefois Paris admira
> Corneille, Racine, Molière;
> Lulli, dans son moindre opéra,
> Trouvait le grand art de lui plaire.
> Ces grands hommes du temps passé
> Par un baudet sont remplacés.[2]

> [Long ago Paris admired
> Corneille, Racine, Molière;
> Lully, in his smallest opera,
> Knew how to please the town.
> These great men of the past
> Are now replaced by a donkey.]

It is in another procès-verbal against the de Baune company by the Comédie-Française on 15 March 1718 that we next encounter the name Molin. Once again, Francisque (more likely than Guillaume, who is known mainly as a tumbler) is working alongside seasoned fair players, Sorin and Dolet. The programme consisted of three one-act pieces, including Louis Fuzelier's *Le Pharaon*, revived from the previous year. A further complaint from the Comédie-Française reveals that they had added Fuzelier's *Les Animaux raisonnables* to the troupe's programme, complete with spoken prose dialogue, stage scenery, orchestra and singers.[3]

---

[1] Parfaict, *Mém*, vol. 1, pp. 202–7.
[2] Emile Raunié, ed., *Chansonnier Historique du XVIIIe siècle*, 10 vols (Paris, 1880), vol. 3, pp. 62–4.
[3] Campardon, *SF*, pp. 403–5.

Since *Le Pharaon* appears in Lesage and d'Orneval's *Le Théâtre de la Foire*, it is possible for the first time to examine a role played by 'Molin sous le nom de Crispin et de vicomte de Badaudancourt', a clear foretaste of the range of non-*commedia* comic characters which Francisque was soon to play. The plot is an abbreviated version of a three-act French comedy (Arlequin and the Italian *tipi fissi* do not appear, though the two other pieces in the programme included Arlequin and Pierrot). Léandre loves Angélique whose aunt, the widowed Comtesse de Sept-et-le-va, is caught up in the craze for the card game Faro, which was sweeping Paris at the time. She is determined to marry off her niece to a provincial gambler from Limoges, Policarpe Maussadinet, reminiscent of Molière's M. de Pourceaugnac. In cahoots with Olivette, the countess's maid, Léandre's valet Crispin disguises himself as a foppish petit-maître, 'le vicomte de Badaudancourt'. By bankrupting the countess in a card game, he is able to persuade her to allow the marriage of Angélique and Léandre in exchange for the return of his winnings.

Simple though it may appear on the page, this brief sketch admirably displays many of the strengths of the newly emerging genre of the opéra-comique at a time when it was still an unofficial and experimental form of theatre. David Trott has rightly argued that criticism of Fuzelier's work by the standards of neo-classical dramaturgy is inappropriate. An important aspect of what he calls the *altérité* (otherness) of this new form was that it was utterly unlike anything at the three licensed theatres.[4] Part of its novelty was its topicality. For example, the name Badaudancourt (a *badaud* is a gawping onlooker/bystander) is also a dig at the playwright Florent Carton (usually referred to as Dancourt) at the Comédie Française.

In *Le Pharaon* character analysis and development are replaced by wittily differentiated stereotypes: the merry widow, the pretentious bumpkin, the foppish petit-maître and the pair of wily servants. Much of the dialogue and action is carried forward in songs, of which there are no fewer than forty-eight. In one of the funniest scenes, Olivette tricks the countess and Maussadinet by convincing each that the other is deaf, so that she can overhear them as they shout at each other their secret plans for Angélique's marriage. In the one scene extraneous to the plot, Pierrot, in drag as an Italian opera singer, ridicules the Italian style of singing, which could, as Lesage and Fuzelier wrote later, stretch out a single vowel for ten pages.[5]

---

[4] David Trott, 'Pour une histoire des spectacles non-officiels : Louis Fuzelier et le théâtre à Paris en 1725–6', *Revue de la Société d'Histoire du Théâtre*, 37:3 (1985), 255–75 at 257.

[5] *Le Temple de L'Ennui* (1716). There are similar scenes in Lesage's *La Ceinture de Vénus* and *Le Monde renversé*.

The Foire Saint-Laurent 1718

By contrast with the limited offerings earlier in the year, the Foire Saint-Laurent of 1718 marks a complete shift in both quantity and quality. With the threat of closure hanging over their heads, the Dame de Baune and the Saint-Edme couple finally saw reason and joined forces.[6] The Opéra granted a licence to a single company formed from the best artists of the old troupes, including the Pierrot Jean-Baptiste Hamoche, the leading Arlequin Marc-Antoine de Lalauze, and the multi-talented Mademoiselle de Lisle (no one seems to know her first name), who had come from the Opéra at Lyon to the Foire in 1716 and soon became popular as Columbine. But new members were also recruited, and this is the point at which the families of Moylin, Sallé and Cochois seem to have come together.

Lesage and d'Orneval provided an entirely new programme of opéras-comiques. Along with the traditional songs, new music composed for the finale was coming to play a more important part, with the involvement of serious musicians. Louis de la Coste (or Lacoste) composed several 'tragédies en musique' and was also chorus master and leader of the orchestra at the Opéra from 1710 to 1714. Jean-Claude Gillier (sometimes spelt Gilliers) had already written incidental songs and dances for some twenty plays by Jean-François Regnard, Dancourt and Charles Dufresny at the Comédie-Française. Between 1713 and 1735 he provided music for at least 70 productions at the Fairs.[7] His contribution to the success of the new genre has still not been fully explored. As Charles Poisot wrote, this now-forgotten composer had 'la gloire de fonder en France le genre national de l'Opéra-comique'[8] [the glory of creating in France the national genre of Opéra-comique].

The combined effort of so many talents was amply rewarded, and the Foire Saint-Laurent of 1718 is described in the Parfaict *Mémoires* as 'la Foire la plus brillante et la plus remarquable de toutes celles dont j'ai déjà parlé' [the most brilliant and remarkable of all those I have already discussed]. This brilliance was in no small measure due to the presence of the Moylin-Sallé-Cochois tribe, a harmonious and talented company within a company, determined to build on the recognition they were at last receiving.[9]

[6] Parfaict, *Mém.*, vol.1, pp. 206–7.

[7] Gillier also visited England on numerous occasions in the first thirty years of the century, composing incidental theatre music for plays including Farquhar's *The Beaux Stratagem*. He was popular enough in London to publish a volume of songs, *Recueil d'Airs français sérieux et à boire, A une, deux, & trois Parties. Composé en Angleterre* in 1723.

[8] Charles Poisot, *Histoire de la musique en France* (Paris, 1860), p. 182.

[9] Parfaict, *Mém.*, give an account of all the members of the family but seem to be unaware that they had been in and out of Paris for at least ten years. Their brief

One reason for the large audiences at the Foire Saint-Laurent in August of that year may have been the unusually hot weather. On 25 August, Madame, mother of the Regent, wrote from the palace of Saint-Cloud,

> Je n'ai jamais vu un été tel que celui-ci. Il n'a pas plu depuis trois semaines, et la chaleur augmente chaque jour; ... Paris est un endroit horrible, puant et très chaud.[10]

> [I have never known a summer like this. It hasn't rained for three weeks, and it gets hotter every day ... Paris is a horrible place, very hot and stinking...]

Unlike Saint-Germain, which was hemmed in by narrow streets near the river, Saint-Laurent was on high ground near the church from which the fair took its name, a fresh and airy spot compared to the crowded medieval city on the insalubrious banks of the Seine. The Fair benefitted further when the intense heat obliged the Comédie-Française to close its doors from 21 to 25 August.[11]

The repertory of the 1718 season occupies almost the whole of the third volume of *Le Théâtre de la Foire*; there were six pieces, one of which was not given through lack of time. All are in one act, apart from *La Princesse de Carizme* which is in three acts.[12] Alongside the well-known traditional airs, de la Coste and Gillier provided original music, mostly for the final scenes.

The opening prologue of the season, *Le Jugement de Paris*, is a parody of the 'pastorale héroïque' of the same name which had premiered at the Opéra in June. In this version, the Olympian gods gather at a French country inn to celebrate the marriage of Thétis and Pelée. La Discorde arrives bearing an apple, not from ancient Greece, but from Vire in her native Normandy. Juno, Pallas and Venus immediately begin to squabble and Jupiter in desperation sends Mercury to find a shepherd to judge their relative merits. Paris (Arlequin-Francisque), after greedily suggesting that he share the apple equally to gain the favours of all three goddesses, finally succumbs to Venus when she promises to introduce him to a young actress who has already ruined many gentlemen (a sly dig at the lax morals of the theatres). They sail off in Venus'

---

mention of Marie Sallé, for those who may not have known that she had begun her career on the fairground stage, is also inaccurate.

[10] Elizabeth-Charlotte, duchesse d'Orléans, *Correspondance complète de Madame duchesse d'Orléans*, ed. M. G. Brunet (2 vols, Paris, 1857), vol. 1, p. 449.

[11] See Lagrave, *TP*, p. 284.

[12] For the full programme, see Lesage, *TF*, vol. 3. Another play, *La Revue des Amours*, is also attributed to Francisque's company by Fuzelier on the title page of the manuscript copy in the Bibliothèque nationale. No other source supports this claim. A further note identifies this play with *Le Camp des Amours*, a play given in 1720 by Lalauze at the Foire St Germain, and this view is supported by Parfaict, *Mém*, vol.1, p. 220.

shell-boat, with the audience probably joining in the chorus of 'Et vogue la galère, / Tant qu'elle pourra voguer.' [And let the boat sail on as much as it can sail.] L'Amour and L'Hymen were probably played by the young Sallé children; a note in the text says of L'Amour, 'Un enfant de six ans faisait ce personnage' [a six-year-old child played this character.] Marie would have been nearer nine.

La Princesse de Carizme, an opéra-comique in three acts, was the fourth occasion on which Lesage borrowed from the Arabian and Persian *Thousand and One Nights and Thousand and One Days*. The orientalist and translator Antoine Galland had introduced *Les Mille et une nuits* in twelve volumes to European readers between 1704 and 1717. *Les Mille et un jours* had been published by François Pétis de la Croix between 1710 and 1712 and Lesage himself had been involved in the preparation of this edition.[13] He and Fuzelier were almost entirely responsible for transforming these oriental stories into colourful onstage spectacle.[14] *La Princesse* is an early example of the combination of a love story with a 'pièce à tiroirs' (the depiction of a sequence of satirised characters).[15] Marcello Spaziani, in his edition of *La Princesse de Carizme*, calls it not only one of the most successful fair comedies but '[U]na di quelle che maggiormente si avvicinano al tipo di opéra-comique quale esso apparirà costante parecchi anni dopo, con Panard e con Favart' [one that most fully resembles the genre of opéra-comique as it appears several years later, with the works of Panard and Favart].[16]

Lesage sets the scene in four airs and just three spoken lines. The Prince of Persia and his 'agent, valet et secrétaire' Arlequin, have been travelling incognito for two years so that the Prince, who wishes to be an enlightened ruler, may learn of the world at first hand. As they arrive at the gates of Carizme, three men are heard singing within the onstage towers. Arlequin sarcastically suggests this may be some new opera, but they quickly realise that the men are all deranged. The keeper of the towers reveals the cause: no man can behold the beautiful Princess Zélica without going mad. This whets

---

[13] For a full discussion of Lesage's involvement see the introduction to François Pétis de la Croix, *Histoire de la sultane de Perse et des vizirs; Les Mille et un Jours, contes persans; les aventures d'Abdalla*, ed. Pierre Brunel, Christelle Bahier-Porte and Frédéric Mancier (Paris, 2006) vol. 8, Sources classiques 54. Christelle Bahier-Porte believes that Lesage was the first to offer a comic treatment of this 'matière orientale': see her *La Poétique d'Alain-René Lesage* (Paris, 2006), p. 71.

[14] For a list of fairground pieces inspired by Oriental themes, see Jean-Noël Laurenti, *Valeurs morales et religieuses sur la scène de l'Académie royale de musique* (Geneva, 2012), p. 649, n. 112.

[15] Pierre Berthiaume, 'Lesage et le spectacle forain', *Études françaises* 15: 1–2 (1979), 125–41 at 130–2. URL: http://id.erudit.org/iderudit/036684ar

[16] Marcello Spaziani, *Il Teatro della Foire* (Rome. 1965) p. 306.

Fig. 2   Frontispiece of *La Princesse de Carizme* by Alain-René Lesage and Joseph de la Font. From Lesage and d'Orneval, *Le Théâtre de la Foire ou l'opéra-comique*, vol. 3 (1723). The roles of Prince Ali and Arlequin were played by Gherardi and Francisque. Photo: Françoise Rubellin.

the Prince's desire to see the Princess, but (in the only spoken scene of any length) a herald announces that to avert further tragedy the Sultan of Carizme has decided to lock up his daughter in the harem. The Prince swears to gain access to it.

In the second act, the Prince and Arlequin are in the house of the Bostangi, the harem gardener, whose fiancée Delira is bribed to introduce them to the Princess. They disguise themselves as women – Arlequin as a virtuous and modest 'actrice de l'opéra du Congo', and the Prince as a 'divinité chantante'. The Grand Vizir pays alarming attention to both of them, but when the Princess arrives, the Bostangi and the Vizir flee her fatal presence. Halfway through the Prince's love-song his sudden attack of madness reveals that he is a man in disguise. All flee as Arlequin, quoting Molière, cries, 'Vous l'avez voulu, Georges Dandin, vous l'avez voulu',[17] [You wanted it, George Dandin, you wanted it] and the raving Prince is carried away.

When, in act three, the guilty parties are brought to the furious Sultan for sentencing, they plead in vain for mercy until Arlequin reveals that it is the King of Persia's only son who is about to be hanged: 'Cela change bien la thèse, n'est-ce pas?' [That alters the case, doesn't it?] A learned Brahmin then pronounces that the cure for amorous madness is to marry the patient to the object of his desire. The High Priest is summoned, then the Prince and the Princess, who is veiled for fear that she might enflame the high priest and his followers. After a burlesque ceremony (reminiscent of Molière) the Prince recovers his senses, Arlequin kisses everyone, and a vaudeville with newly composed music by de la Coste brings the play to a happy end.

The plot is carried forward almost entirely by music and singing, punctuated by occasional dialogue to convey information or underline a witticism. The four interludes of dancing provided a showcase for the talents of Marie and Francis Sallé, making, according to Parfaict, their first recorded appearance on any Paris stage.[18] Spaziani stresses the importance of the musical contribution of de la Coste, with the sheer number and variety of the songs, all perfectly adapted to the libretto. De la Coste combined ninety-seven airs, some forty of which were less frequently used, to create, as Spaziani suggests, something close to a musical score.[19]

Lesage wrote new lyrics for well-known airs (like Arlequin's opening 'Réveillez-vous, belle endormie' and those in the 'mad scenes', grotesque in their new context); the refrains were undoubtedly taken up by the audience as was now usual in fairground productions. The airs are often given to more than one singer, thus allowing the second or third singer to use the last lines as a comic or ironic retort to what has gone before. Sometimes the original

---

[17] Molière, *Georges Dandin*, I.3.
[18] Parfaict, *Mém*, vol. 2, p. 254.
[19] Spaziani, *Teatro*, pp. 305–6.

words buttress or undermine the sense of the new setting. When, at the end, the Prince sings of his nuptial vows to Zélica, the original words of the air 'Par bonheur, ou par malheur', [for better or worse] will have been in the memory of the public.

La Princesse de Carizme is a superb example of the evolving form of opéra-comique. Roger Guichemerre, praising Lesage's addition of humour and characterisation to the original Persian story, concludes that it is 'un petit chef-d'œuvre burlesque, dont les qualités scéniques n'apparaissent qu'imparfaitement à la lecture et auquel une représentation donnerait tout son éclat.'[20] [a small burlesque masterpiece, whose stage qualities appear only imperfectly on reading, and whose brilliance would be revealed in performance.] Although, as we have seen, this was not Francisque's debut as Arlequin at the Fairs, it was his first major success, and, according to the *Mémoires*, the actor Marc-Antoine Lalauze, formerly a leading Arlequin, was on the point of challenging Francisque to a duel for daring to take on the role.[21] Indeed, it may well have been the success of this piece which aroused the jealousy of the official theatres. But their desire for revenge could only have been sharpened by the next piece of the season.

La Querelle des Théâtres, by Lesage and Joseph Lafont, was the first of the many pieces of polemical music-theatre which attest to the growing sense of identity and purpose of Le Théâtre de la Foire, its authors, musicians and actors, and that flourished while the theatres of the fairs remained illegitimate and marginal. For all its apparent levity, it initiated a serious debate that was to continue for many years. Henri Lagrave first discussed this body of material, which he named 'le theatre polémique', in his *Le Théâtre et le Public à Paris*.[22] As Manfred Schmeling explains, this was 'théâtre de combat' in the sense both that it depicted comic fights and that it represents an ideological battle against the protected state theatre: 'Le spectacle devient critique sociale dans la mesure où on considère le conflit entre le théâtre 'bien fait' et le théâtre populaire comme un conflit de classe.'[23] [The show becomes a social critique insofar as the conflict between 'well-made' and 'popular' theatre is seen as a class conflict.]

---

[20] Roger Guichemerre, 'La Princesse de Carizme de Lesage; l'adaptation d'un conte persan au Théâtre de la Foire', in *L'Art du Théâtre; Mélanges en Hommage à Robert Garapon*, ed. Yvonne Bellenger et al. (Paris, 1992), p. 379.

[21] Parfaict, *Mém*, vol. 1, pp. 212–13; vol. 2, p. 254.

[22] See Lagrave, *TP*, chapter 7; Robert M. Isherwood, *Farce and Fantasy: Popular Entertainment in Eighteenth-Century Paris* (Oxford, 1986); and Isabelle Martin, *Le Théâtre de la Foire: des tréteaux aux boulevards* (Oxford, 2002).

[23] Manfred Schmeling, 'Métathéâtre et intertexte: aspects du théâtre dans le théâtre', *Archives des Lettres modernes*, 204 (Paris, 1982), pp. 24–5.

In the prologue to *Turcaret* for the Comédie-Française in 1709, Lesage had already allowed himself a touch of the sarcasm to which he would give full rein in his writing for the Fair. *La Querelle* takes place – literally – on the stage of the Opéra-Comique, a *mise en abîme* which is a regular feature of these polemical pieces. The arguments of the rival companies are brought hilariously to life by actors as burlesque embodiments of L'Opéra (l'Académie royale de musique), Les Français (la Comédie-Française), Les Italiens (la Comédie-Italienne) and La Foire, and the audience, by its very presence, becomes a combattant on the side of the underdog. La Foire, a saucy lass played in drag by Pierrot (Hamoche), calls her company to order; 'Accourez, Troupe Comique,/ Vite assemblez-vous/ De votre lyrique/ Rendez tous les théâtres jaloux.' [Come, comic troupe, Quickly gather round,/ With your songs/ Make all the theatres jealous.] She then sings to a popular air which the audience knew as 'J'entends déjà le bruit des armes.' [I already hear the clash of arms]. By such touches, often lost on the modern reader, the audience of 1718 was alerted to the mood of the impending action. Mezzetin announces the arrival of the two Comédies, Française and Italienne, personified as two grand but angry old dames. Having seen the crowds desert them for the Fairs, they have come to learn why. With mock deference, La Foire gives orders for their welcome, since 'Ce sont mes supérieures, que ces dames-là' [These ladies are my superiors]. Since members of the Comédie-Française regularly went to the fair to gather ammunition for their complaints to the authorities, it is quite possible that this mock- deferential greeting was even funnier on the opening night, if addressed to actual members of the Comédie in the audience, a trick Francisque's company was to use on a number of occasions. La Foire's cry, 'Des fauteuils à ces Dames!' [Chairs for these ladies!] would have provoked horseplay in the auditorium, particularly since the 'visitors' were usually male actors.

La Comédie-Française now totters onto the stage, supported by one of her tragic authors, M. Charitides, accompanied by La Comédie-Italienne. In an instantly recognisable parody of the opening words of Racine's *Phèdre*, and 'dans le goût des héroïnes de théâtre' [in the style of theatrical heroines], she declaims,

> N'allons pas plus avant, demeurons, ma mignonne,
> Je ne me soutiens plus, la force m'abandonne;
> Mes yeux sont étonnés du monde que je vois:
> Pourquoi faut-il, hélas! qu'il ne soit pas chez moi![24]

---

[24] 'N'allons point plus avant, demeurons, chère Œnone./ Je ne me soutiens plus; ma force m'abandonne:/ Mes yeux sont éblouis du jour que je revoi,/ Et mes genoux tremblants se dérobent sous moi.' Racine, *Phèdre*, 1.3.

[Go no further, stay here my dear,
I cannot stand, my strength deserts me;
My eyes are astonished at the sight of these crowds:
Alas! Why are they not in my theatre?]

The Comédie-Italienne, speaking in prose, can offer little help; 'Oh! tâchez de vous soutenir toute seule. J'ai assez de peine à me soutenir moi-même.' [Oh, try to stand up on your own. I'm having enough trouble keeping myself upright.] La Foire and Mezzetin blame La Française for not trying hard enough to please the public with new works. She sings haughtily that she only stages masterpieces: 'Tartuffe et Les Femmes savantes,/ Amphitryon et Le Grondeur,/ Et presque tous les jours L'Avare' [and, almost every day, L'Avare] – to the air known as 'Je ne suis né ni Roi, ni Prince' [I wasn't born a king or prince], mocking the noble characters of the tragic stage. Mezzetin reiterates the common charge that 'l'on sait ces pièces par cœur' [everyone knows these plays by heart]: Molière has been dead for half a century and even the most recent work in the repertoire, *Le Grondeur* by David-Augustin de Bruey, dates from 1691. L'Italienne complains that even her new plays cannot compete with the nonsense of the fairs, but La Foire retorts that even 'l'idiome étranger' [the foreign language] cannot disguise the fact that the Italian repertory is no better than that of La Foire: the two pretentious dames are merely motivated by jealousy.

The cousin of La Foire is now announced, 'Un grand Monsieur de bonne mine qui chante à tort et à travers tout ce qui lui vient dans la tête.' [A big gentleman with a ruddy complexion who sings topsy turvy everything which comes into his head.] Without much cousinly affection La Foire recognises him: 'Ah! C'est l'Opéra! C'est ce fou-là.' [Ah, it's the Opera! It's that fool!] The dames are furious: in 1709 the Comédie-Française had prevented the Opéra from granting any further licences for singing and dancing at the fairs but in 1714–15, these licences had been revived and were now bringing the Opéra a decent income, to the intense annoyance of the other theatres. When the dames threaten to tear l'Opéra to pieces, La Foire quips, 'Mettre en pièces l'Opéra? Oh! laissez ce soin-là à ses poètes et à ses musiciens.' [Tear the Opéra to pieces? Oh, leave that to their poets and musicians.]

When L'Opéra, played by Francisque, enters singing and dancing, he calls for harmonious coexistence. La Française declaims another Racine parody, reflecting her treatment of the fairground players over the previous ten years.

Allons, c'est à nous deux à nous rendre justice.
Que de cris de douleur la Foire retentisse.
Courons chercher main-forte; et, d'un air furieux
Revenons saccager, tout briser en ces lieux.
Nous n'épargnerons rien dans ce désordre extrême,
Tout nous sera forain, fût-ce l'Opéra même.

> [Come, we two must have justice.
> Let the Fair re-echo with cries of pain.
> Let us seek reinforcements and return in fury
> To pillage and smash everything here!
> We shall spare nothing in this extreme disorder,
> All will be fairground, even the Opéra itself.]

The original text ('Allons: c'est à moi seule à me rendre justice': *Andromaque*, 5.2) would have been familiar to many in the increasingly sophisticated audiences. Like Hermione, La Française is hell-bent on revenge, even if she destroys herself in the process. This is just one example of the parodies, musical, literary and topical, which make the plays of the fairs so richly allusive (and sometimes elusive) for the modern reader/audience. L'Italienne's exit line responds to both the on-stage and offstage laughter, saying that she will have the last laugh, and then, 'Vederete, vederete, Razza maladetta.'[25] La Foire, Mezzetin and L'Opéra sing of their determination to please the public but the two Dames return with their actors and begin to destroy the stage (as they had literally done some years earlier). Trumpets and drums announce the counter-offensive of the Forains and L'Opéra (the acrobatic Francisque) easily wins a duel with an elderly actor in Roman costume. (This was a dig at the number of 'Roman' tragedies performed by aging stars at the licensed theatres).

Henri Lagrave saw the onstage conflict as one in which the established theatres were helpless, being unable to use the same weapons as their rivals.[26] But the off-stage battles were fought with very unequal arms. In the very success of the Foire Saint-Laurent of July 1718 lay the seeds of its own destruction.

For the moment, however, Arlequin-Francisque and his company continued their brilliantly successful season. The one-act *Le Monde renversé* takes as its starting point the familiar fairy-tale topos of 'the world turned upside down'. Lesage and his co-writers frequently threw a shipwrecked or kidnapped Arlequin and Pierrot into some faraway land, to become the naïve witnesses, and sometimes the victims, of the strange customs which are, as with Montesquieu, Swift and Voltaire, a thinly disguised moral commentary on those of the real world. In this opéra-comique, Arlequin and Pierrot fly in

---

[25] 'You will see, you will see, accursed race!' Scraps of Italian are often given to the commedia characters at the fairs (especially Arlequin, Scaramouche and Mezzetin). This may have been a last link with the mixed Franco-Italian repertory of the pre-1697 company, some of whose members, as noted earlier, could have taught Francisque more than a smattering of the language. When writing specifically for Francisque and his company, authors often used Italian and even Latin tags.

[26] Lagrave, *TP*, pp. 392–3.

on the back of a griffon, the only example in this season of the use of flying stage machinery.[27] When food and drink come down from the skies, while a ready-laid table rises through a trapdoor, they realise they must be in the kingdom of Merlin. Argentine and Diamantine appear, quite happy to marry them. When Arlequin learns that in this country couples are always faithful, he is certain that it is indeed 'le monde renversé.' Since, in order to spread wealth more equitably, rich folks are forbidden to marry each other, Arlequin and Pierrot are only too happy to describe themselves as 'deux archigueux' [two arch-beggars].

They now meet a series of episodic characters who allow Lesage free rein for a biting satire on contemporary society.[28] These characters include a philosopher who illustrates his skills by singing an aria first in the French style and then in the Italian (another chance for Lesage to mock the latter); a Prosecutor who is noble, virtuous, married, and has never even heard the word cuckold; a Chevalier dressed in sober black and reading 'La Vanité des choses humaines' [the Vanity of all human things]; and a lady-doctor who asks why, since men have made such a hash of medicine, women shouldn't do better by consulting nature instead of Latin and Greek. In this wonderful land, moreover, merchants are scrupulous, judges are incorruptible, and abbés do not indulge in hanky-panky. Amazingly, the acting profession is highly respected; actors frequently present brand-new plays and they are always successful. Authors have the last word, aristocrats are quiet and respectful in the wings, and actresses are vestal virgins.

The arrival of two rival suitors to their betrothed allows Arlequin and Pierrot to perform the *lazzi* of comic weeping. Instead of fighting a duel, the four men play dice. Our heroes lose, but a comic deus ex machina, Merlin, appears and gives his nieces to them anyway on condition they become virtuous. The festivities begin with four upside-down dances; then four lavishly costumed couples perform a ballet. The finale to music by Gillier has a parting jibe at the intolerance of the Comédie-Française (Le Cothurne or buskin):

> Que le Cothurne jaloux
> Blâme ce qu'on fait chez nous,
> C'est le monde à l'ordinaire;
> Mais que, par l'honneur poussé,
> Il s'efforce de mieux faire,
> C'est le Monde Renversé.

---

[27] Walter Rex, *The Attraction of the Contrary: Essays on the Literature of the French Enlightenment* (Cambridge, 1987), pp. 53–4.
[28] Spaziani, *Teatro*, pp. 251–2.

[If the jealous Cothurnus
Condemns what we do here,
That's the ordinary world.
But if, spurred on by honour,
It tries to do better,
That's the world turned upside down.]

As Walter Rex writes, 'behind all the laughter, the conception of this utopia bespeaks a form of social discontent; its perspective is critical.'[29]

The final piece of the season, *Les Amours de Nanterre*, is an example of another opéra-comique type developed at the Fairs, 'Le genre villageois'. In some ways an abbreviated comedy of manners, it presents, often more realistically than on the official stage, a host of characters drawn from village life, or rather a comic stage-version of it, popular both at the fairs and at the Comédie-Française in the works of Dancourt and Dufresny.

Colette is the daughter of Mme Thomas, a rich farmer's widow, and in love with Valère, captain of infantry. Unfortunately, Mme Thomas and Valère's father have quarrelled. Mme Thomas is in fact more eager to remarry herself (preferably to her servant, 'gros Lucas') than to marry off her daughter. Colette reveals her independant spirit by rebuffing Valère's intemperate advances; she is 'paysanne et demie' [a true country lass], not a flighty Parisienne. She asks the village schoolmaster to reconcile the older people but his attempted rapprochement ends in one of the furious quarrels between supposedly civilised folk which fair audiences relished. Colette decides to arouse her mother's jealousy by feigning love for Lucas and he jumps at the offer but finally decides that after all he prefers her mother's money. Arlequin, disguised as a recruiting sergeant, enters singing and beating his drum. He impresses Lucas with the glamour of military life, gets him drunk, then enrols him in the army which is about to leave for Flanders. In a delightful comic crescendo, Mme Thomas offers Captain Valère more and more money to release Lucas. Each time he refuses and demands the hand of Colette, Arlequin beats the drum and marches the hapless peasant further and further away. Finally, Mme Thomas relents; all celebrate the double marriage and dance to the music of a new air by Gillier. Though the freedom to be more sexually explicit was not the least of the elements which gave the fairs the edge over the more conventional village plays at the Comédie-Française,[30] this opéra-comique bears out

---

[29] Rex, *Attraction*, pp. 53–4. *Le Monde renversé* was the vehicle for the arrival of opéra-comique in Germany, in Johann Ulrich von König's translation, *Die verkehrte Welt* of 1728; it was reworked by Gluck as an opera for Schönbrunn in 1758; and given a French revival at the Odéon in Paris in 1899.

[30] See Paul Chaponnière, 'Les comédies de mœurs du théâtre de la Foire', *Revue d'Histoire littéraire de la France*, 4 (1913), 828–44.

Lesage's contention in his Preface to *Le Théâtre de la Foire* that he had been largely responsible for raising the fair above its earlier verbal grossness. The earthy innuendos of Lucas and Mme Thomas are tempered by being sung, in the subtle relationship of old airs with new words.

Lack of time prevented the performance of the last scheduled piece, *L'Isle des Amazones*. But that was not the worst of the company's troubles. At the end of the season, a decree definitively forbade all further theatrical activity at the two Paris fairs. However, as a gesture of support, Madame, the Princess Palatine, mother of the Regent, ordered Francisque to give a command performance on the stage at the Palais-Royal, the home of the Opéra, on Thursday 6 October.[31] This was the first time a fairground troupe had been invited to perform in one of the royal theatres. To mark the occasion, Lesage and d'Orneval provided a new and topical one-act opéra-comique, *Les Funérailles de la Foire*, with mock-solemn music by Gillier.

In this second major example of 'le genre polémique', the two grandes dames who had been routed in *La Querelle* only a few weeks earlier now wreak their revenge. Pierrot again plays La Foire, who confides to Scaramouche that she has been unwell for a week (since the announcement of the closure). After a dream in which 'les deux Comédies' came like wolves to devour her, she has summoned the best doctor from the Faculty of Medecine at Montpellier,[32] who holds out no hope of recovery. Scaramouche goes to alert L'Opéra and the two Comédies so that La Foire may be reconciled with her enemies. Meanwhile, she makes her will. The two Comédies arrive and feign distress as La Foire apologises for emptying their theatres by giving new plays and making all Paris laugh at their expense. They leave when L'Opéra arrives, again played by Francisque, for they hate him even more than they hate La Foire.

Parodying the death of Phèdre, La Foire begins to expire in the arms of her cousin, L'Opéra. They sing a mock-tragic duet to music from Lully's opera *Alceste*, showing that L'Opéra grieves mainly because he will lose his income from selling the Opéra-Comique licence. La Foire's dying words are one last defiant parody of the high tragic style: 'Equitables témoins de mes vives douleurs,/ Plaignez mon infortune, et soyez mes vengeurs.' [Just witnesses of my cruel sorrows, / Bewail my misfortune, and be my avengers.] After a further parody of funereal music from *Alceste*, the two grandes dames re-enter to a march which the audience would have recognised as the song 'Elle est morte, la vache à Panier. Ne faut plus pleurer, mais il faut chanter, il faut danser.' [Panier's cow is dead. We must not weep but sing and dance!] They rejoice that now the public will have no alternative to their boring and lacklustre repertoire. According to the *Mémoires*, the performance was

---

[31] Parfaict, *Mém*, vol.1, p. 215.
[32] Possibly a reference to Francisque's theatre-loving friend, Doctor Michel Procope-Couteaux.

a great success, and the Regent offered the cold comfort of a nicely-turned compliment: 'The Opéra-comique is like the swan, who never sings more sweetly than when it dies.'[33] As Jeanne-Marie Hostiou writes:

> Cette représentation exceptionnelle témoigne de l'attitude ambiguë du pouvoir politique, qui cautionne l'interdiction des spectacles de l'Opéra-Comique tout en lui apportant publiquement des témoignages de soutien. ... La défaite judiciaire des Forains se double ainsi, au terme de cette année 1718, d'une semi-victoire symbolique...'.[34]

> [This exceptional performance testifies to the ambiguous attitude of the political powers, which condone the ban on the performances of the Opéra-Comique while publicly providing marks of support. ... The legal defeat of the Forains is thus coupled, at the end of this year 1718, with a symbolic semi-victory...]

Francisque and his playwrights must have known in advance of the impending closure, and they cleverly solicit the sympathy of the public for the underdog. Even though *Les Funérailles* depicts the Fair's defeat, it also indicts the established theatres, 'qui cherchent davantage à confisquer le public qu'à le conquérir' [which seek to steal the public rather than to win it].[35]

The Revenge of the Comédie-Italienne

Just three days after Francisque's company appeared at the Palais-Royal, on Sunday 9 October, Dominique and François Riccoboni at the Comédie-Italienne responded in kind with the first topical prologue at that theatre, the one-act play, *La Désolation des deux Comédies*, with music by Jean-Joseph Mouret.[36] That it was co-written by Dominique, an erstwhile colleague of Francisque, indicates just how seriously the success of Francisque's 'saison brillante' at Saint-Laurent was being taken by the official theatres.

La Désolation dramatises a situation like that of the Italian players in their early years when there were rumours that, disheartened by their lukewarm reception in Paris, they planned to return to Italy. They had been saved by the success, in April 1718, of their first comedy entirely in French, *Le Naufrage au Port-à-l'Anglais ou les Nouvelles Débarqués* by Jacques Autreau. Now that

---

[33] Parfaict, *Mém*, vol. 1, p. 215.

[34] Jeanne-Marie Hostiou, https://obvil.huma-num.fr/agon/querelles/querelle-des-theatres-en-1718.

[35] For a full discussion, see Hostiou, 'De la scène judiciaire à la scène théâtrale: l'année 1718 dans la querelle des théâtres', *Littératures classiques*, 2013/2 (81), pp. 107-18.

[36] Mary Scott Burnet, *Marc-Antoine Legrand* (Paris, 1938), p. 91.

their existence is again threatened, this time by the success of the fairground players, the stage-set represents a theatre being dismantled, with stage-hands climbing ladders in the background, while the principal actors of the company debate whether they should stay in France or return to Italy. As in the two Lesage plays, the Comédie-Française and the Comédie-Italienne are personified as elderly dames. La Française now enters and the two Dames bewail the emptiness of their theatres. When La Foire comes to bid them farewell, La Française urges l'Italienne to join her in revenge on their common enemies, La Foire and her cousin L'Opéra. A gay symphony announces the arrival of the followers of La Foire: Arlequin and Scaramouche, Polichinelle and Dame Ragonde, who dance a chaconne, then sing a vaudeville on the departure of the Comédie Italienne: 'Notre fortune est certaine, / La Foire désormais à Paris brillera, / La troupe italienne / Faridondaine [...]/ Partira.' [Our fortune is certain,/ From now on La Foire will shine in Paris./ The Italian troupe/ Faridondaine/ .../ Will depart.] But the Italian Arlequin chases them away and declares that the Italians are determined to remain: 'Le public malgré vous me favorisera,/ La troupe Italienne [...] / Restera.' [In spite of you the public will favour me,/ The Italian troupe/ Will remain.] After this good-natured skit, according to the *Mercure* (October 1718), the public left the theatre singing the final refrain.

It would seem, however, that Francisque spent very little time in France after the performance at the Palais-Royal on 6 October. In London, on Thursday 6 November (OS),[37] the *Daily Courant* announced that the following night would see the first performance at the Theatre in Lincoln's Inn Fields, by 'The French Company of Comedians, lately arriv'd from the Theatre-Royal in Paris'. Though Sybil Rosenfeld felt that this advertisement was 'grandiloquently stated', the 'Théâtre du Palais-Royal' had in fact been the last stage on which they had performed.[38]

Thus, Francisque was nowhere near the Comédie-Italienne when Dominique and Riccoboni continued their attack on the fairground players on 20 November (NS). In *Le Procès des Théâtres*, again with music by Mouret,[39] La Foire is put on trial and the Muses of the Comédie-Française and the Comédie-Italienne

---

[37] This was 17 November, NS, in France. England did not adopt the Gregorian calendar until 1752, and was thus 11 days behind continental Europe.

[38] Sybil Rosenfeld, *Foreign Theatrical Companies in Great Britain in the 17th and 18th Centuries*, The Society for Theatre Research Pamphlet Series, no. 4 (London, 1954–5), p. 7.

[39] Jean Auguste Julien, dit Desboulmiers, *Histoire anecdotique et raisonnée du Théâtre-Italien, depuis son rétablissement en France, jusqu'à l'année 1769* ([Paris, 1769] repr. Geneva, 1968), vol.1, p. 254; Antoine-Jean-Baptiste-Abraham d'Origny, *Annales du Théâtre Italien depuis son origine jusqu'à ce jour* (Paris, 1788), 3 vols, vol. 1, p. 54.

take it in turn to attack her in front of the judge, Apollo. While La Foire successfully rebuts La Française's claim that she alone has the right to enflame the passions, l'Italienne maintains that the accused, an illegal novelty born from the ruins of the old Comédie-Italienne, should be deprived of speech and return to her primitive state – that is, acrobatics and rope-dancing. Apollo condemns La Foire to eternal silence and she dies in the arms de l'Opéra. The two Comédies swear sincere friendship and, in the finale of the vaudeville, the Italian Arlequin declares that the public will be the Apollo on whom their fate depends.[40]

At this time, the situation of the Comédie-Française was little better than that of its Italian neighbour: 'Its debts amounted to three hundred thousand livres [...] Sometimes performances were not even given for lack of spectators.'[41] In desperation, the actor-playwright Marc-Antoine Legrand followed the example of the Italians and wrote a polemical prologue for his play *Le Roi de Cocagne*, performed on 31 December at the Comédie-Française. It takes place at the foot of Mount Parnassus in a muddy bog from which the author Géniot struggles to escape. Thalie, the comic muse, tells him that the whole of Parnassus has been alarmed by the success currently enjoyed by 'La Muse Triviale', La Foire; the only solution, Thalie suggests, is for this playwright to beat her at her own game:

> Il me faut pour cela quelque pièce bouffonne
> Qui soit dans le goût à peu près
> De celle qu'elle donne.
>
> [For that, I need some crazy play
> which is pretty much in the taste
> of those she performs.]

In fact, *Le Roi de Cocagne* was a regular three-act verse comedy with a musical divertissement, bearing only slight resemblance to the recent repertoire of the fair.

By now, news of Francisque's success in London will have undoubtedly reached Paris. It seems clear that the established theatres were expecting that the Foire Saint-Germain would open in February 1719, and that Francisque would be granted the licence of the Opéra-comique. Lesage had even written a new prologue, *Le Retour de la Foire à la Vie*, specifically for this occasion.[42]

---

[40] *Mercure*, November, pp. 166–71; also published in Parfaict, *Le Nouveau Théâtre Italien, ou recueil général des comédies* (Paris, 1733), vol. 1, pp. 96–100.

[41] Burnet, *Legrand*, p. 89.

[42] In his introduction to *La Statue merveilleuse* in volume 4 of *Le Théâtre de la Foire* Lesage explains that it and its prologue had been written for 'l'Opéra-comique,

Alarmed, and perhaps hearing of Lesage's new piece, the Italians returned to the 'genre polémique' on 29 January 1719. *La Foire renaissante* (a clear reference to the title of Lesage's new prologue) was preceded by revivals of *Le Proces des Théâtres* and an updated *La Désolation des Deux Comédies* in which the Muse Française explains that a young doctor has cured her with thirty doses of Oedipus. This 'cure' refers to the hugely successful run of thirty performances for Voltaire's tragedy, *Œdipe*, which had opened on 18 November 1718, restoring both the receipts and morale of the Comédie-Française.[43]

In *La Foire renaissante*, la Foire, having been condemned to eternal silence, descends to the underworld and offers to establish an Opéra-comique to entertain Pluto's court. The infernal judge is so disgusted by her performance that he orders her back to earth so that she can do hell better service by corrupting the human race. The Italians learn to their horror that she has been reborn, while her followers rejoice that she has conquered death, singing a parody of Lully's *Alceste*. In the musical finale the Opéra rejoices, La Foire promises to return to the stage, and the Italian actors plead with the public to support them as well. Despite the relatively light-hearted banter of this piece, the Italians were obviously uneasy at the prospect of Francisque at the coming Foire Saint-Germain.[44]

Within a matter of days, however, the situation had changed again. By now it must have been known that Francisque would not be returning from London and that, perhaps as a result, there would be no licensed Opéra-comique at the Foire Saint-Germain. At the next performance of *La Foire Renaissante*, the Italians added a new prologue, set in their own theatre foyer, in which a Gascon and a Lady of Fashion lament the banishment of La Foire.[45] Lélio (Luigi Riccoboni himself) promises that les Italiens will perform plays that are similar to those of the fair but more decent, an astonishing admission from the head of the company.[46]

It is surely significant that in the lists of 'pièces à caractère polémique' drawn up and discussed in detail by Henri Lagrave, the first six at the Fairs were all performed by Francisque and company, while the first three at the Comédie-Italienne (and a fourth which Lagrave does not mention) were all provoked by Francisque. But throughout the winter and spring of 1718–19,

---

dont ils espéraient le rétablissement à la Foire de S. Germain 1719' [at the Opéra-comique which they hoped would re-open at the Foire Saint-Germain in 1719].

[43] For an account of Dominique's production, see *Mercure*, February 1719, pp. 121–2.

[44] The verse finale was printed only in *Le Nouveau Théâtre Italien*, vol. 1, pp. 114–18.

[45] Desboulmiers, *Histoire anecdotique*, vol. 1, pp. 299–303.

[46] *Mercure*, pp. 125–6, and Parfaict, *Dict.*, vol. 2, p. 596. This prologue does not appear in *Le Nouveau Théâtre Italien*.

while the Italians continued to lampoon a supposedly defunct Foire, Arlequin-Francisque and his company were in London, giving performances by royal command and enjoying huge financial success.

3

The first London season: 1718–1719

On 5 October 1717, Nathaniel Mist's *The Weekly Journal or Saturday's Post* reported that Johann Jacob Heidegger, whose management of the opera with Handel at the Haymarket had run into financial difficulties, intended to bring a company of French actors from Paris for the winter season, to replace the opera. This report was contained in a letter 'from an ingenious Hand'– the first of many examples of the xenophobia provoked by the company's visits:

> All English Gentlemen must certainly look with indignation upon Mr. H[eidegge]r's present Undertaking, in sending to France for a sett of Comedians to act French Plays at the [King's] Theatre in the Hay-market. It was formerly thought a scandal to us, for our Taylors to prefer the French Fashions to our own; […] what will be said of us, if we prefer the French Plays and Actors to our own?

The writer concluded:

> The only Plea offered for this Attempt is, that it may tend to his M[ajesty]'s diversion, since he is a perfect Master of the French Tongue; but we have Reason to believe that his M[ajesty] has too great an Affection for his subjects, to prefer the Efforts of another Nation, to the Genius of his own, and that he will be better pleased with Methods for improving himself in the English Tongue, than with any which may keep him longer a Stranger to it.[1]

This was of course ironic: as Nicholas Rogers has written, 'Nothing more disgusted the people of Britain at the Elector [King George I] than his being

---

[1] Nathaniel Mist's *The Weekly Journal or Saturday's Post*, 5 October 1717. The letter reappeared in Mist's own selection of letters, *A Collection of Miscellany Letters Selected out of Mist's Weekly Journal*, Vol 1 (London, 1722). The title, given in the Table of Contents, is 'On the Absurdity of Erecting a French Theatre, with a Prologue and Epilogue to be Spoken at the Opening of It.'

ignorant of their language and his saying he was too old to learn it or change his manners.'[2]

The rumour about French actors almost certainly refers to Francisque; earlier in the year, when King George I had wanted Riccoboni's new Italian troupe to come over, the visit was forbidden by the Regent. Heidegger could have met Francisque in London earlier in 1717 when he hired Marie and Francis Sallé to dance in Handel's *Rinaldo*. But Rich might also have been in touch. In June 1717 Richard Steele wrote to his wife that in the coming season, 'there will be no playhouse but ours [Drury Lane], allowing Rich, who is almost broke, a salary while there is but one house'.[3] Although Rich's theatre did in fact open, he had assigned his patent to managers and was merely a performer in the afterpieces. The success of the Sallé children may have prompted him to turn for help to their uncle. Nothing came of these plans in 1717, and nothing could have come of them, because, in spite of Heidegger's best efforts, the theatre was completely dark (that is, lay empty) throughout the first half of the 1717–18 season. When Francisque's company finally arrived in London in the autumn of 1718, they went not to Heidegger at the King's Theatre but to John Rich's theatre at Lincoln's Inn Fields.

As the press response indicates, this was an ambitious and quite unprecedented visit. The last full-scale French company to visit England, in 1684, had performed only at the court of Charles II,[4] whereas Francisque was proposing to entertain the general public. In 1718 Francisque's company still contained the family members that Parfaict had described a few months earlier at the Foire Saint-Laurent,[5] but he must also have recruited others, as he had done earlier in the provinces.

In London, however, the company did not offer the programme in which they had just triumphed in Paris. Even the most sophisticated London audiences could have known little of the repertoire of the Fairs, for the first volume of *Le Théâtre de la Foire* was not published until 1721; moreover, the polemical plays ('le genre polémique') would have meant nothing to them. On the other hand, the repertoire of the pre-1697 Italian company had been widely available in Evariste Gherardi's *Le Théâtre Italien*, published in London by

---

[2] Nicholas Rogers, 'Popular Protest in Early Hanoverian London', *Past & Present*, 79:1 (1 May 1978), p. 95.

[3] *The Epistolary Correspondence of Sir Richard Steele*, 2 vols (London, 1787), vol.1, p. 168.

[4] Sybil Rosenfeld, *Foreign Theatrical Companies in Great Britain in the 17th and 18th Centuries*, The Society for Theatre Research Pamphlet Series, no. 4 (London, 1954–55), p. 4.

[5] Francisque, Guillaume, and Simon Moylin, Antoni de Sceaux, Nicholas le Tellier, Francis and Étienne Sallé, Michel Cochois; 'Madame Francisque' (Marie Catherine Le Suisse), Jeanne Moylin, Marguerite Cochois, Marie Sallé.

Jacob Tonson in 1714. One of the last foreign players to visit England in the previous century was Giuseppe Tortoriti, the Pascariel in whose footsteps I have suggested Francisque's company began their provincial career. There were those still living who would remember the performances of the Italian players at the Stuart courts, and the season may have been partly designed to attract nostalgic Jacobites among the aristocracy, as well as the King and the gentry, who knew French well.

The Franco-Italian repertoire, which Francisque was the first to present in England, could not have been learned or rehearsed in under a month. It therefore seems likely that Francisque had performed it during his years of training in the provinces. Reworkings of the old Théâtre-Italien were an important part of the repertoire of the Fair performers.[6] George I's earlier invitation to Riccoboni suggests that this repertoire would be warmly received by the court. There may have been (as in later years) some royal involvement in the choice of plays.

The first night curtain went up at 6.00 p.m. on 7 November 1718 for *La Foire de Saint-Germain*, by Charles Dufresny and Jean-François Regnard. The house was packed, with the Prince of Wales (the future George II), conspicuously seated in a side box. With seat prices at five, three, and two shillings, the box office receipt of £157. 12s. 6d. was one of the highest recorded at a time when, as noted earlier, 'anything over £50, except for benefits, was considered a matter for congratulation'.[7] Perhaps it was the response of the first-night audience which prompted the company to repeat the play on their second night, 12 November, when it was advertised 'With the Prologue to the Town, written and spoken by Harlequin'. The takings were almost as good as on the first night, at £147. 14s. 6d. Francisque's prologue was translated by John Ozell, the leading literary translator of the day, and inserted into the preface of his English version, *The Fair of St Germain*, published on 12 November 1718.[8] An advertisement in *The Post Boy* of 27–29 November describes this translation as a record of the play 'as it is Acted (in French) at the Theatre in Little Lincoln's-Inn-Fields, by the French Comedians'.

---

[6] See Anastasia Sakhnovskaia-Pankeeva, 'La Naissance des Théâtres de la Foire: influence des Italiens et constitution d'un répertoire' (doctoral thesis, 2 vols, University of Nantes, 2013), vol.1, p. 14.

[7] C.A.C. Davis, 'John Rich as Lun', *Notes and Queries* 192:11 (31 May 1947), 223–4.

[8] The fact that the playtext was published within two days of the first night, with Francisque's own prologue, is clear evidence that this season was planned well in advance, possibly during another visit to London from Francisque himself in 1718.

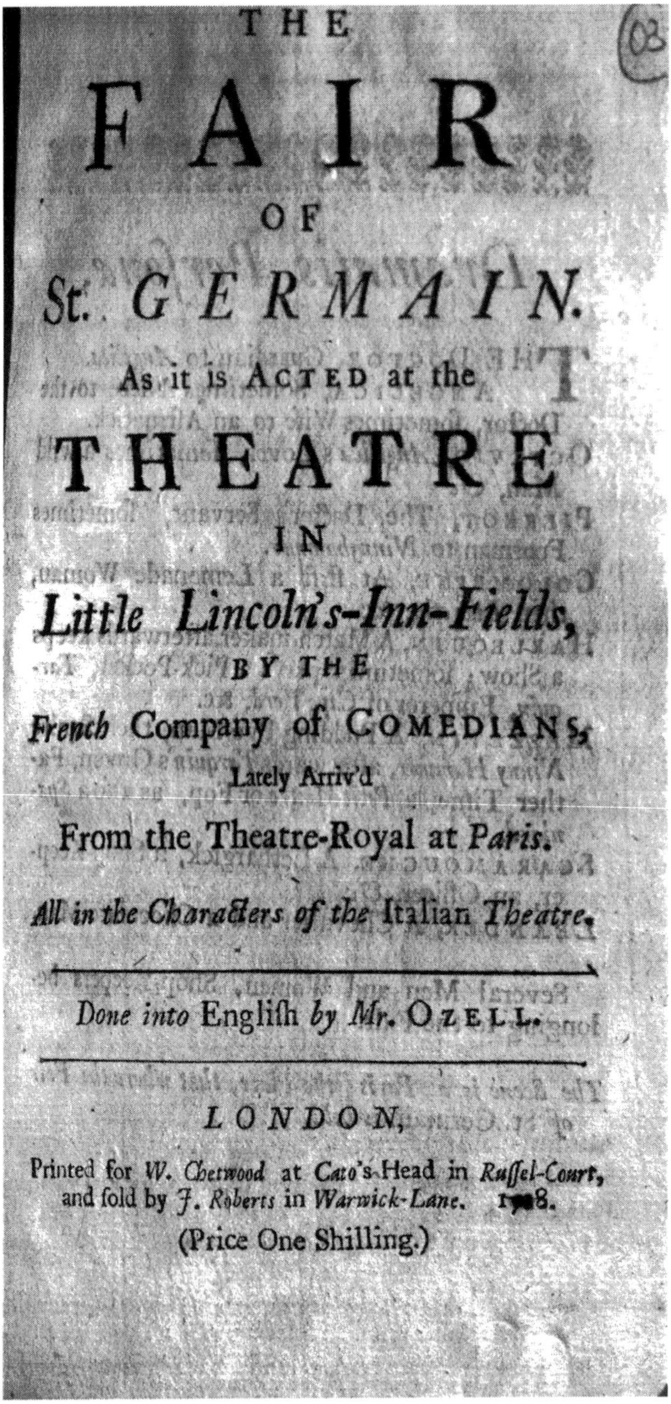

THE FAIR OF St. GERMAIN.

As it is ACTED at the

THEATRE

IN

Little Lincoln's-Inn-Fields,

BY THE

French Company of COMEDIANS,

Lately Arriv'd

From the Theatre-Royal at *Paris*.

All in the Characters of the Italian *Theatre*.

Done *into* English *by Mr.* OZELL.

LONDON,

Printed for W. *Chetwood* at *Cato's*-Head in *Ruffel-Court*, and fold by J. *Roberts* in *Warwick-Lane*. 1718.

(Price One Shilling.)

Fig. 3   *The Fair of Saint-Germain*, title page of the bilingual edition of 1718. Reproduced with the permission of Special Collections, University of Wales Trinity Saint David.

Ozell would seem to have possessed a copy of Gherardi's *Le Theâtre Italien*. His little-known preface is worth quoting:[9]

> The Fair of St Germain is a piece in the Italian Theatre. Like the rest of that collection, its plot is indeed thin, but that defect is supplied by wit and humour. [...]. Most of the scenes are satires upon some character in life; which, by a few masterly strokes, is described, and its vice exposed more fully, than by some more elaborate long-winded performances of this kind.

Ozell adds a personal note about the Prologue to the Town: 'it was sent me written out in Harlequin's own hand, which is as *grotesque* [i.e., 'fantastically extravagant, bizarre, quaint] as his person [...].' Ozell's decision to include this prologue allows us a rare chance to hear, though in translation, the first words spoken (and almost certainly written) by Francisque, performing with his wife (Columbine) and Antoni de Sceaux (Pierrot). It also shows that some of the players wore the traditional masks of the *Commedia* characters and that Scaramouche sometimes spoke French with a mock-Italian accent.

> *Columbine.* But what do you design to do?
>
> *Harl.* To return to France this very Day.
>
> *Col.* You make Use of a good Occasion to fall out with me without any Reason; what Maggot bites you to leave so agreeable a Place as *London*, without having once enjoy'd the Advantage of showing yourself to the noblest City in *Europe*. [...]
>
> *Harl.* The Reason is easy to be explain'd: *Imprimis*, I prognosticate that the Publick will never accommodate themselves to our Way of Playing. The *Doctor* says, that his Figure, and above all his Nose, will fright them most terribly: *Scaramouche* is mad, because he can't speak good *French*: *Pierrot* has not had time enough to let the Niceness of his Wit be known, and *Octavio* is afraid he shall appear too sluggish in his Declarations of Love. Timorous *Isabella* is dying with Apprehensions of appearing before so illustrious an Assembly, and there's the Devil to do with *Marinetta*, who will certainly run stark mad, if her singing should be hiss'd.

Pierrot assures her that 'we are all resolv'd to do our best to gain Applause and the Guineas.' The prologue concluded with a direct appeal to the audience, modestly complimenting their host John Rich, who had recently begun to play Harlequin:

[9] I have modernised the spelling.

Harl. Convinced as we are of the particular Merit of several famous Actors who have had the good Fortune to please the Ladies and Gentlemen of this polite Nation, *we* can scarcely hope to please in the Habit of Harlequin.

Col. Unless you have as much Goodness to pardon our Defects, as you have Understanding to discern them. [...]

Harl. Do you, indulgent, grant some small Applause;
'Tis generous to support the Stranger's Cause:
The Glory of the Act with you remain,
While we content ourselves with – all the Gain.

The whole piece, simultaneously cheeky and modest, is a well-judged *captatio benevolentiae*.

So 'pleased' was the Town that, when the Company's contract with Rich ended on 26 December, they entered into a new contract with Christopher Bullock, sub-lessee of the theatre, for another twelve performances to 5 February. Perhaps Francisque originally intended to return to Paris for the Foire Saint-Germain. Was a Parisian licence granted and then revoked, or did Francisque turn it down, preferring to stay in London, where the Town still seemed more than eager 'to support the Stranger's Cause'?

Whatever the reason, on 12 February the company moved to the King's theatre in the Haymarket and remained for a further five weeks. The opening night – given 'By Command, for the diversion of the three young Princesses', in the presence of the King and 'a great number of Nobility and Gentry'[10] and featuring a new prologue spoken by Arlequin and Colombine – was a very grand affair in the very grand setting of Vanbrugh's theatre.

Members of the royal family were present at performances at both Lincoln's Inn and the Haymarket on at least nine nights. The Prince of Wales was at the opening night, and on 29 November the *Original Weekly Journal* reported, 'On Wednesday, his Majesty, accompanied by the Duke of Richmond, came to the New Play-House in Little Lincoln's-Inn Fields, and saw a Farce acted in French by the Company of Comedians lately come from Paris; and we hear, his Majesty gave a 100 Guineas.'[11] The Prince of Wales returned on four further occasions and the young Princesses had two command performances. The first five nights were Rich benefits, as were six later nights (eleven out of forty); the manager Bullock received three; the Comedians received two benefits and Francisque, Antoni de Sceaux and the Sallés, one each. On 12 March, the company announced that it would give only five more performances at the King's theatre. The season closed on 19 March.[12]

---

[10] *The Weekly Journal or British Gazetteer*, 14 February 1719.

[11] A guinea was one pound and one shilling (21 shillings, 105 modern British pence). The Duke of Richmond was the father of the second Duke who, in the 1730s, supported and encouraged both Marie Sallé and her uncle Francisque.

[12] *London Stage*, Pt 2, 1700–1729, p. 505.

Fig. 4   Façade of the King's Theatre in the Haymarket (the Opera House) (Alamy).

The Repertoire:

1. Franco-Italian comedy

In 1717 the anonymous author in the *Weekly Journal* had claimed that French actors were incapable of playing anything except farce. He added verses in broken English, supposedly intended to be spoken by a French actor 'at the opening of the House'. Admitting that the English had defeated France on the battlefield, the speaker gloated over the prospect of making audiences swallow inferior exports:

> Oh very pretty Vellows you be Gar,
> Ve Conquer more in Peace dan you in Var.

The following week the same journal printed an 'Epilogue' in similar vein, promising a season of brainless entertainments which the actors themselves understood no better than their audience ('Ve're versed in every Ting, but Vit and Sense').[13]

---

[13] See p. 41, n.1.

It is not, then, surprising that during Francisque's visit there was nothing in the English press which could be called objective criticism of the plays or the performers. The main criticism is suggested in a parodic letter, purporting to be from a Puritan, which attacks the current craze for all things French, as exemplified by 'the *Devil's Tabernacle* or *School of Vanity* in the Fields of *Lincoln's-Inn*, sinfully nam'd a *Playhouse*'.[14] Near the end of the season, the *Mirrour* of 12 March 1719 was still giving an equally false impression of the French company's repertoire and the audience's taste:

> A gentle Salute with spitting in the Face, tweaking by the Nose, and Baise-Ma-Cue, are the only Scenes the Gentlemen are pleased with, and Agility in Tumbling, Steadiness of Posture, and ready Extension of Limbs, the Ladies.
>
> > [...] Degenerate Age: (Incurably diseas'd)
> > Only with Nauseous, Foreign Folly Pleas'd!
> > Why need you round the Globe for Nonsense roam?
> > Both Stages furnish out enough at Home [....]
> > Will nothing do? – Then Harlequin! Next Farce,
> > Spare le Docteur and bid them kiss your A—.

It was perhaps his awareness of the negative image of French theatre that made Francisque open his season with a 'Farce in three acts' which was no mere Harlequinade or slapstick, but one of the jewels in the crown of the old Franco-Italian repertoire. The brief cast list for *La Foire de Saint-Germain* in the press hides the multitude of colourful episodic characters and caricatures, disguises and travesties which each player took on in the course of the action.[15] The plot is the very simplest Italian scenario: Arlequin and Columbine help the lovers Angelique and Octave to escape from the clutches of the jealous old Doctor. The story, however, takes place at the Foire Saint-Germain, allowing a procession of outlandish minor characters to submerge the main plot in a welter of comic interludes. The protean Arlequin appears as Polyphemus in a parody of Lully's opera *Acis et Galatée*; as Tarquin in a parody of Racinian tragedy (with mock-heroic alexandrines); as the Emperor of Cap-Vert with his exotic retinue; and as a pretentious coquette, la Dame du Bel-Air, who has to

---

[14] A letter from 'Hezekiah Headstrong' to the editor of *The Weekly Journal or British Gazetteer*, 14 February 1719.

[15] No cast list was given for this play but one can attempt an approximate reconstruction, based on a comparison with the cast list given for *Le Tartuffe*, and other indications in the press: Arlequin – Francisque; Scaramouche – Michel Cochois; Pierrot – Antoni de Sceaux; Octave – Guillaume Moylin; Mezzetin – Simon Moylin; Le Docteur – Nicolas le Tellier; Léandre – Étienne Sallé; Colombine – Mme Francisque; Angélique – Marguerite Cochois.

strip down to her corset to pay for a piece of cloth. Another much appreciated interlude was the *scène des deux carosses* (immortalised in the famous painting by Claude Gillot, c. 1707) in which Arlequin and Mezzetin as *grandes dames* block the street with their carriages and refuse to back down.[16] The comic dialogue was the work of Dufresny and Regnard – of whom Voltaire declared that 'Qui ne se plaît pas à Regnard n'est pas digne d'admirer Molière.'[17] [He who does not enjoy Regnard is not worthy to admire Molière.] These authors, and others from the same repertory, frequently figured in this season.[18]

Anne Mauduit de Fatouville, the first author (in 1681) to write regular French scenes for the old Italians, was represented by *Arlequin Grapignan ou La Matrone d'Ephèse*, *Colombine avocat pour et contre*, *La Précaution inutile* and *Colombine fille savante ou La Fille [Isabelle] capitaine*; in the last of these, Arlequin-Francisque played the scene of the 'professeur d'amour, à visage découvert, habillé proprement à la française'[19] [the professor of love, unmasked and elegantly dressed in the French style]. An engraving in volume three of Gherardi's *Le Théâtre Italien* shows Arlequin in this role, without the motley which normally protruded beneath his various disguises.

Fatouville's *Arlequin empereur dans la lune* was well known in England in Aphra Behn's English adaptation (1687). The English company at Lincoln's Inn performed Behn's version four times during this season. Perhaps tactfully, Francisque waited until his company had moved to the King's Theatre before giving three performances of the French play in rapid succession on 7, 10, and 12 March 1719, 'Performed after the French Manner. With New Scenes and Decorations proper to the Play. In which will be seen a Battle on Horseback between the Knight of the Sun and the Emperor of the Moon, call'd in French La Cavalcade Espagnol [*sic*], a Performance never yet seen in England.'[20]

Four further pieces complete the list from the published volumes of *Le Théâtre Italien*: Gherardi's *Le Retour de la Foire de Bezons*, N. de Boisfranc's *Les Bains de la Porte Saint Bernard*, Dufresny's *L'Opéra de campagne*, and

---

[16] Jean-François Regnard, *Comédies du Théâtre Italien*, ed. A. Calame, Textes Littéraires Français (Geneva, 1981), p. 594.

[17] Quoted in Regnard, *Comédies,* ed. Calame, p. 10.

[18] Dufresny and Regnard, *La Baguette de Vulcain* and *Les Chinois*; Regnard alone, *Arlequin, Homme à bonne fortune*, *Le Divorce* and *Les Filles errantes*. There were plays by other writers from Gherardi's *Le Théâtre Italien*: Brugière de Barante's *La Fausse Coquette* (which gave Francisque another opportunity for travesty), Biancolelli and Dufresny/or Brugière de Barante's *Les Pasquinades Italiennes ou Arlequin médecin des mœurs* [Pasquin et Marforio] and, from the same authors, *Arlequin misanthrope*. See Evariste Gherardi, *Le Théâtre italien ou le recueil général de toutes les comédies et scènes françaises jouées par les comédiens italiens du roi* ([Paris, 1741], repr, 1969)

[19] This entire repertoire is discussed in the later chapters of Virginia P. Scott, *The Commedia dell'arte in Paris, 1644–97* (Charlottesville, 1990).

[20] *Daily Courant*, 7 March 1719.

Eustache Le Noble's *Les Deux Arlequins*. This last piece was published in London with a parallel English translation in 1718. The French title page describes it as a 'Comédie' whereas the English one reads as follows: 'The Two Harlequins, a Farce in Three Acts, Written by Mr. Noble and acted by the King's Italian Comedians at Paris. And now perform'd by the French Comedians at Lincoln's Inn Fields.' The word 'farce', here and elsewhere, seems to have made earlier scholars assume that the repertoire was made up largely of slapstick and tumbling. In fact, this lively and polished work was written in alexandrine and octosyllabic verse. There is a scripted Night Scene for the two Arlequins, one short improvised scene *à l'italienne*, a quarrel between Arlequin and Colombine, and – the only extended *lazzi* – a comic recognition scene when the two Arlequins at last come face to face. Francisque's repertoire also included a few *scènes détachés* not published by Gherardi, which probably lent themselves to *lazzi*. Francisque's association with Dominique and Paghetti had undoubtedly made him familiar with the Italian techniques of *commedia all'improvviso*. Two other pieces, *Arlequin larron, juge et grand prévôt*, by Fuzelier and Dominique, and *Arlequin jouet de la fortune*, by Vivier de St-Bon, were opéras-comiques from the Foires Saint-Germain of 1713 and 1714. *L'Enfant prodigue* must have been the anonymous three-act 'comédie en vaudevilles' given there on 9 March 1714.[21] None of these had been published, so Francisque must have possessed manuscript copies.

Francisque himself was aware of the English misperception of French performers, as is clear from the prologue he wrote for the company's opening night. When Pierrot accuses Harlequin of 'always prognosticating ill Luck' and is apparently about to say that the company's tumbling, at least, will be a success, Harlequin interrupts him: 'Devil take you and your Tumbling; 'tis the very Thing that has made us contemptible.' Even modern scholars sympathetic to Francisque's troupe seem to have believed that 'Tricks and feats played a large part in the entertainments.'[22] The company has recently been referred to as 'Francisque Moylin's French commedia pantomime troupe'.[23] In fact, as Mitchell Wells long ago pointed out, 'these comedies were in no sense pantomimes, were never referred to as such, and should not be confused with the special type of nonsense and spectacle that Rich brought to such

---

[21] The text is contained in BnF, Ms. fr. 25480, ff. 381–400.

[22] Rosenfeld, *Foreign Theatrical Companies*, p. 7. Similar views were expressed by Emmett L. Avery in 'Foreign Performers in London Theaters in the Early Eighteenth Century', *Philological Quarterly*, 16 (April 1937), 105–23, at p. 107.

[23] Paul Boucher and Tessa Murdoch, 'A French household in London, 1673–1733', in Debra Kelly and Martyn Cornick, eds, *A history of the French in London: liberty, equality, opportunity* (London: Institute of Historical Research, 2013), pp. 43–68, at p. 65.

popularity'.[24] While there were clearly feats of purely physical dexterity, other routines were inspired by the *lazzi*, the elaborate physical and mimetic theatre for which the Italians were renowned. Gherardi's *Le Théâtre Italien* is seriously undervalued by references to 'its sawdust origins' and its 'deplorable debasement of the English stage'. [25] Tricks and feats were also performed in the English theatre, even after *Hamlet* and *King Lear*.[26]

We earlier noted the popularity at the beginning of the century of the Alard brothers and the revival of their act as late as 1716 by Sorin and Baxter. On two occasions after the play, Francisque advertised 'A new entertainment in imitation of the Elards [*sic*]' (21 November) and, on 26 December, in the presence of the Prince of Wales, 'Tumbling by Harlequin, Scaramouche, Mezzetin and Pierrot. Scene in imitation of Elard and his two sons'. Francisque was emulating performers whose routines were woven into silent *commedia*-style scenarios, especially Night Scenes. Their popularity is borne out by the higher than usual box office receipts on the nights these entertainments were advertised. On many other evenings, the afterpieces are simply described as 'Vaulting and Tumbling', often with the brilliant Antoni de Sceaux. These silent scenes, and improvised scenes 'à l'Italienne', allowed Francisque to display the skills he had learned directly from the last of the old Italian performers and their offspring, linking their tradition with the beginnings of English pantomime in the hands of Weaver and Rich.

Francisque's royal command benefit was on 8 January, consisting of 'A Farce of Two Acts, in French, call'd *Arlequin esprit folet*. To which will be added, a Farce of Three Acts, call'd *Les Filles errantes*. With several new Entertainments of Vaulting and Tumbling, never yet perform'd in England.'[27] On 17 March, the *Daily Courant* announced *Arlequin prince par magie*, followed by a curious statement: 'During these two last Days Arlequin will Tumble.' If Francisque Moylin was principally an acrobat, why would such

---

[24] Mitchell P. Wells, 'Some Notes on the Early Eighteenth-Century Pantomime', *Studies in Philology*, 32:4 (October 1935), 598–607, at p. 600. Wells was discussing Avery's article 'Dancing and Pantomime on the English Stage, 1700–1737', *Studies in Philology* 31 (1934), 417–52. The pantomime harlequinades of Rich and Weaver are discussed in Papetti, *Arlecchino a Londra*, and in John O'Brien, *Harlequin Britain: Pantomime and Entertainment, 1690–1760* (Baltimore and London, 2004).

[25] Robert F. Storey, *Pierrot: A Critical History of a Mask* (Princeton, 1978), pp. 83–4. Storey claims that Francisque's programme was made up of 'staples of the Foire repertory', whereas it contained almost nothing from the Paris Fairs, and he wrongly attributes to Ozell Arlequin's anxieties concerning tumbling, though Ozell makes it clear that he is merely the translator of Francisque's words.

[26] E.g., on 4 April 1719 Drury Lane offered *The Dumb Farce* after *Macbeth*, while Lincoln's Inn Fields advertised that *1 Henry IV* would be followed by 'an epilogue by Spiller riding on an ass': *London Stage*, Vol.1, pt 2, p. 534.

[27] *Daily Courant*, 8 January 1719.

an announcement have been necessary? The press advertisements in fact indicate that the main tumblers throughout the season were Antoni and Octave. 'Octave' may have been the stage name of Francisque's brother Guillaume who is listed by Campardon as 'chef de la troupe des Sauteurs du Roi, qui donnait des représentations à la foire Saint-Germain en 1720'[28] [leader of the troupe of royal acrobats, who performed at the Foire Saint-Germain in 1720]. Parfaict also speaks of him at this time as 'Molin, excellent voltigeur [...] et frère de Francisque'[29] [excellent tumbler [...] and brother of Francisque]. Francisque was a highly gifted acrobat, but he was also the director of the troupe and its most important actor. He therefore needed to limit his involvement in the tiring and dangerous afterpiece entertainments. The advertisement 'Arlequin will Tumble' suggests that this was something extraordinary, reserved for the company's farewell performances.

2. Music and Dance

Singing and dancing were essential elements of the Gherardi repertoire. Francisque's company had performed songs and dances by Jean-Claude Gillier and others six months earlier at the Foire Saint-Laurent. Ozell's *The Fair of St Germain* contains many of Gillier's songs for characters including Arlequin-Francisque, and although his vaudeville finale was not translated by Ozell, it seems unlikely that it was entirely omitted, since other performances were advertised in the press as including singing and '*Dancing proper to the plays*'.[30] The 1718 London translation of *Les Deux Arlequins* reveals that the musical finale was almost certainly given and may have included the Sallé children: 'four little Harlequins dance with Scaramouch'.[31]

Francisque's players were free to adapt and incorporate elements of the dancing at all the official Paris theatres, thus creating a richer, freer dance style which may well have been admired and emulated at Drury Lane and Lincoln's Inn. Moira Goff has shown that the presence of French dancers in John Rich's companies (including the Sallés, both as children and adults) meant that his dancers knew French music and French dancing techniques.[32] As Rebecca Harris-Warrick writes, 'Arlequin and his cohort may have deliberately transgressed stylistic conventions, but, no matter on which stage they

---

[28] Campardon, *SF*, vol. 2, p. 146.

[29] Parfaict, *Mém*, vol. 1, p. 222.

[30] For the music, see Jean-Claude Gillier, *Airs de Monsieur Gillier pour la Comédie de la Foire S. Germain, représentée sur le théâtre des Comédiens Italiens* (Paris, 1696).

[31] Eustache Lenoble, *The Two Harlequins* (London, 1718), p. 43.

[32] See Moira Goff, 'John Rich, French Dancing, and English Pantomime', in Joncus and Barlow (eds), *The Stage's Glory: John Rich, 1692–1761* (Newark, DE, 2011), pp. 85–98.

danced, they relied on a common technique with the dancers from the Opéra.'[33] Francisque's company combined elements of both serious and comic dance in their programmes. The Sallé children were being trained in the formal dancing of the Opéra and may well have shared their special skills with other members of the company. Antoni de Sceaux had danced at the 'Grandes Nuits de Sceaux' of the duchesse du Maine and had performed his famous comic 'Danse de l'ivrogne' not only at the Paris Fairs but on the prestigious stage of the Opéra and at Lincoln's Inn on at least three occasions. He was no mere grotesque: 'Sa danse était noble et aisée'[34] [His dancing was noble and effortless].

While the company was at Lincoln's Inn Fields, the dancing was sometimes shared with Rich's own resident dancers, including Louis Dupré and Charles de la Garde (or Delagarde) and his sons, in grand ensemble dances.[35] The 'new Dance by 8 persons: Arlequin, Punchanello, Spanish Man and Woman, Country Man and Woman, Arlequin Woman, Dame Ragonde' which was performed on 3 March seems to be related to a dance with the same characters performed by Dupré at Drury Lane in March and October 1716. The dance styles of the various companies, although with minor national variations, must, then, have been compatible.

Despite the immense acclaim and financial gain which Marie and Francis had secured for John Rich only two years earlier, he seems to have made very little attempt to publicise their presence in the new company, except in a royal command performance.[36] When the company moved to the Haymarket, the children were mentioned twice by name; but the theatres thrived on novelty, and 'The Children', as they were often simply called, were now well known and well-enough patronised. Moreover, on the nights when his English company took the stage, Rich was busy promoting the two young sons of one of his own French dancers.

One of Francisque's most popular entertainments combined music, singing and dancing. On 30 December, the entertainment included '*Carillon* by Harlequin and others' and on 16 March '*Le Carillon* with the scene of the Monkey'. This entertainment seems to be based on a comic ballad, *Le Carillon du ménage entre Maître Gervais le savetier et Dame Alison la ravaudeuse*, published in 1706, telling of a bawdy quarrel between a drunken peasant couple. The word Carillon was used figuratively for the noise of a domestic

---

[33] Rebecca Harris-Warrick, *Dance and Drama in French Baroque Opera: A History* (Cambridge, 2016), p. 390.

[34] Parfaict, *Dict.*, vol. 1, p. 152

[35] On Louis Dupré see Moira Goff, 'The "London" Dupré', *Historical Dance*, 3:6 (1999), 23–6.

[36] Stanley Vince, 'Marie Sallé, 1707–56', *Theatre Notebook*, 12:1 (1957), 7–14 at p. 10.

dispute. A version of this piece seems to have become one of Francisque's afterpiece specialities and it stayed in his repertoire until the 1730s.[37]

The frequent 'Entertainments' of dancing, the songs in the *divertissements* at the end of many of the plays and the advertised solo singing, all presuppose the existence of a more than rudimentary orchestra. As early as 1715, Antoine Duményhad been described as a 'symphoniste dans la troupe du sieur Francisque' [musician in the company of Sieur Francisque], so it is possible that Francisque brought some musicians with him. However, as music must have been required every night, he may also have engaged the services of London theatre musicians, many of whom were French. On 2 March the advertisement for *La Précaution inutile* at the King's theatre lists various entertainments, followed by this announcement, 'The band of music will perform all French music that night, compos'd by the famous Mr Baptist Luly [Lully]. At the desire of several persons of quality.' A 'band of music' capable of giving an all-Lully programme must have included accomplished performers. French musicians and composers, including Jean-Baptiste Lœillet ('the London Lœillet'), and the prolific Fair composer Jean-Claude Gillier, were in plentiful supply in early eighteenth-century London. As Vanessa Rogers has pointed out, 'French instrumentalists populated all of the London theatre bands in the early eighteenth century, and frequently made their living teaching or publishing music as well.'[38] With the music of Lully, and 'Dancing proper to the plays', Francisque was offering the London public an entertainment worthy of the Sun King himself.

3. 'London Plays': Le Parisien Dupé and Arlequin Balourd

The most original feature of the season was Francisque's performance of two plays set in London, which reveal his awareness of the ongoing cultural debates about the distinction between French and English national character. On 1 January 1719, the press announced '*Le Parisien dupé dans Londres ou La Fille à la mode*, never acted before.' There is no known play called *Le Parisien dupé*, but the subtitle makes clear that this play must be Nicolas Barbier's *La Fille à la mode* which was first performed and published in Lyon in 1708.[39] Francisque may have discovered Barbier's plays in Lyon through

---

[37] An air called 'Le Carillon de Maître Gervais' was used in *La Grand-Mère amoureuse* by Lesage and d'Orneval, Foire Saint-Germain, 1726.

[38] Vanessa L. Rogers, 'John Gay, Ballad Opera and the Théâtres de la Foire', *Eighteenth-Century Music*, 11:2 (2014), 173–213, at pp. 181–2.

[39] Nicolas Barbier, *La Fille à la mode, Comédie mise au Théâtre par M. B*** (Lyon, 1708). The Parfaict *Dictionnaire* (Vol. 7, p. 391) makes clear that Barbier's plays were little known and rarely performed in Paris.

Dominique's company which performed them in that city.[40] *La Fille à la mode*, a *comédie italienne* with young lovers, the Doctor, Arlequin and Colombine, is set in Lyon and contrasts the elegance and sophistication of all things Parisian with the rustic ways of the provinces. The play's sub-title, *Le Badaud de Paris,* refers to Monsieur Godinet (a kind of Monsieur de Pourceaugnac in reverse), a young Parisian man-about-town who comes to Lyon to marry Isabelle.[41] Arlequin's role, on behalf of his master, who loves Isabelle, is to sow suspicion between the father, the daughter and Godinet, then, as he puts it, 'à coups de pied au cul, renvoyer Monsieur Godinet à Paris.' [with a kick up the backside, send Godinet back to Paris.]

Francisque must have realised that a rivalry between Paris and Lyon would mean little to London audiences, so *Le Badaud de Paris* became *Le Parisien dupé dans Londres*,[42] a new comic twist on the relative merits of Paris and London. Arriving in London, the ridiculous Godinet praises Paris as the home of all elegance and pleasure and calls London outmoded, boring and unfashionable, its inhabitants gross and clumsy. Many specific references to Lyon must have been changed: the hill at Fourvière might have become Richmond Hill, and Lyonnais patois could have been transformed into Cockney. Arlequin impersonates the Parisian Godinet in order to ensure his rejection by Isabelle and her father. When the real Godinet arrives, he has a delightful exchange with Arlequin. Since Francisque's version was never published, I have tried to recreate the effect by replacing 'Lyon' and 'Lyonnais' of the published text with 'Londres' and 'Anglais'.

> *Godinet.* Au reste, C'est une espèce de Ville assez jolie que votre Londres.
>
> *Arlequin.* Monsieur vous êtes bien obligeant.
>
> *God.* Comment? Il y a une Rivière comme à Paris!
>
> *Arl.* Ne trouvez-vous pas qu'elle ressemble à la Seine comme deux gouttes d'eau?

---

[40] The links between Dominique and Barbier are examined in the preface to Dominique's play *La Promenade des Terreaux de Lyon*, J. Rittaud-Hutinet, et al. (eds), and by Sakhnovskaia-Pankeeva in *La Naissance,* especially vol.1, pp. 103–13.

[41] The *Dictionnaire de l'Académie Française* (1798) defines 'badaud' as a negative term for idle Parisian bystanders who gape at everything.

[42] Dominique had set Francisque an example by sometimes setting his own comedies in the town where he was performing, as in Bordeaux in 1713 with *Les Salinières ou La Promenade des Fossés*. See Charles Mazouer, *Le Théâtre d'Arlequin: comédies et comédiens italiens en France au XVIIe siècle* (Paris, 2002), p. 317.

God. Il y aussi des Rues, des Boutiques, et des Carrosses. Dame, j'aurais cru que ce n'était qu'à Paris qu'il y avait de toutes ces choses-là.

Arl. À votre retour vous désabuserez ceux de vos compatriotes qui n'ont point voyagé, et qui s'imaginent qu'à deux lieues de Paris on trouve le bout du monde. […]

God. Au moins, Monsieur, ne croyez pas que je vienne ici comme ces Badauds de notre Pays qui n'ont jamais rien vu. Je suis dégourdi, oui.

Arl. Il y paraît.

God. Et même déjà je sais parler un peu l'Anglais. 'Monsieur, *voula vous venir buva* fouïlletta?'

[*Godinet.* Besides, it's quite a pretty town, this London of yours.

Arlequin. You are most kind sir.

God. What? There's a river just like in Paris!

Arl. Don't you think it looks just like the Seine?

God. And there are streets, shops, and carriages. Good Lord, I would have thought you only had all those things in Paris.

Arl. When you return you must enlighten all those among your compatriots who have never travelled and who imagine that the world ends two leagues from Paris. […]

God. At least sir, don't think I come here like those gawpers from back home who have never seen anything. I'm smart, me.

Arl. So it would seem.

God. And I can even speak a bit of English already. 'Monsieur, *voula vous venir buva* fouïlletta?'][43]

Godinet is outwitted by the tricks of the 'provincial' Londoners led by Arlequin; Isabelle rejects the Parisian and returns to her first love Octave,

---

[43] 'fouïlletta: Chopine, petite mesure pour le vin' [a small measuring glass for wine]. Louis Pierre Gras, *Dictionnaire du patois forézien* (Lyon, 1863), p. 74. This must have been changed to something in English such as, 'Sir, will you take a glass of beer?'

who in this version must have been an honest Englishman. Eventually Godinet is forced to admit that London is just as sophisticated as Paris, a clever compliment to Francisque's London audience.

On 16 February 1719 an event took place which may well be unique in the annals of French and British theatre history. *Arlequin balourd*, a prose comedy in five acts, was written specifically for Francisque.[44] Its author, Michel Procope-Couteaux (1684–1753), a son of the proprietor of the famous Parisian literary café Le Procope, was a doctor currently residing in London and also a passionate theatregoer, playwright and critic. Though by all accounts small in stature, hunched, swarthy and physically unprepossessing, he was a renowned wit and conversationalist, and women apparently found him irresistible.[45] He was reputed to have had a liaison with a rich Englishwoman, which may account for his presence in London at this time.[46] In the preface to his play, Procope (as he was often called) tells the story behind its creation. Having suffered 'une vapeur hypochondriaque, qu'on appelle ici la Spleen' [a hypochondriac state, which here is called Spleen], he had attended performances by Francisque's visiting troupe and was inspired to begin writing a comedy himself:

> Je voyais souvent M. Francisque qui a infiniment de l'esprit et du goût. Je puis dire, sans le flatter, que sa moindre qualité est d'être excellent Arlequin. Je lui parlai de ma pièce, il m'inspira l'envie de la faire représenter, et il me donna même plusieurs idées qui n'ont pas peu contribué à la réussite.[47]

> [I often met M. Francisque, who has infinite wit and taste. I can say, without flattering him, that his least quality is that he is an excellent Arlequin. I spoke to him about my play, he encouraged me to have it performed, and he even gave me several ideas which contributed not a little to its success.]

---

[44] For a fuller account of *Arlequin Balourd*, see Robert V. Kenny, 'A French Première on the London Stage: *Arlequin Balourd*, 1719', *Society for Theatre Research Occasional Essays* (2024): https://www.str.org.uk/publications/theatre-notebook/occasional-essays/arlequin-balourd-a-premiere-in-london-1719/.

[45] *The Anti-Theatre* of March 1720 (written by 'Sir John Falstaffe') mentions the presence of 'a little witty French physician in this town.'

[46] As a prominent Freemason, he may have been involved in the setting up of the Grand Lodge of England in 1717. He remained in London until c. 1723.

[47] See the Preface to Michel Procope-Couteau, *Arlequin Balourd, comédie italienne en cinq actes comme elle a été representée sur le Theatre Roial de Hay-Market devant Sa Majesté* (London, 1719). This may be one of the earliest examples of the use of the word spleen in French. Littré gives no example earlier than Voltaire, who may have learned the word when he came in 1726 to London.

As a theatre-lover Procope would undoubtedly have been familiar with most of Francisque's repertoire. But *La Fille à la Mode,* on which *Le Parisien Dupé* was based, would almost certainly have been new to him, as it had not been performed in Paris; he would have been impressed by Francisque's ingenious transformation of the original setting, which may well have led him to set his own comedy in London. *Arlequin balourd* was first performed by Francisque's company six weeks after Barbier's play.[48]

Before the Prologue to *Arlequin balourd* an unusual 'happening' took place: Léandre appeared on the stage to announce that Arlequin was ill and could not perform. There followed an angry exchange between the actor and a voluble Frenchwoman in one of the boxes who finally leapt onto the stage and offered to play the role herself. This was of course none other than Francisque in drag. He went on to perform this *lazzi* in Brussels and London as late as 1733–5,[49] but its first appearance seems to have been as a curtain-raiser to *Arlequin balourd*. This comic scene, together with a verse prologue spoken by Arlequin and Colombine and a verse epilogue spoken by Arlequin alone, were printed in the 1719 London edition of *Arlequin balourd*, dedicated to the young Princess Anne. In his preface Procope thanks 'Monsieur Vézian' for both the prologue and epilogue. Judging by the prologue's lavish praise of the House of Hanover, 'Vézian' was probably Anthony Vézian, a member of the large French Huguenot community in London; he was a clerk at the War Office and an ardent Hanoverian.[50]

Vézian's prologue for the King's Theatre, written entirely in alexandrines and octosyllabics, is very different from the one spoken at the company's first night in Lincoln's Inn Fields in November 1718. Some lines may show that, as I suggested earlier, Francisque had initially negotiated with Heidegger, and now regretted his deal with John Rich:

> Que franchement j'aurais eu tort
> De ne pas de ces lieux m'être assuré l'entrée,
> Et plût au Ciel que l'eussé-je fait d'abord. (p.16)

---

[48] When Procope-Couteaux returned to Paris he wrote for both of the official theatres, beginning with the prologue *L'Assemblée des Comédiens* for the Comédie-Française in 1724. See *Encyclopédie méthodique, ou, par ordre de matières*, vol.6, pt 1 (Paris, 1804), pp. 278–9. The *Dictionnaire des Théâtres* claims that *Arlequin balourd* was based on an Italian canovaccio, *Gli Sdegni* (*Les Amans brouillés par Arlequin messager balourd*). A comparison of the resumé with the text of *Arlequin balourd,* while revealing superficial similarities of plot, also highlights the originality of Procope-Couteaux's first play. Parfaict, *Dict.*, vol. 1, pp. 62–3.

[49] See pp. 173, 209, below.

[50] See *The Postman*, 8 August 1717. Vézian's name also appeared in the subscription list to a volume of Jean-Claude Gillier's French songs in 1723. He later celebrated the accession of George II and Queen Caroline in his *Ode au roi sur son avènement à la couronne* (London, 1727).

> [That frankly I would have been wrong
> Not to have gained entry to this place,
> And would to heaven I had done so first.]

Since the French actors are now standing on the stage of the very theatre where the efforts of Heidegger and Handel to keep the Italian opera alive had foundered in 1717, Colombine mockingly suggests that they should perhaps try to perform opera themselves. Arlequin retorts with a rant against opera, quoting a notorious denigration of the genre by Saint-Évremond.

Having sent Colombine off to dress, Arlequin then delivers a *Compliment* which concludes by offering to cure the English of their 'noirs chagrins':

> Si je puis remporter l'honneur de vos suffrages,
> Objet de mon ambition,
> J'animerai par-là, les plus grands Personnages,
> Et les plus renommés de ma Profession,
> Qui viendront tous les ans vous rendre leurs hommages,
> Avec moi, dans cette Saison. (p.17)

> [If I can win the honour of your favour,
> Sole object of my ambition,
> I will inspire the greatest and most renowned
> Members of my profession,
> To come here with me every year
> To pay their respects in this Season.]

It was a bold move in 1718 to prescribe a French cure for what George Cheyne was to christen in 1733 'The English Malady',[51] but no adverse comment appeared, probably because Francisque had carefully prefaced his remarks with a fulsome apostrophe to the King, who was sitting a few feet away:

> Peuple chéri du Ciel, le plus heureux du monde,
> Qui goutez les plaisirs dans une paix profonde,
> Sous l'empire d'un Roi dont les grandes vertus
> Le fait craindre, admirer jusqu'aux bouts de la terre,
> Heureux Peuple de l'Angleterre ...

> [People beloved of heaven, the happiest in the world,
> who enjoy their pleasures in perfect peace,
> Under the rule of a king whose great virtues
> Make him feared and admired to the ends of the earth,
> Happy people of England....]

---

[51] See Eric Gidal, 'Civic Melancholy: English Gloom and French Enlightenment', *Eighteenth-Century Studies*, 37:1 (2003), 23–45.

Apart from the tact of this gesture, Francisque had a personal reason to thank the King who had given him one hundred guineas in November. His company was now at the very heart of the British courtly and cultural establishment. Moreover, his promise to furnish the London stage with 'the greatest and most renowned members of my profession' shows that Francisque was already seeing himself, not only as a successful *chef de troupe,* but as an international *entrepreneur.*

Russell Goulbourne sees *Arlequin Balourd* as an anglophile work:

> Despite occasional references to the dreadful English weather and the characteristic boorishness of Englishmen, the play offers a largely positive and comfortingly recognisable vision of England for the home audience [...] and the one English character, a newspaper seller, comes to embody, together with his wares, all that is good about England – a country of freedom, and in particular freedom of information...[52]

But the English *gazetteer*, whatever he may symbolise, is shown to be a cheat, as are most of the other characters. Throughout the play there is more emphasis on libertinage than liberty, and still more emphasis on money. In the opening scene, Marinette, masquerading as a countess from the Indies, shamelessly reveals that she had stolen 4000 guineas' worth of gold and jewels from her elderly employer Geronte before fleeing to London, where she intends to seduce gullible fools at theatres and gambling dens and steal the heart of Isabelle's beloved Léandre. Arlequin later claims that a purse of money opens any London door, and the penniless servant Pierrot tells Scaramouche that his one true mistress is 'Mademoiselle Guinée'.

The plot, loosely based on an old Italian scenario, *Gli Sdegni*, consists of Arlequin's various attempts to help Léandre free his mistress from the clutches of the Doctor, attempts which always make matters worse, until at the end all is forgiven and a double wedding is followed by the usual singing and dancing. The words of the songs are included in the published text but there is no mention of the music, which might have been composed by Gillier, a regular visitor to London. As was traditional, the final verse was sung by Arlequin to the public.

> Messieurs, bon soir,
> Je vous dis un adieu fort tendre,
> Mais ce n'est que jusqu'au revoir.
> Venez m'entendre
> Jeudi prochain,
> Je ferai mieux il est certain.

---

[52] Russell Goulbourne, 'The Comedy of National Character: Images of the English in Early Eighteenth-Century French Comedy', *Journal for Eighteenth-Century Studies*, 33:3 (2010), 335–55, at pp. 14–15.

[Gentlefolk, good evening,
I bid you a tender farewell
But only until we meet again.
Come and see me
Next Thursday,
I'll do better for sure.]

Vézian's epilogue, which Francisque spoke at the King's visit to the theatre on 24 February, was written for Procope's benefit and praises his many qualities:

Il possède en effet des talents merveilleux,
Et quoi qu'il soit de petite stature,
Pour l'en dédommager, Madame la Nature
A formé son Esprit avec de si bons yeux,
Qu'il connait des Humains quel est le Ridicule,
De même que les maux qui font languir leurs Corps.

[He has wonderful talents,
And though he's small in stature,
To compensate him, Mother Nature
Has blessed him with such good insight
That he perceives the follies of men's minds
As well as the ills that make their bodies sicken.]

Finally, Arlequin reminds the audience that 'Les Balourds fourmillent partout' [Blunderers swarm everywhere] and defends the role of comedy in correcting mankind's foolish ways: 'Souvent d'un simple badinage / On peut tirer un grand profit' [Often from simple bantering/ We may learn great things]. The play received four performances, and the Prince of Wales was present on the last night.

4. Regnard, Poisson and Molière

Four plays from the repertoire of the Comédie-Française appeared after Christmas, perhaps in order to give the company time to prepare this more elevated material. Molière's *George Dandin, or The Wanton Wife* was given on 27 January with Raymond Poisson's one-act *Le Baron de la Crasse* (1661) as the afterpiece.[53] Francisque played both Poisson's Baron (a country bumpkin) and the travesty role of the ridiculous Mme de Sotenville in *George Dandin*, another display of his exceptional range.[54] Also from the Comédie-Française,

---

[53] The actor-playwright Raymond Poisson was a rival of Molière and a founder member of the Comédie-Française.

[54] A complete playlist for this season appears in the appendix to Papetti, *Arlecchino a Londra*, pp. 253–6, but it contains some inaccuracies and omissions. For instance,

Regnard's *Les Folies amoureuses* (1704), given on 14 March 1719, is a classic three-act comedy in alexandrines (*petite pièce*, as opposed to the five-act *grande pièce*).

More surprising than these three plays is the inclusion of *Le Tartuffe* in the repertory. The single performance on 13 January 1719 was the first time that a play by 'the famous Monsieur Molière' was seen in the original on the London stage. Francisque himself played the eponymous hypocrite.[55] The choice of this play, which had created such a stir in France only half a century earlier, may well reflect Francisque's awareness of the mood and preoccupations of his current audience. In the wake of the Jacobite rebellion of 1715, the actor-playwright Colley Cibber wrote and starred in *The Non-Juror*, a loose adaptation of *Le Tartuffe*. First performed at Drury Lane on 6 December 1717, the play received 25 performances in the following twelve months, was published in January 1718 with a dedication to the King and went through six editions before the year was out. It had been annotated to ensure that not a single allusion would be missed, and the prologue by Nicholas Rowe was deliberately provocative:

> We mean to souse old Satan and the Pope;
> They've no Relations here, nor Friends, we hope. [...]
> Good Breeding ne'er commands us to be civil,
> To those who give the Nation to the Devil;
> Who at our surest, best Foundation strike,
> And hate our Monarch and our Church alike.

The first non-jurors were the Anglican clergy who refused to swear loyalty to William III either as legitimate sovereign or as head of the Church of England. Later non-jurors were accused of disloyalty to the House of Hanover and the Protestant succession. In 1718 some non-juring Anglican parsons were convicted, fined and pilloried for preaching that 'King George is an Usurper, King James (meaning the Pretender) is our lawful King.'[56] In transforming Molière's hypocritical *dévot* into a Catholic priest in disguise, and thus implying that all non-jurors were Catholic and Jacobite sympathisers in disguise, Cibber

---

Papetti believed *La Fille capitaine* to be the 1672 play by Montfleury (Zacharie Jacob). In fact, the play in Gherardi's *Théâtre Italien* is completely different.

[55] The rest of the cast: Mme Pernelle – Antoni de Sceaux, *en travesti* (older and grotesque women, as well as ridiculous coquettes, were frequently played by men in both the French and Italian companies); Orgon – [either Nicolas or Jean-François; see p. 129, n. 65] Tellier; Cléante – Étienne Sallé; Valère – Guillaume Moylin; Damis – Simon Moylin; Loyal – Michel Cochois; Elmire – Madame Francisque; Mariane – Madame [Guillaume] Moylin; Dorine – Marguerite Cochois. Flipote, Mme Pernelle's non-speaking servant, may have been played by the nine-year-old Marie Sallé.

[56] *The Weekly Journal or British Gazetteer*, 6 December 1718.

had angered non-juring Anglicans, Jacobites, and Catholics.[57] In opposition to *The Non-Juror*, Rich's company produced Christopher Bullock's *The Perjuror* at Lincoln's Inn in December 1717,[58] and the anti-Hanoverian press denounced Cibber for making 'a Farce of a Matter of Conscience'.[59] Beginning on 27 December 1718, the *Daily Courant* carried several announcements of the publication of '*Tartuffe*, or *The French Puritan*. Written in French by Molière and render'd into English with Improvements by the late Mr Medbourne.' The purpose of this re-publication of an old translation is clear from the rest of the announcement: 'in which Play may be seen the Plot, Characters, Incidents, and most part of the Language of *The Non-Juror*.'

This ongoing controversy may explain why Francisque chose, or was persuaded, to give the original French version of '*Le Tartuffe ou l'Imposteur* (As it is represented in Paris)'. The company would thus gain the distinction of presenting, in its original language, the suddenly topical play. By restoring Tartuffe to his status as a layman, they would counteract what many considered Cibber's gross slander of the non-juring clergy. Moreover, while the unseen King whose messenger appears at the end of Molière's play could be taken by Hanoverians to represent George I, the Jacobites were free to interpret praise for 'un Prince ennemi de la fraude' as a reference to the Pretender, the unseen 'King across the water.'

The performance of these controversial plays indicates the extent to which, as John Loftis wrote, 'Actors frequently were made the spokesmen of party and faction.'[60] Protestant Hanoverians saw their conflict with Catholic Jacobites as one of sturdy free-born Britons versus degenerate French and Spanish slaves in the pay of the Pope and the Pretender, and critics argued that the French had taken advantage of the recent peace to invade Britain culturally, corrupting its taste and manners.

Francisque's Franco-Italian repertoire, although it satirised morals and manners, was not overtly political. The liberty of expression taken for granted in London would have been very dangerous in Paris, as Voltaire was to point out a few years later. However, the fact that the players were appearing at Lincoln's Inn Fields automatically gave a political colour to whatever they did. The residence of the Portuguese ambassador, not far from the theatre, contained

---

[57] For a summary of the *Non-Juror* controversy see Helene Koon, *Colley Cibber: A Biography* (Lexington, KY, 1986), pp. 86–9. See also Dudley Miles, 'A Forgotten Hit: *The Nonjuror*', *Studies in Philology*, 16:1 (1919), 67–77, and Rodney L. Hayley, 'Cibber, Collier, and *The Non-Juror*', *Huntington Library Quarterly*, 43:1 (1979), 61–75.

[58] Allardyce Nicoll, *A History of Early Eighteenth Century Drama: 1700–1750* (Cambridge, 1925), p. 212.

[59] *Mist's Weekly Journal*, 28 December 1717.

[60] John Loftis, 'The London Theaters in Early Eighteenth-Century Politics', *Huntington Library Quarterly*, 18:4 (1955), 365–93.

a private Catholic chapel, the scene of anti-Catholic riots from the Popish Plot of 1679 to the Gordon Riots of 1780. The chapel was discreetly frequented by London's recusant Catholics and Jacobites, and more openly by visiting French and Italian performers. The nearby theatre was sometimes attacked as anti-Hanoverian and Jacobite, in opposition to Drury Lane, a bastion of Protestant Whigs.[61] Plays and prologues at Lincoln's Inn Fields frequently countered these attacks with protestations of loyalty to Church and State.[62]

The mere fact of being Italian or French in London at this time invited suspicion. In his epilogue to *The Tender Husband* (1705) Richard Steele had jokingly warned that the 'eunuch' Nicolini (Nicolò Francesco Leonardo Grimaldi) at the opera was secretly a friar:

> No more th'Italian squalling tribe admit,
> In Tongues unknow'n; 'Tis Popery in Wit.
> The Songs (their selves confess) from *Rome* they bring,
> And 'tis High-Mass for aught you know they sing [...].[63]

The four comedies by Poisson, Molière and Regnard are the first examples of Francisque's company attempting the elevated register and formal diction of the Comédie-Française. With so many old Italian plays at their command, there would have been no need to include these pieces unless it was Francisque's intention to vie with the official theatres on their own ground. The company was becoming ever more fluent in a repertoire embracing the distinctive and, in Paris, utterly different traditions of the four stages: La Française, L'Italienne, La Foire and even L'Opéra, which was the home of dance as well as singing. By omitting everything from their last Fair season, Francisque was demonstrating that his company were genuine actors and not merely fairground entertainers. They offered not only high culture but, at the other end of the spectrum, parodies of that culture. Sophisticated spectators might have recognised, in Lenoble's *Les Deux Arlequins*, Arlequin's parody of Rodrigue's famous soliloquy from *Le Cid*. They might even have realised that Francisque was parodying the style of the veteran French actor Michel Baron, who, still performing at the age of seventy, was the frequent butt of mocking impersonations.

---

[61] Emmett L. Avery et al., eds, *The London Stage*, Pt 3 (Carbondale, 1961), p. lxxxii.

[62] In *Traveling Tunes: French Comic Opera and Theater in London, 1714–1745* (Ph.D., Cornell University, 2017) Erica Pauline Levenson makes the interesting suggestion that Francisque's company may have removed a song from their London performance of *La Foire St Germain* because its music was by a composer associated with the court of the exiled James II (pp. 77–8).

[63] See also Ruth Smith, *Handel's Oratorios and Eighteenth-century Thought* (Cambridge, 1995), pp. 205–8.

So the repertoire of Francisque's 1718–19 season had something to satisfy all tastes, from the polished alexandrines of Molière and Regnard, to the baroque verbal extravagance and outlandish plots of the Franco-Italian plays, to the elegance and grace of the dancing with the Sallé children and Antoni de Sceaux and the courtly music of Lully. Thanks to what Viola Papetti has called 'la presenza vivificante' [the invigorating presence] of this ground-breaking company,[64] Rich, and Weaver at Drury Lane, were able to see, and learn from, the full range of Francisque's talents as Arlequin, and London audiences heard for the first time not only the comedies of Molière and Regnard in their original tongue, but also the *speaking* Arlequin of the Franco-Italian repertoire of Gherardi's *Le Théâtre Italien*. As Max Fuchs wrote, 'Porter des spectacles français en Angleterre était, à vrai dire, une entreprise ingrate […]. Pour une tentative aussi périlleuse, trois conditions au moins étaient indispensables: une prudence diplomatique, des talents hors de pair, des mœurs privées irréprochables.'[65] [Bringing French theatre to England was, in truth, a thankless task … For such a dangerous enterprise to succeed, at least three conditions were indispensable: diplomatic prudence, unparalleled talents, and irreproachable private lives.] That Francisque and his company fulfilled these conditions is borne out by the evidence of the box office. Despite the hostility or indifference of the English press, and despite the strangeness of a genuinely literary repertoire in a foreign tongue, the average night's takings, throughout a long season, never fell much below £100, a level which must have been the envy of Cibber at Drury Lane. Facilitated at the political level by the end of hostilities between England and France, the way was now open for further visits of foreign (mostly French) players, led by Francisque and his extended family.

---

[64] Papetti, *Arlecchino a Londra*, p. 55.

[65] M. and P. Fuchs, 'Comédiens Français à Londres (1738–1755)', *Revue de Littérature Comparée* (Paris, 1933) 43–72, at pp. 69–70.

4

The open road between London and the Paris Fairs: 1720–1721

When Francisque and his company left England shortly after Easter 1719, they had probably learned from Paris that little theatrical activity had been tolerated at the Foire Saint-Germain, and that this was likely to be the case at Saint-Laurent in July. It seems that the company set its sights on Holland, where they gave a season in The Hague in a theatre on Casuariestraat. Among the actors were Louis de Verneuil and his wife Marie-Louise Chabot, Charles Lesage, and Marie Antoinette de Tourneville, all of whom were to be associated with Francisque's companies for many years.[1] According to Jan Fransen, this venture collapsed because of competition from a rival theatre on the Voorhout.[2] Francisque and his company must then have returned to Paris.

At the Foire Saint-Germain of 1720, while the Opéra maintained its ban on singing and dancing, fair performers were to be allowed pieces with 'prose' (spoken) monologues and jargon. But there was a darker reason for this apparent tolerance. Despite the wary alliance through which the two official theatres had destroyed the Opéra-comique of 1718, the Comédie-Française was becoming unhappy about the inroads that the new Comédie-Italienne was making into its audience and its box office, once it started performing in French as well as Italian. It therefore attempted to divide and rule the opposition.[3]

The Foire Saint-Germain of 1720

Two companies were tolerated at this fair, one led by Marc-Antoine Lalauze and one by Francisque. Animosity between the two leaders went back to 1718, when Francisque had supplanted Lalauze as the Arlequin of the fairs. Lalauze had little success with three plays by Fuzelier, whereas Francisque's season

---

[1] Jan Fransen, *Les Comédiens français en Hollande au XVII et XVIIIe siècles* (Paris, 1925; Geneva, 1978), pp. 257–69.

[2] The rival theatre manager, Jean Francisque, was not related to Francisque Moylin. See R. L. Erenstein, 'De invloed van de commedia dell'arte in Nederland tot 1800', in *Scenarium*, 5 (1981), 91–106.

[3] Parfaict, *Mém*, vol. 1, p. 219.

opened with the highly topical prologue, *L'Ombre de la Foire*, a mixture of monologue and jargon, the latest addition to the 'genre polémique'. The text recalls the fact that the company had been silenced throughout 1719, and it makes clear that Francisque (alone) had spent some part of the winter of 1719–20 in England. True to his promise to return to England with the finest French players, Francisque was undoubtedly preparing the visit of a new French company. He must have intended to remain in England, leaving his brothers in charge at the Foire Saint-Germain. But when the company learned that only one speaking actor would be tolerated, they wrote in desperation to London, begging Francisque to return.

He did indeed return, and, in the opening scene of *L'Ombre de la Foire*, Arlequin-Francisque is all alone beside a lake, lamenting the contrast between his present unhappy state and the comfortable situation he had enjoyed in the 'charmant pays des Guinées':

> Vous m'écrivez en Angleterre, où j'étais comme un rat en paille,[4] de venir vous joindre à Paris, pour jouer à cette malheureuse foire de Saint-Germain. Je quitte aussitôt ce charmant pays des Guinées pour vous rejoindre, et quand j'arrive, je ne vous trouve plus. On m'apprend que ces deux fameuses magiciennes (conjurées depuis longtemps à notre perte) vous ont enlevés, sans qu'on ait pu savoir où elles vous ont mis, ni ce qu'elles ont fait de vous. [...][5]

> [You write to me in England, where I was as snug as a bug in a rug, asking me to join you in Paris, to play at this unhappy Fair of Saint-Germain. I immediately leave the charming Land of Guineas to join you, and when I arrive, I cannot find you. I am told that those two famous magicians (who have long conspired to ruin us) kidnapped you, and no-one knows where they put you or what they did to you.]

Comedy, he says, is 'le seul bien que me reste' [all that is left to me]. Spectators who recognized classical references could have capped these words with the second half of the well-known alexandrine from Racine's *Andromaque*: 'Le seul bien qui me reste, et d'Hector et de Troie' [All that is left to me of Hector and of Troy].

---

[4] The *Dictionnaire de l'Académie française* (1798) explains that this expression 'se dit des gens qui sont dans un lieu où ils ont tout à souhait, où ils font bonne chère sans qu'il ne leur en coûte rien' [is said of people who find themselves in a place where they have the best of everything, eat well, and pay for nothing].

[5] *L'Ombre de la Foire*, in *Théâtre de la Foire: anthologie de pièces inédites, 1712–1736*, ed. Françoise Rubellin (Montpellier, 2005). Available online: L'Ombre de la Foire http://cethefi.org/doc/ombre_foire_1720.pdfhttp://cethefi.org/doc/ombre_foire_1720.pdfhttp://cethefi.org/doc/ombre_foire_1720.pdf.

The ghost of La Foire appears and hands Francisque a paper which says that in a hole beneath a stone he will find a rope to put an end to all his woes. When he lifts the stone, two vicious cats spring out and run off. Then, instead of the hangman's noose which he expects to find, a fishing line emerges from the hole and Francisque starts to fish, but, instead of catching fish, he pulls out his entire troupe, one by one, each with the name of a different fish. He is obliged to communicate with them through mime, as the two cats have struck them all dumb. A legal injunction is thus transformed into an effective comic device, and, as Jeanne-Marie Hostiou has pointed out in her perceptive introduction to the text, the figurative vocabulary of fish and fishing runs cleverly throughout the rest of the prologue, culminating in Francisque's final address to the audience: 'Messieurs, nous allons faire tout ce que nous pourrons pour vous faire avaler le goujon'[6] [Gentlemen, we will do all we can to make you swallow the bait].

The company next performed the two-act *L'Isle du Gougou*, by d'Orneval, possibly with Lesage, an example of the 'island-castaway' genre. Here, the authors have delved into the accounts of the earliest French explorers of Canada. In *Des sauvages ou Voyage fait en la France Nouvelle* of 1603, Samuel Champlain described the fear among local tribes of 'Un monstre espouvantable que les sauvages appellent Gougou'[7] [A dreadful monster that the savages call Gougou]. The Gougou and the 'savages' from La Nouvelle France are transformed into a typical fair scenario. Léandre, seeking his mistress Argentine, and Arlequin, seeking Marinette, are shipwrecked near the Isle of the Gougou and captured by the wild inhabitants, who lead them to the Sagamo, their sovereign. The Sagamo receives the strangers politely but orders Arlequin to be fed to the Gougou. Fortunately, an eunuch sent from Princess Tourmentine, daughter of the Sagamo, interrupts in jargon: 'Arrêtic, arrêtic; L'Infantic Tourmentinic désiric parlic à Léandric; la regardic de son balconic, voulic l'empêchic d'estric mangic.' Only Arlequin and Marinette speak, in separate scenes, in normal French; Léandre and Argentine play in mime, and everyone else speaks 'jargon' in which real French words are deformed with the endings '-ac, -ec, -ic, -oc, -uc.'[8] Léandre, led before the

---

[6] See Jeanne-Marie Hostiou, *Notice* to *L'Ombre de la Foire* in Rubellin, ed., *Théâtre de la Foire*, pp. 221–227. For a general discussion of *l'Ombre de la Foire* and the 'pièces en monologues' of 1720–1723 see Frédérique Offredi, *Monologues en France du Moyen Age à Raymond Devos* (Ph.D. thesis, Queen's University Kingston, Ontario, Canada, 2010), pp. 115–19.

[7] Quoted in Gilbert Chinard, *L'Amérique et le rêve exotique dans la littérature française au XVIIe et XVIIIe siècle* (Paris, 1913), p. 98.

[8] The complete text is available at http://www.theatre-classique.fr. The manuscript of the monologue ends with the note that the play could easily be divided into three acts, or expanded and made into a comédie italienne, a pantomime or an opéra-comique.

princess, refuses to marry her and Arlequin refuses to marry Tourmentine's ugly servant Carabosse; both would prefer to be eaten by the Gougou. At the end of Act 1, a young boy and girl, probably Marie and Francis Sallé, dance and sing the praises of the Gougou in jargon:

> [Cantou Cantou,] Deou Gougou,
> Qui fa vivou lou sauvageou,
> Qui da panou, qui da vivou,
> Cantou Cantou, Deou Gougou.

The monster is led in by Pierrot, but Tourmentine takes pity on Léandre and Arlequin, ordering her elves to take them to the Black Island. In Act 2, Argentine and Marinette are already on the island, to which the Sagamo has sent them, furious at their rejection of his advances. The four lovers are briefly reunited and a genie informs them that in order to escape they must steal Tourmentine's magic ring. Arlequin manages to steal the ring and subdues the Princess and her followers; the Sagamo reluctantly agrees to provide a ship for them all to return home. The play ends with a ballet by the elves, probably led by Francis and Marie Sallé.

After the first two pieces of the season, the company's fortunes improved dramatically. With the increased tolerance of the Comédie Française, they were now allowed to perform, in normal prose dialogue, the prologue *Le Diable d'argent*, followed by *Arlequin roi des ogres* and *La Queue de vérité*, both in one act.[9] *Le Diable d'argent* was highly topical in the period of wild financial speculation that led to the collapse of the French banking system of John Law. Money, as the title suggests, can be the root of all evil, especially when the devil has rejected La Raison as his assistant, and is guided by La Folie, granting money to a procession of clients (another *pièce à tiroirs*) who will squander it and cause trouble. An honest philosopher is turned away penniless, and when Arlequin's turn comes, he too remains penniless because, as he points out, Le Diable d'argent does not come knocking at the doors of the poor. But, thanks to La Folie, his mind is filled with nonsense to be used in new plays. In a final comment on the unfairness of his situation, Arlequin says he will starve if the speculators and financiers do not patronise his theatre, whereas Les Français are paid even when their theatre is half-empty.

---

[9] These three pieces were included in Lesage, *TF*. Their authorship is rather unclear, but they were either by d'Orneval alone or d'Orneval and Lesage. For further discussion of this point see Loïc Chahine, *Louis Fuzelier, Le Théâtre et la Pratique du Vaudeville: établissement et jalons d'analyse d'un corpus* (doctoral thesis, 3 vols, University of Nantes, 2014), vol. 1, pp. 88–89.

The next piece, *Arlequin roi des ogres*, returns to the theme of dangerous islands. The impressive stage set represents an island in a stormy sea from which the shipwrecked Arlequin emerges, clinging to a plank.[10] Arriving onshore, he is fearful of wild beasts and, finding an animal skin, wraps himself in it, making the first of the play's moral reflections: 'Les animaux me prendront pour un animal; et comme ce ne sont pas des hommes, ils respecteront leur semblable.' [The animals will take me for an animal; and as they are not men, they will respect their fellows.] But, when a tom cat mistakes Arlequin for another cat, he is obliged to rebuff its amorous advances. Two ogres, Sastaretsi and Adario – the latter a reference to the Baron de Lahontan's *bon sauvage*[11] – now confront Arlequin, who explains that, 'Je viens de Paris. J'en étais parti avec deux cents jeunes gens d'élite tant mâles que femelles que la police avaient choisis par prédilection pour aller fonder d'honnêtes familles au Mississippi.' [I come from Paris. I left with two hundred elite young men and women whom the police had specially chosen to go and found honest families in Mississippi.] This refers to the highly topical subject of the current wave of apparently random police arrests and the rumour of child kidnappings and transportation to the newly founded city of New Orleans.[12]

Adario tells Arlequin that custom demands that, as a stranger, he should be their new king. Arlequin is delighted until he learns that custom also demands that they eat their new king. All assemble and sing in the jargon-language of Ogrélie. Arlequin is already stewing in the cooking pot when Scaramouche arrives to save him and Arlequin forgives the ogres on condition they renounce human flesh. Along the way there are further caustic social comments. When, for instance, Arlequin expresses his disgust at the ogres' cannibalism, Adario (*le bon sauvage*) unexpectedly points out that human beings behave like cannibals when they eat the flesh of harmless animals who have served them well:

> Nous, en mangeant des hommes nous croyons en même temps purger la terre de mauvais animaux, de monstres pleins de malice qui ne songent qu'à nous nuire.
>
> [By eating men, we believe we are purging the earth of bad animals, of monsters full of mischief who think only of harming us.]

---

[10] For a discussion of the inspiration for this piece see Anastasia Sakhnovskaia-Pankeeva, *La Naissance des Théâtres de la Foire: influence des Italiens et constitution d'un répertoire* (doctoral thesis, 2 vols, University of Nantes, 2013), pp. 675–9.

[11] Louis Armand de Lom d'Arce, Baron de Lahontan, *Dialogues curieux entre l'auteur et un sauvage de bon sens qui a voyagé* (The Hague, 1703). See Réal Ouellet, 'Adario: Le Sauvage philosophe de Lahontan', *Québec français* 142 (2006), 57–60; doi: id.erudit.org/iderudit/49755ac.

[12] A-P. Herlaut, 'Les enlèvements d'enfants à Paris en 1720 et 1750', *Revue historique*, 139 (1922), 43–61.

This budding *philosophe* continues,

> Vous, qui pensez avoir en partage toute l'humanité, comment en usez-vous les uns avec les autres? Vous vous querelez, vous vous chicanez, vous vous pillez, chez vous le plus fort ôte au plus faible sa subsistance; cela ne s'appelle-t-il pas se manger? Et les ogres vous en doivent-ils beaucoup de reste?
>
> [You, who think you have all the humane qualities, how do you apply them with each other? You quarrel, you fight, you steal, the strongest among you rob the weakest of their livelihood; is that not devouring? And are the ogres any worse than you?]

When a giant with seven-league boots fetches dancers from the Paris Opéra, the girls fear they too may be eaten, but Arlequin reassures them sarcastically: 'Ne craignez rien mes déesses; les ogres n'en veulent qu'à la chair fraîche' [Fear not, my goddesses, the ogres only go for fresh meat] – another dig at the immorality of the Opéra dancers. In the end Arlequin and Scaramouche settle down on an island henceforth given over to love and feasting, a far cry from the Foire Saint-Germain.

The last of the three prose pieces, *La Queue de Vérité*, also reflects on honesty and falseness in human relationships. Arlequin, jester to the King of Tunis, restores the monkey Cascaret to his true form as the magician Padmanaba. As a reward, he is given the monkey's tail which, when pulled, has the power to make everyone instantly reveal their true feelings. After several comic interludes demonstrating this property, the tail finally helps to restore the King's son to love and liberty, and to reveal the base duplicity of two courtiers who are renegade Frenchmen. Arlequin remarks how much better all sovereigns would govern if they had the benefit of this compass of complete honesty. But beneath this pious surface, the suggestive double meaning of 'queue', the ambiguous stage directions, and the actors' gestures combine to create an extremely erotic subtext which Nathalie Rizzoni describes as 'une apologie de l'onanisme à peine voilée par le biais d'une intrigue orientale'[13] [an apologia for onanism barely disguised in an oriental plot]. The fact remains that the main message of this play is a highly moral one about truth and falsehood in general.

The last play of the season, the one-act *L'Âne du Daggial*, never appeared in print and we know of its content only from a summary.[14] Arlequin, jester

---

[13] Nathalie Rizzoni, 'Féerire à la foire', *Féeries*, 5 (2008), URL: http://feeries.revues.org/691, para. 60.

[14] J.-A. Desboulmiers, *Histoire du Théâtre de l'Opéra-Comique* (2 vols, Paris, 1769), vol. 2, p. 158.

of the Caliph of Baghdad, has been dismissed by his prince but luckily is hired by the enchanter Friston who sends him to Argentine, a relative of the Doctor. Mounted on the ass of the Daggial, he arrives in the land of the Caliph where the Doctor and Argentine live. The Doctor captures him, locks him in a cupboard, and offers him for dissection to two Fraters (assistant surgeons). As soon as the cupboard is opened, Arlequin flies into the air, and, releasing a firecracker from his backside, makes everyone flee.[15] Thus, this season ends with Arlequin's defiant breaking of wind in the face of his enemies. It was performed on Passion Sunday, 17 March, and Parfaict notes that the piece was not particularly well received, one of the few negative judgements on an item in Francisque's repertoire.

The play's curious title refers to the monstrous false prophet of Islamic theology. The term *Al-Masih ad-Dajjal* is Arabic for 'the false messiah', an evil figure directly comparable to the Antichrist in Christian eschatology.[16] He is expected to appear, pretending to be *Masih* (the Messiah), before *Yawm al-Qiyamah*, The Day of Resurrection. Some versions of this belief maintain that this evil creature will reign over the earth for forty days of sorrow, before being defeated by the Mahdi who will usher in a time of justice and happiness. Both the enchanter Friston and *l'âne du Daggial* had appeared in 1712 in the story, *Les Avantures d'Abdalla fils d'Hanif*, where a footnote (which Lesage would have known) explains the nature of the Daggial.[17]

But what was the Daggial doing at the Foire Saint-Germain on Passion Sunday? To lovers of literary puzzles, there was an obvious parallel between the Daggial and the Mahdi on the one hand and Lent and Easter on the other. The fair opened at the beginning of Lent and closed just over forty days later, a week before Easter Sunday. In fact, these rather bizarre plays of early 1720 can be fully understood only in the context of the 'genre polémique', which, as Henri Lagrave pointed out, was at its fiercest between 1718 and 1721. Although moments of comic terror are regular features of the Fair repertoire (often in the *lazzi* of Arlequin), they are normally softened by fantasy, laughter, music and dance. In this season, with no singing and dancing, and plays almost bereft of 'normal' dialogue, there is an insistence on the monstrous, and the monsters often come in pairs: a pair of ferocious cats, eager to devour the

---

[15] Parfaict, *Dict.*, vol. 1, pp. 143–4.

[16] *Les Avantures d'Abdalla fils d'Hanif, envoyé par le Sultan des Indes à la découverte de l'ile de Borico, où est la fontaine merveilleuse dont l'eau fait rajeunir* (Paris, 1712), p. 351.

[17] See the introduction by Christelle Bahier-Porte to François Pétis de la Croix, *Histoire de la sultane de Perse et des vizirs; Les Mille et un jours, contes persans*; and *Les Aventures d'Abdalla,* ed. Pierre Brunel with Christelle Bahier-Porte and Frédéric Mancier, Bibliothèque des Génies et des Fées, vol. 8, Sources classiques 54 (Paris, 2006).

poor dumb fishes; the cannibalistic ogres, who point out that human beings exceed even them in cruelty; cruel Tourmantine and the hideous Carabosse; and the two 'Fraters' who intend to dissect the body of Arlequin. Bleakness and anxiety prevail throughout the season: Arlequin all alone and visited by a ghost; Arlequin in the ogres' pot, about to be eaten; Arlequin in the Doctor's cupboard, about to be dissected; Arlequin collapsing in terror at the sight of Carabosse. Moreover, both *La Queue de Vérité* and *Le Diable d'argent* contain sustained reflections on the conflict between honesty and avarice. The playwrights (who had been silenced at the end of 1718 and throughout 1719) made full use of the freedom this fair gave them to lampoon the official theatres. The ubiquitous ugly pairs of monsters in this season are all clearly embodiments of the official theatres who were the cause of forty days of Lenten suffering at this Foire Saint-Germain, a mere shadow of its former self: *L'Ombre de la Foire*.

When the fair closed on 23 March, Francisque's company headed north to Lille, where, on 26 April 1720, Martin Simon, son of Guillaume Moylin and Jeanne Gaillardet, was baptised in the church of Saint Étienne.[18] His godmother was Francisque's sister, Marguerite, who was presumably accompanied by her husband Michel Cochois and the rest of the family. The company may have been heading for Brussels, where the Verneuil couple, who had been part of the company in the Hague in 1719, have been located in 1720.[19] However, it is almost certain that Francisque himself had already left the company in the hands of his siblings and had returned to 'The Land of Guineas.'

The King's Theatre in the Haymarket: March–June 1720

In the prologue spoken at the King's Theatre in February 1719, Francisque had promised to return to London every year bringing with him 'les plus renommés de ma profession' [the most renowned members of my profession]. His stay in London in late 1719 or early 1720, for which the text of *L'Ombre de la Foire* seems to provide reliable evidence, strongly suggests that he played a part with John Jacob Heidegger in setting up a 1720 visit. On 5 February the *Daily Post* reported: 'There is upon the road from Paris a Company of French Comedians, which, 'tis said, are to perform at the [King's] Theatre in the Haymarket twice every Week the Remainder of this Season; and we hear that £1000 is already subscribed towards their encouragement.' Francisque, who was known and trusted by London society, was probably responsible for raising this not inconsiderable subscription during his recent London visit. He

---

[18] AM Lille (St-Étienne) 1GG/75 1719 – 1730.
[19] See Fransen, *Comédiens français en Hollande* ([Paris, 1925] repr. Geneva, 1978), p. 259.

probably had a hand in choosing the programme as well, since, of the total number of pieces presented, over half had already figured in his 1718–19 season.

But Francisque's urgent recall to Paris must inevitably have disrupted his preparations and obliged him to leave things in the hands of a company manager who was less than ideal. Jean-Baptiste de Grimberghs had been living in London since 1715 and may have known Francisque during the 1718–19 season. Though de Grimberghs had experience of management – at the Brussels Théâtre de la Monnaie from 1710 to 1715 – his tenure there had ended in financial disaster, and he seems to have moved to London to escape his creditors.[20] Not surprisingly, therefore, the company got off to a shaky start. The February announcement of its arrival was premature and they did not appear until March. Even then, the troupe seems to have been incomplete and disorganised. Information in the press (for which the manager was responsible) is scant compared to the previous year; there were no cast lists, few actors were named, and players arrived in dribs and drabs rather than as a unified group.[21]

The company finally announced its opening play, *Arlequin Grand Provost et Juge*, for 5 March, with no information about its cast. The popular Mlle de Lisle was not named until the eighth performance. On 29 March and 4 April the press announced performers 'just arrived from Paris' (from the fair that had just finished); and other new acrobats and tumblers are named on 26 and 29 April. On 3 May Roger 'who plays the part of Pierrot' was named among the dancers. This was the versatile Anthony Francis Roger (singer, dancer, violinist, and composer), the third of the company's stars, who came up through the Paris fairs. Several critics have claimed that he performed only in mime.[22] But in London with Francisque, Roger took a full part in the *spoken* repertoire. Confusion may have arisen because Roger stayed on in

---

[20] Henri Liebrecht, *Histoire du Théâtre Français à Bruxelles au XVIIe et au XVIIIe siècle* (Paris, 1923), p. 138.

[21] Just ten performers were named in the press, two of whom, Dangeville and Mlle Deschaliers, were dancers, and two, Dubroc and Madame Violanta, were acrobats; Dulondel, Mlle de Gremont and Mlle de Livrey were the only actors named apart from the star trio of Francisque, Mlle de Lisle and Roger the Pierrot. For a complete list of plays performed in this season, see Papetti, *Arlecchino a Londra*, pp. 256–258.

[22] See Judy Sund, 'Why So Sad? Watteau's Pierrots', *The Art Bulletin*, 98:3 (2016) 321–47, at p. 330. Sund's claim is based on Jean-Baptiste Dubos, *Réflexions critiques sur la poésie et sur la peinture: Nouvelle édition revue, corrigée et considérablement augmentée*, 2nd ed. (Paris, 1733), pp. 288–9. This text, however, clearly refers not to the London seasons of 1720–21 but to Paris visits by dancers from London, including Roger, in 1729–31. There is no mention of Roger in the original 1719 edition. On Roger's career in both London and Paris see Highfill et al., *A Biographical Dictionary of Actors, Actresses, Musicians, Dancers, Managers, and Other Stage Personnel in London, 1660–1800*, 16 vols (Carbondale, 1973–93) vol. 13, pp. 61–2.

England through the 1720s and, no longer acting in French, became a dancer-choreographer at Drury Lane until his death in Paris late in 1731.[23]

Finally on 9 May 'the famous Monsieur Francisque who had the honour to be so much applauded last year' is advertised in *L'Etourdi*.[24] This can hardly have been Francisque's first appearance in this season; if another performer had played Arlequin for two whole months, it would have been odd not to name him in the press or reward him with a benefit. Because of the difference between the English and French calendars, Francisque could have left Paris in mid to late March and have arrived in London around the opening of the season. This view is supported by the performance on 19 March of *Harlequin a Blunderer*, probably Procope-Couteaux's *Arlequin balourd*, written for Francisque the previous year; it was followed by Regnard's *Attendez-moi sous l'orme*, in which Francisque may have played the Officer Dorante, as he was to do in London in 1735.[25] After this first mention on 3 May, which may have been at his insistence, Francisque was named in the press no fewer than six times in under four weeks, always in plays which he had already introduced to London audiences.

On 20 March Molière's *Le Bourgeois Gentilhomme* was advertised as a Benefit for Mlle de Lisle, including 'the Great Turkish Ceremony' with music by Lully. Francisque's Benefit, 'by their Royal Highness's command', took place on 31 May: *Les Deux Arlequins* and 'a French Farce call'd *Le Baron de La Crasse*. With variety of Dancing by Mons. Dangeville and others.[26] And extraordinary Tumbling by Mons. Francisque and others.' Francisque had already performed the main roles in both of these plays in London in 1718–19. On 9 June the performance, attended by the Prince of Wales,[27] was 'For the benefit of Mons. Roger who acts the part of Pierrot.' The programme included the only opéra-comique from the Paris fairs in this season, Fuzelier

---

[23] Ifan Fletcher suggested that Roger was English, but, given his ability to perform in French, this seems highly unlikely. See Ifan Kyrle Fletcher, 'Ballet in England, 1660–1740', in Fletcher, Selma Jeanne Cohen, and Roger H. Lonsdale, *Famed for Dance, Essays on the Theory and Practice of Theatrical Dancing in England, 1660–1740* (New York, 1959), p. 17.

[24] This was not the Molière play of that name but an Italian scenario, *Les Fourberies d'Arlequin*.

[25] Two more Regnard comedies from the Comédie-Française were also given in this season.

[26] *Daily Courant* Tuesday 2 May 1721. Dangeville would appear to be Jean-Baptiste, the younger brother of Antoine-François Dangeville; both had danced at the Opéra. See Parfaict, *Dict.*, vol. 2. pp. 246–9. Among the dancers was 'Mlle Descheliez;' although there is one mention of dancing by 'Mlle Vaurenville, and Mlle des Challiers', this would seem to be Louise Deseschaliers de Vaurenville who appears in the Hague in 1722 and in Poland in 1724–6

[27] *The Weekly Journal or Saturday's Post*, 11 June 1720.

and Legrand's *Les Animaux raisonnables*,[28] containing roles for both Arlequin and Pierrot; it was first performed in 1718 but not published until 1721, so the company must have obtained the script from their friends at the fairs. The other piece must have been *Les Chinois* by Regnard and Dufresny (Comédie-Italienne, 1692), a four-act comedy which wittily exploits the differences between the French and Italian theatres, with the three stars all in drag.

After eleven nights the company left King's on 29 March to make way for the Opera. On 4 April they moved to Lincoln's Inn Fields for just two performances. Then, after an unexplained absence of three weeks from the playbills, they reappeared on 26 April at King's where they alternated with the Opera to the end of the season. On the company's last night, 21 June, Francisque, Mlle de Lisle and Roger took their leave of the Town in 'Les Adieux d'Arlequin, Pierrot et Colombine'. The sheer length of this four-month season indicates that, after a shaky start, the company, bolstered by its three 'stars', had been fairly successful – which may explain Francisque's willingness to work with de Grimberghs again at the end of 1720. But there had also been evidence of poor management. On 12 March at the fourth performance the public was asked to forgive the failure to send tickets to subscribers; on a single night, de Grimberghs announced both that Madame Violanta was unable to perform through illness and that Dangeville had refused to dance, 'being puft up by the Applause he had the good Fortune to meet with; fancying he hath a Right to do so whenever he pleases.'[29] The manager's willingness to go public with his exasperation makes one wonder whether there was some sarcasm even in his first mention of 'the famous Monsieur Francisque'.

Compared to Francisque's earlier visit, the London response to this one was rather mixed. The king was present just once (on the second night). Mlle de Lisle's appearance at the eighth performance was by command of the Prince of Wales, and the ninth night was for the entertainment of the Prince's daughters, 'the young princesses.' Thereafter there were only two further royal commands, both by the Prince of Wales, for the benefits of Francisque and Roger. As for the press reaction, Richard Steele's journal, *The Theatre*, set the tone for much anti-French criticism in the first half of the century. With Addison, Steele had long conducted what Viola Papetti described as a crusade against the theatre of mime and gesture, as opposed to intellectual and verbal drama.[30] By the date when his essay appeared (12 March), the French had given only three performances ('to a crowded audience of gentlemen and ladies'), none of which he seems to have seen himself. Nevertheless, he describes them as 'very extraordinary':

---

[28] Based on Montfleury's one-act verse comedy *Les Bestes Raisonnables* of 1661.
[29] *Daily Courant*, 2 May 1720.
[30] Papetti, *Arlecchino a Londra*, p. 23.

> Harlequin appears as a Lady dressing at her looking-glass, and there goes through the beginning, progress, and consummation of a courtship, against all sense of decency [...]. To acquaint women of honour with what is more filthy than could be seen at a brothel; to entertain our wives and daughters with what their whole education tended to make them abhor, is something more monstrous than I believed even this age of contradictions could ever produce.[31]

Steele's article later takes off into the realm of the absurd:

> The undertakers design to get a subscription for representing on the stage the nuptials of a stone horse. [...] I cannot but think it may endanger the House, if they should go on in the intended *Opera Marine*, wherein, to raise the horror of the fair sex, they represent the meeting of an he and she whale [...].

Steele was answered in *The Anti-Theatre* (14 March 1720) by 'Sir John Falstaffe' who claimed that Steele's attack on indecency was more indecent than the performance and questioned Steele's claim that English theatre had been innocent before the French arrived, but added: "In this remark I would not be supposed an advocate for Harlequin. The French farces are full of base and insipid ribaldry, equally shocking to good sense and good manners [...] their actions [...] may be too free and unpolite for a British audience."

Mary, Countess Cowper, who was present at Francisque's Benefit, does not seem to have found the plays indecent, but she wrote disapprovingly in her diary: 'A most dismal Performance. No Wonder People are Slaves who can entertain themselves with such Stuff.'[32] Another disapproving note was sounded by the clergyman Thomas Rundle, who wrote to a friend on 24 March, bewailing the popularity of the French players over 'old SHAKSPEARE, at Drury Lane' and Steele's own *The Conscious Lovers*.[33] All these critics reveal, if inadvertently, the popularity of the French players.

But the company's 1720 visit may have left other, less obvious, traces. Francisque undoubtedly played parts on nights for which no cast lists were recorded and may well have continued his forays into the classical repertoire by appearing in the two performances of Molière's *Le Malade imaginaire* (13 and

---

[31] Steele, *The Theatre*, ed. J. Loftis (Oxford, 1962) pp. 90–1.

[32] *Diary of Mary Countess Cowper* (London, 1864), p. 172. Lady Cowper was also present at a later performance, probably Roger's Benefit.

[33] Thomas Rundle, *Letters of the late Thomas Rundle, LL D. Lord Bishop of Derry in Ireland, to Mrs. Barbara Sandys, of Miserden, Gloucestershire* (Dublin, 1789), p. 20, quoted in Sybil Rosenfeld, *Foreign Theatrical Companies in Great Britain in the 17th and 18th Centuries*, The Society for Theatre Research Pamphlet Series, no. 4 (London, 1954–5), p. 9.

17 June). In London, also in 1720, the dancer François Le Roussau wrote down 'the only notated dance for a Harlequin to survive in the English repertoire in the early eighteenth century', a *chaconne* set to music from Marc-Antoine Charpentier's first *Intermède* in Molière's *Le Malade imaginaire*; Jennifer Thorp has suggested that 'it is possible that Le Roussau may have seen a production of this work' in that London season.[34] If this was indeed the case, the *chaconne* would almost certainly have been danced by Francisque, and one of the most famous early images of Harlequin in London must be a sketch of Francisque Moylin at work.[35]

A still more exciting possibility is that the company was immortalised by one of the greatest artists of the period. Jean-Antoine Watteau, suffering from the tuberculosis that was to kill him a year later, came to London in 1719 to consult Dr Richard Mead, returning to France in the following summer.[36] Both Judy Sund and Craig Hanson make clear that the famous painting, 'Les Comédiens Italiens' (now in the National Gallery of Art in Washington, D.C.), was painted specifically for the doctor, who was not only a respected physician but a connoisseur and collector.[37] The work has been seen as purely imaginary and allegorical, or as a collection of portraits of various non-acting professionals in *Commedia* costume. Watteau had painted many subjects based on the Comédie Italienne in Paris, but the only actors performing Italian comedy in London at this time were those in the de Grimberghs company, often called the Italian company because of their repertoire.[38] As one of Watteau's biographers has pointed out, the artist could

[34] See Jennifer Thorp, 'From Scaramouche to Harlequin: dances "in grotesque characters" on the London stage', in *The Lively Arts of the London Stage, 1675–1725*, ed. Kathryn Lowerre (Farnham and Burlington, 2014), pp. 11327, at pp. 116–19.

[35] As Rebecca Harris-Warrick points out, at the first performance of *Le Bourgeois Gentilhomme*, the chaconne d'Arlequin 'was performed by the Arlequin of the Italian troupe, Domenico Biancolelli [Dominique]': *Dance and Drama in French Baroque Opera: A History* (Cambridge, 2016), p. 425. Dominique must have danced a similar role in *Le Malade Imaginaire*. It thus seems clear that Francisque, the Arlequin of his company, was Le Roussau's 'Arlequin' in 1720.

[36] Sund, 'Why So Sad?', p. 328 and n.77; Gilbert W. Barker, *Antoine Watteau* (London, 1939), p. 107.

[37] See Sund, 'Why So Sad?', p. 328; Craig Hanson, 'Dr. Richard Mead and Watteau's "Comédiens Italiens"', *Burlington Magazine* 145 (April 2003), 265–72, at p. 266.

[38] Robin Simons makes this point (although he thinks that Francisque's and de Grimberghs' were two different companies) in *Hogarth, France, and British Art: The Rise of the Arts in 18th-Century Britain* (London, 2007), 71, cited in Philip Conisbee and Aaron Wile, "Antoine Watteau/The Italian Comedians/probably 1720," French Paintings of the Fifteenth through Eighteenth Centuries, p. 4, *NGA Online Editions*, https://purl.org/nga/collection/artobject/32687.

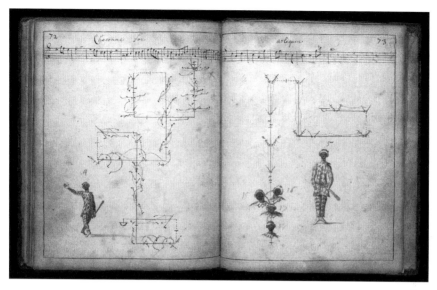

Fig. 5   'Chaconne pour Arlequin', noted by the dancing-master F. le Roussau. MS *Collection of Ball and Stage Dances*, pp. 72–3. Reproduced by permission of the University of Edinburgh Library (La.III.673).

have met the performers in Slaughter's Coffee House in St Martin's Lane, a popular resort for foreign artists.[39] The painting is unusual in the motley assortment of figures crowding the left-hand side, including an English jester in cap and bells. Moreover, as Judy Sund says, 'The centrality of Pierrot in the Washington Italian Comedians is seemingly at odds with de Grimbergue's [*sic*] Harlequin-heavy offerings.' Her suggestion – that the painting commemorates the benefit performance for Pierrot-Roger on 9 June 1720 – seems to me entirely plausible.[40]

Two further events of this London season deserve mention. On 29 March 1720, the *Daily Courant* reported that four new performers from Paris had just given 'An Act of extraordinary Entertainment, call'd, in French, Pantomims.' As Sybil Rosenfeld pointed out, 'This appears to be the earliest use of the word in reference to a contemporary entertainment.'[41] The afterpiece would appear to have been a balletic performance in mime, perhaps like the 'mimick scenes' of Sorin, Baxter and the Alards, and the word 'extraordinary' indicates that, the activities of Rich and Weaver notwithstanding, such embryonic *ballets*

---

[39] Barker, *Watteau*, pp. 100, 104.
[40] Sund, 'Why so sad?', p. 329.
[41] Rosenfeld, *Foreign Theatrical Companies*, p. 8.

Fig. 6 Antoine Watteau's *Les Comédiens Italiens* (c. 1720), almost certainly depicting the company of Arlequin-Francisque. Harlequin can be seen to the left of Pierrot, in his black mask and diamond-patterned costume (National Gallery of Art, Washington, D.C., PD).

d'action were clearly seen as French, almost ten years before the proliferation of supposedly 'English' pantomimes at the Paris fairs.

Another intriguing footnote is to be found in *The Ludlow Postman or The Weekly Journal* for 4 March: 'We hear that Mr. Laws has got a subscription of many thousand pounds, to encourage the chiefest actors of the Drury-Lane Theatre to go and perform at Paris during their vacation next summer, and 'tis said they'll have permission to go thither.'[42] This project did not materialise, but it is fascinating to speculate on what might have happened if Parisian audiences had been exposed to Shakespeare in the original over one hundred years before the visit of William Abbot's company in September 1827. It may well be that the jester in cap and bells who, surprisingly, figures in

---

[42] Was this the French financier, John Law, at the very moment when his bank was about to collapse?

Watteau's painting, looking more English than French or Italian, symbolises the reciprocal influence of Franco-Italian and English acting styles at this time, the short-lived marriage of two great traditions.

The Foire Saint-Laurent of 1720

Although the *Mémoires* say that only Francisque's troupe performed at the fair in July, in fact his rival Lalauze was present with a troupe which included Antoni de Sceaux. But, even though the Opéra maintained its ban on singing and dancing, it seems clear that Francisque was again more successful, because the tolerance of the Comédie-Française allowed him to perform plays with complete dialogue.[43] Originally written for Saint-Laurent in 1718 but not given through lack of time, Lesage's *L'Isle des Amazones* was performed in prose, stripped of all its songs and thus of the coded intertextuality which so frequently governed the choice of airs. Alert as ever to subjects of topical interest, Lesage must have been aware of the publication in 1718 of Mlle de Villandon's story *L'Amazone française* and the translation from Latin of Pierre Petit's *Traité historique sur les Amazones*. In the popular imagination, Amazons hailed from the islands of the New World or 'Les Indes', and were cannibals, perfect characters for the mock-horror of the island-shipwreck genre; interestingly, *L'Isle des Amazones* was written the year *before* Defoe's *Robinson Crusoe*.

The play begins with Arlequin and Pierrot in chains, having been captured by two Amazon pirates. Misinterpreting the overheard remark, 'Ce gros garçon est à manger' [That big chap is fit to eat], they are terrified. They are joined by Scaramouche, to whom Lesage frequently gives dialogue in pidgin Italian. The men fear they will be 'marinés' [marinated] before being eaten, then learn to their relief that they will be 'mariés' [married], but only for three months, as Amazon custom demands. The female children of Amazon unions will be cherished while the males will be bartered against girls from neighbouring islands, at the rate of two to one. Arlequin remarks that many a Parisian father would be only too glad to get rid of his female offspring in this manner. In this 'monde renversé', a reversal of the real condition of many a long-suffering French wife, women rule their husbands.

Mary Ellen Ross claims that the Fair comedies always return things to the *status quo ante*: 'l'ordre est rétabli au terme de l'action: l'homme domine de nouveau la femme, ayant vaincu la fière Amazone.'[44] [order is re-established at the end of the action: having conquered the proud Amazon, man again

---

[43] Parfaict, *Mém*, vol. 1, p. 221.

[44] Mary Ellen Ross, 'Amazones et Sauvagesses: rôles féminins et sociétés exotiques dans le théâtre de la foire', *Miscellany/Mélanges*, ed. Haydn Mason, Studies in Voltaire and the Eighteenth Century, 319 (Oxford, 1994), p. 111.

dominates woman.] But is this really the case here? In the final scene, Arlequin and Pierrot joyfully accept their three months of marriage, but the Amazons insist on remaining free from the legal chains which elsewhere (i.e., in France) can bind a woman to a tyrant for a hundred years. As followers of Bellona, Amazon women are the equals of Mars. As Anne Richardot notes, Lesage, although in parodic form, treats a serious issue, which will be fully elaborated later in the century.[45]

The next play of this threadbare season was *La Statue merveilleuse*, originally written as an opéra-comique for the Foire Saint-Germain at which all speaking, singing and dancing remained forbidden. Like the preceding piece, it was now performed entirely in prose. Lesage's note on the title page, 'Tirée de l'Arabe' [taken from the Arabic], acknowledges once again his familiarity with Antoine Galland's *Les Mille et une nuits* (published, in twelve volumes, between 1704 and 1717) and François Pétis de la Croix's *Les Mille et un jours* (1710–12). However, there is nothing unexpected here; the play confirms the contemporary view of women as fickle and faithless in love. This alternation between subversion and conventional stereotypes allowed the former to slip through unnoticed and unchallenged by the authorities.

The King of the Genii, Féridon, reveals to Zéyn, King of Kashmir, a secret room in the palace containing six statues of ideal women. A seventh plinth remains empty and Féridon promises to fill it if the King sacrifices a twenty-year-old virgin. Her identity will be revealed by a magic mirror, which will turn opaque if a girl has even had thoughts of love or marriage. The three acts are taken up with Arlequin and Pierrot's search for such a Vestal virgin. There follows a procession of lovely candidates who make the mirror turn cloudy. Even the thirteen-year-old Loulou, undoubtedly played by Marie Sallé, causes it to mist over slightly. In despair, the King orders his old Vizir Mobarec to produce Rézia, the daughter he has kept hidden at home. The King falls in love at first sight, though he sadly prepares to sacrifice her. Back in the statue chamber, Rézia has magically become the occupant of the seventh plinth; she steps down, and the King takes her for his bride. The magic mirror theme was reworked by several later authors, including Lesage's son, the provincial actor known as Pittenec.[46]

The Marquis d'Argenson noted that *La Statue merveilleuse* was poorly performed – hardly surprising, in the circumstances.[47] This opéra-comique

---

[45] Anne Richardot, 'Cythère redécouverte: la nouvelle géographie érotique des Lumières', *CLIO: Histoire, femmes et sociétés* 22 (2005), pp. 3–4 & 12. URL: https://journals.openedition.org/clio/1747.

[46] See Isabelle Martin, 'Usage et esthétique du miroir dans une pièce orientale: "La Statue merveilleuse" de Lesage', *L'Esprit créateur*, 39:3 (1999), 47–55.

[47] René-Louis de Voyer de Paulmy, Marquis d'Argenson, *Notices sur les Œuvres de Théâtre*, ed. H. Lagrave (Geneva, 1966), p. 606.

was intended to move forward almost entirely in song and contains no fewer than 162 airs, with spoken links acting almost as operatic recitative. The airs themselves become dialogue, with different characters singing successive lines of the same air. All this would have been lost when the song lyrics were given as spoken dialogue, without music or dance.

However, towards the end of the fair, there must have been greater tolerance from the Opéra, because Francisque was emboldened to restore both pieces to their original opéra-comique format, with music, airs and dances. It was probably to these performances that the *Mémoires* refer in glowing terms: 'Mademoiselle MOLIN femme de [Guillaume] MOLIN, excellent Voltigeur de cette Troupe, & frère de Francisque, joua d'original, & avec beaucoup d'applaudissements le rôle de la *Statue*, dans la Pièce de ce nom. Mademoiselle COCHOIS très-jolie Comédienne, y représentait une Soubrette brillante, qu'elle rendit au gré du public.'[48] [Mademoiselle Molin, wife of [Guillaume] Molin, excellent tumbler of this troupe and brother of Francisque, was the original and much applauded player of the role of the statue, in the play of that name. Mademoiselle Cochois, a very pretty actress, played a dazzling Soubrette role, to the great satisfaction of the public.]

Lady Pennyman meets Francisque

An obscure volume published in London in 1740 contains a little-known account of a visit by an Englishwoman to the Foire Saint-Laurent of 1720. Lady Margaret Pennyman travelled to Paris in August of that year, hoping to salvage what she could of her shares in John Law's collapsing Mississippi Company. She kept a journal throughout her voyage, vividly describing the sights of Paris, Versailles and Saint Germain. At the Comédie-Française, she saw '*The Woman Judge,* and *The Cuckold in Imagination*' (Montfleury's *La Femme juge et parti* and Molière's *Le Cocu imaginaire*), which she judged to be 'two dull and insipid Pieces, and what would be hissed off the *English* Stage.' Going on to the Foire Saint-Laurent, she had an extraordinary reunion with Francisque Moylin whom she claims to have seen 'on the Stage of the *French* Playhouse in the *Hay-Market*'. In fact, when Lady Pennyman set out for Paris on 5 August, the Little Theatre in the Haymarket had not yet been built (it opened on 29 December 1720, three months after her return). However, Francisque had been at the King's Theatre across the road in 1719 and again from March until June 1720; as she speaks of seeing him 'the year before', she must have seen him in that theatre.

Her account of her meeting with Francisque in Paris not only gives a rare glimpse of his ebullient personality but also throws new light on performance

---

[48] Parfaict, *Mém*, vol. 1, pp. 222–3.

practices at the fairs and provides further proof of Francisque's aristocratic patronage:

> August 1720. But the best Diversion I met with of this Kind [of Theatre], was at *St Lawrence* Fair, which is kept every Year without *St Martin's* Gate: Here are great Numbers of Shops, with all Sorts of Nicknacks and Curiosities, with Raffling, Gaming, and Lotteries, and abundance of Booths for Farces, Rope-dancing, and Tumbling, which is the best they can perform, as everyone knows the *French* have the best Jack-puddings in the World. There was a famous Harlequin, whose Name was *Francisque,* who had been in *England* the Year before, and had been mightily caressed by our *English* Quality; he had got a Booth there, and as everyone had their Inscriptions, with some Encomiums on their Perfections, he had wrote himself in large Capital Gold Letters, *Here is* FRANCISQUE *the famous* English *Harlequin, who has had the Honour to perform before his* Britannique *Majesty, and all the* English *Quality, to their entire Satisfaction, being the most perfect* English *Harlequin in the World.* I own my Curiosity led me to see my Countryman, as I thought, but when I came in, to my no little Surprise, I found him to be the same Gentleman who I had seen on the Stage of the *French* Playhouse in the *Hay-Market;* but here we found the Booth so crowded, with the best Quality, that there was no Room for us, without we would sit on the Stage, which was also very full; after some Reluctancy, we seated ourselves, but in a little Time when Harlequin found us out to be *English,* he fell into such a Rapture, before the whole Audience, to see his Countrywomen, as he called us, and with his Cap in his Hand he came spluttering to us with all his *English,* which consisted of five or six Phrases, as *How do you do ? I love you; You lye, I won't kiss you, No, no.* This set the whole Audience in so great a Laughter, that I thought they would have split my Brains with their clapping and noise, if they did not bring the House over our Heads; and thus he did every now and then between the Acts, and they again clapping him, so that I heartily wished myself out; but it was almost impossible to stir a Hand, the House was so crowded: He afterwards came to us, and begged Pardon, making us a World of fine Speeches, assuring us we had done him a great Service, for now his Audience was convinced he was an *Englishman.* I thought in this I saw the Spirit of my own Country, who are ambitious, and flock to *Italian* Operas they do not understand; and thus it was with them, for I question if any one there but ourselves, understood one Word of his *English.* From his Booth we went to several others, some of whom I thought much more dextrous and entertaining than him: It is true, they were all full, but none so crowded as his Booth, neither was there any Appearance of Quality in them.[49]

---

[49] Margaret Pennyman, *Miscellanies in Prose and Verse by the Honourable Lady Margaret Pennyman, containing her late Journey to Paris* (London, 1740), pp. 42–4.

This rare evidence of players interacting with the audience between the acts also reveals the hitherto unrecorded fact that Francisque was advertising himself as 'the most perfect English Harlequin in the World.' Perhaps he wished to be seen as the successor to Richard Baxter, the English Arlequin who retired from Lalauze's company the following year, leaving Francisque as the undisputed leading Arlequin of the fairs. Lady Pennyman's observation that the 'Quality' patronised only Francisque's booth is clear evidence (from an unusual source) that Francisque rather than Lalauze had the protection of people in high places. This may account for the belated return of singing and dancing at the end of the fair, a moment of respite in what otherwise was, in the words of Jeanne-Marie Hostiou, '[une] année noire pour les forains'[50] [a black year for the fairground players].

[50] Hostiou, Notice to *l'Ombre de la Foire*, in Rubellin, *Théâtre*, p. 224.

5

Success and failure in London and Paris: 1721

After the Foire Saint-Laurent, Francisque made his way to London to join a new troupe led (again) by de Grimberghs. The French were the first actors to appear at John Potter's newly-built theatre, as the *Daily Courant* announced on 15 December 1720: 'At the New Theatre in the Haymarket, (between Little Suffolk Street and James Street) which is now completely finished, will be acted French Comedies, as soon as the rest of the actors arrive from Paris.' What was generally referred to as 'The new French Theatre' was built on the site of The King's Head Inn in the Haymarket, almost opposite the King's Theatre (or Opera House); it was the third public theatre in the West End, but never had a full licence (or royal patent). The company again included the Pierrot Roger who both acted and danced with Mlle Deschaliers de Vaurenville. The season opened on 29 December with *La Fille à la mode, ou le badaud de Paris*. This must have been the original version of the Barbier comedy that had been adapted and performed in Francisque's first London season as *Le Parisien Dupé dans Londres*.

The company's third performance was Regnard's *La Foire de Saint-Germain*, the opening play of Francisque's first London season. One of Francisque's comic travesty afterpieces, *Arlequin Dame Alison ou Le Carillon*, was given on 3 February following Molière's *L'Avare*. Once again, scarcely any cast lists were published; Francisque was mentioned only twice in the press, and never in the glowing terms of previous visits. After just four weeks, on 21 January, the *London Journal* reported an ominous rumour: ''Tis said the Company of French Comedians, newly arrived from Paris, are preparing to return home for want of Encouragement; neither his Majesty, nor any of the Royal Family, having been, as yet, to countenance their Performances.' On 31 January de Grimberghs insisted in the *Daily Courant* that 'the said Report is totally groundless, for they will remain here all the Winter Season'. The same advertisement announced the second performance within a week of Molière's *Le Tartuffe*, with *Le Tombeau de Maître André* as afterpiece. No cast list was given apart from the fact that 'Arlequin will play a part', a reassurance that Francisque (who had played Tartuffe in 1719) was not 'on the point of departing'. Despite their patronage of Francisque in earlier seasons, no member of the royal family commanded or attended a single performance. Sybil Rosenfeld suggested that this was because the new theatre was not

Fig. 7   Façade of the Little Theatre in the Haymarket,
also known as the French Theatre (Alamy).

licensed, but another French company received royal visits in the same theatre at the end of the year. The second performance of *Le Tartuffe* was advertised as 'At the Desire of several Ladies of Quality', suggesting that Francisque himself had not entirely fallen from grace.

Just as late arrivals had been a feature of de Grimberghs' earlier season, two new performers came over from Paris on 16 January, followed by Mlle de Lisle on 9 February; one can only wonder why they had not been present from the start. On Tuesday 14 February, the playbill contained an unusual postscript: '*Les Fourberies d'Arlequin ou l'Étourdi*. Wherein Arlequin will make a Speech to the Audience on a Matter of Consequence'. Nothing is known of the speech but three days later a performance of *Arlequin Major Ridicule* was cancelled, and the following day, 18 February, the *Daily Courant* announced: 'The French Company of Comedians give Notice, that Monsieur Francisque, alias Harlequin, did refuse to perform last Night, which obliged the master to dismiss the Audience; but they will perform on Monday next and continue as before.' In fact, on Monday, 20 February, the same journal advertised '*Arlequin et Scaramouche déserteurs, Arlequin Major Ridicule* and *The Scene of the Hat* by Arlequin' as 'At the Desire of several Persons of Quality', followed by an announcement in garbled French explaining that Francisque had not refused to perform but was in fact unwell. We have no further evidence on the reasons for these three announcements in the space of a week, but they are clearly a sign that all was not well.

There were three performances of Barbier's *Arlequin cru Colombine et Colombine cru Arlequin; ou, l'Heureux Naufrage*. The press notes on 25 February that Francisque and Mademoiselle de Lisle starred in its travesty roles 'At the Desire of several Persons of Quality' and that it was 'never acted in England before'. Francisque was probably responsible for the inclusion of Barbier's plays, which he had first come across performed by Dominique's company in Lyon. After this, there were no further performances at the desire of 'Persons of Quality'. Francisque was given a benefit on 20 March, with boxes and pit together at the special higher price of five shillings. The programme consisted of *Les Deux Pierrots* and *Les Quatre Arlequins*. The first piece, a three-act opéra-comique written by Dominique for the Foire Saint-Laurent of 1714, has in fact only one Pierrot, but Arlequin, unmasked, also disguises himself as Pierrot. The second piece, an old Italian *canovaggio* (scenario), allowed Francisque to display his remarkable physical daring, on a par with the Arlequin-Thomassin of the Comédie-Italienne, who, according to Desboulmiers, performed such terrifyingly dangerous acrobatic routines that his admirers begged him to stop.[1] Roger's benefit took place three days later; it included *Arlequin Perroquet* and, as in 1720, *Les Animaux raisonnables*, but there is no record of a benefit for Mademoiselle de Lisle. This is surprising given that the trio of Francisque, Roger and Mademoiselle de Lisle had been so admired a year earlier.

The theatres closed for Easter from 3 to 8 April. On 18 April, the *Daily Post* reported that in *Les Disgraces d'Arlequin* and *Arlequin limonadier*, 'a new Arlequin will perform that Part, who has had the Honour of representing in several foreign Courts with Applause, the late Arlequin, Mons. Francisque, being gone for France'. This highly irregular changeover so late in the season seems to me further evidence of Francisque's profound disagreement with de Grimberghs; he had simply walked out. The company performed on just four more nights. On 2 May, the *Daily Courant* announced grandly – in French, perhaps belatedly to impress the gentry –

---

[1] Desboulmiers, *Histoire anecdotique et raisonnée du Théâtre Italien depuis son rétablissement en France, jusqu'à l'année 1769*, 7 vols ([Paris, n.d.], repr. Geneva, 1968), vol.1, p. 70.

Le Sieur Soulard, qui a fait autrefois les rôles d'Arlequin en France et en Flandres, ayant pris ledit emploi vendredi dernier à la place du dernier Arlequin, duquel s'étant si bien acquitté qu'il a eu l'honneur d'avoir l'applaudissement général de toute l'assemblée, représentera mardi 2 mai pour la première fois *Arlequin Empereur dans la lune*.[2]

[M. Soulard, who has played the role of Arlequin in France and Flanders, took the role last Friday in place of the last Arlequin; he acquitted himself so well that he had the honour of the applause of the whole assembly, and he will perform *Arlequin Empereur dans la lune* for the first time on Tuesday May 2.]

If the enthusiastic puff truly reflected the mood of the Town, it seems odd that *Arlequin Empereur dans la lune*, given on 4 May, proved to be the company's final performance. The company may have stayed on in London for some time; on 8 July the *London Journal* commented disdainfully, 'The French strollers, who appeared on the stage last winter in the Haymarket, have thought proper to withdraw. We condole the misfortunes of those who may have been losers by them, but congratulate the Town on a good riddance to those apish impertinents[…]'.

From the start, the company seems to have been dogged by mismanagement and misfortune. Actors arrived late and departed early in the course of the oddly truncated season, and signs of disharmony within the troupe found echoes in the press. To its credit, the season offered nine comedies by Molière and two by Regnard, but it was not successful financially. It seems likely that there was a clash of personalities between Francisque and the company's leader. De Grimberghs retreated to Brussels, where he died in 1722. He left behind a legacy of ill-feeling and considerable debts which may account for the abrupt ending of the season and were to cause problems in the following year for the theatre management.[3] This probably explains the *Daily Journal*'s reference to 'those who may have been losers by them'.

Perhaps because of these two highly unsatisfactory seasons under de Grimberghs, Francisque did not return to London for thirteen years. However, in fulfilment of his promise (at *Arlequin Balourd* in 1719) to send French players to London annually, he almost certainly helped Jean-Baptiste Hamoche and his wife to secure a five-month season at the Little Theatre in the Haymarket from 4 December 1721 to 10 April 1722. Francisque was on excellent terms

---

[2] *Daily Courant*, 2 May 1721.

[3] For a full account of these difficulties, see Sybil Rosenfeld, *Foreign Theatrical Companies in the 17th and 18th Centuries*, The Society for Theatre Research Pamphlet Series, no. 4 (London, 1954–5), pp. 11–13. A list of the season's performances is printed in Papetti, *Arlecchino a Londra, la pantomima inglese, 1700–1728 (studi e testi)* (Naples, 1977), pp. 258–263.

with Hamoche, who had played with him at the Paris fairs. If he had warned Hamoche against an undiluted diet of Franco-Italian comedy, this could account for the appearance in Hamoche's London season of no fewer than eleven tragedies, by Corneille, Racine, Crébillon, Campistron, and Voltaire. These were the first original-language performances of French tragedy on the English stage, although several were well known in English adaptations, such as Ambrose Phillips' *The Distres't Mother (Andromaque)*. But the season also contained many of the comedies which Francisque had made popular during his earlier visits, including a single performance of Molière's *Le Tartuffe* on the opening night.

After Hamoche, only two companies of French players visited London (in the winter of 1724–5 and the spring of 1726),[4] both with clear links to Francisque in personnel and repertoire. Neither of them received royal commands. All three of these last companies were dogged by quarrels with management over debts and goods, which may be why there were no further French visits until Francisque himself returned in 1734. Erica Levenson has suggested that this gap may be connected with the death of George I.[5] More likely, the new hybrid form of English pantomime (including important French dancers such as the Sallé siblings and Nivelon) satisfied theatre-goers' appetite for spectacle. By this time, in any case, most of the royal family knew English well enough to have less need for foreign-language entertainers.

The Foire Saint-Germain 1721

While Francisque was in London, the Foire Saint-Germain of 1721 opened with his company under the direction of his younger brother Simon. At this fair, though still unlicensed by the Opéra, the companies of both Lalauze and Francisque enjoyed unusual freedom.[6] Lalauze's opening piece was a complete failure and he was obliged to fall back on familiar old repertoire. Francisque's company secured the services of Lesage and d'Orneval, collaborating for the first time with Fuzelier on a new programme of two prologues and four opéras-comiques. Lady Pennyman had already noted the presence of many aristocrats at Francisque's performances, and this patronage seems to have continued: as Lesage wrote, 'Quelques personnes de la plus haute distinction s'étant intéressées pour cette troupe, on la laissa jouer ce prologue

---

[4] See Rosenfeld, *Foreign Theatrical Companies*, pp. 13–15. See also Papetti, *Arlecchino in Londra*, pp. 63–4; a complete playlist of these companies appears on pp. 263–74.

[5] Erica Pauline Levenson, *Traveling Tunes: French Comic Opera and Theater in London, 1714–1745* (Ph.D. dissertation, Cornell University, 2017), p. 60. George I died in June 1727.

[6] Parfaict, *Mém.*, vol. 1, p. 223.

et les deux pièces qui le suivent en prose mêlée de vaudevilles.'[7][Several persons of the highest distinction having taken an interest in this troupe, it was allowed to perform this prologue and the two spoken plays with vaudevilles.]

The prologue to which he refers takes the form of a conversation among three of these highly distinguished spectators, which allows Lesage to conduct a light-hearted review of the strategies for survival which the Fairs had been forced to adopt over the preceding ten years. The comtesse de Vieux-Château confesses to the Marquis that she is bored at the Opéra but loves opéras-comiques: if she had her way the fairs would last all year. The Marquis agrees that 'ces pauvres diables mériteraient bien qu'on les laissât jouer tranquillement, puisqu'ils plaisent au public' [these poor devils should be allowed to play in peace, since they entertain the public]. The Marquis likes the spoken plays but the Countess, who does not want the Forains to end up sounding like the actors at the Comédie-Française, prefers the jollier sung plays. They ask the Chevalier de la Polissonière (Arlequin-Simon Moylin) to settle the debate but he astonishes them by preferring the days of the *pièces à écriteaux*, in which two cupids lowered the song-sheets from above: 'Dès que l'écriteau était déroulé, l'orchestre donnait le ton, et l'on entendait un chorus discordant le plus réjouissant du monde.' [As soon as the song sheet was rolled down, the orchestra struck up, and you'd hear the jolliest out-of-tune chorus in the world.]

By way of demonstration, the first two begin to declaim and sing, while the Chevalier mimes the lowering of the song sheet and sings along to the popular air 'Réveillez-vous, belle endormie'. Colombine enters to announce the programme on the playbill which the aristocrats have not condescended to read. 'Hé, pensez-vous, ma mie, que les personnes de qualité s'amusent à lire une affiche? [...] Fi! cela ne convient qu'à des Bourgeois.' [My girl, do you imagine that people of quality bother to read a poster? [...] Fie! That's only suitable for the bourgeoisie.] The Chevalier, disappointed to learn there will be no song sheets, goes off to the Marionettes, and the others take their places for the performance. The prologue's portrayal of the idle and scatter-brained aristocracy, which harks back to Molière as well as to the chevalier and marquis in Lesage's own *Turcaret*, holds up a rather unflattering mirror to the growing numbers of aristocrats in the Fair audiences during the final years of the Regency.

The two plays which followed mark Lesage and d'Orneval's return to the light-hearted style of their best pieces from 1718, creating almost uninterrupted music-theatre. The first, *Arlequin Endymion*, was an irreverent skit on *Diane et Endymion ou l'Amour vengé*, which Les Italiens had performed at court on 25 and 27 January.[8] The entirely nocturnal setting on Montmartre (still a bare hill outside the city) recalls the 'night-scenes' of the *commedia*. The authors

---

[7] Lagrave, *TF*, vol. 4, p. 213.
[8] Parfaict, *Dict.*, vol. 2, p. 388.

exploit their freedom to carry the action forward almost entirely in song; in the first scene alone, a dialogue between the goddess Diana and Night, there are no fewer than nineteen airs. Woven into the intrigue of the chaste Diana's passion for a fickle shepherd lad (Arlequin), a series of detached scenes depicts various ne'er-do-wells who are abroad at night. Magic and mystery are present when Night calls for darkness to descend ('Larves, fantômes, loups-garous!' [Shades, ghosts, werewolves]). Later, Diana, angry at Arlequin's dalliance with the pastry cook Madame Tartiflette, makes herself invisible and torments him. His repentance air, 'Pardon, pardon, adorable déesse', is sung to the popular air 'Les Folies d'Espagne', and the opéra-comique ends with the reconciled lovers singing suggestively, 'Moi je ferai la pleine lune, et toi tu feras le croissant' [I'll be the full moon and you'll be the horned one], to a popular refrain, 'Et vogue la galère', which was taken up by the audience.

The parody of mythology continues in *La Forêt de Dodone*. The oracular oak trees of ancient Greece are re-situated on the outskirts of a French village on the wedding day of Colin and Colinette. In the first scene, two wise old oaks are played by actors concealed inside the tree-trunks, with a green mask and moss for hair. They chide a couple of dancing baby oak saplings, probably played by the Sallé children, and lament the fact that no-one these days consults them. Within this framework, various wedding guests slip away into the forest to indulge in extra-marital flirtation. When Arlequin and Scaramouche, a pair of itinerant thieves, first meet, Scaramouche's mixed jargon of French and Italian is constantly misunderstood by Arlequin, a reminder of the degree to which the latter has become a naturalised French character. The two friends decide to abduct the bride. The village apothecary Monsieur Bolus and his mistress Mlle Suzon appear, followed by an irate Mme Bolus. The astute Mlle Suzon calls her bluff and when M. Bolus consults the oak trees, they reply that Madame is as faithful (i.e., unfaithful) as Monsieur. The sheepish trio make their uneasy peace and return to the feast. Enter Damis and Céphise, who is accused of flirting with her dancing-master. When Damis asks the oaks if Céphise is misleading him they reply in the affirmative. The wily Céphise saves her skin by assuring Damis that oracles always mean the opposite of what they say.

Arlequin and Scaramouche now enter with the kidnapped bride and convince her that they are part of a wager with Colin, but on hearing the villagers calling for Colinette Scaramouche flees and Arlequin climbs into an oak-tree where he sings a parody of the aria 'Bois épais' from Lully's *Amadis*. To his horror the oak tree starts to move and shakes him to the ground. Arlequin and Scaramouche are arrested, but when the bride assures Colin that they have not tried to steal her 'jewels', all is forgiven and everyone joins in the singing and dancing finale. These two charming opéras-comiques, lightly seasoned with pungent comments on marital infidelity, are in marked contrast to the lugubrious fare of the previous year.

The remaining three pieces from this season were not included in *Le Théâtre de la Foire*, perhaps because the Arlequin role was played by Simon rather than Francisque. Parfaict says that Simon, in the role of Arlequin-Endymion, 's'en acquitta parfaitement'[9] [acquitted himself perfectly] but he seems never to have attracted the same kind of adulation as his older brother. In *L'Ombre d'Alard*, the ghost of the title could have been Alard *pére* or his son Charles, who had died after an onstage fall in 1711. The next piece, *Magotin*, was set in the visually spectacular world of orientalism and magic so popular with playwrights and the public. The hideous magician Magotin falls in love with a portrait that he has found and insists on possessing the original. His aunt, the equally hideous magician Bédra, kidnaps the woman in the portrait – the Princess of Moussel, who is about to be married to a prince. Each magician is armed with a bouquet which has the power to make its wearer appear beautiful, and the Princess is given a potion which makes her forget the Prince her lover. But, just as Magotin and the Princess are being married, the Genie Féridon, protector of the Princess, destroys Bédra's spell, and takes the Princess back to her Prince.[10]

But it is the final piece of the season, another lost manuscript, which offers the most tantalising possibilities for speculation. This was the one-act *Robinson* or *L'Isle de Robinson*; Parfaict notes its immense success, which he attributes to the popularity of Daniel Defoe's *Robinson Crusoe* (1719), translated into French in 1720.[11] The story fitted perfectly the desert island theme already so popular at the Fairs. Lesage and d'Orneval could not have foreseen the enduring influence of Defoe's novel, second only to the Bible in its numerous editions, and they probably omitted it from *Le Théâtre de la Foire* as a piece whose relevance would fade. Nevertheless, to them must go the credit for the first adaptation of Defoe's novel, with the young Simon Moylin in the first portrayal of Robinson on any stage. Sadly, not only has the manuscript not been located, but neither the Parfaict *Mémoires* nor the Parfaict *Dictionnaire des Théâtres* gives a résumé. It is interesting to note that the (probable) appearance of the gentle 'Man Friday' at the Foire Saint-Germain pre-dates by four months Delisle's comedy *Arlequin Sauvage*, which introduced the figure of the philosophical 'bon sauvage' to the stage of the Comédie-Italienne; Delisle may have been partly inspired by *L'Isle de Robinson*.

[9] Parfaict, *Mém.*, vol. 1, p. 225.
[10] The summary in Parfaict's *Dict.*, vol. 3, pp. 290–1, paraphrased here, was all that was known of this play until the edition by Julie Tinant in 2014. See her preface at https://jtsbook.blogspot.com/search?q=Magotin/. See full text at Fanny Prou, https://archive.bu.univ-nantes.fr/pollux/show.action?id=ecd6aa75-91e9-42d2-b359-ac7a73bcbf52.
[11] Parfaict, *Mém*, vol. 1, pp. 226–7. See Daniel Defoe, *La Vie et les Avantures [sic] surprenantes de Robinson Crusoe, Contenant entr'autres événemens, le séjour qu'il a fait pendant vingt & huit ans dans une isle déserte, située sur la côte de l'Amérique, près de l'embouchure de la grande rivière Oroonoque. Le tout écrit par lui-même*, trans. Justus van Effen and Thémiseul de Saint-Hyacinthe (Amsterdam [Rouen], 1720).

At the same fair, Antoni de Sceaux also opened a theatre, but his unauthorised use of music and dancing provoked an official complaint from the Opéra. It may be that Simon Moylin allowed Antoni (who had been with Francisque's London company in 1718) to employ Francis and Marie Sallé, since the *procès-verbal* against Antoni mentions elaborate dancing by two young people.[12] What is certain is that on 10 July 1721, Marie Sallé unexpectedly found herself dancing at the Palais-Royal, when she replaced her teacher, Françoise Prévost, in the leading role of Terpsichore in 'Les Caractères de la Danse', and was widely praised. This ballet, which was to become one of her specialities, marks the moment when Marie first rose from the rough boards of the fairgrounds to the classical world of *belle danse*.[13]

At the close of this lacklustre Fair, Francisque rejoined his family and it would seem that the company spent the early summer in Holland, from which they returned in time for the Foire Saint-Laurent.

The Foire Saint-Laurent

On 30 April 1721, the directors of the Opéra had granted to 'Marc-Antoine Delalauze' [*sic*] and his associates a nine-year licence, covering both fairs, for the establishment of 'un opéra-comique composé de vaudevilles, de danses, de machines, de décorations et de symphonies'[14] [opéras-comiques composed of vaudevilles, dances, stage machinery, decorations and orchestras]. Lesage, Fuzelier and d'Orneval were unhappy that the licence had not been given to Francisque, as they had hoped, and they refused to write for Lalauze. The Fair opened on 24 July and the first play for Lalauze's troupe, which was composed mainly of old-timers (including Alard, Baxter, and Sorin), was provided by a newcomer, Denis Carolet. It was poorly received and the company was obliged yet again to fall back on older repertoire. Matters were further complicated by the Comédie-Italienne who, faced with declining receipts, decided to present a summer season at the Fair in a magnificent theatre constructed at vast expense by Jacques Pellegrin.[15] They opened on the same day as Lalauze, with the comedy *Danaé*, written by Saint-Yon for the old Italian company and lavishly

---

[12] Campardon, *SF*, vol. 1, p. 16.

[13] *Mercure*, July 1721, p. 7.

[14] https://francearchives.gouv.fr/en/search?q=Delalauze&es_escategory=archives Interestingly, a document of the same date in the same archive suggests that Lalauze was helped by 'François Parfaict, seigneur de Boisredon' (one of the authors of the *Mémoires*) who was granted 20,000 livres a year for his services.

[15] Parfaict, *Mém.*, vol. 1, p. 237. The Chevalier Jacques Pellegrin was the brother of the better-known Abbé (Simon-Joseph) Pellegrin.

restaged by Dominique and François Riccoboni as a 'pièce à grand spectacle' with music by Mouret.[16]

Francisque's company finally arrived on the 31st of July, bringing with them two of the Fair's most popular actors, Mademoiselle de Lisle and Jean-Baptiste Hamoche. As the *Mercure* put it, 'la Dlle de Lisle, connue sous le nom d'Olivette, et Hamoche, le bon Pierrot, tâcheront d'obtenir *gratuitement* du public le *privilège* de l'amuser' [Mlle de Lisle, known as Olivette, and Hamoche, the good Pierrot, will try to obtain from the public *free licence* to entertain it] [emphasis added].[17] As Lalauze held the costly licence, the choice of words showed where this writer's sympathies lay. The reaction of the Comédie-Française to all this is described in Lesage's preliminary notice to the season's plays: 'Ce qui augmenta le bonheur de Francisque, fut le silence des Comédiens Français, qui, animés contre les Italiens […] lui laissèrent paisiblement représenter ces pièces'[18] [What increased Francisque's good fortune was the silence of the French Players, who were exasperated by the Italians […] and left him in peace to perform these plays].

Francisque's company opened with an entirely new repertoire of opéras-comiques by Lesage, Fuzelier, and d'Orneval. Lalauze immediately made a legal complaint against his unlicensed rivals.[19] The complaint was upheld and Francisque was again forbidden the use of stage decor, music, and special effects. But his opening prologue already contained a wicked lampoon against Lalauze's company, and one from which it never recovered.

La Fausse Foire

The prologue, *La Fausse Foire*, a new *pièce polémique*, dramatises the current state of affairs.[20] To the sound of a funeral march (two instruments were officially tolerated but at the first performance Francisque in fact had 'quatre violons et deux basses' as well as trumpets and drums), Arlequin, Colombine, Scaramouche, Mezzetin and le Docteur assemble at the tomb of La Foire. Mezzetin's lament, parodying a line from Lully's opera *Amadis,* also makes a serious point:

---

[16] 'On vanta beaucoup une décoration, qui représentait le Palais de la Fortune' [A stage set representing the Palace of Fortune was highly praised]. Parfaict, *Mém.*, vol. 1, p. 238.

[17] *Mercure*, August 1721, p. 113.

[18] Parfaict, *Mém.*, vol. 1, p. 231.

[19] Campardon dates this document 1720, but it clearly refers to the events and the repertoire of July-August 1721.

[20] Desboulmiers, *Histoire du Théâtre de l'Opéra Comique* (2 vols, Paris, 1769), vol. 2, p. 315.

> Toi, qui dans ce tombeau n'est plus qu'un peu de cendre;
> Des spectacles réglés, toi qui fus la terreur...[21]
>
> [You who are now but ashes in the tomb;
> You who were the terror of the official theatres. ...]

La Foire had terrified the official theatres precisely because she was irregular, outside the rules and norms of the establishment. Suddenly La Fausse Foire bursts in. While Carole Fabre appears to believe that La Fausse Foire represents the Italian troupe,[22] and Marcello Spaziani holds her to be L'Opéra,[23] it is clear that the battle is between Francisque and Lalauze who held the *privilège* from the Opéra. It was Lalauze, not the Italians, whose *procès-verbal* first called for the closure of Francisque's theatre and La Fausse Foire was clearly understood at the time to be the troupe of Lalauze.[24]

Comic repetition is very effectively used in the confrontation between Francisque and La Fausse Foire (a vulgar fishwife, probably played by Michel Cochois in drag). By this time, Francisque has become so important that the playwrights make La Fausse Foire address him by his own name rather than that of the character he plays.

> *La Fausse Foire à Arlequin avec un ris [sic] moqueur.* Ha, ha! Monsieur Francisque. C'est donc vous?
>
> *Arlequin.* C'est moi-même. [...]
>
> *La Fausse Foire.* Ha, ha, ha! Je vois bien que vous ne me connaissez pas.
>
> *Arlequin.* Ma foi, non; et je n'ai nulle envie de vous connaître.
>
> *La F. Foire (se grattant les fesses).* Il faut pourtant bien que vous me connaissiez. Je suis la Foire.
>
> *Le Docteur.* La Foire!
>
> *Mezzetin.* La Foire!

---

[21] Cf/ Lully's opera *Amadis* (Act 3): 'Toi qui dans ce tombeau n'est plus qu'un peu de cendre/ Et qui fut de la terre autrefois la terreur.'

[22] Carole Fabre, *La Problématique du jeu et son architecture dans le théâtre de Lesage* (PhD., City University of New York, 2007), pp. 175–6.

[23] Marcello Spaziani, *Il Teatro della Foire* (Rome, 1965), p. 227.

[24] A point made by Desboulmiers, *l'Opéra-Comique*, vol. 2, p. 315, though he confuses Lalauze with Alard.

Colombine. La Foire!

Scaramouche. La Foire!

Arlequin. Vous, la Foire!

[*La F. Foire.* Ha, ha, ha! I see you don't know who I am.

Arlequin. Good Lord, no, and I don't want to know you.

La F. Foire (*scratching her backside*). But you must know me. I am La Foire.

Le Docteur. La Foire!

Mezzetin. La Foire!

Colombine. La Foire!

Scaramouche. La Foire!

Arlequin. You, La Foire!]

When La Fausse Foire and her servants threaten to attack Francisque, the ghost of the true Foire, played by Pierrot-Hamoche, arrives and, in a wicked parody of the words of the ghost in Lully's opera *Amadis* ('Ah! tu me trahis, malheureuse' [Ah, you betray me, unhappy wretch]), commands her insipid rival to desist and leave her children in peace:

>Va, retire-toi, malheureuse;
>Ne viens point dans ces lieux, détestable chanteuse....
>
>[Go, withdraw, unhappy wretch;
>Do not come here, hateful singer....]

La Fausse Foire claims that everything at her theatre is newer and better. Le Docteur retorts, 'Puisque tout est si merveilleux chez vous, il me semble que vous ne devriez faire aucune attention à nous autres bateleurs.' [Since everything of yours is so marvellous, it seems to me you should pay no attention to us mountebanks.] In a series of replies in ever more rustic and ungrammatical French, La Fausse Foire shows the extent of her malice.

La Fausse Foire. ... Vous avez beau avoir votre *Hamoche* et votre *Delisle*, ils ne vous serviront de rien. [...] Vous n'aurez personne, et je crèverons de monde, nous.

Arlequin. Cela est-il aussi dans le contrat?

La Fausse Foire. Assurément, tout y est. Vous n'aurais ni violons, ni décorations, pas même une tapisserie. Ça y est encore, au moins.

[*La Fausse Foire.* ... You may have your Hamoche and your Delisle, they won't help you. [...] You won't have an audience, and I will be stuffed with people.

Arlequin. Is that also in the contract?

La Fausse Foire. Assuredly, everything is in it. You'll have no violins, no scenery, not even a tapestry. That's all in it, and more.]

As Francisque and his friends prepare to starve to death, 'un air gracieux' is heard; the muse Thalie (Mlle de Lisle) appears and, declaiming in the 'style noble', offers her children the protection of 'Les Romains' (the Comédie-Française):

>Je vais leur inspirer de la bonté pour vous.
>Vous parlerez pendant la Foire.
>Bien loin de s'en montrer jaloux,
>Ce serait pour leur cœur un plaisir assez doux,
>Si sur tous vos voisins vous aviez la victoire.
>
>[I will inspire them with kindness for you.
>You will speak during the fair.
>Far from being jaloux,
>It will be a heartfelt pleasure for them,
>If you win a victory over all your neighbours.]

Lesage makes clear that defeating the Italians rather than just Lalauze was the real motive of 'Les Romains'. Thalie advises La Fausse Foire that only good material can assure a troupe's success, a dig at Carolet's inferior pieces for Lalauze.

Carole Fabre rightly stresses the serious subtext to this prologue:

>[...] ce prologue donne un raccourci saisissant du réseau des intrigues qui se nouent entre théâtres. Au demeurant, celui-ci est fort complexe.

Une telle présentation permet au spectateur de suivre l'évolution des événements [...].[25]

[this prologue provides a striking résumé of the web of intrigues between theatres. Moreover, as the web is very complex, such a presentation allows the audience to follow the evolution of events].

Francisque was already a central figure in the 'querelle des théâtres', between David and Goliath. With *La Fausse Foire* he takes his place in the less edifying internecine 'querelle des Forains.' As Barberet long ago pointed out, 'Lesage, sans perdre de vue l'ennemi commun, était souvent fort occupée à combattre les entreprises rivales de la sienne, et le public s'intéressait vivement à ces querelles mesquines.'[26] [Lesage, without losing sight of the common enemy, was often very busy fighting rival undertakings to his own, and the public was highly interested in these petty quarrels.]

La Boîte de Pandore

After the prologue came *La Boîte de Pandore*, in which the mythological setting became a French village on the eve of the marriage of Pierrot and Olivette (Pandore), played by Hamoche and Mlle Delisle. Francisque-Arlequin (as Mercury) has been sent to warn Pandora not to open the box Jupiter gave her. Pandora's family arrives and all is sweetness and light until she insists on opening the box (which she and Pierrot are convinced must be full of jewels). Mercury echoes Molière's George Dandin; 'Vous l'avez voulu, Madame Pandore, vous l'avez voulu!' [You wanted it, Madame Pandore, you wanted it!] The evil passions contained in the box immediately affect all the characters, as Francisque-Mercury comments: 'Cela ne va pas mal; la Jalousie, la Haine, l'Envie, la Médisance, la Coquetterie. Parbleu, la boîte fait une belle évacuation.' [It's not a bad start; Jealousy, Hatred, Envy, Back-biting, Coquetry. Goodness me, the box is emptying very nicely.] In scenes which Desboulmiers described as worthy of Molière, Coridon, a rich farmer, invents the first prison, dubs himself 'Monsieur de la Coridonière' and creates hierarchy, subordination and envy based on rank; before the play ends, he has risen to 'Monseigneur' and the once-innocent Olivette is now his snobbish wife.[27]

As a finale the company prepares to dance a Ballet of the Vices, but Arlequin reminds them, and the public, of the ban imposed by Lalauze: 'Messieurs, nous vous avions préparé un Divertissement complet; mais l'Envie qui est

---

[25] Carole Fabre, *La Problématique du jeu*, p. 178.
[26] Victor Barberet, *Lesage et le Théâtre de la Foire* ([Nancy, 1887] repr. Geneva, 1970), p. 248.
[27] Desboulmiers, *Opéra-Comique*, vol. 1, p. 75.

sortie de la boîte de Pandore pour aller à l'Opéra, nous oblige à vous donner des comédies toutes nues.' [Ladies and Gentlemen, we had prepared a full *divertissement* for you; but Envy, which came out of Pandora's box and went to the Opéra, forces us to give you stark naked plays.] Instead of the cast singing the verses of the vaudeville-finale, Arlequin announces bitterly, 'Ainsi, Messieurs, cette pièce finira un peu froidement; puisque nous n'avons pas la permission de vous chanter les couplets que nous allons vous réciter.' [And so, Ladies and Gentlemen, this play will end rather coldly since we do not have permission to sing you the verses which we will now recite]. And he speaks:

> Les danses et les chants font, dit-on, le mérite
> De nos voisins les Histrions.
> Plaire à l'esprit est donc notre unique ressource;
> Si nous nous tirons bien d'un si grand embarras,
> Ce ne sera, par ma foi, pas
> Voler l'argent de votre bourse.

> [Song and dance, they say, are the charms
> of our histrionic neighbours.
> The only resource we have left is to please the mind.
> If we can succeed in such straitened circumstances,
> Then, heaven knows,
> We won't be stealing your money.]

The actors probably exaggerated this spoken doggerel to make the ban on singing seem as ridiculous as possible. The *Mercure* reported that in the Ballet of Vices Antoni de Sceaux would have performed his famous Drunkard's dance, but that too was of course forbidden.[28]

In spite of the adverse conditions in which it was first staged, the play received high praise from Parfaict.[29] Echoing him, Desboulmiers asserted, 'Cette pièce qui réunit la plus grande gaîté à la plus excellente morale, est digne d'être jouée sur le Théâtre Français'[30] [This play, which combines great jollity and excellent morality, is worthy of the stage of the Comédie-Française]. Raymond Trousson notes that *La Boîte de Pandore* is the first play to use the myth of Pandora as a vehicle for social criticism: 'L'inégalité, l'oppression, le goût de la propriété opposés à l'innocence et à la pureté primitives, n'y a-t-il pas là de quoi faire songer à Rousseau trente ans avant le premier *Discours*?'[31] [inequality,

---

[28] *Mercure*, June-July 1721, vol. 2, p. 116. This is the only mention of Antoni in this company. His sister Agathe was the wife of Lalauze.

[29] Parfaict, *Dict.*, vol. 4, p. 67.

[30] Desboulmiers, *Opéra-Comique*, vol. 1, p. 79.

[31] Raymond Trousson, *Le Thème de Prométhée dans la littérature européenne* (Geneva, 2001), pp. 263–5.

oppression, the love of possessions, against primitive innocence and purity, is it not enough to make us think of Rousseau thirty years before the first *Discours*?]

La Tête Noire

The plot of the next play, *La Tête noire*, was, as Lesage explains in the printed text, loosely based on a rumour concerning a girl in a Paris convent whose face resembled a death's head, or skull. A reward was offered to any man who would marry her and crowds of suitors besieged the convent. With Arlequin and his black mask in mind, Lesage changed 'tête-de-mort' to 'tête-noire' and created a one-act comedy based on an assumption no longer acceptable to most readers.

Arlequin has left the service of Clitandre because he is tired of paying his master's bills. Marinette introduces him to her employer Monsieur Jérôme, and the servants hope to profit from their positions. Jérôme confides in Arlequin that his orphaned niece Argentine has returned from the New World with an immense fortune. His sister, Mme Candi, has not yet seen their niece but has already promised her hand to Clitandre. Greedy Jérôme, however, has other ideas. Arlequin is to disguise himself as a girl whose black mask will so disgust Mme Candi that she will abandon her niece to Jérôme who will then put the real Argentine in a convent and steal her fortune. However, Arlequin, enjoying his role, behaves so shockingly that Mme Candi fears that such a person would corrupt the convent; she instead insists on giving 'her', dowry and all, to any man who will take her.

The disguised Arlequin then receives a procession of suitors, horrifying each in turn, until Clitandre comes to see his betrothed and immediately recognises his valet. They insist on signing the marriage contract at once. Marinette brings in the real Argentine, Jérôme is exposed, and the young lovers are united. In the finale the actors were again obliged to recite rather than sing the verses of the vaudeville, but the *Mercure* printed the musical score, thus giving it a far wider distribution than it would otherwise have had.

During the first three weeks of August a dramatic change took place. On 10 August, by royal decree, the *privilège* of the Opéra-comique was withdrawn from Lalauze and granted to Francisque who, the decree noted, was succeeding better in pleasing the public:

> Sa Majesté a permis et permet à Francisque et sa troupe de continuer ses représentations auxdites foires, même d'y mêler les agréments de l'opéra comique en payant à l'acquit de Lalauze et sa troupe, à la caisse de l'Académie royale de musique, le prix entier convenu par le traité du 30 avril dernier [...].[32]

---

[32] Campardon, *SF*, vol.1, p. 341.

> [His Majesty has now allowed and will allow Francisque and his troupe to continue their performances at the said fairs, and even to add all the features of opéra-comique by paying as an acquittal to the Royal Academy of Music, the entire price agreed with Lalauze and his troupe by the treaty of 30 April [...]].

By an act dated 22 August, Jean Francine, the director of the Opéra, granted Francisque and his associates (Hamoche and Hyacinthe [Jacinthe]) a full nine-year licence to perform opéras-comiques.[33] On the same day, an agreement was drawn up and signed between the authors Lesage, Fuzelier et d'Orneval and the three actors, to provide plays for both fairs.[34]

For the first time since 1718 Francisque was within the law. Lalauze, who was allowed to continue performing, appealed and on 31 August the courts ordered Francisque's theatre to close, but, according to the *Mémoires,* on 1 September, '[il] ouvrit son Théâtre plus glorieusement que ci-devant, en vertu d'un nouvel ordre.'[35] [he opened his Theatre more gloriously than before, by virtue of a new order.] As if to rub salt into the wounds of Lalauze, Francisque now revived *Les Funérailles de la Foire* (1718), followed by *Le Rappel de la Foire à la Vie* (1721). In doing so, he was proclaiming that the true Foire had died in 1718, and that only now, with Francisque, did it rise again.

Le Rappel de la Foire à la vie

Lesage's note to the printed text of *Le Rappel de la Foire à la Vie* explains that he had originally hoped to stage its first version at the opening of the Foire St Germain in February 1719; as no licence was granted for the Fair, he was obliged to withhold the play. He then hoped to present it at the beginning of the Foire St Laurent in July 1721, but since the Opéra unexpectedly granted that season's licence to Lalauze, Lesage was obliged to wait until August. After the licence was transferred to Francisque, Lesage was finally able to present *Le Rappel* with his chosen players, updating the final scene to refer to the presence of Les Italiens at the fair.[36] In *Le Rappel*, Francisque, as L'Opéra, plays the sympathetic rôle of a new Orpheus who rescues La Foire from Hades (albeit, he admits, only in order to profit from her box-office). But in the face of Pluto's refusal to give back La Foire, all hell is put to sleep with an aria and Cerberus is stupefied with a scrap of recitative! The

---

[33] https://francearchives.gouv.fr/en/facomponent/e5a1d920994089d428fa78e6304 1b9fb468f2260.

[34] https://francearchives.gouv.fr/en/facomponent/81282763bee7d5fb6158f6fa5b0a 289edfb22648.

[35] Parfaict, *Mém.*, vol. 1, pp. 231–2

[36] Lagrave, *TF*, vol. 3, p. 411.

resurrected Foire is greeted by Monsieur Vaudeville, with a reminder that the last officially licensed Opéra-comique had been Francisque's company at the Foire Saint-Laurent of 1718.

> J'ai passé trois ans sans vous voir,
> Plus cruels qu'on ne pense.
> Je disais dans mon désespoir,
> Avec toute la France:
> Foire folette mes amours,
> Êtes-vous morte pour toujours?

> [I have spent three years without seeing you,
> More cruel than you think.
> With all France
> I said in my despair,
> Crazy little Fair, my love,
> Are you dead forever?]

La Foire restates her vision of her own distinctive theatrical vocation: 'Aiguisons bien nos traits; / Sur la folie humaine / Lançons mille traits.' [Let's sharpen our barbs;/ Let's launch a thousand darts/ Against human folly.]

The two Comédies feign friendship for the reborn Foire. La Française, having first whispered 'c'est ce monstre odieux!' [it's that odious monster!], declaims, 'Ah! Que votre retour, ma bonne, nous est doux!' [Ah! My dear, how sweet to us is your return!] L'Italienne offers to embrace La Foire but whispers that she would rather strangle her. And the goodwill of La Française is equally short-lived. Le Public enters and chides the two Comédies for their intolerance; he insists there should be room for all three theatres and urges them to compromise. Finally, to everyone's amazement, L'Italienne announces that she is to set up her stall at the fair; La Foire mockingly invites La Française to join them, but the latter leaves in disgust. By the time this piece was performed in September 1721, the Comédie-Italienne was already at the fair, but the forced cordiality between La Foire and L'Italienne at the end of *Le Rappel* was short-lived. Once again, the 'genre polémique' puts the actors on a stage within a stage, in a comic yet serious debate.

Le Régiment de la Calotte

The sheer stupidity of this relentless and petty warfare inspired the last piece of the season, *Le Régiment de la Calotte*. The mock 'regiment' of the title was founded by a group of officers and gentlemen towards the end of the reign of Louis XIV, and it admitted to its ranks people who were judged to have committed acts of egregious stupidity for which they were awarded a *brevet* or certificate, usually in satirical verse.[37] Here, its principal officers are Momus and La Folie who interview a procession of candidates. Alongside familiar types like the aging and luckless coquette Dorimène and the flighty spendthrift Céphise, there are references to contemporaries like the man who lost all his money by wagering it would rain for forty days after the feast of St Gervais. The climax is the arrival of Pantalon, representing Les Italiens. He explains their qualification for this dubious award: they have spent vast amounts on lavish décors for this fair, thinking that mere show would please the public. To crown it all, they have, like the Opéra and the Comédie-Française, held balls twice a week[38] – but during the summer heatwave, which meant that they had to be discontinued after a couple of weeks.[39] Mocking their failure, Lesage sets words to an air whose refrain makes ribaldry inevitable:

> Mais le trait original,
> C'est d'imaginer un bal
> Dans la ca, ca, ca,
> Dans la ni, ni, ni,
> Dans la cu, cu, cu,
> Dans la ca, dans la ni, dans la cu,
> Dans la canicule. Chose ridicule!

> [But the original thing
> is to dream up a ball,
> in the ca, ca, ca,
> in the ni, ni, ni,
> in the cu, cu, cu,
> in the ca, in the ni, in the cu,
> In the *canicule* [heatwave]. Ridiculous!]

This vulgar chorus would have been taken up with gusto by the audience, only the grammatical gender of 'dans la cu' adroitly saving it from utter grossness. Having thus established his credentials, Pantalon and his troupe are admitted to the regiment in a mock-Latin ceremony deliberately recalling Molière's *Le Malade imaginaire*:

> Quando vestræ pieces novæ
> Vous sembleront trop frigidæ,
> Pour bien illis rechaufare,
> Quid illis facere?

---

[37] For the history of the Régiment see Antoine de Baecque, 'Les éclats du rire. Le Régiment de la calotte, ou les stratégies aristocratiques de la gaieté française (1702–1752)', *Annales*, Histoire, Sciences Sociales, vol. 52:3 (1997), 477–511.

[38] *Mercure*, June-July 1721, vol. 2, p. 26.

[39] See Lagrave, *TP*, p. 373.

To this, and further questions in dog-Latin about how to warm up a 'frigid' repertoire, Pantalon keeps replying, with mounting comic effect, 'Theatrum decorare,/ Postea cantare, /Ensuita dansare.' The company are granted cap and bells with one final twist in readily decipherable mock-Latin: 'Plenum puissantium dono/ Decorandi, / Cantandi, / Balandi, / Baragouinandi, / Et ennuiandi, /Tant in villa, qu'au faubourgo.' Despite this play's extreme topicality, it is not difficult, once it is re-contextualised, to imagine the glee with which this public ridicule was received by audiences at the time. Les Italiens were so incensed that in *Les Terres australes*, a one-act comedy by Dominique and Legrand performed on 23 September, the characters L'Opéra-Comique and Le Régiment de la Calotte were banished from an imaginary utopian island along with other social undesirables. Desboulmiers reports that this skit was badly received and was never published.[40]

In mid-September 1721 Lalauze tried to revive his fortunes with new parodies: *La Réforme du Régiment de la Calotte*, *La Décadence de l'Opéra-comique l'Aîné* and *Le Jugement de Pan et d'Apollon par Midas*. According to Parfaict, this 'critique assez ennuyeuse de la troupe de Francisque, et des pièces qu'elle représentait' [rather irksome criticism of Francisque's troupe and the plays they presented] had only a few performances.[41]

After this, Lalauze, virtually bankrupt and further disheartened by the recent death of his wife (Agathe de Sceaux), left Paris forever.[42] Some other members of his troupe, Joseph Sorin and Pierre Alard (who was married to Lalauze's sister Marguerite), retired from the stage for good and, according to Campardon, Alard became a dentist. The English Arlequin Richard Baxter, like Sorin a veteran of the fairs and the London stage, withdrew to a hermitage and died a pious death in 1747.[43] With the demise of these veterans of the first generation's struggle to create the genre of opéra-comique, a chapter in the history of the fairs came to an end.

At the close of the fair, Madame, the mother of the Regent, once again, as in 1718, showed her support for Francisque. On 2 October, she commanded a performance of three plays at the Palais-Royal, where Francisque, Hamoche and Mlle de Lisle were heartily applauded.[44] But once again Francisque's enemies were lying in wait. The *Mercure* in December reported that, at the insistence of Les Deux Comédies, Francisque's theatre had been closed down again and two of his stars had left, Hamoche taking a company to London and Mlle de Lisle disappearing temporarily from view. It glumly concluded:

---

[40] Desboulmiers, *Histoire anecdotique*, vol. 7, pp. 441–2.
[41] Parfaict, *Mém.*, vol. 2, p. 2. All three plays are lost.
[42] Parfaict, *Dict.*, vol. 3, pp. 258–9.
[43] Parfaict, *Mém.*, vol.1, p. 229; Campardon, *SF*, vol.1, p. 4, p. 101.
[44] Parfaict, *Mém.*, vol. 1, pp. 232–3. The plays were Les Funerailles de la Foire, Le Rappel de la Foire à la Vie, and Le Régiment de la Calotte.

'On ne verra plus dans la Foire Saint-Germain prochaine, que des danseurs de corde, des marionnettes et des curiosités.'[45] [At the next Foire Saint-Germain we shall see only rope dancers, puppets and curiosities.]

Between 1718 and 1721 the Opéra granted just two licences and Francisque's company was the principal holder of both. No further licence was granted to any troupe until the Foire Saint-Laurent of 1724. As a result, in 1722, Francisque and his company were to face even greater challenges.

---

[45] *Mercure*, December 1721, p. 164.

6

The fight goes on: Francisque and the first plays of Alexis Piron: 1722–1723

The Foire Saint-Germain 1722

Forbidden to perform anything with dialogue or songs, Francisque opened his season on 3 February with *Ourson et Valentin* and *Les Fourberies d'Arlequin*, probably given in a mixture of mime and jargon in order to stay within the law; these old plays were not successful.[1] Refusing to work for Francisque under such restrictions, Lesage, Fuzelier and d'Orneval wrote instead for the marionettes of Charles Dolet and Antoine Delaplace. Marionettes had always enjoyed free speech at the fairs, and they now performed opéras-comiques with the offstage voices of Dolet's actors. All Paris flocked to see *Pierrot Romulus, ou Le Ravisseur poli*, a parody of La Motte's tragedy *Romulus*, and Fuzelier proudly noted that 'avec ces acteurs de bois, on fit tomber Francisque qui jouait à la muette dans le même préau' [with these wooden actors we beat Francisque who was playing in dumbshow nearby].[2] After much pleading, Francisque obtained permission to perform with a single speaking actor.

Deserted by his previous collaborators, and desperately needing new material, Francisque turned to the virtually unknown thirty-two-year-old Alexis Piron, who had come to Paris from his native Dijon in 1719. Penniless and without patrons, Piron found work as a copyist and ledger clerk, while assiduously frequenting theatres and cafés in the hope of entering the literary world. Before long he was a welcome visitor to the house of the Marquise de Mimeure,[3] where he first crossed swords with Voltaire and also met his future wife, Marie-Thérèse Quenaudon, known as Mlle de Bar. According to Piron's biographer, Rigoley de Juvigny, Francisque, who had heard of Piron's reputation for wit, burst into his lodgings and explained his predicament:

---

[1] Parfaict, *Mém*, vol. 2, pp. 1–2.
[2] Quoted in Françoise Rubellin, ed., *Théâtre de la Foire: anthologie de pièces inédites, 1712–1736* (Montpellier, 2005), p. 86.
[3] On the Marquise de Mimeure, an important literary patron, see Alain Niderst, *Charlotte-Madeleine de Mimeure: une muse des lumières* (Paris, 2010).

> Je suis Francisque, entrepreneur de l'opéra-comique; la police me défend de faire paraître plus d'un acteur parlant sur la scène ; MM. Lesage et Fuzelier m'abandonnent ; je suis ruiné si vous ne venez à mon secours ; vous êtes le seul homme qui puissiez me tirer d'affaires; tenez, voilà cent écus, travaillez, et comptez que ces cent écus ne seront pas les seuls que vous recevrez [...].[4]
>
> [I'm Francisque, director of the opéra-comique; the police forbid me to put more than one speaking actor on stage; Lesage and Fuzelier abandon me; I'm ruined if you don't come to my aid; you're the only man who can rescue me; look, here are a hundred crowns, work, and you can be sure that these hundred crowns won't be the only ones you'll receive [...].]

Three days later, Piron had completed *Arlequin Deucalion*, a monologue for Francisque and a dozen non-speaking actors. Francisque not only kept his promise but also invited Piron to help him cast the play. Piron, for his part, was touched by the generosity of a mere actor, and the two men, having struck up an instant friendship, now collaborated on the staging of one of the longest and most literary texts ever spoken by Arlequin at the Fairs.

On 25 February – after just two days of rehearsals, according to Juvigny – the three-act monologue *Arlequin Deucalion* gave Francisque the perfect vehicle to revive his fortunes. As Paul Chaponnière put it, 'Jamais rôle plus apte à ses qualités de souplesse, de volubilité, de mimique, ne fut plus vite appris.'[5] [Never was a role more quickly learned, or more suited to his gifts of suppleness, loquacity and mimicry.] It was a turning point for Piron as well: *Arlequin Deucalion,* his first staged work, 'established his reputation as a playwright decisively for the rest of the century'.[6] Piron could have known only the first three volumes of *Le Théâtre de la Foire* which were published in 1721, and the absence of licensed performances throughout 1719 meant that his knowledge of live performance was largely limited to Francisque's four seasons in 1720–21. Although he could have seen only one monologue, *L'Ombre de la Foire*, Piron in *Deucalion* reveals a complete mastery of the genre. Juvigny was among the first to marvel at the brilliance of Piron's theatrical début: 'Il fallait l'imagination

---

[4] Alexis Piron, *Œuvres Complètes*, ed. Jean-Antoine Rigoley de Juvigny (7 vols, Paris, 1776), vol.1, pp. 39–45. All Piron's works, and his own annotations on them, are quoted from this edition. Biographical information is taken from de Juvigny's *Vie de Piron* in vol.1. https://www.google.co.uk/books/edition/_/fKkaA236ZW4C?hl=en&gbpv=1 All seven volumes of this edition are now available online in Google Books.

[5] Paul Chaponnière, *Piron: sa vie et son œuvre* (Geneva, 1910), pp. 38–9.

[6] Walter Rex, *The Attraction of the Contrary: Essays on the Literature of the French Enlightenment* (Cambridge, 1987), p. 65.

riante et féconde, et peut-être même tout le génie de Piron, pour jeter tant de traits brillants et une variété si piquante, dans un sujet qui parait en être si peu susceptible....'[7] [It required the happy and fertile imagination, and perhaps even the genius of a Piron, to fill out such a seemingly unpromising subject with so many brilliant features and such piquant variety], and all this in the form of a monologue. Derek Connon has called *Deucalion* an 'anti-fair play',[8] but neither Piron nor Francisque had any quarrel with the fairs; if anything, *Deucalion* is a protest against the arbitrary restrictions on the players' ability to speak.

Arlequin Deucalion

Arlequin Deucalion opens with a musical storm and shipwreck scene, a device already used by Lesage, as in *Le Roi des Ogres,* to allow Arlequin to be stranded on a foreign shore, all alone *après le déluge*. Since Piron had anticipated a dearth of spectators and a lukewarm reception, Deucalion declaims, in a parody of the tragic style: 'Me voilà délaissé! Je suis seul en ce monde!/ Il n'est plus à ma voix personne qui réponde!' [Here I am, abandoned! I'm alone in this world! No one is left to answer me!] Then, in prose, he adds, 'N'importe, parlons toujours; ne fût-ce que pour n'en pas perdre l'habitude. Ah! Que nous allons faire un beau soliloque! Quel dommage de n'avoir point d'auditeurs! Que de bons mots perdus!' [Never mind, let's go on talking if only so as not to lose the habit. Oh what a fine soliloquy I'm going to deliver! Too bad no one is listening! What a waste of fine words!] This tonal variety from sublime to grotesque characterises the entire play.

Arlequin-Deucalion realises that he has landed on Mount Parnassus, home of Apollo and the Muses. Piron, who had seen the official theatres personified at the Foire Saint-Laurent in 1721, brings on the Tragic Muse Melpomène (la Comédie Française), sighing and groaning, followed by the Comic Muse Thalie (l'Italienne), singing jargon and dancing; both try to speak but Arlequin prevents them. The act ends as acrobatic dancers appear from nowhere, rejoicing that the flood has passed.

Act 2 opens with Deucalion's wife Pyrrha (probably played by Mme Francisque) arriving on the back of Pegasus. Believing she is the sole survivor of the flood, she mimes her despair, and then falls asleep. Apollo, representing the Opéra, arrives, playing the 'sleep aria' from Destouches' opera *Issé* on his flute. Arlequin returns from visiting the other Muses, all of whom have refused his offer to help them repopulate the earth. He claims that he is the only remaining healthy male because 'Apollon n'est qu'un efféminé. Depuis des

---

[7] See *Piron*, ed. Juvigny, vol.1, pp. 39–45.

[8] See Derek F. Connon, 'Piron's Arlequin-Deucalion: Fair play or Anti-fair Play?', in *Essays on French Comic Drama from the 1640s to the 1780s*, ed. Derek Connon and George Evans (Berne, 2000), pp. 127–38.

siècles qu'il est avec neuf filles, ne sont-elles pas encore pucelles?' [Apollo's just a pansy. For centuries he's been with nine girls, and they're still virgins?] Seeing Apollo paying court to the sleeping Pyrrha, he drives the god away with a hail of blows. The mimed recognition between Deucalion and Pyrrha which follows parodies the recognition scene from Crébillon's tragedy *Rhadamiste et Zénobie*. When Pyrrha explains in gestures that she is dumb, Arlequin indulges in comic misogyny: 'Hé bien, j'avais le bonheur d'être veuf; je ne le suis plus: patience! Elle est muette; du moins, il n'y a que demi-mal.' [Well, I was lucky to be a widower; now I'm not one any longer. Be patient! She's mute at least; that's the glass half-full.]

While Pyrrha mimes her joy, Arlequin exits and re-enters mounted on a mock-Pegasus, a turkey covered with playbills including those for two recent failed tragedies, Marivaux's *La Mort d'Annibal*, and Voltaire's *Artémire*, from which Arlequin declaims some lines. The unruly Pegasus carries him into the sky and Francisque returns with a daring leap from high above the stage. Believing that only they are left to re-populate the earth, the couple seek advice from the oracle at the temple of Themis. When the temple doors open: 'L'Amour & une jeune Grâce exécutèrent un pas de deux qui fut fort applaudi: c'était le début de Mademoiselle Sallé & de son Frère, devenus depuis si célèbres.'[9] [Cupid and a young Grace performed a *pas de deux* that was much applauded; this was the début of Mlle Sallé and her brother, who have since become so famous].

At the opening of act 3, Francisque can make no sense of the oracle's command that he and Pyrrha should throw their grandmother's bones over their shoulders: 'C'est-là de l'algèbre.' [It's all algebra.] Oracles, Arlequin suspects, speak clearly only in return for ready cash; this is the first of Piron's many anti-clerical jibes. Arlequin offers to forgive Apollo for flirting with Pyrrha if he can explain the oracle, but the god is so unhelpful that Arlequin again drives him off with a beating.

Unlike a traditional comedy, the final act suddenly becomes darker in tone. Arlequin now examines the contents of the barrel on which he had arrived. Finding an *Almanac of the Nobility of Thessaly*, he hopes that his new post-flood family will laugh at the many social inequalities of the past. Finding a pair of pistols, he ponders on mankind's need to kill, but then, terrified when one gun accidentally goes off, he hurls the pistols into the sea, with a pun on the name of Louis Fuzelier ('fusil', or pistol). He is about to do the same with the next object from the barrel, a bag of money which provokes even darker reflections on the crimes committed in its pursuit, but

---

[9] 'Note de Piron'. This is how Juvigny cites the notes Piron made to his manuscripts, to be cited henceforth as '(Piron)'. *Arlequin-Deucalion* was not in fact the children's debut. Piron had not yet arrived in Paris when they first appeared at the Foire Saint-Laurent in 1718.

he is halted by the thought that the money might move the Oracle (the greedy clergy) to help him further.

The last object to emerge is the puppet Polichinelle, who immediately begins to speak in the high-pitched, strident voice created by the 'sifflet-pratique' in the mouth of an actor beneath the stage,[10] a trick, Piron gleefully records, which no one had expected, as puppets had always had free speech at the fairs. Polichinelle introduces himself as Momus, the god of fools and madmen, and explains that the oracle refers to the earth as grandmother and the stones are her bones. Arlequin thanks Polichinelle for his unexpected wisdom; the latter replies, with a pun on the name of rival playwright Lesage: 'Pourquoi le fou, de temps en temps, ne dirait-il pas de bonnes choses, puisque Le Sage, de temps en temps, en dit de si mauvaises?'[11] [Why should not the fool, from time to time, say wise things since the wise man [Lesage], from time to time, says such bad things?] Tired of talking nonsense, Polichinelle begs to be thrown into the sea and Arlequin obliges.

Following Polichinelle's instructions, Arlequin-Deucalion and Pyrrha now set about repopulating the earth by throwing the stones over their shoulders. Five men and four women appear. The first four men are clearly recognisable as a peasant, a tradesman, a swordsman, and a lawyer. The men fight, until separated by Arlequin. He expresses admiration for the innocent, hard-working ploughman; warns the artisan against the corruption of city life; scolds the swaggering soldier; and is revolted by the sight of the fourth man, the ugly and grasping lawyer. The identity of the fifth man is at first far more puzzling. He wears:

> une large calotte sur la tête,[12] une perruque à la cavalière en bourse, une longue barbe de capucin,[13] un petit collet,[14] un habit de couleur, une épée au côté, un paquet de plumes à la main, un bas blanc, un bas noir, une culotte rouge d'un côté, noire de l'autre, etc., etc., etc.

---

[10] The device is known in English as a swazzle, still to be heard in British seaside Punch and Judy shows.

[11] 'M. le Sage, dont on jouait alors les Pièces, dans la loge voisine, aux Marionnettes' [Monsieur Lesage, whose plays were then being given in the next booth, by marionnettes] (Piron).

[12] 'Espèce de petit bonnet qui est surtout en usage parmi les gens d'Église' [type of small bonnet which is chiefly used by churchmen]: *Dictionnaire de l'Académie Française* (1878).

[13] The Friars Minor Capuchin are distinguished by their long beards.

[14] 'Les petits collets, se disait des ecclésiastiques. On disait aussi figurément, Le petit collet, pour désigner la profession ecclésiastique' [small bands, a term used of churchmen. 'The small band' is also used figuratively to designate the ecclesiastical profession.]: *Dictionnaire de l'Académie Française* (1878).

[a large cap on his head, a wig with side curls and tail, a long capuchin beard, a small white neck band, a coloured coat, a sword at his side, a packet of quill-pens in his hand, one white stocking, one black stocking, breeches red on one side, black on the other, etc., etc., etc.].

Although dangerous satire is veiled by this bizarre costume, Arlequin suddenly realises that the fifth man represents the clergy, and he explains the absence of a fifth woman with a contemptuous reference to priestly celibacy:

> Ah! J'y suis! Il n'en a que faire pour se multiplier. La race n'en sera que trop nombreuse, sans que le mariage s'en mêle. Ainsi que Prométhée, mon grand-père, ils se perpétueront sans avoir jamais chez eux de femme en couche.

> [Ah! I have it! He doesn't have to do anything in order to multiply. There will be far too many of this race, without marriage getting involved. Like my grandfather Prometheus, they will perpetuate themselves without ever having a woman in bed.]

Comparing a scene in Piron's later comedy *Les Enfants de la Joie* (1725), Walter Rex convincingly suggests that 'l'épée', 'la calotte', and 'la plume' 'combine to make sense if one assumes that Piron is attacking not only the priesthood, but the entire Church in its cruellest role as persecutor – *l'infâme* – at its most infamous.' Piron is clearly implying that the Catholic Church is a protean monster, endlessly transforming itself through a variety of disguises: the small white neckband of the society abbé; the scarlet and black of the secular priests, canons, deans, bishops, archbishops and cardinals; and the various habits of the religious orders. Rex comments 'How the Commissaire, who we know was present at performances of this play, can have let this derogation of the priesthood pass uncensored, we may never quite understand.'[15] However, I believe Piron goes even further in his denunciation of the clergy than Rex has suggested. Arlequin distinguishes two types among these men without women:

> J'ai connu de ces gens-là à milliers avant le déluge. Les uns nous en menaçaient de la part des dieux offensés: les autres nous chantaient les mœurs innocentes des premiers temps; et tous accumulaient les crimes et grossissaient l'orage.

> [I knew thousands of these types before the flood. Some of them threatened us in the name of the offended gods; others sang the praises of the innocent manners and customs of ancient times; and they all piled up their crimes and swelled the storm.]

---

[15] Rex, *Attraction*, pp. 70–1.

Here, the preachers of punishment for sinners are distinguished from a very different class, those who praise the 'innocent' customs of ancient times. Just a year after the première of Delisle's immensely popular *Arlequin sauvage* at the Comédie-Italienne, and at a time of growing curiosity about the unusual sexual customs of 'les sauvages', the words 'les mœurs innocentes des premiers temps' must have suggested not only harmless Edenic pastimes but, more disturbingly, the sexual licence associated with the New World 'sauvages', especially practices such as the ritual abduction of boys by older men.[16] Contemporary writers, including the baron Lahontan and Jean-François Lafitau, had given the public an appetite for accounts of 'la vie sexuelle des sauvages', which were received with a mixture of fascination and revulsion.[17] Arlequin's reference to the crimes that had led to the flood suggests not only Deucalion's deluge but Noah's Flood and the destruction of Sodom and Gomorrah. At this point, Piron was clearly attacking the sexual deviance of the contemporary clergy,[18] and very probably the reputation of one man in particular.

In 1719, the ex-Jesuit writer Pierre-François Guyot Desfontaines was in the service of the Abbé d'Auvergne: Saint-Simon records that Henri-Oswald de La Tour d'Auvergne was so notorious a pederast that even the libertine regent, the duc d'Orléans, was shocked when asked to nominate him as Archbishop of Tours.[19] When Piron arrived in Paris he may well have heard among the café gossips that, although distinguished as a journalist and man of letters, Desfontaines was also notorious because of his predilection for 'les petits Savoyards', the young ragamuffin chimney-sweeps of Paris.[20] In the early 1720s it was widely known that Desfontaines had been placed under police surveillance, denounced by an informer, accused of sodomy, flogged, and imprisoned.[21] Voltaire and Piron shared a mutual loathing for Desfontaines,

---

[16] See Jean-Noël Laurenti, *Valeurs morales et religieuses sur la scène de l'Académie royale de Musique (1669–1737)* (Geneva, 2002), p. 203. Jean-François Lafitau's *Mœurs des sauvages Américains comparées aux mœurs des premiers temps* was submitted for publication in 1722, and appeared in 1724.

[17] See Rudi Bleys, *The Geography of Perversion: Male to Male Sexual Perversion outside the West and the Ethnographic Imagination, 1750–1918* (New York, 1995), especially Chapter 1.

[18] On the relevance of this topic see D. A. Coward, 'Attitudes to Homosexuality in Eighteenth-Century France', *Journal of European Studies*, X (1980), 232–55.

[19] Duc de Saint-Simon, *Mémoires sur le siècle de Louis XIV et la Régence* (Paris, 1858), vol. 12, p. 247.

[20] 'L'abbé Duval des Fontaines, attire chez lui des jeunes gens pour les corrompre, et il en fait souvent coucher avec lui.' [The Abbe Duval des Fontaines attracts young men to his house to corrupt them, and he often makes them lie with him.]: François Ravaisson, *Archives de la Bastille*, vol. 12 (Paris, 1881), pp. 102–3.

[21] See Thelma Morris, *L'abbé Desfontaines et son rôle dans la littérature de son temps* (Oxford, 1961), pp. 25–7.

whom Voltaire called 'ce pesant abbé, /Brutalement dans le vice absorbé' [this heavy abbé sunk brutishly into vice].[22] Voltaire also approvingly quoted one of the over fifty epigrams that Piron later wrote against Desfontaines: 'Il fut auteur, et sodomite, et prêtre.../ Bien fessé fut, et jamais corrigé.' [He was an author, a sodomite, and a priest[...],/ He was well thrashed, and never corrected.].[23] It seems to me that, if Piron had one example of the perverted clergy in mind at this time, it must surely have been the abbé Desfontaines.

La Harpe, in his *Cours de Littérature* (1760), was among the first to point (disapprovingly) to the revolutionary implications of the closing scenes of *Deucalion*.[24] On the other hand, Sainte-Beuve, writing in the 1860s, lightly dismissed any such serious intent: 'Malgré ces boutades d'un bon sens bariolé d'humeur, il ne faut voir en toutes ces pages que de la gaieté gauloise...'[25] [Despite these sensible quips shot through with good humour, we should see in these pages only Gallic gaiety and mockery]. With specific reference to the end of *Deucalion*, Walter Rex vehemently disagrees with Sainte-Beuve:

> What an extraordinary comedy to compose in 1722! Piron's dramatic *renversement* amounts to an overthrow of the entire social structure, something like the great Revolution *en germe* [...] There was nothing else like it at the time. Even his "rival," Voltaire, never launched such a broadside attack on the upper classes.[26]

But the sheer virulence of Piron's attack on the social order and, especially, clerical perversion, is carefully masked and interrupted by a sudden change of tone. On hearing the sound of a cuckoo Arlequin reproaches the first four men for not waiting even one generation before reintroducing cuckoldry into this brave new world. In the final *divertissement*, the Sallé children reappear and all ends with singing and dancing. According to Juvigny's *Vie de Piron*, the Marquise de Mimeure and Voltaire were in the audience at the first performance of *Deucalion,* and Voltaire expressed his displeasure at Piron's

---

[22] 'Le Anti-Giton', *Œuvres Complètes de Voltaire*, vol. 20A, *Œuvres de 1739–1741*, ed. Nicholas Cronk et al. (Oxford, 2003), p. 521, lines 47–8.

[23] 'A M..., sur le Mémoire de Desfontaines', *Œuvres Complètes de Voltaire*, vol. 28A, *Œuvres de 1742–1745*, ed. Oliver Ferret, Russell Goulbourne, et al., Oxford, 1968–2010) p. 60.

[24] As Auguste Font put it, 'peu s'en faut qu'il ne rende responsable des massacres révolutionnaires l'auteur de cette curieuse bagatelle ...' [he comes close to blaming the author of this curious trifle for the massacres of the Revolution]: Auguste Font, *Favart, L'Opéra-comique et la Comédies-Vaudeville aux XVIIe et XVIIIe siècles* ([Paris, 1894] repr. Geneva, 1970), p. 94.

[25] *Œuvres choisies de Piron*, ed. Jules Troubat; introduction by Charles-Augustin Sainte-Beuve (Paris, 1866), pp. 14–15.

[26] Rex, *Attraction*, p. 72.

ironic quotation of a line from one of his unsuccessful tragedies.[27] News of Piron's theatrical début and Francisque's one-man *tour de force* spread rapidly. *Deucalion* ran for thirty performances, a figure previously unrivalled at the fairs and only ever again equalled by Piron himself with *Le Caprice* in 1724.

L'Antre de Trophonius

Several writers wrongly assume that the official theatres were closed throughout 'the season of Lent'.[28] In fact it was on the eve of Palm Sunday (one week before Easter) near the end of Lent that they were obliged to close for two weeks, reopening a week after Easter Sunday. At Saint-Germain, an ancient ecclesiastical dispensation allowed the fair and the players to continue into Holy Week. Thus, for one week, the fair players had no competition, something of which they and their spectators took full advantage.[29] In the circumstances, as Piron wrote, quoting Lully's opera Amadis, 'Je brillais seul en ces retraites' [I shone alone in this solitude]; his new work, *L'Antre de Trophonius*, was bound to benefit from the lack of competition. After the success of *Deucalion*, Piron wrote that he wanted to see whether he could move from monologue to dialogue, which the authorities were now prepared to allow; the result was his very first opéra-comique, a remarkably assured début for a mere beginner.

L'Antre de Trophonius is loosely based on the Greek legend of the treasure-filled cave and oracle of Trophonius in Boeotia. The opening scene finds Arlequin and Scaramouche sitting in the middle of a forest with a money box which Arlequin has stolen from his master, the rich old financier Agrippain. Arlequin gloats that, thanks to this new wealth, he will soon be as courted and flattered as he was avoided and despised when he was poor – a comment that may well reflect Piron's own feelings on his experience in Paris in 1719.

Arlequin still loves the fickle Marinette, even though she had flirted with Monsieur Agrippain, and now that he is rich he will ask her to leave the old man and return to him. As two thieves approach brandishing pistols, Scaramouche runs away. Replying to the classic challenge of 'La bourse ou la vie!' [Your money or your life!], Arlequin asks, 'Êtes-vous procureur? Êtes-vous Médecin?' [Are you lawyers or doctors?] Like Molière, Piron is saying that lawyers rob you and doctors kill you. When the thieves claim to be taxing those they meet in the forest, Arlequin claims that as a nobleman he

---

[27] Piron, *Œuvres complètes*, ed. Juvigny, vol. 1, pp. 43–5.

[28] See Derek Connon, *Identity and transformation in the plays of Alexis Piron* (London, 2007), p. 18, n.19; Chahine, 'Fuzelier', vol.1, p. 181.

[29] 'Ce mince privilège était ressenti comme une revanche ironique par les forains eux-mêmes et par les spectateurs [qui] accouraient nombreux à ces spectacles' [This slender privilege was felt to be an ironic revenge both by the fairground performers and by the crowds who flocked to these spectacles]: Lagrave, *TP*, p. 266.

is exempt from taxes. The thieves' reply that they are 'des espèces d'Arabes vivants sous la loi d'innocence. Noblesse et roture chez nous, sont synonymes' [a kind of Arabs living under the law of innocence. Among us, nobleman and commoner are synonymous]. Then they make off with the money box. Scaramouche returns with belatedly drawn sword, and as night falls the penniless friends begin a comic *lazzi* of lamentation. The thieves reappear, now disguised as priests with high pointed hats and long beards. Arlequin and Scaramouche accept an invitation to become ministers of Trophonius, and there follows a cynical exchange exemplifying Piron's anticlericalism. The fake priests openly admit that 'L'habit ici fait le Ministre' [here, clothes make the minister] and demonstrate how to act the part: 'Allongez vos mines; soyez graves, et tenez les yeux baissés' [Make long faces, look serious, with downcast eyes]. They reveal the cynical strategies employed by the clergy to rob the credulous faithful, 'nos dupes': after the pilgrims have made an offering, they are drugged and dragged down into a cave, where they are subjected to frightful images. The priests then dismiss their hapless victims and gloat over their ill-gotten gains. Doctors and lawyers could be mocked on the stage with impunity, but this denigration of the clergy was both daring and dangerous in 1722.

Agrippain arrives to ask the oracle about his stolen money box and his plan to marry Marinette. As the disguised Arlequin and Pierrot drag the old man into the cave, Marinette and Olivette arrive. Marinette is furious that Arlequin has deserted her and declares that she would like to hang him. Arlequin, who has been eavesdropping, throws off his priest disguise and offers his belt as a noose; the couple enact a parody of the scene in Corneille's *Le Cid* in which Rodrigue begs to die by the hand of his beloved Chimène.[30] Once they are reconciled, Arlequin explains the Trophonius swindle and Olivette tells them they owe a votive candle to Mercury, patron of thieves. At once, the god himself appears, providing an excuse for Piron to introduce a completely extraneous topical scene playing on the name of the journal *Le Mercure*, whose editor, the playwright Fuzelier, had abandoned Francisque's troupe. Arlequin learns that he has recently been mentioned in the press:

Arlequin. J'étais Arlequin-Deucalion; et Deucalion-Arlequin était moi; et moi lui? ...A-t-il réussi? Ai-je réussi? Avons-nous réussi?

Mercury. Réussi, coussi, coussi.[31] Vous parliez trop morale, et disiez trop de vérités. Cela n'a pas plu également à tout le monde.

---

[30] Piron's note on this scene: 'On doit ici se rappeler l'irrégularité d'un Théâtre Forain, où l'Acteur et le Spectateur, à tout moment se confondaient dans l'action, et se supposaient réciproquement instruits de la bonne ou mauvaise plaisanterie du moment.' [Here we must remember the irregularity of the Fair Theatre, in which Actor and Spectator were constantly mixed up in the action, and both were supposed to be reciprocally aware of the latest good or bad joke of the moment.]

[31] Coussi coussi; Comme ci, comme ça, from the Italian cosí cosí.

[*Arlequin.* I was Arlequin-Deucalion; and Deucalion-Arlequin was me; and I him? Did it succeed? Did I succeed? Did we succeed?

Mercury. Succeed, so so. You spoke too much morality and told too many truths. That did not please everyone equally.]

Piron was clearly aware of the critical reactions of fellow playwrights to his biting satire and, by way of revenge, he made Mercury ridicule all the plays in the contemporary Paris theatres. He later wrote that, although this scene was greeted with laughter, the authors mentioned in it never forgave him. After this topical interpolation, Agrippain, who has been shown terrifying visions of cuckoldry in the cave, agrees to let Arlequin keep the money box and marry Marinette, and he offers the young lovers the wedding feast he had prepared for himself. In the brief vaudeville finale, with music by l'Abbé, Arlequin bemoans the straitened circumstances of his beleaguered troupe: 'La Foire est pour nous cette année,/ L'Antre de Trophonius.'[32] [This year the Fair is for us/ The Cave of Trophonius].

The Fire at Lyon

At the close of the Foire Saint-Germain at the end of March, Francisque's company made its way to Lyon. Proof of their presence there is to be found in the baptismal certificate of Jeanne Malter, daughter of Jean-François Malter, 'maître à danser', on 25 April 1722, in the Church of St Croix.[33] Signatories at the baptism were Francisque himself and Étienne Sallé. The register contains the extraordinary statement that the archbishop of Lyon had given permission for Antoine Jassinte and Jeanne Gaillardet, wife of Francisque's brother Guillaume, to be godparents, although they are listed as 'comédiens' and their status as actors would normally have disqualified them.[34] The fact that Guillaume's wife Jeanne had been asked to be the child's godmother suggests an already close relationship between the Moylin and Malter families.

During the night of Monday 8 June, fire broke out in the theatre in the Hôtel du Gouvernement in the old town of Lyon. A contemporary account in

[32] In the first edition of the play, Piron headed the text 'Francisque', not 'Arlequin', revealing the extent to which, for him, the two were interchangeable.

[33] Two years earlier, at the wedding of Jean-François, his brother had signed the register, listed simply as 'Malter frère'. The brother is most likely to have been Aubin-Jean-Michel, or Jean-Baptiste-Nicolas, usually known as Jean-Baptiste Malter. This is the first of many references to links between the Moylin family and the Malters, who were also a dynasty of performers.

[34] AM Lyon, registre 415 (Ste-Croix). The Archbishop of Lyon, François Paul de Neufville de Villeroy, was one of a long line of distinguished Villeroy family members who supported music and theatre. When one considers that the great tragedienne Adrienne Lecouvreur was to be denied Christian burial in Paris in 1730, the Archbishop's permission is no small matter.

Léonard Michon's manuscript *Journal de Lyon* blames it on 'les Comédiens Italiens étrangers' and on the negligence of the concierge, noting that the city would have to bear the full cost of the repairs, including damage to nearby properties, since they had no way of getting anything from 'ces misérables Comédiens dont la plupart même se sont sauvés'[35] [these wretched actors, most of whom have fled]. The gravity of the situation was reflected in the minutes of the City Council in 1723, which mention paying 7,836 livres for public expenses and another 8,000 livres to the theatre's proprietors whose furnishings were largely destroyed, as were the actors' own possessions.[36] This was the first recorded theatre fire to affect Francisque's company, but not the last.

When Francisque returned to Paris in the summer of 1722, Piron made the disastrous fire the subject of an amusing prologue to his next play, *Tirésias*, with which Francisque hoped to reestablish his fortunes. However, the company found that they did not have permission for even a single speaking actor. Juvigny's introduction to the play makes it clear that, after several unsuccessful attempts to bend the authorities, Francisque and Piron decided to take the law into their own hands, despite their awareness of the danger of this act of defiance.[37]

In the prologue to *Tirésias* the members of the company appear as themselves and it begins with Francisque-Arlequin and his wife arriving from Lyon, ruined by the fire. A passing gentleman commiserates with them and Francisque jokingly attributes his black mask to the effects of the fire. When asked to describe the scene, Francisque replies simply '*Infandum*'. The classically educated gentleman at once catches the allusion to Virgil's *Aeneid* and retorts, 'Va te promener avec ton *renovare dolorem*.'[38] [Go to hell with your *renovare dolorem.*] Like Aeneas, telling Queen Dido of the destruction of Troy, Francisque continues, '*Quamquam animus meminisse horret...incipiam.*'[39] On that dreadful night, says Francisque, he dreamed that the company was performing *Le Jeune Vieillard* and the public were throwing smoke bombs in disgust. (*Le Jeune Vieillard* – by Fuzelier, Lesage, and d'Orneval, with music

---

[35] *Journal de Lyon, ou Mémoires historiques et politiques de ce qui s'est passé de plus remarquable dans la ville de Lyon et dans la province depuis le commencement du XVIIIe siècle*, 7 vols in folio. MS, Musée Gadagne, Lyon, Inv. N 24811.

[36] *Inventaire-Sommaire des Archives Communales antérieures à 1790: Ville de Lyon*, ed. M. F. Rolle (Paris, 1865), Vol. 1, pp. 185–6.

[37] Piron, *Œuvres Complètes*, vol. 4, pp. 339–40. Juvigny's biography claims that at the time of *Deucalion* Francisque had already been the victim of a fire in Lyon. In fact, the fire occurred four months after *Deucalion* and before *Tirésias*.

[38] 'Infandum, regina, jubes renovare dolorem.' 'O Queen, you order me to renew unspeakable grief.' Virgil, *Aeneid*, Book 2, line 3.

[39] 'Though my mind shudders to remember ... I will begin.' (lines 12–13).

by Mouret –was the opening play of the Italians' rival season at Saint-Laurent on 25 July. Piron obviously added this topical detail months after the fire at Lyon.) Then he awoke to find a real fire, but hadn't the heart to wake his sleeping wife, although she would have burned to death: a typical misogynist joke. He now quotes Boileau:

> Car le feu, dont la flamme en ondes se déploie,
> Fait de notre quartier une seconde Troie. [40]

> [For the spreading waves of fire and flame,
> Make our neighbourhood a second Troy.]

The gentleman, taking pity on the actors, gives them the money he had intended for an opera girl.

Le Docteur arrives and Francisque greets him with more Virgil; '*Quibus, Hector, ab oris, expectate, venis?*'[41] Le Docteur happily quotes even more Virgil but Colombine puts a stop to what she calls 'votre chien d'argot' [your damned lingo]. With the arrival of Scaramouche, Latin is replaced by Italianised French; 'nous avons hourousement escapé du fou' [We luckily escaped the *fou* (madman) / *feu* (fire)]. Pierrot arrives happy to have escaped, thanks to the fire, not from girls (*pucelles*) but from fleas (*puces*) which had been plaguing him.

A poet, Monsieur Sans-Pair, offers them his new play about the Danaids. But, on learning that the play requires not only the barrel on which Arlequin arrived onstage in *Deucalion*, but fifty nuptial beds, fifty daggers, fifty princes and princesses, and so on, the exasperated Francisque tells Sans-Pair to take his play to the 'Quinze-Vingts' (the madhouse). Le Docteur now reveals that he had written a play called *Tirésias* for the company to perform in Lyon. Francisque agrees to present it but warns the actors that, although it might have been good enough for the suburbs of Lyon, in Paris they might face another roasting.

Arlequin Tirésias

The play opens with largely spoken scenes of sexually suggestive banter between Tirésias and the Innkeeper Mopse; the main plot of Tirésias' transformation does not get underway until the appearance of Jupiter late in act one. The god, who had once impersonated Amphitryon in order to seduce his

---

[40] Boileau, *Œuvres* (2 vols, Paris, 1969), Vol.1, Satire 6, *Les Embarras de Paris*, lines 107–8.

[41] 'From what shores, long-awaited Hector, do you come?' *Aeneid*, Book 2, lines 282–3.

wife, wants to repeat the trick with Tirésias' fiancée Cariclée. When Tirésias refuses, Jupiter punishes him by changing him into a woman. Cariclée, who suspects Tirésias of infidelity, disguises herself as a man and pursues him. The transformed couple meet but do not recognise each other. Tirésias, now Tirésie, is coquettish and flirtatious, has already had a serious dalliance with Mopse, and now makes advances to the disguised Cariclée. In the meantime, Juno has pursued her fickle husband and the two gods argue about who receives more pleasure in sex, men or women. Juno argues for men, Jupiter for women. Tirésias who has been both man and woman, is called upon to arbitrate and he sides with Jupiter. As a punishment, Juno turns him back into Tirésias. After further complications, Cariclée in turn sheds her disguise and is reconciled with Tirésias.[42]

Much of what has been written about *Tirésias* is inaccurate. The *Mercure* refers to it as '*la Vengeance de Tirésias ou le Mariage de Momus.*'[43] There is no such play as *La Vengeance de Tirésias*; *Le Mariage de Momus* is a separate comedy, performed later, and it has nothing to do with *Tirésias*. The Parfaict *Mémoires*, followed by Pascale Verèb, are equally misleading in stating that *Tirésias* was performed with life-sized marionettes.[44] In fact, Francisque's marionettes were not made until the first performance of *Le Mariage de Momus* and they could not have been used in *Tirésias*. Furthermore, Piron's footnote makes it clear that, at the moment of Francisque's transformation into the female Tirésie, 'Son masque tombe, et Francisque paraissait à visage découvert. Comme il était jeune et beau garçon, la métamorphose faisait beaucoup d'effet.'[45] [His mask falls, and Francisque appeared with his face uncovered. As he was a handsome young man, the transformation was very effective.] (In 1722, Francisque would have been in his early thirties.)

Paul Chaponnière maintained that '*Tirésias* est la plus grivoise des farces de foire'[46] [*Tirésias* is the most ribald of the fairground farces]. It does indeed have many examples of ribaldry: most notably, the conversation between the innkeeper Mopse and Tirésie leaves no doubt that in their illicit nocturnal rendezvous their *coitus* was far from *interruptus*. As a result, Tirésie fears she may have to let out her belt: 'Que dira-t-on de moi? N'avoir pu être vingt-quatre heures honnête fille.' [What will people say about me? Couldn't remain

---

[42] For a fuller synopsis, see Jean Baudrais, *Petite Bibliothèque des Théâtres contenant un Recueil des meilleures Pièces du Théâtre François, Tragique, Comique, Lyrique et Bouffon, depuis l'origine des Spectacles en France, jusqu'à nos jours* (78 vols, Paris, 1783–88), vol. 52, pp. 143–5.

[43] *Mercure*, September 1722, p. 181.

[44] Parfaict, *Mém.*, vol. 2, p. 8; Pascale Verèb, *Alexis Piron, poète (1689–1773): la difficile condition d'auteur sous Louis XV* (Oxford, 1993), p. 100.

[45] Piron, *Œuvres Complètes*, vol. 5, p. 273.

[46] Chaponnière, *Piron*, p. 40, n. 4.

an honest girl for twenty-four hours.] Along with lively comic dialogue for the lower orders (with echoes of Piron's native Burgundy in the peasant speech of Mopse), much of the play's originality lies in Piron's surprisingly subtle examination, particularly in the exchanges between Jupiter and Juno, of the notions of male and female psycho-sexual identity, the only elements of the Tirésias legend which he retained. The delicately handled scenes of seduction between Tirésias-Tirésie and Cariclée, with both lovers in travesty, are years ahead of their time in both tone and content.[47] Although there are many sung airs, as befits an opéra-comique, the growing predominance of spoken dialogue suggests that Piron already aspired to move towards a more elevated genre. Parfaict says that *Tirésias* 'n'eut pas un succès trop marqué' [was not particularly successful] and the playwright Carolet mocked it with a parody, also unsuccessful, written for the marionettes of Dolet.[48] Juvigny on the other hand claims that the play provoked uproarious laughter from every corner of the theatre. The commissaire, whose job it was to ensure that the actors did not speak, reported that respect for the distinguished audience (which must have included the aristocracy) prevented him from interrupting the play.[49]

But the many qualities of this witty and original comedy have been overshadowed by the offstage drama that followed its first and only performance. According to Juvigny, the moment the curtain fell, Francisque and his entire company were arrested and imprisoned on the grounds of the play's obscenity. Although Piron wrote a long letter in Francisque's name to the Lieutenant of Police, the marquis d'Argenson, this was not, as scholars have hitherto believed, a plea to release him from prison. Although he refers to *Tirésias,* internal evidence in his letter makes it clear that it was written many weeks later, after his next play had been shut down. Piron insists that he would never have submitted *Tirésias* to the censor (who had evidently read and passed it) if he had thought there was anything offensive in it. Arguing that the official theatres ought to be held to higher standards than the fairs, he then offered examples of greater indecency in the 'Théâtre réglé, ou soi-disant tel' [the so-called regulated theatre], such as Legrand and Riccoboni's *Polyphème* at the Comédie-Italienne. Since *Polyphème* was first performed on Monday

---

[47] Piron may well have seen Francisque's performance in 1720 in Barbier's *Arlequin cru Colombine et Colombine cru Arlequin; ou, l'Heureux Naufrage*, in which an enchanter transforms Arlequin into Colombine and Colombine into Arlequin.

[48] Parfaict, *Mém.*, vol. 2, p. 9.

[49] *Tirésias* vanished without trace from the French stage but, faithful to his old friend, Francisque gave three performances of it in London at the Little Haymarket in 1734–5.

31 August, and Piron's letter refers to a performance 'il y a quinze jours' [two weeks ago], he could not have written his letter before mid-September.[50]

If Francisque had been in prison (for which, apart from Juvigny's claim, there is no documentary evidence), he was soon released, but with a total ban on speaking. In despair, he ordered a set of marionettes (Fuzelier in the *Mercure* says that they were almost life-sized) and asked Piron for a new play. Piron hurriedly wrote *Le Mariage de Momus, ou La Gigantomachie*. However, these large marionettes were so clumsily handled on the full-sized stage that the performance was greeted with hoots of derision. The playbill outside the theatre proclaimed '*Quae sit rebus fortuna videtis!*' [you see the state our affairs are in], yet another quotation from the *Aeneid* (2.350). In the *Mercure*, Fuzelier mocked the use of a Latin quotation on a fairground poster,[51] and Piron replied in a long letter. He had, he declared, used the grandiloquent quotation out of 'une indulgence aveugle que j'eus pour le pauvre Francisque, qui veut toujours jeter quelque héroïsme sur ses guenilles' [blind indulgence on my part for poor Francisque, who always wants to drape his rags with heroism]. But he then pointed out that Fuzelier had misunderstood the quotation, taking the word *fortuna* to mean good fortune, whereas in both its Virgilian and its present context it meant something like 'sorry plight' – in this case, the fact that the superbly eloquent Francisque had been reduced to acting with marionettes. Fuzelier chose not to publish Piron's letter but it was included in Juvigny's *Œuvres Complètes*.

Le Mariage de Momus ou La Gigantomachie

Piron's borrowing of the story of *La Gigantomachie* is probably the first example of the influence of his friend (later his wife) Marie-Thérèse Quenaudon, Mademoiselle de Bar. She was renowned for her knowledge of early French literature and may well have introduced Piron to Scarron's *Typhon ou la Gigantomachie* (1644), a burlesque version of the battle between the gods and the Titans. In Piron's retelling, the gods of Olympus are asleep from boredom. Momus wakes them with the warning that the Titans are preparing to depose them. The gods ignore the warning and the irreverent mockery of Momus makes Jupiter decide to put an end to his jollity by marrying him off. When the Titans approach, the frightened gods flee in all directions. Jupiter and Momus go to Egypt where they interview a series of people who want to change their lot; but their complaints are rejected as ridiculous. Meanwhile, Silenus and his donkey, unaided, put the Giants to flight, and the gods return to Olympus. Jupiter, still intending to marry off Momus, offers him a vast

---

[50] All quotations from this letter are from Piron, *Œuvres Complètes*, ed. Juvigny, vol. 4, pp. 442–6.
[51] *Mercure*, September 1722, p. 180.

choice: Diana, the three Graces, and the nine Muses. Momus rejects all of them, especially the old-fashioned tragic and comic Muses, Melpomène and Thalie. In their place he chooses 'une Muse encore toute neuve, jolie comme l'Amour, gaie, badine, amusante' [a brand-new Muse, pretty as love, gay, amusing and playful], namely La Foire. 'C'est dommage pourtant qu'elle soit muette' [But it's a pity she's dumb]. For this, he declares, the Italians are to blame: the jealous Thalie cut out her tongue. But Momus still chooses La Foire because she embodies the best qualities of her parents, Bacchus and Vénus.[52] It is clear that the real slayer of giants (the official theatres) is this brave new goddess, La Foire.

Towards the end of the fair, Francisque obtained permission to perform this play with live actors and it then fared better. But this latest permission was short-lived, and on 25 September the Lieutenant Général ordered Francisque's theatre to be closed. This dramatic event is described in a *procès-verbal*, reproduced by Campardon, in which we get a rare glimpse of Francisque's wife, Marie-Catherine. When the officials had made their announcement, closed the doors of the theatre, and stationed two guards at the doors, they were confronted by a woman, 'laquelle s'est mise à crier et tenir des discours insolents contre nous' [who began to shout and insult us]. Ordered to contain herself, she instead provoked such a disturbance that the guards arrested her and several other women in order to prevent a full-scale riot.[53] The women were finally released after apologizing for their behaviour. It seems clear that it is to this event, not to the opening night of *Tirésias,* that Piron was referring in the latter part of his letter to d'Argenson:

> Son ardeur à me nuire, l'affectation de venir fermer la loge, avec tout l'éclat qu'il a pu, & à main armée, quand tout se serait anéanti à l'aspect de l'ordre qu'il cachait malicieusement, la violence enfin, qu'il exerce sur mes Camarades & sur moi; tout cela marque bien moins un Officier amateur de l'ordre, qu'un homme emporté, qui se sert odieusement des armes sacrées de la Justice, pour satisfaire un mécontentement particulier.
>
> [His keenness to harm me, the affectation of coming to close the theatre, with all the show which he could muster, and armed with weapons, when all would have been settled on sight of the order which he maliciously concealed; lastly, the violence with which he treated my comrades and me; all this is less the mark of a lover of good order than of a man out of control who odiously uses the sacred weapons of Justice to satisfy a personal grudge.]

---

[52] For a longer summary, see Baudrais, *Petite Bibliothèque*, vol. 52, pp. 149–50.
[53] Campardon, *SF*, vol.1, pp. 342–3.

Francisque describes himself (in the words Piron wrote for him) as 'un malheureux [...] contraint, par sa misérable profession, à errer de pays en pays' [an unhappy fellow [...] constrained by his wretched profession to wander from land to land], then begs for the protection of the great and the good. According to Juvigny, d'Argenson was annoyed by the tone of this letter but took no further action.

After this troubled season at the Foire Saint-Laurent, the Cochois family, with Marguerite Cochois in the advanced stages of pregnancy, went ahead (probably with the rest of the company) to Metz, a garrison town on the eastern border of Lorraine, where they may have performed for the troops. The Cochois' eldest daughter, Barbe (known as Babet), was born there on 23 January 1723.[54] Francisque did not accompany his family to Metz but, probably with his brother Guillaume, joined forces with Antoni de Sceaux and the performers from all the Paris theatres who took part in a lavish entertainment known as Les Fêtes de Chantilly, given by the duc de Bourbon to celebrate the coronation of Louis XV.[55] *Le Mercure* for November 1722 describes the contribution of the fairground performers, which took place at the end of the King's visit to the menagerie of wild animals. The Duke's music master, Aubert, dressed as Orpheus, played his violin in a woodland setting and the acrobats, disguised as the wild animals that the young king had just seen, gave a remarkable imitation of their cries and movements. Dacier claims, though without giving his source, that Francisque was much admired for his agility in the role of a bear leaping from branch to branch to escape from pursuing dogs.[56] After Chantilly, he did not rejoin his family, but stayed on in Paris for the Foire Saint-Germain.

The Foire Saint-Germain of 1723

Although 1722 had been a difficult year for both Francisque and Piron, Piron's gifts as a comic dramatist were by now so appreciated that he was invited to write for each of the three companies which performed at the Foire Saint-Germain.[57] Only one of these companies concerns us here and it reveals a surprising realignment of forces. Dolet and Delaplace abandoned the marionettes with which they had mocked Francisque just months earlier and joined forces with him. Although no company was granted a licence from the Opéra,

---

[54] AM Metz, GG 64 (St-Gorgon).
[55] Parfaict, *Mém.*, vol.1, p. 20.
[56] Dacier, pp. 16–17.
[57] See Parfaict, *Mém*, vol. 2, p. xx. Arthur Heulardt thought it doubtful that Francisque performed at this fair: Heulhard, *La Foire Saint-Laurent, son histoire et ses spectacles* (Paris, 1878), p. 176. Piron's own notes on the text of *L'Endriague*, however, prove that Francisque remained in Paris until February 1723.

Dolet's troupe and Piron were given an unusual commission by no less a person than the director of the Opéra himself, Nicolas Francine. Francine asked Piron for a work including recitatives, arias, and a chorus in the grand manner, to enable a young singer, Mlle Petitpas, to demonstrate her skill in the tragic genre as a test piece for her entrance to the Opéra. This was the origin of Piron's next piece, *L'Endriague*. Piron called on the services of a fellow Burgundian recently arrived in Paris, the still unknown Jean-Philippe Rameau, whose music (his first for any theatre) must have been among the grandest ever heard at the fairs. The score is lost, but scholars believe that some pieces were incorporated into Rameau's later works.[58]

Like the monster of its title, Piron's *L'Endriague* is a hybrid of styles and genres thrown together partly as a vehicle for Mlle Petitpas and partly to annoy the official theatres. The plot is a lighthearted send-up of the mythological and chivalric themes of tragic opera: innocent virgins sacrificed to a hideous monster, a sinful people punished by a cruel god (Popocambéchatabalipa), and a maiden rescued by a knight errant (the chevalier Espadavantavellados), with the *commedia* characters Arlequin, Scaramouche, Le Docteur and Marinette thrown into the mixture. The inspiration for the mock-medieval aspects of the plot almost certainly came, again, from Piron's friend Mlle de Bar. The monster of the title, L'Endriague, takes its name from the old Spanish romance *Amadis de Gaule*.[59] The name Espadavantavellados combines the Spanish original of the knight *Amadis*, 'el Caballero de la verde espada', with a joke on French 'avant' and Spanish 'al lado', with a Spanish 'llosa' thrown in for good measure. In the account of the play given in the *Dictionnaire des Théâtres de Paris*, probably based on a lost manuscript, the Chevalier has the much simpler French name of Percemaroufle [Pierce-booby]. This name gives more point to Popocambéchatabalipa's remark to Arlequin that the Chevalier will accomplish 'la plus grande aventure qui fut mise onc à fin par les Perceforêt, les Perceval et tous les grands Perceurs de l'univers' [the greatest adventure that was ever accomplished by the Perceforêts, the Percevals and all the great Piercers of the universe].

The High-Priest who feeds the maidens to the monster is Caudaguliventer, a mock-Latin mixture of tail, gullet and stomach, perhaps an echo, again thanks to Mlle de Bar, of Rabelais' Grandgousier. The name of the High-Priest's son Elfridérigelpot is less easy to deconstruct. In the *Dictionnaire des Théâtres* this character's name is given as Nicaise, an old French saint's name; the word Elfridérigelpot may conceal a private joke to which we have lost the

---

[58] See C. Girdlestone, 'Rameau's Self-Borrowings', *Music and Letters* 39:1 (1958), 5, and Graham Sadler, 'Rameau, Piron and the Parisian Fair Theatres', *Soundings* 4 (1974), 13–29.

[59] *Le Tiers Livre de Amadis de Gaule*, trans. Nicolas Herberay, le Seigneur des Essarts (Paris, 1542), Bk 3, chapters 9 and 10.

key. The outlandish name of the invisible genie Popocambéchatabalipa certainly has Latin-American echoes (Popocatepetl, Atahualpa); Scarron's *L'Héritier ridicule* (1649) also refers to Attabalippa and Arlequin uses the form 'Popocambêche Atabalipa' when comically mispronouncing the name of the genie.

The action takes place on the island of Vazivéder (Vas-y/Vedere, or Go and See), where the beautiful young prisoner Grazinde (played by Mlle Petipas) is about to be sacrificed to the monster Endriague. Grazinde prays to be rescued by her devoted knight errant and bewails her fate in an aria by Rameau. Rameau also composed the 'horror' music for the sacrifice scene, which must have been an impressive spectacle. (Piron had probably seen a similar one in *L'Isle du Gougou*.) When the monster appears the chorus sings in a kind of pidgin Italian-Latin jargon, 'Ouvra la bocca, Signor Endriaga! ouvra la bocca. Gorgibus avala, devora barbara!' Piron's footnote describes the enormous monster, which had the body of a crocodile and filled nearly the whole stage. Four men inside it moved its giant legs and opened its jaws (nine or ten feet high) to devour Grazinde.

Arlequin-Francisque does not arrive until Act 2, when he is surprised to find everyone, including his friend Scaramouche, turned to stone. This is because Popocambéchatabalipa, after expressing his rage in a grand aria by Rameau, has chosen to punish his people for their subservience to the monster. From this probably sublime music, Piron deliberately descends to the grotesque: a chorus praising the god in the vulgar refrains of a typical opéra-comique:

> Vive notre gran papa,
> Le brave Atabalipa:
> Po, po, po, ca, ca, ca [...]

Arlequin learns that Grazinde is in the belly of the monster and that when her knight errant rescues her all the frozen inhabitants will return to normal, except for the spot they were touching at the moment of petrification, which only Espadavantavellados can heal. When the monster next appears, the acrobatic Francisque makes a daring leap into its mouth, which closes at once. Piron's note explains what happened next:

> L'Endriague s'en allait. Mais à peine avait-il le dos tourné, qu'au moyen d'un culbute, Arlequin, sortant par-derrière, se présentait en face du spectateur.

> [L'Endriague went off, but hardly had he turned his back when, with a leap, Arlequin came out from behind and presented himself to the audience.]

Francisque gets Popocambéchatabalipa to release Scaramouche and the reunited friends steal food from the petrified townsfolk. Scaramouche wanders among them and offers a series of thumbnail sketches of a range of dubious characters. Meanwhile, Arlequin has found his master, the chevalier Espadavantavellados. The outlandish French in which the Chevalier addresses him was probably the work of Mlle de Bar, who, according to Juvigny,[60] could imitate medieval French authors perfectly: 'Or me narre en brief l'émerveillable devis du gentil & courtois Enchanteur, & comme aussi, sans détourbier aucun, tu sus de ce corps tien transpercer le Diable, en qui m'Amie a son tripeux manoir' [Pray now tell unto me in brief words the tale most wondrous of yon noble and courtly Enchanter, and also tell how thou, without trouble to thy person, didst with this thy body transpierce yon Devil, within whose bowels my beloved makes her dwelling]. When the monster reappears, Arlequin re-enters it from behind and eventually exits by 'une route plus honnête que la première fois' [a more decent route than the first time]. After killing the monster, the Chevalier is reunited with Grazinde and the townsfolk are reanimated – though even Espadavantavellados cannot melt the lawyer's heart of stone. Finally, Terpsichore appears and begs the knight to help the Comédie-Française, where the latest boring comedy has turned its audience to stone. The final singing and dancing (probably led by Francis and Marie Sallé, who had remained in Paris with their father) is set to new music by Rameau, and the vaudeville warns the ladies to beware of human 'croqueurs de pucelles' [devourers of virgins].

Though *L'Endriague* was described as 'Pièce en trois actes, en monologues',[61] and though, as Françoise Rubellin points out, it is largely made up of long speeches by single speakers,[62] it cannot strictly be said to be a monologue. From the very first scene, Piron signals his intention to create something more complex, using the monologue form to denounce the restrictions placed upon Francisque over the preceding three years, especially by the Italians. Piron draws attention to the artificiality of the genre in the conversation between two commedia characters, le Docteur who tries to maintain silence, and the 'dumb' Marinette who is determined to speak. Her outburst, ostensibly a lament for the fate of Grazinde, could equally be (like

---

[60] Piron, *Œuvres complètes*, vol. 1, p. 108. Honoré Bonhomme reproduces a letter that she wrote to Piron 'en vieux gaulois' which bears a striking resemblance to the mock Middle French of Piron's *Chevalier Espadavantavellados*: see Piron, *Œuvres inédites, prose et vers, accompagnées de lettres adressées à Piron*, ed. H. Bonhomme (Paris, 1859), p. 77, n. 2.

[61] Parfaict, *Dict.*, vol. 2, p. 395.

[62] I am grateful to Professor Françoise Rubellin of the University of Nantes for allowing me to read the manuscript of her forthcoming edition.

the reference to the cutting out of La Foire's tongue in *Le Mariage de Momus*) an attack on the repeated prohibitions:

> Je veux parler coûte que coûte ... Si j'étais muette, véritablement muette, je ferais ce que je pourrais pour ne point parler; mais avoir à la contrefaire en toute occasion, cela me passe ... Enfin, dussé-je être jetée au monstre, mangée, croquée, avalée, digérée, je veux parler, je parlerai.

> [I want to speak whatever the cost ... If I were mute, really dumb, I would do all I could to stay silent; but constantly having to pretend, it's too much ... Anyway, even if I'm thrown to the monster, eaten, chewed up, swallowed and digested, I want to speak, I will speak.]

Piron exaggerates to the point of caricature the various monologue scenes. At one point when le Docteur and Marinette are warned, 'Et surtout ne dites mot de ceci à personne!' [And above all, say nothing of this to anyone!], the 'dumb' Marinette replies 'Ne craignez rien! Vous ne songez donc pas que nous sommes des muets!' [Have no fear! Have you forgotten we are dumb?] However, throughout the scene in which Arlequin and Scaramouche are reunited, all pretence of monologue is abandoned, and the same is true of the Chevalier's exchanges with Arlequin which, despite the Middle-French, are not mere jargon. *L'Endriague* can only be described as true opéra-comique, using no fewer than twenty-five popular airs to take the action forward.

Piron had quickly absorbed the styles and techniques of Lesage, Fuzelier and d'Orneval and in many ways surpassed them. But behind his seemingly effortless wit, there was, from the outset, a preoccupation with more serious matters: an unjustly hierarchical society, the construction of gender psychology, and the financial greed and sexual perversions of the clergy. His moments of absurd hilarity distracted the censor, who passed even *Tirésias* without a murmur. Piron had a horror of overt moralizing and firmly believed in the corrective power of laughter. But his quips and epigrams can be as bitterly incisive as those of his sparring partner Voltaire. Goethe was among the first to note, in his brief but perceptive essay on Piron, the originality of these early works for the fairs;[63] more recently, Derek Connon has also called them the best examples of Piron's 'wit and invention' and 'moral and psychological subtlety'.[64] In spite of severe opposition, Alexis Piron, aided and abetted by Francisque, had gone overnight from provincial nonentity to Parisian playwright.

---

[63] Johann Wolfgang Goethe, 'Alexis Piron', *Goethes Werke* (Stuttgart, Tübingen, 1830), vol. 36, pp. 195–8.

[64] Derek Connon, *Identity and Transformation in the Plays of Alexis Piron*, p. 170.

Francisque left Dolet's troupe after the performances of *L'Endriague* and in March 1723, accompanied by a certain Le Tellier,[65] he arrived in Metz where his sister Marguerite and his new-born niece awaited him. According to Henri Tribout de Morembert, Francisque's company gave fifty performances in Metz, a lengthy season by any standard, and, as the theatre had to close for Easter from 20 March to 5 April, the company must have stayed on throughout April in order to achieve that number.[66] No account of the repertoire has survived but it would surely have been drawn from the company's performances in London and Paris between 1718 and 1722.

Emile Dacier claimed that in 1723 the Sallé children left for the provinces with their uncle.[67] According to the *Nouveaux Mémoires*, however, they were with their father at the Foire Saint-Laurent in the summer of 1723. This is confirmed by the fact that they appeared in Dolet's company in August 1723 and in 1724 they danced in Piron's *Le Claperman* and *La Conquête de la Toison d'or* by Lesage and d'Orneval.[68] It would seem that both children continued to dance at the fairs and to train at the Opéra until they returned to London in 1725.

Having left Paris in March 1723, Francisque did not return until July 1726. But although he was gone, Francisque-Arlequin was, as we shall see, far from forgotten.

---

[65] This appears to be Jean François Letellier, whose family had worked at the Fairs since the 1680s as actors, puppeteers, and authors. A Nicolas Le Tellier had been present at the wedding of Guillaume Moylin in Lyon on 1 July 1715 and the Letellier family were at the Foire Saint-Laurent later that month alongside Francisque. See Campardon, *SF*, vol. 2, pp. 73–6.
[66] Henri Tribout de Morembert, *Le Théâtre à Metz* (Paris, 1952), vol. 1, p. 39.
[67] Dacier, p. 17.
[68] *Ibid.*

7

A provincial interlude and a Paris triumph: 1724–1726

The Foire Saint-Laurent 1724

Francisque Moylin and his company are mentioned nowhere in contemporary published accounts of the Foire Saint-Laurent of 1724. And yet his presence hovers ghostlike in the repertoire of that fair in a way which has never been analysed or explained. After three not particularly successful seasons (1721–23), the Comédie-Italienne did not return to the Foire Saint-Laurent.[1] The splendid theatre they left behind was taken over by Maurice Honoré, a man with no theatrical experience apart from supplying candles for the stage. At great expense, he obtained a licence from the Opéra, the first such licence since 1721. Honoré embellished the premises even further and put together a new company, described in some detail in the *Mémoires*,[2] for which he secured the services of Fuzelier and Piron. Fuzelier's opening prologue on 25 July stressed the link with the former tenants: *Le Déménagement du Théâtre ci-devant occupé par les Comédiens Italiens, et à présent réuni au Domaine de la Foire* [*The Vacating of the Theatre formerly occupied by the Italian Players, now reunited with the Domain of the Fair*].

But Honoré's new enterprise did not go unchallenged; Dolet and Delaplace had managed to acquire the right to speak and Lesage and d'Orneval agreed to write three prose plays for them, *Les Captifs d'Alger* (prologue), *La Toison d'or* and *L'Oracle muet*. These were so successful that on the third day Honoré obtained an order forbidding Dolet's troupe to speak; but a few days later Dolet was given permission to perform *par écriteaux*. As Anastassia Sakhnovskaia-Pankeeva writes, 'Nous sommes en pleine guerre – une de ces petites guerres qui animaient perpétuellement la vie théâtrale foraine et que la grande guerre

---

[1] Their one brief moment of triumph was Dominique's *Agnès de Chaillot*, a parody of de la Motte's tragedy *Inès de Castro*. For more on this play, see below, pp. 228–9.

[2] Parfaict, *Mém.*, vol. 2, pp. 19–20.

avec les Comédiens Français fait souvent oublier.'[3] [We are in the middle of a war – one of those little wars that constantly animated the theatrical life of the fairs and which the major battles with the Comédie-Française often make us forget.]

Only one element of the season's internecine comic warfare directly concerns us here, namely Fuzelier's prologue *Les Dieux à la Foire*, first performed by Honoré's troupe on 22 September. The list of roles given at the head of Fuzelier's manuscript contains a curious feature.[4] Opposite three of the characters' names are written the names of three contemporary actors: 'Jupiter – M. Jacinte; La Fortune – Mlle de Lisle; Gilles – M. Cauchois.' *Mercure* is listed as played by 'Arlequin' and Pierrot is left blank. Loïc Chahine, in his brief mention of this text, takes the list of actors at face value, and cites in support a note in one of the two known versions of the manuscript, stating that it seems to have been played by Francisque's company.[5] However, this presumption cannot be correct, and this cast list cannot be factual. Fuzelier wrote this prologue for Honoré's troupe, and not one of these extremely well-known players, including Francisque himself, is mentioned in Parfaict's five-page account of Honoré's new company for this fair.[6] Francisque and his company had been far away in the French provinces since early 1723. It is therefore impossible that, as claimed by Léon Chancerel and others, Pierrot's ass in Piron's *L'Âne d'or*, performed at the Foire Saint-Laurent on 16 August 1724, was played by Francisque.[7] Of the performer of this role, Piron wrote that 'cet Arlequin' [this Arlequin], as he called him, had the unusual gift of braying like an ass.'[8] Piron would never have called his friend 'cet Arlequin'; it is clear from the Parfaict *Mémoires* that Honoré's Arlequin was Le Bicheur.[9]

---

[3] Anastassia Sakhnovskaia-Pankeeva, 'Chronique d'une petite guerre. Autour d'une parodie inédite de Lesage: *La Reine des Péris*', in *Séries parodiques au siècle des Lumières*, eds Sylvain Menant and Dominique Quéro (Paris, 2005), pp. 41–54, at pp. 48–9.

[4] Ms. BnF fr 9336 ff. 34–5.

[5] (Ms. BnF fr 9336 & Musique Rés. Th 8) Loïc Chahine, *Louis Fuzelier, le théâtre et la pratique du vaudeville* (doctoral thesis, 3 vols, University of Nantes, 2014), vol. 1, p. 177. Chahine suggests that Jacinte was in Honoré's troupe in 1724, but, given the fact that Mlle de Lisle, Francisque and Cochois were not there, I believe this is highly unlikely.

[6] Parfaict, *Mém.*, vol. 2, pp. 19–24.

[7] Léon Chancerel, *Les Animaux au Théâtre* (Paris, 1950), vol. 1, p. 29. This claim has been repeated by others, e.g., Isabelle Martin, *L'Animal sur les planches au XVIIIe siècle* (Paris, 2007), p. 235.

[8] Piron, *Œuvres Complètes*, vol. 3, p. 405.

[9] Parfaict, *Mém.*, vol. 2, pp. 20–1.

What, then, is one to make of the presence of the names of members of Francisque's company at the head of the manuscript of *Les Dieux à la Foire* and of Francisque's own name in the text? I believe that it is possible to throw new light on some aspects of this unusual prologue. To begin with its supposed cast list: the role of Jupiter is attributed to Jacinte. Antoine Hyacinthe had been part of Francisque's companies at the fairs since 1718 and was with Francisque's troupe in Lyon in the summer of 1722. He is mentioned nowhere else in the 1724 season, nor does his name appear in the list of players Loïc Chahine gives for the following year. Mercure, played by 'Arlequin', must have been Le Bicheur, but is evidently intended to represent Francisque Moylin, who, as Fuzelier would remember, had played Mercure in *La Boîte de Pandore*. No performer's name is given for Pierrot, but Jean-Baptiste Hamoche, who had been Francisque's Pierrot at the Foire Saint-Laurent of 1721, was in Honoré's company. According to the *Mémoires* he became ill and only recovered towards the end of the fair;[10] but as *Les Dieux à la Foire* came late in the season it seems likely that Hamoche played Pierrot, an important role containing the longest speeches in the prologue. Perhaps his name was not given because the other names were part of an *imaginary* cast list. Paradoxically, Pierrot-Hamoche was the only member of the old 'troupe du Sieur Francisque' who was *literally* present in 1724.

The 'Cauchois' playing Gilles (a character who makes only a brief appearance) is clearly meant to be Francisque's brother in law, Michel Cochois, who was first listed as the Gilles of Francisque's company in 1718 in both Paris and London. The name Cochois/ Cauchois appears nowhere else in the 1724 seasons.[11] Mademoiselle de Lisle, supposedly playing La Fortune, was certainly *not* present at this fair; had she been, the *Mercure* (and later the *Mémoires*) would surely have informed their readers of the fact. When she did join Honoré's troupe the following year at the Foire Saint-Germain in February 1725 her appearance in the role of L'Occasion in *L'Audience du Temps* led the *Mercure* to comment approvingly, 'L'Occasion est représentée par la Dlle de Lille [sic], qui *en reparaissant sur ce Théâtre-là*, [emphasis added] lui a rapporté des agréments qui lui manquaient.'[12] [L'Occasion is played by Mlle de Lille [sic], who *by reappearing on this stage*, brings back to it the graces it lacked.] This comment would hardly make sense if Mlle de Lisle had already been part of the company in the previous year.

---

[10] *Ibid.*, p. 24.

[11] The Cauchois spelling is found elsewhere. Michel was present at the baptism of his daughter Barbe in Metz in January 1723, and presumably played a part in the long season given there by Francisque and Le Tellier, remaining with Francisque's company in the provinces.

[12] *Mercure*, March 1725, pp. 559–60. Cf. Campardon, *SF*, p. 239.

The first scene of *Les Dieux à la Foire* is set in the fairground, where Jupiter meets Mercury and tells him how, on the lookout for amorous adventures, he had wandered near a dark and deserted theatre, where he saw an old yellowing playbill and heard ghostly Italian voices which, mistaking him for the Jupiter of the Italian theatre, called him to return. They also cried, 'Nos chandelles brûlent' [Our candles are burning], which was both a way of saying the stage was ready and a dig at Honoré, the former 'maître chandelier'. Terrified of being asked to behave like a god, Jupiter has fled to the nearby marionette theatre and swapped his divine robes for a dressing gown and slippers. In this first scene, there is no explanation of the darkened theatre, old playbill, or Italian voices. It gradually becomes clear, however, that the action is not taking place in the present but is referring back to the opening of the Foire Saint-Laurent of 1721, when the Italians first came to the fair, Lalauze held the *privilège* of the Opéra-Comique, and Francisque and his company, including Hamoche, Jacinte, Mlle de Lisle and Michel Cochois, were (at first) merely an unlicensed troupe of Forains.

> *Mercure.* Dites-nous s'il vous plaît de quelle troupe vous êtes?
>
> *Pierrot.* De quelle troupe je suis! Belle demande! Il n'y a qu'une troupe à la foire. […]
>
> *Jupiter.* Compte, maraud, compte! L'Opéra-Comique, Les Italiens, et la troupe deFrancisque.
>
> *[Mercure.* Please tell us which troupe you belong to?
>
> *Pierrot.* Which troupe I belong to? What a question! There is only one troupe at the Fair. […]
>
> *Jupiter.* Count, you fool, count! The Opéra-Comique, the Italians, and Francisque's troupe.]

Pierrot insists that, because both the Italians and Lalauze had given themselves grandiose titles in 1721, Francisque's company is the only genuine *troupe foraine*.

> *Pierrot.* Compte toi-même, vieux fou, et compte bien. Primo, l'Opéra-Comique n'est point une troupe, cela s'appelle l'Académie Foraine de Musique.[13] […] Il est vrai que la Comédie Italienne est une troupe, mais elle n'est point à la foire quoi qu'elle soit à deux pas de nous.

---

[13] A play on the official title of the Opéra; 'l'Académie royale de musique.'

Jupiter. La Comédie Italienne n'est pas à la Foire?

Pierrot. Non, elle est au faubourg St. Laurent, lisez plutôt ses affiches.[14]

Mercure. Ma foi! Pierrot a de la logique.

Pierrot. Ergo, il n'y a à la foire que la troupe de Francisque et vous en voyez un échantillon.

Jupiter. Vous êtes de la troupe de Francisque? C'est fort bien fait à vous.

Mercure. On dit que je ressemble à ce coquin-là.

Pierrot. Assurément vous vous ressemblez comme deux gouttes d'encre.

[*Pierrot.* Count for yourself, you old fool, and count properly. Primo, the Opéra-Comique is not a troupe, it is called the Fairground Academy of Music.[…]. It is true that the Comédie Italienne is a troupe, but it is not at the fair although it is just a couple of steps away.

Jupiter. The Comédie Italienne is not at the fair?

Pierrot. No, it is in the Faubourg St Laurent, just read their posters.

Mercure. My word! Pierrot is logical.

Pierrot. Ergo, at the fair there is only Francisque's troupe and you see a sample of it before you.

Jupiter. You belong to Francisque's troupe? Well done.

Mercure. They say I look like that rascal.

Pierrot. For sure, you are as alike as two drops of ink.]

Pierrot's line, which varies the standard phrase 'comme deux gouttes d'eau' [like two drops of water], is not only an allusion to Arlequin's black mask, but also, surely, an admission that Francisque was present only in the ink of Fuzelier's text. One of the many curious aspects of *Les Dieux à la Foire* is that scenes 4 and 5 are devoted to a discussion of someone (Francisque) who is not even present. There is absolutely no evidence that Francisque was in

---

14 The Italians called themselves 'Le Théâtre du Faubourg S. Laurent.'

Paris, and yet Fuzelier makes him *textually* present in ways whose significance would not have been lost on contemporary audiences.

When Jupiter asks what Francisque's troupe does, Pierrot replies that 'Nous sommes tous orateurs' [We are all orators] – because they were forbidden to sing or dance. Urging the gods to enter the show, he adds:

> Vous n'y courez aucun risque de vous casser le cou. Nous ne voiturons pas les dieux en l'air dans des machines de sapin, ils arrivent sur notre théâtre en pantoufles.
>
> *Jupiter.* Cela est fort commode. J'aime mieux être piéton que de m'exposer dans ces chars de carton doré qui brillent chez nos voisins, une corde n'a qu'à manquer...
>
> *Mercure.* ... et voilà le dieu à tous les diables.[15]
>
> [*Pierrot.* You run no risk of breaking your neck. We don't send the gods flying through the air in pinewood contraptions, they come on stage in slippers.
>
> *Jupiter.* Very comfortable. I'd rather go on foot than appear in those gilded cardboard chariots which glitter at our neighbours' place; a rope only has to break ...
>
> *Mercure.* ... and the god goes to the devil...]

Having firmly established the date and place of the action as the Foire Saint-Laurent of 1721, Fuzelier makes a further reference to the repertoire of that season with the arrival of La Fortune, 'played by' the absent Demoiselle de Lisle.

> *Jupiter.* Que vois-je? La Fortune à la Foire St Laurent! [...]
>
> *Pierrot.* Eh! quoi Madame Fortune! Vous avez abandonné ce riche palais à colonnes dorées qu'on allait voir comme les Tableaux changeants?[16]

---

[15] In a footnote to *Le Mariage de Momus* Piron says that such an accident had just taken place at the Opéra.

[16] 'Tableaux changeants' were a novelty invented by Jean Boinard: painted scenery which could be altered by means of sliding parts. C. Dugasseau, *Notice des tableaux composant le musée du Mans: précédée d'une notice Historique* (Le Mans, 1870), p. 28. There is a comic scene concerning the tableaux changeants in Legrand's *La Foire de Saint-Laurent* (Comédie-Française, 1709). See Joseph La Porte and J. M. B. Clément, *Anecdotes dramatiques* (Paris, 1775), vol. 1, p. 385.

[*Jupiter.* What do I see? Madame Fortune at the fair! [...]

Pierrot. What, Madame Fortune! Have you deserted that rich palace with its gilded columns which people went to see like the Moving Pictures?]

Fuzelier here refers to the lavish sets and decorations for *Danaé,* the Italians' opening play of their first season at the fair in 1721. Parfaict noted that the set representing the Palace of Fortune, was highly praised;[17] as the *Mercure* wrote: 'douze colonnes torses, cannelées, rehaussées d'or, forment un riche vestibule; elles tournent continuellement entre leurs bases & leurs chapiteaux; symbolisant l'instabilité de la Fortune'[18] [twelve twisted, fluted columns, embellished with gold, form a rich vestibule; they rotate continually between their bases and capitals, symbolizing the instability of Fortune].

When Fortune says that she wants to visit 'le théâtre du pauvre Francisque' [the theatre of poor Francisque], Pierrot retorts:

Pierrot. Pauvre vous-même, Madame La Fortune. Si nous ne faisions pas de dépense pour divertir le public, c'est qu'on nous ordonne de le divertir *in puris naturalibus.*[19]

La Fortune. Ne vous fâchez pas, mon cher Pierrot, je ne viens pas insulter à vos malheurs, je viens plutôt les soulager.

Mercure (à Pierrot). On n'exige de vous ni pluie de clinquant ni roue de Tombac; on ne veut seulement que de la dépense d'esprit.

[*Pierrot.* Poor yourself, Madame Fortune. If we don't spend money to entertain the public, it's because we've been ordered to entertain them *in puris naturalibus.*

La Fortune. Don't be angry dear Pierrot, I haven't come to mock your misfortune but rather to relieve it.

Mercure (to Pierrot). We don't ask you for showers of tinsel or wheels of cheap glitter; we only want you to dispense your wit.]

---

[17] Parfaict, *Mém.,* vol. 2, p. 238.
[18] *Mercure,* August 1721, p. 111.
[19] I.e., naked. Arlequin-Mercure, played by Francisque in *La Boîte de Pandore* (Foire Saint-Laurent 1721), had said that the company is obliged to 'donner des comédies toutes nues.'

They are of course referring to Jupiter's mythological golden shower and the glittering wheel of Fortune which were part of the stage set for *Danaé*. The very stage on which Fortune's gilded temple had appeared now merely represents the fairground, 'le préau de la Foire', a witty twist to the *mise en abîme* which often occurs in polemical plays at the fairs. Honoré's actors are pretending to be Dolet's actors pretending to be Francisque's company, and they are caricatures rather than characters.

The contrast between ostentatious wealth and unadorned talent is a recurring theme of this season in the troupes of both Honoré and Dolet, but nowhere more so than in the end of this prologue which almost imperceptibly shifts back to the present. The gods have come down firmly on the side of the underdog. Jupiter agrees with Mercury that the actors don't need the elaborate décor of Honoré's troupe: 'vous donnez des pièces sans décorations et vos voisins donnent des décorations sans pièces.'[20] [You give plays without décor and your neighbours give décor without plays.] Pierrot laments the fickle nature of audiences who are easily won over by mere spectacle and goes on to announce the evening's entertainment as *La Matrone de Sève* and *La Revue du Régiment de la Calotte*. In reality, the two plays which followed this prologue were *Les Bains de Charenton* and *Les Vendanges de Champagne*. This discrepancy has puzzled commentators.[21] But, as I hope to have shown, the prologue began not in current real time but in an 'espace imaginaire.'[22] It is a parody within a parody, and Pierrot-Hamoche is simply playing with words, as his description of the setting for the *imaginary* play *La Matrone de Sève* makes clear.[23] Pierrot, now seemingly on behalf of the rival troupe of Dolet, asks the gods and the audience to use their imaginations to conjure up the lavish décor which he *describes* in painterly detail: Fuzelier may have been making another ironic point here, since it was well known that Le Bicheur, the Arlequin of Honoré's troupe, was a painter, and married to a painter's daughter. No doubt in keeping with this supposed performance *in puris naturabilis*, the prologue contains no sung airs and ends without the customary vaudeville.

---

[20] In *La Boîte de Pandore* (Foire Saint-Laurent, 1721), Francisque had told the audience that, 'Plaire à l'esprit est donc notre unique ressource.' [Pleasing the mind is therefore our only resource].

[21] See Chahine, *Fuzelier*, vol. 1, p. 177.

[22] Francisque's 1721 season did not, of course, take place in Pellegrin's theatre which, as Pierrot reminds the gods, was occupied by the Italians.

[23] Pierrot offers no comment on *La Revue du Régiment de la Calotte*, apparently a playful reminder of *Le Régiment de la Calotte* from Francisque's repertoire of 1721 which Fuzelier had co-written with Lesage and d'Orneval.

The one high point of Honoré's programme was Piron's *Le Caprice,* which ran for thirty performances.[24] Fuzelier's last play of the season, *L'Assemblée des Comédiens,* features a personification of La Discorde, which may reveal that the author himself was unhappy with the internecine squabbles of the rival troupes.[25] But he had already voiced his disquiet, for *Les Dieux à la Foire* is a rare kind of historical retrospective, in which the author rises above the petty quarrels to be found in parts of the Lesage-d'Orneval repertoire for Dolet, and looks back wistfully to the presence of Francisque's company at the Foire Saint-Laurent of 1721.

Lesage and d'Orneval's prologue, *Les Captifs d'Alger,* performed at the opening of Dolet's season, may contain a further clue to Fuzelier's curious decision to 'revisit' the fair of 1721. At the end of *Les Captifs,* we are told that the two bourgeois who had bought la Foire from its true owners, les Forains, had taken her onto a boat; the boat capsized and la Foire was drowned. Her body is carried in procession across the stage, followed by the grieving actors. Arlequin cries, 'Au diable les malheureux qui n'ont pas su gouverner la barque.'[26] [To hell with the wretches who could not steer the boat.] This funeral is a clear echo of *Les Funérailles de la Foire,* which Francisque had first performed in October 1718, and revived with *Le Rappel de la Foire à la vie,* when he won the licence from Lalauze in 1721.[27] The contemporary relevance of the funeral theme is evidenced by the fact that both *Les Funérailles* and *Le Rappel* were revived yet again at the Foire Saint-Laurent in 1725.

Sylvain Menant stresses that 'La parodie est par excellence inséparable d'une série, elle exige une lecture 'palimpsestueuse', selon le mot amusant de Philippe Lejeune. Car elle ne peut être que parodie d'un autre, ou d'autres textes.'[28] [Parody is above all inseparable from a series, and it requires, in the amusing word of Philippe Lejeune, a "palimpsestuous" reading, because it can only be a parody of another, or other texts.] There is another 'palimpsestuous' allusion to Francisque in Lesage and d'Orneval's prologue for Dolet's troupe,

---

[24] Juvigny and later critics have misunderstood a manuscript note by Piron concerning the success of *Le Caprice* as referring to *L'Âne d'or.* Parfaict makes clear that '*L'Âne d'or* fut faiblement reçu ... [*Le Caprice*] eut un grand succès': Parfaict, *Dict.*, vol. 2, p. 25.

[25] The title surely echoes *L'Assemblée des Comédiens,* a (lost) prologue written by Francisque's old friend Michel Procope-Couteaux and given at the Comédie-Française in September 1724.

[26] Parfaict, *Dict.*, vol. 2, p. 39.

[27] Cf. Pierrot's mock title, *La Revue du Régiment de la Calotte.* The point may be that in 1721 it was Pantalon, representing La Comédie-Italienne, who was admitted to the Regiment.

[28] Sylvain Menant and Dominique Quéro, eds, *Séries parodiques au siècle des lumières* (Paris, 2005), p. 10.

l'*Oracle muet*. The opening scene finds Arlequin as a fisherman, alone at the water's edge, hoping to catch something to revive his fortunes. This is an exact echo of the opening of the same authors' prologue from 1720, *l'Ombre de la Foire*, in which Arlequin-Francisque fished his dumb comrades from the lake into which their cruel enemies had cast them.

As Anastasia Sakhnovskaia-Pankeeva points out, the ludic nature of much of the onstage warfare of 1724 may be inferred from the fact that the following year Lesage and d'Orneval wrote for Honoré's troupe alongside Fuzelier, whom they had ridiculed throughout the previous Fair season. She notes the difficulty of distinguishing:

> les phrases dictées par l'antipathie personnelle d'un auteur envers l'autre, des passages "obligés" adressés au concurrents et où les railleries réciproques tiennent presque la place d'une échange de politesses; il est tout aussi difficile de les démêler des phrases dictées par un certain entrain ludique qui fait que les auteurs oublient les cibles réelles de leur satire et se livrent au jeu de l'invention et de l'imagination ...[29]

> [remarks dictated by the personal antipathy of one author towards the other from the "obligatory" passages addressed to competitors, in which the mutual jokes almost function as an exchange of courtesies; it is just as difficult to separate them from remarks dictated by a kind of playfulness that makes authors forget the real targets of their satire and engage in games of invention and imagination ...'.]

These points could not be more perfectly exemplified than in Fuzelier's bizarre and fascinating *Les Dieux à la Foire*, in which Francisque is both absent and present.

Parfaict reported that the Foire Saint-Laurent of 1724 overall was not successful.[30] In spite of the rather petty textual squabbles between Fuzelier (for Honoré) and Lesage and d'Orneval (for Dolet), it seems to me that there was on all sides an element of genuine distaste for the internecine warfare, and that Francisque and his company had become the symbolic embodiments of all that was best in the Théâtre de la Foire.

A year later, also because of Francisque, Honoré's company was able to end its season on a brighter note. September 1725 saw the unusual re-appearance of four plays by Lesage, Fuzelier and d'Orneval from Francisque's earlier successful seasons: *Les Funérailles de la Foire*, the *Rappel de la Foire à la Vie*, *Le Monde renversé* and *Les Animaux Raisonnables*. Such revivals were unusual: Piron himself pointed out that 'Les pièces de foire, en ce temps, une

---

[29] Sakhnovskaia-Pankeeva, 'Chronique d'une petite guerre', pp. 48–9.
[30] Parfaict, *Mém.*, vol. 2, p. 25.

fois passées, ne reparaissaient jamais.'[31] [In those days, plays at the Fair, once performed, never reappeared.] It could be that the revival of these topically significant pieces saved Hamoche and Honoré from disaster at a time when the fate of the Opéra-Comique once again hung in the balance. The performances were attended by the Duchess of Orleans and other members of the royal family.[32] The fair players had rarely been patronised by royalty since Francisque's performances for Madame at the Palais-Royal in 1718 and 1721. If indeed the memory of Francisque had come to the rescue of Honoré's company in 1725 it might help to explain why Honoré went into partnership with him at the Foire Saint-Laurent of 1726.

A Wedding in Marseille, 1725

In the summer of 1725 the Moylin company was in Marseilles, where they must have been performing in the crumbling old *jeu de paume* in the rue Pavillon, a narrow and insalubrious building which was the only theatre in the city until 1735. On 19 June they attended a grand family wedding. Francisque's niece Catherine Dussoye/Dusuisse of Toulouse, known as Catherine Labbé, married Jean-Baptiste Malter, 'maître à danser' from Bordeaux, in the church of St Ferréol. Catherine was the daughter of Elizabeth Dusuisse, sister of Francisque's wife Marie Catherine. Three years earlier, members of Francisque's troupe had been witnesses in Lyon at the baptism of a child of Jean-Baptiste's older brother. The Malter family was well-known in the world of dance, both at the Paris Opéra and in the French provinces.

The marriage certificate is an unusually detailed and informative document. It reveals that legal power of proxy to consent to the marriage was granted by the parents of the groom to Jean-Baptiste Gherardi on 14 May in Bordeaux, and, for the bride, proxy was granted in Toulouse by her widowed mother on 1 June to the Sieur Boniolo.[33] The wedding was also witnessed by 'François Moylin, oncle de l'épouse' and four of his musicians. Francisque seems to have been as close to his niece Catherine Labbé as to his other niece, Marie Sallé; with this marriage he also acquired a longstanding colleague. The Malter couple remained with Francisque's troupe for many years, and the locations

---

[31] Note to line 9 of 'Épître a Francisque' in *Piron: complément de ses œuvres inédites*, ed. Honoré Bonhomme (Paris, 1866), pp. 277–9.

[32] Parfaict, *Mém.*, vol. 2, pp. 31–2.

[33] Campardon records the presence of a member of the Bognolo/Bognoli family at the Comédie-Italienne. See *Les Comédiens du roi de la troupe italienne pendant les deux derniers siècles* ([Paris,1880]; repr., Geneva, 1970), vol. 1, pp. 50, 52, 216.

of the births and deaths of their numerous children probably indicate the presence of that troupe where no other evidence exists.[34]

The appearance of the name Gherardi is particularly interesting as it reveals a link between Francisque and the families of the old Comédie-Italienne. Jean-Baptiste Gherardi (b. 1696) was the son of Evariste Gherardi, member of the old Italian troupe and editor of *Le Théâtre Italien*. According to Campardon, Gherardi performed at the fairs from 1726 to 1734.[35] Not only was he in Francisque's company in 1726, but the wedding in Marseille indicates that his association with Francisque predates this by at least one year. And Gherardi must have already been a close friend of the Malter family to be invited to stand *in loco parentis*. He retained links with the Moylin family until at least 1736.

While he was in the south-west of France, Francisque wrote to his friend Piron. Although almost every written trace of Francisque (apart from his signature) seems to have disappeared, Piron's papers were preserved. In reply to Francisque's letter, he wrote a verse epistle which was first published by Honoré Bonhomme in 1866.[36] Bonhomme dated the *Epître à Francisque* to 1723 and Pascale Verèb followed him in her recent study.[37] But evidence within the text makes this date impossible, since the *Epître* mentions both Piron's *Le Claperman* (staged February 1724) and his triumphant run of *Le Caprice* for Honoré's company in August 1724. It could not, then, have been written before October 1724 at the earliest and probably dates from 1725 rather than 1723, 3 and 5 being two easily confused digits in manuscript. Piron's own long title explains the occasion:

> A Francisque, entrepreneur de l'Opéra-Comique, à qui j'avais promis d'accomoder pour lui en vers français et pour les théâtres de Province la Tragédie de Samson, en Italien, et qui, n'en ayant pas de nouvelles, m'écrivait que Samson était mort
>
> [To Francisque, director of the Opéra-Comique, to whom I had promised a French verse rendering for the provincial theatres of the Italian tragedy Samson, and who, having heard nothing from me, wrote to say that Samson was dead.]

---

[34] The known birth locations are: Tours (1726), Montpellier (1728), Grenoble (1729), Montpellier (1730), Montauban (1731), Rouen (1732), Brussels (1733), Lille (1734), and Toulouse (1740).

[35] Campardon, *Les Comédiens*, pp. 241–2.

[36] *Piron: complément*, ed. Bonhomme, pp. 277–9.

[37] Pascale Verèb, *Alexis Piron, poète (1689–1773): la difficile condition d'auteur sous Louis XV* (Oxford, 1993), pp. 106–9.

Piron explains that, after he had written one act of the verse tragedy that he had promised Francisque, the goddess of famine (rather than the tragic muse) had forced him to dash off a series of fairground plays, which he enumerates with disparaging comments. He ends by urging Francisque to return from the south. As part of the record of a remarkable friendship between the playwright and the actor who had launched his career, this Epistle deserves to be quoted in full.

Non, ne crois pas, ami, que je t'aie oublié:	No, friend, do not think that I have forgotten you:
Compte sur mon travail et sur mon amitié.	Count on my work and my friendship.
Ne crois pas Samson mort ; tu le verras paraître;	Do not believe Samson is dead; you will see him appear;
Comment le serait-il, étant encore à naître?	How could he be dead, as he is not yet born?
Pardonne, si je mets ta patience à bout:	Forgive me if I exhaust your patience:
Le sort, et non mon cœur, a disposé de tout.	It was fate, and not my heart, which decided everything.
Et jour et nuit pour toi puisant dans l'Hippocrène,[38]	For you by day and night, with draughts of Hippocrene,
Suivant tantôt Thalie, et tantôt Melpomène,	Inspired now by Thalia now by Melpomene,
Je mêlais, en cothurne ainsi qu'en brodequin,	I mingled, with the buskin and the comic sock,
Les fureurs de Samson aux lazzis d'Arlequin.	The fury of Samson and the tricks of Harlequin.
Déjà, du premier acte héroïque et burlesque,[39]	In my mind I had already woven
J'avais dans mon cerveau tissu le plan grotesque,	The heroic and grotesque plan of act one,
Lorsqu'une Déité, trop connue au rimeur,	When a goddess poets know too well,
Tout à coup, malgré moi, suspendit mon labeur.	In spite of me, suddenly interrupted my work.
Cette divinité, du Pinde est citoyenne;[40]	This goddess dwells on Mount Pindus

[38] Hippocrene: the sacred spring of the Muses, created when it was struck by the hoof of Pegasus.

[39] 'Je donnai ce premier acte en vers français à Romagnesy, qui le mit à la sauce qu'il voulut dans celui qu'il a donné en vers français au Théâtre-Italien.' (Piron) [I gave this first act to Romagnesi, who put it in the sauce he wanted in the French verse play that he gave to the Théâtre-Italien.]

[40] Pindus, a distant mountain in northern Greece, contrasts with Mount Olympus, home of gods and muses.

Il n'est si sainte loi qui ne cède à la sienne.	And no sacred law can defy her decrees.
C'est la FAIM qui vers moi tristement s'avança.	It was HUNGER which sadly bore down on me.
En vain j'aurais voulu me révolter contre elle:	In vain would I have resisted her advances:
Sous le poète à jeun Pégase n'a plus d'aile.	Under the hungry poet, Pegasus has no wings.
Celle qui sait des bois faire sortir les loups,[41]	She who lures the wolf from the woods
Du Sacré Mont aussi fait descendre les fous.	Can also bring mad poets down from the sacred mountain.
Laissant donc pour un temps Thalie et Melpomène,	So, leaving for a while Thalia and Melpomene,
J'abandonnai ma verve à la muse foraine,	I abandoned my wit to the Muse of the Fair,
Plus lente à me conduire au chemin de l'honneur,	Slower to lead me to the field of honour,
Mais plus prompte à payer du moins le voyageur.[42]	But quicker at least to pay the traveller's bills.
La froide *Nitétis*,[43] la fade *Philomèle*,[44]	Cold *Nitétis*, and dreary *Philomèle*,
L'insensé *Claperman*,[45] mainte autre bagatelle	The ridiculous *Claperman*, and many another trifle
(Enfants de mes besoins plus que de mon esprit),	(The fruits of my needs rather than my wit),

---

[41] The French proverb, 'La faim fait sortir le loup du bois' [Hunger drives the wolf from the woods].

[42] The four opéras-comiques mentioned in the text are: *Colombine-Nitétis*, Saint-Germain 1723; *Philomèle*, Théâtre-Italien, July 1723; *Le Claperman*, Saint-Germain 1724; and *Le Mariage du Caprice et de la Folie*, Foire Saint-Laurent, August 1724.

[43] *Parodie de l'opéra de* [librettist Pierre-Charles] *Roy*. (Piron).

[44] *Parodie de la tragédie de Danchet*. (Piron) [Parody of Antoine Danchet's tragedy.] Juvigny states wrongly that *Colombine Nitétis* was performed by Francisque's marionettes at Saint-Laurent in 1722. However, evidence in the Prologue to *Nitétis* makes it absolutely clear that it was given at Saint-Germain in 1723, not by Francisque but by the marionettes of Bienfait. In the prologue, the Doctor says he is off to see *Les Trois Commères*, also premiered at Saint-Germain in 1723, in which Piron joined forces with Lesage and Fuzelier.

[45] 'Pièce bizarre qui eut un grand succès et qui ne valait rien.' (Piron) [Strange play which was a great success and which was worthless.]

Presque en un même instant et mourut et naquit;[46]	In barely an instant were born and died;
Tous ces riens, toutefois, ont amusé la scène,	However, all these nothings amused the stage,
Et de leur peu de vie entretenu la mienne.	And with their brief lives they nourished mine.
De l'opéra comique enfin ressuscité[47]	Finally, the resurrected Opéra-Comique,
Et retombé déjà presque à l'extrémité,	Already tottering on its last legs
(Pour le triumvirat jugez l'affreux déboire!)[48]	(What a disgrace for the Triumvirate!),
Par un caprice heureux j'ai relevé la gloire,	I restored to glory with a happy *Caprice*,
Et je reprends haleine à l'ombre d'un laurier	And I catch my breath in the shade of a laurel bough,
Qui, dans ce nouveau champ, est cueilli le premier.	The first I have gathered in this new field.
À la cour, à la ville, ami, veux-tu complaire?	Friend, will you delight the Court and the Town?
Viens joindre à mon talent, qui commence à leur plaire,	Come and join to my talents, which begin to please them,
Et qu'à te dévouer je me sens résolu,	
Viens y joindre les tiens qui leur ont toujours plu.	Your own which have always pleased them.
Préférant désormais la Seine à la Garonne,[49]	Preferring henceforth the Seine to the Garonne,

---

[46] 'Les pièces de foire, en ce temps, une fois passées, ne reparaissaient jamais.' (Piron) [In those days, plays at the Fair, once performed, never reappeared.]

[47] 'Les sieurs Honoré et Picard avaient entrepris l'Opéra-Comique et ouvert leur théâtre par trois pièces de Le Sage, Fuselier et Dorneval. Elles tombèrent. Je donnai *L'Âne d'or* et *Le Caprice*; *Le Caprice* eut trente représentations. C'est le premier succès que j'aie eu de ma vie; je ne m'y devais pas plus attendre qu'à mes autres pièces.' (Piron) [Messrs Honoré and Picard had undertaken the Opéra-Comique and opened their theatre with three plays by Le Sage, Fuselier and d'Orneval. They were a failure. I gave *L'Âne d'or* and *Le Caprice*; *Le Caprice* had thirty performances. This was the first success I ever had in my life; I did not expect it any more than for my other plays.]

[48] Piron often jokingly referred to Lesage, Fuzelier, and d'Orneval as the triumvirate, as their plays dominated the Paris fairs.

[49] 'Il était alors avec sa troupe en Gascogne.' (Piron) [He was then with his company in Gascony].

Viens dans nos deux faubourgs partager ma couronne;	Come share my crown at the two Fairs.
Accours et nous rapporte un style fanfaron	Hurry back, bringing with you your crazy style,
Où je trouve à finir le rôle de Samson.	In which I'll find a way to finish my *Samson*.

But, as Piron himself reports, Francisque did not return to Paris and the unfinished manuscript of *Samson* underwent a fascinating transformation, which I will discuss in chapter nine.

8

Farewell to the Fairs and return to the provinces: 1726–1734

Francique's company returned from the southwest to Paris early in 1726. Parfaict's marginal note at the head of the entry for the Foire Saint-Laurent of 1726 refers to the 'Opéra-Comique du Sieur Honoré associé avec Francisque'.[1] 'L'Opéra-Comique du Sieur Francisque' is also named in the reports of the fair which appeared in the *Mercure*,[2] and the words appear on the title page of *Les Pèlerins de La Mecque*, published separately in September 1726, although not when the play was included in the sixth volume of *Le Théâtre de la Foire* in 1728. There can therefore be little doubt that the 'Opéra-Comique du Sieur Honoré associé avec Francisque' (*Mémoires*) and 'L'Opéra-Comique du Sieur Francisque' (*Mercure*) were one and the same thing. The large casts of this season's productions indicate that Francisque probably retained many of Honoré's actors, along with his own family and old associates. This is the first season in which all four major fair authors – Lesage, Fuzelier, d'Orneval and Piron – wrote for Francisque and his company.

The season opened on 3 July with a prologue by Fuzelier, *Les Dieux travestis*, which was not published in its day.[3] Fuzelier's 1724 prologue *Les Dieux à la Foire*, fraught with resentment and rivalry, had been set in a half-deserted fairground. By contrast, his new prologue is set in the fairground tavern of Monsieur Canarie, where the gods of love and wine join crowds of merrymakers. Fuzelier, like Piron, seems to have known that Francisque and his company had recently been in Gascony, which is probably why the tavern drinkers include the Chevalier de Criccrac, a stereotypically boastful Gascon nobleman with comic pronunciation (confusing b and v) and mock-Gascon

---

[1] *Mém*, vol.2, pp. 35–8. Although Loïc Chahine claims that 'Les Parfaict n'indiquent pas que Francisque ait disposé d'un théâtre' [The Parfaicts do not state that Francisque had the use of a theatre], he seems to have overlooked these contemporary references: Chahine, *Fuzelier*, vol.1, p. 143.

[2] *Mercure*, September 1726.

[3] Unpublished manuscript, with title page saying that it was 'Représenté par la Troupe du Sr. Francisque à la Foire St Laurent le … 1726.' The full text is followed by a *canevas* (scenario) version entitled *L'Amour et Bacchus à la Foire*, available in Gallica (Ms. BnF fr. 9336 ff. 209–24) and reproduced in Chahine, *Fuzelier*.

oaths, 'Sandis!' and 'Cadédis!' The Chevalier hails a member of Francisque's troupe, Le Docteur, who tells him the titles of the evening's plays. Something is clearly missing from the MS at this point, since the Chevalier replies to this information as if he had been asked whether he knew of Francisque:

> *Le chevalier.* Si je connais Francisque, moi. Allez, Docteur, Francisque me faisait respectueusement sa cour à Vordeaux, je le protégeais, demandez-lui ce que c'est que le chevalier de Criccrac.[4]
>
> *Le docteur.* Le chevalier de Criccrac!
>
> *Le chevalier.* Oui, c'est un nom... Vaste, je suis modeste. Adieu, Docteur, puisque bous possédez ce cher Francisque, je caracolerai jour et nuit sur botre théâtre et par conséquent bos loges seront vien meublées.
>
> [*Le chevalier.* Do I know Francisque? Come on, Doctor, Francisque paid me his respects in Bordeaux where I patronised him. Just ask him who is the chevalier de Criccrac.
>
> *Le docteur.* The chevalier de Criccrac!
>
> *Le chevalier.* Yes, it's a huge name. I'm a modest man. Farewell Doctor; as you have that dear Francisque among you, I will prance day and night on your stage and your boxes will be full.]

The Chevalier sings a jolly air promising to attract the cream of society to the theatre, and in the concluding chorus the whole company agrees that 'La Foire sera bonne!' Although there is no spoken role for Pierrot in this prologue, Hamoche is named in the manuscript as one of the singers in the concluding vaudeville.

The prologue was followed by *Le Saut de Leucade* and *Le Galant brutal*. These were plays over which Fuzelier took very little trouble and of which he himself did not think highly: in the prologue, the Chevalier de Criccrac is equally unenthusiastic about their subject-matter.[5] In *Le Saut*, Francisque played an Arlequin who reluctantly agrees to leap from a cliff into the sea to prove his love but is saved by the substitution of a (literal) straw man; in *Le*

---

[4] Onomatopoeic in French as well as English; see *Dictionnaire de l'Académie Française* (1762). On the figure of the comic Gascon, see Pauline Beaucé and Françoise Rubellin, '« Vos pièces sont farcies de Gascons »: enjeux d'une figure comique sur les scènes parisiennes du XVIIIe siècle', *Littératures classiques,* 87:2 (2015), 301–15.

[5] Parfaict, *Mém*, vol. 2, p. 165. These plays can be found in Chahine, *Fuzelier*, vol. 2, and, edited by Isabelle Degauque, on http://cethefi.org/memoire_master.htm.

Galant brutal, a parody of Bertin de la Doué's opera *Ajax* (1716), he played a cruel king and lover. Perhaps the Chevalier was right; there are gloomy elements in both of these mythological stories which, even when parodied, would not have appealed to a popular audience. *Le Galant brutal* ends with a storm and shipwreck from which Ajax-Arlequin manages to save himself. In the final verse of the vaudeville, he hopes 'Que le vent de la Critique / Epargne un vaisseau Comique / Égaré depuis longtemps'[6] [May the winds of the Critics/ Spare our little comic vessel which has wandered for so long']. But even Francisque's powers of persuasion could not save the play: the title page of the manuscript contains the note 'joué le 3 juillet avec *Le Saut de Leucade*, n'a pas réussi' [played on 3 July with *Le Saut de Leucade*, unsuccessful]. Both pieces disappeared within two weeks.

On 17 July, the company gave *Pierrot fée*, a new piece by Joseph La Font, with music by Jacques Aubert; the Pierrot in fairy costume was probably played by Hamoche in drag.[7] The company also revived two older plays from 1716, both of which appeared in volume 2 of *Le Théâtre de la Foire*: *L'École des Amans* by Lesage and Fuzelier and *Les Arrêts de l'Amour* by d'Orneval. On 29 July came a new collaboration between Lesage, Fuzelier, and d'Orneval, *Les Pèlerins de la Mecque*, with music by L'Abbé.[8] This three-act opéra-comique was the first major success of the season. Set in the imaginary Orient already exploited by Lesage and d'Orneval, it was based loosely on the tale of Atalmulc and Princess Zélica from *Les Mille et un jours*. Prince Ali (played by Gherardi) has fled Balsora to escape from his brother, who has just seized power.[9] While taking refuge with the Sophy of Persia, he fell in love with Princess Rézia. But her father had promised her to the Great Mogul, and when Rézia died of grief, Prince Ali fled to Cairo, where the action takes place. Now both he and his valet Arlequin are penniless. In desperation, Arlequin becomes a Calender, a mendicant Dervish, and urges his master to follow suit. When the chief Calender, who recognises the Prince, asks why he is in such a sorry state, Arlequin replies, 'Je vais vous le dire, moi. C'est aux Ecuyers des Chevaliers Errans à faire ces sortes de récits.' [I will tell you why. It's the job of the squires of Knights Errant to tell these kinds of stories.] This is an in-joke, alluding to Piron's *L'Endriague* (1723), when Francisque-Arlequin had been the 'écuyer du chevalier errant'.

Ali is informed that the Sultan's favourite, having caught sight of him, has invited him into her magnificent house. Ali, still grieving for Rézia, rejects the offer, but Arlequin forcibly carries his master inside. The favourite turns out to be Rézia herself, who has only feigned death. The lovers' attempt to

---

6 Ms. BnF fr. 9336 ff. 295–7.
7 Chahine, *Fuzelier*, vol. 1, p. 143.
8 *Mercure*, August 1726, p. 1879. Fuzelier's name is missing from some accounts.
9 For Gherardi, see Parfaict, *Mém.*, vol. 2, p. 96.

escape is foiled by the Sultan's unexpected return from hunting. They seek shelter in the Caravanserai of the Calenders, passing for pilgrims to Mecca, and Arlequin, disguised as a female Pilgrim (another of Francisque's travesty turns), has several scenes of flirtation. But the Sultan invades the Caravanserai and sentences the couple to be tortured. When Rézia's servants and Arlequin tearfully reveal the true identity of the Prince and Princess, the Sultan pardons them and offers them asylum. All the pilgrims take their partners and, with much singing and dancing, prepare to depart for Mecca.

Les Pèlerins de la Mecque held the stage throughout August and early September and, according to the *Mémoires*, added to the reputations of Lesage, Fuzelier and d'Orneval. The play went on to have an illustrious afterlife, contributing to the growing fashion for 'Turquerie'. In Rameau's opera *Les Indes galantes* in 1735, with its libretto by Fuzelier, the noble Osman Pasha clearly owes much to the Sultan in *Les Pèlerins*. In 1763, the opéra-comique formed the basis for Louis Dancourt's libretto for Gluck's longest and finest comic opera, the three-act *La Rencontre imprévue, ou Les Pèlerins de la Mecque*.[10] In 1775, with new music by Haydn, *La Rencontre* became *L'Incontro improvviso* and the 1780 Vienna revival of Gluck's version seems to have inspired the plot of Mozart's *Die Entführung aus dem Serail* in 1784.

Francisque next presented a new opéra-comique by his old friend Piron, who, during Francisque's absence from Paris, had experienced both triumph and disaster at the fairs. Despite the success of *Le Caprice,* his relations with Honoré and Hamoche had reached a low point late in 1725 and at the Foire Saint-Germain of 1726 he gave Honoré's troupe three plays with, said the *Mémoires*, 'peu de succès'.[11] In *La Robe de dissention ou le faux prodige*, a satire on the Spanish obsession with honour, Piron created an exceptionally witty and facetious Arlequin, written specifically for Francisque. Claiming to be the sorcerer Balivernos, Arlequin produces a magic coat, saying that it is multicoloured but will appear black to those whose women are unfaithful. The coat is of course black, so this trick leads to many scenes of comic embarrassment. In surprisingly modern language, the women finally denounce the machismo of their suitors and the play ends with the reconciliation of all the couples.[12] The divertissements that end each act (for which the music may have been composed by Rameau) are far more elaborate than was usual at the fairs, and this was surely due to the presence in the company of the *maître de ballets,* Jean-Baptiste Malter, now the husband of Francisque's niece Catherine. Arlequin-Balivernos is frank about the arbitrary nature of these

---

[10] See Larry Wolff, *The Singing Turk: Ottoman Power and Operatic Emotions on the European Stage* (Stanford, 2016), pp. 65–71.

[11] Parfaict, *Mém.*, vol. 2, p. 37.

[12] For a modern edition, see Alexis Piron, *L'Antre de Trophonius et la Robe de Dissention ou le faux prodige* ed. Derek Connon (Cambridge, 2011).

interludes, claiming that the Act 1 finale proves his magic powers: 'Je vais faire tomber des nués un divertissement.' [I shall make an entertainment fall from heaven.] Marie and Francis Sallé, who had danced in London during the winter season of 1725–6, but not in the summer, may have returned to Paris and could have taken part in these interludes.[13] Sophisticated dancing clearly played a part in the growing popularity of opéra-comique.

The second of Piron's contributions to Francisque's season, the one-act *Olivette juge des enfers*, exists today only as a manuscript scenario and a plot summary in the *Dictionnaire des Théâtres de Paris*, where it is wrongly listed as the work of 'M. Fleuri.'[14] Françoise Rubellin and Isabelle Degauque in their edition establish that Piron is the undoubted author of *Olivette*, which slightly resembles his contribution to *Les Trois Commères*, a collaboration with Lesage and d'Orneval. Pluto is having an affair with Olivette, Proserpine's lady-in-waiting, and persuades her to impersonate Minos, judge of the dead, promising that she can resume her own form at will. Recent arrivals in hell appear before her in a series of cameos: a penniless Gascon who wants to pay the ferryman on credit, the incompetent doctor who killed him, an amorous Abbé, a lovelorn young girl, a gallant who has exhausted himself in the pursuit of voracious women, and two pretentious aristocrats who complain of the lack of amenities in hell. Olivette sentences them all without respect for rank. When the ghost of her husband Pierrot appears, not recognizing his own wife, he proudly boasts of his amorous conquests under the influence of drink; furious, she reveals her identity. The couple finally allow Pluto to reconcile them, if only for the pleasure of quarrelling again. The bare resumé that has come down to us does little justice to Piron's opéra-comique which contains no fewer than thirty popular airs and a concluding vaudeville-divertissement. It was an amusing vehicle for Mlle de Lisle and Hamoche, who played Olivette and Pierrot, as they had in *Les Trois Commères* and *La Robe de dissention*.

La Rose

The next new piece Piron wrote for the fair was *La Rose, ou le Pucelage*. Francisque's role in its convoluted history has never been fully explained. The opéra-comique was initially passed for performance by the censor. However, the Lieutenant of Police disagreed with this judgement and submitted the play to another censor who banned it on the grounds of indecency.[15] Copies must

---

[13] At Lincoln's Inn Fields, in February 1727, in Rich's *The Rape of Prosperpine*, they created similar roles to those they might have danced in the interludes. See *Daily Journal*, Monday 13 February 1727.

[14] The surviving version of Piron's *Olivette juge des enfers*, edited by Jeanne-Marie Hostiou and Isabelle Degauque was published in *Théâtre de la Foire, Anthologie de pièces inédites*, ed. Françoise Rubellin (Montpellier, 2005), pp. 291–305.

[15] See Victor Hallays-Dabot, *Histoire de la censure théâtrale en France* (Paris, 1862), p. 55; Verèb, *Piron*, p. 107; and Lagrave, *TP*, p. 64. For a discussion of the

have circulated among Piron's friends because by November it had been read by the Parisian lawyer and man of letters Mathieu Marais who, in a letter to his friend Jean Bouhier, president of the parlement de Bourgogne, neatly sums up the simple plot:

> J'ai lu une petite comédie qui devait être jouée par les danseurs de corde et qui a été refusée à la police. Elle a pour titre *la Rose*; cela est en chansons, et l'idée est prise du *Roman de la Rose*: il y a des choses très-fines, mais d'autres un peu fortes.[16]

> [I've read a little comedy which was to be performed by the rope dancers and which was banned by the police. It is called *La Rose*; it is all in songs, and the idea is taken from the *Roman de la Rose*: there are some very fine things, but other parts are a bit strong.]

Marais also comments on a brief exchange between Rosette and a 'bel esprit', probably to be played by Francisque, who mocks the Académie Française. As Sainte-Beuve noted, this was the first version of the famous quip: "Ils sont quarante et ils ont de l'esprit comme quatre" [There are forty of them but they have enough wit for four]. Piron was later to write a mock-epitaph for himself, 'Ci-gît Piron qui ne fut rien, / Pas même Académicien' ['Here lies Piron who was nothing,/ Not even a member of the Academy.]

Jean Monnet, who visited Rouen in 1743, learned from a local bookseller of a single performance of *La Rose* in Rouen, apparently in 1729. Members of the Moylin family were in Rouen often enough to suggest that it was one of their regular calling points. Piron himself spent months there in 1728–9 in order to complete his tragedy *Callisthène*, and it seems possible that Francisque passed through and gave a belated première of *La Rose* as a favour for the old friend who had written it for him. In 1744 Monnet, who was in Rouen recruiting for his company at the Foire Saint-Laurent, acquired the still-unpublished manuscript,[17] which finally got a Paris performance, as *Les Jardins de l'Hymen ou La Rose*, at the Foire Saint-Germain on 5 March of that year. Francisque certainly performed it twice on his last known visit to Piron's hometown of Dijon in 1750–1.

---

sexual language in *La Rose* and *Tirésias*, see Robert M. Isherwood, *Farce and Fantasy: Popular Entertainment in Eighteenth-Century Paris* (Oxford, 1986), pp. 69–72.

[16] Letter of 18 Nov., 1726, Jean Bouhier, *Correspondance littéraire du président Bouhier*, ed. Henri Duranton, 14 vols (St Étienne, 1988), 9:2: *Lettres de Mathieu Marais*, p. 100. This letter is not from Bouhier to Marais as Pascale Verèb claims in *Piron*, p. 107.

[17] Jean Monnet, *Supplément au Roman comique, ou Mémoires pour servir à la vie de Jean Monnet* (London, 1772), vol. 1, pp. 48–9.

Les Comédiens Corsaires

On 20 September 1726 Francisque's company performed a new opéra-comique by Lesage, Fuzelier and d'Orneval, *Les Comédiens Corsaires,* in which they returned to the 'querelle des théatres'. In November 1725 hostilities had broken out between the three official theatres. The Comédie-Française produced a highly successful entertainment, *La Française Italienne,* an *ambigu-comique* (three plays, each in a different style) which mimicked the fairs and the Italians, and in which Legrand's daughter played Arlequin. The lavish singing and dancing drew a complaint from the Opéra and the Italians responded with a skit of their own, *L'Italienne Française.*[18] An explanatory notice in volume six of *Le Théâtre de la Foire* makes it clear that *Les Comédiens Corsaires* was a response to a play given by the Italians on 10 August, *Les Comédiens esclaves,* as the prologue to another *ambigu-comique* by Dominique, Romagnesi and François Riccoboni. In *Les Comédiens esclaves,* the Italian players are captured by pirates and taken to the court of the bloodthirsty King of Morocco.[19] Pantalon explains to the King that in Paris there are four kinds of theatre and the actors will give brief samples of three, leaving out l'Opéra as too boring. The performance which follows wins them their freedom.

Les Comédiens corsaires cleverly turns the theme of piracy on its head: the two official theatres become the pirates and their victim is the Théâtre de la Foire, once again represented by 'La Troupe du Sieur Francisque.' In the opening scene, set on an island off the coast of Provence, Monsieur Desbroutilles (Legrand of the Comédie-Française) defends his borrowings from the fairground repertoire against the snobbish complaints of Mlle Piaulard, a haughty French actress of the old school.[20] The Italian players' ship appears. Cliclinia (Flaminia of the Comédie-Italienne) disembarks and tells Desbroutilles that she has seen the ship of the Opéra-Comique sailing nearby. Scaramouche, again showing that the new Italian company still spoke imperfect French, adds, 'Ils vont passer à la voue de cet ile per se rendre à Marseille.' [They will pass within sight of this island on their way to Marseille.] Desbroutilles launches into a tirade in alexandrines, beginning with a parody of Racine's *Mithridate* (3.1) and ending with an echo of Hermione's rage in *Andromaque*:

---

[18] For a full discussion of this quarrel, see Jeanne-Marie Hostiou, 'Querelle de La Française Italienne', https://obvil.huma-num.fr/agon/querelles/querelle-de-la-francaise-italienne.

[19] The idea is less far-fetched than it might seem: piracy was still a serious threat and the dramatist Regnard was captured and briefly enslaved by pirates in 1678–9.

[20] *Des broutilles* are scraps, trifles; *piauler* is to squeak or squawk.

Fig. 8 Frontispiece of *Les Comédiens Corsaires* from Lesage and d'Orneval, *Le Théâtre de la Foire ou l'opéra-comique*, vol. 6, 1726. Photo: Françoise Rubellin.

Le Comique Opéra, pour se rendre à Marseille,
Va passer par ici. Vite, qu'on appareille.
Attaquons son vaisseau, pillons tous ses effets,
Ses morceaux polissons, ses burlesques ballets ...
Il faudra dans la suite en faire un tel usage,
Que le Parisien, voyant le batelage
Dans sa ville régner de l'un à l'autre bout,
Doute où sera la Foire, et la trouve partout.

[The Opéra Comique, bound for Marseille,
Will pass through here. Quickly, let us go aboard,
Attack their ship, pillage all their effects,
their tricks, their burlesque ballets ...
Later we must make such use of them,
That the Parisian, seeing tomfoolery
Reign in his city from one end to the other,
Will wonder where the Fair is and will find it everywhere.]

Battle is joined and the Forains are quickly overcome. The pirates not only steal costumes and roles but demand a lesson in dramatic art from their supposedly despised rivals. At the end of the Prologue, the French and Italians sing a typical fairground vaudeville and order the Forains to perform *L'Obstacle favorable* and *Les Amours déguisés*.

But why was the Opéra-comique en route for Marseille? The answer to this hitherto unasked question is, I believe, another reference to Francisque and his family. When Francisque returned to Paris from the south of France in 1726, his company included the newly married Malter couple. News of their grand wedding in Marseille in the summer of 1725 must already have spread among Parisian theatre folk. By setting the scene in Provence, the authors of *Les Comédiens corsaires* seem to be claiming that Francisque's company remains the true embodiment of the Opéra-comique, even when as far away as Marseille. Cliclinia, with scant regard for geography, tells Desbroutilles that before being captured by Barbary pirates, the Italians had been sailing to England in search of guineas. They were clearly hoping to emulate Francisque's success in what he long ago had called 'le pays des guinées.'[21]

The message of *Les Comédiens corsaires* is that, despite the Italians' performance of an opéra-comique in *Les Comédiens esclaves,* and Legrand's presenting his daughter as Arlequin at the Comédie-Française, neither company was in fact capable of performing an opéra-comique in the authentic style of La Foire. The words of Pierre Larthomas concerning Les Français are equally true of Les Italiens at this time: 'Pendant une dizaine d'années (de 1718–1728) les comédiens français tentèrent d'imiter les Forains, pastichant non seulement

[21] See p. 67, above.

le style de leurs œuvres, mais encore le jeu de leurs acteurs'[22] [For ten years (1718–1728) the French actors tried to imitate the Forains, copying not only the style of their plays, but also the performance style of their actors].

L'Obstacle Favorable

In *l'Obstacle favorable*, Francisque's company now proceed to show their rivals how things should be done. The scene is a village near Paris. The doctor, M. Trousse-Galand (a mocking allusion to doctors' reputation for killing their patients, since Trousse-galand was a common name for fatal illnesses such as cholera), had angrily left Paris for his country chateau when the surgeons rebelled against the Faculty of Medicine. His daughter Argentine is in love with Dorante, a young surgeon, and his son Valère loves Dorante's sister Spinette, but Trousse-Galand hates the surgeons so much that he refuses any alliance with them. The lovers therefore enter the chateau in disguise: Spinette as a shepherd, Dorante and Arlequin as a Duenna and her Spanish maidservant (Francisque in a double drag act). The Doctor is called away to a patient who dies, and whose angry servants follow the doctor to take their revenge. The Doctor is hit on the head and the disguised Dorante, examining the wound, exaggerates its seriousness; then, revealing his identity, promises to save the Doctor's life if he will consent to the two marriages. Trousse-Galand grudgingly agrees, crying out: 'Aux Chirurgiens je vais devoir la vie ! / N'ai-je donc tant vécu que pour cette infamie !' [I shall owe my life to the surgeons!/ Have I lived so long only for this disgrace?] The comic rage of Monsieur Trousse-Galand is both a parody of Don Diègue's 'Ô rage! Ô désespoir! Ô vieillesse ennemie!/ N'ai-je donc tant vécu que pour cette infamie?' in Corneille's *Le Cid* (1.4) and a reference to the age-old quarrel between physicians and surgeons. In October 1726 the *Mercure* would describe the renewal of this quarrel, also comically featured in scene ten of Fuzelier's *Les Songes*.

I believe that Monsieur Trousse-Galand is in fact a comic portrait of Francisque's old friend Michel Procope-Couteaux, Doctor of Medicine and a Regent of the Paris Faculty of Medicine. Procope, who had now returned from London, wrote for the Comédie-Française in 1724 and the Comédie-Italienne in 1725; like Trousse-Galand, he had a country house outside Paris and had been heavily involved in the quarrel with the Surgeons. In 1726 the Dean of the Paris Faculty of Medicine (in a letter published in the *Mercure* in February) had felt obliged to dissociate his Faculty from a scathing anonymous attack on the surgeons which had recently appeared in print. If, like many, Lesage and d'Orneval suspected that Procope was the author of that attack, they would have had still more reason to make him the object of their parody.

---

[22] Pierre-Henri Larthomas, *Le Théâtre en France au XVIIIe siècle* (Paris, 1980), pp. 9–10.

Some years later the distinguished surgeon François Quesnay would call Procope 'un médecin comique' and wittily allude to the fact that in 1716 Procope's brother Alexandre had taken over the running of the café Procope from their father, François Procope: 'Tandis que son frère rafraîchit le parterre de la Comédie-Française, il glace celui de la Comédie-Italienne'.[23] [While his brother refreshes the patrons of the Comédie-Française, he is chilling those of the Comédie-Italienne]. Perhaps it was Piron or Francisque, whose own father had been an army surgeon, who encouraged Lesage, Fuzelier and d'Orneval to lampoon their little doctor friend; the name Trousse-Galand may also allude to his small stature and reputation for gallant adventures; at this time the expression 'un petit homme bien troussé' meant 'a clever, dapper, tight little fellow.'[24] All of this is a reminder of the complex topical and intertextual references to be found in the fairground theatres, references which are often lost on modern audiences.

Les Amours déguisés

Les Amours déguisés is loosely based on a ballet of the same title with music by Bourgeois and libretto by Fuzelier, first performed in 1713, and revived in September 1726. It takes place in the palace of Venus, who orders her cupids to bring before her all those who refuse to recognise that they are in love. The *Mémoires* note that the piece was well-received.[25] Although it parodies the ballet (especially the entrée entitled 'L'Amitié'), the main reason for its success was probably its inclusion of recognisable parodies of Marivaux, whose *La Surprise de l'Amour* was first performed at the Comédie-Italienne in 1722. Having been ordered to teach their rivals to act, Francisque's company must have enjoyed parodying scenes originally played by Silvia, Flaminia, Dominique and Thomassin, in a convoluted exaggeration of the prose style which came to be known as 'le Marivaudage'.

The subject-matter of Marivaux's theatre was described by d'Alembert in his *Eloge* at the Académie Française many years later:

---

[23] François Quesnay, *Œuvres économiques complètes et autres textes* (Paris, 2005), vol. 2, p. 815. Procope had already been mocked by Lesage in his novel *Gil Blas de Santillane* as 'le docteur Cuchillo, petit avorton de la Faculté' [Doctor Cuchillo [Spanish for knife], a little pipsqueak of the faculty]. In 1732 he was caricatured again in a satirical play, *Le Docteur Fagotin*. See Gustave Desnoiresterres, *La Comédie satirique au XVIIIe siècle* (Geneva, 1970), pp. 69–70.

[24] *The Royal Dictionary*, ed. Abel Boyer (London, 1699), pt.1, n.p.

[25] Parfaict, *Mém*, vol. 2, p. 37.

toutes les niches différentes où peut se cacher l'amour, lorsqu'il craint de se montrer [...]: c'est tantôt un amour ignoré des deux amants, tantôt un amour qu'ils sentent et qu'ils veulent se cacher l'un l'autre; tantôt enfin un amour incertain et comme indécis, un amour à demi né.[26]

[all the different corners where love can hide, when it fears to show itself: it's sometimes a love of which the two lovers are unaware; sometimes one that they feel but want to hide from each other; finally, an uncertain and undecided love, a love only half born.]

In *Les Amours déguisés* Arlequin interrogates a procession of motley characters who offer a parody of just these types. First, Colette claims not to understand her strong feelings for her 'friend', the handsome officer Léandre, for which her uncle mockingly suggests an obvious explanation. Then a rich old widow claims to be lodging a poor but handsome young man in her house purely out of compassion and resents Arlequin's suggestion that this is really 'un amour déguisé.' A drunken *Suisse* thinks he loves a tavern hostess whereas he really loves her barrels. A modern précieuse, Mademoiselle Rafinot, elaborately describes her friendship for Dorimon, a fellow 'Bel-Esprit', and then insults Arlequin in sub-Marivaudian phrases:

Allez, Mon Cher. Vous jugez mal de la figure de mes sentiments. La lorgnette de votre pénétration est trouble. [...] Vous êtes un insolent. Si les femmes portaient à leur côté un fardeau secourable [une épée], je vous le passerai au travers du corps.'

[Come, come, my dear. You misjudge the features of my feelings. The eyepiece of your penetration is cloudy. ... You are an insolent fellow. If women carried a helping burden [a sword] at their side, I would pass it through your body.]

Refinement is quickly banished with the entrance of Pierrot-Hamoche in drag as a fat baker's wife who has an unacknowledged passion for her strapping kitchen boy, and a cuckolded Procureur, M. Pié-de-mouche, who blindly believes in his wife's fidelity until Arlequin reveals that, far from hating her husband's chief clerk, Madame Pié-de-mouche is madly in love with him. In the closing scenes, Colette and Léandre act out a mock farewell which uncannily foreshadows the denouement of *Le Jeu de l'Amour et du Hasard*, not performed until 1730. Léandre admits that Colette had always had first place in his heart: '(*Lui baisant la main*) Ah! ma chère Colette, vous l'avez toujours eue, et vous ne la perdrez jamais.' [(*Kissing her hand*)

---

[26] Reprinted in Pierre Marivaux, *Théâtre complet*, ed. Bernard Dort, préface de Jacques Scherer (Paris, 1964).

O my dear Colette, you have always had my love and you will never lose it.] Colette sighs, 'Que j'étais folle d'attribuer à la simple amitié tout ce que je sentais pour Léandre.' [How foolish I was to think all I felt for Léandre was simple friendship.] The play ends with a ballet danced by a troupe of lovers of all nations and a troupe of loves and pleasures, followed by a vaudeville with music by l'Abbé. Once again, the elaborate dancing may be due to the presence of Jean-Baptiste Malter.

It seems that Fuzelier's *Le Bois de Boulogne* was given a single performance on 8 October.[27] This rather shapeless one-act opéra-comique may have been intended as a prologue, but to what remains unclear. The rich, elderly Orgon woos Argentine, while Arlequin, disguised as the Baron de Groupignac, pays court to Madame Orgon. But the young people are really in league to defraud the old couple, who quarrel over their passion for Arlequin and Argentine. Another unhappy couple, La Foire and L'Opéra, sing of their mutual misfortunes. Monsieur Orgon persuades La Foire to provide an entertainment in which Madame Orgon demands a role, and the piece finishes abruptly with a vaudeville on the antics of lovers in the Bois de Boulogne.[28]

Although the script had some comic potential, and music by Mouret, it was such a flop that, according to the *Mémoires,* the finale was drowned out by hissing.[29] One reason may be that the audience recognised an egregious example of plagiarism by Fuzelier, who, as Anastasia Sakhnovskaia-Pankeeva has pointed out, 'borrowed' the plot, and even the name of le baron de Groupignac, from Regnard and Dufresny's *Les Momies d'Egypte* [*The Egyptian Mummies*] (1696) in Gherardi's *Le Théâtre Italien*.[30]

Le Retour de la Chasse du Cerf

The final play of the season, *Le Retour de la Chasse du Cerf* [*The Return from the Stag Hunt*], was better received, probably because of its links to the ongoing 'querelles des théâtres'.[31] The play to which it alludes, Legrand's *La Chasse du cerf* [*The Stag Hunt*], was loosely based on the tale of Diana and Actaeon, but also contained a rather tasteless subplot about a lover who disguises himself as an amorous pet monkey. It was first performed at the Comédie-Française on 14 October 1726, with little success even after the

---

[27] Parfaict, *Mém.*, vol.2, pp. 37–8.

[28] There is a full synopsis in Parfaict, *Dict.*, vol. 1, pp. 474–8.

[29] Parfaict, *Mém.*, vol. 2, p. 185.

[30] Sakhnovskaia-Pankeeva, *La Naissance des Théâtres de la Foire: influence des Italiens et constitution d'un répertoire* doctoral thesis, 2 vols, University of Nantes, 2013), vol.1, pp. 679–82.

[31] Parfaict, *Mém.*, vol. 2, p. 185.

author had revised it.[32] Even the Italians had fun at the expense of Legrand's stag in their parody of the opera *Pirame et Thisbé,* given on 9 November.[33] At the moment when Thisbé comes to meet Pyrame but flees in terror from a lion, a stag arrives instead, and Pyrame exclaims: 'Quel monstre vient ici me couper le chemin?/ C'est un cerf échappé du Faubourg Saint Germain.'[34] [What monster comes hither to bar my way? / It's a stag escaped from the Faubourg Saint Germain.]

Le Retour de la Chasse du cerf, given at the Palais-Royal on 22 October,[35] is not really a parody, in that it does not follow Legrand's plot but is a lampoon on the author himself. Already mocked as Monsieur Desbroutilles in *Les Comédiens corsairs*, Legrand now becomes Monsieur Crottin (horse dung rather than goat's cheese), who, after the failure of his latest play, is holed up in a tavern trying to revise it. The tavern waiter sings to him in thieves' jargon, arguing that a plagiarist is little better than a common robber. The hiding place is then invaded by a procession of characters mocking his work. The insults culminate with the arrival of Arlequin and Columbine, dressed as a 'petit maître' and a 'femme de qualité', who advise Crottin/Legrand how best to please the public. The final irony of this amusing piece is that the Colombine and Arlequin who promise to create a better impression than the 'mauvais auteurs' of the Comédie-Française are in fact Francisque and Mlle de Lisle from the fairs, now on the stage of the Palais-Royal. This was the second time this season that the fairground players were depicted as telling the Comédie-Française how to do its job.

At the end of this unusually long season Francisque's company gave several performances at the Palais-Royal, including *Les Pèlerins de la Mecque, Les Comédiens corsaires, L'Obstacle favorable, Les Amours déguisés* and *Le Retour de la Chasse du cerf.* The final performance, on 23 October, ended with 'un Compliment prononcé par Francisque.' The *Mercure* printed the speech in full, a speech ('fort applaudi') which, for all its conventional courtesies, nevertheless had a sting in its tail, reminding the playwrights that Francisque's company would have needed even greater skill to make some of the season's plays succeed:

---

[32] Pierre-François Godard de Beauchamps, *Recherches sur les Théâtres de France* (Paris, 1735), p. 494.

[33] 430 *Pirame et Thisbé*, by Dominique, Riccoboni, Romagnesi, 9 November 1726, Comédie-Italienne. The lovers were played by Arlequin-Thomassin and Silvia (Gianetta-Rosa Benozzi).

[34] Nicolas Chamfort, *Dictionnaire Dramatique*, ed. Joseph and Sébastien Laporte (Paris,1776), vol. 2, p. 498. The Comédie-Française was still located in what today is the rue de l'Ancienne Comédie near the abbey of Saint-Germain.

[35] Isabelle Martin attributes it to Joseph La Font in *Le Théâtre de la Foire: des tréteaux aux boulevards* (Oxford, 2002), p. 370.

MESSIEURS, Permettez-nous de vous rendre de très-humbles grâces de l'extrême indulgence que vous avez eue pour nous pendant le cours de la dernière Foire. Satisfaits des efforts que notre Troupe faisait pour vous plaire, vous avez excusé nos fautes, et votre bonté a prévalu sur la délicatesse de votre goût. Aussi ne sommes-nous pas assez vains pour regarder comme une justice les applaudissements dont vous nous avez quelquefois honorés. Nous savons bien que vous nous les avez donnés, seulement pour nous encourager à les mériter; et c'est ce qui fera désormais toute notre attention. Oui, Messieurs, nous allons nous appliquer, mes Camarades et moi, à vous rendre plus contents de nous à la Foire prochaine. Puissent nos Auteurs nous donner de si bonnes Pièces, qu'elles vous dérobent nos défauts, ou puissions-nous devenir assez habiles pour faire valoir les médiocres.[36]

[Ladies and gentlemen, permit us to give you very humble thanks for the extreme indulgence you have shown us during the last Fair. Satisfied with the efforts our troupe has made to please you, you excused our faults, and your kindness prevailed over the delicacy of your taste. We are not, therefore, vain enough to regard as our just deserts the applause with which you have sometimes honoured us. We know that you gave it only to encourage us to deserve more; and that, henceforth, will be the object of all our care. Yes, ladies and gentlemen, my comrades and I will strive to make you even happier at the next Fair. May our authors give us such good plays that they disguise our faults, or may we become skilful enough to make their mediocre plays triumph.]

To the best of my knowledge, these were the last words spoken by Francisque onstage at the Paris fairs or the Palais-Royal. He did not keep his promise to return. Instead, leaving behind the incessant wrangles with authority in which he had been a central figure for over ten years, he went back to the provinces, where he was already known and admired. At the end of 1726, Francisque and company were in Tours where, on 13 December, Jeanne Elizabeth Malter, daughter of Jean-Baptiste and Catherine Malter, was baptised in the church of Saint Venant.[37] Jeanne Gaillardet, wife of Guillaume Moylin, was godmother and the register was signed by Jean-Baptiste Malter, Francisque and several other members of the company.[38] One of these, Desessars ('Barthélemy Durocher dit Des Essars'), went on to play leading comic roles; he and his

---

[36] *Mercure*, October 1726, p. 2347.

[37] This was in fact their second child. The first, Catherine, must have been born early in 1726, probably in Paris; her existence is known only from the certificate of her death in Toulouse, 12 June 1731, at the age of five.

[38] AM Tours (Saint-Venant). They were Guillaume Moylin, Drouin, Louis Tourteville, Desessars, and Pierre Rosidor, a musician who had signed the register at the Malters' wedding in 1725.

wife, also a comic performer, were among many new actors who were still with the company as late as the season of 1734–5.

The next family affair was the wedding of Francisque's younger brother Simon (at the unusually late age of thirty) in Bordeaux, on 18 March 1727. The register was signed by Michel Cochois but no other members of the family. From Bordeaux, Simon wrote to Marseille on 24 March, requesting permission to perform, which he clearly received, since in July he wrote from Marseille about a return to Bordeaux.[39] This is the second time that Simon is recorded as taking a managerial role; he had already taken over the company (and played Arlequin) at the fair in 1721, when Francisque was in London. The birth of the Malters' daughter Charlotte in Montpellier in 1728 may give some indication of the company's whereabouts in that year.[40]

Dancing in London and Paris

Meanwhile, however, Francis and Marie Sallé were no longer 'the Sallé children'. In 1725 they had returned from the fairs to be John Rich's leading dancers at Lincoln's Inn Fields. In 1727, the last year in which Étienne Sallé is recorded as their manager, Francis was twenty-two and Marie eighteen.[41] For the first time, the siblings went their separate ways: Marie returned to the Opéra, while Francis stayed on in London, continued to dance for Rich, and married an English actress who was a member of the Lincoln's Inn company. His wife, whose name I have not been able to discover, played Molly Brazen in the original cast of *The Beggar's Opera* first performed in January 1728, where she is listed as Mrs Sallé. Francis did not cut his ties with France, however. In July 1728, he and Rich's other star dancer François Nivelon returned to dance at the Foire Saint-Laurent and in 1729 they brought fellow dancers Anthony Francis Roger, and the English actor-dancers Haughton and Rainton (or Rinton or Renton) as well as Mlle Rabon, who performed dances in Scottish and Dutch costume. When Marie Sallé came back to London in 1730 she joined her brother at Lincoln's Inn Fields. For a brief period, she, her brother, and her new sister-in-law may all have been performing on the same stage: while Mrs. Sallé was acting in *The Beggar's Opera*, 'Rich billed entr'acte dances by the French dancer Marie Sallé and her brother in another attempt to draw fresh audiences for the now too-familiar piece.'[42]

---

[39] AM Marseille, FF 307.

[40] Another daughter, Marie, had been born in 1727, but the place of her birth is unknown.

[41] Nothing further is known of Étienne Sallé after that year.

[42] Jeremy Barlow and Moira Goff, 'Dancing in Early Productions of "The Beggar's Opera"', *Dance Research: The Journal of the Society for Dance Research*, vol. 33:2 (2015), 143–158, at p. 145.

An important Anglo-French link continued when Roger, Houghton and Rainton returned to the Foire Saint-Laurent in 1730 and 1731, apparently without Sallé or Nivelon. These visiting dancers, whom Parfaict consistently describes as 'les danseurs pantomimes anglais', advertised the Englishness of their entertainment when they danced in two 'ballets pantomimes', *La Noce anglaise*, and *La Guinguette anglaise*, 'Un divertissement composé de Scènes muettes figurées en Ballet' [an entertainment made up of a silent scenes expressed in ballet].[43] Here at the fairs, the training ground of both Francis and Marie Sallé, we already have the beginnings of the narrative *ballet d'action* which only found its way later and with difficulty into the official theatres. So great was the success of these seasons that on 18 September 1731 the whole company of 'Les Danseurs Anglais Pantomimes' were summoned to perform before the queen at Versailles.[44] In fact, most of the dancers who came over from London between 1728 and 1731 – Roger, Nivelon, Mlle Rabon, Sallé and Boudet – were French.[45] Anthony Roger had worked with Francisque in London; Francis Nivelon and Francis Sallé were the highest-paid dancers in Rich's company. Boudet (known as 'le Petit' to distinguish him from his father, who had been a dancing master at the Paris fairs) had begun to dance at the age of four at the Foire Saint-Laurent, with a parody of the clog dance that was a speciality of the Nivelons; Mlle Rabon was also a fairground performer: they and the visitors from London must have shared a common performance style. In 1732 Houghton, the dancer-choreographer John Essex and his pupil, 'Miss Robinson', visited Paris; a London journal reported: 'We hear from Paris that Miss Robinson, the fine dancer of Drury-lane, has danced before an Assembly of the first Quality with vast Applause'. In an interesting example of cross-cultural influence in reverse, when these three English dancers returned to Drury Lane in the autumn of that year, they performed a ballet which was described as 'composed in the taste of Monsieur Dumoulin and Mademoiselle Camargo of the Opera at Paris'.[46]

In her discussion of the development of pantomime, Nathalie Rizzoni claims that these visiting dancers 'contribuèrent d'une façon décisive à l'introduction de la pantomime en France à partir de 1729'[47][made a decisive contribution

[43] Parfaict, *Mém.*, vol.2, pp. 55–56.
[44] Parfaict, *Mém.*, vol. 2, p. 74.
[45] This list is certainly incomplete; records generally name only the best-known dancers.
[46] *London Stage*, Pt 3, vol.1, p. 233. See also the entry on 'Robinson, Miss, later Mrs. Campbell Price', in Philip H. Highfill et al., *A Biographical Dictionary of Actors, Actresses, Musicians, Dancers, Managers, and Other Stage Personnel in London, 1660–1800*, 16 vols (Carbondale, 1973–93), vol. 13, pp. 20–21.
[47] Nathalie Rizzoni, 'Le Geste éloquent: la pantomime en France au XVIIIe siècle', in *Musique et Geste en France de Lully à la Révolution: études sur la musique, le théâtre et la danse*, ed. Jacqueline Waeber (Bern, 2009), pp. 129–47, at p. 137.

to the introduction of pantomime into France from 1729]. However, it might be more accurate to say that the French actor-dancers simply brought back to Paris from London the skills which they had taken with them in the first place. These skills, as Rizzoni rightly points out, were already present in embryo at the fairs and were ultimately a fusion of the old Italian *lazzi* and the silent performances 'à la muette' and 'par écriteaux'. As Erica Levenson points out, the 'British' traditions of ballad opera and pantomime 'were formed through recurring contact with France'.[48] While the work of Weaver at Drury Lane and Rich at Lincoln's Inn was undoubtedly innovative, the contribution of their French colleagues was indispensable to what might best be termed a creative fusion of English and French styles and techniques in the world of dance. We have already noted *The Daily Courant's* reference, as early as March 1720, to 'An Act of extraordinary Entertainment, call'd, in French, Pantomims', and, thanks to the journal of Lady Margaret Pennyman, we know that in that year Francisque was taking advantage of fashionable Anglophilia by advertising himself as 'the most perfect *English* Harlequin in the World'. There was indeed an upsurge of English pantomime dancers at the fairs after 1729 but it was the subject-matter (e.g., *La Noce anglaise*) which they imported, not the genre or its techniques.

Grenoble, September–October 1729

In September 1729, while the Paris fairground was demonstrating 'son zele et la joie universelle' caused by the birth of the Dauphin,[49] Francisque's troupe was taking part in celebrations at the other end of France. Grenoble, like every major French city, held several days of civic and religious ceremonies with processions, bonfires, illuminations, fireworks, feasting, music and dancing, presided over by the High Steward of the Dauphiné, Gaspard de Fontanieu. The official account states that on 27 September, Fontanieu gave a magnificent banquet lit by two thousand candles in the vast Hôtel de Lesdiguières, after which Francisque's company gave a performance for the guests, paid for by Fontanieu.[50] Alongside this official account in French,[51] François Blanc la Goutte, a local poet, published a narrative poem, far more vivid, in Franco-Provençal under a French title page: *Épître en vers, au langage vulgaire de Grenoble, sur les Réjouissances qu'on y a faites pour la Naissance de Monseigneur le Dauphin* [*Verse epistle, in the local speech of Grenoble, on*

---

[48] Levenson, *Traveling Tunes: French Comic Opera and Theater in London, 1714–1745*. Ph.D. dissertation (Cornell University, 2017), p. 2.

[49] Parfaict, *Mém.*, vol. 2, p. 56.

[50] *Ibid.*, p. 14.

[51] *Relation des réjouissances faites à Grenoble au sujet de la naissance de Monseigneur le Dauphin* (Grenoble, 1729).

the rejoicings held for the birth of the Dauphin]. In a tone of naive wonder he recounts the grandiose, quasi-theatrical events, beginning with a solemn Mass of thanksgiving, processions through the streets, accompanied by all the local dignitaries and the townsfolk. The Provençal poet also shows that, before the private event, Francisque's company had already been performing in the usual *jeu de paume* near the Hôtel de Ville, on the site of the present-day theatre, where he gave a free performance for the people of Grenoble. Blanc la Goutte delights in describing the mixture of people of all classes and conditions who filled the theatre:

> Tout lo Peuplo ceu jour intrave pe paren,
> I n'ouron de long temp m'et avi tan de Gen,
> Que si vit d'Ecolié, de Clerc, de Revendouze,
> De Cousouze de Gan, et de poure Piquouze.[52]

> [That day all the people entered without paying.
> Not for a long time were so many people seen,
> for there were scholars, clerks, clothes sellers,
> glove makers and poor rag pickers.]

The feast, and Francisque's contribution to it, were also reported in the *Mercure* in October. From this account we learn the names of the two plays that were performed (with iced refreshments served in the interval).[53] *La Surprise de l'amour* is particularly noteworthy, as the first known example of Francisque performing a work by Marivaux, and the only known example before 1734.[54] The comedy had premiered at the Comédie-Italienne in May 1722, and this must have been one of its earliest performances in the provinces. As an afterpiece the company gave *Le Carillon*, one of Francisque's comic travesty afterpieces. In the words of de la Goutte, 'Ne se farat Jamey una Feta si bella.' [Never was there such a gorgeous feast.]

Pierre Monnier and Jean Sgard make unjustifiably negative assumptions about Francisque's traveling troupe:

> En ce début de siècle, la ville ne peut guère s'offrir que des 'bateleurs',
> des 'farceurs', des 'opérateurs', parfois des troupes ambulantes comme
> on en rencontre dans *Le Roman Comique* de Scarron.[55]

---

[52] [François Blanc, dit la Goutte], *Épître en vers, au langage vulgaire de Grenoble, sur les Réjouissances qu'on y a faites pour la Naissance de Monseigneur le Dauphin* (Grenoble, 1729).

[53] *Mercure*, October 1729, p. 2385.

[54] It is also the first recorded example in France of Francisque going beyond the repertoire of the Théâtre de la Foire. In London in 1718–19 he had presented works from both the Comédie-Italienne and the Comédie-Française.

[55] Anon., *Les Plaisirs de La Tronche, 1711* (attributed to Pierre-François Biancolelli), ed. Pierre Monnier and Jean Sgard (Grenoble, 2006), p. 7, n. 31.

[At the beginning of this century, the city could afford little more than mountebanks, clowns, tumblers, sometimes travelling troupes such as one finds in Scarron's *Roman Comique*.]

However, High Steward Fontanieu must have been aware that Francisque's company were far more than mere provincial mountebanks. Having severed links with the Paris Fairs, the troupe was becoming one of the finest in the kingdom, worthy of mention in the *Mercure de France*. They were still in Grenoble on 16 October when François, son of Catherine and Jean-Baptiste Malter, was baptised in the parish church of St Hugues.[56]

From Rouen and Bordeaux to Brussels, 1730–33

There is little detailed documentary evidence for the company's whereabouts over the next few years; that evidence, however scant, will at least provide a rudimentary chronology. On 9 September 1730, Jeanne Gaillardet, wife of Guillaume Moylin, gave birth to a son in Rouen. The child was named Jean-Baptiste Constantin after his godfather Gherardi, who, as we have already noted, had an even grander theatrical lineage than the Moylins. Gherardi's presence as part of the Moylin company went back at least as far as 1725 and he was still with the company in Toulouse in 1736.[57] The child's godmother was 'Françoise Moylin au lieu et place de Damoiselle Marie Sallé' [in place of Mlle Marie Sallé]. The Françoise Moylin who deputised for Marie was Guillaume's young daughter.

By the end of the year, Francisque's company was in Bordeaux. In January 1731, the twenty-four-year-old Georges-Louis Leclerc, Comte de Buffon, arrived there and wrote to a friend in Dijon telling of his visits to the theatre surrounded by the pretentious fops whom he amusingly describes as traipsing through the mud in their red high heels. Commiserating with his friend about the dearth of entertainment in Dijon, he comments on the presence in Bordeaux of an excellent troupe: 'Francisque et sa troupe y représentaient, avec un succès et un applaudissement infinis.'[58] [Francisque and his company were

---

[56] AM Grenoble, registre GG 104 (Saint-Hugues). Malter is described in the register as 'maître à danser.' Both Francisque and Desessars signed the register.

[57] Sept. 1730: 'Jean Baptiste Constantin né du jour d'hier du légitime mariage de Guillaume Moylin et de Jeanne Gaillardet a été baptisé. Son parrain a été Monsr Jean Baptiste Constantin Gherardi et sa marraine Françoise Moylin au lieu et place de Damoiselle Marie Sallé. [signé] Guillaume Moÿlin — JB Gherardi — Françoise Moylin pour Mlle Marie Salé.' Rouen, Bibliothèque municipale, registre 640 (St-Vincent) The infant died in Rouen aged seven months on 29 April 1731.

[58] Georges-Louis Leclerc Buffon to Richard de Ruffey, 22 January 1731, *Correspondance annotée de Buffon (1729–1779)*, vol 13 of *Œuvres complètes de Buffon*, ed. J-L. de Lanessan (Paris, 1884); édition électronique, http://www.buffon.cnrs.fr/ Lettre IV.

performing there with infinite success and applause.] The fact that Buffon simply writes 'Francisque et sa troupe' rather than 'un certain Francisque' is further evidence of the company's reputation at this time. The Dijon diarist Claude Micault in fact had placed Francisque's troupe in Dijon in the 1720s when Buffon was a student.

Francisque's successful Bordeaux season was interrupted on the night of 13 January by the curse of the theatre in all ages: fire. The play on the night of the fire was *Le Festin de Pierre*, almost certainly the five-act verse comedy by Nicolas Drouin (known as Dorimond or Dorimon), first performed in Lyon in 1685 (and which the company performed in London in 1734–5); the Don's comic servant Briguelle would have been played by Francisque. At the climax the Don is dragged down to hell through a stage trap-door, engulfed, as Buffon makes clear, in clouds of very real smoke and flames:

> [[Le feu] fut mis par un feu d'artifice allumé sous le théâtre pour brûler don Juan dans *le Festin de Pierre*. Les pauvres comédiens ont perdu toutes leurs hardes; à peine Francisque put-il se sauver en robe de chambre. Pour surcroît de malheur, on voulait les poursuivre et leur faire payer, par la prison ou autrement, le dommage du feu; mais tant de gens se sont intéressés pour eux, on leur a fait tant de présents par les quêtes, qu'on dit qu'ils seront bientôt en état de représenter encore dans la salle du concert, qu'on leur donnera pour rien.[59]

> [[The fire] was started by a firework that was set off under the stage to burn Don Juan in *Le Festin de Pierre*. The poor actors lost all their costumes; Francisque barely escaped in his dressing gown. Worse still, there was a desire to pursue them and make them pay for the fire damage, with imprisonment or otherwise, but so many people took their part and made collections for their benefit that it is said they will soon be in a fit state to act again in the concert hall, which they will be given gratis.]

A brief account in the Bordeaux *Annales* adds to Buffon's information:

> Cette salle fut entièrement brûlée, ainsi que quatre maisons voisines. Au mois de Février suivant, on construisit en planches une nouvelle salle des spectacles sur le pont de l'Hôtel-de-Ville.[60]

> [This hall was entirely burned, as were four neighboring houses. In the following February a new wooden theatre was built on the bridge of the Hotel de Ville.]

---

[59] *Ibid.*

[60] Pierre Bernadau, ed., *Annales politiques, littéraires et statistiques de Bordeaux* (Bordeaux, 1803), pt 2, pp. 119–20.

Once again, Francisque was protected and remunerated, and it seems that he was determined to carry on, in the concert hall and later in the new theatre, despite the fact that this was his second theatre fire in eight years. The building in which the fire took place was situated in the narrow rue du Chai des Farines, not far from the Porte Cailhau which still stands today, one of the few remnants of Bordeaux's medieval city walls. The makeshift theatre had opened in 1717 and was the fourth such temporary theatre to be destroyed by fire, a fact which finally determined the authorities to bring from Holland some special fire-fighting equipment.[61] One of Francisque's oddest claims to fame is that he was directly responsible for the founding of the Bordeaux Fire Brigade.

Francisque probably remained in Bordeaux until the end of Lent and then followed his usual route toward Montauban and Toulouse (where the death of the Malters' five-year-old daughter Catherine is recorded in June 1731).[62] On 28 October 1731 Simon's son Fréderic was born in Besançon, which suggests that Simon may have been leading a separate company further north, and in fact there is a record of him (with de Fompré) in Dijon in 1731.[63] On 14 November 1731 the authorities in Grenoble received a letter from one Francisque, 'Italien de nation, danseur, sauteur et voltigeur de corde', requesting permission to perform and stating that he had already appeared there several years ago.[64] This could refer to Francisque's visit during the celebrations for the birth of the Dauphin; 'Italien de nation', as usual, describes repertoire rather than nationality. However, given that on that visit he had been the director of a Marivaux play, not a dancer, tumbler, and tightrope-walker, I suspect that this letter is not from Francisque Moylin. Moreover, there is evidence of the company's presence in Rouen in November, where Guillaume Moylin's twelve-year-old daughter Françoise died. When she was buried on 27 November 1731 the parish register was signed by 'Jean Baptiste Guerardy, Tellier Rosidor et autres.'[65] Two of these signatories were actors in Francisque's troupe, and, just a year earlier, Gherardi had been present (along with Françoise) at the baptism of Guillaume's son in Rouen, which suggests that the company (or part of it) was in Rouen rather than Grenoble. At the end of the year Francisque seems to have returned to Bordeaux; according to Lagrave, he built a temporary theatre where he performed in the winter of 1731–2.[66]

By June 1732, Francisque had certainly moved on to Metz in eastern France, where the director Guillaume Robard engaged his company of thirty-six players to give a summer season. Francisque had performed there at least once

---

[61] *Histoire des Maires de Bordeaux* (Bordeaux, 2008), p. 219.
[62] AM Toulouse, GG 308 (Saint-Étienne).
[63] Louis de Gouvenain, *Le théâtre à Dijon, 1422–1790* (Dijon, 1888), pp. 83–4.
[64] AM Grenoble, FF 43.
[65] AM Rouen, GG 104 (Saint-Éloi).
[66] Henri Lagrave, *La Vie théâtrale à Bordeaux, des origines à nos jours*, vol. I, *Des origines à 1799* (Paris, 1985), p. 135.

before, in 1723, in the old and dilapidated theatre in the Nexirue.[67] At the end of the year, 'la troupe de Molin' moved on to Nancy, not to the court theatre but to a provisional building in the town, which was little more than a barn.[68] According to Christian Pfister, Moylin's troupe gave a few performances in the bitterly cold winter of 1732–3, but, according to the journal of a local bookseller, Jean-François Nicolas, the company gave far more: 'La troupe de Molin, fameux comédien, passa l'hiver ici. Elle fut très suivie. Elle donnait des comédies dans le magasin de la ville proche la Visitation; on leur avait préparé un théâtre.'[69] [The troupe of the famous actor Moylin spent the winter here. They drew considerable crowds. They gave plays in the city storehouse near the Visitation; a theatre had been set up for them.] It is possible that the 'Molin' troupe at Nancy was that of Simon Moylin, because on 9 February 1733 Francisque wrote from Rouen requesting permission to perform for two months at Amiens from the first Sunday after Easter, 'Quasimodo Sunday.'[70] No details survive of Francisque's repertoire in these towns, but by late 1733 his ambitious playlists were drawn almost entirely from the repertoires of the official Paris theatres, and include comedy, tragedy, tragicomedy, music and ballet. Most of the actors in his troupe were capable of performing all of these genres.

While Francisque remained in the north, in July 1733 Simon was recorded as 'chef de troupe' on the point of leaving Grenoble.[71] By the end of the month Simon was in Marseille, where he signed a contract to present 'la comédie italienne à la salle d'opéra' until 15 October.[72] The grandly-styled 'salle d'opéra' must have been the old *jeu de paume* in the rue Pavillon, the only venue in the town; its owner, the widow Châteauneuf, was rumoured to have made considerable profit from her monopoly.[73] Simon was authorised to perform in Avignon from 21 October to 28 November 1733,[74] and again in Marseille from 23 January 1734 until Palm Sunday.[75]

[67] Gilbert Rose, Metz et la musique au XVIIIe siècle (Metz, 1992), p. 54; Henri Tribout de Morembert, *Le Théâtre à Metz,* vol 1: *Du moyen age à la revolution* (Metz. 1952), p. 45.
[68] C. Pfister, 'Le Théâtre à Nancy au XVIII siècle', *Le Pays Lorrain*, 7 (1900), 98.
[69] Jean-François Nicolas, *Journal de ce qui s'est passé à Nancy depuis la paix de Ryswick conclue le 30 Octobre 1697 jusqu'en l'année 1744 inclusivement*, ed. C. Pfister (Nancy, 1900), p. 86.
[70] AM Amiens, FF 1307, 9 février 1733. Signed by Leduc, 'comédien, au nom du Sr Francisque, chef de la troupe à présent à Rouen.'
[71] AM Grenoble, FF 57.
[72] AM Marseille, FF 308.
[73] Jeanne Cheilan-Cambolin, 'Notes sur les trois premières salles d'Opera et de Comédie de Marseille', *Provence Historique*, 40:160 (1990), 147–55 at p. 152.
[74] AD Avignon, 3E9(2) /215 Notaire Mounier.
[75] AM Marseille, FF 308.

In June 1733 the *Journal de la Cour & de Paris* had reported that 'L'Opéra-Comique vient d'être donné à Francisque qui y est né et qui saura bien le faire valoir.'[76] [The Opéra-Comique has just been given to Francisque who was born into it and will know well how to make it thrive]. The item is interesting in that it reinforces the contemporary perception that he embodied all that was best in the Fair theatres. But by the summer of 1733, Francisque, who had enjoyed great success in the provinces and beyond, had far more ambitious projects in mind than simply returning to the fairs.

---

[76] *Journal de la Cour & de Paris depuis le 28 novembre 1732 jusques au 30 novembre 1733*, ed. Henri Duranton (Saint-Étienne, 1981), p. 100.

9

Monsieur Francisque in Brussels and London: 1733–1734

In July 1733 Francisque went to Brussels to hire the Théâtre de la Monnaie for the winter season of 1733–4. On 3 August, he signed a detailed contract with the manager of La Monnaie, Jean-Baptiste Meeus, who, having no resident company, regularly let the theatre to French and Flemish touring companies. The contract, preserved in the Archives Générales du Royaume in Brussels, shows that Francisque was granted permission:

> pour le terme à commencer le premier octobre prochain finissant au premier jour du Carême prochain pour le prix de quatre mille florins pour le dit terme pour y pouvoir donner toutes sortes des comédies Opéra Comiques et ballets avec la troupe lui appartenant [...].[1]

> [for the term to begin the first of October next ending on the first day of Lent next, for the price of four thousand florins for the said term, to give all kinds of plays, opéras-comiques and ballets with the troupe belonging to him].

The Brussels Season 1733–4

In 1733 Brussels was the capital of the Austrian Netherlands under the governorship of the Archduchess Marie-Elisabeth of Austria. After Louis XIV's bombardment of the city in 1695, a magnificent new theatre with a capacity of almost 1300 had been built in 1700 on the site of the ruined Mint. The theatre was at the centre of a larger building and through a series of communicating doors it opened onto covered corridors housing cafés, shops, and gaming rooms.

The company opened as planned on 1 October, which happened to be the birthday of the Austrian Emperor. Most unusually, the opening performance was not a comedy but one of the grandest of French tragedies, Racine's

---

[1] I have modernized spelling and accents. The full contract is reproduced in Appendix 1.

Athalie.[2] The choice of this biblical tragedy may have been dictated by the Archduchess's well-known piety and taste for solemn or biblical drama, although she also attended Francisque's performances of comedies. *Athalie* was not a novelty for the Brussels audience; the Archduchess had seen it on 7 November 1730. Francisque's casting of the tragedy was made easier by the fact that his nephew Francis Cochois was at that time about fourteen years old and perfectly suited to the part of Joas, the boy-king of Israel; eighteen months later in London, he played the part at the Haymarket Theatre.

We have nothing like a complete programme for this major season of over five months. The Brussels journal *Relations véritables* seems to have included only those performances deemed worthy of report because of the presence of the Archduchess and her retinue. They were again present on 15 October (the feast of St Theresa) for *Rhadamiste et Zénobie,* by Crébillon *père*, one of the most popular of eighteenth-century tragedies. On 22 and 28 October the court attended what is merely listed as 'la Comédie' (here meaning simply the theatre). On 4 November, the feast of St Charles Borromeo, again in keeping with the solemnity of the occasion, the court was present for 'une Tragédie'. The journal also records that on 11 November Her Serene Highness saw *L'Embarras des richesses* by d'Allainval (Léonor Jean-Christine Soulas, abbé d'Allainval). This highly popular comedy, first performed at the Comédie-Italienne in 1725, seems to have been a favourite of Francisque's and it remained in his repertoire for many years. This is his first recorded performance. On 19 November, the feast day of her namesake St Elizabeth, the Archduchess was present at a performance of Racine's tragedy *Andromaque*. The company gave Romagnesi's tragicomedy *Samson* on 5 January 1734, and there were two further tragedies on 'Christian' themes in the same month: Voltaire's *Zaïre*, widely considered the most touching of all French tragedies, and Corneille's *Polyeucte martyr*. Towards the end of the season Marivaux's comedies *La Double Inconstance* and *Le Prince travesti* were performed, and the last recorded performance was *Arlequin maître et valet* [*Le Jeu de l'Amour et du Hasard*] on Shrove Tuesday, 9 March.[3] The presence of so many serious plays says something about Francisque's ambitions and also about the nature of the company that he had been gathering around him since his departure from the fairs. Since much of the Brussels repertory was repeated in London in the following year, it is likely that many performers mentioned in London cast lists were already present in Brussels. Desessars and his wife had been with the company since 1726 and Dubuisson since 1732, but the Lesages, along with the

---

[2] 'Relations véritables', in Frédéric Faber, *Histoire du Théâtre Français en Belgique*, 5 vols Paris and Brussels, 1877–82), vol. 4, p. 28. Faber reproduces entries only up to 20 November 1733.

[3] Two of the four performances in London in 1734–35 were advertised as *Le Jeu de l'Amour et du Hasard, ou Arlequin maître et valet.*

Fig. 9 *L'Embarras des Richesses*, frontispiece of 1735 London edition. Reproduced with the permission of Special Collections, Leeds University Library, Brotherton Collection [BC Lt d/EMB].

Verneuil couple, may have been recruited for Brussels.[4] Jean-Baptiste Lesage (called Lesage Jr. to distinguish him from Charles Lesage, who was either his father or elder brother) played the young lovers in most productions; in 1740 he would be described as a fine actor with a beautiful voice and would soon be involved in the running of the company. Verneuil was clearly an impressive actor as well: he played parts like the raisonneur Cleante in *Tartuffe* and the pathetic elderly Lusignan in *Zaïre*; his wife played dignified or comic elderly women, and his daughter, usually known as Mimi, would soon be playing ingénue roles.[5] There is no specific mention of Marie Châteauneuf being in Brussels, but her guardian the dancer Étienne Châteauneuf was there and it seems probable that she was there with the man who later became her husband.

At a performance of Le Noble's *Les Deux Arlequins* attended by the Archduchess, Francisque re-used one of his most amusing and dramatically effective *lazzi*, which had already formed the Prologue to Procope-Couteaux's *Arlequin balourd* in London in February 1719: the audience was told that Arlequin was ill, then a female spectator, after angrily protesting, finally leaped onto the stage and insisted that she would play the role herself: 'C'était l'Arlequin lui-même. Mais on avait eu soin de prévenir l'archiduchesse'[6] [This was Arlequin himself. But they had taken care to warn the Archduchess]. Francisque's contract was due to expire on the first day of Lent. In Paris the theatres played on through Lent almost up to Holy Week, but it may be that the pious Marie-Elisabeth went into retreat for Lent as she had done for Advent.[7] In 1734 Ash Wednesday in Brussels fell on 10 March (New Style), by which time Francisque had already gone ahead of his company to London.

Despite the incompleteness of the Brussels records, much of the missing repertoire may be suggested by the programme for the London season of the

---

[4] Lesage Jr. was not the son of the playwright Alain René Lesage, as is sometimes claimed. Lesage's third son was indeed an itinerant provincial actor, but his name was François-Antoine and he was always known simply as Pittenec. During the London season, cast lists published in the press included the names of Lesage Senior (Charles), Lesage Junior (Jean-Baptiste), and their wives, showing that this Lesage family was in no way related to the author of *Turcaret*, but belonged to an acting family possibly originating in Lyon.

[5] When the Malters' son, Étienne-Joseph, was baptised on 9 October in the church of Notre-Dame du Finistère, his godparents were the company members Étienne Châteauneuf, and 'Marie-Josèphe de Pré dite Verneuil.' Bruxelles, Archives de la Ville, Registres paroissiaux, paroisse Notre-Dame du Finistère, registre 439 p. 116.

[6] Jean-Nicolas Servandoni d'Hannetaire, *Observations sur l'art du comédien* (Paris, 1775), p. 148. The episode is also recorded by the Abbé Prévost,in *Le Pour et contre: ouvrage périodique d'un goût nouveau* (Paris, 1734–5) for 1735, and by Henri Liebrecht, *Histoire du Théâtre Français à Bruxelles au XVIIe et au XVIIIe siècle* (Paris, 1923), p. 165.

[7] See Liebrecht, *Histoire*, p. 121.

same year. Romagnesi's *Samson*, for instance, reappears for three performances in London, and *Les Deux Arlequins* for five. If the company performed only twice a week during their five-month stay, then they will have given around forty performances, usually with two plays at each, a considerable repertoire. In Francisque's contract for La Monnaie, ballets and dancers are both mentioned twice; it seems therefore clear that dancing featured prominently in the Brussels programmes, as it was to do six months later in London.

An anonymous pamphlet from many years later describes a brief war between Francisque and his public over ticket prices, a war which he eventually won. Though it contains a number of inaccuracies, it could well refer to the winter of 1733–4. The story certainly fits what is known of Francisque's temperament, and, according to the author of the pamphlet, he made a huge profit (more than 8000 florins).[8] The Brussels season must have been a financial as well as artistic success because, later that year in London, the Abbé Prévost mentions rumours of considerable wealth surrounding Francisque, and another source confirms the fact that 'il fit assez bien ses affaires'[9] [he did good business]. Further weight may be given to the story by his sudden appearance (alone) in London in January 1734. Francisque, perhaps following this dispute over seat prices, left his company in the hands of his associates while he went ahead to London to plan his next winter season. It could be that Simon Moylin joined his brother's Brussels company at that time and took over the role of Arlequin as he had done in the past.[10]

Piron, Romagnesi, and the Genesis of *Samson*

Thanks to the title-page of a Brussels edition, we know that on 5 January 1734 Francisque's company performed Jean-Antoine Romagnesi's five-act verse tragicomedy, *Samson*.[11] The genesis of this work, first given at the Comédie-Italienne on 28 February 1730 and almost forgotten today, is unusually complicated. It has been thought that Romagnesi's *Samson* was merely a French adaptation of Luigi Riccoboni's earlier *Sansone,* a prose Italian-language

---

[8] Faber, *Histoire*, quoting a pamphlet, *Spectacles français à Bruxelles, ou Calendrier historique du théâtre pour l'année 1767*. The inaccuracy of the dating is pointed out in Liebrecht, *Histoire*, p. 165.

[9] *Annuaire Dramatique de Belgique pour 1840* (Paris, 1840), p. 32.

[10] 'Sa famille se chargea de sa Troupe qui a toujours passée sous son nom.' [His family took charge of his troupe which always used his name]. *Dictionnaire Historique de la Ville de Paris et de ses environs*, ed. Pierre Hurtaut and Magny (Paris, 1779), vol. 4, p. 704.

[11] See, online: https://www.google.co.uk/books/edition/Samson/3QUUAAAAQ AAJ?hl=en&gbpv=1&dq=Samson+Romagnesi++Bruxelles&pg=PA1&printsec=front cover.

tragicomedy, which was given its first Paris performance by the recently-arrived Italian company on 28 February 1717. However, the relationship between the two plays, which has been called 'l'affaire des deux *Samsons*',[12] needs further discussion, as it directly concerns both Francisque Moylin and his friend Alexis Piron.

Why did Romagnesi, sometime in the mid-1720s, turn to the subject of Samson? The answer lies in Alexis Piron's *Épître* to Francisque (see p. 142, above). In it, Piron makes clear that, though Francisque had commissioned him to write a verse tragedy on the subject of Samson, he had broken off his work in order to write pieces for the fairs, which brought instant money. Having admitted that he never got beyond the first act of *Samson,* Piron added the following footnote to his *Épître*; 'Je donnai ce premier acte *en vers français* [emphasis added] à Romagnesi, qui le mit à la sauce qu'il voulut dans celui qu'il a donné en vers français au Théâtre-Italien.' [I gave the first act in French verse to Romagnesi, who served it up in his own fashion in the play in French verse that he presented at the Theatre-Italien]. Francisque's loss was Romagnesi's gain. It seems unlikely that Romagnesi would have looked a gift horse in the mouth by deviating significantly from Piron's generous offering. Although Romagnesi must be given credit for the highly effective completion of *Samson*, many of the scenes which he was later credited with adding or altering must in fact already have been elaborated in Piron's first act, where the characters are introduced and the broad lines of the plot are set in place. In other words, it may not be too fanciful to assert that Piron was more or less the author of the first act of Romagnesi's *Samson*, and that he wrote it with Francisque's company in mind.

Riccoboni's *Sansone*, in Italian, received only about seven performances in all, many of these to audiences of just a few hundred spectators. It was revived on 3 and 5 July 1727, at which time, it seems clear, Romagnesi's *Samson* was ready for production. Riccoboni, however, had argued in a petition to the Duc de Gesvres that the Romagnesi play was merely a translation of his *Sansone,* and the Duke had granted him, as head of the company, the right to cast the French play. Nothing seems to have come of this. By this time, according to his biographer, Riccoboni, whose attempts to create a purer Italian theatre on the Paris stage clashed with the public perception of what *Les Italiens* stood for, had lost faith in Italian-language tragicomedy based on Spanish models (he described his own *Sansone* in its first edition as a monster).[13] In the end, his loss of interest in the whole affair left Romagnesi free to mount his own

---

[12] Xavier de Courville, *Un Apôtre de l'art du théâtre au XVIIIe siècle, Luigi Riccoboni dit Lélio* (Paris, 1945), pp. 284–5. Claudio Vinti, *Jean-Antoine Romagnesi al 'Théâtre Italien'* (Naples, 1988), pp. 35–6.

[13] Courville, *Un Apôtre de l'art du théâtre*, p. 65.

production, first given on 28 February 1730. It was an instant and huge success, playing regularly to enormous audiences almost throughout the century. At the last four performances between 22 February and 7 March 1761 *Samson* was seen by an average of about a thousand people per performance.[14]

Both the *Mercure de France* and Parfaict agree that Romagnesi had improved Riccoboni's play to the point where he could be called an author rather than a translator.[15] The two plays are indeed very different in structure, tone and characterisation. Riccoboni dramatised the entire story of Samson, including both Philistine women who, successively, betray him. Thus, the Italian Dalila does not appear until the beginning of Act Four, where she is presented as a heartless coquette. On meeting Samson she immediately recognises that she has an opportunity to make a conquest of 'il terrore dei Filistei' [the terror of the Philistines]. When she has the secret of the Nazarite's hair, she gloats 'Qual trionfo per la mia bellezza!'[What a triumph for my beauty!]'[16]

Romagnesi, undoubtedly following Piron's reworking, introduces Dalila in the opening scene. This Dalila is already in love with Samson and is tormented by the conflict between love and duty. Her avowal to her confidante of her guilty passion for an enemy is expressed in verse of great delicacy:

> *Armilla.* Confiez à ma foi le feu qui vous dévore.
> *Dalila.* Hélas! C'est un Hébreu que ta Princesse adore.
> Les Dieux pour l'accabler du sort le plus cruel,
> En ont fait triompher le fils d'Emanuel.
> *Armilla.* Samson ...?
> *Dalila.* Oh jour fatal! malheureuse victoire![17]

> [*Armilla.* Entrust to me the passion that devours you.
> *Dalila.* Alas! He whom your Princess adores is a Hebrew.
> To overwhelm her with the cruellest fate,
> The gods have made the son of Emanuel her conqueror.
> *Armilla.* Samson ...?
> *Dalila.* Oh, fatal day! unhappy victory!]

---

[14] In this period an audience of a thousand was rarely reached except at premières, and in the whole of 1761 the audience for Samson was only equalled on six other nights. See Clarence D. Brenner, *The Théâtre Italien, its repertory 1716–1793* (Berkeley, 1961) and Lagrave, *TP*, pp. 603–5.

[15] *Mercure*, April 1730, p. 794, Parfaict, *Dict.*, vol. 5, p. 29.

[16] *Le Nouveau Théâtre Italien* (Paris, 1718), vol.1, pp. 89–99, 101. A French translation accompanied Riccoboni's Italian original.

[17] J.-A. Romagnesi, *Samson* (Paris, 1730), pp. 4–5.

There are clear echoes of *Phèdre* in this scene. Moreover, even though it is Armilla who betrays Samson, Dalila, like Racine's heroine, commits suicide out of remorse.

Riccoboni had created two comic servant roles; Piron, in the role he wrote for Francisque, conflated these as well. Ascalon-Arlequin, like the Spanish *gracioso,* brings the tragic characters down to earth with his unheroic actions and dialogue. None of this dialogue could have been found in Riccoboni, since, in the Italian tradition, his comic scenes were only unscripted scenarios on which the actors were expected to improvise. Some of Ascalon's behaviour even parodies that of the hero, as when, after Samson has killed a lion and carried the city gates on his back, the servant fights with a turkey and then carries it off in the same manner. Whether this was Piron's idea or Romagnesi's, it fits Piron's description of his first act as 'héroïque et burlesque'.

The critics admired the play, particularly the changes made to the character of Dalila. But the *Mercure*'s largely positive review refused even to discuss the comic scenes involving Arlequin-Ascalon, which it described as tasteless and out of place, redeemed only by the fine performance of Thomassin.[18] Mention of Thomassin reminds us that the cast of *Samson* must have been virtually identical to that of Marivaux's *Le Jeu de l'amour et du hasard*, which had been premiered at the Comédie-Italienne almost exactly one month earlier in January 1730. Judging by audience numbers for *Samson*, the public did not share the reservations of the critics. At the Comédie-Italienne they were used to seeing a mixture of genres, long since proscribed at the Comédie-Française.

When (as he surely did) Francisque saw Romagnesi's play in 1730, he must have felt a twinge of legitimate resentment at the fact that Marivaux's Arlequin, 'le gentil Thomassin', was delighting Paris audiences in a role originally conceived for him. Given the gaps in documentation, we cannot know for certain when he first performed in *Samson* himself, but we can be sure that he was responsible for the appearance of the Brussels edition of 1734, whose title page says that it was 'performed for the first time on 5 January 1734 by the French and Italian comediens on the Grand Theatre of Brussels'[19] Romagnesi's publisher Delanoe had a seven-year exclusive *privilège* for *Samson*. But beyond the borders of France, the French *privilège* did not apply, so Francisque could reclaim what he may well have thought of as his own. He seems to have wanted through such publications to associate his name with certain plays and playwrights, thereby leaving tangible evidence of the considerable achievements of his little company.

---

[18] *Mercure*, April 1730, pp. 800 and 803.
[19] The title page and full text can be viewed at: https://www.google.co.uk/books/edition/Samson/3QUUAAAAQAAJ?hl=en&gbpv=1&dq=Romagnesi+Samson+Bruxelles&pg=PA1&printsec=frontcover.

Thanks to the cast list given in the London press at the end of this same year, we may even suggest the probable Brussels cast for *Samson* in January 1734: *Samson*, Lesage Jr.; *Phanor*, Verneuil; *Acab*, Lesage Sr.; *Emmanuël*, Dessessars; *Azaël*, Delisle; *Zamec*, Dubuisson; *Ascalon*, Arlequin-Francisque; *Dalila*, Mme Malter; *Armilla*, Mme Francisque. The Mrs Malter who played Dalila in London was Francisque's niece Catherine; her *confidente*, Mrs Francisque, was in real life her maternal aunt.

I have found six recorded performances of Francisque's *Samson*: in Brussels, London, Compiègne, and finally in Dijon in 1739. Three of these records survive because their prestigious location and royal patronage ensured their mention in the press. The Dijon performance is recorded in a diary, still in manuscript, kept by the theatre-loving magistrate Claude Micault.[20] Francisque had undoubtedly given many more performances in the towns through which he passed. Félix Gaiffe has pointed out that the play's enormous popularity is proved by the many editions which appeared throughout the eighteenth century, and not only in Paris;[21] moreover, its stage sets are mentioned in the inventories and managers' contracts of many provincial theatres at this period.[22] Francisque's request for a verse tragedy on the subject of Samson had inspired Piron to attempt his first serious drama, and Francisque deserves much of the credit for the dissemination and popularity of Romagnesi's *Samson* in the provinces and abroad throughout the eighteenth century.

Marie Sallé, Francisque, and the Malters

In the autumn of 1733, shortly before her family left for Brussels, Marie Sallé was in Paris, but it was reported both in London and Paris that she was on the point of returning to London, where she was to dance for the first time at Rich's new Covent Garden theatre. In a letter of 1731 to the Duchess of Richmond, Sallé had indicated that she was already planning her return but was delayed by 'une maladie dangereuse' [23] [a dangerous illness]. She had also made it abundantly clear that she did not like John Rich, whom she described as 'un

---

[20] Archives Municipales de Dijon, MS 742 bis, microfilm 555, reproducing ff 2v–3r (troupe de Moylin) and 9v–10r (troupe de Francisque) from Part 2 of the *Mercure dijonnois de Claude Micault*. See Appendix 3.

[21] A search of the Catalogue Collectif de France on the website of the Bibliothèque Nationale gives over thirty locations for *Samson* in the provinces, with the BnF itself holding at least eight copies. There are also contemporary copies in Paris, The Hague and Amsterdam. It was published in a Dutch translation (Rotterdam, Hofhout) in 1803.

[22] Félix Gaiffe (citing Fuchs), *Le Rire et la Scène Française* (Paris, 1931), p. 173.

[23] Sarah McCleave, 'Dancing at the English Opera: Marie Sallé's letter to the Duchess of Richmond', *Dance Research*, 17:1 (1999), 22–46, at p. 41.

homme impoli et injuste, dont j'ai souffert trop de mauvais traitemens'[24] [a rude and unjust man at whose hands I have suffered too much ill treatment]. Her plans were almost certainly further delayed by the news of the sudden death of her brother at the age of twenty-seven. Francis, who had danced leading roles in pantomimes in Rich's company, died on 9 June 1732 and was buried at St Augustine's, Hackney.[25] Sallé might have been expected to travel to London for the opening of the 1732 season, but she stayed at the Opéra until December 1732, the date mentioned in her contract; then, for a year, she remained in Paris, dancing by private invitation only. An item in a news sheet in February 1733 – 'Mlle Sallé a pensé mourir, et toute la vertu de l'Opéra avec elle!'[26] [Mlle Sallé almost died, and with her all the moral decency at the Opéra] – suggests that her long-delayed departure may have been due to serious illness, possibly a recurrence of the earlier 'maladie dangereuse' of 1731, perhaps also with a psychological element.

No record exists of her whereabouts between mid-September 1733 and her opening night on 8 November at Covent Garden, apart from a disparaging news item in the *Journal de la Cour & de Paris* dated 12 October: 'Parlons de Mlle Sallé pour la dernière fois. Elle part le 16 pour Londres, mignaudant [sic] d'avance sur la peur que le trajet lui donne.'[27] [Let us speak of Mlle Sallé for the last time. She is leaving for London on the 16th, whinging in advance about her fear of the journey]. But on 12 September 1733, the same journal had revealed that she had already chosen as her London dancing partner 'un petit Maltaire *qu'elle emmène avec elle en Angleterre* [emphasis added]. Ce Maltaire n'est connu que dans les provinces, ou il a mieux aimé tenir le premier rang que d'être confondu ici parmi les autres danseurs.'[28] [a little Malter fellow *whom she is taking with her to England* [emphasis added]]. This Malter is known only in the provinces, where he has preferred to be in the first rank rather than be lost here among the other dancers].

---

[24] McCleave, 'Dancing', p. 37.

[25] See p. 161. For the effect of her brother's death on Sallé, see Parmenia Migel, *The Ballerinas, from the Court of Louis XIV to Pavlova* (London, 1972), p. 29.

[26] *Journal de la Cour et de Paris depuis le 28 novembre 1732 jusques au 30 novembre 1733*, ed. Henri Duranton (Saint-Étienne, 1981), p. 61.

[27] *Journal*, ed. Duranton, p. 161. 'Simpering' in modern French is 'minaudant'.

[28] *Journal*, ed. Duranton, p. 155. It is therefore impossible to support J.-P. van Aelbrouck's claim that Jean-Baptiste made his début at the Paris Opera in 1734 (*Dictionnaire des danseurs, chorégraphes et maîtres de danse à Bruxelles de 1600 à 1830* (Liège, 1994), p. 176). Arthur Pougin also wrongly claimed that Malter was one of Sallé's 'meilleurs camarades de l'Opéra': Pougin, *Un ténor de l'Opéra au XVIIIe siècle: Pierre Jélyotte* (Paris, 1905), p. 143.

This reporter obviously was unaware either that Jean-Baptiste Malter was Francisque's *maître de ballet* or that he was Sallé's cousin by marriage. Furthermore, Marie Sallé had been a pupil of Ballon and Prévost, two of the finest dancers at the Paris Opéra, and she was renowned, some said notorious, for her impeccably high artistic standards. Despite her close family ties to Malter, it seems to me highly unlikely that she would have consented to partner him if his ability did not at least come close to her own. The company which was leaving for Brussels included all the closest family members left to Sallé after the death of her brother Francis and she would have known that the relatives with whom she had performed since childhood were hoping to return to London the following year. Since Catherine Labbé was pregnant and had been unable to dance for several months, Malter was temporarily without his regular dancing partner at the very moment when Sallé was about to face London without her beloved brother.

It therefore seems to me both possible and plausible that Marie did not travel directly from Paris to London but accompanied or followed her uncle's troupe to Brussels. The troupe certainly included the pregnant Catherine Malter and, presumably, Malter himself. The Malters' newborn son, Étienne-Joseph, was baptised on 9 October in the church of Notre-Dame du Finistère and his godparents (who gave him their names) were the company members Étienne Châteauneuf, and 'Marie-Josèphe de Pré dite Verneuil'.[29] Thus, as late as the end of October (N.S.), Marie and Malter could have travelled on from Brussels to London while Catherine and her new-born child remained in Brussels until she was fit to travel.

The London season began in October, which is also the period from which contracts normally began; however, Marie and Malter did not arrive in London before November. If my hypothesis is correct, it would also have been possible for Marie, in Brussels, to begin teaching her cousins, Francis, Babet and Marianne Cochois, now aged around twelve, ten and nine, and the twelve-year-old Marie Châteauneuf, who, like Marie, had lost her mother at an early age.[30] When Marie Châteauneuf came to London with Francisque's company in 1734 she gave three performances of one of Sallé's early specialities, Jean-Féry Rebel's *Les Caractères de la danse*, beginning on 30 October, the third night of Francisque's season. Her ability to take on this work supports my suggestion that Sallé began to teach Châteauneuf in Brussels, as it would

---

[29] Archives de l'État en Belgique, Registres paroissiaux, Notre-Dame du Finistère, registre 439 p. 116.

[30] According to the Drury Lane prompter William Chetwood, who knew her well, Marie Châteauneuf was born on 15 April 1721. Chetwood reveals that she sang as well as she danced; he coached her for the part of Polly in *The Beggar's Opera*. W. Chetwood, *A General History of the Stage* (London, 1749), pp. 129–30. See also van Aelbrouck, *Dictionnaire*, pp. 89–90.

have been a remarkable achievement to teach this ballet to a thirteen-year-old girl in just a couple of days in London. Even more intriguing is the possibility that in October 1733 Sallé and Malter took part, however briefly, in the dancing at the Théâtre de la Monnaie as a kind of dress rehearsal for Covent Garden. As we have already noted, Francisque's contract for the Théâtre de la Monnaie specifically mentions the company's intention to give 'toutes sortes des comédies, Opéra Comiques ... et ballets.'

Francisque and the Drury Lane Rebels 1734

In January 1734, while his company continued to perform in Brussels, Francisque came to London where he was undoubtedly welcomed by Marie Sallé, Jean-Baptiste Malter and Francis Nivelon, who had been a friend and colleague of Marie's recently deceased brother.[31] Marie and Malter had been dancing at Covent Garden since November 1733, and it is possible that Marie was in some way instrumental in facilitating her uncle's return to England. Sarah McCleave's publication of Marie's letter to the Duchess of Richmond in 1731 – one of only two known Sallé letters, and the only one concerned with artistic matters – throws light on the network of powerful associations built up by the extended Moylin-Sallé-Cochois family. As McCleave writes, 'The letter is couched in such terms of respect and affection as to suggest a very solid relationship.'[32] It is therefore hardly surprising that Francisque's contract for the winter season of 1734–5 is preserved in the archives of the Dukes of Richmond.

The Richmond contract was signed on 6 March 1734. In January, however, Francisque had made a rather surprising move by joining a company of English actors led by Theophilus Cibber. Cibber had quarrelled with the managers of the Drury Lane Theatre and had set up a breakaway company at the Little Theatre in the Haymarket in the autumn of 1733. Along with most of the best Drury Lane actors, it included the influential dancer and choreographer John Essex, Nivelon, and the actor-dancers Haughton and Miss Robinson, all of whom had recently danced in Paris.[33] Music was provided by the composer Thomas Arne, whose sister and brother, Susanna and Richard Arne, acted, danced, and sang. The company opened on 26 September 1733 and continued to

---

[31] Malter's wife Catherine must have accompanied Francisque, since the Malters' next child, Jean-Louis, baptised in Lille on 10 September 1734, must have been conceived in London.

[32] McCleave, 'Dancing', p. 31.

[33] Parfaict, *Mém*, vol. 2, p. 74, and the entries on Haughton and 'Robinson, Miss, later Mrs. Campbell Price', in Philip Highfill et al., *A Biographical Dictionary of Actors, Actresses, Musicians, Dancers, Managers, and Other Stage Personnel in London, 1660–1800*, 16 Vols (Carbondale, 1973–93), vol. 7, p. 178; vol. 13, pp. 20–1.

perform until 9 March 1734, attracting larger and more appreciative audiences than the remnant company at Drury Lane. Theophilus Cibber had scored a remarkable coup in October 1733 when the press announced 'A comic dance by Mr Nivelon from the Theatre in Covent Garden, being the first Time of his appearing on this Stage.'[34] Nivelon had been one of John Rich's leading French dancers but their relations had often been strained, and in 1725 Nivelon had sued Rich for non-payment of salary.[35]

Francisque made his debut with Cibber's company on Saturday 12 January 1734. On that night the programme announced in *The Daily Journal* consisted entirely of new productions. The main play was John Banks' blank-verse tragedy *The Albion Queens, or the Death of Mary, Queen of Scotland*, followed by Thomas Arne's 'Dramatic Masque', *Dido and Aeneas*, another work depicting a tragic and iconic queen. Arne re-used Barton Booth's libretto *The Death of Dido*, which had already been set to music by Johann Pepusch, a composer principally remembered today for his arrangement of the airs for Gay's *The Beggar's Opera*. The original masque was first performed at Drury Lane in 1716. Pepusch's music and Booth's published libretto have survived, but most of Arne's setting has been lost, apart from two airs published in a contemporary song-book.[36] The loss of Arne's setting of *Dido* is a matter for serious regret since Arne was probably the finest native British composer of the eighteenth century. It would have been fascinating to hear the music which Thomas wrote for his fourteen-year-old soprano brother Richard, who sang Cupid, and his sister Susannah in the role of Dido.[37]

The Haymarket playbill in *The Daily Journal* for 12 January states, however, that *Dido* was to be 'intermix'd (by particular Desire) with a Grotesque Pantomime, *The Burgomaster Trick'd*'. This pantomime was clearly modelled (probably by Nivelon himself) on an entertainment of the same name by Theobald, *The Burgomaster Trick'd*, first performed at Lincoln's Inn Fields in 1726, with music by Johann Ernst Galliard.[38] (The cast lists given in the

---

[34] *The Daily Journal*, 13 October, 1733.

[35] See Jennifer Thorp, 'Pierrot strikes back: François Nivelon at Lincoln's Inn Fields and Covent Garden, 1723–1738', in Berta Joncus and Jeremy Barlow, eds, *The Stage's Glory: John Rich, 1692–1761* (Newark, 2011), pp. 138–46.

[36] *The British Musical Miscellany, or The Delightful Grove* 4 vols (vols 1–2, London, 1734, vols 3–4, London 1735), vol.1, pp. 102–3, 123–4. It has been claimed that only at Handel's English oratorios 'did the patrons actually have the words in front of them during performance': Ruth Smith, *Handel's Oratorios and Eighteenth-Century Thought* (Cambridge, 1995), p. 76, but *The Daily Journal* also announced, 'NB. The Masque will be printed and delivered gratis at the Theatre.'

[37] Aeneas was sung by 'Miss Jones', and Mercury by 'Mr Kelly'.

[38] Rich's Burgomaster is fully discussed in Viola Papetti, *Arlecchino a Londra: la pantomima inglese, 1700–1728 (studi e testi)* (Naples, 1977), p. 159.

press for the two versions are virtually identical.) Nivelon had created the title role in that highly popular production, given forty-four times in its initial season alone, and Harlequin was played by Lun (John Rich). In the classical section of the plot, Marie Sallé had danced the role of Daphne with her brother Francis as Apollo, a role he reprised many times. Beyond the presence of Nivelon as the Burgomaster and Cibber himself as a servant,[39] what makes this new production of *The Burgomaster Trick'd* exceptionally interesting is the presence of 'Mons. Francisque', for the first and only time, as a *silent* Harlequin, fully integrated into an English company, in a pantomime performed in the peculiarly English or, perhaps more accurately, Anglo-French, manner. The evening concluded with 'The Grand Ballet', *Les Ombres des amants fidèles*, for which *The Daily Journal* lists eight dancers, including the Miss Mann who played Colombine to Francisque's Harlequin, and the Miss Robinson who had danced in Paris in 1732. Thomas Arne may have written the music for the songs and dances and for the concluding ballet. If so, these have also been lost.[40]

I have already suggested that Sallé and Malter accompanied Francisque's troupe to Brussels and, while there, began the experimentation that led to the creation of *Pygmalion* in London. The start of Sallé's London season seems to have been briefly overshadowed by the success of Manon Grognet from the Paris fairs, dancing as a 'petit-maître' [fop] in 'mens' cloaths' at Drury Lane and attracting a glittering crowd. On 1 December 1733 Mathieu Marais reported on her success and suggested that Sallé was jealous. But, he added, 'c'est une autre danse, et il y en aura pour tout le monde'[41] [it's another kind of dance and there's enough for everyone]. There was in fact no reason for jealousy, since what Marais meant by 'une autre danse' was that Grognet was performing in a completely different style from the *belle danse* of the Opéra-trained Sallé.[42]

Émile Dacier noted that for their first two months at Covent Garden, Sallé and Malter danced only simple, conventional solos and *pas de deux*, familiar stock-in-trade character dances. He offered no explanation for the curious imbalance of what he described as a season 'commencée de la façon la plus

---

[39] Other named cast members were 'Miss Mann' as Columbine, Janno (?), Tench, and, surprisingly, Mrs. Pritchard as a peasant woman.

[40] When Nivelon eventually agreed to rejoin Rich's company at Covent Garden in 1735–6, he took back many of his old roles, including the Burgomaster.

[41] Letter to Bouhier, *Correspondance Littéraire du Président Bouhier*, ed. Henri Duranton, 14 vols, vol. 6: Lettres de Matthieu Marais (1733–1735) (Saint-Étienne, 1988), 9:2, p. 26.

[42] For a full discussion of these different dancing styles, see Sarah McCleave, *Dance in Handel's London Operas* (Rochester, NY, 2013), pp. 9–21.

terne et terminée en apothéose'[43] [beginning drably and ending with an apotheosis]. The apotheosis to which Dacier refers was the first of Marie's two landmark choreographic innovations, *Pygmalion*, with Sallé as Galatea and Malter as Pygmalion, on 14 January 1734. It was then that, as Sarah McCleave puts it, 'a woman born into a family of itinerant fairground performers enabled, through prodigious talent, a new aesthetic to emerge'.[44] It is surely no coincidence that this première took place just two days after her uncle Francisque's opening performance in *The Burgomaster Trick'd* at the Haymarket. Given Marie's extreme timidity and her personal dislike of John Rich, it seems to me highly likely that, perhaps even by agreement with Francisque in advance, she delayed the première of her most daringly innovative creation until the reassuring presence of her famous uncle and Malter's wife Catherine gave her and her dancing partner the courage to face the public – in the newest theatre in the most important capital in Europe – in what Dacier called Sallé's first real 'danse d'action'.[45]

A description of the action of the ballet makes it clear that Malter was no mere supporter in a *pas de deux* but played an important solo role in the scenes before the statue comes to life.[46] Even after that point, it is he who teaches Galatea her first faltering steps. It may even be that, while rehearsing in Brussels, Marie and Malter *together* developed the freer style and costume which eventually led to the creation of this ground-breaking ballet. Marie's family could have reminded her that, back in 1717, the young actress Adrienne Lecouvreur, fresh from the provinces, had caused a sensation at her début at the Comédie-Française in Crébillon's tragedy *Électre*.[47] Breaking with the tradition of elaborate gowns and ornate plumed headdresses, Lecouvreur appeared with her own hair worn loose; she was dressed in a plain white satin Greek tunic and adopted a simpler and more natural acting style. This is very much how Sallé's Covent Garden appearance as Galatea would be described.[48]

Sallé's *Pygmalion* reconquered her London public, and on 21 March 1734, 'by their Majesties' Command', she enjoyed a Benefit in the presence of the

---

[43] Dacier, p. 146. Dacier wrongly gave the date of the creation of *Pygmalion* as 14 February.

[44] Sarah McCleave, 'Marie Sallé and the development of the ballet en action', *Journal of the Society for Musicology in Ireland* 3 (2007–8), 1–23, at p. 23.

[45] While Rich may well have had a hand in the date of this performance, this does not diminish the importance of Francisque's arrival only two days before.

[46] A full account of the action appeared as a letter dated 15 March in the April issue of the *Mercure*. For an English translation see Moira Goff, https://danceinhistory.com/2019/12/31/the-first-ballet-at-covent-garden/.

[47] See Jack Richtman, *Adrienne Lecouvreur: The Actress and the Age* (Englewood Cliffs, N.J., 1971), p. 59.

[48] The example of Lecouvreur predates that of Hester Santlowe, who has also been suggested as a model for Sallé's appearance.

Prince of Wales and the Prince of Orange; the King and Queen reluctantly stayed away, fearing the oppressive overcrowding. The Abbé Prévost raved about the enthusiasm of the audience and calculated that it had resulted in a fortune for Sallé. He added that she might have earned even more if, as was rumoured, she had not rejected an offer of two thousand guineas to 'grant her favours'.[49]

Drury Lane had never quite equalled Rich's success in pantomime, but suddenly at the Little Haymarket, Cibber and the Drury Lane rebels enjoyed the services of both 'the Adroit and Elegant Monsieur Nivelon',[50] creator of many of Rich's best pantomimes, and 'the famous Monsieur Francisque', the Harlequin from whom Rich had learned his craft almost twenty years earlier. *Dido and Aeneas* and *The Burgomaster Trick'd*, which combined the talents not only of Nivelon and Francisque but also of the Arne family, had a very successful run of seventeen performances. These must have caused Rich considerable anxiety in view of the fact that the Theobald version of *The Burgomaster Trick'd* with *Apollo and Daphne* was still being given at Covent Garden, with Laguerre as the Burgomaster and Rich himself (Lun) as Harlequin.[51] Lun and Francisque must have been seen as in direct competition, and in a satirical poem published a year later the English and French Harlequins are compared to a couple of squabbling dogs.[52] The other great success of Cibber's season was James Miller's new comedy *The Mother-in-Law or The Doctor the Disease*, largely an adaptation of Moliere's *Le Malade imaginaire*, which received eighteen performances at the Haymarket. This was the first time that Francisque and Miller crossed paths, but it was not to be the last.

Francisque's final appearance with Cibber's company was on 18 February 1734, which was also the last advertised performance of Arne's *Dido and Aeneas*.[53] He remained in London until the 6th of March, when he signed the agreement already mentioned with the Duke of Richmond for the winter season at the little Haymarket. The agreement reads as follows:

---

[49] Prévost d'Exile, Antoine-François [L'Abbé Prévost], *Le Pour et contre: ouvrage périodique d'un goût nouveau* (Paris, 1734–5), vol. 3 (39), p. 216.

[50] See Moira Goff, 'The Adroit and Elegant Monsieur Nivelon', in *Dancing Master or Hop Merchant: The role of the Dance Teacher through the Ages*, ed. Barbara Segal (London, 2008), pp. 69–77.

[51] In her otherwise excellent account of Nivelon's career, Jennifer Thorp makes no mention of Arne's *Dido and Aeneas* or the Haymarket *Burgomaster Trick'd*, or Francisque and Nivelon's part in it. See 'Pierrot strikes back' in *The Stage's Glory*, ed. Joncus and Barlow, pp. 138–43.

[52] See below, pp. 235–6.

[53] Shorn of Arne's 'intermix'd' masque, *The Burgomaster* featured in the Drury Lane programme in the 1734–5 season, with Nivelon still in the title role but with the dancer Lebrun in the role of Harlequin.

> Proposals by Francisque Moylin Director of the French Theatre in the Hay Market, for furnishing a complete set of French comedians for the Winter season 1735 in manner following /viz/ He, the said Francisque Moylin, does hereby promise and engage himself to furnish out a complete set of French Comedians, and to provide the theatre in the Haymarket now called the French Theatre or some other place at least as convenient as the said theatre, and in such theatre or place to act French plays one hundred nights in the winter season of the said year 1735. And the said Francisque Moylin does hereby likewise promise that such Gentlemen and Ladies or their assigns shall be free of such house in which the said one hundred French plays are to be acted, at all times during the continuation of the performance thereof, except the night wherein the said Francisque Moylin's benefit shall happen, on producing a silver ticket to be delivered by the said Francisque Moylin for that purpose, which ticket is to admit but one person at a time on payment of the sum of ten guineas in manner following / viz/ Three guineas part thereof on subscribing these presents and the farther sum of seven guineas, the residue thereof, on delivery of the silver ticket the week before the first night of acting.

On a second sheet of paper is the heading for a subscription list:

> We whose names are underwritten being desirous to give all due encouragement to the French theatrical performances and especially to the endeavours of the said Francisque Moylin, do hereby each of us promise to pay to the said Francisque Moylin the sum of ten guineas at the time and in the manner above proposed in consideration of the above freedom. [54]

This second sheet contains no signatures. Like the first sheet it is in pristine condition and would seem to be a fair copy retained for the Duke's records.

In his biography of Marie Sallé, Emile Dacier stated rather condescendingly that Francisque found himself in London in 1734 'au hazard de ses pérégrinations'[55] [by chance in his wanderings]. Max Fuchs, more accurately, noted:

> L'Arlequin de la Foire n'est point un bohème: c'est un homme d'affaires entendu; sa troupe, qui parcourt toute la France, ne se met certainement pas en route sans avoir assuré au moins ses principales étapes, et longtemps à l'avance.[56]

---

[54] West Sussex County Record Office, Goodwood Ms145. I am grateful to the trustees of the Goodwood estate for permission to reproduce this manuscript document.
[55] Dacier, p. 142.
[56] Fuchs, *VT*, p. 124.

[The Arlequin of the Fair was no bohemian: he was a sound businessman; his troupe, which travelled all over France, certainly did not set out without having agreed at least its main stopping places well in advance.]

The Richmond document fully supports Fuchs' view, as does the contract drawn up in Brussels in August 1733, both of them months ahead of the proposed seasons. As the contract reveals, the French season was just as professionally organised as the costlier seasons at the two rival operas. Judith Milhous and Robert Hume have shown that in a slightly earlier season, Handel was counting on around 122 opera subscribers among the nobility and gentry at 15 guineas per subscription. In the light of this information the 10 guineas asked by Francisque is by no means an insignificant sum for the less costly business of spoken theatre.[57] Francisque also employed the practice, common with opera subscribers, of the 'silver ticket.' This special ticket was distributed to all paid-up subscribers one week before performances began. It could be used at no further cost to secure admission for the holder on any night, with one exception which also reveals Francisque's business acumen: 'except the night wherein the said Francisque Moylin's benefit shall happen.' This contract, and the one signed in Brussels the previous year, are valuable as the only known examples from Francisque's career, but they surely indicate the degree of legal formality which the impresario expected and received elsewhere.

Having finalised these arrangements, Francisque rejoined his company in France. In July 1734 he requested permission to perform in Amiens and, for the first time, described himself as 'chef de la troupe des comédiens privilégiés du Roy'[58] [leader of the company of actors licensed by the king]. It seems most unlikely that the company had already received such a title from Louis XV because he was to grant it to them in 1739, but Francisque had performed in London by command and in the presence of the British royal family, so perhaps this was a reference, not to the king of France but to the king of the country to which the company was about to return.

---

[57] Judith Milhous and Robert D. Hume, 'Handel's Opera Finances in 1732–3', *The Musical Times*, 125:1692 (Feb. 1984), 86–9.
[58] AM Amiens, FF. 1307.

10

The London season, 1734–1735: Part One

At a time when in Paris there were just three licensed theatres and the seasonal theatres of the fairgrounds, London theatregoers in 1734–5 had an 'embarrassment of riches',[1] with performances from six professional companies. As early as July 1734 *The London Evening Post* announced the impressive roster:

> We hear that the Town will be entertain'd next season with an Opera at the Haymarket [The King's Theatre], and with another under the direction of Mr. Handel (twice a week) at the new Theatre in Covent-Garden [...].The former will consist of Signor Senesino, Signora Cuzzoni, Signora Celesti, Signora Bertolli, and Signora Montagnana, with the addition of the famous Signor Farinelli, who is now on the road from Italy, and is expected to land shortly at Dover. [...] The Opera under the direction of Mr. Handel will be compos'd of Signor Carestini, Signora Strada, The Signore Negre, and some celebrated voices who have been sent for over from Italy. We also hear that Mademoiselle Sallé is to dance in the said Opera at Covent-Garden theatre. And that a company of comedians from Paris have taken the little Playhouse in the Haymarket, in order to act French Comedies there.[2]

As this quotation makes clear, Francisque's company was to be part of a season when a large number of prestigious French and Italian artists were working on, and indeed dominating, the London stage. Summing up the season as it drew to a close in June 1735, the Abbé Prévost wrote, 'Les dernières nouvelles du Théâtre de Londres contiennent trois Articles qui surpassent tout ce qu'un sujet si fécond m'a fourni jusqu'à présent.'[3] [The latest news from

---

[1] An expression derived from the title of d'Allainval's comedy *L'Embarras des Richesses* (1726).

[2] *London Evening Post*, 11–13 July 1734. This news item makes it clear that all these contracts must have been drawn up almost six months in advance of the new season.

[3] Antoine-François Prévost d'Exile [L'Abbé Prévost], *Le Pour et contre: ouvrage périodique d'un goût nouveau* (Paris, 1734–5), 6 (87), pp. 283–8. Jean Sgard dates the preceding number of *Le Pour et contre* to early June 1735. Jean Sgard, *Le 'Pour et contre' de Prévost. Introduction, tables et index* (Paris, 1969), p. 55. No. 87 would seem to date from late June, see p. 33.

the London theatre contains three items that surpass everything that so rich a subject has furnished me hitherto.] The three items he had in mind were Farinelli, Marie Sallé, and Francisque Moylin.

The careers of Farinelli and Sallé are well documented. They earned enormous sums of money during this season, a fact on which Prévost and many others commented disapprovingly. These two artists were the stars of two rival companies. In 1733, a group of aristocrats, tiring of the high-handedness of Handel (the King and Queen's favourite), had lured most of his best singers to what is usually called The Opera of the Nobility, directed by Nicola Porpora and patronised by Frederick, Prince of Wales. At the opening of the 1734–5 season Heidegger brought Porpora's company to King's and Handel moved to share Covent Garden with Rich's company. At this time Porpora had just succeeded (where Handel had failed) in acquiring the services of the castrato Carlo Broschi, known as Farinelli and hailed throughout Europe as the finest singer of the day. It was partly as a counter-attraction to this operatic superstar that Rich and Handel engaged Marie Sallé, at a fee rumoured to be three thousand francs.[4] If this sum is anywhere near correct, it puts Sallé in the same exclusive financial bracket as Farinelli. Sallé was the choreographer for Handel's 1734–5 opera season at Covent Garden. Between them, the two operatic factions, one with the exquisite 'siren-pipe' voice of Farinelli, the other with the dancing and choreography of Marie Sallé, provided the London public with an exceptional season of music and dance.

Farinelli made his eagerly awaited London début on Tuesday 29 October in Hasse's opera *Artaserse*, directed by Porpora.[5] *The Daily Advertiser* reported that 'All the Royal Family were at the Opera, when Signior Farinelli perform'd [...] with prodigious applause.' By 7 June 1735 the company had given 64 performances, with the King and Queen present on three occasions. Handel opened his season at Covent Garden on 9 November with the *opera seria, Il Pastor Fido*, preceded by *Terpsicore*, an opéra-ballet in the French style, a starring vehicle for Marie Sallé, who was also its choreographer. The King and Queen were present at Covent Garden on nineteen evenings throughout this season, which included the spectacular premières of *Ariodante* and *Alcina*, with choreography and dancing by Sallé. In spite of this conspicuous royal patronage, Sallé was overshadowed by the new castrato,[6] and her season with Handel marked both the high point and the end of her association with

---

[4] Sarah McCleave, *Dance in Handel's London Operas* (Rochester, NY, 2013), p. 73.

[5] See Thomas McGeary, 'Farinelli's Progress to Albion: The Recruitment and Reception of Opera's "Blazing Star"', *Journal for Eighteenth-Century Studies*, 28:3 (December 2000), 339–60.

[6] Graham Cummings, 'Handel's Organ Concertos (HWV 290–93) and Operatic Rivalry', *The GFH Journal*, 1 (2007), 21.

Fig. 10 Marie Sallé, detail from engraving of the painting by Nicolas Lancret (Alamy).

the London stage. Meanwhile, Farinelli's glamorous and sexually ambivalent personality launched a kind of hysteria, the *morbus farinellicus*.[7]

Modern scholars have paid little attention to the third of Prévost's 'three items', the ambitious programme of French theatre given between October 1734 and June 1735 by Francisque Moylin's company at the Little Theatre in the Haymarket, which by now had come to be known as the French Theatre. Yet an online search of the Burney newspaper collection reveals that the names of Francisque and Farinelli appeared in the press roughly the same number of times, and were discussed at much the same length, during that season.[8] Moreover, the French company was patronised by the entire royal family: King George II and Queen Caroline, their sons Frederick, Prince of Wales and William, Duke of Cumberland, and their daughters the Princesses Anne, Amelia, Caroline, Louisa and Mary.

Francisque and his company arrived on 18 October and his season opened on 26 October with *L'Embarras des richesses* and *Arlequin Hulla*, both starring Francisque as Arlequin.[9] The company performed on Mondays, Wednesdays, Thursdays, and Fridays; two or three plays were given each evening, normally beginning at six o'clock. Seat prices were similar to those at Drury Lane and Goodman's Fields: boxes at 5 shillings, pit at 3 shillings, and gallery at 2 shillings.

Detailed playbills appeared almost daily in the press, and the cast lists which (infrequently) appeared give the names of the following actors: Michel Cochois, Master [Francis] Cochois, De Lisle, Deshayes, Dessesars, Dubuisson, Francisque, Malter, Charles Lesage (Lesage Sr.), Jean-Baptise Lesage (Lesage Jr.), and Louis-Joseph Verneuil; (Actresses) Marguerite Cochois, Mrs. Dessesars, Marie-Antoinette Fompré, Mimi Verneuil (later Fourcade), Marie-Catherine Moylin, Catherine Malter, Mrs. Lesage Jr., Mlle Villepierre,[10] Marie-Louise Verneuil. Those named as dancers were Baudoin, Castiglione, Granier, Roland, Villeneuve; Mlle Chateauneuf, Mlle Grognet. The list of dancers should also include Michel Cochois' 'Lilliputians', a team of at least eight of the company's children. But, as Barlow and Goff point out with regard to the English theatre,

---

[7] The Farinelli phenomenon has been discussed in all its bizarre detail by Thomas McGeary, 'Farinelli and the English: 'One God' or the Devil?', *Revue LISA/LISA e-journal*, vol. 2:3 (2004), https://doi.org/10.4000/lisa.1130. Cf. Judith Milhous and Robert D. Hume, 'Construing and Misconstruing Farinelli in London', *British Journal for Eighteenth-Century Studies*, 28:3 (December 2005), 361–85.

[8] 'After Farinelli's debut, recorded commentary is fairly scattered': Milhous and Hume, 'Construing', 362.

[9] *The London Evening Post*, 19–22 October 1734.

[10] This performer may not have been a company member. She was dancing at Covent Garden in 1734–5 while Marie Sallé was performing there, and her only appearance at the Haymarket was on 23 April 1735, as Lisette in *La Double Inconstance*, where she appeared for her own Benefit 'at the particular desire of several persons of quality.'

'The importance of dancing at both theatres [Covent Garden and Drury Lane] meant that each employed between fifteen and twenty dancers alongside the actors and actresses. The men usually specialised in dancing, whereas the women were very often actresses as well.'[11]

As the same was true of Francisque's company, separating the performers into actors and dancers thus gives a false impression.

Because newspaper announcements for this season sometimes give cast lists, it is possible to infer the particular 'lines' of most company members.[12] For example, 'Mrs Fompré' (Marie Antoinette Tourneville, a widow whose married name had been Fompré) played young leading roles in both comedy and tragedy, including Inès in *Inès de Castro*, Zaïre in *Zaïre*, and Marianne in *Le Tartuffe*. The Verneuil couple played leading tragic roles and the dignified roles in comedy; Charles and Jean-Baptiste Lesage both played leading roles as lovers. In Molière's *Amphitryon* Jean-Baptiste played Jupiter and Charles was the husband whose shape the god takes on.

The company, unlike the one Francisque had brought to London in earlier years, no longer included his brothers Guillaume and Simon, who continued acting in the provinces, or the popular Mlle de Lisle and Hamoche, who continued to perform at the Paris fairs. After partnering Marie Sallé at Covent Garden in the 1733–4 season, Jean-Baptiste Malter had rejoined Francisque's company, where the standard of dancing must have been at least as high as that of the other London theatres.[13] He was an actor as well as a dancer and his other roles included Pierrot, which he played opposite Arlequin-Francisque, the Columbine of Mme Francisque, and Michel Cochois as Scaramouche.[14] As in Francisque's 1718–19 season, the extensive programme of singing and dancing, including the challenging score of Rebel's 'Les Caractères de la Danse', would have required a more than competent band of musicians. The widowed Mrs Fompré married the musician Jean-Baptiste Foulquier at some point before 1738 (their first known child was born in January 1739). It is therefore likely that Foulquier too was present in Brussels and London, where he may well have played an important role in the musical programme; he later went on to become a member of the orchestra of the Comédie-Italienne and composed music for several ballets.

---

[11] Jeremy Barlow and Moira Goff, 'Dancing in Early Productions of "The Beggar's Opera"', *Dance Research: The Journal of the Society for Dance Research*, vol. 33:2 (2015), 143–58.

[12] For these cast lists, see Appendix III.

[13] Still at Covent Garden, Sallé reprised the roles she had danced with Malter, now with the English dancer Michael Lally.

[14] He was given a Benefit as 'Malter the Pierrot' on 3 March 1735.

The repertoire

The presence of the name Arlequin in many titles of Francisque's repertoire is perhaps responsible for the assumption of later scholars that his season consisted only of 'the usual French comedies and farces'.[15] Even Allardyce Nicoll, who recognised the influence of the French and Italian comedians on English theatre, says only that they 'taught the English dramatists many a stage trick, stage character and stage situation.'[16] In fact, Francisque's repertoire was a major cultural contribution. The company performed some seventy-two plays on a total of a hundred and nineteen nights, and their programme was drawn from the repertoires of all the Paris theatres: the Comédie-Française, the pre-1697 Ancien Théâtre Italien, the post-1716 Comédie-Italienne, and the Théâtre de la Foire, along with music and dance from the Opéra. As if to stress his company's versatility, Francisque gave one performance of *Arlequin et sa troupe de comédiens esclaves*. It was advertised in the press as 'Composed of three different plays representing an idiom of the French stage, in General, beginning with a prologue: the first piece called *Arcagambis*, a Tragedy, the second *L'École des Maris*, a comedy in three acts, written by Molière. The third *Harlequin always Harlequin*, of the Italian Theatre.'[17]

Almost a decade had elapsed since Francisque was merely 'l'Arlequin de la Foire' and he offered only four plays from his fairground repertoire: *Les Animaux raisonnables*, *Les Amours de Nanterre, Arlequin Tirésias* and *L'Allure*.[18] The only comic pantomime afterpiece was *Le Carillon de Maître Gervaise et Dame Alison*, given four performances, with Francisque as the grotesque dame that he had played in the 1719–20 London season. Comedy from the official theatres accounted for over one hundred performance nights. Twelve comedies by Molière were given thirty-two performances, the highest *overall* number for any playwright in Francisque's repertoire. Eight comedies by Regnard, who wrote for both the Comédie-Française and the Old Italian Theatre, received a total of fourteen performances.

---

[15] Emmett L. Avery, 'Foreign Performers in the London Theaters in the Early Eighteenth Century', *Philological Quarterly* 16 (1937), 105–23, at p.118. See also Sybil Rosenfeld, *Foreign Theatrical Companies in Great Britain in the 17th and 18th Centuries*, The Society for Theatre Research Pamphlet Series, no. 4 (London, 1954–55), p. 17; Esther J. Ehrman, 'Huguenot participation in the French theatre in London, 1700–50', *Proceedings of the Huguenot Society*, 24:6 (1988), 480–92, at p. 481.

[16] Allardyce Nicoll, *A History of Early Eighteenth Century Drama, 1700–1750* (Cambridge, 1925), p. 146.

[17] This ambigu was a clever adaptation of *Les Comédiens esclaves* by Dominique, Romagnesi and Riccoboni, first performed at the Théâtre Italien in August 1726.

[18] A fifth piece, *Arlequin Hulla*, was either a one-act opéra-comique by Lesage and d'Orneval, from the Foire Saint-Laurent of 1716, or, more probably, a one-act piece of the same name by Dominique, Riccoboni and Romagnesi from the Comédie-Italienne in 1728.

Even more importantly, this season was responsible for the introduction into England of the plays of Pierre Carlet de Marivaux, previously known there only as a journalist and writer of prose fiction.[19] Early instalments of Marivaux's prose works were being advertised in the London press at this time, and an English translation of *Le Paysan parvenu* was published in 1735, but none of his plays were commercially available in Britain until many years later.[20] Francisque gave twenty-one performances of seven of Marivaux's comedies. This new form of comedy, with its emphasis on refined language, was entirely new to most audiences and must have made a strong impression: the actress Kitty Clive, who apparently saw Francisque's single performance of Marivaux's *L'Ile des esclaves* on 21 February 1735, persuaded Garrick in 1761 to produce it (in a translation done at her request) for her benefit.[21] Between October 1734 and May 1735 the company gave four performances of Marivaux's *Le Jeu de l'amour et du hasard*, and Lady Mary Montagu may have attended one of these.[22] As Lynne Long notes, 'she certainly obtained a copy of the original play shortly afterwards' and set about writing *Simplicity*, a free adaptation.[23]

[19] Arthur Sells discusses Oliver Goldsmith's debt to Marivaux, principally as journalist and author of *Le Spectateur Français*, in *Les Sources Françaises de Goldsmith* ([Paris, 1924] repr. Geneva, 1977).

[20] In 1749–50 in Dublin there was a sudden spate of publications of fairly recent comedies in the original French. Within the space of twelve months, the printer and bookseller S. Powell of Crane Lane published the following comedies in separate volumes: Marivaux, *La Double Inconstance*, *Le Jeu de l'amour et du hasard*, *L'Isle des esclaves*; Delisle, *Arlequin sauvage*, *Timon le misanthrope*; Boissy, *L'Homme du jour*; Nivelle de La Chaussée, *Mélanide*, *L'Ecole des amis*. In 1749 Powell published *Recueil de Pièces de Théâtre*. Volume 1 contained *Timon le Misanthrope*, *Le Jeu de l'amour et du hasard*, *Mélanide*, *Arlequin sauvage*, *L'Homme du jour*. As late as 1968 Oscar Mandel pointed out that 'in over two centuries, only five of Marivaux's plays have been translated into English.' See *Seven Comedies by Marivaux*, trans. O. and A. Mandel (Ithaca, 1968), p. 2.

[21] See Robert Halsband, 'The First English Version of Marivaux's "Le Jeu de l'amour et du hasard,"' *Modern Philology* 79:1 (1981), 16–23, at p. 22; Berta Joncus, *Kitty Clive, or The Fair Songster* (Woodbridge, 2019), pp. 212–13n. These were the only performances of *L'Ile des Esclaves* in England, in French or English, until the twentieth century.

[22] Isobel Grundy, *Lady Mary Wortley Montagu* (New York, 1999), pp. 321–3. See also Robert Halsband, '"Condemned to Petticoats," Lady Mary Wortley Montagu as Feminist and Writer', in *The Dress of Words: Essays on Restoration and Eighteenth Century Literature in honour of Richmond P. Bond* (Lawrence, KS, 1978), pp. 46–7.

[23] Lynne Long, 'Lady Mary Translates Marivaux: A Female Perspective?', *Palimpsestes* 22 (2009), 129–47. As there is no record of Marivaux's plays in London bookshops until 1760–64, copies must have been sent from Paris. Lady Mary's adaptation was not published and performed until the twentieth century. It is possible

The company repertoire also included the works of Marivaux's contemporaries at the Comédie-Italienne – d'Allainval, François-Antoine Jolly, Pierre-François Godard de Beauchamps, and Louis François Delisle de la Drevetière – whose plays, with their emphasis on interiority and their transformation of the comic servant into 'Arlequin philosophe', have been called 'School of Marivaux'.[24] Three of Delisle's prose comedies received an impressive total of twenty-three performances: *Arlequin sauvage* (1721), *Timon le misanthrope* (1722), and *Le Faucon et les oies de Boccace* (1725). Apart from *Timon in Love* (John Kelly's adaptation of Delisle's *Timon,* given at Drury Lane in 1733), nothing by these four dramatists had ever before been seen on the London stage.

Francisque gave six performances of *Arlequin balourd*, advertised as by the 'late' doctor Michel Procope-Couteaux and 'Calculated for the Meridian of London.'[25] Four performances of the play were given in the presence of members of the royal family, and the last, on 15 May, was a royal command performance. Francisque also played Arlequin in nine performances of Fatouville's comedy from the old Italian Theatre, *La Fille savante ou Isabelle fille capitaine* (1690), with its scene of the Professeur d'Amour in which Arlequin wore neither his mask nor his usual motley. From the seventeenth-century French repertoire there was one performance of Montfleury's one-act verse comedy *Don Pasquin d'Avalos* and three performances of Raymond Poisson's *Le Baron de la Crasse*, advertised in London as *My Lord Sloven* and *My Lord Scrub*. As in 1719, Francisque played the title-character. Overall, the single most popular play from the Comédie-Française was Louis Michel de Boissy's *Le Français à Londres* (1727) with eight performances.

Particularly significant, as we shall see later, were four verse tragedies from the repertoire of the Comédie-Française: Racine's *Athalie*, Houdart de la Motte's *Inès de Castro*, Voltaire's *Zaïre*, and Piron's *Gustave Vasa*; the tragicomedy *Le Festin de pierre ou l'athée foudroyé*, by Dorimond; and two verse plays from the Comédie-Italienne: Romagnesi's *Samson*, a tragicomedy, and Boissy's *La Vie est un songe*, a comédie-héroïque based on Calderón's *La Vida es Sueno*.

---

that Lady Mary was struck by the parallel between the heroine's predicament and that of her own daughter, whose marriage to the son of her friend John Perceval, first Earl of Egmont, was currently the subject of protracted bargaining.

[24] Gustave Attinger, *L'Esprit de la Commedia dell'arte dans le Théâtre Français* (Neuchâtel, 1950), pp. 395–400.

[25] Procope-Couteaux, who had written this play for Francisque in 1719, was certainly not dead but had long since returned from London to Paris.

Patrons and Supporters

Twenty years after the arrival of the Hanoverians, the royal family had learned the English language; nevertheless, French was the language of the court and Francisque's company benefitted from its patronage. Members of the royal family were present in various combinations at no fewer than thirty-four performances by his company, twenty-six of which were given by royal command. A further twenty performances were advertised as 'At the particular desire of several Persons [or Ladies] of Quality [or Distinction] '. Francisque's Benefit was 'by order of Their Majesties' Command'. Only one press report mentions the Prince of Wales, at a single command performance of *Harlequin Astrologer* on 28 April. Although Frederick was a cultured Francophile, it is possible that the French players were favoured by supporters of the King and Walpole rather than by the opposition now gathering around the Prince of Wales.

Princess Anne and Princess Caroline were present at the opening night of *L'Embarras des richesses* and *Arlequin Hulla*, both starring Francisque as Arlequin. They were present again on the company's second night, when *Arlequin Sauvage* and *La Sylphide* were given at their command, and at the company's fifth performance, on 1 November. The presence of Princess Anne calls for special comment. As a girl of ten she had often attended Francisque's first London season, and she was the dedicatee of Procope-Couteaux's *Arlequin balourd*. In March 1734 Princess Anne had married the Prince of Orange. She visited London that summer and, when in the autumn it was believed that she was pregnant, she prepared to return to Holland. Her three visits to the Haymarket, days before her return, suggest that she must have had a high regard for Francisque. His programme on 1 November followed Molière's *L'Avare* with what might have been seen as his belated contribution to the celebrations for her marriage. Marivaux's *La Réunion des amours*, first performed at the Comédie-Française on 5 November 1731, is set on Mount Olympus and depicts a battle for supremacy between tender 'l'Amour', and sensual 'Cupidon'.[26] The gods, along with La Vérité and La Vertu, join in the debate until Minerva commands the two kinds of love to join together as one.

Along with the regular patronage of the royal family, Francisque had secured the support of the nobility and gentry well in advance. Lady Margaret Pennyman had already described Francisque as 'mightily caressed by our *English* Quality',[27] and this statement is confirmed by Robert Seymour's description of the two theatres in the Haymarket at this time. After calling the vast sums paid to Italian singers at Vanbrugh's Haymarket 'an Extravagance

---

[26] Valentini Papadopoulou Brady, *Love in the Theatre of Marivaux* (Geneva, 1970), pp. 17–19.

[27] See above, pp. 83–5.

that will perhaps not be believed in the next Age', he adds: 'The other Theatre is at present taken up by a pack of French Strollers, who are likewise much caressed and followed by Persons of the greatest Quality. So much do we admire at this Time everyThing that is Foreign!'[28]

John Percival, Earl of Egmont, is the only aristocrat who has left a written record of his presence at the Little Theatre, to which he paid seven visits between 6 January and 21 May 1735. A distinguished parliamentarian and a confidant of both the King and Queen, Egmont was a regular theatre-goer. As noted in chapter three, misunderstanding of the word 'farce' has led to disparagement not only of Francisque's repertoire but also of the taste of his patrons. Emmett Avery argues that English spectators 'preferred the farcical', as indicated by the predominance of farce and comedy in the offerings of the visitors and by the taste displayed by the Earl of Egmont in an entry in his diary: 'In the evening I went to the French play, where the farce that followed it, called *Le Français à Londres* was very diverting and well-acted.'[29] Egmont's diary, however, proves that his taste was not purely for the farcical;[30] he called *L'Embarras des Richesses* 'an excellent satire' and among his other choices was Boissy's *La Vie est un songe*.

The Critics

If the 'quality' admired Francisque, the opposite was true of the professional critics. Because the actors were patronised by those who knew the language and theatre of France – that is, the court and the upper classes – the French performers attracted the animosity of the less well-off class to which most journalists belonged. The company's emphasis on comedy and dance made it popular even with those who did not know French well, but also led to accusations of triviality. Critical reactions were also affected both by the unfamiliarity of drama in alexandrines and by the assumption that these 'strolling' actors must be inferior to those of the authorised Paris theatres. Early in the company's season, 'Patriophilus' sent an account of the November 1st double

---

[28] Robert Seymour, *A Survey of the Cities of London and Westminster, Borough of Southwark, and parts adjacent* 2 vols (London, 1734–35), vol. 2, p. 664. The volume was announced in *Read's Weekly Journal* in December 1735 but was written during the 1734–5 season, shortly after Farinelli's Benefit in March.

[29] Avery, 'Foreign Performers', p. 120.

[30] John Perceval, first Earl of Egmont, *Manuscripts of the Earl of Egmont, Diary*, vol. 2, pp. 140–79. Mon. 6 Jan.; Mon. 20 Jan.; Tues. 21 Jan.; Mon. 24 Feb.; Thurs. 6 March; Wed. 26 March; Wed 21 May. Comparison of these dates with *The London Stage* makes clear that the plays he saw were *Arlequin Astrologue*, *Les Filles Errantes*, *Les Amants Réunis*, *Arlequin Sauvage* (twice), *La Fausse Coquette*, *Le Français à Londres*, *La Vie est un Songe*, *Arlequin Cartouche*, *L'Étourdi* (twice), *Timon le Misanthrope*, and *Arlequin Esprit Follet*.

bill (*L'Avare* and *La réunion des amours*) to *The Grub-Street Journal*.[31] The writer complains, among other things, of 'The continual return of the same tone at the end of every sentence'.

> This runs through all the actors, except those who acted Harpagon and Frosine [in *L'Avare*]; who were the only two who entered perfectly into their parts; and who, I must own, perform'd extremely well.[32] As for the rest, tho' some did not act so ill as others, yet they all performed in so ordinary a manner, as plainly shew'd, that they had undertaken a trade which they had never learned; and which, if our own actors should exercise no better, they would be continually hissed off the stage.

> But tho' I cannot think any of these to be tolerable comedians, yet I will not deny, but that there may be among them extraordinary singers, dancers, Arlequins, Scaramouches, &c., tho' I had not the pleasure of hearing or seeing any of them perform in any of these characters.

As for Marivaux's play, Patriophilus found it 'insipid': though 'the parts of the two Amours [the main characters of the piece] were perform'd very prettily'; the gods and goddesses 'made a very scurvy and ridiculous appearance', and Mercury had a voice 'as hoarse as the great string of a bass viol.' He concluded: 'In short, Sir, I look upon this Company of French Comedians to consist chiefly of strollers: who, if ever they acted upon a theatre in Paris, (which I must question) performed the lowest parts.' Princess Anne evidently did not share this view of the company, since she had braved the draughty, smoky theatre to attend the very same performance.

Another important visitor to the 'French Playhouse' was the playwright and journalist Aaron Hill, whose short-lived theatrical journal *The Prompter* (1734-6) is one of the few places in which Francisque's season is discussed in relatively serious terms. On 7 December Hill wrote disparagingly of 'the *Ginger-bread French* Theatre [i.e., all show and no substance]; or its soft Neighbours, the *Sillininnies* [Senesino] and the *Foolinellos* [Farinelli].' But, despite his contempt for 'the Monsieurs, and the Mademoiselles', on 24 December Hill admitted that Francisque, 'the General of these Foreign Troops', had 'shewn himself not only an able *Actor* at the Head of his little *Corps*, but a most consummate *Politician*', by which he meant that Francisque never performed on Opera nights, as he would have been competing for the

---

[31] *The Grub-Street Journal*, 5 November 1734. Rosenfeld, *Foreign Theatrical Companies*, wrongly calls this an account of the company's opening night.

[32] No cast list was given for this performance. Harpagon was probably played by Francisque.

same elite audience. Hill then advised British theatre managers (including John Rich, the silent Harlequin and manager of Covent Garden):

> to fight this *assuming Foreigner* with *his own* Weapons, and give their *Harlequins* TONGUES, as well as Feet. [...] *Le Théâtre Italien,* as well as other Foreign Magazines, opens a large Field for Plunder. For my part, I do not see why *Harlequin* should not speak *English,* as well as *French.* An *English* Joke, has as much *Salt* in it, as a *French* one; and *English* Sense, at least, is as good *Sterling,* as *French.*
>
> As true a Lover of my Country as I am, I must confess I have been both Instructed, and Diverted, by the *French* Harlequin. Why may not I be equally moved by an *English* one?

He pointed out that a *speaking* Harlequin, acting in English, would provide competition if the French tried 'to expand their Empire more City-wards' (he meant into the theatre at Lincoln's Inn Fields, currently dark). And he railed against what he saw as the Francomania of the upper classes:

> The Butterflies that used to display their gilded Wings at both the Theatres, direct their Flight towards the *Hay-market,* as the Rendezvous of the better Company. People of Quality already study *French, for the sake of understanding what* Harlequin *says.* If the *Middling Gentry* and *Trades-Folks* should follow their Example, and take it in their Heads, to look upon the *French* Theatre, as a *Nursery* of Language, to breed their Children in, by making them *improve* by *Diversion,* I am not a little apprehensive of a Success very detrimental to our *English* Theatres.[33]

On 17 January 1735, Hill published a letter under the name of 'Q. in the corner', in which he pretended to argue against his own view in order to ridicule John Rich: '[I]n your 13th Paper, you are for *opening our Harlequin's Mouth* – But, alas! He ought *never* to *speak*: since his tongue wants those *Documents,* to which his *Heels* have been *Educated.*' By contrast, the writer praises Francisque, 'his Elder Brother of *France*; who, they say, never *moves*, without *Meaning*, never *speaks*, without *Wit*, never *looks* without *Humour*', and in March Hill was still arguing for a speaking Harlequin: 'Ev'ry Body must own, the *French Harlequin* is infinitely more entertaining than the *English* one.'[34]

---

[33] *The Prompter*, 24 December 1734.
[34] *The Prompter*, 18 March (wrongly dated 14 March). That 'the English Harlequin' is John Rich is supported by other contemporary press references: *The Craftsman* of 22 February suggested that if thespian Nero were living now, he 'might have outdone even Messieurs Lun and Francisque themselves.' See also the 'Two Dogs' poem discussed below, pp. 235–6.

Another of his pseudonymous letters, published 31 January 1735, is evidence of the real nature of his animosity:

> I was seated, the other Night, close by two Dukes, an Earl, and a Foreign Minister, at the *French* Theatre, but could not hear a single Word of the facetious Mr. *Francisque*: On which I moved to the other Corner of the Pit, under the Side-Boxes, where I had observed three very attentive Ladies; but I soon found I had not changed to Advantage; for they (I presume) thought it necessary likewise to MANIFEST their QUALITIES the same OBSTREPEROUS way.

Much of Hill's apparent dislike of the 'French theatre' had to do, in fact, with his hostility toward its aristocratic patrons.

The Roast Beef Affair

On 27 December, Hill, on more obviously 'patriotic' grounds, had attacked:

> those Malapert French Dappers in the Hay-market, who have not blushed to Ridicule (in England, and under an English Character, called ROAST BEEF) the Nerves and Genius of our Country, I must be bold to inform those Comic Satirists, that their Countrymen have felt the Effects of such sound Diet, in some of the saddest and most serious Tragedies, that ever were acted in their Nation.

The 'Tragedies' to which he refers are the French defeats at Crécy and Agincourt, which Hill (author of a Henry V play) often mentions, while the '*English* Character' to whom he refers is Jacques Rosbif in Boissy's *Le Français à Londres*. One can only wonder if Hill actually saw or understood the play, which is not a farce and does not ridicule roast beef.

Boissy's play contrasts the marquis de Polinville, who has just come from Paris to London, with the cousin he is visiting, the baron de Polinville. The baron is the very model of the civilised and cultured French aristocrat, whereas his newly arrived cousin is the kind of *petit-maître* (fop) well known from the comedies of Molière onwards. A young English widow, Eliante, is wooed by the marquis but drawn towards the more polite baron. Eliante's father, Lord Craff, comes to town hoping to marry his daughter to a bluff and taciturn English merchant, Jacques Rosbif. He also wishes to cure his son, Lord Houzey, of aping the foppish French. In a scene between Jacques Rosbif and the marquis de Polinville, Boissy contrasts the stereotypical silent Englishman and the stereotypical garrulous Frenchman, who, claiming that the English have no 'esprit', gives young Lord Houzey a lesson in fashionable French manners, all insolence and condescension. When Lord Craff retorts that the French have no 'raison', he and the marquis almost come to blows, but the day is saved by the baron, who maintains that the French can be moderate and reasonable. Won over by the baron's sound sense, Lord Craff gives him the hand of Eliante, and Jacques Rosbif accepts the situation with grace: 'Adieu, je vous pardonne de m'avoir refusé. Ce Français-là mérite d'être Anglais, vous ne pouviez pas mieux choisir.' [Farewell, I forgive you for refusing me. That Frenchman deserves to be English; you could not have made a better choice.] Only the foppish marquis remains unchanged. The concluding exchange between the baron and Lord Craff is a model of Anglo-French diplomacy and mutual respect.

> *Le baron, au Lord Craff.* Vous venez, Monsieur, de me convaincre que rien n'est au-dessus d'un Anglais poli.
>
> *Le Lord Craff.* Et vous m'avez fait connaître, Monsieur, que rien n'approche d'un Français raisonnable.[35]
>
> [*The Baron, to Lord Craff*: Sir, you have just convinced me that nothing surpasses a polite Englishman.
>
> *Lord Craff.* And you, sir, have made me aware that none can compare with a French man of reason.]

Most negative contemporary responses to *Le Francais à Londres*, and most modern assumptions about the English reaction to it, clearly derive from Aaron Hill's journal rather than from a reading of the play. Russell Goulbourne has even suggested that Francisque revived *Arlequin Balourd* as an antidote to the annoyance caused by *Le Français à Londres*. In fact, the first performance of *Arlequin Balourd* took place on the same day (27 December 1734) as Hill's complaint about Jacques Rosbif. Francisque could hardly have responded to a complaint which had not yet been published and he would never have given eight performances of Boissy's play if it had caused serious offence to the Town.

But the fuss surrounding Jacques Rosbif had a more lasting consequence, namely the resurgence of Roast Beef as a symbol of a proudly muscular British identity in opposition to all things flimsy and French.[36] In the opening scene of John Kelly's *The Plot* (Drury Lane, 22 January 1735), a 'Frenchman'

---

[35] For a discussion of this play in the context of national stereotypes see Russell Goulbourne, 'The Comedy of National Character: Images of the English in Early Eighteenth-Century French Comedy', *Journal for Eighteenth-Century Studies*, 33:3 (2010), 335–55. The intellectual background has been explored in Gábor Gelléri, *Philosophies du Voyage, visiter l'Angleterre aux 17e-18e siècles* (Oxford, 2016).

[36] The association of England and roast beef was far from new, but Boissy's 'Rosbif' is an early example of what became a derogatory French term for an

sings, 'Roast Beef! Marbleu let's taste Roast Beef!' In the same month, James Miller prolonged the saga with *The Man of Taste*, a satire on the merchant classes of the City who had caught from the aristocracy the taste for all things foreign. In 1734 both Francisque and Miller had been attached to Cibber's company. *The Man of Taste* (with a cast that included Theophilus Cibber and Kitty Clive) premiered on 6 March, ran at Drury Lane for 25 performances and went rapidly through three editions in London and Dublin in 1735. Its prologue says that Miller intends:

> To lash the reigning Follies of the Land:
> Blushing to see *Britannia*'s Sons become
> Dupes to each Vagabond from France and Rome.

The 'vagabonds' are, of course, Francisque and Farinelli, and the play shows how thoroughly their names were linked in the public mind. In an episode based on Molière's *Les Précieuses Ridicules*, two rejected suitors get their servants, Martin and Reynard, to present themselves, disguised as Lord Apemode and Colonel Cockade, to Maria and Dorothea, affected City women:

> *Martin*. But come Ladies, what say you of making a Party for the *French* Players? There's a charming piece perform'd there tonight.
>
> *Reynard*. Where our unpolish'd Beef-and-Pudding *English* Clowns are so roasted!
>
> *Maria*. I have neglected my French so shamelessly of late, I shouldn't understand 'em enough to find out the Sense of the Play.
>
> *Martin*. The Sense of the Play; ha, ha, ha, – Why, Madam, you may find out all the Sense that's in it, without understanding a single Syllable.
>
> *Maria*. Well, that's pure!
>
> *Martin*. Besides, 'tis being ten times more Polite, Madam – 'tis quite out of Fashion to go to any thing one understands. [...] Well, Ladies, if you are not for regaling on *Francisque*, what think you of a Taste of *Faronelli* to Night?
>
> *Doro*. Oh! That charming Creature *Faronelli*! ...[37]

Englishman. The Oxford online dictionaries give the origin as 'early 19th century', https://en.oxforddictionaries.com/definition/rosbif.

[37] James Miller, *The Man of Taste* (London, 1735) [Act 4, Scene 2], pp. 61–2.

This sarcastic reference to *Le Français à Londres* was heard on 25 nights by audiences at Drury Lane and probably contributed more to negative views of it than Hill's article or the play itself, which, after all, was seen only by audiences who understood French.

The symbolism surrounding the very words 'Roast Beef' culminated in an event of major cultural significance on 15 April at Covent Garden. For the Benefit of the singer-songwriter Richard Leveridge, the press announced 'Leveridge's new song in praise of Old English Roast Beef.' Henry Fielding had written two verses to the tune of 'The Queen's Old Courtier' for his unperformed *Grub Street Opera* in 1731, and later included them in his *Don Quixote in England*, performed at the Little Haymarket in 1734. This first version, telling of Sancho Panza's preference for English Roast Beef above all foreign delicacies, seems to have provoked little reaction, but when Leveridge composed a new air for it in 1735, and added five new verses, it became an instant hit.[38] Just weeks after its first performance, *The Weekly Amusement, or The Universal Magazine*, announced, 'The following Song being universally esteemed by the Public we are willing to entertain and oblige our Readers with a correct Copy of it.'[39] Before the end of the year it had been published in two collections of ballads,[40] and its patriotic words rapidly made it a popular anthem. *Le Français à Londres* had inadvertently played a major role in reinforcing this image of British identity, and it is surely no coincidence that John Rich founded his Beefsteak Society in 1735 with the motto 'Beef and Liberty.'

Benefit Nights: Sallé, Farinelli, Francisque

An important source of income was the theatrical Benefit, at which the beneficiary received the full amount from the sale of tickets once the expenses of the theatre had been deducted. Sometimes it was a fund-raiser for someone in need. This was probably the case when, on 18 March 1735, the company gave a performance of *L'Embarras des Richesses* for the widow of Marie Sallé's brother Francis. *The London Stage* does not list Marie as dancing at Covent Garden that night, so she would have been free to attend her sister-in-law's Benefit, another sign of the continuing closeness of this theatrical family.[41]

---

[38] See Edgar V. Roberts, 'Henry Fielding and Richard Leveridge: Authorship of "The Roast Beef of Old England"', *Huntington Library Quarterly*, 27:2 (1964), 175–81.

[39] *The Weekly Amusement, or The Universal Magazine* (London, 1735) vol. 3, 12 July 1735, p. 918.

[40] *The British Musical Miscellany or The Delightful Grove* 4 vols (London, 1735), vol. 3, p. 121; *A complete collection of old and new English and Scotch songs, with their respective tunes prefixed* 4 vols (London, 1735), vol. 2, pp. 5–6.

[41] On 7 May 1734 the young widow had been given another Benefit at Covent Garden, at which both Sallé and Malter danced, though it was shared with the actress

But the most famous, and lucrative, Benefits of 1735 were those for the foreign celebrities. Two of them – those for Farinelli on 15 March and Sallé herself on 24 April – have been extensively studied. The third, that of Francisque on 27 February, has never been given the attention it deserves. A brief examination of the other two Benefits may help to set its importance in context.

Farinelli's first London Benefit, which has been called 'quite possibly the most celebrated and stellar single musical event of the century',[42] took place at the King's theatre when the mania surrounding his person and his performance was at its height. Unlike Sallé's equally glamorous Benefit of the previous year, Farinelli's 'London apotheosis', in Hasse's *Artaserse*, was not given by command of any member of the royal family, and the King and Queen were notably absent. Two days before the occasion, *The Daily Advertiser*, listing the lavish presents showered on the singer, reported ''Tis expected that Signor Farinello [*sic*] will have the greatest Appearance on Saturday that has been known. We hear that a Contrivance will be made to accommodate 2000 people.'[43] Judith Milhous and Robert Hume show that, 'With the building packed to the rafters, as many as 900 people might have crammed into the King's Theatre. For this Benefit, scenery was removed, and stage movement was probably close to non-existent.'[44] There is some evidence in the press of numbers seated onstage:

> the Pit and Galleries were full by four o'clock, and the Stage being done up without any Scenes, as at a Ridotto, and curiously adorned with gilt Leather, there were several hundreds of People in the Seats erected there; so that it is reckoned he had a most extraordinary Benefit.[45]

Even if one were to add a very liberal estimate of two hundred onstage seats to the 'crammed' nine hundred and forty, this only gives eleven thousand and forty places.

Sallé's 1735 Benefit, by command of the Prince of Wales, took place one week after the première of Handel's *Alcina*. Whereas in 1734 Sallé had been the unrivalled darling of London audiences, she now had to contend with a

---

Mrs. Cantrell. Philip Highfill et al., *A Biographical Dictionary of Actors, Actresses, Musicians, Dancers, Managers, and Other Stage Personnel in London, 1660–1800*, 16 vols (Carbondale, 1973–93), vol. 3, p. 41.

[42] Thomas McGeary, *The Politics of Opera in Handel's Britain* (Cambridge, 2013), p. 152.

[43] McGeary, 'Farinelli and the English', paras 20–1.

[44] Milhous and Hume, 'Construing Farinelli', p. 363.

[45] *The Political State of Great Britain*, January-June 1735, pp. 365–6. https://babel.hathitrust.org/cgi/pt?id=osu.32435073201899&seq=7.

new Drury Lane dancer from Paris, Catherine Roland, and with Francisque's dancers, including the vivacious Marie Châteauneuf and the saucy Manon Grognet. Furthermore, in February Sallé was absent from some performances of *Ariodante* because of an injury. The date of her Benefit might have had to be delayed until after those of the two other foreign stars, and, although her personal popularity had not waned, audiences may have been suffering from what might be called Foreign Star Benefit Fatigue.[46] The Abbé Prévost said that her financial gains had been less than half of those in the previous year. By contrast, he mentioned Francisque and 'les dix mille écus qu'il a déjà gagnés' [the ten thousand écus (crowns) that he has already earned].

Francisque's Benefit, originally scheduled for Monday 24 February, was postponed 'by order of their majesties' to Thursday 27 February,[47] perhaps because someone noticed that Monday was the night of the tenth (and penultimate) performance 'by His Majesty's Command' of *Ariodante*, Handel's first new opera for Covent Garden. In spite of what Charles Burney called the 'intrinsic and sterling worth' of the music, and Marie Sallé's dramatically integrated danced scenes, Handel was struggling to compete with Porpora's company and, above all, with Farinelli. The King and Queen may not have wanted to do anything which might further reduce audiences for *Ariodante*, already 'so thin that in six of its eight weeks, there was only one performance rather than the customary two.'[48]

Robert Hume has estimated that the Little Haymarket's maximum capacity must have been six- to seven-hundred, whereas Lincoln's Inn Fields and Covent Garden each held around fourteen hundred,[49] several hundred more

---

[46] Sarah McCleave notes (citing the *Bee* and the *Daily Advertiser* for 7 February 1735) that Sallé was reported to have been injured during an early performance of *Ariodante* but that she has recovered enough to 'perform again next week'. Her name does not appear in the bills between 17 January and 13 March, though apparently she danced in the last performance of *Ariodante* on 3 March. Handel seems to have made some changes to his score to take account of her absence. McCleave, *Dance in Handel's London Operas*, pp. 102–3.

[47] *The London Daily Post*, 15 February 1735.

[48] Graham Cummings, 'Handel's Organ Concertos', p. 15. The King and Queen attended the Opera of the Nobility in the Haymarket just three times in the 1734–35 season, whereas they went nineteen times to hear Handel at Covent Garden.

[49] Robert D. Hume, 'Henry Fielding and Politics at the Little Haymarket 1728–1737', in J. M. Wallace, ed., *The Golden and the Brazen World: Papers in Literature and History 1650–1800* (Berkeley and Los Angeles, 1985), pp. 79–124, at p. 81. See also Judith Milhous, 'The Capacity of Vanbrugh's Theatre in the Haymarket', *Theatre History Studies*, 4 (1984), 38–46; Milhous and Hume, 'Handel's London – the Theatres', in *The Cambridge Companion to Handel*, ed. Donald Burrows (Cambridge, 1997), pp. 55–63, at pp. 55–7; and Robert D. Hume, *Henry Fielding and the London theatre, 1728–1737* (Oxford, 1988).

than the King's theatre. It seems clear that the Little Haymarket was thought to be far too small for the expected crowds at Francisque's Benefit. For this reason, it took place at Lincoln's Inn Fields. On 26 and 27 February traffic directions were printed on the playbills: "'Tis desir'd that all coaches will come on Lincoln's-Inn Fields side, and the Chairs on Carey-street side.'[50] All of this must have infuriated John Rich. Suddenly, for one night in honour of his rival, his old theatre, empty for much of the season, was to be filled with high society, led by the king and queen, and he himself would receive little or nothing of the box-office takings. What Aaron Hill had feared in December 1734 had in fact occurred: the French players had extended their 'Empire' to Lincoln's Inn Fields, attracting the audience that he had called 'the Butterflies that used to display their gilded Wings at both theatres'. On Francisque's Benefit night, the whole of the Haymarket was dark, and there was no opera at Covent Garden; Marie Sallé was almost certainly at Lincoln's Inn to applaud her family. In contrast to Farinelli's Benefit, Francisque's Benefit was by command of both of their Majesties, and all the royal family were present.[51] Farinelli's Benefit was preceded by what Thomas McGeary called 'an unprecedented series of seven advertisements in the London newspapers.' In fact, the precedent had been set just two weeks earlier by *nine* advertisements for Francisque's Benefit, beginning on 15 February.[52] Farinelli's press advertisements humbly requested subscribers not to use their silver tickets on his Benefit night, whereas the astute businessman Francisque had already insisted in his contract of March 1734 that those tickets would not be accepted.

Francisque's Apotheosis

Given the richness of Francisque's London repertoire, the programme of two plays chosen for his Benefit might not at first appear impressive: *Arlequin Astrologue*, followed by '*Harlequin always Harlequin*, with Several entertainments of Dancing.' But, on this Benefit night, the principal honours were to go, not to Molière, Regnard, Racine or Voltaire, but to 'Monsieur Francisque, the famous Harlequin'. Significantly, both plays had originally been performed by 'le gentil Thomassin' of the new Italian company of 1716. Thomassin, like all the members of the new Comédie-Italienne, had had to learn French rapidly

---

[50] The front of the theatre was in present-day Portugal Street facing Carey Street, with Lincoln's Inn Fields to the rear. Similar traffic instructions were issued on 17 February for crowds attending the last wildly popular ball of the season at the King's theatre in the Haymarket, but not for Farinelli's Benefit there.

[51] *London Stage*, pt 3, vol. 1, p. 464.

[52] McGeary, 'Farinelli and the English', pp. 19–28, at para. 20. Advertisements for Francisque's Benefit appeared in *The London Daily Post* on 15, 18–22, 25–7 February 1735, including an assurance that printed tickets for the 24th would be accepted on the 27th.

to retain dwindling audiences with a new repertoire. He had surprised Paris audiences by abandoning the nasal voice common to the Arlequins of the pre-1697 Italian theatre and the fairs, which Louis XIV's Arlequin, Dominique Biancolelli père, had originally adopted to overcome a speech impediment. As Jacques Scherer put it, 'au lieu de parler de la gorge et d'affecter un ton de perroquet, il s'exprimait sur un mode naturel qui, à la balourdise et bien entendu à l'acrobatie, savait allier la finesse et même la grâce'.[53] [instead of talking from the throat and affecting a parrot-like tone, he spoke in a natural way that managed to combine blundering and, of course, acrobatics with refinement and even grace.] Francisque, although trained in the old school, had probably adopted Thomassin's example, using a 'normal' speaking voice in all his roles. In his *Journal*, Charles Collé recalled that Thomassin was capable of moving an audience to tears in some of Marivaux's plays, 'ce qui m'a toujours paru un prodige sous le masque d'Arlequin'[54] [which has always seemed to me a miracle under the mask of Arlequin].

The choice of *Arlequin Astrologue* may have reflected the tastes of Francisque's royal patrons, since it was given seven performances in the season, five of them at the desire of members of the royal family. It is an Italian *canovaccio* which the new Italian players had given in Italian during their opening Paris season in August 1716. In the simple *commedia* plot, the lovers Lélio and Mario command Arlequin to deliver letters to their mistresses who are jealously guarded by their father Pantaloon. So Arlequin visits Pantaloon's house in the series of disguises mentioned in the advertised title: '*Statue, Enfant, Ramoneur, Nègre et Squellette*, with two new scenes viz. *The Elbow chair* and *The Dog*'. The list could be extended *ad libitum* at the whim of the actor until it was time for the happy ending. The fact that this play was primarily a vehicle for the talents of Arlequin was recognised by critics when Thomassin first performed it in Paris:

> Quoique cette pièce soit un peu farce, cependant Arlequin, par tous les déguisements qu'il prend, la rend si agréable, qu'elle a été représentée plusieurs fois avec succès, tant il est vrai qu'un excellent Acteur, peut faire lui seul un spectacle amusant.[55]

> [Although this play is rather farcical, thanks to all the disguises he adopts Arlequin makes it so pleasing that it has been successfully performed several times, so true is it that it only takes a single excellent actor to create an amusing performance.]

---

[53] Preface to Marivaux, *Théâtre complet*, ed. Bernard Dort (Paris, 1982, 1964).
[54] Charles Collé, *Journal et Mémoires de Charles Collé sur les hommes de lettres*, ed. H. Bonhomme (3 vols, Paris, 1868), vol.1, p. 328.
[55] Parfaict, *Dict.*, vol. 1, pp. 240–1.

Arlequin toujours Arlequin was a one-act prose comedy by Dominique, Romagnesi and Riccoboni, first performed at the Comédie-Italienne in 1726. Francisque had played it on 18 December in the presence of 'the Duke [of Cumberland] and the young princesses' and a further six times, at three of which members of the royal family were present. The plot is a light-hearted echo of Calderón's *La Vida es Sueno*. Arlequin, about to marry Colette, is drugged and abducted by the servants of the King of Naples, who tell him that he is King Alphonse, married to Rosalde. Though they place him on the throne, he keeps trying to return home, first to join his friends in feasting and then to keep the angry Colette from marrying his rival. Instead, he is forced to receive a stuttering ambassador, then to lead his subjects into war. Finally he escapes to his village, just in time to prevent Colette's marriage. He receives a thousand écus from a grateful King, whose melancholy son has been cured by laughter, and the play ends with Arlequin and Colette's wedding feast. The airs and vaudeville sung at the end of the play to music by Mouret were printed in volume I of *Le Théâtre Italien* in 1733. Perhaps a touch ironically, given the royal and aristocratic audience at the Benefit, the second air spurns wealth ('Des Grandeurs la suite opportune' [The inviting parade of grandeur]) and celebrates the pleasures of rustic village life, a recurrent theme in comedies featuring 'Arlequin philosophe'.

Many of Thomassin's other roles were also in Francisque's repertoire, including the Arlequins of Delisle, d'Allainval and Marivaux, and the role of the slave Ascalon in Romagnesi's *Samson*. The distinguished audience at Francisque's Benefit would have known (some at first hand) of Thomassin and the Comédie-Italienne, and Francisque was clearly not afraid of the inevitable comparison with the actor whom Aaron Hill later called 'the best Harlequin in Europe.'[56] Perhaps, also, in the very theatre where he had made his London debut almost twenty years earlier, Francisque wanted to remind the Town (and John Rich) that he was the original inspiration for the many comic routines for which Rich as Lun was now so famous.

Like Farinelli and Sallé, Francisque was a celebrity, long before the term, or even the concept, came into use. The Abbé Prévost reported that:

> On parle avec beaucoup d'éloges du talent de Francisque pour le rôle d'Arlequin. Il invente, il compose, il exécute, avec le même succès, et dans ce goût que les Anglais appellent *humour*, et qui réussit toujours à Londres.

> [They speak with much praise of Francisque's talent for the role of Arlequin. He invents, composes and performs equally successfully, with what the English call humour, which always goes down well in London.]

---

[56] *The Prompter*, Tuesday March 14 [should be 18], 1735.

As an example of Francisque's versatility, he describes the comic prologue that had preceded *Arlequin Balourd* in 1719 and was repeated in Brussels in 1733–4, in which Arlequin impersonates an irate lady spectator before jumping onto the stage and offering to play Arlequin himself. If it was part of the entertainment at his Benefit, it would have been a further example of his ability to surprise as well as amuse.

Thanks to a long letter published in *The Grub-Street Journal* on 13 March 1735 and signed by 'True Briton', we have what purports to be an eye-witness account of Francisque's Royal Benefit. The epistolary convention was as prevalent in the press as in novels, and letters to the press indicated their partisan nature by their *noms de plume*: Misogallicus, Anglicus, Patriophilus, True Briton, Staunch Old Briton, etc. Despite his attitude, some solid facts may be gleaned from 'True Briton's' letter. This no-nonsense Englishman informs readers that he comes up from the country each winter and relies on his friends to recommend worthwhile entertainments:

> At this time, wherever I went, I could hear nothing but a profusion of praise on the French Theatre, and the inimitable Monsieur FRANCISQUE, the delight of the *Beau Monde*. These high recommendations of him raised my curiosity so far, that I went to his Benefit.

'True Briton' is impressed by the grandeur of the occasion, but he goes on to disparage the repertoire:

> From the exaggerated encomiums of *Monsieur* FRANCISQUE, and from the magnificence, rank, and number of the audience at his Benefit, before the drawing up of the curtain, I fed myself with the pleasing hope, that this French operator (his Harlequinship must excuse me, If I think the name of actor too dignified for his character) had contributed to the reforming of the many abuses, which had so long prevailed on our English stages, by introducing the best plays of CORNEILLE, MOLIERE, RACINE, and other celebrated French poets.[57] [...]

He is disappointed to find that the plays on offer are lightweight rubbish. Nevertheless, 'True Briton' cannot help but reveal that the distinguished spectators were tightly packed (even in the large space of Lincoln's Inn). On the following day, he claims to have met in a coffee house a French actor who seems only too happy to dismiss his own company's repertoire as ancient unprinted pieces out of Italy. He is delighted with their reception in London:

---

[57] 'In fact, Molière had already figured prominently in the repertoire.

'we act pieces here with the greatest applause, which, if we attempted at home, we should be stoned off the stage. But the English are indulgent; they must be amused: FRANCISQUE can do what he will with them; he can suit their palate with *drollery* and buffoonery; so that it may be justly said, with them *'Every rank fool goes down.'*

'True Briton' deplores the fact that lovers of great English literature could let themselves be entertained by 'the monkey tricks or grotesque postures of a Merry-Andrew, tho' disguised under the name of *Monsieur* FRANCISQUE, or *Monsieur* LUN, *senior* or *junior*.'[58]

The fictitiousness of this coffee-house discussion is revealed by the words 'Every rank fool goes down', a quotation from Otway's tragedy, *The Orphan* (1680) which a French actor (even a good one) would not have known. Equally ridiculous was his coupling of Francisque and Lun (Rich), given that the latter was only a mime artist. James Hillhouse accurately summed up this letter and others like it as 'insular, even parochial, fulminations.'[59] 'True Briton' also takes Aaron Hill to task for having praised

'the *wit, humour, and marvellous talents of Maître* FRANCISQUE, tho' he and all his troupe of strollers, declaim in a tone as disagreeable, as the proverbial harshness of a French Capuchin, without the least tincture of fine elegance of diction, or justness of action.'

The declaration of 'True Briton's' French actor that 'Francisque can do what he will' with an English audience is, like many of Aaron Hill's comments, an attack on the leisured classes more than on the performers. Hill's reply was, 'If ... Mr *True Briton* can find any means of driving all *Harlequins* from the stage, I'll join Forces with him, readily, in so laudable an Undertaking.' Clearly, the views of 'True Briton' and Aaron Hill were not shared by the audience on the night of 27 February 1735. Moreover, had 'True Briton' chosen to visit the Little Haymarket the day before or after the Benefit, he could have seen three of the finest recent plays from the new Théâtre Italien in which Arlequin had become a *philosophe*: Delisle's *Arlequin Sauvage*, Marivaux's *La Double Inconstance*, and d'Allainval's *L'Embarras des richesses*, all three offering enough refinement of language and content to make nonsense of 'True Briton's' allegations.

---

[58] The name 'Lun junior' was given to the actor Henry Woodward when he played Harlequin at Goodman's Fields.

[59] James T. Hillhouse, *The Grub-Street Journal* (Durham, NC, 1928), p. 224.

'Indian kings' and 'noble savages'

The success of *Arlequin Sauvage*, in particular, is evidence of Francisque's ability to respond both to the taste of the Town and to contemporary topical events. In June 1734, James Oglethorpe, founder of the colony of Georgia, had returned to London from America, bringing with him a delegation of nine Yamacraws, headed by Chief Tomochichi and his wife, Senauki. Chiefs from North American tribes had already visited London in 1710 and 1730, but this was apparently the largest such group yet seen, and they attracted considerable interest at all levels of society: 'Bells rang in honour of the colourful visitors; there was a tremendous bonfire, and many demonstrations of welcome. Their every move was reported by the newspapers.'[60] The Earl of Egmont, as chairman of the Georgia Trustees, formally welcomed the group to Whitehall and the occasion was recorded in a painting by William Verelst. They were entertained at Egmont's country estate and shown the sights of London, Eton and Windsor, formally received at Kensington Palace by the whole royal family, and at Lambeth Palace by the Archbishop of Canterbury. The Princess of Orange commanded a performance at Lincoln's Inn Fields on 1 October 'for the Entertainment of TomoChachi [*sic*] and Queen Senauki.' In all, between 7 August and 25 October, the Yamacraw delegation visited the theatres on 11 occasions, and audiences watched them as much as they watched the play.

According to press reports and the diary of the Earl of Egmont, the Yamacraws were extensively questioned about their society, their manners and beliefs. Although at first it was their strange appearance and customs which appealed to the town, by the time they departed on 30 October 1734, 'Londoners, much impressed with the dignity, conduct and intelligence of the Indians, no longer considered them savages.'[61] Tomochichi declared that although the English knew many things his people did not know, he doubted they were any happier, and he observed that 'nothing is done without money.' In his journal, Egmont expressed his admiration for the group at length, noting their modesty and 'their discomfort with the rude crowds that flocked to see them'.[62]

As Francisque had arrived in London in mid-October, he may well have seen the Yamacraws in town or at the theatre; he would surely have recalled a similar

---

[60] Carolyn Thomas Foreman, *Indians Abroad, 1493–1938* (Norman, OK, 1943), p. 60.

[61] Helen Todd, *Tomochichi, Indian friend of the Georgia Colony* (Marietta, GA, 2005), pp. 21–2. See also Alden T. Vaughan, *Transatlantic Encounters: American Indians in Britain, 1500–1776* (Cambridge, 2006), pp. 150–61.

[62] Julie Anne Sweet, *Negotiating for Georgia: British-Creek Relations in the Trustee Era, 1733–1752* (Athens, GA, 2005), p. 53. The *Daily Journal* for Tuesday, 13 May 1735 announced the publication of *A new voyage to Georgia* [...] to which is added, a curious account of the Indians, by an honourable person; and a poem to James Oglethorpe, esq., on his arrival from Georgia (London, 1735).

visit to Paris in 1725 of a group from Louisiana led by Chief Agapit Chicagou of the Mitchigamea. This delegation had been received at court by Louis XV and on 10 Sept 1725 a group of them performed a traditional song and dance of war and peace on the stage of the Comédie-Italienne, to music specially written for them by Jean-Philippe Rameau, an event reported by the *Mercure* as 'une nouveauté des plus extraordinaires' [the most remarkable novelty].[63]

Francisque's company gave no fewer than fourteen performances of Delisle's *Arlequin Sauvage*, a play partly inspired by the writings of Baron Lahontan and his description of the 'noble savage' Adario.[64] Francisque played the unusually complex role of a 'savage' Arlequin brought from the New World to France. His naïve misunderstanding of 'civilised' conventions is sometimes comic, as when he discovers that he cannot make love to a pretty woman 'à la sauvage' (Delisle borrows from Lahontan the custom of wooing by the lighting and blowing out of a match) and gets into trouble because he does not see why he should pay for the merchandise he was offered. But the social commentary sometimes goes deeper, as in the famous dialogue with his master, Lelio (2.4), where he learns that, as Tomochichi reportedly said in 1734, nothing can be done without money. In distress, Arlequin confronts his master in a surprisingly moving speech:

> Pourquoi donc, scélérat, m'as-tu tiré de mon pays pour m'apprendre que je suis pauvre? Je l'aurais ignoré toute ma vie sans toi; je ne connaissais dans les forêts ni les richesses, ni la pauvreté: j'étais à moi-même mon Roi, mon Maître et mon valet; et tu m'as cruellement tiré de cet heureux état, pour m'apprendre que je ne suis qu'un misérable et un esclave. [...] [*Il pleure.*]

> [Then, why, you scoundrel, did you take me from my own country to teach me that I am poor? Without you, I would have gone all my life without knowing it: in the forests I knew neither wealth nor poverty; I was myself king, master, and servant, and you have cruelly taken me out of that happy state to let me know that I'm only a wretch and a slave [...]. [*He weeps.*]

---

[63] *Mercure*, September 1725, vol. 2, pp. 2774–6. Rameau was inspired to write the dance *Les Sauvages*, in which, he claimed, 'j'ai caractérisé le chant et la danse de ces sauvages qui parurent sur le Théâtre Italien' [I have characterized the song and dance of these savages who appeared on the Théâtre Italien]. See Sylvie Bouissou, *Jean-Philippe Rameau* (Paris, 2014), p. 180.

[64] Louis Armand de Lom d'Arce, Baron de Lohantan, *Mémoires de l'Amérique Septentrionale ou la suite des voyages de Mr. le baron de Lahontan*, ed. Réal Ouellet ([The Hague, 1703] Montreal, 2003). As noted in chapter four, p. 70, Lesage borrowed the name of Lahontan's noble savage Adario in his *Arlequin roi des ogres*.

At its première at the Comédie-Italienne in 1721, Delisle's comedy was praised by the marquis d'Argenson: 'On corrige ici nos mœurs en général, tandis que les comédies ordinaires ne reprennent que quelque vice en particulier.'[65] [Here our manners in general are corrected, whereas ordinary comedies deal only with some particular vice.] Olive Dickason notes the historical distinction between two stereotypes: 'This purging of *l'homme sauvage* of his bestial and demonic aspects resulted in his idealisation into *'le bon sauvage'*, a fate which he shared with the Amerindian during the 18th century.'[66] Susan Castillo argues that the theories of Jean-Jacques Rousseau 'would not have enjoyed such an enthusiastic response' if readers in Enlightenment France had not been familiar with ideas 'such as the basic goodness of Man in a state of nature and the corrupting effects of social institutions such as private property, laws and matrimony'[67] – all of which is on display in this play long before Rousseau.[68]

The curiosity engendered by the visit of the chiefs, coupled with the novelty for London audiences of hearing Arlequin s*peak* as both *sauvage* and *philosophe*, made *Arlequin sauvage* as popular in London as it had been in Paris. It held the stage throughout the whole of Francisque's season, including the company's last two nights. There were three command performances (on 28 October, 12 December, and 10 February) for members of the royal family who had met the Georgia delegation at Kensington. The Earl of Egmont saw *Arlequin sauvage* twice.

James Miller must have been more favourably impressed by the French repertoire than one would guess from the comments in his comedy *The Man of Taste*. In 1738 he adapted *Arlequin sauvage* as *Art and Nature*; the philosophical Arlequin became 'Julio, a savage', played by Theophilus Cibber. Miller's play was 'damned' on the first (and only) night at Drury Lane by a cabal, in which Aaron Hill may have played a part.[69] In his published preface

---

[65] René-Louis de Voyer de Paulmy, marquis d'Argenson, *Notices sur les œuvres de théâtre*, ed. Henri Lagrave (Geneva, 1966), p. 657.

[66] Olive Patricia Dickason, 'The Concept of l'homme sauvage and early French colonialism in the Americas', *Revue française d'histoire d'outre-mer*, 64:234 (1977), 5–32, at p. 25. https://www.persee.fr/doc/outre_0300–9513_1977_num_64_234_1990. The English usually said 'noble savage', a term originally used in the opening scene of Dryden's *The Conquest of Granada, Pt One*.

[67] Susan P. Castillo, *Colonial encounters in New World writing, 1500–1786: performing America* (London, 2005), p. 186.

[68] See also Robert V. Kenny, 'The Edifying Spectacle: Images of Le Sauvage and La Nouvelle-France in the Theatre World of Early Eighteenth-Century France', in *Focus on Québec 2: Further Essays on Québécois Society & Culture*, ed. Ines Christine Molinaro and Christopher Rolfe (Edinburgh, 2000), pp. 15–29.

[69] Miller had many enemies who, as Berta Joncus writes, 'would go on to wreck the reception of all works known to be his': Joncus, *Kitty Clive*, p. 71. Hill was certainly one of these enemies: he had written a long and scornful review of Miller's previous

to the play, Miller lamented the audience's rejection of 'scenes, which in Paris, for several years past, have charm'd the Gay and Polite from all Parts of Europe, nay, which lately perform'd in this very Town, in a foreign tongue, brought together and delighted crowded audiences'.[70]

Over twenty years later, when John Cleland published *Tombo-Chiqui, or The American Savage* (1758), he acknowledged in his 'Advertisement' that he was adapting *Arlequin sauvage* (wrongly attributed to d'Allainval), 'which was received in France with highest applause.' He also referred to the 'unequal success' of Miller's version.[71] Probably in order not to recall that failed adaptation, he called his hero (Miller's Julio) Tombo-chiqui, an exotic concoction surely designed to remind readers of Chief Tomochichi's visit in 1734 and Francisque Moylin's fourteen much-applauded performances in *Arlequin sauvage*.

---

play in *The Prompter* of 11 March 1735 and Miller, in his poem *A Seasonable Reproof* (London, 1735), had called him 'blust'ring Aaron' who 'mouths the same coarse Fustian o'er and o'er' (lines 35, 37). Interestingly, although Miller also attacks a number of well-known theatrical figures like Farinelli and Henry Carey in this poem, he does not mention Francisque.

[70] James Miller, *Art and Nature, a comedy* (London, 1738), p. ii.

[71] John Cleland, *Tombo-Chiqui, or The American Savage, A Dramatic entertainment in Three Acts* (London, 1758), 'Advertisement', n.p.

11

The London season, 1734–1735: Part Two

Plots and the Press

French dramatists were as committed as their English contemporaries to the view that the duty of comedy was to correct morals through laughter: indeed, the Latin tag *Castigat ridendo mores* was coined by a French seventeenth-century poet, Jean-Baptiste de Santeul. This ethical motivation was particularly visible in the plays of the new Italian theatre known as the école de Marivaux. *Arlequin Sauvage* was as popular in London as in Paris, and London audiences clearly appreciated its relevance to recent events and its blend of comedy with socio-political questioning. However, other plays in Francisque's season, possibly with the connivance of some of his aristocratic patrons, may have had more dangerously topical resonance.

Recent scholarship has emphasised the importance of religion in the cultural and political controversies of this period.[1] The twin spectres of Catholicism and Jacobitism haunted both the national psyche and the daily papers in the 1730s. The Gunpowder Plot and the 'Glorious Revolution' were far from forgotten, and the extensive official celebrations of the Fifth of November now had a double significance, commemorating not only the foiling of the Gunpowder Plot but the arrival of William of Orange in 1688 to guarantee the Protestant Succession. Two Jacobite plots were still fresh in the minds of the public. The Atterbury Plot of 1722, led by Francis Atterbury, Bishop of Rochester, was 'the most serious challenge to the Hanoverian regime before the '45 rebellion',[2] while the much feebler Cornbury Plot of 1733 was foiled by lack of support from the French. Throughout 1734 and early 1735, the London press was filled with warnings of the immediate danger of Popery. Colin Haydon has identified more than a dozen different 'anti-Papist panics'.[3]

---

[1] See Linda Colley, *Britons: Forging the Nation 1707–1837* (New Haven and London, 1992) and Colin Haydon, *Anti-Catholicism in Eighteenth-century England, c. 1714–80: A political and social study* (Manchester, 1993).

[2] Eveline Cruickshanks and Howard Erskine-Hill, *The Atterbury Plot* (Basingstoke, 2004).

[3] Haydon, *Anti-Catholicism*, p. 128.

In August 1734, the *Gentleman's Magazine* published a letter alleging that there were more than 30 'Mass-houses' in the city and more than 300 priests, and that 'daily great numbers are sent over hither [i.e., from France]'.[4] In December both the Bishop of London[5] and Protestant Dissenters[6] warned in sermons and in the press of an influx of popish priests, stressing the link between Catholicism and Jacobitism; similar warnings continued to appear in the press through the spring of 1735.[7]

As I noted in chapter three, the Catholic chapels of several foreign embassies were frequented by many of the high-profile French and Italian performers, including Francisque's company, the Italian opera singers, and the French dancers. Gatherings of foreign Papists in London would have created an alarming spectacle. At the Portuguese Embassy Chapel in Warwick Street Farinelli and others sang a *Te Deum* in late February 1735;[8] on 19 March, Mimi de Verneuil and Léonard de Forcade [Fourcade], were married there, probably attended by Francisque and other Catholics from the various companies.[9] The *Weekly Miscellany* of 29 March made a (false) announcement that, in gratitude for the immense sums received at his Benefit, Farinelli was going to sing in the church of St James, Westminster, for the benefit of poor children. This unlikely story was probably invented to set up an anti-Catholic riposte in *The Prompter* on 8 April: 'Whereas it was invidiously reported [...] that Senor C.B.F-r-o was to have sung at St James's Church, for the Benefit of the poor Children of That Parish; These are to certify, that he never had any such intention; and that it is a high insult done to him to suppose he could be so criminal, as to prostitute his ROMAN CATHOLICK Voice, to raise Charity for PROTESTANT BOYS and GIRLS.'

---

[4] *The Gentleman's Magazine*, August 1734, pp. 450–1.

[5] *The London Daily Post*, 23 December 1734. For an alternative view of the perceived threat, see E. P. Thompson, *Whigs and Hunters. The Origin of the Black Act* (London, 1975), p. 258.

[6] *The London Daily Post*, 28 December 1734.

[7] See, e.g., *The Free Briton*, 2 January 1735, *The Old Whig or the Consistent Protestant,* March 1735, and *The London Evening Post*, 11–13 March 1735.

[8] Announced in *The London Daily Post*, 21 February 1735.

[9] The Register states that the wedding took place in the presence of the bride's parents (the leading tragedians of the company), along with Charles Lesage and his wife Marianne Pettite, and Marie Antonette Tourneville. *Registers of the Catholic Chapel Royal and of the Portuguese Embassy Chapel, 1662–1829, Catholic Record Society Publications*, vol.38 (Leeds, 1941), p. 164. Léonard Fourcade's name does not appear in any cast list, but he was associated with the company for the next ten years.

Joshua Ward, Francisque-Arlequin, and John Kelly's The Plot

Responses to the press's anti-Popery propaganda ranged from the grotesquely farcical to the more sinister. Francisque was indirectly involved in several of these, which can be understood only through awareness of their intertextual and topical cross-references. In 1734 there was a brief Plot scare over Joshua Ward, a quack doctor whose disgrace in 1717 had led to his exile in France. Ward had recently returned to London and his offer of his 'pill and drop' as a cure for all ills, given free to the poor, had provoked considerable discussion. On 28 November, the *Daily Courant* published a letter that filled its entire front page. The writer claimed that Ward was a Papist agent who was being assisted by a Catholic 'Lady of Fashion and great Gaiety' in a plot to bring in the Pope and the Pretender. This 'revelation' led to a flurry of responses. *The Gentleman's Magazine* for December 1734 printed 'The Pill Plot', comic verses by Sir William Browne of the Royal College of Physicians. Its title summed up the *Courant*'s overblown argument: 'The Pill Plot; or *The Daily Courant*'s miraculous discovery, upon the ever-memorable 28th day of November 1734, from the Doctor himself being a Papist, and distributing his pills to the poor gratis, by the hands of the Lady Gage also a Papist, that the Pill must be beyond all doubt a deep-laid plot, to introduce Popery'. The poem sarcastically praised the journal for uncovering a second Gunpowder plot:

> Auspicious Month, be ne'er forgot,
> May ev'ry age remember;
> That both the Pill and Powder-Plot
> Were baffl'd in *November*. [10]

A poem published in December as a separate volume provides a curious link to Arlequin-Francisque. Its enormously long title, like that of 'The Pill Plot', makes its sarcasm obvious: *Ward's downfal: or, the plot detected. A poem. Being a full and true account of a most horrid, barbarous, and bloody plot, to undermine the Hanover succession, bring in the Pretender, and blow up all true Protestants. As it was carrying on between the celebrated Mr. J—a W-rd, a L–y of Quality, and a Jesuit behind the Curtain; had it not been happily discovered by one of the Enlightened Authors of the Daily Courant. Now Published as a Warning to all True Britons, how they suffer themselves to be deluded by the Treasonable and Ill-Designing Cures of any bloody-minded Papist*. The preface comments: 'Neither that of the Dog *Harlequin*, or of *Signior Belloni*, come within a Bow-Shot of [this plot].' The allusion here is

---

[10] The verses were also printed in *The London Magazine, or, Gentleman's Monthly Intelligencer*, December 1734, *The Weekly Amusement: or, The Universal Magazine*, January 1735, and *The Craftsman*, Saturday, 4 January, 1735.

to the Atterbury plot which had involved the Pretender's banker Belloni and a spotted dog called Harlequin, sent from France to Bishop Atterbury's wife. The dog had been mentioned in Jonathan Swift's verses of 1723, 'Upon the horrid PLOT discovered by *Harlequin* the B[ishop] of R[ochester]'s *French dog*, in a Dialogue between a *Whig* and a *Tory*':[11]

> His name is *Harlequin*, I wot,
> And that's a name in evr'y *Plot*....

Clearly echoing Swift, *Ward's Downfall* looks back to the time 'When the Dog *Harlequin* / Once a plotter was seen'. The *Craftsman* on 14 December announced that 'This *Plot*, indeed, hath been turn'd to Ridicule, as most *Plots* commonly are.' The *Courant* hurriedly claimed that its report was merely a jest, though also a warning, and on 10 January insisted again on the dangerous '*Growth of Popery*'.

The whole saga was turned to ridicule in John Kelly's ballad opera, *The Plot or Pill and Drop, A New Tragi-Comi-Farcical Operatical Grotesque Pantomime*, first performed at Drury Lane on 22 January 1735: 'a temporary [topical] trifle interspersed with songs'.[12] No commentator has hitherto made much sense of it, beyond noting that it concerned Joshua Ward and the medical profession. Allardyce Nicoll claims that it satirises 'continental innovations of the pantomimic kind',[13] while Jean Kern argues that its satire on physicians is weakened by the inclusion of 'irrelevant interludes of French comedians who have nothing to do with The Plot.'[14] In reality, these apparently 'irrelevant interludes' parallel and ridicule two recent arrivals from France: Ward and Francisque's troupe. The point of the satire has been missed because Ward's name is absent from the cast list. 'The English Harlequin' who appears at the beginning of the play clearly refers to John Rich, a fact that is further reinforced because the part is played by Lebrun, who, like Rich, was a dancer, not an actor. But the impersonation is more complicated than that. Rich simultaneously stands for Joshua Ward and Francisque, both of whom have come over, supposedly, to give the English health. (In the 1735 Drury Lane revival of *The Burgomaster Trick'd*, Lebrun took over the role of the

---

[11] Jonathan Swift, 'Upon the Horrid Plot', in *Poems on Several Occasions* (Dublin, 1735), pp. 149–51.

[12] John Kelly, *The Plot. As it is Performed by His Majesty's Company of Comedians at the Theatre-Royal in Drury-Lane, with the Musick prefix'd to each Song* (London, 1735). It was given just three times in all.

[13] Allardyce Nicoll, *History of Early Eighteenth Century Drama: 1700–1750* (Cambridge, 1925), p. 256.

[14] Jean B. Kern, *Dramatic satire in the age of Walpole, 1720–1750* (Ames, IA, 1976), p. 66.

silent Harlequin that Francisque had played early in 1634.) As Rich was a non-speaking Harlequin, in *The Plot* his 'French' valet (the actor Thomas Salway) sings for him, referring both to Ward's philanthropic project and to Francique's lean and hungry players who are desperate for English roast beef:

> Je scai you come not here for Wealt,
> Mais vor to give relief:
> But ere you give the *Englis* Healt
> Morbleu lets taste der Beef. [...]

> Relieve the Sick, de tout mon Cœur,
> Assuage de Patient's grief:
> But still, ma foi, mon cher Monsieur,
> Me hungar for Roast Beef!

The 'Plot' of the title satirises both the false alarms in the press and the London doctors' hostility to Ward. A writer in *The Grub-Street Journal* of 9 January 1735 had claimed that Ward was loved by the doctors and 'the undertakers, coffin makers and sextons of this city', for his ability to kill with just one drop, a valuable service in an over-populated metropolis. Kelly, on the other hand, claims that Ward's pill actually works and has deprived the physicians and others of their livelihoods.[15] (One of the doctors, Misoquackus, has written against Ward – possibly a reference to Browne and his 'Pill Plot' verses.) Ward's enemies hire ruffians to kill him, and the climax was apparently a pantomime chase, ending with his escape. After the disappearance of this bizarre comic conflation of Ward and Harlequin, the play is rounded off with the triumphal entry of 'the French players' led by the 'French Harlequin' who of course is Francisque again, parodied by the actors who had worked alongside him in the previous year.[16] Kelly, an admirer and translator of French plays,[17] could have known about Francisque's earlier London seasons and the actor's promise that his players would cure the English spleen. The memory of this promise may lie behind the words given to 'Francisque':

> Begar, me take no Pill, no Drop,
> Me vaite vid Patience for de Crop [financial gains].

---

[15] Kelly was familiar with Molière on doctors: 'Thus, when Molière an Empirick attacks,/ He finds no censure, but among the Quacks' (Prologue).

[16] The French Arlequin was played by John Laguerre, who had been a member of Rich's company before moving with his wife to Drury Lane. One of the Frenchwomen was played by Charlotte Charke (Colley Cibber's daughter).

[17] In 1732, Kelly had produced an English version of Destouches' *Le Philosophe marié* and, in 1733 at Drury Lane, *Timon in Love or the Innocent Theft*, based on Delisle's *Timon le misanthrope*.

> Me ave come here one Time before,
> And me be den – as now, ver poor [...].

Two French actresses gloat over the prospect of extorting money from their aristocratic patrons and triumphing over the more intellectual English drama of the two licensed theatres:

> *2nd Woman.* Dere be Lors, great Vits, Monsieur,
>   Vill starve de Englis, de bon Cœur,
>   Dey'll let dem walk vid empty Poche,
>   And us, mes Chères, dey'll put in Coach.
>   Dere playing Sense dey'll find is vain,
>   We'll down vid Rish [Rich] and Drury Lane

This final scene indicates how thoroughly the French actors at this point were part of the London landscape, recognisable figures in a highly topical play.

'Application Plays'

1. Le Tartuffe, Le Festin de Pierre, and Zaïre

But Francisque's company itself became involved in topical issues in a far more serious way. It is possible that not only *Le Tartuffe* but a number of verse tragedies and tragicomedies from the Comédie-Française and Comédie-Italienne had been requested in advance when Francisque was in London early in 1734. Whatever the case, their relevance to current events could hardly have gone unnoticed by contemporary audiences.

In his discussion of politics in the theatre in the 1730s, Robert D. Hume makes a useful distinction:

> Topical allusion plays refer openly to current events ... generally in a snide or hostile way. Application plays rely on the audience to draw parallels and see connections: for example, applying the lessons of Scanderbeg, the Earl of Essex, or Charles I to the times and court of George II.[18]

Related to Hume's concept of application is that of 'personation', which, as Thomas McGeary says, relies on the comparison of characters in a play

---

[18] Robert D. Hume, 'Henry Fielding and Politics at the Little Haymarket 1728–1737,' in J. M. Wallace, ed., *The Golden and the Brazen World: Papers in Literature and History 1650–1800* (Berkeley and Los Angeles, 1985), pp. 79–124, at p. 96.

with contemporary figures.[19] Hume's view is that 'After 1731 the theaters did not stage application plays unless they stuck to fairly general parallels and ideology.'[20] However, in his discussion of Handel's oratorio revivals of this period, Lawrence Zazzo points out that the 1735 performances of *Esther*, *Deborah* and *Athalia*:

> coincided with a particularly highly-charged anti-Government climate, almost a campaign, in some London theatres. This was mostly directed at the person and ministry of Robert Walpole, but was also at times anti-Court and even dangerously anti-Hanoverian, due to the alliance of a diverse number of disaffected minorities.[21]

Francisque's 1734–5 season included eighteen performances of eight plays (evenly spaced throughout the season) that fall squarely into the categories of both application and personation. It is worth noting that the press carried unusually full cast lists for all these plays, as if to indicate that these performances would not be a reduction of the original.

Francisque's revival of *Le Tartuffe*, which he had performed during his first London season in 1719, exemplifies the way in which application is affected by context. The performances given early in the reign of George I took place shortly after Colley Cibber's anti-Jacobite adaptation of Molière's play. While the non-jurors were still topical in 1734–5, the remarkable total of six performances could also have been seen in terms of the obvious parallel between Orgon's dysfunctional household and the English court.[22]

At the Little Haymarket in 1731, *The Fall of Mortimer*, with its clear 'application' to Prime Minister Walpole of the over-powerful favourites of Edward II's reign, had been banned.[23] *Majesty Misled, or the Overthrow of Evil Ministers*, also set in the reign of Edward II, was banned in 1734 before it even reached the stage. It was however printed and had been on sale since January of that year.[24] But, although the relationship between Tartuffe and his

---

[19] Thomas McGeary, *The Politics of Opera in Handel's Britain* (Cambridge, 2013), p. 45.

[20] Hume, 'Henry Fielding', p. 104.

[21] Lawrence Zazzo, *"Not Local Beauties": Handel's Bilingual Oratorio Performances, 1732–1744* (Ph.D dissertation, Queen's University, Belfast, 2015), p. 124.

[22] Another interesting difference in *Le Tartuffe* is that the role of the comic elderly lady, Mme Pernelle, played by a man in 1718, was taken in 1734 by Mme Verneuil. This casting may simply reflect the strength of the company, but it may also indicate a more general shift in theatrical practice.

[23] William Hatchett, *The fall of Mortimer. An historical play. Reviv'd from Mountfort, with alterations.* (1731).

[24] Anon [Philathes], *Majesty Misled: Or, the Overthrow of Evil Ministers, as intended to be Acted at one of the theatres, but was refused for certain reasons*

misled benefactor Orgon could have suggested that of Walpole and George II, the disturbing parallels went even further than politics. Just as Tartuffe attempts to seduce Orgon's wife, Elmire, it was whispered that Walpole enjoyed, or sought to enjoy, the favours of the Queen. The waspish Lord Hervey called Walpole 'The Queen's Minister' and Walpole was perceived by some as having succeeded where even Tartuffe had failed, in ruling the husband through the wife. But other religious and dynastic allusions are almost certainly present. Orgon is saved at the end of the play by the direct intervention of a king who is never named and who never appears.[25] Jacobites and non-jurors would undoubtedly think of James III, the 'king across the water'.

Le Festin de Pierre was advertised in *The London Daily Post* on 8 January with a full cast list, which, though no author is named, makes it clear that what Francisque presented was the tragicomedy of 1658 by Dorimond.[26] The version of the Don Juan legend known to London audiences, Thomas Shadwell's *The Libertine* of 1675, was derived mostly from *Le Nouveau Festin de Pierre* by Rosimond, which, like Molière's play, depicts a Don far more godless than Dorimond's. The Restoration libertinage of Shadwell's play was too strong for a more moral age, and the play had been performed just once in 1731 and twice early in 1733. Perhaps not coincidentally, two performances were also given in August and September of 1734, just a month before the arrival of Francisque's troupe.

Dorimond's play was published in Lyon in 1659 with the subtitle *Le Fils criminel*. In the Paris edition of 1665 the subtitle was changed to *L'Athée foudroyé*, translated in the London press advertisement as 'The Libertine destroy'd', perhaps in order to remind theatregoers of Shadwell's play, at the same time shifting the stress to divine retribution. Given the well-known conflict between Frederick, Prince of Wales and his parents, the play's original subtitle could have been seen in the context of Queen Caroline's view (recorded by Lord Hervey) that the feckless, gambling and whoring Frederick was 'the greatest ass and the greatest liar and the greatest canaille and the greatest beast in the whole world, and I heartily wish he were out of it.' The Don's

---

(London, 1734). The advertisement in *The Craftsman* clarifies the 'certain reasons' by linking the play to another which openly mocks Walpole and his hold over the royal family. 'This day is also published ... The NORFOLK GAMESTER, or the Arts of Managing the whole pack, Even King, Queen, and Jack.' The Walpole family's country seat was at Houghton in Norfolk.

[25] Cf. Andrew Calder: 'If ... *Le Tartuffe* is a political play translated into a domestic context, an unconventional ending involving a political solution is appropriate. The ending is a reminder to the audience of the wider meaning of the play.' *Molière: The Theory and Practice of Comedy* (London, 1993), p. 177.

[26] For a detailed comparison of the Dorimond play with Molière's *Dom Juan*, see C. Bourqui, *Les Sources de Molière* (Paris, 1999), pp. 375–82.

fate might have inspired another outburst by the queen, which shocked even the unshockable Lord: 'I wish the ground would open this moment and sink the monster to the lowest hole in hell.'[27]

The performance of Voltaire's *Zaïre* on 9 January, given by command of the Duke of Cumberland and all the royal princesses, was advertised in *The London Daily Post* as 'Never Acted before in England'. Again, the play was open to opposing interpretations. Although the performance was by royal command, the character of Corasmin, the Sultan's chief officer who, like Iago in *Othello,* encourages his master's jealousy with tragic results, could have been seen by the political opposition as a reference to Walpole, the evil minister of a misled monarch. At a time when the treatment of religion on the stage was dangerous, the play's comparatively sympathetic treatment of Islam was daring enough in Paris, but in London it could have been interpreted as a veiled plea for greater tolerance for Catholics. Similarly, Ruth Smith describes the original libretto of Handel's *Esther*, revived in April 1735, as a plea 'for tolerance of minority views and the repeal of anti-Catholic legislation.'[28]

Aaron Hill's silence in *The Prompter* on the performance of *Zaïre* calls for comment. After translating the play in 1733 (as *Zara*), he had been trying in vain for two years to get his version staged, printing passages from it in *The Gentleman's Magazine*, and eventually presenting it himself with an amateur cast in the spring of 1735.[29] At last, in *The Prompter* of 4 July 1735, a convoluted postscript to his Epilogue to *Zara* complimented the good taste of the Duke and the four Princesses who had bespoken *Zaïre* at the Haymarket, though he did not name the play. This is the total extent of Hill's acknowledgement of Francisque's January performance; his remarks also indicate that, surprisingly, he did not attend this performance of a play which he had been praising to the skies for the preceding eighteen months.[30]

---

[27] John Walters, *The Royal Griffin, Frederick Prince of Wales 1707–51* (New York, 1972), p. 133, p. 161.

[28] Ruth Smith, *Handel's Oratorios and Eighteenth-Century Thought* (Cambridge, 1995), p. 280.

[29] Christine Gerrard, *Aaron Hill: The Muses' Projector, 1685–1750* (Oxford, 2003), p. 176.

[30] In fact, both Francisque and Hill had been pre-empted by schoolboys. As early as 8 May 1733, when Hill was still struggling with *Zara*, *The Daily Journal* announced that 'Mr. Voltaire's new Tragedy, entitled ZAIRE, which has been received with so much applause on the Theatre at Paris, is, we hear, to be acted Tomorrow, by the young Gentlemen at Mr. Dorey's Boarding-School, at Chelsea.'

2. *Gustave Vasa*

On 11 and 17 January 1735, *The London Daily Post* reported:

> We hear that the Tragedy of Gustavus Vasa, or the story of Gustavus the Great, which was lately written at Paris, and acted there with great Applause, is now in rehearsal by the Company of French Comedians at the New Theatre in the Hay-market; and that they design to use their best Endeavours to oblige the Town with the Representation of the same in a few days.

Francisque's plays were usually advertised just a couple of days before each performance, but the first announcement of Piron's tragedy appeared almost a full month before the single performance at the Haymarket on 5 February, allowing plenty of time for speculating about its possible topical application. The play was advertised again in the same newspaper on 21 January. Two days later the play was postponed, 'on Account of the Indisposition of one of the principal Performers.'[31] As if to further heighten expectations, the play was re-advertised, with a full cast list, on 3 and 4 February, and finally performed on 5 February. Whatever might have been the real reasons for the unusually early announcement in January, or the postponement to February, the result was that this single performance was advertised on seven separate occasions over the course of a month.

Gustave was by far the most recent item in Francisque's programme, probably the most rapid transfer of a new play from Paris to London in the early eighteenth century. First performed at the Comédie-Française on 3 February 1733 (N.S.), it was so successful that *The Daily Courant* reported on 6 February (O.S. – 17 February N.S.): 'Never did Play meet with so universal an Applause; the Boxes are all taken up a Week before-hand; and it is thought this new play will be acted every other Night till the House is shut up.'

Piron's acknowledged source for the story of King Gustavus Vasa of Sweden (1496–1560) was the Abbé Vertot's *History of the Revolutions in Sweden*, which had been available in English translation since 1696 and was the source for a long-forgotten tragedy by Catherine Trotter, *The Revolution of Sweden* (1706). In 1735, however, there was considerable interest, largely thanks to Voltaire, in another Swedish ruler, Charles XII (1682–1718). As Ian Higgins points out, disaffected 'Tory' writers could find an anti-type to the ruling Hanoverian in this 'enemy of George I and Protestant hero of the Jacobites.'[32] In 1717, in the wake of the 1715 Jacobite rebellion, there had been widespread rumours of a complex plot of Sweden, France and Russia to invade

---

[31] The only other known postponement in Francisque's season was his Benefit (see p. 205, above).

[32] Ian Higgins, *Swift's Politics: A Study in Disaffection* (Cambridge, 1994), p. 39.

England via Scotland and restore the Pretender. The affair led to the arrest by the British government of the Swedish diplomat, Carl Gyllenborg, with serious diplomatic repercussions.[33] Many Jacobites believed that Charles XII did not die in battle, but at the hands of agents of George I.

Another King Gustavus of Sweden must also have been fresh in the minds of the many aristocratic Freemasons of the Grand Lodge of England who were also regular theatregoers, including past Grand Master Charles Lennox, Duke of Richmond, patron of Francisque and of Marie Sallé. In 1729, Thomas Howard, Duke of Norfolk, was elected Grand Master of the Grand Lodge of England. He was England's leading aristocratic Roman Catholic. Before the Church became hostile to Freemasonry, many Catholics were Masons and the English Catholic and Jacobite diaspora was crucial to the spread of Freemasonry in continental Europe, while the 'Lodge of Free Masons' in Rome was described as 'a nest of Jacobites.'[34] In 1731, the Duke of Norfolk was in Venice, from where he sent, as a gift to the Grand Lodge, 'the old Trusty Sword of King Gustavus Adolphus of Sweden, which was ordered to be the Grand Master's Sword of State for the Future'.[35] This symbolic gesture, linking the Catholic Duke of Norfolk with the avenging sword of the Protestant King Gustavus Adolphus the Great (1594–1632), 'Father of modern warfare' and 'the Lion of the North', would certainly have sent alarming signals to those who understood its cultural and political implications.

Thomas Howard had married Maria Shireburn, a member of the staunchly recusant Catholic and Jacobite family of Stonyhurst Hall in Lancashire. Thomas's brother Edward narrowly escaped death for high treason in the Jacobite rising of 1715. Despite Thomas's submission to the House of Hanover, in October 1722 he was held in the Tower for over six months, suspected of involvement in the Atterbury plot. The Duchess of Norfolk, disgusted by her husband's 'truckling' with 'the Usurper', abandoned him for a Catholic Jacobite, and the deserted Duke died heirless in 1732, suspected by both sides and trusted by neither.[36] It must have been with a keen awareness of these complex issues that Francisque's audience of diplomats, ministers and aristocrats gathered on 5 February to witness a classical French tragedy in

---

[33] The affair is discussed in great detail in several chapters of Marsha Keith Schuchard, *Emanuel Swedenborg, Secret Agent on Earth and in Heaven* (Leiden, 2012). See also Frederik Dhondt, *Balance of Power and Norm Hierarchy: Franco-British Diplomacy after the Peace of Utrecht* (Leyden, 2015), pp. 84–90.

[34] Andrew Lang, *A History of Scotland from the Roman Occupation* (Edinburgh, 1907) vol. 4, pp. 434–5.

[35] A. Mackey and H. L. Haywood, *Encyclopedia of Freemasonry* ([Chicago, 1912] Kessinger Reprints, 2010), vol. 2, p. 1000.

[36] See Jacques Monod, *Jacobitism and the English people, 1688–1788* (Cambridge, 1989), pp. 133–5.

which a brave native King is restored from exile to his rightful throne and the occupying foreign usurper and his wicked advisor are vanquished. Many must have been forcefully struck by its powerful theatrical evocation of the theme of 'Majesty Misled' and one can only assume that a public performance of Piron's *Gustave* was tolerated because it was in French and its political implications would be grasped by very few – although the few who *would* grasp it were those who might be in a position to act on it.

One of these was the aspiring young Irish writer Henry Brooke. He had come to London to study law at the Temple and had gained a certain celebrity with his ambitious 'philosophical' poem, *Universal Beauty*, published in monthly instalments from February 1735 and much admired by Pope and his circle. Brooke, who had been introduced to the Prince of Wales and his oppositional entourage, could have seen Piron's *Gustave* which was advertised in the press at the same time as his own poem, and the inspiration for his *Gustavus Vasa or the Deliverer of his Country* may have come from Francisque's production. There is little need here for a comparison of the two plays; what matter are the broader themes. Both Piron and (later) Brooke depart from the Abbé Vertot's historical account in several ways, and Brooke does not follow Piron's changes. One enormous liberty in Piron is the unhistorical presence of the Prince Frédéric. The historical Frederick was King Christian's uncle, who took the throne of Denmark when Christian was deposed. Partly for the sake of a love interest, Piron depicted Frédéric as a virtuous alternative to his usurper nephew. A major difference between Piron and Brooke is that Piron's Gustave is re-united at the last with his beloved, whereas Brooke's Gustavus renounces love in favour of service to his people, a change possibly inspired by the Prince of Wales's recent espousal of Masonic ideals. What Ian Higgins says of Jacobite propaganda around this time also holds good for the disaffected groups around the Prince of Wales who 'used strategies of disguise, indirection, innuendo, allusion and analogy in disseminating anti-Establishment views while seeking to evade prosecution'.[37] Brooke's Epilogue ends with a protestation of loyalty to the Protestant succession: deliberate and protective ambiguity, to be found everywhere in the cultural production of these years.

In spite of Brooke's protestations, his *Gustavus Vasa* was the first play to be banned under the Licensing Act (1737), and it could well be that the ban in 1739, which apparently came only in the late stages of rehearsal, was provoked in part by someone's sudden recollection of the disturbing implications of Piron's *Gustave Vasa* just four years earlier. What Ruth Smith said of Brooke's play applies with equal force to Piron:

---

[37] Ian Higgins, *Swift's Politics: A Study in Disaffection* (Cambridge, 1994), p. 161.

[I]t could be read not just as being heavily imbued with Patriot opposition themes (a king misled by an evil chief minister, a national hero saving his country from corruption and oppression, the restoration of national integrity) but as propagating Jacobitism: as proposing not only reform of the government but a change of monarchy. The king from whom Gustavus delivers his country, Sweden, is a usurping Dane, while Gustavus himself belongs to the old, native, ousted royal family.[38]

3. Inès de Castro and Agnes de Chaillot

Houdart de la Motte's subject, the tragic story of Inès de Castro, was well known in England, thanks to Aphra Behn's novella *Agnes de Castro, or the Force of Generous Love* (1688), which had its eighth edition in 1735. At the fourteenth-century court of King Alfonso IV of Portugal, the heir to the throne, Don Pedro, has had a passionate affair with Inès de Castro, lady-in-waiting of his wife Constantia. When Don Pedro is condemned for leading a rebellion against his father, Inès tries to move the King to pity by presenting their three children to him. But Alfonso, for both personal and political reasons, orders her murder. Succeeding to the throne on the death of his father, King Pedro declares that he and Inès had been secretly married. He orders her body to be exhumed and crowned, and the courtiers are obliged to do homage to the dead queen.

La Motte, however, in keeping with the French *bienséances*, removed any suggestion of adultery or illegitimacy and omitted the post-mortem coronation. La Motte's Don Pedro (played by Francisque) is betrothed to Constantia but secretly married to Inès. When he revolts against his father he is condemned to death by the King's counsellors. In a touching scene in the last act Inès succeeds in moving King Alfonso to pity and pardon by one of the rare appearances of children on the French tragic stage.[39] But Alfonso's jealous queen, mother of Constantia by her first marriage, has already poisoned Inès, and the star-crossed lovers expire together in the final scene. *Inès de Castro* was one of the earliest sentimental French tragedies; like Voltaire's *Zaïre*, it moved audiences to tears throughout the century.

La Motte's *Inès*, although sanitised, would still have recalled the dysfunctional family relationships of the House of Hanover: the conflict between George I and his son and the equally strained relations between George II and Prince Frederick. Don Pedro's affair with Inès may have reminded the audience of George II's many affairs, or of his mother Sophia Dorothea's

---

[38] Smith, *Handel's oratorios*, p. 290.

[39] The (non-speaking) children in Francisque's production must have been drawn from Cochois' Lilliputians.

blighted affair with Count Philip Christoph von Königsmark, which led to her imprisonment by George I for over thirty years. George II's distress over the imprisonment of his mother was one of the earliest reasons for the mutual hatred between him and his father. Sophia Dorothea never came to England and was never crowned queen. When she died in 1726, George I forbad court mourning in Hanover and London, but, to his fury, the Prussian court, led by the queen who was the daughter of George and Sophia, went into full mourning, as if the uncrowned Sophia, like Inès, had reigned after death. The pathetic plight of Inès and Pedro's sequestered children was reminiscent of George I's treatment of his son's children, which George II repeated with the children of the Prince of Wales. The two performances of *Inès de Castro* (30 December 1734 and 10 April 1735) were given 'By command of His Royal Highness', presumably the Prince of Wales, since his younger brother the Duke of Cumberland was normally referred to in playbills as 'His Royal Highness the Duke.' If Prince Frederick did indeed command these performances, the parallels with contemporary events, which go well beyond the conventions of genre, must have been provocative.

But Francisque also regaled London audiences with a very different version of the story. On 17 January, 'By Special Command of His Royal Highness', Francisque's company performed '*Agnès de Challiot* [sic]; being a critick and paradox upon *Inès de Castro*.' This one-act verse parody of La Motte's tragedy, written by Dominique and Legrand, was first performed by the Comédie-Italienne at the Foire Saint-Laurent in 1723. It was a huge success, as the marquis D'Argenson wrote, 'S'il y a jamais eu une parodie, à aucun théâtre, qui ait eu un grand succès, c'est celle-ci.'[40] [If ever there was a successful parody in any theatre, this was it.] The parody highlighted and mocked flaws in the tragedy pointed out by critics at the time. Although in alexandrines, it shifts from the sublime to the grotesque, even when quoting La Motte's original. The scene is the village of Chaillot: the King becomes Trivelin, a bailiff, and his wife is a baker's widow. Agnès is the bailiff's servant, and her secret husband is Pierrot. Don Pedro's aristocratic judges become the schoolmaster, the village beadle, the churchwarden, and the bell-ringer. At the climax, like Inès, Agnès introduces her children:

> Venez, pauvres enfants, qu'on veut rendre orphelins;
> Venez faire parler vos soupirs enfantins.
>
> [Come, poor children, soon to be orphans;
> Come and let your childish sighs speak for you.]

---

[40] René-Louis de Voyer de Paulmy, marquis d'Argenson *Notices sur les œuvres de théâtre*, ed. Henri Lagrave, Institut et musée Voltaire (Geneva, 1966), pp. 723–4.

The parody is enriched by the fact that these lines are an exact quotation from Racine's comedy *Les Plaideurs*, in which a dog is on trial and, as a plea for pity, the defence introduces a litter of puppies. Some spectators would also know that Racine had borrowed this scene from *The Wasps* by Aristophanes. The four children cry out, 'Mon papa, mon papa, mon papa, mon papa.' This perfect alexandrine with a caesura at the sixth syllable is also a line from Molière's *comédie-ballet, Monsieur de Pourceaugnac*, at the point when the provincial bumpkin is surrounded by shrieking children, the supposed fruits of his bigamy.

Agnès, far from being poisoned, suffers a bout of colic and thinks she is about to die. Arlequin waves an enormous handkerchief, signalling the arrival of the 'scène larmoyante' [the tearful scene]: 'Tirons tous nos mouchoirs, voici la belle scène.' [Let's all get our hankies out, here comes that lovely scene.] The *Mercure* reported that 'Tous les acteurs tirent de leurs poches des serviettes et des nappes. On peut juger facilement que tout le monde rit à ce burlesque spectacle.'[41] [All the actors pulled napkins and tablecloths from their pockets. As one might expect, everyone laughed at this burlesque scene.] The scene effectively made it impossible to produce a handkerchief on the French tragic stage for almost a century.[42] Pierrot deepens the comic intertextuality by parodying Corneille's *Le Cid*:

> Pleurez, pleurez mes yeux, et fondez-vous en eau,
> Puisque ma chère Agnès va descendre au tombeau.

> [Weep, weep, my eyes, and melt all into tears,
> For my beloved Agnès is going to her grave.]

But when Pierrot administers a splash of eau de toilette, Agnès suddenly recovers, and the play ends with all the peasants singing and dancing to the music of Mouret. Both the tragedy and the parody must have been well received in London in December and January because they were performed again, this time together, and once again 'by Command of HIS ROYAL HIGHNESS', on 10 April. The playbill added the information that the Bailiff in *Agnès de Chaillot* was played by Arlequin [Francisque]. Thus, in a single night, Francisque was seen both as the passionate Don Pedro, Prince of Portugal, and as the pompous and bumbling Bailiff of a French village.

---

[41] *Mercure*, July-December 1723, p. 211.

[42] For more on the 'mouchoir' (which is relevant to later French treatments of *Othello*) see Hans Mattauch, 'Inès, Agnès, Inesilla: Parodies françaises et espagnoles d'Inès de Castro', in Sylvain Menant and Dominique Quéro, eds, *Séries parodiques au siècle des Lumières* (Paris, 2005), pp. 29–40.

4. *La Vie est un songe* and *Samson*

La Vie est un songe and *Samson* were 'tragi-comédies', which in Paris could be seen only at the Théâtre-Italien. With these two plays Francisque gave London audiences a rare opportunity to see examples of this mixed genre, with its comic subplot – a genre frequently reviled by French critics but enjoyed by the French public, and perhaps more easily appreciated by London audiences. Louis de Boissy's *La Vie est un songe, ou Arlequin bouffon à la cour de Pologne*, was based on Calderón de la Barca's verse drama, *La vida es sueño* (1635). At the Comédie-Italienne in 1717, Luigi Riccoboni had given a performance in Italian of *La vita è un sogno*, adapted from a text by Cicognini which closely followed Calderón but was in prose. *La Vie est un songe* follows Calderon's play, but, like Riccoboni, renames Calderón's comic servant, the 'gracioso' Clarín, as Arlequin. Boissy's three-act play is in *vers libres* and eliminates the important character Rosaura and her sub-plot of wronged honour. In the view of the Marquis d'Argenson, 'Cette pièce est intitulée tragi-comédie, quoiqu'elle soit bien assez sérieuse pour être tragédie'[43] [This play is called a tragicomedy, although it is certainly serious enough to be a tragedy].

Boissy's version may be briefly summarised: Basile, King of Poland, warned in a prophecy that his son Segismond would depose his father and wreak havoc as a ruler, has imprisoned his child from infancy and had him brought up unaware of his true identity. Eventually, Basile brings the boy to court in the hope that Segismond will defy fate and behave nobly. But when Segismond learns the truth he behaves so wildly that he is returned to his prison. The two presumed heirs to the throne are his cousins Federic and Sophronie. The king has promised the cousins to each other in marriage, but Sophronie is drawn to Segismond, who loves her in return. When he awakens in chains, he ponders the nature of dreams and reality. Princess Sophronie sacrifices her own claim to the throne and rouses the people in support of the true heir. Thanks to her efforts and those of his jailor Clotalde, Segismond is restored to power. Having learned from his experience, he forgives his enemies, replaces the crown on his father's head and marries Sophronie.

Haymarket audiences at the three performances of *La Vie est un songe* must have been struck by the numerous parallels with the House of Hanover: the animosity between a king and his heir, imprisoned royalty, the importance of the king's advisor. The deposition of King Basile might have struck Catholic Jacobites as a justification of the people's right to depose or even murder a despotic king.[44] The outlandish behaviour of Segismond could have been

---

[43] d'Argenson, *Notices*, p. 722.
[44] See the discussion of Juan de Mariana's *De rege et regis institutione* (1599) in Murray N. Rothbard, *Economic Thought before Adam Smith* (Aldershot, 1995), pp. 117–18.

understood by the anti-Frederick faction as reflecting the King and Queen's low opinion of their boorish son. However, the effusive final reconciliation between King Basile and Prince Segismond, and the Prince's acceptance of the King's good and faithful minister, were a far cry from the behaviour of King George, Prince Frederick, and Walpole.

I have already discussed the genesis of Jean-Antoine Romagnesi's *Samson* and its special place in Francisque's repertoire. However, the play's reception in London would have been coloured by preoccupations of a peculiarly British order. Ever since Milton's poem *Samson Agonistes* (1671), 'captive Israel' had been taken to represent England after the collapse of the Commonwealth. But, by 1734, the figure of Samson had become a broader symbol of British nationhood, a noble, Protestant hero, willing to lay down his life to defeat the heathen. In this context, the wily seducer Delilah could well have been seen as the embodiment of the Whore of Babylon, the Catholic Church. Those familiar with Milton's 'serpent' Delilah would have been surprised by Romagnesi's sympathetic portrayal of a tragic heroine, torn between love and duty, and by the comic relief provided by Francisque as the servant Ascalon. Given the ambiguity noted elsewhere, both Jacobites and Hanoverians could have seen in the defeated Samson and the tormented Delilah the embodiment of their conflicting political ideals. But perhaps most surprisingly, despite the ban on biblical drama in the English theatre, Francisque's production was fully staged and costumed, and the press promised 'all new scenes, machines and decorations, as much as the theatre will admit of.'

5. Athalie

On Monday 14 April *The London Daily Post* announced a forthcoming production of Racine's *Athalie,* claiming that the tragedy had never before been seen outside Paris. The advertisement went on to remind the Town of the versatility of 'Monsieur Francisque, who by his extraordinary Performance, is esteem'd by the best Judges a most just Actor, both in Tragedy as well as Comedy.' The choice of Racine's biblical tragedy had a particular significance in London, as its single performance on 16 April came immediately after five performances at Covent Garden (1–3, 9 and 12 April) of Handel's oratorio *Athalia*, based on Racine's tragedy. Like spoken theatre, Italian operas and Handel's English-language oratorios often reflected contemporary politics.[45] In his verse satire *Harlequin-Horace* (1731), James Miller had attacked Handel and his 'foreign *Songsters*' but he removed the composer's name in the fourth edition of the poem in 1735. Leslie Robarts suggests that this 'airbrushing' was a response to Handel's choice of English rather than Italian texts for his

---

[45] Heather McPherson 'Theatrical Riots and Cultural Politics in Eighteenth-Century London', *Eighteenth Century: Theory and Interpretation*, 43:3 (2002), 236, 237.

libretti, and his movement from mythological to Biblical themes.[46] At Covent Garden, the composer had revived two Old Testament oratorios in English, *Esther* (also based on Racine) and *Deborah*, and, in April 1735, a modified version of his 1733 oratorio *Athalia*.

Queen Athalia, the idolatrous worshipper of Baal, has seized the throne of Judah, and ordered that the children of the Jewish royal house be put to death. Her grandson Joas, rightful heir to the throne, is saved by Joad the High Priest and his wife Josabeth and raised in the temple as their own son. When Joas is old enough to assume kingship, the Israelites defeat Athalia and install Joas as the true king of Judah. At this point in Handel's setting, with trumpets and drums deliberately recalling the coronation anthems of 1727, the exultant chorus sings:

> Reviving Judah shall no more
> Detested images adore;
> We'll purge with a reforming hand
> Idolatry from out the land.
> May God, from whom all mercies spring,
> Bless the true church and save the king!

Despite this unambiguously Protestant declaration, scholars have found the subject an odd choice for the loyal Hanoverian Handel, especially since the oratorio was first performed in Oxford, a bastion of non-jurors and Jacobites. The story of resistance to a tyrant had been evoked as far back as 1657, in the pamphlet *Killing no Murder*, calling for the overthrow of Cromwell and the restoration of the Stuarts. After the deposition of James II in 1688 the oppositional narrative became firmly associated with the Stuarts, the Catholics and the non-jurors.

As Donald Burrows reminds us, in his discussion of Handel's *Athalia*, 'eighteenth-century British political life is not amenable to simplistic interpretation.'[47] Deborah Rooke suggests that Handel's treatment may have been an 'astute compromise', as 'the Jacobites were not alone in claiming that *Athalia* embodied their political aspirations',[48] and Stanley Pelkey agrees that 'the same classical and Biblical figures were used as object lessons by both sides in political debates.'[49] Ruth Smith, however, has argued:

---

[46] Leslie Michael Martin Robarts, 'A bibliographical and textual study of the wordbooks for James Miller's *Joseph and his Brethren* and Thomas Broughton's *Hercules*, oratorio librettos set to music by George Frederic Handel, 1743–44'. Ph.D. thesis (University of Birmingham, 2008), p. 140.

[47] Donald Burrows, *Handel* (Oxford, 1994), p. 175.

[48] Deborah W. Rooke, *Handel's Israelite Oratorio Libretti: Sacred Drama and Biblical Exegesis* (Oxford, 2012), pp. 53–74, especially n. 15.

[49] Stanley Pelkey, 'Political discourse and the Representation of Authority in the music of Handel', *Newsletter of the American Handel Society*, 13:3 (1998), p. 5.

If this libretto constitutes a Hanoverian allegorical takeover it is peculiarly inept ... and its ideological ambition is foolhardy: one could hardly find a more challenging part of the Bible to reclaim or a more hostile venue [Oxford] for the first performance.[50]

Lawrence Zazzo has claimed that Handel's revisions for the London version of 1735 'place *Athalia* even more comfortably within the 1730s' London theatrical vogue for evil minister plays critical of the Walpole regime'.[51] Zazzo also points out that, in that otherwise English-language production, the Italian castrato Carestini sang the role of the High Priest Joad in Italian, possibly 'reinforcing identifications of Italian opera singers, especially castrati, with Catholic priests, and thus contributing to the already strong Jacobite application in the plot of an oppressed religious minority and the restoration of their true king.'[52]

It seems to me that Francisque's single performance of *Athalie* in the original French should be seen as the climax of this series of theatrical events. In 1691 the exiled James II saw one of the earliest performances of Racine's play, which from the outset was read politically as a lament for the plight of the Stuarts. The tragedy was already in Francisque's repertoire; he had performed it in Brussels in 1733, and he must have realised that staging it in London would achieve something which had been denied to Handel. The Bishop of London's ban in 1732 on any attempt to give a staged performance of *Esther* had forced Handel to present biblical oratorios in concert form. Four days later, Francisque's company gave (as for *Samson*) a fully staged and costumed performance of *Athalie*, in which he himself played the small role of the Chief Priest Azarias.

The story of the boy-king Joas had a further striking contemporary resonance: in 1735 Charles Edward Stuart, the eldest son of the Old Pretender, was a youth of fifteen, about the same age as Joas. Those who followed newspaper reports of continental wars would have read in *The London Evening Post* of 10–13 August 1734 that the young Prince Charles had arrived at the siege of Gaeta 'to learn the Art of War' during the War of the Polish Succession. The commander of the troops, the Jacobite Duke of Berwick, wrote to his brother: 'I wish to God that some of the greatest sticklers in England against the family of the Stuarts had been eyewitnesses of this prince's resolution during that siege, and I am firmly persuaded that they would soon change their way of thinking.'[53] Another, anonymous, admirer wrote,

---

[50] Smith, *Handel's Oratorios*, p. 287.

[51] Laurence Zazzo, *"Not Local Beauties": Handel's Bilingual Oratorio Performances, 1732–1744* Ph.D. dissertation (Queen's University, Belfast, 2015), p. 236.

[52] *Ibid.*, p. 124. Cf. the joke about castrati in Steele's prologue to *The Conscious Lovers*, quoted above, p. 64.

[53] *The Scots Magazine*, 50 (1788), p. 314.

> Never was any Prince endowed with so much vivacity nor appeared more cheerful in all the attacks. [...] You may easily conclude that a young Prince, so affable and of so charming a behaviour, cannot fail of being adored both by officers and soldiers.[54]

As Paul Langford has pointed out, popular loyalty 'was more to the Protestant Succession than the current incumbent'[55] and the first two Georges survived principally because they were neither French nor Catholic. Accounts of this alternative Prince of Wales, more appealing than Hanoverian Frederick, were widely disseminated among Jacobites. When, at the Haymarket theatre, the chief Priest Azarias, played by Francisque, vowed to restore young Joas to the throne of his fathers, he would have expressed the heartfelt desire of some of his audience.

> Oui, nous jurons ici pour nous, pour tous nos frères,
> De rétablir Joas au trône de ses pères,
> De ne poser le fer entre nos mains remis,
> Qu'après l'avoir vengé de tous ses ennemis.
>
> [Yes, we swear here for ourselves, for all our brothers,
> To restore Joas to the throne of his fathers,
> To sheath the sword we were given
> Only after avenging him against all his enemies.]

In the role of Joas, Francisque's nephew, young Francis Cochois, must have seemed to many the very embodiment of 'the lad who was born to be king'. In act five, this extreme example of personation reaches its shattering climax when the High Priest Joad urges the boy to appear wearing his crown and to lead his troops into battle:

> Venez, cher rejeton d'une vaillante race,
> Remplir vos défenseurs d'une nouvelle audace;
> Venez du diadème à leurs yeux vous couvrir,
> Et périssez du moins en roi, s'il faut périr.
>
> [Come, dear scion of a valiant race,
> Inspire your followers with new bravery;
> Come, appear before them wearing the crown,
> And if you must die, at least die as a king.]

---

[54] Alexander Charles Ewald, *The Life and Times of Prince Charles Stuart, Count of Albany* 2 vols (London, 1875), vol. 1, pp. 48–9.

[55] Paul Langford, *A Polite and Commercial People: England, 1727–1783* (Oxford, 1989), pp. 35–6.

Ten years later, Prince Charles promised his father that he would reclaim the crown for the Stuarts or die in the attempt. In the end, he did neither. But in April 1735, after five (at the least, ambiguous) performances of Handel's *Athalia* and the one performance of Racine's *Athalie* (in the language of the protector of the exiled Stuarts), many Catholics, Jacobites and non-jurors may well have believed that their hour was at hand. Among loyal Hanoverians, however, these performances could only have aroused anger and suspicion, contributing to a growing belief in government circles that the theatres needed stricter control.

Rich foreigners and English critics

The 'dog Harlequin' of Swift and of *Ward's Downfal* had a further incarnation on 13 March 1735, when *The Grub-Street Journal* published a poem called 'The Two Dogs', referring to the English and French Harlequins. The poem was preceded by a Greek epigraph from book eight of *The Iliad*, which prays that the gods will 'expel hence those dogs brought here by evil fate'. Clearly, the author has little time for either the English or the French Harlequin, but his verses are worth quoting in full for their explicitness about the animosity between Rich and Francisque:

> Since dogs had of old,
> As Aesop has told,
> Both reason and speech like mankind;
> I'll sing in this age,
> How two dogs of the stage
> In a comical dialogue join'd.
> Of these Harlequin foes,
> One in Britain first rose;
> Who cou'd sneak, fawn, howl, cut a caper;
> The other from France,
> Hither taking a dance,
> Grew sawcy, and loudly did vapour.
> This provoked the spleen,
> Of English Harlequin,
> To bark out his passionate spite thus:
> Such a pack of sad dogs,
> Let loos'd from their plogs,
> How dar'd you bring over to bite us?
> When first you came o'er,
> You looked mangy and poor;
> And only your bitches were fat:
> But now, stuff'd with good cheer,
> You, like them, plump appear;
> And grin, bark, and dance with éclat.

> To this the Mounsieur,
> Reply'd with a sneer;
> Your sad case, my dear friend, I bemoan:
> But the true English taste,
> Is now changed at last,
> To prefer foreign curs to your own.
> Then, good brother Spot,
> Be content with your lot;
> 'Tis in vain to fret, snarl, or to frown:
> For a French Harlequin,
> Be he ever so mean,
> Will now charm the bright part of your Town.

In January Kelly had depicted the French as lean and starving (longing particularly for roast beef) and hoping to profit from the gullibility of English audiences. In March the whole company, once 'mangy and poor', is said to be 'stuffed with good cheer'. Francisque's Benefit had taken place on 27 February and word of its success had obviously spread.

In November 1734 Lord Hervey had commented: 'there are no less than two Italian Operas, one French playhouse, and three English ones. Heidegger has computed the expense of these shows, and proves in black and white that the undertakers must receive seventy-six thousand odd hundred pounds to bear their charges, before they begin to become gainers.'[56] In the case of the two opera companies, these gains failed to materialise. Despite the lure of Farinelli, Porpora's company was not much more financially successful than Handel's. As Graham Cummings wrote, 'Even without detailed financial records, it is possible to observe that the 1734–5 season represents the peak of the financially disastrous rivalry between the two companies.'[57] Despite a similar lack of financial records for Francisque, contemporary sources like the Abbé Prévost indicate that of all the companies in this season it was his that enjoyed the most robust financial health.

However, the company's success, many felt, was at the expense of English performers. Dedicating the published text of *The Man of Taste* to Lord Weymouth, Miller laments the age in which 'Husbands are ruin'd, Children robb'd, and Tradesmen starv'd, in order to give Estates to a French Harlequin, and Italian Eunuch, for a Shrug or a Song'. Kelly's *The Plot* showed the French company gloating that audiences will 'pay for vat none understand,/ While *Englis* Players starve'.

---

[56] Lord Hervey to Henry Fox, 2 November 1734: John Hervey, *Lord Hervey and his Friends 1726–38*, ed. Earl of Ilchester (London, 1950), p. 211. Quoted in Emmett L. Avery et al., eds, *The London Stage*, pt 3, vol. 1, p. 428.

[57] Graham Cummings, 'Handel's Organ Concertos (HWV 290–93) and Operatic Rivalry', *The GFH Journal*, 1 (2007), p 6. http://www.gfhandel.org/gfhjournal/cummings.pdf.

> Chorus: To France ven we return again,
> We'll be great Lors, and dey poor Men.

April 1735 saw the publication of *The Happy Courtezan: Or, the Prude demolish'd*, verses supposedly written by Constantia Phillips, a notorious courtesan and bigamist,[58] which sarcastically praise Farinelli's wealth and pretend indifference toward the unpaid tradesmen and out-of-work actors left in his wake:

> In short, sweet Boy! thy Fortune must be made;
> No Matter, let the Tradesman go unpaid;
> Let Children starve, let Fathers, Husbands break,
> 'Tis all well done, if done for thy dear sake.

Mrs Phillips makes one notable, if unflattering, exception:

> But let's at any rate preserve *Francisque*,
> At instant Repartee, so pat so brisk;
> What tho' his Troop are but a strolling Crew,
> It is enough, they're Foreigners, and new;
> No Matter how Abroad they were esteem'd.
> With us they're excellent Comedians deem'd: [...]
> Our Hospitality is always shewn,
> To any Nation's Vagrants, but our own.[59]

On 31 May 1735, Francisque and Farinelli were again coupled in 'An *Epilogue*, spoken by a young Gentleman, when the Tragedy of *Cato* was acted at York-Buildings:'

> Our English stages labour now in vain,
> Francisque and Farinelli, with less pain,
> Are more in favour, and have greater gain.

He urged all true Britons to rise and 'Banish th'Italian quav'rer, French buffoon'.[60] The line echoes the prologue to Henry Fielding's *The Universal Gallant*, which had premiered in February that year:

---

[58] See Thomas McGeary, 'Verse Epistles on Italian Opera Singers, 1724–1736', *Royal Musical Association Research Chronicle*, 33 (2000), 29–88.

[59] *The Happy Courtezan: Or, the Prude demolish'd. AN EPISTLE From the Celebrated Mrs. C-P TO THE Angelick Signior Far-n-li* (London, 1735), pp. 10–11.

[60] *The Weekly amusement: or, The Universal Magazine* (London, 1735), vol. 2, pp. 780–1.

> Do not your native entertainments leave;
> Let us at least our share of smiles receive,
> Nor while you censure us, keep all your boons,
> For soft ITALIAN airs, and FRENCH buffoons.

A song printed in 1737 but clearly dating from this period laments that '*Englishmen* starve while the *Foreigners* gain',[61] and, moreover, acquire their vices:

> The Voice of an *Eunuch* what Clown won't obey?
> Sound Sense for *Francisque* you've bartered away […]
> Our Heroes, like *Italians* now impotent grow,
> Our Elders all weak as *Francisque* in his Show,
> And our Statesmen short-sighted, alas! as a *Beau* […].[62]

After their final performance on the 4th of June Francisque's company returned to Paris, but the press did not forget its animosity. On 18 December 1735, having heard a rumour of a new invasion of performers from Paris, 'Staunch Old Briton' wrote in *The Grub-Street Journal*: 'Have not the *Faronellies*, the *Cuzzonies*, the *Sallés* and the *Francisques* chous'd us of money enough of late; but we must have pour'd in upon us a fresh shoal of *Jack Puddings* and *Tumblers* to pick our pockets with *wry faces* and *distorted limbs*?' He urged: 'Let us drive these Vermin from the British Stage, and return them to the tumbling Skip-frog nation from whence they came.' If 'those who call themselves *People of Distinction*' want such entertainment, he suggests, they should go abroad for it.

More invidiously, in January 1736, Aaron Hill, bewailing the general debasement of the London stage, contrasted it with that of Paris:

> They have indeed a Theatre on which Harlequin exerts his talents: but their Harlequin might, at times, make some of our comedies blush, in being more *moral*, more *chaste* and more *rationally pleasing*; and what is now called The New Italian Comedy, treads on the heels of true Comedy. […] I forbear the parallel of our conduct with theirs.[63]

---

[61] The 'Song Occasion'd by the FOREIGNERS meeting with so much Encouragement here' first appeared in *A Collection of Miscellany Poems* (London, 1737), p. 120. It is also found in *The Delights of the Muses* (London, 1738), *The Aviary: or Magazine of British Melody* (London [1745?], repr. 1765), and *The Merry Man's Companion and evenings agreeable entertainer* (London, 1750).

[62] Cf. James Miller's *Seasonable Reproof* (London, 1735): 'When thro' a Glass the gaudy Coxcombs stare,/ Or squint a superficial sidelong glare…'

[63] *The Prompter*, Friday, 30 January 1736.

'More *moral*, more *chaste* and more *rationally pleasing*': all of this Aaron Hill could, and should, have said of Francisque Moylin and his presentation of the longest and most successful season of French theatre *ever* seen on the English stage, unequalled even by the first visit to London of the Comédie-Française in 1871.

The enthusiasm of London audiences had sustained the French players for six whole months in the face of competition from three English theatre companies and two Italian operas. But there were signs that this very success would have dangerous consequences. More ominous than all the banter in the newspapers, a 'Bill for the Regulation of the Stage' was presented to the House of Commons in March 1735 by Sir John Barnard. Its targets included the vast sums earned by 'Eunuchs and Signoras' and the corrupting influence of 'our fluttering, fiddling Masters the French'. Although the Bill failed, it was widely discussed in the press and, no doubt, in the coffee houses, where Francisque would certainly have heard of it.[64] Within two years the freedom of the London stage would be drastically curtailed by the Licensing Act, and Francisque was to become one of its first and most spectacular victims.

---

[64] The Bill became the subject of a song published in May 1735 as 'Song on the Bill preferred in Parliament for suppressing of Players and Playhouses by John Phoenix, Commedian': *The Gentleman's Magazine*, May 1735, p. 279.

12

Brief scenes from the French provinces: 1736–1737

In the period before Francisque's next visit to London, information on his family and company is relatively scarce. I have already suggested that Marie Sallé may have come to London via Brussels in 1733, and in 1735 she was still more in need of the support of her extended family, since her Covent Garden season, despite its moments of triumph, had ended prematurely and unhappily.[1] It seems clear therefore that Sallé and Francisque's entire company left London together in June 1735.[2] When Sallé arrived in France, she was clearly unwell: on 15 July Voltaire wrote to Sallé's ardent but frustrated admirer, Nicolas-Claude Thieriot, 'Vous voilà donc vengé de votre nymphe; elle a perdu sa beauté' [So, you are avenged; your nymph has lost her beauty].'[3] Her unhappiness and illness may have led her, or her family, to seek out a companion for her. Emile Dacier was the first to identify this companion as Rebecca Wick,[4] and I have found more details in her naturalization papers in the Archives Nationales.[5] Born in London in 1703, and raised an Anglican, Wick was brought to France at the age of sixteen (for reasons never explained) and placed in an institution known as 'Les Nouvelles Catholiques', a religious society devoted to the conversion of non-Catholic women. She left the institution on 19 July 1735, shortly after Sallé had returned to Paris, and I believe that it was at this time that the two women first met. She became Sallé's

---

[1] For a new interpretation of Sallé's final season and its ending, see R. V. Kenny, 'Mademoiselle Sallé and Her Discontents', https://blogs.qub.ac.uk/dancebiographies/tag/marie-salle/.

[2] The company included Manon Grognet, but there are no grounds for the inferences that Deirdre Kelly has drawn from the fact that, as she puts it, the two women travelled 'openly' together. See Kelly, *Ballerina: Sex, Scandal, and Suffering Behind the Symbol of Perfection* (Vancouver, 2012), p. 34.

[3] D893. Voltaire to Nicolas Claude Thieriot, c. 15 July 1735, *The Complete Works of Voltaire. 87: Correspondence and Related Documents*, vol. 3, *May 1734–June 1736*, ed. Theodore Besterman (Geneva, 1969), pp. 174–5.

[4] See Dacier, pp. 267–70.

[5] Rebecca Wick, 'Lettres de naturalité' [French naturalization papers]: https://francearchives.fr/en/search?q=WICK+Rebecca.

companion for the next twenty years.[6] In August 1735, Sallé had recovered enough to dance at the Opéra and all her known stage appearances after this date were in Paris or at the French court.

After June 1735 Francisque's company disappear from the records until their arrival at the beginning of 1736 in the duchy of Lorraine. Little would be known of their visit to Nancy in that year were it not for the fact that, as on several other occasions, Francisque seems to have had a hand in the publication of a new play. *L'Hymen vainqueur* reveals on its title page that this 'Petite Pièce Héroïque, ornée de Spectacles, de Chants et de Danses' was performed by Francisque's company on 18 February 1736, for the festivities surrounding the marriage of Francis III, Duke of Lorraine, with the Archduchess Maria-Theresa of Austria. The wedding itself had taken place in Vienna on 12 February and Nancy, the administrative capital of the duchy of Lorraine, and nearby Lunéville, known as 'le Versailles lorrain', marked the occasion with lavish displays of loyalty, presided over by the Duke's mother, Elisabeth-Charlotte d'Orléans. A magnificent temple to Hymen and Peace was constructed in the town. A local bookseller, Jean-François Nicolas, gave an account in his journal of the month-long celebrations at Nancy and Lunéville, with a brief reference to Francisque performing seven or eight times at the grand court theatre, closing on 11 March.[7] The court theatre at Nancy was far from the humble *jeux de paume* in which Francisque frequently played. Opened in 1709, it had been built by Francesco Bibiena for Léopold I and was considered one of the finest in Europe.

The title page of *L'Hymen vainqueur* also mentions the 'Compliment' spoken (and probably written) by 'le Sieur Verneuil' to announce its performance, which followed Marivaux's *Le Prince Travesti*. Verneuil noted that the author of the entertainment had modestly concealed his name, which suggests that either he or Francisque might have had a hand in its creation. The cast list reads as follows: 'Mars – M. [François] Deshayes; L'Hymen – Mlle. Cochois la Jeune [Marianne]; L'Amour – M. Cochois le Jeune [Francis]; La Déesse de la Paix – Mlle. Cochois [Babet].' Jean-Baptiste Malter was the ballet master;[8] the music was by Ruault, probably 'le célèbre Ruault, flûtiste

---

[6] Dacier notes (p. 245) that she must be the person referred to as 'mon aimable amie' in Sallé's letter to Titon du Tillet, which he dates to 1742.

[7] 'Journal de Jean-François Nicolas', ed. C. Pfister, *Mémoires de la Société d'archéologie lorraine et du Musée historique lorrain*, 49 (1899), 216–386, at p. 311.

[8] He therefore could not have danced at the Opéra late this year, as is claimed in the entries for 'Malter' in Philip Highfill, et al., *A Biographical Dictionary of Actors, Actresses, Musicians, Dancers, Managers, and Other Stage Personnel in London, 1660–1800*, 16 vols (Carbondale, 1973–93) and Jean-Philippe van Aelbrouck, *Dictionnaire des danseurs, chorégraphes et maîtres de danse à Bruxelles de 1600 à 1830* (Liège, 1994).

au Concert Spirituel', who was active as a composer and flautist in Paris at this time.'[9] The three older children of Michel and Marguerite Cochois, Francis, Babet and Marianne, who had performed in London as Cochois' 'Lilliputians', all sang, danced and acted the leading roles, and were probably joined in the ballet by the children of other company members who had been among the London Lilliputians. Deshayes, who played the god Mars, had also been in the London company.[10] The presence of Michel Cochois is confirmed by the fact that Francis is referred to as 'M. Cochois le Jeune.'[11]

The entertainment uses familiar tropes for celebrating a royal wedding which is also part of a peace treaty. A dance of Mars and his warriors is followed by the arrival, first of Cupid, then of Hymen. Both reproach Mars for glorifying war. Iris, who appears on a rainbow, brings news of the peace that will be assured by the forthcoming marriage. Mars's rage is appeased by the goddess of Peace, and a scene change reveals the royal couple, in the Temple of Peace, holding the coats of arms of Lorraine and Austria, and surrounded by personifications of the benefits of peace. The goddess presides over songs and dances celebrating Hymen's triumph over war, and Cupid speaks a cheeky epilogue.[12]

In his 'Compliment' Verneuil obliquely refers to the difficulties the company seems to have experienced during their stay and indicates that they were aware of the geo-political significance of the dynastic marriage they were celebrating and of which they were honoured to be witnesses. In the flowery style characteristic of this genre, he added:

---

[9] A. Choron and F. Fayolle, *Dictionnaire historique des musiciens* 2 vols (Paris, 1817), vol. 2, p. 441. Rualt's first name seems not to be known.

[10] The Deshayes in Francisque's company could not have been (as suggested by the *Biographical Dictionary of Actors*) the choreographer Jean-Baptiste de Hesse (sometimes known as Deshayes). At this time de Hesse was a member of the Comédie-Italienne. On 5 March 1735 he danced in Riccoboni and Romagnesi's *Les Sauvages*, a parody of Voltaire's *Alzire*, and so could not have been the Deshayes in the cast of *Athalie* at about the same time in London. The latter is more likely to be the François Deshayes in whose troupe Martin Moylin was to appear in Lorient in 1751 and in Amsterdam in 1753.

[11] Both Fuchs and Emile Dacier mistakenly refer to the children's mother Marguerite Moylin as 'la veuve Cochois' in Nancy in 1736, but she was first called 'la veuve Cochois' in a document of 1756. In fact, Michel Cochois was to live for another fifteen years.

[12] Francis Cochois had already played a Cupid ('prettily', admitted the otherwise hostile English critic) in *La Réunion des Amours* in Francisque's 1734–5 London season. See pp. 197–8.

et nous, Messieurs, renfermés dans notre Sphère, occupés du soin de vos plaisirs, nous ne pouvons dans ces heureuses circonstances donner d'autres preuves de notre zèle, qu'en redoublant notre étude à vous rendre les Représentations, que S. A. R. MADAME Régente a bien voulu nous accorder sur ce Théâtre, plus dignes de votre attention.

[And, gentlemen, we who are enclosed in our own sphere, dedicated to your pleasures, can give no other proof of our zeal than by redoubling our study to make the performances which her royal highness Madame the Regent has kindly allowed us on this stage, more worthy of your attention.]

At the company's last performance, the 'Compliment' was again spoken by Verneuil. After lengthy and florid thanks to the Regent and the city of Nancy, he refers more directly to the uncertain political atmosphere of the time:

L'idée que nous nous étions formés de la Ville de Nancy, nous avait fait concevoir la douce espérance d'y passer des jours sereins; mais des nuages épais se sont élevés que la force seule du soleil pourra dissiper.

[The idea we had formed of the city of Nancy had made us hope to spend pleasant days here, but dark clouds have gathered which only the power of the sun can dispel.]

He hopes that the company that follows them may feel the happy effect of the 'sun'. This curious mixture of effusive thanks and rueful regret suggests that the marriage celebrations may have been 'clouded' (like the scene in *L'Hymen*) with anxiety about the future of the province. As part of a complex political settlement, in exchange for the Grand Duchy of Tuscany, Francis had reluctantly ceded the Duchy of Lorraine to Stanisław Leszczyński, former King of Poland and father of Louis XV's queen. For Francisque, as Christian Pfister put it, 'Les circonstances n'étaient pas favorables: c'était le moment où la Lorraine perdait son indépendance.'[13] [Circumstances were not favourable: it was the moment when Lorraine was losing its independence.]

On leaving Nancy in the spring of 1736, Francisque's company made its way to Toulouse, where a daughter of 'Jean-Charles' [*sic*] and Marianne Petit Lesage (the 'Lesage senior' couple in Francisque's London company in 1734–5) was baptised on 19 May. Jeanne Gaillardet, the wife of Guillaume Moylin, was godmother to the child, and there are two other family signatures, 'Moylin' and 'M. Moylin.' These must have been Guillaume and his son Martin, now aged sixteen. Another notable signatory was Jean-Baptiste Gherardi, who had

---

[13] Christian Pfister, ed., *Histoire de Nancy* (Paris, 1908), vol. 3, p. 423.

been involved with Francisque's troupes since at least 1725.[14] There is no further evidence of Guillaume's presence in the company after this date. He and his wife Jeanne Gaillardet may have retired to Bordeaux soon after this time, though their son Martin remained with the company.

In June 1736 Francisque and company arrived in Avignon where the magistrate authorised his troupe to perform 'dès aujourd'hui, à finir quand le Sr Franchisque [*sic*] le voudra'[15] [starting today and finishing whenever he wishes]. At the end of the year the company was in Marseille. Much had happened in the theatrical life of that city since their last visit. In March 1733, the city authorities had decided to build a new theatre to replace Mlle Châteauneuf's shabby old Jeu de Paume in the rue Pavillon, which however remained open. The new theatre had a Doric façade, a parterre which could hold 500 people, an amphitheatre, two rows of nineteen boxes and a *paradis* ('the gods'), all set off with a fresco-painted ceiling from which the chandeliers were suspended: for almost fifty years the theatre was considered one of the finest in France.[16] Evidence that Francisque performed here is to be found on the title page of a comedy, *Le Fortuné Marseillais*, by a local man, Jean-Baptiste Audibert, which says that the play was first given in 1735 by the local company of Antoine de Loinville on the stage of the new theatre and revived there by Francisque's troupe in the following year.[17] A curious feature of this play is its example of theatrical diglossia: two characters speak (and sing) entirely in Provençal while the others speak French, and they all understand each other perfectly.[18] It would be interesting to know if the two Provençal roles were taken by members of Francisque's troupe or by the local actors who had played them the previous year. Provençal was part of the wider Langue d'oc which Francisque's players encountered throughout the south of France.

In Marseille on 25 November 1736, Francisque's niece Catherine Malter gave birth to a son, Pierre. The child was baptised on 3 December in the church of St Ferréol, the same church in which the Malters were married in 1725. The child's godmother was Francisque's younger sister Marguerite Moylin (Madame Cochois).[19] The company may well have spent the winter in Marseille; then, at some point in 1737, they began to move up the Rhône valley.

---

[14] AM Toulouse, GG 313 (St-Étienne).

[15] AD Avignon, ROTE 199 and AD 3E9(2)/218 Notaire Mounier.

[16] See Jeanne Cheilan-Cambolin, 'Notes sur les trois premières salles d'Opera et de Comédie de Marseille', *Provence Historique*, 40:160 (1990), 147–55, at pp. 153–4.

[17] Jean-Baptiste Audibert, *Le Fortuné Marseillois, comédie, par Audibert, en un acte, en Provençal et en Français* (Amsterdam, 1736; 2nd edn Marseille, 1775).

[18] For the implications of this diglossia, see René Merle, *Une mort qui n'en finit pas?: L'écriture de l'idiome natal de la fin de l'Ancien régime à la naissance de Félibrige* (Nimes, 1990), p. 131; and https://renemerle.com/remembranca/.

[19] AM Marseille, GG 320 (St-Ferréol).

Francisque and Rousseau in Grenoble: August-September 1737

Francisque's company arrived in Grenoble in the summer of 1737. On 5 August a licence to perform was granted by the Consuls to 'Francisque, comédien du Roy françois et italien' [French and Italian player to the king]. This document also contains the information that 'la Troupe est en partie arrivée en cette ville, le reste arrive incessamment pour faire les représentations dans le Jeu de Paume accoutumé ...'.[20] [In part, the troupe has already arrived in town, the rest are about to arrive to give performances in the Jeu de Paume as usual.] The Jeu de Paume was located next to the medieval Hôtel de Ville in the picturesque centre of old Grenoble, and the word 'accoutumé' indicates that Francisque was a regular visitor to the town, where many will have remembered his participation in the celebrations for the birth of the Dauphin in 1729. He may also have visited in January 1736 before going on to Nancy.

In the autumn of 1737, the young but already valetudinarian Jean-Jacques Rousseau left Les Charmettes, the idyllic country retreat near Chambéry of his friend and patron Madame de Warens, and set out for Montpellier where he hoped to be treated for what his morbid fascination with medical text books had convinced him was a growth on his heart ('un polype au cœur').[21] In his poem 'Le Verger de Madame de Warens' [Mme de Warens' Orchard], published in 1739, Rousseau singles out two playwrights whose tragedies had moved him as a young man.

> Et vous trop doux la Motte, et toi touchant Voltaire,
> Ta lecture à mon cœur restera toujours chère.[22]

> [And you, too sweet la Motte, and you, touching Voltaire,
> reading you will always remain dear to my heart.]

Rousseau's lines make it clear that he had read rather than seen their works. The 'trop doux la Motte' refers to Houdard de la Motte's sentimental tragedy *Inès de Castro* of 1723. The 'touchant Voltaire' was probably *Zaïre* (1732).

On 12 September, during a three-day stop at Grenoble, Rousseau attended a performance of *Alzire* by Francisque's company,[23] and the play, with its deathbed Christian conversion of the villain Gusman and the happy reunion of the lovers, so profoundly moved him that on the following day he wrote to Madame de Warens:

---

[20] AM Grenoble, FF 43, fol. 297.

[21] See Jean-François Cordier, 'Le Polype au Cœur de Jean-Jacques Rousseau', *Bulletin de l'Académie Nationale Médicale*, 202:1–2–3 (2017), 485–93.

[22] Jean-Jacques Rousseau, 'Le Verger de Madame de Warens', *Œuvres Complètes*, 5 vols, ed. Bernard Gagnebin and Marcel Raymond (Paris 1959–95), vol. 2, p. 1129.

[23] *Alzire* had first been performed at the Comédie-Française in January 1736 and published in the same year, but Rousseau may not yet have possessed a copy, or known the text.

> Permettez encore, madame, que je prenne la liberté de vous recommander le soin de votre santé. [...] La mienne fut fort dérangée hier au spectacle. On représenta *Alzire*, mal à la vérité, mais je ne laissai pas d'y être ému jusqu'à perdre la respiration; mes palpitations augmentèrent étonnamment, et je crains de m'en sentir quelque temps.

> [Allow me, madam, to take the liberty once again to advise you to look after your health. Mine was greatly upset yesterday at the play. They were performing *Alzire*, badly it's true, but this did not prevent me from being so moved as to be unable to breathe; my heart pounded amazingly, and I fear that I shall feel the effects for some time.]

In fact, as his letter also reveals, Rousseau was well enough to go to supper after the play: 'Hier M. Micoud me donna à dîner avec plusieurs de ses amis, et le soir, après la comédie, j'allai souper avec le bonhomme Lagère'[24] [Yesterday M. Micoud invited me to dinner with a few of his friends and in the evening, after the play, I went to supper with good old Lagère.]

Rousseau's negative comment on the performance is open to question. In his native Geneva, public theatrical performances (with rare exceptions) were banned by law. Rejecting a request from a travelling troupe for permission to perform in 1732, the Calvinist Conseil de la Ville declared, 'Il n'est pas de notre usage ni conforme à nos mœurs de recevoir des comédiens dans notre ville.'[25] [It is not our practice nor in keeping with our customs to receive actors in our city.] Thus, the provincial Rousseau, with little or no experience of live theatre before he came to Paris in 1742, was not ideally equipped in 1737 to pass judgment. If the performance of *Alzire* was really of such poor quality, it is difficult to understand why he should be so deeply moved, rather than disappointed or angry on seeing the work of an admired author so poorly staged. What is certain is that Francisque was the catalyst for one of Rousseau's most formative emotional experiences, which also provoked the famous rhetorical question, in his letter to Madame Warens: 'Pourquoi, madame, y a-t-il des cœurs si sensibles au grand, au sublime, au pathétique, pendant que d'autres ne semblent faits que pour ramper dans la bassesse de leurs sentiments?' [Why, madam, are some hearts so touched by all that is

---

[24] Jean-Jacques Rousseau, *Correspondance complète de Jean Jacques Rousseau*, ed. R. A. Leigh 52 vols (Geneva, 1965), vol. 1, p. 49. Rousseau was also well enough to leave Grenoble the following day, 14 September, and continue his journey.

[25] In 1738, thanks to increasing French political influence in Geneva, the troupe of Francisque's friend and colleague Jean-Baptiste Gherardi was licensed to perform in the city for several seasons, but the experiment was short-lived, and the ban was reimposed. See R. Markovits, *Civiliser l'Europe: Politiques du théâtre français au XVIIIe siècle* (Paris, 2014), pp 166–70. In 1739–40 Gherardi moved on to Grenoble, Lausanne and Bern.

great, sublime and tender, while others seem only fit to wallow in their baser feelings?] Rousseau clearly counted himself among the 'cœurs sensibles', and so intense was his response to *Alzire* that he claimed that he felt obliged to eschew tragedy until his health improved.

Thanks to this letter, another brief episode in the career of Francisque Moylin was saved from oblivion. While *Alzire* is generally recognised as an inspiration for the libretto of Rousseau's lost 'opéra-tragédie', *La Découverte du Nouveau Monde*,[26] Henri Gouhier points specifically to the effect of seeing the play in performance: 'Il reste que la soirée grenobloise du 12 septembre a laissé des traces dans l'imagination du poète-compositeur'[27] [The fact remains that that evening in Grenoble on 12 September left its mark on the imagination of the poet-composer].

By the end of September Francisque and his company had moved on, and they were probably all in Avignon when on 28 September 1737 a licence was granted to 'les enfants de Michel Cochois'.[28] In October 1737 Francisque acquired the lease of the old theatre in Marseille for the winter.[29] The news reached the ears of François and Barthélemy Hus, the leaders of another important provincial troupe, who were planning to take the new theatre in the rue Vacon. On 9 October 1737 they wrote ahead anxiously from Le Havre to the city magistrates: 'le Sr Francisque vient en concurrence dans la petite salle' [Mr. Francisque is going to be competing with us in the small theatre], adding a warning: 'Il n'est pas nécessaire, Messieurs, de vous rappeler les désordres, et la triste situation où cette concurrence fatalle a jetté les spectacles dans Marseille.'[30] [It is hardly necessary, gentlemen, to remind you of the

---

[26] See, e.g., David Charlton, *Opera in the Age of Rousseau: Music, Confrontation, Realism* (Cambridge, 2012), p. 316.

[27] Henri Gouhier, *Rousseau et Voltaire: portraits dans deux miroirs* (Paris, 1983), p. 23.

[28] In a letter of 20 January 1737 Voltaire had written to the marquis d'Argens, then in Holland, referring to the Marquis' current mistress, a local actress, as the 'Mademoiselle Lecouvreur d'Utrecht' (an ironic comparison with Adrienne Lecouvreur, the finest tragic actress of the Comédie-Française): Letter D1263, *Œuvres Complètes de Voltaire*, ed. Besterman (Oxford, 1985) vol. 88:4. The Garnier edition of Voltaire's letters *Œuvres Complètes* (Paris, 1880), vol. 34, p. 205, identified this actress with Babet Cochois, who later married the Marquis. Babet Cochois was at this time barely 13 years old and the Marquis had not yet met any of the family. The error is repeated in many subsequent publications, e.g., the 'Key to Pseudonyms and Nicknames' in the recent Oxford edition (vol. 135) and Julia Gasper, *The Marquis d'Argens: A Philosophical Life* (Plymouth, 2014). p. 43 fn. 2. Jean Sgard, in his *Dictionnaire des Journalistes* (1600–1789), rightly rejects this erroneous identification.

[29] AM Marseille, FF 308.

[30] AM Marseille, FF 308 & GGL 202. I am grateful to Jean-Philippe Van Aelbrouck for giving me a copy of the Hus letter. The troupes of François Hus (1695–before 1774)

disorder and the unhappy situation into which this dangerous competition has thrown the theatre life of Marseille]. Possibly aware of this, Francisque seems not to have made use of the Marseille theatre, and by February he was already in northern France.

Taking the road to London

It would seem that Francisque had considered coming to London for the season of 1737–8. On 28 September 1737 *The Daily Gazetteer* reported: 'We hear that the famous *Francisco*, and his Company of French Comedians, have obtained Leave to come over hither this Winter.' The news was also printed in the *Grub St Journal* on 29 September, followed by an account of a theft of several guineas, to which the witty journalist added, 'This *Fellow* [the thief] seems to be the forerunner of *Francisco*.' Surprisingly, the proposed visit provoked no further comment in the press. And yet this news came only three months after the passing of the Licensing Act, which closed all non-patent theatre spaces, leaving only Covent Garden and Drury Lane, and throwing many actors out of work. Perhaps Francisque had come to London, as in earlier years, to seek a contract; but, being warned of the effects of the Act, decided it would be unwise to return to 'the land of guineas'. Whatever the case, he would have been obliged to postpone his visit, since after the death of Queen Caroline on 20 November 1737 the court went into mourning and the theatres were closed for six weeks.

On 2 February 1738, Francisque wrote to the authorities at Amiens requesting the right to perform there, explaining that he and Jean-Baptiste Lesage (who appears to have been joint manager with him) were 'entrepreneurs d'une troupe de Comédiens qu'ils peuvent dire sans témérité être des meilleurs Comédiens de province' [the managers of a troupe of actors who they can claim without fear of contradiction to be the best actors in the provinces]. Currently performing in Lille, they were preparing to take 'la route d'Angleterre'[31] [the road to England]. Later that month, Francisque and Lesage came to London and presented themselves to the French ambassador, Louis Dominique, Comte de Cambis, seeking his aid in obtaining permission to perform.[32] Given the contract which Francisque had signed in 1734, it may well be that the Duke and Duchess of Richmond, patrons of Marie Sallé, were

---

and Barthélemy Hus-Desforges (1699–1786) visited Marseille, Avignon, Montpellier, Perpignan, Toulouse, Bordeaux, Lyon, Chambéry, Grenoble, Rennes, Nantes, Le Havre, Rouen, Douai, Ghent and Brussels. See Fuchs, *Lexique*, pp. 117–20.

[31] AM Amiens, FF 1308.

[32] Sybil Rosenfeld claims that it was Francisque's younger brother Simon who led the company in London. (*Foreign Theatrical Companies in Great Britain in the 17th and 18th Centuries*, The Society for Theatre Research Pamphlet Series, no. 4 (London, 1954–5), p. 22. However, Francisque's name appears not only in all English

among those who supported the proposed season. Richmond was an ardent Francophile and had recently invited de Cambis to spend several months at his summer residence. The enterprise clearly had the eager assent of George II. In his letters to Paris de Cambis reported that the king was looking forward to attending the theatre as soon as royal mourning for the Queen ended in November; he had chosen some thirty plays that he wanted to see and the whole royal family were preparing for an enjoyable winter.[33] Armed with de Cambis's assurances, as the company leaders were later to write, 'we ... returned into France, and collected together the best Company that were to be had.'[34] In June they were in Avignon, where permission to perform was granted to Francisque and Desessars and their players, 'français et italiens'.[35] Finally, in October, at the head of a large company of actors, singers and dancers, Francisque set out for London, hoping to repeat his success of 1734–5.

---

accounts but also in the Amiens authorisation of February 1738, where there would have been no point in subterfuge.

[33] F. Baldensperger, 'Un Incident théâtral franco-anglais au XVIIIe siècle', *Revue de Littérature comparée* (1929), 573–8, at p. 576. The King would have seen French plays on his visits to Hanover, where there was a resident French theatre company.

[34] *The London Daily Post and General Advertiser*, 7 Nov. 1738.

[35] AD Avignon, B ROTE 199.

13

'A sharp and bloody battle': the Haymarket riot: October 1738

Francisque was the head of the first foreign company to come over to England since the passing of the Licensing Act, which had ended the careers of all actors not engaged at one of the patented theatres. He had been present in London in March 1735 when the earlier bill was introduced in the House of Commons and French players were cited as examples of 'lewd and idle diversions' in need of regulation.[1] During his visit in February 1738, when he and Lesage were petitioning the Lord Chamberlain for permission to perform, he must have heard of players made redundant by the Act. Indeed, during that time, *The London Daily Post* had reported that an actor from Fielding's disbanded company had been sent to prison for attempting to perform a 'shew' at York Buildings. Yet ambassador de Cambis seems to have foreseen no problems. In a dispatch sent later to the French foreign minister, he reported that 'La chose, effectivement, ne fit aucune difficulté, et le Duc de Grafton, après avoir eu l'ordre du Roi d'Angleterre, fit expédier la permission'[2] [This, in fact, was no problem, and the Duke of Grafton [the Lord Chamberlain], having received his orders from the King of England, had the permission sent]. The ambassador, who had arrived in London only in September 1737, may not have been aware of the feelings aroused by the Licensing Act which had come into force three months earlier. The Lord Chamberlain would have known of the popular reaction, but he may have had no choice in the matter. Although Sybil Rosenfeld found no authorisation in the Lord Chamberlain's records,[3] Arthur Scouten points out that the Licensing Act gave the King the personal

---

[1] *The Gentleman's Magazine*, May 1735, p. 777.

[2] De Cambis's letters of 23 October NS [12 October OS] and 13 November NS [2 November OS] are quoted in F. Baldensperger, 'Un Incident théâtral franco-anglais anglais au XVIIIe siècle', *Revue de Littérature comparée* (1929), 573–8. A version of this information appeared in November in the *Mercure Historique et Politique* (The Hague, 1738), p. 572, and the *Lettre Historique et Politique* (Amsterdam, 1738). Baldensperger consistently misspells the ambassador's name as de Cambris.

[3] Sybil Rosenfeld, *Foreign Theatrical Companies in Great Britain in the 17th and 18th Centuries*, The Society for Theatre Research Pamphlet Series, no. 4 (London, 1954–55), p. 22.

authority to grant letters patent for performances in Westminster, within the vicinity of the royal palaces. As the Haymarket was close to the Palace of St James, the King, for the first time since the passing of the Act, had made use of his privilege. But, as Scouten writes, giving the company a licence was 'a tremendous blunder': 'practically any Londoner could have predicted a serious explosion if foreigners were authorised to play when English companies had been restricted.'[4]

Feelings were running high in the press as early as April 1738 in a letter purporting to be from 'Rusty Bacon', a country gentleman:

> When I heard of an act against plays and the players of interludes &c.,
> I thought it was to forbid these foreigners acting, and to send them,
> with their useless unnatural pipes, back to their own country. I little
> thought my own countrymen were to starve to support them [...].[5]

Old hostilities gained a new and much sharper focus with the publication on 12 May 1738 of Samuel Johnson's *London: A Poem in Imitation of the Third Satire of Juvenal*. It proved to be so popular that a second edition appeared within a week, a third was published in July, and a fourth appeared in Dublin. Johnson transformed Juvenal's satire on Roman city life into an anti-Walpole satire and an attack on the fashion for all things foreign, especially in the theatre. Juvenal's Latin original: 'Non possum ferre, Quirites, Graecam urbem' 'I cannot bear a Greek city] became 'I cannot bear a French metropolis.' Neither Johnson nor his friend David Garrick can have seen Francisque's 1734–5 season at the Little Haymarket; they did not arrive in London until March 1737. But Johnson, as an avid reader of the London press while still in Lichfield, knew all about Francisque's visit. He and Garrick might just have heard Farinelli at the King's theatre before the singer left for Spain in June, and Johnson was in London when the Licensing Act came into force. (He later altered the line 'With warbling eunuchs fill our silenc'd Stage' (line 59), changing 'our silenc'd Stage' to 'a licens'd Stage.'[6]) The short extracts from *London* printed in *The Gentleman's Magazine* for May 1738 included lines 93–8:

---

[4] Emmett L. Avery et al., eds, *The London Stage*, pt 2, vol. 2, p. clxxv.
[5] Reproduced, from *Common Sense*, in *The London Magazine* for April 1738.
[6] The first version of this line has been called 'the best Irish bull Johnson ever committed in print.' See the *Yale Edition of the Works of Samuel Johnson: Poems*, ed. E. L. McAdam, Jr. (New Haven, 1964), p. 51. But Johnson's point is that Henry Fielding was silenced by the Licensing Act whereas the castrati Senesino and Farinelli were free to warble on in Italian at the Opera.

> London! the needy Villain's gen'ral Home,
> The Common Shore of Paris and of Rome;[7]
> With eager Thirst, by Folly or by Fate,
> Sucks in the Dregs of each corrupted State.
> Forgive my Transports on a Theme like this,
> I cannot bear a French metropolis. (93–8)

This linking of Paris and Rome as sources of sewage, like the reference to 'warbling eunuchs', recalls the negative press comments in 1734–5 that link 'th'Italian warbler' and 'the French buffoon'. However, Johnson's poem as a whole directs nearly all its hostility at the French. To some extent, this was inevitable. As one editor writes, Johnson 'had no choice but to make the Frenchman represent the Greek of the classical satires.'[8] Johnson could have read the Francophobic responses to Francisque's last season, and he sharpens his own text by invoking the warrior kings Edward III and Henry V, conquerors of the French at Crécy and Agincourt:

> Illustrious EDWARD! from the Realms of Day,
> The Land of Heroes and of Saints survey;
> Nor hope the British Lineaments to trace,
> The rustic Grandeur, or the surly Grace;
> But lost in thoughtless Ease, and empty Show,
> Behold the Warriour dwindled to a Beau;
> Sense, Freedom, Piety, refin'd away,
> Of France the Mimic, and of Spain the Prey. (99–106)
> Ah! what avails it, that, from Slav'ry far,
> I drew the Breath of Life in English Air;
> Was early taught a Briton's Right to prize,
> And lisp the Tale of HENRY'S Victories;
> If the gull'd Conqueror receives the Chain,
> And what their Armies lost, their Cringes gain? (117–22)

Juvenal had been far more vicious in his attack on the Greeks as born actors, but there was an obvious topical appropriateness in Johnson's adaptation, widely read throughout the summer of 1738.

> Studious to please, and ready to submit,
> The supple Gaul was born a Parasite [...]. (123–4)
> Besides with Justice this discerning Age,
> Admires their wond'rous Talents for the Stage:
> Well may they venture on the Mimic's Art,
> Who play from Morn to Night a borrowed Part. (132–5)

---

7 Some versions give 'sewer.' John Oldham's imitation of Juvenal (1682) has 'the common-shore,/ Where France does all her filth and ordure pour.'

8 *The Poems of Samuel Johnson*, ed. David Nichol Smith and Edward L. McAdam, 2nd edn (Oxford, 1974), p. 62.

One 'Tale of Henry's Victories', Aaron Hill's Shakespeare adaptation, subtitled *The Conquest of France by the English*, first acted in 1723, had been revived at Goodman's Fields in 1735 and 1736. Written with the avowed aim of making 'the Harrys' more popular than 'the Harlequins', it was, as Louise Marshall says, 'overtly Francophobic.'[9] Hill had not forgotten that his first attempt to produce his *Henry V* at the Little Haymarket Theatre in 1720 had been thwarted by the presence there of what he later called 'the French vermin'.[10] Perhaps in response to Hill's *Henry*, on 23 February 1738, Shakespeare's *Henry V* was staged at Covent Garden. Its appearance was partly thanks to the Shakespeare Ladies' Club which was praised (in a letter supposedly sent by Shakespeare from Elysium) for having turned the Town away from 'Harlequin and his Harlot Columbine'.[11] Fiona Ritchie has stressed the 'substantial anti-French sentiment' in the revival of Shakespeare performance in 1735–8.[12]

Thus, well before the French company's return, the press had already begun a hostile campaign. On 5 September *The London Evening Post* reported the Company's intention 'to take off some of our Fools Pence this winter.' On 25 September *The Daily Gazetteer*, in its shipping news, reported that the *Jemima* had arrived at Gravesend from Calais 'with fifty French Comedians' on board, a figure which by the end of the week had become seventy. A week later, the *Evening Post* asked why a horde of foreigners was being allowed to re-open one of the theatres closed by the Licensing Act. 'If several of our own countrymen are almost starv'd by being debarred acting without a licence, it's presum'd French Strollers won't be allowed to come and eat the bread out of their mouths.'[13] The word 'strollers', frequently used in the past to denigrate the French actors, had taken on a new meaning since the Licensing Act, equating them with vagrants. Whether by chance or design, a news item on the same page announced that 'Mr Rich, Master of The Theatre Royal in Covent-Garden, has discharg'd several of his performers, both men and women.' A few days later, the same paper notes the support given the French actors by the nobility and condemns 'the gross Partiality shown in their Favour, even to the DISHONOUR of a *British Act of Parliament*'.[14]

---

[9] Louise Marshall, *National Myth and Imperial Fantasy: Representations of British Identity on the Early Eighteenth-Century Stage* (London, 2008), p. 90.

[10] Letter to John Rich, 9 September 1721. In J. Milhous and R.D. Hume, eds, *Register of English Theatrical Documents 1660–1737* (Carbondale, 1991), vol. 2, p. 646, no. 3070.

[11] *The Daily Advertiser* for 4 March 1737, quoted in Emmett L. Avery, 'The Shakespeare Ladies Club', *Shakespeare Quarterly*, 7:2 (1956), 153–8, at p. 155.

[12] Fiona Ritchie, *Women and Shakespeare in the Eighteenth Century* (Cambridge, 2014), pp. 144–5.

[13] *The London Evening Post*, 30 September–3 October 1738.

[14] *The London Evening Post*, 5–7 October 1738.

The company's opening night at the Little Theatre in the Haymarket was advertised in *The London Daily Post and General Advertiser* on Saturday 7 and on Monday 9 October, the day of the first performance:

> By Authority. By the French Company of Comedians at the new Theatre in the Hay-Market, this day, Oct. 9, will be presented a Comedy called *L'Embarras des Richesses*: the character of Harlequin by Mons. Moylin Francisque. To which will be added, *Arlequin Poli par L'Amour*; with several entertainments of dancing, by Mons. Pagnorel, Mademoiselle Chateauneuf, Mons. Le Fevre, Madm. Le Fevre, and others.

The biography of Thomas de Veil (or Deveil), the Justice of the Peace at the centre of the drama which followed,[15] stresses the effect of the language of the advertisement:

> printed bills being stuck up in all parts of town, with the words BY AUTHORITY in over-grown capitals; this provoked to the last degree, the wits that were already enough out of humour.[16]

The very choice of venue, the Little, or French, theatre in the Haymarket, of no great significance in 1734–5, had now become a further provocation. It was there that Henry Fielding in 1736–7 had staged the outspoken political satires that made Walpole finally push through the long-threatened Licensing Act. In 1737 Fielding's preface to *The Historical Register for the Year 1736* stated his commitment to the theatre as a voice for the opposition. Announcing his intention to launch a subscription 'for beautifying and enlarging [the Little Haymarket] and procuring a better company of actors',[17] he concluded, 'If Nature hath given me any Talents at ridiculing Vice and Imposture, I shall not be indolent, nor afraid of exerting them'.[18] This manifesto could not fail to incur the wrath of the authorities. Robert D. Hume unearthed evidence of some very underhand machinations:

---

[15] DeVeil was a naturalized Englishman of French Huguenot ancestry. Although Protestants, the Huguenots were not popular in London: scholars have pointed out that the central figure in Hogarth's painting 'Night' is a tipsy Thomas de Veil and those pictured in 'Noon' are clearly distant from the English people around them.

[16] *Memoirs of the Life and Times of Sir Thomas Deveil, Knight, one of His Majesty's Justices of the Peace* (London, 1748), p. 43. This is an anonymous biography, not an autobiography.

[17] Robert D. Hume, 'Henry Fielding and Politics at the Little Haymarket 1728–1737', in J.M. Wallace, ed., *The Golden and the Brazen World: Papers in Literature and History 1650–1800* (Berkeley and Los Angeles, 1985), pp. 79–124, at pp. 109–10.

[18] *Henry Fielding: Contributions to 'The Champion', and Related Writings*, ed. William B. Coley (Oxford, 2003), p. xxix.

Walpole and Lord Chamberlain Grafton seem to have persuaded Potter [John Potter, the proprietor] to turn Fielding out of the Little Haymarket. If we can believe some MS. notes by J. Payne Collier, Potter took the precaution of piling the theatre high with lumber and bricks to make sure that it could not be forcibly entered and used without authorisation. ... Collier's notes include a copy of a bill dated 13 June 1737 and evidently submitted by Potter to the Duke of Grafton, the Lord Chamberlain. The bill includes £12 12s. 'To the taking down the scenes and decorations so that the Theatre was Rendered Incapable of haveing any Play or other performance, and men's time and Carts to fill the same with deal and timber Bricks and Lime.'[19]

Knowledge of these facts would have added considerably to the general mood of grievance. Fielding's theatrical career had been ended by the Act; he was not merely evicted from the Little Haymarket but saw the theatre locked and barricaded against his re-entry. One can readily understand the anger of passers-by in 1738 who observed that, in order to gain entrance to the Little Haymarket and prepare the stage, Francisque's company, or John Potter's men, had to demolish the brick and timber barricades set up to keep out the popular company of Henry Fielding.

In the period immediately preceding Francisque's opening night, press comments became more inflammatory. As de Veil's biographer later noted, 'the wits' were giving 'broad hints, that upon this occasion, *the town* would interpose their Authority, in order to reform an abuse tolerated by the superior powers'[20] *The Daily Advertiser* of 4 October 1738 remarked, 'It seems to be a little unnatural that French Strollers should have a superior privilege to those of our own country; and it were to be wish'd, that these should meet with no more encouragement here than ours would in France.' Two days before the first night, when the playbill headed 'By Authority' appeared in the press, *The London Daily Post and General Advertiser* printed a long letter from 'Anglicus', falsely claiming that the French authorities had recently refused an English troupe permission to perform in Paris.[21]

---

[19] Robert D. Hume, *Henry Fielding and the London Theatre, 1728–1737* (Oxford, 1988), pp. 109–10. Although Collier was a notorious forger, there seems little reason to doubt the authenticity of this particular document. Apart from a few brief interludes, as under Charles Macklin in 1744, the Little Theatre remained dark and semi-derelict for many years.

[20] *Memoirs of the Life and Times of Sir Thomas Deveil*, p. 43.

[21] The visits of the dancers from London in 1729–31 contradict this claim, and, in the summer of 1737, just after the closure of all the unlicensed theatres, a group of English dancers from Drury Lane had performed at the Foire St Laurent to enthusiastic applause. See Parfaict, *Mém.*, vol. 2, pp. 121–2, which also notes that their programme was advertised in English on the playbills. Just a few weeks before Francisque's arrival

[I]nsolent it is, I think, that foreign vagrants and *French* Papists, should dare attempt to follow that very profession which is deny'd our own countrymen. [...] Could any senator or peer, without compunction, conduce to the support of a parcel of Gascoon stage-players, who has given his voice to a bill which deprives his own countrymen of the same liberty? And would it not be a reflection on the generosity, as well as good sense, of our *English* ladies, to countenance with their presence a foreign band of strollers, and leave *Shakespear, Otway, Congreve, &c.* for the mimicry of a Harlequin?

This article later appeared, in French translation, in the November issue of the *Mercure Historique et Politique*, with the comment: 'On avait déjà sonné contre eux le tocsin dans nos feuilles publiques.' [The alarm bell had already been sounded against them [the French players] in our public press]. With hindsight, what happened at the opening of Francisque's season, on the evening of Monday, 9 October, was totally predictable.

The Haymarket Riot

There are a number of accounts of the riot of 9 October.[22] What follows is based on these contemporary reports and other sources previously unexamined by modern scholars. A hitherto unknown account, by the journalist Antoine de la Barre de Beaumarchais, appeared in French in the *Amusemens Littéraires* published in Frankfurt in 1739 and The Hague in 1740. Written in epistolary form, and drawing extensively on the London press, it includes details which appear nowhere else and (although stylistically embellished) may contain eye-witness testimony.[23] The most reliable versions seem to be those in the

---

in London, another English troupe had received high praise at the Foire St-Laurent. See Campardon, *SF*, vol. 1, p. 227.

[22] Contemporary accounts appeared in *The London Daily Post and General Advertiser*, 7, 9, 10 and 12 October, *The Gentleman's Magazine*, VIII (1738), pp. 532, 545, 592; *The Historical Register for the Year 1738*, 23 (92), pp. 279–95; *Read's Weekly Journal*, 14–25 October. The monthly digests, *The Gentleman's Magazine* and *The London Magazine*, also reproduced accounts from other papers. Their versions, many from apparently identical sources, in fact differ considerably from each other. Two recent discussions are Richard Gorrie, *Gentle riots? theatre riots in London 1730–1780*, Ph.D. thesis (The University of Guelph, 2000), pp. 235–44, and Thomas Lockwood, 'Cross-Channel Dramatics in the Little Haymarket Theatre Riot of 1738', *Studies in Eighteenth-Century Culture*, 25 (1996), 63–74. Lockwood seriously underestimates the political significance of the riot but emphasizes its theatricality.

[23] Antoine de la Barre de Beaumarchais, *Amusemens Littéraires: ou Correspondance Politique, Rhétorique, Philosophique, Critique, et Galante pour l'Année MDCCXXXVIII*, 2 vols (Frankfurt, 1739 and The Hague, 1740), vol. 2, pt 2, Letters 39, 42, 44, and 48.

dispatches of ambassador de Cambis, and Benjamin Victor's *History of the Theatres of London and Dublin*.[24] De Cambis, an eye-witness, sent his reports to the foreign minister in Paris in November. As Philip Woodfine points out, Walpole's agents routinely intercepted these dispatches;[25] awareness of this fact must have affected the tone of the letters. Victor's lively account provides the quotations below where no other source is given, but it should be noted that he was not an impartial observer but a participant in the disturbance;[26] moreover, writing over twenty years later, he based much of his 'history' on printed sources. An anonymous biography of Thomas de Veil, who was also present at the riots in his capacity as Justice of the Peace and who was later to be attacked in the press for his conduct, also contains some useful information.

The curtain was due to rise at 6 o'clock, but by 4 o'clock the theatre was packed from the pit to the gallery. Since footmen and servants often came early to reserve boxes on behalf of their masters, some rougher elements of the mob may have been hired from among them. Those who could not get in milled around in the Haymarket and amused themselves by breaking windows, or selling rotten fruit at the doors, where they eventually broke in.

No member of the Royal Family could be present, as the court was still in mourning, but, towards six o'clock, the French and Spanish ambassadors and their families took their places in the stage boxes, along with other foreign ministers and their wives, as well as Sir Thomas and Lady Gage (well known as recusant Catholics, which may be why Victor names them). The presence of the wives of the gentry suggests that the risk of trouble was seriously underestimated.

The crowd, inside and outside the theatre, was clearly well-organised. One of the ringleaders called for the singing of 'The Roast Beef of Old England', and 'a gentleman', obviously ready for this request, sang it; the audience joined in the chorus, cheering loudly at the end.[27] By the time the performance was due to begin, the theatre management must have been expecting trouble, because, when the curtain rose, the spectators saw not only the French

---

[24] Benjamin Victor, *A History of the Theatres of London and Dublin*, 2 vols (London, 1761), vol.1, pp. 53–61.

[25] See the chapter 'Mechanisms of Diplomacy' in Philip Woodfine, *Britannia's Glories: The Walpole Ministry and the 1739 War with Spain* (Woodbridge and Rochester, NY, 1998), pp. 19–46.

[26] 'A Person of Distinction, now living, told me next Day, that he had read my Name that Morning in a List of Leaders, who had opposed the French Players, lying on the Table of a great Duke. [...] I thought myself honoured by being in that List': Victor, *History*, p. 61.

[27] Leveridge's patriotic ballad 'was so popular in the late 1730s that London theatre audiences at every play demanded renditions of it before and between acts': Woodfine, *Britannia's Glories*, p. 131.

performers but two ranks of guards, with fixed bayonets, on either side of them. This was not absolutely unusual (since 1722, 'militia were a common if problematic recourse if a manager had reason to expect trouble')[28] – but the sight of them made the audience even more furious. Justice de Veil reminded the audience that the play was being performed by the King's command and that if the hullabaloo continued he would be forced to read the Riot Act. The Riot Act of 1714 made refusal to disperse, in a crowd of more than twelve people, a felony carrying the death penalty (and thus could have authorised the soldiers to fire on the crowd). The Justice had already read it at Drury Lane in February 1737 and he was now about to do so again, when a bystander begged him not to risk the loss of life. De Veil ordered the soldiers to withdraw, hoping that this would mollify the crowd. Instead, all hell broke loose: the rioters had brought bells and whistles, and the theatre resounded with 'not only catcalls, but all the various portable instruments that could make a disagreeable noise'. They hurled missiles, which knocked some of the candles from their sconces. Ambassador de Cambis reported that the mob completely surrounded the front of the theatre, 'et elle n'a cessé d'y jeter des pierres que lorsqu'elle a eu cassé les lanternes et les vitres, et démoli entièrement les façades, et ceux qui étaient dans la salle rompirent les lustres et jetèrent des pierres et des couteaux sur les acteurs.'[29] [and they did not stop throwing stones until they had broken the lanterns and the windows, and completely demolished the façade; and those who were in the auditorium broke the chandeliers and threw stones and knives at the actors.] The noise was carefully orchestrated, and specifically anti-French:

> The cry on one side the galleries was, *No soupe maigre*, and the other side answered in a different tone, *Beef and pudding*; and the general cry was, *Pray remember the poor English players in gaol*; *No French Strollers*.[30]

The opposition of thin soup (French) to beef and pudding (English) was, like the singing of 'the roast beef of old England', a typical jibe at the supposedly starved and skinny French that can be traced at least as far back as Shakespeare's *Henry V* and would be immortalised ten years later in Hogarth's 'The Gate at Calais, or, The Roast Beef of Old England'. The reference to English players in gaol was a reminder that in February an actor had been sent to prison. The French were called 'strollers' as a way of indicating their status as rogues and vagabonds with no 'settlement' within the terms of the Licensing Act.

---

[28] Daniel O'Quinn, Kristina Straub and Misty G. Anderson, 'The Chinese Festival Riots', in *The Routledge Anthology of Restoration and Eighteenth-Century Performance* (Abingdon and New York, 2019), pp. 397–422, at p. 400.

[29] *Read's Weekly Journal* (14 October) adds another detail of the violence: 'One Mr Hewet, a Fencing Master, had the side of his face cut off with a Sword, in the Pit.'

[30] *The London Evening Post*, 10–12 October, 1738.

Fig. 11 *The Gate at Calais, or, the Roast Beef of Old England* (1748), engraved by C. Mosley and William Hogarth from the painting by William Hogarth. Open Access Image from the Davison Art Center, Wesleyan University (http://www.wesleyan.edu/dac/openaccess). Photo: T. Rodriguez.

Unable to make themselves heard, the actors sent on the dancers, hoping that they might be more acceptable. But the rioters had planned for this too, and they threw onto the stage 'a bushel or two of [dried] peas, which made their capering very unsafe.' Anger was increasing on both sides of the proscenium. As for the company's reaction to this violence, accounts varied. 'To please the audience, one of the French Mademoiselles fairly shew'd her A***, but it being foreign goods, gave no content.' *The Craftsman* (14 October) nastily claimed: 'It is confidently reported, that General *Harlequin* was seiz'd with a violent Disorder in his Bowels upon the first Onset; and that one of his *Mademoiselles* hath since miscarry'd by the Fright.' Another journalist gloated: 'Oh! Had you but seen poor *Harlequin!* He look'd as simple as *Pierrot.*'[31] On the other hand, de la Barre quoted an anonymous correspondent who wrote, 'Je dois avouer que le Général Arlequin soutint le premier assaut avec

---

[31] *The Historical Register for 1738*, 23 (92), p. 281.

assez de constance, quoi que plus de cent œufs se fussent déjà brisés sur son masque' [I must admit that General Harlequin sustained the first assault bravely enough, although more than a hundred eggs had already broken on his mask].[32] He added, however, that Francisque was probably counting on the support of the militia.

Standing on his seat in the middle of the pit, Justice de Veil momentarily silenced the crowd, promising them that if they would let the play proceed that night he would, on his honour, lay their grievances before the King. This offer was greeted with shouts of 'No treaties! No treaties!' One last attempt was made to begin the play and, according to the ambassador, confirmed by the *London Evening Post,* the players managed to get to the end of the first act, but not a word could be heard. The newspaper adds that the crowd:

> continued hissing and pelting them [the actors] in such a manner that the strollers were drove out of back windows into Suffolk Street, crying out *Morblieu, Morblieu*; and several of the company [i.e., the audience] were forc'd to go out the same way.

In front of the theatre the mob had cut through the harnesses and traces of the ambassadors' coaches, and the ferocity of the crowd forced some of the audience, along with the actors, to clamber down through the windows at the back of the stage.[33] It was now getting dark outside and, in the confusion, the mob was throwing dirt at friend and foe alike. As the reporter wrote, 'happy therefore was he that could prove himself a TRUE ENGLISHMAN, then he escaped unmolested.'[34]

According to Ambassador de Cambis, 'Lorsque je commençai à m'apercevoir de l'opiniâtreté de cette cabale, j'engageai toute ma compagnie à nous retirer, ce que nous fîmes' [When I began to perceive the obstinacy of this cabal, I urged my company to leave, which we did].[35] De la Barre had heard a different (and romanticised) account of this moment:

> Madame l'Ambassadrice de [Cambis] craignit si bien qu'on ne manquât de même aux égards qui lui étaient dus, qu'elle exhorta le Comte son Époux à se retirer. Elle ne fut pas écoutée cette fois-là. *Vous pouvez partir, Madame,* lui dit ce Seigneur. *Pour moi, la dignité de mon caractère exige que je garde ma place jusqu'à la fin.* Effectivement il tint bon et ne sortit qu'avec les derniers.[36]

---

[32] De la Barre, *Amusemens,* Letter 39, p. 266.
[33] Suffolk street is immediately behind the present Haymarket theatre.
[34] *The London Evening Post*, 10–12 October, 1738.
[35] *Read's Weekly Journal* (14 October) adds another example of the violence: 'One Mr Hewet, a Fencing Master, had the side of his face cut off with a Sword, in the Pit.'
[36] De la Barre, *Amusemens*, p. 335.

[Madame de [Cambis], the ambassador's wife, was so afraid that she might not be treated with the respect which was her due that she begged her husband to leave. She was not heeded on this occasion, '*You may go, Madame*', said de Cambis. '*As for me, the dignity of my character demands that I remain in my place to the end.*' Indeed, he stood his ground and was among the last to leave.]

When the curtain finally fell, after the crowd had been calling for it for some time, Victor compared their shouts to the joy at any 'battle gained over the French by the immortal Marlborough'. *The Craftsman* for October 14 called the whole event 'a sharp and bloody Battle [...] between the new Company of *French Strollers*, and the *Gentlemen of London*', concluding: 'The *English Forces* maintained their Charge with so much Vigour and Conduct, that they soon obliged the *Enemy* to retire with great Precipitation, and kept the Field of Battle all Night.' De la Barre's account, partly based on this one but purporting to be written by a member of the rioting English faction, takes the military imagery even further: 'Don Francisque parut, et son arrivée fut le signal du combat. À l'instant notre Musique guerrière se fait entendre de toutes parts.'[37] [Don Francisque appeared, and his arrival was the signal for the fight. At once our warlike music was heard on all sides.] In the same vein, he later reports another hitherto unnoticed detail about the behaviour of the mob:

> Imaginez-vous, Monsieur, que leur impatience ne put attendre jusqu'au lendemain à recevoir les applaudissements dont un si beau fait d'armes méritait d'être payé. Tout échauffés encore du combat, ils coururent à la Comédie Anglaise, imposèrent silence aux Acteurs, racontèrent leurs exploits aux Spectateurs et aux Comédiens.[38]

> [Imagine, sir, that their impatience could not wait until the next day to receive the applause which such a fine feat of arms deserved. Still hot from battle, they ran to the English Theatre, imposed silence on the actors, told the actors and the audience of their exploits.]

To the best of my knowledge, the story of the performance at another theatre being interrupted by protesters was not reported in the British press, but in the *Mercure Historique et Politique* the 'Comédie Anglaise' to which the rioters ran is named as the 'Théâtre du Commun Jardin' – clearly a reference to Covent Garden, where on that night Francisque's old rival John Rich was playing Harlequin-Faustus. At 'about eight in the evening', one of the longest riots in English theatre history finally drew to a close.[39]

---

[37] De la Barre, *Amusemens*, pp. 265–7. There is a striking similarity between the language of the letter quoted in de la Barre and that of Benjamin Victor's later account.
[38] *Ibid.*, pp. 335–6.
[39] *The Historical Register for the year 1738*, 23 (92) pp. 278–9.

The Aftermath

Possibly because of the presence of foreign ambassadors, the riot was widely reported in continental journals, including the *Gazette d'Amsterdam*, the principal European journal of political information. Its article of 28 October, also reproduced by de la Barre, reveals the extent of the repercussions: there was (finally) an attempt to track down those involved in the riot; the theatre manager wanted reparations for the damage done to his building, and the Lord Chamberlain for the insult to his authority. De la Barre's correspondent wrote:

> Peut-être alors avez-vous regardé cette affaire comme chose peu importante. On n'en juge pas de même en Angleterre. Chacun s'y intéresse pour ou contre le Seigneur Francisque Arlequin. La décision de son sort est devenue une affaire nationale. Il a pour lui la Cour, et contre lui la Nation. Aurait-il jamais cru dans ses plus forts accès de vanité qu'il était un personnage si important![40]

> [Perhaps you thought of this matter as unimportant. This is not how it is judged in England. Everyone is interested in it, either for or against Don Francisque Arlequin. The decision on his fate has become a national affair. He has the Court for him, and against him the Nation. Could he ever have believed in his greatest flights of vanity that he was such an important figure!]

De Cambis was said to have made a formal complaint to the king,[41] and *The Evening Post* of 10–12 October reports that 'a Noble Lord has waited on the French Ambassador, to assure him no Affront was intended, either against him, or the French Nation'. *The Craftsman* for 14 October wondered, only half-jokingly, 'if the *French* Court should look upon it as a *national Hostility*'. In an effort to cool down what might indeed have become an international incident, de Cambis's dispatches to Paris put the blame for the riot on the Licensing Act: 'Ce n'était point aux comédiens français personnellement que la Nation veut du mal; mais qu'elle ne saurait souffrir l'acte du Parlement qui en restreignant les théâtres lui fait craindre qu'il ne soit le présage de la suppression de la liberté de la presse.'[42] [The Nation wished no harm to the French actors personally; but they could not tolerate the Act of Parliament which, by restricting the theatres, makes them fear a restriction of the freedom of the press.]

---

[40] De la Barre, *Amusemens*, pp. 282–4.
[41] Jacques-Elie Gastelier, *Lettres sur les Affaires du Temps: 1738–1741*, ed. Henri Duranton (Paris-Geneva, 1993), p. 167. Cf. *London Evening Post*, 10–12 October.
[42] Baldensperger, 'Un Incident', p. 557.

Throughout October, newspapers made the most of the ironic inappropriateness of the title of the opening play, *L'Embarras des Richesses*, writing of *The Plague of Players* and '*The Plague of Returning.*'[43] 'Misogallicus' in *The London Daily Post and General Advertiser* of 12 October, traces the influence, ever since Charles II's Restoration, of 'all the pernicious Customs of that Destroyer of Happiness, *France*', and argues that those who protect and encourage the French actors 'are Traitors, and Enemies to their Fellow-Subjects. [...] If we go on in this Manner, if Foreigners are encouraged even in Opposition to the Laws of our Country, we shall soon find *London* a French Metropolis. [...] I hope *Britain* will be no more the Mimic of *France* and the Prey of *Spain.*' Similarly, an anonymous writer in *The Craftsman* of 21 October thanks God that:

> an English Audience hath shewn that We are not to be driven, even by military Force, to applaud *French* Mummery; and turn our Eyes from the glorious Deeds of our Henries and our Edwards, to the Tricks of Harlequin, and his beggarly Train.

Given these striking intertextual parallels with *London* ('a *French Metropolis*', '*Of France the Mimic, and of Spain the Prey*', the references to Edward III and Henry V), I wonder if either or both of these letters might have come from the pen of the Francophobe Johnson himself.

As de Veil said, 'the case of the *French*-players became with some folks a point of law, and with others a point of state'. The pro-government *Daily Gazetteer* insisted that the players had no Licence to perform and were therefore vagrants, while on 28 October Charles Molloy, the Jacobite editor of the opposition journal *Common Sense*, insisted that the French actors, 'being unacquainted with our disputes, could not think they should give offence'; the crowd's animosity had really been directed at the Lord Chamberlain and the new Act, which he himself hoped would be repealed. 'I consider them in the Condition of Persons shipwreck'd upon our Coast, that have lost both Ship and Cargo, and, Therefore, are entitled to so much Succour as will enable them to go back to their own Country.' This attempt to win sympathy was countered by November's *London Evening Post*, which said that the riot was fair retaliation for 'the treatment the British subjects in Paris met with, just this time four years when they were termed VAGABONDS in the French King's edict'. (I have found no reference to this alleged incident in any contemporary French or English source.) Throughout October and November, *The Daily Gazetteer* for the Government and *Common Sense* for the opposition continued to argue over the legality of the performance and the role of de Veil.

---

[43] *The Historical Register for 1738*, 23 (92), pp. 281–2.

Amid the controversy, the plight of the players was increasingly lost to view. A few days after the riot *The London Evening Post* wrote of a collection being taken up 'for *the French Strollers*, who we hear will speedily embark for Boulogne on their way home; tho' *some Papists* pretend to give out they will act again'.[44] Both these reports may have been true. The company members who had already left had presumably been discharged and paid off with the money raised by sympathetic supporters. On the other hand, the rumour that 'they will act again' suggests that the remaining strollers and their partisans were putting up more of a fight than has hitherto been realised. There seems to have been support from the royal family and some of the aristocrats, possibly led by the Duke of Richmond. *The London Evening Post* for 17–19 October reported, 'Yesterday the remaining Part of the French Strollers were at Kensington, to take leave of such of the Nobility, &c. as were their Friends.' In other words, the actors had been received at court. In the following week (26–28 October), the *Post* reported that two dancers had performed before the princesses at Kensington Palace 'and were graciously receiv'd'. They would have been paid generously for these private performances.

However, the fact that no further help could be expected from the court is clear from de Cambis' letter to Paris, dated 13 November (NS, 2 November OS):

> Les comédiens français sont encore ici, *la Cour les a absolument abandonnés* [my italics], on m'a dit cependant que quelques seigneurs projetaient de faire entre eux une espèce de collecte pour les renvoyer. J'ai su que le roi d'Angleterre avait été extrêmement piqué du peu de respect que le peuple avait marqué pour ses ordres ou pour son autorité à ce sujet, mais qu'on lui avait fait entendre qu'il fallait ménager la Nation, et ne point augmenter ses murmures pour une troupe de comédiens étrangers.[45]

> [The French players are still here; the Court has completely abandoned them. I was told, however, that some lords were planning to make a sort of collection to send them back. I learned that the King of England had been extremely piqued by the lack of respect the people had shown for his orders or his authority on this subject, but he had been made to understand that it was necessary to mollify the nation and not to increase its hostility for the sake of a troupe of foreign actors.]

Thomas de Veil's biographer confirms that the King and court were made to realise the political danger involved: 'they very wisely judged that supporting players of any sort, was much beneath the dignity of persons of their rank; that *French* players made this more unworthy, and more unpopular, and that

---

[44] *The London Evening Post*, 10–12 October 1738.
[45] Baldensperger, 'Un Incident', p. 578.

the consequences which might attend it were not to be risked upon so trifling an occasion.'[46]

Molloy's *Common Sense*, on 28 October, had approved of a rumoured suggestion that the company would be allowed to recoup their losses by giving a few performances at the patent theatres. Perhaps remembering the involvement of Francisque and Nivelon in Cibber's breakaway company in 1734, he added:

> When they are thus incorporated with our own Actors, they will be receiv'd according to their Merits in Acting; and they will find that an *English* Audience, however jealous they may be of their Privileges, don't want Humanity [...].

But the *Post* on 26 October, perhaps hearing of this forthcoming article, insisted that, 'if ever they presume to perform here again, they must expect the same treatment as formerly'.

Abandoned by the court, the managers now threw themselves on the mercy of the town. Someone must have penned (or at least translated) the appeal which appeared in *The London Daily Post and General Advertiser* on four successive days, from 7 to 10 November:

The Case of the FRENCH COMEDIANS

> Whereas we, Moylin Francisque and John Baptist Lesage were in England in the Month of February last, and having then obtained Leave to bring over a French Company of Comedians, for to represent the same in the Little Theatre in the Hay-Market this season; we, for that Purpose, returned into France, and collected together the best Company that were to be had; being wholly ignorant of any Affairs transacted in England relating to the Regulation of the Stage, and not in the least doubting but that the Company would meet with the same Encouragement as heretofore, made us engage with several Performers abroad, at very great Expenses, to come into England; and the Night the said Company were to have acted, they met with such an Obstruction from the Audience, that a Stop was put to the Performance, and the said Company discontinued, and laid aside all Thoughts of making the least Attempt, since the same was not agreeable to the Publick. Notwithstanding we the said Undertakers, by the Contracts we made, have been obliged to pay each Performer the same Monies hitherto, and liable to the same Obligations for the Remainder of this whole Season, as if the Company had performed the whole Time, and have besides expended large Sums of Money, and contracted several Debts here, which we are not in Circumstances to

---

[46] Deveil, *Memoirs*, p. 45.

pay: so that we are obliged to lay our case before the Publick, in hopes that they will be so indulgent as to permit us to perform three nights only in one of the Patent Theatres, so as to enable us to discharge those Debts we have contracted here, and we will then humbly take our Leaves, and return to France, with grateful Acknowledgement for the Favour done to us. (Signed) Moylin Francisque. J. B Lesage. Suffolk Street, Nov 6, 1738.

The tone and language of this appeal are so reminiscent of Molloy's article in *Common Sense* on 28 October as to suggest that he may have been involved in its composition. The most striking similarity is the claim that the players were wholly ignorant of the new law and its implications. Throughout this controversy, the view that the actors were legally entitled to perform was hardly entertained. Government circles would surely have known that, as the French ambassador's correspondence makes clear, the King had exercised his royal prerogative to grant 'Authority' for the entire season. Given the widespread unpopularity of George II, however, it may well be that the company leaders were strongly advised, even ordered, to feign aggrieved innocence and say nothing of what really took place during Francisque's February visit to London.

The press response to the appeal was unsympathetic. If John Rich at Covent Garden had ever considered agreeing to the requested run of three nights, he would have been warned off by the threat a few days later in *The London Evening Post*:

Two of the *French strollers* having desir'd Leave of the Town to act three Nights at one of the *Patent Theatres*, the Master of that House is desir'd to consider, whether if he lends it to those *Foreigners*, he can ever hope to have it fill'd with an *English Audience*, who will *chastise* the *Abuse* of Power in an *ungrateful Patentee*, as they did the *Want* of it in a *French Harlequin*.[47]

On 13 November Rich placed an advertisement in *The London Daily Post and General Advertiser*:

Whereas it has been industriously reported that the French Comedians are to perform in One of the Theatres belonging to Mr. *Rich*, this is to certify to the Publick, that nothing of that kind was ever intended, or wou'd have been permitted by him, unless the same had been with the general Consent of the Town.

The sharp rejection in the press of Francisque's appeal to the Town, and Rich's unwillingness to defy public opinion, finally put an end to further support from any quarter.

---

[47] *The London Evening Post*, 7–9 November 1738.

As we have already noted, the press reported that shortly after the riot some of the company had left for France via Boulogne. The remaining members finally set sail on 17 November, a date with ironic significance. Long after the death of Elizabeth I the date of her Accession was still being celebrated with feasting, bell-ringing and pageantry to give thanks for England's deliverance from a return to Popery under 'Bloody' Mary Tudor.[48] Leveridge's *Song of Roast Beef* was by now an essential part of the demonstrations of patriotic fervour. As *Common Sense* reported, the day 'was observed as a solemn Holiday at Westminster School, the Scholars on the Foundation being entertain'd, according to annual Custom, with Roast Beef and Plum Pudding'. In the midst of the Protestant festivities all over London, a band of 'French Papist vagrants' made its way from Suffolk Street to board the *Jemima* at Tower dock and set sail for Ostend. In its issue of 23–25 November *The London Evening Post* reported one last ignominy: 'The Day before they embarked, their Goods were seized for £100, which Sum was paid by some Persons of Quality, their Encouragers.' The same journal had already reported (16–18 November) that some £600 had been collected for the French 'strollers', at least half of it from the court. If this sum is correct, it would have more than covered the proceeds of the three performances Francisque had begged leave to give.[49]

Despite de la Barre's occasional insistence on the triviality of the whole episode, he leaves no doubt as to its symbolic importance:

> Après tant de nouvelles, que je vous ai écrites sur le fait des Comédiens Français de Londres, je me trouve comme engagé à vous mander la suite de leurs aventures. Elles sont finies. L'Angleterre l'a emporté sur la France, ou si vous voulez, le Parti Anglais opposé à la Cour a triomphé du Parti qui est pour elle. On ne jouera plus à Londres de Comédies en langage non entendu ... [50]

> [After giving you so much news about the French Players in London, I feel obliged to tell you what happened next. It's all over. England has prevailed over France or, if you like, the English Party has triumphed over the Party which favours the Court. No more plays will be performed in London in languages that no one understands.]

The intensity of the passions aroused by the Haymarket riot is brought home most forcefully in the collection of lengthy letters and articles republished in

---

[48] See the entry for 17 November in Robert Chambers, *Chambers' Book of Days* (Edinburgh, 1864).

[49] In 1736, 'according to the *Grub Street Journal*, the nightly receipts at Drury Lane, Covent Garden and the Haymarket came to £80, on average, at each house': Louis D. Mitchell, 'Command Performances During the Reign of George II', *CLA Journal* 31:2 (December 1987), 223–39, at p. 223.

[50] De la Barre, *Amusemens*, p. 334.

The Historical Register for the Year 1738. As the editor wrote: 'the Dispute they raised while here did not die with [the French players'] departure, as would naturally have been expected; but became rather more serious than ever.' One final excerpt from his selection (many examples of which have already been quoted) will make it clear that I have not exaggerated the political and religious ramifications of this 'Dispute'.

> BUT it is said, the Consequence of this Affair was not great enough to merit the Regard which hath been shewn it. [...] [Y]et I cannot help thinking, that those who talk thus have not thoroughly weigh'd what would follow on such an Indulgence as hath been demanded for these Foreigners. [...]
>
> We do not stile the *French* Barbarians; we do not deride their Customs; we do not question their Abilities; but we are of Opinion, that however advantageous, however excellent, they may be in Respect to themselves, it is not expedient they should be copy'd by us; we conceive, that a different Religion, a different Constitution, and different Interests, require different Manners; and we are apprehensive, that our exchanging Manners with the *French,* may induce a Change of Religion, Constitution, and Interests; and therefore we are afraid of taking any Steps of so hazardous a Nature.[51]

The same cultural nationalism is reflected in verses *On the French Players' coming to England,* published in *The London Magazine* for November 1738:

> Long, ah! Too long soft Farinelli reign'd,
> Seduc'd the wise and ev'n the brave enchain'd [...].
> No sooner this unmanly songster gone,
> But foreign strollers crowd to gull the town;
> Their dowdy actresses come o'er from France,
> To show their a—s in immodest dance;
> Think Harlequin's grimace would please the town,
> And anything, if foreign, would go down;
> Expect each dull insipid farce would please,
> And peals of thunder-claps each night would raise;
> But now they find that Dryden's sterling wit,
> And Shakespear's beauties please a British pit.
> Assist, ye gales, with expeditious care,
> To waft these vagrants to their native air;
> Let Gallia know that Britons are born free,
> And will maintain their right and liberty.

---

[51] *The Historical Register for the Year 1738*, 23 (92), pp. 291–2.

These anonymous lines have a long intertextual history. In 1714 Richard Steele had called for the departure to Italy of the famous castrato, Nicolò Francesco Leonardo Grimaldi, known as Nicolini:[52]

> Long, ah! too long the soft Enchantment reign'd,
> Seduc'd the Wise, and ev'n the Brave enchain'd;
> Hence with thy Curst deluding Song! away!
> Shall British Freedom thus become thy Prey?

Steele tells the winds to 'Waft this prepost'rous Idol of the Fair' who 'stole from Shakespeare's self our easie Hearts.' Imitating him, Ambrose Phillips in May 1724 published his often-anthologised lines to Francesca Cuzzoni: calling her an 'empty warbler' and 'Bane of every manly art', he urges her to 'Leave us as we ought to be, / Leave the Britons rough and free'. The *London Magazine* verses echo both these poems in their language and their emphasis on the emasculating effect of music and its danger to British freedom and national character. The cult of Farinelli in 1734–5 had revived memories of the enormous success of the earlier 'warbling Eunuch'; once again, the French players were firmly linked in the press and the popular imagination to the Italian castrati of the opera.

Francisque's London visits had occurred in an interval of comparative peace between the War of the Spanish Succession, which ended in 1715, and the War of the Austrian Succession which began in 1740, but the Haymarket riot and the controversy which surrounded it eerily foreshadowed the resumption of warfare. The conflict between England and France became, for a time, synonymous with the contrast between 'high culture' Shakespeare and 'low culture' Harlequin. David Garrick's pantomime *Harlequin Student*, given at Goodman's Fields Theatre to mark the unveiling of Shakespeare's statue in Westminster Abbey in 1741, looked forward to a time when 'Farce and Harlequin shall be no more.' In the final scene, depicting the new statue, Jupiter and Minerva issue a command to Britons which echoes the many verses linking Francisque and Farinelli in joint opprobrium just a few years earlier:

> Doat on Shakespear's manly Sense,
> Send th'invading Triflers home,
> To lull the Fools of France and Rome.[53]

---

[52] In 1711, he sang the leading role in Handel's *Rinaldo*, the work which confirmed the popularity of both opera and Handel in England. Steele's verses appeared in *Poetical Miscellanies, consisting of original poems and translations by the best hands. Publish'd by Mr. Steele* (London, 1714), p. 44.

[53] *The Plays of David Garrick: Garrick's own plays, 1740–1766*, eds Harry Pedicord and Frederick Bergmann (Carbondale, 1980), p. 406. 'Rome' is used for

Audiences were all too willing to obey. Riots greeted Jean Monnet's ill-judged and aborted season of French plays in 1749. The riots in 1755 at the dancer Noverre's equally disastrous *Chinese Festival* marked, as Max Fuchs noted, the third failure in twenty years of attempted cultural exchanges between 'le pays de Molière et le pays de Shakespeare' [the land of Molière and the land of Shakespeare].[54] In a prologue written in 1756, Garrick, whose Drury Lane theatre had sustained thousands of pounds of damage in the riots of the previous year, reassured his audience about the play they were to see:

> No smuggled, pilfer'd Scenes from France we shew,
> 'Tis ENGLISH – ENGLISH, Sirs! – from top to toe.[55]

As John O'Brien puts it in *Harlequin Britain*:

> Garrick's indefatigable efforts to promote Shakespeare as the singular figure who simultaneously represents and transcends the British stage and, by extension, British culture itself rely to a great extent on his positioning of the figure of Harlequin as Shakespeare's demonic Other, the rival whose illegitimate usurpation of the stage must be exposed and repulsed.[56]

The title of Garrick's 1759 afterpiece, *Harlequin's Invasion, or A Christmas Gambol*, must surely have reminded some audience members of the high drama of the invasion and expulsion in 1738 of 'Don Francisque Arlequin.' To quote O'Brien again:

> Shakespeare's ascendancy in [Garrick's] play needs to be understood as a sign of British cultural pre-eminence designed to rhyme with a military puissance that Britain demonstrated in the year of its first production.[57]

---

the rhyme, but it is also a reminder of press reports that Farinelli had been a member of the papal chapel.

[54] M. and P. Fuchs, 'Comédiens Français à Londres (1738–55)', *Revue de Littérature Comparée* 13 (1933), 43–72, at p. 72. See also Heather McPherson, 'Theatrical Riots and Cultural Politics in Eighteenth-Century London', *The Eighteenth Century* 43:3 (2002), 236–52, and, for the Chinese Festival, O'Quinn et al., 'The Chinese Festival Riots', pp. 397–421.

[55] Prologue to Arthur Murphy's *The Apprentice* (London, 1756).

[56] John O'Brien, *Harlequin Britain: Pantomime and Entertainment, 1690–1760* (Baltimore and London, 2004), pp. 221–2.

[57] *Ibid.*

1759 had been hailed as 'the year of victories', when the British military defeated French forces at Quiberon Bay, Quebec, and Minden. In this context it is not surprising that the parallel defeat of Arlequin-Francisque – which the press at the time had called 'a sharp and bloody battle' – was remembered with satisfaction. In 1761 Victor's *History of the Theatres* was published, and *The London Magazine* reprinted his account of the riot under the heading 'The French Strollers routed'.[58] Arlequin-Francisque and his troupe had inadvertently become victims of the clash of two great cultures, and an association which had lasted more than twenty years was at an end.

---

[58] *London Magazine*, August 1761, p. 426.

14

'Comédiens du Roi': last years and final curtain: 1739–1770

At the end of 1738, Francisque's company was financially ruined. In place of the lucrative Benefits that they had been promised in the Land of Guineas, they were reduced to receiving charitable donations to cover their debts and expenses. Their final departure was reported by de la Barre:

> Le pauvre Dom Francisque Arlequin s'embarqua le vingt-huit du mois passé avec sa Troupe pour Ostende. Il remporte pour tout fruit de son voyage cent cinquante guinées qu'on a collectées pour lui. Assurément c'est bien peu de chose.[1]

> [Poor Francisque Arlequin and his troupe set sail for Ostend on the twenty-eighth of last month [NS]. He takes with him just the one hundred and fifty guineas that were collected for him. A paltry sum.]

Although de la Barre says that it was Francisque himself who led the company to Ostend, when the company arrived in Ghent it was Simon Moylin and Jean-Baptiste Lesage who made a contract with the Confraternity of St Sebastian in Ghent, which granted them permission to perform from 18 December until Palm Sunday, 21 March 1739 (NS). The explanation, it seems to me, is that in the immediate aftermath of the riot, Francisque had decided to divide the company and to call for the help of his brother Simon. If indeed the company had consisted of seventy players, as had been rumored in the press, two companies of thirty-five would have been perfectly viable. It seems most likely that, leaving Simon in charge of the company in the north, Francisque followed the part of the troupe that had gone to France via Boulogne. On 14 December (NS) he was granted the lease of the theatre in Toulouse for the winter.

Their hastily arranged seasons in Ghent and Toulouse meant that the companies of Francisque and Simon spent the winter of 1738–9 far apart. No trace of the programme of the two long winter seasons has survived, but the

---

[1] Antoine de la Barre de Beaumarchais, *Amusemens Littéraires: ou Correspondance Politique, Rhétorique, Philosophique, Critique, et Galante pour l'Année MDCCXXXVIII, 2 vols* (Frankfurt, 1739, and The Hague, 1740), vol. 2, pt 2, pp. 334–5.

playgoers of Ghent and Toulouse were undoubtedly treated to the extensive repertoire which had been prepared for George II and the London élite. In his *Amusemens Littéraires* de la Barre reported a rumour that the company in Ghent would open with Boissy's *Le Français à Londres*, and noted the irony of its celebration of the marriage of 'la politesse Française' with 'le bon sens Anglais'.[2] Francisque's troupe seems firmly placed in Toulouse in January 1739, when Marie-Catherine Foulquier, eldest daughter of Jean-Baptiste Foulquier, was baptised there.[3] Foulquier's wife, Marie-Antoinette Tourneville, had been with Francisque's company in London in 1734–5. Simon's company was in Ghent until Palm Sunday and his movements in subsequent months are unknown. However, the summer of 1739 brought a spectacular revival of Francisque's fortunes and, almost certainly, a reunion of the two companies.

The season at Compiègne 1739

In the summer of 1739 Louis XV decreed that thousands of French troops would take part in military manoeuvres at a summer camp created on the vast estates of the chateau at Compiègne.[4] Work on the construction of fortifications and earthworks for war games began in April, and the news that the court and the entire royal family would be present at these extraordinary events attracted visitors from all over Europe.[5]

Evidence of Francisque's involvement in these events first appears in June 1739 in a letter from Mme de Graffigny to François-Antoine Devaux:

> À propos, la troupe de Francisque fait fortune. Le roi lui donne 12 mille francs pour Compiègne et Fontainebleau, et les jours qu'il ne va pas à la comédie, ce qui arrive souvent, ils tirent et font beaucoup. Les pauvres Italiens d'ici [la Comédie-Italienne] sont désolés, car le voyage de Fontainebleau leur valait beaucoup et ils n'iront pas.

> [By the way, the troupe of Francisque is making a fortune. The King is giving them 12,000 francs for Compiègne and Fontainebleau, and on the evenings when he does not attend the theatre, which often happens, they pull in crowds and make a lot. The poor Italians here [the Comédie-Italienne] are distraught, because the trip to Fontainebleau was worth a lot to them and now they won't be going.]

---

[2] De la Barre, *Amusemens*, p. 335.

[3] AM Toulouse GG 316 (Saint-Étienne). The godmother, Marie-Catherine Fompré, was presumably a relative of Tourneville's late husband.

[4] There were fourteen royal military camps at Compiègne between 1666 and 1769, notably Louis XIV's 'camp de Coudun' in 1698, recorded by Saint-Simon in his *Mémoires sur le siècle de Louis XIV et la Régence* (Paris, 1858).

[5] Jean Pellassy de l'Ousle, *Histoire du Palais de Compiègne* (Paris, l'an II [1793–4], p. 224.

Devaux's reply to this news on 5 July was less than enthusiastic: 'Comment! La troupe de Francisque est au roi? Oh, ma foi, c'est quitter le vin de Bourgogne pour la piquette.' [What! Francisque's troupe has gone to the king? Good Lord, that's like swapping Burgundy wine for plonk.][6] While de Graffigny's information concerning Francisque and Compiègne was correct, she was wrong about Les Italiens. Both the Comédie-Française and the Comédie-Italienne performed at Fontainebleau as usual in November and there is no evidence that Francisque ever appeared there.[7] The official theatres did not normally accompany the court to Compiègne but de Graffigny may have heard a rumour that, given the exceptionally distinguished gathering, the Italians might have hoped to be invited. The King's gift of 12,000 francs to Francisque was a rare privilege for an itinerant troupe. As I have already noted, the French ambassador had kept Louis XV's ministers fully informed of events in London in October 1738 and this large sum was surely a public act of reparation for the perceived insult to French honour as well as financial compensation for the losses Francisque had incurred.

In July the *Mercure* reported, 'On mande de Compiègne qu'il y a une assez bonne troupe de comédiens, le Roy ayant bien voulu permettre qu'elle y restât pendant le séjour que la cour y fera.' [It is reported from Compiègne that they have a fairly good troupe of actors, the King having allowed them to remain during the stay of the court.] It gave its readers a detailed description of the theatre Francisque had built near the river, including precise measurements: 102 feet long by 33 wide, with a ceiling 22 feet high, balconies on two levels, a parquet, and a parterre that could hold 400 people.[8] Such a purpose-built structure is impressive when one remembers that 400 seats (in the parterre alone) is about a third of the capacity of each of the three official Parisian theatres.

A document never quoted before in this context offers new information on Francisque and company and further insight into the social life of the court. The journal *Le Camp de Compiègne de 1739* was written by a Parisian bourgeois, Gabriel Scellier, an avid non-military observer, who recorded the events of that summer in the form of a series of letters to the wives of his friends back in Paris. Describing Francisque's theatre, he gives the reason for its solid construction:

---

[6] Françoise de Graffigny, *Correspondance de Mme de Graffigny* ed. English Showalter, Peter Allan and J. Alan Dainard. 15 vols (Oxford, 1985–2016), vol. 2, p. 18. Devaux plays on the name of the building which housed the Comédie-Italienne, the Hotel de Bourgogne. 'Piquette' is watery wine.

[7] *Mercure*, November 1739, p. 2704.

[8] *Mercure*, June 1739, pp. 1399–1400.

Ces comédiens ont fait bâtir une loge, partie sur ce rempart, partie dans le fossé, tout près du cours, qui est la plus belle et la plus fréquentée promenade de la ville. Cette loge est faite de charpente et de plâtre, couverte de tuiles. Elle a été travaillée solidement, parce que cette troupe compte y venir tous les ans, si le Roi continue à y prendre ses plaisirs.[9]

[These actors have built a theatre, partly on the rampart, partly on the moat, near the Cours, which is the most beautiful and busiest promenade in the city. The theatre is constructed of plaster on a wooden framework and it has a tiled roof. It has been solidly built, because this troupe intends to return every year if the King continues to take his pleasure here.]

Though the *Mercure* (not an eye-witness) calls the company 'une assez bonne troupe', Scellier, on the spot, is far more laudatory: 'Les acteurs y sont excellents, principalement l'Arlequin, qu'on estime approcher beaucoup du fameux Thomassin de la Comédie-Italienne. L'orchestre est passable, mais les danseurs et les chanteurs y sont admirables.' [The actors are excellent, especially the Arlequin, who is thought to be about as good as the famous Thomassin of the Comédie-Italienne. The orchestra is passable, but the dancers and singers are admirable.] That Francisque should be compared to 'Thomassin [...], l'interprète incomparable des Arlequins de Marivaux' [the incomparable interpreter of the Arlequins of Marivaux], was indeed rare praise.[10]

Although the troupe did not perform inside the royal residence at Compiègne, Henri Lagrave gave them a special place in his chapter on 'Le Théâtre à la Cour' because they were performing essentially for a court audience and during the period when the court was present in the chateau.[11] The August number of the *Mercure* mentions 'Moylin cadet' [i.e., Simon] and 'Lesage cadet' as the leaders of the troupe, but Madame de Graffigny's letter to Devaux and Francisque's own words in a letter of September 1739 make it clear that he was present in Compiègne and in overall charge of the company there. The *Mercure* reports that Francisque's company numbered about twenty-five. This number, which seems to be a serious underestimation, may not have included

---

[9] Baron Xavier de Bonnault-d'Houët, ed., *Le camp de Compiègne de 1739, suivi d'un menu royal: extraits des Mémoires de Scellier avec introduction et notes par le Baron de Bonnault-d'Houët* (Compiègne, 1897), pp. 30–1.

[10] Anon., *Les Plaisirs de La Tronche, 1711*, ed. Pierre Monnier and Jean Sgard (Grenoble, 2006), p. 30. By the summer of 1739, Thomassin was gravely ill and he died in Paris on 19/20 August aged 57.

[11] Lagrave, *TP*, p. 163. Lagrave, who does not make the connection between this troupe and Francisque Moylin, gives the managers' names as Moulin and Lesage, wrongly identifying the latter as the son of the famous writer.

the musicians and the excellent singers and dancers mentioned by both Scellier and the *Mercure*; the latter also remarks that Compiègne seat prices were the same as those paid at the Comédie-Française in Paris. Following the *Mercure*, Lagrave notes that, for the convenience of the courtiers, on the days when they were obliged to follow the King on a long day's hunting, plays began at 10pm, as opposed to 6pm on other days. This fact led him to speculate that the theatre, exceptionally, catered at the same time for the court and the general public. However, Scellier's account contradicts this over-egalitarian impression, revealing that the company gave two performances in the same evening to satisfy the differing needs of two very different audiences: early, for the townsfolk, but as late as 11pm for the courtiers.[12] This arrangement seems unique in the annals of eighteenth-century French theatre, and it is yet another example of the ingenuity and resourcefulness of Francisque. Although the King apparently went only twice to the theatre, Scellier's account suggests that his courtiers regularly attended the late-night performances and balls.

Before going on to examine the company's repertoire, it seems appropriate, with the help of Scellier's journal, to show just how extravagant every aspect of this magnificent international gathering was. Scellier considered the court 'bien plus brillante et plus nombreuse qu'à Versailles' [much more brilliant and crowded than at Versailles] because it included the whole of the royal family and the court, whereas when the King was at Versailles many of his courtiers could remain in Paris. The breathless catalogue of events could easily be dismissed as the over-enthusiastic outpouring of a loyal and impressionable bourgeois; but it seems to be an accurate summary of the six-week season which, Scellier says, attracted more than a hundred thousand visitors. He describes choreographed military exercises, of which some even included marionette-like wooden soldiers, for extra dramatic effect during staged explosions, and a series of dinners, balls, and fêtes champêtres worthy of the brush of Watteau.

> des repas superbes donnés par des princes dans des tentes magnifiques; des illuminations de toutes façons; des danses, des concerts dans les camps; des revues de régiments; des batailles représentées; [...] une chasse royale trois à quatre fois par semaine [...] dans la plus belle forêt de France, embellie de plus de douze cents allées ou avenues garnies de rendez-vous; une troupe de comédiens du Roi; enfin un air de gaîté et de joie partout.[13]
>
> [superb meals given by princes in magnificent tents; illuminations of all kinds; dances and concerts in the camps; regimental reviews; staged battles; [...] a royal hunt three to four times a week [...] through the

---

[12] Bonnault-d'Houët, ed., *Le Camp*, p. 29.
[13] *Ibid.*, pp. 60–1.

most beautiful forest of France, embellished with more than twelve hundred avenues with arbours for assignations; a troupe of royal actors; finally, a mood of joy and jollity reigned everywhere.]

During the daily military exercises, the King and his chosen party (an honour reserved for the bluest of blue blood) would often go hunting, returning around six to inspect the latest fortifications, earthworks and explosive devices. Senior military commanders vied with each other as much off the battlefield as on it. On several occasions after dinner, the King's Lieutenant-Colonel, Louis Charles de Bourbon, comte d'Eu, gave lavish entertainments. Scellier reports that the first of these was reputed to have cost 25,000 livres and his tent, surrounded by beds of flowers, was lit with twenty thousand lamps and various kinds of illuminations. There were games and dances until three in the morning.[14] Scellier gleefully reveals the unexpectedly comic dénouement of these festivities as bewildered peasants found periwigs, slippers, shawls, brooches, earrings and gold watches, lost during nocturnal scenes of passion in the cornfields.[15] The all-pervading sense of theatricality extended even to the local church and the Royal Mass on 16 July. On the same night, comte d'Eu gave an even more lavish entertainment for the whole royal family, this time with an orchestra and singers, who must surely have been drawn from Francisque's company. Once again the festivities lasted until dawn.

Scellier, a respectable bourgeois, must have been as aware as anyone else of the gossip of the day. The editor of his journal, the puritanical Baron de Bonnault d'Houet, pointed out in 1897 that the diarist had failed to mention the 'honteux scandale' of the King's mistresses, Mme de Mailly and Mademoiselle de Nesle, on view even in the queen's carriage, or the satiric songs that must have been circulating in Compiègne as in Paris.[16] These songs are mentioned by Edmond Barbier in his journal for November of the previous year, which goes into salacious detail about the King's liaison. The scurrilous popular song, 'La Béquille du Père Barnaba', which was all the rage in Paris included the words:

> Mailly dont on babille,
> La première éprouva
> La royale béquille
> Du Père Barnaba.[17]

---

[14] *Ibid.*, p. 16.
[15] *Ibid.*, p. 17.
[16] 775 *Ibid.*, p. 4.
[17] Edmond Jean François Barbier, *Chronique de la régence et du règne de Louis XV (1718–1763), ou Journal de Barbier*, fifth series (1731–1753), 8 vols (Paris, 1857) vol. 3, p. 112. For more on this song see the entry on the website 'Satires du XVIII Siècle', Université de Saint-Étienne: https://satires18.univ-st-etienne.fr/texte/

[Mailly of whom we gossip,
Was the first to feel
The royal stick
Of Father Barnaba.]

Scellier's *Le Camp de Compiègne*, far richer in detail than the *Mercure*, evokes the sensual indulgence and self-conscious theatricality to which Francisque's company seems to have made a significant contribution.

The company gave its first performance in the newly built theatre on 21 June, and it may not be a coincidence that they opened with the play which London had refused to hear on 9 October 1738, d'Allainval's *L'Embarras des richesses*. Performances of twenty-seven plays have been recorded. This may not be an exhaustive list, but if the company gave just over thirty performances in six weeks, it may not be far short. In his choice of repertoire Francisque benefitted from a liberty unknown to the two Comédies, and his programme was drawn from them both.

Fourteen plays came from the recent repertoire of the Comédie-Italienne. There were four comedies by Marivaux,[18] the three by Delisle that had been seen in London, and one each by d'Allainval and Jolly (*La Femme Jalouse* again); the most recent were Marivaux's *L'Heureux stratagème* of 1733, and *Les Fées* from 1736 by Romagnesi and Francisque's old friend Procope-Couteaux. Perhaps rather surprisingly in the midst of such frivolity, the company performed two verse tragicomedies, Romagnesi's *Samson* and Boissy's *La Vie est un songe*. Only four pieces were drawn from the old pre-1697 Italian repertoire: Fatouville's *La Fille savante* [*Isabelle Fille Capitaine*], Lenoble's *Les Deux Arlequins* and two 'canevas', *Arlequin, enfant, statue et perroquet* and *Les Intrigues d'Arlequin*. Just two plays from the Théâtre de la Foire were given, the one-act opéra-comique *Les Animaux raisonnables* (1718, Fuzelier and Legrand), and Lesage's *La Statue merveilleuse* (*Le Miroir sans fard*).

Seven plays are recorded from the repertoire of the Comédie-Française. With Regnard's *Les Folies amoureuses* and *Les Ménechmes*, comedies in the elegant and mellifluous verse for which Regnard was renowned, Francisque seems to be inviting comparison with the best from the past. The Comédie's repertoire from the 1730s is also well represented, with Destouches' *Le Glorieux* and two plays by Nivelle de la Chaussée, creator of sentimental comedy: *Le Préjugé à la mode* and *L'Ecole des amis*, which was barely two years old. The appearance of the two de la Chaussée comedies in 1739 shows that Francisque was eager to take the newest plays on the Paris stage to the provinces.

Perhaps the most curious feature of the programme is the performance on 19 July, by royal command, of Scarron's seventeenth-century comedy, *L'Héritier ridicule*. In a letter of 28 July to the marquis d'Argenson Voltaire

---

[18] *Arlequin poli par l'amour, Le Prince travesti, La Double Inconstance*, and *L'Heureux stratagème*. The other plays from the Théâtre Italien were *Arcagambis* and *Arlequin Hulla*, both by Dominique and Romagnesi.

explains that, having heard that Louis XIV and his brother had watched this play twice in one day, Louis XV had ordered the Comédie-Française to revive it but they refused to do so. With rare exceptions, Scarron's plays were now considered too vulgar for polite audiences. (In his 'Notices sur les œuvres de théâtre', the marquis d'Argenson commented that *L'Héritier ridicule* with its 'ordures' [filth] and 'gros mots français' [foul French words] was too coarse for modern tastes, although he admits that 'cette gaîté naïve et outré peut encore plaire une fois'[19] [this naïve and outrageous humour may still be found amusing one more time]). In the end, says Voltaire, when the king finally saw it performed by 'les bateleurs de Compiègne' [the mountebanks of Compiègne], he and his party were bored to death.[20] The *Mercure* contradicts Voltaire's grudging account, saying that the play was 'très bien représentée'[21] [very well performed], and Scellier, who was actually present in Compiègne, describes the event:

> A onze heures de la nuit, le roi alla à la comédie pour la première fois qu'il est à Compiègne. Il prit pour sa cour le théâtre, un côté des loges, l'amphithéâtre et la moitié du parterre. Il abandonna le reste aux comédiens qui en firent, comme vous en pouvez juger, bien de l'argent.
>
> [At eleven o'clock at night, the King went to the theatre for the first time at Compiègne. He took for his court the stage, one side of the boxes, the amphitheatre, and half of the parterre. He left the rest to the actors who made, as you can imagine, a lot of money out of it.]

These remaining seats were probably sold at exorbitant prices to the many visiting dignitaries. The King was again present on 31 July for *Les Intrigues d'Arlequin* and *Les Animaux raisonnables*. It was on this occasion that he formally bestowed on Francisque and company the title of 'Comédiens du Roi.'

> Le roi a paru s'y amuser et a bien voulu permettre à cette troupe de prendre le titre de Comédiens du Roi. Sa Majesté a même ordonné au duc de Gesvres, Premier Gentilhomme de sa Chambre, d'en délivrer un Certificat aux deux chefs de la troupe, et de recommander aux Gouverneurs, Maires, Échevins et autres Officiers de la Police, que sa Majesté souhaitait que cette troupe fût protégée, et qu'ils donnassent leurs soins pour empêcher qu'elle ne soit troublée dans ses exercices.[22]

---

[19] René-Louis de Voyer de Paulmy, marquis d'Argenson, *Notices sur les œuvres de théâtre*, ed. Henri Lagrave, 2 vols (Geneva, 1966), vol. 1, p. 401.
[20] Voltaire, *The Complete Works of Voltaire*, ed. Theodore Besterman (Geneva, 1968), vol. 90, p. 438.
[21] *Mercure*, July 1739, p. 1639.
[22] *Ibid.*, p. 1640.

[The King seems to have enjoyed himself and he granted the troupe the title Comédiens du Roi. His Majesty even ordered the Duke of Gesvres, First Gentleman of the Bedchamber, to issue a Certificate to the two heads of the company, informing Governors, Mayors, Aldermen and other Officers of the Police, that His Majesty wished this troupe to be protected, and that care should be taken to prevent it being troubled in its work.]

Perhaps there is deliberate political irony in King Louis' insistence that the company should not be 'troublée dans ses exercices'; in London, King George's 'By Authority' had proved powerless against the fury of the mob. According to Scellier, the actors were also generously rewarded with at least three thousand livres, and by the following day they had already put their new title on their handbills.[23]

Francisque's season also included late-night theatre balls like those at the Opéra, and the one given on 12 July was reported in Gastelier's *Lettres sur les affaires du temps*: 'On dit qu'il s'est rendu une affluence de monde extraordinaire' [It is said to have had attracted an extraordinary crowd]. The *Mercure* also stresses that nearly all the plays were followed by excellent performances of serious and comic dances.

The most impressive and unexpected item in the Compiègne programme was *La Princesse d'Élide*, the first collaborative work of Molière and Lully, a 'comédie héroïque mêlée de Musique et d'Entrées de Ballet'. The important comic role of Moron the jester, originally played by Molière, was probably taken by Francisque. This elaborate comédie-ballet, set in the realm of Ariosto's enchantress Alcina, had been part of the week of 'Les Plaisirs de l'île enchantée', the first of Louis XIV s grandiose entertainments at Versailles in 1664, and the king himself in a costume of gold and jewels played the part of the knight Roger. Music, singing and dancing were integral parts of the spectacle. The Comédie-Française had dropped *La Princesse d'Élide* from its repertoire in 1738; the ballet scenes, now being performed at the Opéra, may have been beyond the resources of the actors in the 'Maison de Molière'. A successful performance of this sophisticated work would have required a highly gifted company of actors, singers and dancers, undoubtedly led by the ballet-master Jean-Baptiste Malter.[24]

Coincidentally, in July 1739 the young Horace Walpole on his Grand Tour was staying nearby at Rheims. In a letter to Richard West dated 20 July (N.S.)

---

[23] Bonnault-d'Houët, ed., *Le Camp*, p. 52.

[24] Although they are not mentioned by name in any of the press reports, the Malters must also have been with the company; their presence is not recorded anywhere else until they appear with Francisque in Toulouse in the following year.

he reported on the spectacular entertainments at the royal camp and said that on leaving Compiègne the actors were to visit Rheims:

> They have balls twice a week after the play, and ... the Count d'Eu gave the king a most flaring entertainment in the camp ... We are going to have all manner of diversions. The comedians return hither from Compiègne in eight days;[25] and in a very little of time one attends the regiment of the King, three battalions, and an hundred of officers; all men of a certain fashion, very amiable, and who know their world. Our women grow more gay, more lively, from day to day in expecting them.[26]

The season closed on 2 August with Marivaux's *Arlequin poli par l'amour*, *Arlequin Hulla* and *Arcagambis* by Dominique and Romagnesi. In its August number the *Mercure* further underlined the reputation of the company at Compiègne: 'fort connue dans différentes Villes du Royaume, où elle a toujours joué avec beaucoup de succès' [very well known in various towns of the kingdom, where it has always performed with great success]. 'Au reste cette Troupe est très bien assortie, le Sr Moylin, qui en est le chef, est l'Auteur de la dernière Pièce que le Roy a vu. Il y a joué le rôle d'Arlequin avec beaucoup d'intelligence et de légèreté' [Moreover, this troupe is very well made up: Mr. Moylin, the leader, is the author of the last play that the King saw. In it, he played the role of Arlequin with great intelligence and lightness]. Francisque is presumably called an author because of his commedia-style improvisation in *Les Intrigues d'Arlequin* on 31 July. The *Mercure* goes on to give other useful details about Francisque's fellow actors:

> il a été très bien secondé par les autres Acteurs, en Scaramouche, Pierrot, etc. qui ont mérité les applaudissements qu'ils ont reçus. Le Sr Lesage s'est aussi distingué dans les Rôles sérieux, ayant d'ailleurs l'avantage d'une fort belle voix. La Chanteuse a exécuté différents Cantates qui ont fait beaucoup de plaisir. Les Srs Lefèvre et Pacorel sont les principaux Danseurs, de même que les Dlles Lefèvre et Dupuis, et chacun dans leur genre ont fait paraître leurs différents talents.[27]

---

[25] Walpole seems not to have known that these were the same comedians whom he had undoubtedly seen in London in 1734–35 and who had been driven out of the Haymarket in 1738.

[26] Horace Walpole, *The Yale Edition of Horace Walpole's Correspondence* 48 vols (New Haven, 1937–83), vol. 13, p. 178. His previous letter to West had commented that constant speaking of French was affecting his epistolary style. In a footnote the editors wrongly assume that the visiting troupe was the Comédie-Française.

[27] *Mercure*, August 1739, p. 1851.

[he was very well supported by the other actors as Scaramouche, Pierrot etc., who received well-earned applause. Mr. Lesage also distinguished himself in serious roles and has the advantage of a very beautiful voice. The singer performed various cantatas and she gave great pleasure. Messrs Lefèvre and Pacorel are the principal dancers, along with Mlles Lefèvre and Dupuis, and each of them in their different genres displayed their various talents.]

The Lefèvre couple and Pacorel (spelt Pagnorel in the English press) were probably star dancers who had been newly recruited for the 1738 London season.[28] Along with Mlle Chateauneuf, they had been among the twelve dancers whose Haymarket appearance had been greeted with a hail of dried peas. As the *Mercure* was read in all foreign courts and capitals, one cannot help wondering if this article was aimed at the court of George II.

Despite their unofficial status and their precarious and itinerant lifestyle, the Moylin company (led by both Francisque and Simon) were now entitled to call themselves 'Comédiens du Roi'. The royal ordonnance made clear that this title was not intended merely for the duration of the season at Court but also for the prestige it would give them when they again took to the road. If this title had not been considered well deserved, it would have invited derision from the press, the public, and the memoirs of contemporaries. Then there is the evidence of the box-office. The company would hardly have dared to ask, nor would the court have agreed to pay, seat prices comparable to those of the Comédie-Française, unless the standard of performance at least approached that of the official theatres. Although he was unaware that this was the company of Francisque, and although his reference to the 'morne séjour du château' is contradicted by two sources which he did not know, Scellier's lively narrative and the letter in the August *Mercure*, Lagrave was otherwise correct in his summary of the achievements of the 'Comédiens de Compiègne':

La troupe de Moulin [Moylin] se montrait capable de rivaliser non seulement avec la Comédie-Française et la Comédie-Italienne, mais aussi avec l'Opéra et les forains. [...] Ils avaient su, fort intelligemment, faire du morne séjour du château une brillante saison parisienne. [...] Quelle que soit, au demeurant, la valeur de ces artistes, la variété du répertoire, la liberté des programmes confèrent à leurs représentations une originalité certaine.[29]

---

[28] A member of the Pacorel family was maître de ballet in Metz from 1754 to 1762. Gilbert Rose, *Metz et la Musique au XVIIIe siècle* (Metz, 1992), pp. 73, 98, 184.

[29] Lagrave, *TP*, pp. 164, 165, 167.

[The troupe of Moulin [Moylin] proved itself capable of competing not only with the Comédie-Française and the Comédie-Italienne, but also with the Opéra and the fairgrounds.[…] They had managed, very cleverly, to make of the gloomy stay at the chateau a brilliant Parisian season. […] Moreover, whatever the quality of these performers may have been, the variety of their repertoire and the freedom of their programmes gave their performances a definite originality.]

Thanks to Horace Walpole's letter, we know that Francisque's company moved from Compiègne to Rheims in August. Then, in September, the comte d'Eu, perhaps as a token of gratitude for Francisque's help with his nocturnal entertainments at Compiègne, wrote from Versailles to Bordeaux, ordering the city authorities to grant a year-long exclusive theatrical licence to 'Moylin et Lesage.' As very few such documents exist from the period, I shall quote it in full, in all its formality:

Aujourd'hui, onzième jour de septembre de l'année mil sept cent trente-neuf, Son Altesse sérénissime Mgr le Comte d'Eu, étant à Versailles, a accordé aux sieurs Moylin et Le Sage, comédiens, et à leur troupe, la permission de représenter dans la ville de Bordeaux pendant une année, à compter depuis Pâques de l'année 1741, sans que pendant ladite année aucune autre troupe de comédiens puisse s'établir dans la dite ville de Bordeaux. À l'effet de quoi mon dit seigneur le comte d'Eu charge et prie MM. les maires, sous-maires et jurats gouverneurs de la ville de Bordeaux de faire jouir les dits sieurs Moylin et Lesage et leur troupe de l'effet des présentes, et de tenir la main à ce que les dits comédiens se conforment en tout aux règles de la police, et qu'il ne se commette aucun désordre aux dites représentations. En foi de quoi, Son Altesse sérénissime m'a commandé d'expédier le présent brevet, qu'elle a signé de sa main, et l'a fait signer par moi, secrétaire de ses commandements, maisons et finances.[30]

[Today, the eleventh day of September in the year one thousand seven hundred and thirty-nine, His Serene Highness the Comte d'Eu, being at Versailles, granted Messrs Moylin and Le Sage, actors, and their troupe, permission to perform in the city of Bordeaux for a year, starting from Easter 1741; during that year no other troupe of actors may settle in the said city of Bordeaux. In consequence of which my Lord the Comte d'Eu charges and prays Messrs the mayors, deputy mayors and governors of the city of Bordeaux to grant the said Moylin and Lesage and their troupe enjoyment of the effect of these presents,

---

[30] Arnaud Detcheverry, *Histoire des Théâtres de Bordeaux* (Bordeaux, 1860), pp. 306–7. No modern source reproduces this document, which seems to be lost.

and to ensure that the said actors comply with all the rules of the police, and that there is no disorder in the said performances. In virtue whereof, His Serene Highness has commanded me to send this patent, which he has signed with his hand, and has had it signed by me, secretary of his household.]

Bordeaux, Compiègne and Dijon 1739–40

At the end of the summer of 1739, Francisque and his company returned to Toulouse. Earlier in 1739 Duchemin and Brémont, the theatre directors of Bordeaux and Toulouse respectively, were associated in a joint venture to perform in both cities, but, Arnaud Detcheverry reports, this arrangement did not save them from financial ruin.[31] Their companies had been performing in the temporary wooden theatre built in 1735 in the gardens of the Hôtel de Ville, which was by now in a dilapidated condition unworthy of one of the great cities of the kingdom. In June 1738 the jurats voted to create the first purpose-built theatre in the history of Bordeaux, a magnificent structure that was completed in September 1739.[32] Its opening night coincided with the visit of 'Madame de France'. Shortly after her return from Compiègne to Versailles in August, the twelve-year-old Princess Louise-Elisabeth had been married to a son of the King of Spain by proxy and, as 'Madame Infante', was now on her way to Spain.

As Henri Lagrave makes clear in his history of the theatre in Bordeaux, all the troupes in that city between 1736 and 1742, with two exceptions, can be shown to have been associated with the Moylin family.[33] Since the 1720s the theatre lovers of Bordeaux had known and admired Francisque's company, which contained several natives of Bordeaux, including his wife and Jean-Baptiste Malter. Buffon had spoken of the troupe's huge success and applause in 1731 (see p. 165); in 1737, the jurats had written to the director of the theatre at Angers, negotiating for a visit from the Moylins, 'Il ne nous faut ici que du choisi en tout genre.'[34] [Here we want only the choicest of every kind.] Lagrave did not note the link between 'Moylin' at Compiègne and 'Francisque' at Bordeaux, and he seems not to have known of a letter from Francisque to the jurats written from Toulouse in September 1739 requesting permission to perform in the new theatre.[35] Francisque's letter is not mentioned in any modern study, and in correspondence with me M. Frédéric Laux, the

---

[31] Detcheverry, *Histoire*, p. 22.
[32] Detcheverry, *Histoire*, p. 220. This theatre was destroyed by fire in 1755.
[33] Henri Lagrave, *La Vie théâtrale à Bordeaux, des origines à nos jours*, vol. 1, *Des origines à 1799*, p. 137.
[34] Detcheverry, *Histoire*, p. 229.
[35] Lagrave, *VT*, vol. 1, p. 137.

director of the city archives of Bordeaux, has confirmed my suspicion that the original letter, along with the brevet from the duc de Bourbon, must have disappeared in the disastrous fire at the Hôtel de Ville in June 1862.[36] Fortunately, an extract from Francisque's letter was published in 1847, thus saving from oblivion another important episode in his career and providing a glimpse of his (public) personality:

> Un grand prince m'honore de sa protection, c'est Mgr le duc de Bourbon. De plus, j'ai un privilège du roi. On m'a assuré que vous faisiez bâtir un théâtre superbe. Je désire avec ardeur y paraître [...]. Si je ne puis jouer sur le théâtre neuf, je me contenterai de celui qui est actuellement existant, ou bien permettez-moi de bâtir aux Salinières ou au Chapeau-Rouge; je ferai faire une cabane. Vous voyez bien que je ne suis pas glorieux. Je le réitère, c'est la nécessité de ma route qui m'oblige à cela. De plus, nous ne sommes pas forts dans le genre français; c'est l'italien que nous jouerons. Ainsi Bordeaux aura tous les jours du spectacle (italien et français); cela deviendra un petit Paris. P.S. S'il y a quelque irrégularité dans ma lettre, pardonnez à mon caractère arlequinéqui, qui dit la vérité comme il pense.[37]

> [A great prince, the duc de Bourbon, honours me with his protection. In addition, I have a licence from the King. They tell me that you are building a splendid theatre. I ardently desire to perform there ... If I cannot perform in the new theatre, I will content myself with the one that currently exists or else allow me to build a cabin at Salinières or Chapeau-Rouge [two suburbs of Bordeaux]. You see, I'm not vainglorious. I repeat, my planned itinerary obliges me to come. Moreover, we are not strong in the French repertoire; it's the Italian repertoire that we will perform. Thus, Bordeaux will have plays every night (French and Italian style); it will become a little Paris. P.S. If my letter is somewhat irregular, please forgive my arlequinéqui character who speaks the truth as he sees it.]

As is clear from his earlier repertoire, Francisque's company was perfectly capable of performing the 'genre français'. He probably emphasised their experience with the Comédie-Italienne because he knew that there was already another troupe in the city (perhaps that of Duchemin or Brémont) specialising in the repertoire of the Comédie-Française.

---

[36] Email from Frédéric Laux to R. V. Kenny, 5 September 2018.

[37] M. E. Dégranges, 'Mémoire à consulter sur l'état général des théâtres en provinces, et sur celui de Bordeaux en particulier', *Recueil des actes de l'Académie Royale des sciences, belles-lettres et Arts de Bordeaux, neuvième année* (Bordeaux, 1847), pp. 469–524, at pp. 490–1, and p. 491, n. 2.

The historian Patrice-Jean O'Reilly knew of Francisque's letter and summarised its contents in 1860 in his monumental *Histoire complète de Bordeaux*. He may have had access to further documentation lost in the fire of 1862, since he seems to assume that Francisque was indeed given the use of the new theatre.[38] Francisque's mention of the King and the Comte d'Eu in his letter must have impressed the jurats, especially since the city was shortly to welcome 'Madame'. When they received the Count's letter, they would already have read in *Le Mercure* of Francisque's exceptional season at Compiègne where he had given twice-weekly balls 'dans le goût de ceux de l'Opéra' [like those of the Opéra] and may have organised those which the comte d'Eu had given for the royal family. Furthermore, the jurats had invited the painter-designer Jean-Nicolas Servandoni to provide the scenery for the inauguration of the new theatre,[39] an expense which they would surely not have wasted on inferior local troupes. Scant though the surviving evidence may be, it seems clear that Francisque's 'Comédiens du roi' were the troupe which opened the new theatre, described by a contemporary as:

> une des plus belles et des plus vastes et des mieux entendues du royaume [...] Elle fut extraordinairement parée et éclairée. On ne voyait partout que des glaces, ce qui, joint à une nombreuse assemblée de dames et seigneurs magnifiquement parés, formait un spectacle des plus brillants [...][40]

> [one of the biggest, most beautiful and well-designed in the kingdom. It was magnificently decorated and brilliantly lit. There were mirrors everywhere which, along with the crowds of lords and ladies in all their finery, made a most splendid sight [...]]

The following day, amid great pomp and circumstance, 'Madame' attended a command performance of Dancourt's comedy, *Le Chevalier à la Mode*.[41]

At the end of the year, Francisque returned to Toulouse, where he had been granted the lease of the theatre for the winter of 1739–40. The Malters must still have been with his company at this time; their daughter Marie-Antoinette was baptised in Toulouse on 1 March 1740.[42] Thus, the 'Troupe de Moylin' which began performing in Dijon at the end of December 1739 seems more likely to be Simon's. Simon's daughter Nicole was baptised in Rouen on 7 December 1739, but his wife need not have travelled with him to Dijon.[43]

---

[38] Patrice-Jean O'Reilly, *Histoire complète de Bordeaux* 7 vols (Bordeaux, 1860), pt 1, vol. 3, p. 342.

[39] Pierre Bernadeau, *Annales Politiques, Littéraires Et Statistiques De Bordeaux* ([1803] repr. Kessenger, 2010), p. 134.

[40] Detcheverry, *Histoire*, p. 23.

[41] *Ibid*.

[42] AM Toulouse, GG 317 (Saint-Étienne).

[43] Rouen, Bibliothèque municipale, registre 640 (St-Vincent).

'Troupe de Moylin:' Dijon, December 1739–March 1740

As in many French provincial towns and cities at this period, the theatre in Dijon had been a makeshift affair. In 1718 the city had bought and converted a building in what is today the Rue Buffon, where a fragment of its façade can still be seen. Claude Micault, a lawyer in the Parlement de Dijon, was an avid theatre-goer and for many years he kept a diary, *Le Mercure dijonnais*, in which he recorded the visits of the various itinerant troupes, with the dates and details of their programmes.[44] Thanks to a still-unpublished manuscript list of Micault's, headed 'Troupe de Moylin', a record exists not merely of the company's authorisation to perform but also of the plays given in 1739–40,[45] which enable a comparison with the repertoire of earlier Moylin seasons.[46]

There were performances of thirty-five plays on nineteen nights. The repertoire was largely drawn from the Nouveau Théâtre Italien with just four from the Ancien Théâtre Italien and four popular comedies from the Comédie-Française. The erratic gaps in dating suggest that there may have been other performances that Micault did not see or record. The programme also contained seven plays from the Comédie-Française, including Boissy's *Le Français à Londres*, Fagan's *La Pupille* (1734) and *Le Préjugé à la mode* by Nivelle de la Chaussée (1735), which had also featured in the summer programme at Compiègne. There were no tragedies, but there was one five-act verse tragicomedy from 1643, *La Belle Esclave* by Claude de l'Estoile, a curious throwback to the taste of an earlier age. A couple of favourites remained from the old Théâtre Italien, such as *Arlequin Misanthrope*, and Fatouville's *La Fille savante [Isabelle Fille capitaine]*. But pride of place went to the new Italian repertoire, including the works of Delisle, d'Allainval, Boissy and Marivaux. The most recent of these pieces was Boissy's *La xxxx, Comédie anonyme* which was first performed at the Comédie-Italienne two years earlier in August 1737. Simon's Dijon season ended on 12 March with an 'ambigu comique' by Dominique and Romagnesi: *La Foire des poètes, L'Isle du divorce*, and *La Sylphide*.[47]

As I have already noted, in early March Francisque was still in Toulouse, but by May he had moved on to Nantes, where he is recorded in association

---

[44] *The Mercure Dijonnais* was first published by the Académie des sciences, arts et belles lettres de Dijon in 1887.

[45] I am extremely grateful to the staff of the Archives Municipales de Dijon for supplying me with copies of these manuscripts: Dijon, AM, réf: 2011/287.GR microfilm 555, reproducing f° 2 v°-3 r° (troupe de Moylin) et 9 v°-10 r° (troupe de Francisque) from Part 2 of the *Mercure dijonnois* (Ms 742 bis).

[46] Max Fuchs' reading of Micault's ms. gives the date '2 décembre' and adds 'à cette date il a déjà donné 18 représentations' [at this date he had already given 18 performances]. Fuchs misreads the date of the opening performance as 2 rather than 20. Micault's '18/19 représentations', refers to the total number of nights, not plays.

[47] Three unattributed performances in May which, in the manuscript, follow the list of Moylin company plays, seem to me unlikely to be by that company.

with Antoine Loinville.[48] The Foulquiers were still with the company and their younger daughter Suzanne-Antoinette was baptised in Nantes on 29 May 1740.[49] That summer, the company (almost certainly under the reunited leadership of Francisque and Simon) returned to Compiègne, as the duc de Luynes noted in his Mémoires on 4 August: 'Il y a ici une troupe de comédiens qui y sont établis dès l'année passée dans les fossés.'[50] [There is a troupe of actors here, who first set up last year by the moat.] The season ran from 17 July to 21 August. The *Mercure* gives fewer details, but it does dignify the company with the title which had been bestowed on it in 1739:

> La troupe des comédiens du roi [...] firent l'ouverture de leur théâtre, le dimanche 17 juillet, par les comédies des *Comédiens esclaves*, d'*Arcagambis*, de *l'Occasion*, et d'*Arlequin toujours Arlequin*, d'un acte chacune, avec des agréments de chants et de danses. Ils ont continué tous les jours leurs représentations jusques et compris le 31 juillet, par différentes comédies du Théâtre Français, de l'ancien et nouveau Théâtre Italien et de celui de l'Opéra-Comique, qu'ils ont représentées au gré des spectateurs.

> [The troupe of The King's Players [...] opened their theatre on Sunday, 17 July, with the comedies *Les Comédiens esclaves*, *Arcagambis*, *L'Occasion*, and *Arlequin toujours Arlequin*, all of one act, with songs and dances. They continued their performances every day up to and including 31 July, giving various comedies of the Théâtre Français, the old and new Théâtre Italien and the Opéra-Comique, which they performed to the satisfaction of their audiences.]

This account, though brief, stresses yet again the remarkable range and diversity of the company's repertoire. The opening performance was an ambigu-comique which had first been performed at the Comédie-Italienne in August 1726. During that season, in *Les Comédiens corsaires* at the Foire Saint-Laurent, Francisque had mocked the official theatres' growing tendency to plagiarise the style and content of the fair theatres. Now Francisque was brazenly borrowing from all the theatres of Paris, both official and marginal, and this important point would not have been missed by contemporary readers

---

[48] Fuchs, *Lexique*, p. 142, quoting Étienne Destranges, *Le Théâtre à Nantes depuis ses origines jusqu'à nos jours, 1430?–1893* (Paris, 1893), p. 38.

[49] AM Nantes, GG 243 and 748. By the 1750s, when Foulquier was a member of the orchestra of the Comédie-Italienne, his daughters were received into the company. In 1760 Suzanne-Antoinette married the Arlequin Carlo Bertinazzi (Carlin), the greatest Arlequin after the death of Thomassin.

[50] [Charles-Philippe d'Albert, 4th duc de Luynes], *Mémoires du duc de Luynes sur la cour de Louis XV* (Paris, 1860), vol.3, p. 225.

of the *Mercure*. Again, singing and dancing were a significant feature of the programmes, as the *Mercure* points out in its report of the King's visit on 12 August. 'Le roi honora cette troupe de sa présence, à la représentation des comédies d'*Arlequin valet étourdi* et du *Miroir sans fard*, qui furent suivies d'une pantomime anglaise très bien exécutée et applaudie.' [The King honoured this troupe with his presence at the performance of the comedies *Arlequin valet étourdi* and *Le Miroir sans fard*; these were followed by an English pantomime which was very well performed and much applauded].[51] On this occasion, the King was at the theatre from 11pm until 1am. The duc de Luynes notes that once again special performances for the court were given late at night, after the earlier performances for the lesser orders.

The term 'pantomime anglaise' is interesting, given the fact that all the company members were French. As has already been shown, 'English' in the title often referred to the fashionable content, but it also suggests a narrative such as that of *The Burgomaster trick'd* which Francisque and Nivelon had performed in the Haymarket in 1734 and which had come to be regarded as a peculiarly Anglo-French development of the silent fairground repertoire 'à la muette.' It probably also refers to the kind of ballet d'action which Marie Sallé had pioneered during her seasons in London and introduced on her return to the Paris Opéra with her 'Acte des Fleurs' in Fuzelier and Rameau's *Les Indes galantes* in 1735. The Moylin-Sallé-Cochois clan had been instrumental in the evolution of both the pantomime anglaise and the ballet d'action on both sides of the channel and, characteristically, were bringing the latest Parisian novelties to the provinces. In fact, while Francisque's company was performing a 'pantomime anglaise' for the King, a troupe of 'Danseurs Anglais' were performing 'pantomimes' and 'un ballet anglais' at the two Paris fairs, further giving the lie to English press claims of cultural Anglophobia in Paris.[52]

On leaving Compiègne, a company led by Simon Moylin and Lesage made its way north to Douai from where, on 19 October, they requested permission to spend the winter at Ghent, from 15 November 1740 until Palm Sunday 1741, which in that year fell on 27 March.[53] On 23 March 1741, [Simon] Moylin and Lesage, styling themselves 'Comédiens du Roy', received an authorisation to perform at Amiens 'depuis le dimanche de Quasimodo jusqu'au voyage du roi à Compiègne' [54] [from the Sunday after Easter until the king's travel to Compiègne]. The company clearly wanted to advertise the fact that they were on their way to perform for the King, but there is no record of their having performed at Compiègne in 1741 and no further reference in the *Mercure*. On 10 May, Nicolas-Jean-Baptiste-Simon, son of Simon Moylin, was baptised in

[51] Luynes, *Mémoires*, p. 237.
[52] For these claims, see above, pp. 255–6 and n. 21.
[53] Fuchs, *Lexique*, p. 1584.
[54] Fuchs, *Lexique*, p. 1584.

the church of St Firmin in Amiens.[55] That they did not return to Compiègne in 1741 is further confirmed by a passing reference, in another context, in the *Mercure* of 14 August to 'la troupe qui était à Compiègne l'année dernière [my italics][.]'[56] [the troupe which was in Compiègne last year].

Between 1744 and 1748 the extensive rebuilding of the palace meant the court did not go to Compiègne, so there was no reason for the Moylin company's presence. And their nine-year leasing arrangement on the theatre would anyway have ended in 1747. The later disparaging references to the theatre at Compiègne (e.g., 'L'on s'ennuie mortellement à Compiègne ... La Comédie y est jouée par une troupe de campagne qui est assez mauvaise.'[57] [We are bored to death at Compiègne ... Plays are performed by a country troupe which is rather bad.]), would certainly not fit 'la troupe du Sieur Francisque'.

In a letter of 1741 discovered by M. E. Dégranges, 'femme Moylin' [Francisque's wife], 'Maltère' [Jean-Baptiste Malter], and 'Chapuis' [who had been at Compiègne]', wrote ahead from Dijon to the magistrates of Bordeaux, proposing to visit that city rather than Rouen, 'pour profiter de l'honneur et de la gloire de vous assurer du profond respect' [for the honour and glory of paying you our deepest respects].[58] Given the presence of Malter's name in this document, this seems an appropriate point at which to correct another misunderstanding about the Malter couple. Both the *Dictionary of Actors* and van Aelbrouck's *Dictionnaire des Danseurs* state that the Malters 'came and went' between London and Paris.[59] However, although in November 1740 the London press reported that a 'Mons. and Mlle. MALTERE' had 'lately arriv'd from the Opera at PARIS' to dance at Drury Lane, this cannot refer to Jean-Baptiste and Catherine Malter: they never danced at the Opéra and in any case were almost certainly still in Francisque's company at this time. The Malter who danced in London in 1741 was not Jean-Baptiste but the dancer who was later known at the Paris Opéra as 'Malter l'Anglais.'

As the Comte d'Eu had commanded in 1739, a troupe led by 'Moylin et Lesage' did indeed have a long season in Bordeaux in 1741. All that is known of their stay is an anecdote recorded in Patrice-Jean O'Reilly's history of Bordeaux. Apparently, after the managers had dismissed an actress whom

---

55 AM Amiens, registre 15 (St-Firmin-en-Castillon).

56 *Mercure*, August 1741, p. 1885.

57 Barbier, *Chronique de la régence*, p. 64. Lagrave discusses these as if they still refer to the Moylin-Lesage company.

58 Dégranges, 'Mémoire', p. 490. This 1847 extract is the only source; the full letter was presumably destroyed in the fire of 1862.

59 Philip Highfill et al., *A Biographical Dictionary of Actors, Actresses, Musicians, Dancers, Managers, and Other Stage Personnel in London, 1660–1800*, 16 vols (Carbondale, 1973–93) vol 10, pp. 63–64; Jean-Philippe van Aelbrouck, *Dictionnaire des danseurs, chorégraphes et maîtres de danse à Bruxelles de 1600 à 1830* (1994), p. 176.

they found unsatisfactory, one of her admirers created a disturbance during the play by loudly calling for her. He was arrested, but finally let off with a one-month ban on attending the theatre.[60]

After visits to Nantes in 1740–1, Francisque's name disappears from the records until 1750.[61] It may be that during this decade he handed over the running of the company completely to Simon. Evidence of this can be seen from a number of signed letters and documents in municipal archives and church registers throughout the 1740s. On 18 April 1742, Simon Moylin and a certain 'Labat' wrote to the Échevins (city councillors) of Marseille from Montpellier,[62] and on 7 July the local magistrate in Avignon authorised performances by 'Moulin'.[63] On 29 September 1742 Simon hired the theatre in Marseille, planning to begin performances as soon as it was free.[64] After a one-year gap in records, Simon wrote to the Échevins of Marseille in September 1743 from Arles.[65] During his stay in Arles, Simon gave the première of *La Vangeance Trompée* [sic], by Pierre de Morand, a native of Arles who had become a minor literary figure in Paris. The title page of the published play states that it was first performed at Arles on 15 September 1743 'par la Troupe du 'Sieur Molin, Comédien Ordinaire du Roi.'[66] This play is further evidence that the Moylins were continuing to move away from the Italian and fairground styles which had earlier been staples of their repertoire.

On 21 December 1743, an unusually negative view of the Moylins was expressed in a letter from the Maréchal de Richelieu, Lieutenant-Général of Languedoc. Writing from Montpellier, he urges the Secretary of the Academy of Bordeaux to engage actors for the region, especially Toulouse:

> j'ai défendu de recevoir Moylin; aussi il faut y suppléer, et que Ebrard y envoie au plutost une bonne troupe de comédiens. Je vous prie de vouloir bien veiller à ce qu'ils ne diffèrent pas, parce que l'on m'en demande à Toulouse et que j'ai promis d'y en faire aller une incessamment. […]Tout ce qu'il y a à Toulouse m'a sollicité pour permettre que Molins jouast la comédie jusqu'à l'arrivée de la troupe d'Ebrard, on tiraille; j'ai résisté jusqu'à présent […][67]

---

[60] O'Reilly, *Histoire*, vol. 1, parts 3–4, p. 342.

[61] The company received permissions to perform in Nantes in May 1740 and March 1741. Destranges, *Le Théâtre à Nantes*, p. 17.

[62] AM Marseille, GGL 202.

[63] AD Avignon, B ROTE 200.

[64] AM Marseille, FF 309.

[65] AM Marseille, GGL 202.

[66] Pierre de Morand, *Théâtre et œuvres diverses de M. de Morand*, 3 vols(Paris, 1751), vol.2 p. 127.

[67] Letter to Jean-Baptiste de Navarre, in *Archives historiques du département de la Gironde* (Paris, 1864), vol.6, p. 154.

> [I have forbidden the hiring of Moylin; so we must make up for this, and let Ebrard send them a good troupe of actors. I beg you to see that they do not delay, because I am asked to send a troupe to Toulouse and I have promised to send one soon. [...] Everyone who is anyone in Toulouse is begging me to allow Molin to perform until the arrival of Ebrard's troupe. They are nagging me. I have resisted so far [...]]

The Moylin in question here is almost certainly Simon. One can only speculate as to the reason for Richelieu's disapproval of a company for whose presence the theatregoing public of Toulouse was apparently begging. Had the actors offended the Maréchal in some way? More likely, they were caught up in a local power struggle. Dégranges notes that in Languedoc for many years there had been serious differences of opinion between the City Councillors and the Provincial Governors and Commandants as to their relative powers of jurisdiction over theatrical troupes.[68] The 'Ebrard' mentioned by Richelieu is François Hébrard who had a long and not particularly successful association with provincial itinerant opera and theatre companies. Richelieu's faith in this troupe was sadly misplaced.[69] According to the jurats of Bordeaux, 'ces messieurs [Hébrard and Loinville] ne cherchent qu'à tromper la ville et le public'[70] [these gentlemen seek only to defraud the city and the public]. Yet despite Hébrard's constant failure to honour his contracts or pay his debts, the authorities allowed him to continue to extort money from theatre troupes to support his moribund opera company; by 1749 he owed the Paris Opéra 6,067 livres. The objections to the Moylin troupe seem all the more puzzling in the light of what we know about Hébrard. Max Fuchs, who gives a full account of his shady dealings, suggests that only corruption could explain the authorities' willingness to allow him to get away with such behaviour.[71]

The few remaining Moylin documents for the 1740s, which principally concern Simon, involve authorisations and baptisms mostly in northern and eastern France. On 2 July 1744, 'Simond Molin, comédien du Roy, français et italien' was in Grenoble.[72] A number of letters to the authorities in Marseille (where he may have hoped to establish himself as the resident company) show that in September 1745 he was in Besançon, on 26 October 1745 in Lyon, and in Montpellier between 17 April and 14 June 1746.[73] He had been in Lyon in March 1746 when his son Joseph-Henry was born. Simon is described in

---

[68] Desgranges, *Mémoire*, pp. 496–500.
[69] See E. Isnard, 'Notes sur la vie théâtrale à Marseille au XVIIIe siècle', *Bulletin de la société des historiens du théâtre*, 3:1–2 (1935), 5–13 and 37–49, at pp. 6–7.
[70] Detcheverry, *Histoire*, p. 223.
[71] Fuchs, *VT*, pp. 135–8.
[72] AM Grenoble, FF 44.
[73] AM Marseille, AM GGL 202.

the register as 'Officier du Roy.'[74] By the end of 1748 he and his wife had settled in Toulouse where in the baptismal register for his last known child he is described simply as 'Bourgeois.'[75]

Meanwhile, Francisque's troupe had largely dispersed. In 1742 his sister Marguerite Cochois and her family were recruited by the Marquis d'Argens to perform at the court of Frederick the Great in Berlin. By that year, also, Catherine Labbé and Jean-Baptiste Malter had given up the touring life and settled with their children in Nantes. It was there that their son Jean-Louis died on 3 December 1743, aged 10. Catherine Labbé died on 29 January 1747 and Jean-Baptiste remarried in 1749. Mimi Fourcade (nee Verneuil) and her husband Léonard also seem to have settled in Nantes (it was there that Léonard died, aged only about forty, in 1746).[76] Nantes was France's largest and richest port city and capital of the duchy of Brittany. Perhaps because of the presence of the Malters, perhaps because of the city's pleasant climate and easy transport links, Francisque and Marie-Catherine Moylin also settled there at some point early in the 1740s. But Francisque seems to have come out of retirement, if that is what it was, for one more season in Dijon.

La Troupe de Francisque: Dijon 1750–1

It is thanks to Claude Micault's manuscript diary that the repertoire of Francisque's last fully documented company has been preserved. The sheer number of plays performed, which could not have been prepared solely for this season, suggests that a Moylin company had continued to tour, whether or not Francisque was appearing personally in it. However, Micault, who refers to the visiting company as 'La troupe de Francisque', recalled that Francisque had performed in the city some thirty years ago, perhaps in the spring and summer of 1722 on the way to and from Lyon. (The fact that Micault does not mention the 1740 season may confirm my view that that season's company was led by Simon.) There are no cast lists for this season, but the 1750 company must have contained a new generation of actors, possibly including some of the Malter children. Francisque himself may by now have been playing nobles and elders.

The company opened with Piron's *Gustave Vasa*, followed by a comedy (*L'Epoux par Supercherie*) by Boissy. Both plays were applauded, and Micault declared that the actors:

---

[74] AM Lyon, registre 620 (St-Pierre St-Saturnin).
[75] AM Toulouse, GG 325. (St-Étienne).
[76] The death certificate shows that 'Léonard Dubois, dit Forcade' was buried in the presence of his wife, née Marie Despré de Verneüil (Mimi): AM Nantes, GG 247 (Saint-Nicolas).

réussirent également dans la tragédie et dans le comique. Ils sont magnifiquement habillés et on dit que Francisque, chef de cette troupe, a environ dix mille livres de rentes. On croit qu'ils seront suivis.[77]

[were equally successful in tragedy and comedy. They are splendidly attired, and it is said that Francisque, the master of the troupe, has an income of some ten thousand livres a year. It seems that they will be well patronised.]

As in 1739–40, performances took place in the 'salle de l'Ancienne Comédie', on average twice a week, a total of twenty-seven nights during their stay of some fourteen weeks. Each evening a main play was followed by a shorter comic afterpiece and dancing. Ten years separate this programme from that of the company's last Dijon season. During these ten years the repertoire had changed radically. Almost completely gone are the plays of the Théâtre Italien, both Ancien and Nouveau, and, as a result, almost completely gone too is Arlequin, whose name appears in only one title, *Arlequin Misanthrope* by Brugière de Barante.[78] Now, most of the major plays are five-act comedies from the repertoire of the Comédie-Française.

But there are also no fewer than nine tragedies; Racine's *Phèdre et Hippolyte*, *Andromaque*, *Esther* and *Athalie*; Crébillon's *Rhadamiste et Zénobie*; Voltaire's *Oedipe* and *Sémiramis*, and *Venise sauvée*, an adaptation of Otway's *Venice Preserved* by Pierre-Antoine de La Place. *Gustave Vasa* was given two performances, probably because, as Micault notes with pride, it was a 'fort belle tragédie de M. Piron, notre compatriote' [a very fine tragedy by M. Piron, our fellow Dijonnais].[79] Although Francisque's comic repertoire had evolved, of the eight tragedies, five were in his 1733–4 season at Brussels, and two were in the 1734–5 London season. The tragic repertoire is also noticeably older than the comic; the three Racine plays date from the seventeenth century, the rest from the early eighteenth century; the two latest were *Gustave Vasa* from 1733, and *Venise sauvée* from 1746.

Among the comedies, Molière is represented by *Le Bourgeois Gentilhomme*, and Lesage by *Turcaret*. Three other earlier comedies are Jean Desmarets' *Les Visionnaires*, first acted at the Hotel de Bourgogne in 1637, Campistron's five-act verse comedy *Le Jaloux désabusé* from 1709, and Simon Joseph Pellegrin's *Le Nouveau Monde* from 1722. In sharp contrast, over a third

---

[77] *Le Mercure dijonnais*, reproduced in *Mémoires de la Commission des antiquités du département de la Côte-d'Or* (Dijon, 1885), p. 327.

[78] Regnard's *L'Homme à bonne fortune* (1690) is also an Arlequin play from the old Italian theatre.

[79] I have been unable to decipher the title of a further probable tragedy, *La Mort de Protas/Procris*, from Micault's manuscript.

of the plays are later than 1738. The repertoire shows that Francisque was fully aware of recent theatrical activity in Paris, and it provides an example of the rapid dissemination of new works beyond the capital. All the recent plays (apart from *Venise sauvée*) are comedies or opéras-comiques. Apart from four pieces by Charles Favart, of the Opéra-Comique, all were from the current repertoire of the Comédie-Française, and the rest were five-act 'grandes comédies'. *La Force du naturel*, a five-act verse comedy by Phillippe Néricault (known as Destouches), had first been performed at the Comédie-Française in February 1750. Surprisingly, the company also staged Piron's opéra-comique, *La Rose*, written in 1726 and subsequently banned. It had finally been staged by Monnet's company at the Foire Saint-Germain in 1744 (see p. 151); perhaps, as with his performance of *Samson* in Brussels in 1734, Francisque was reclaiming ownership of a piece originally written for him.

But most remarkable is the performance at the end of the season (28 March 1751), of Mme de Graffigny's five-act prose comedy, *Cénie*, which had premiered at the Comédie-Française on 25 June 1750, barely six months earlier. The first printed copies of the play were ready only in November 1750, and Mme de Graffigny writes about sending them to her friends.[80] The edition on sale in the bookshops is dated 1751. Francisque was already in Dijon in December 1750, where he remained until April, and could not have bought a copy in Paris before his departure. Mme de Graffigny may have known Francisque personally;[81] he could have received one of the copies that she sent out in November, or someone in Paris could have sent him a copy by post. The inclusion of the latest plays from Paris had been a regular feature of Francisque's seasons in the French provinces and beyond.

An interesting development is the complete absence from the programme of the plays of Marivaux which had figured prominently in Francisque's seasons from 1729 to 1741. During Francisque's visit to Dijon in 1739–40, Marivaux was represented by four comedies. Ten years later, all have disappeared. As the theatre critic Francisque Sarcey wrote in 1900, 'Marivaux ne fut pas estimé de son temps à sa juste valeur' [in his own day Marivaux was not valued at his true worth].[82] The Paris fairs are represented only by the ballet-pantomime *L'Œil du maître*, of 1742, by Florimond Boizard de Pontau, and three examples of the work of Charles Favart.[83] Under the direction of Favart the Opéra-Comique had long since moved away from the satirical vein

---

[80] See J.-A. McEachern and D. Smith, 'The First Edition of Mme de Graffigny's *Cénie*', in David Garrioch et al., eds, *The Culture of the Book. Essays from Two Hemispheres in Honour of Wallace Kirsop* (Melbourne, 1999), pp. 201–17.

[81] See her letter to Devaux in 1739 (p. 273, above).

[82] Francisque Sarcey, *Quarante Ans de Théâtre*, 8 vols (Paris, 1900), vol. 2, p. 414.

[83] *La Nièce*, also listed by Micault, may be *La Nièce vengée*, Foire Saint-Laurent 1731. *Les Quatre Spectacles* was probably an ambigu comique.

of Lesage, Fuzelier and d'Orneval, towards a more sentimental, frequently pastoral, genre in which elegant vocal music and dancing were becoming ever more important.

On two evenings at the end of the season, on either side of the single performance of *Cénie*, Francisque gave an entertainment called *Le Spectacle brillant*. As Max Fuchs notes, this evening was one of only two occasions on which Micault's *Mercure* thought it worthwhile to comment on the lighting.[84] Instead of the usual smoky, greasy, and malodorous tallow candles or oil lamps, there were at least two hundred of the beeswax candles normally reserved for special occasions in churches and palaces, all reflected in large mirrors placed around the theatre. Micault's account makes it clear that Francisque's company also provided an unusually grand gala of acting, singing and dancing:

> Il y eut beaucoup de monde et la représentation valut bien 700 livres; ils donnèrent *Le Nouveau Monde*, comédie en trois actes, et *Le Magnifique*, comédie en deux; il y eut six intermèdes de chants et de danse, et le tout sans interruption.[85]

> [There were many people present and the performance made 700 livres; *Le Nouveau monde* [by Pellegrin], a comedy in three acts, and *Le Magnifique* [by Houdart de la Motte], a comedy in two, were performed; there were six interludes of singing and dancing, and all without interruption.]

This event proved so popular that the company's final performance on 2 April is described by Micault simply as *Le Nouveau Spectacle brillant*. Saturday 3 April was the eve of Palm Sunday when the theatres were obliged to close for Easter, so the *Spectacle brillant* was also *Le Spectacle de clôture*, the last performance before Holy Week.

After this season, there are no further known records of performances by Francisque's company. In 1751 Francisque was in his early sixties and, as Micault's diary shows, he was reputed to be extremely rich. It would not be surprising if he now decided to put an end to his travels round the provinces. If this was the case, his 'spectacle brillant' would have been a fitting end to a brilliant career.

---

[84] Fuchs, *VT*, p. 89, p. 216. Micault in fact mentions three occasions. The first was 25, not 27 March, and Fuchs failed to note that Francisque's *Spectacle brillant* was repeated on 2 April.

[85] *Mercure Dijonnais*, p. 122.

15

Francisque's legacy and family fortunes

Perhaps because he had no children of his own, Francisque was intimately linked to the lives and careers of his siblings' children. During his retirement in Nantes (which may not have been complete), he could have observed their careers benefitting from what contemporaries recognised as an explosion of enthusiasm for the theatre. The years 1740 to 1770 saw an enormous expansion in the construction of permanent theatre buildings and in the public demand for entertainment. In particular, the prestige of French culture meant competition for the best French performers,[1] and the next generation of the Moylin-Sallé-Cochois family, at least six of whom became actors and/or dancers, were pursuing careers that carried their uncle's legacy to every corner of Europe.

Marie Sallé

Unlike all her cousins, however, Marie Sallé was to be firmly rooted in Paris. By the late 1730s, after years of restless coming and going between Paris and London, she finally made her peace with the Opéra, where she was given the freedom to choreograph several memorable roles. When she formally retired in June 1740 at the age of thirty-one, she was granted a special royal pension, though she had nowhere near the required years of service. She continued to make occasional appearances, though only by royal command, and only in the Paris region. She probably trained younger dancers at the Opéra-comique,[2] and it has been suggested that she contributed to Favart's *L'Ambigu de la folie ou Le Ballet des dindons*, choreographed by Lany and given at the Foire Saint-Laurent in August 1743. This work, which includes a parody of Sallé's

---

[1] See Lauren R. Clay, *Stagestruck: The Business of Theatre in Eighteenth-Century France and Its Colonies* (Ithaca, 2013). Rahul Markovits, 'L'« Europe française », une domination Culturelle? Kaunitz et le théâtre français à Vienne au XVIIIe siècle', *Annales. Histoire, Sciences Sociales* 2012/3, pp. 717–751, at p. 740.

[2] Sarah McCleave informs me that an unpublished manuscript by Stanley Vince, now in her possession, gives evidence that Sallé was invited to teach at the fairs.

Ballet des Fleurs in the Fuzelier-Rameau *Les Indes galantes*,[3] was something of a Lilliputian affair: the young Jean-George Noverre was sixteen, but two of the leading female dancers were only ten and eight years old. Two years later both Noverre and Lany were recruited for Berlin.

Did Sallé ever return to England? Dacier notes that some of her contemporaries thought this, though he could find no evidence of it.[4] An unsubstantiated and uncorroborated account, written some ten years after the event it claims to describe, was included in an anonymous article (*Mémoires d'un Musicien*) which appeared in three numbers of the *Journal Encyclopédique* in May–June 1756, just a month before Sallé's death in obscurity:

> Mlle. Sallé, Danseuse Françoise, qui scavoit unir les mœurs les plus respectables aux plus rares talens, faisoit assez admirer sur le Théâtre de Londres des graces que les Anglois n'avoient pas encore connues, & qui ne naissent, & ne peuvent s'acquerir qu'en France. Je l'y avois connue, elle parut fort aise de me voir, & je fus temoin du sacrifice qu'elle n'hésita point de faire de plus de mille Louis qui auroient dû lui revenir de son engagement avec Hendel, quoique sollicité par les plus grands Seigneurs de Londre de le rompre, pour en prendre un nouveau avec un entrepreneur qu'un caprice leur faisoit espérer plus agréable.
>
> [Mlle Sallé, the French dancer in whom the most respectable morals were united with the rarest talents, caused admiration on the London stage for graceful qualities which the English had not hitherto seen, and which are created and acquired only in France. I had known her there; she seemed most content to receive me, and I was witness to her unhesitating sacrifice of over a thousand *louis* which ought to have accrued from her engagement with Handel, even though she was solicited by the greatest lords in London to break it off, which a caprice led them to speculate would be more desirable.][5]

In a 1996 article by David Charlton and Sarah Hibbard, these few lines became the subject of scholarly speculation on the possibility of Sallé's return

---

[3] See Edward Nye, 'L'Allégorie dans le ballet d'action: Marie Sallé à travers l'écho des parodies', *Revue d'Histoire littéraire de la France* 108:2 (2008), 289–309, at pp. 299–300.

[4] Dacier, p. 253.

[5] *Journal encyclopedique*, 14 (1756), 47–48, as translated in David Charlton and Sarah Hibbard, '"My father was a poor Parisian musician": a memoir (1756) concerning Rameau, Handel's Library and Sallé', *Journal of the Royal Musical Association*, 128:2 (2003), 161–199, [47–48 in the original], at p. 197.

to London in 1746, a discussion taken up and amplified by Sarah McCleave.[6] Whatever the facts of this matter may be, one thing is clear: after leaving London in June 1735, Marie Sallé was never again to dance on the English stage.

Away from the stage, Sallé avoided the limelight and lived quietly and modestly in the rue Saint-Honoré with her companion Rebecca Wick. The two women made their wills in 1751, each leaving her entire estate to the other. Marie Sallé's last known performances were at Fontainebleau in the autumn of 1752. Even in these last years, however, there are further examples of her unpredictable behaviour. Dacier notes her unexplained disappearance between 1747 and 1750, and her equally unexplained reappearance on the stage in 1752.[7] The fact that she had made her will in the previous year might be suggestive of recent illness, and this seems the most viable explanation for a history of behaviour which would have been tolerated in very few other performers.

She died, after another long illness, on 24 July 1756, and was buried in the church of Saint-Roch in the rue Saint-Honoré, in the presence of her uncle Francisque.

> L'an mil sept cent cinquante-six, le vingt-neuf juillet, a été inhumé en cette église le corps de Marie Sallé, fille, décédée avant-hier en cette paroisse, rue Saint Honoré, âgée de quarante-neuf ans environ.[8] Présents: François Moylin, bourgeois de Paris, oncle de la défunte, demeurant susdites rue et paroisse, et Denis de La Noue, marchand de vin, demeurant mêmes rue et paroisse, qui ont signé à la minute. Collationné à l'original par moi prêtre soussigné, dépositaire desdits registres, ce 22 novembre 1757. Lourdes [prêtre].[9]

> [In the year 1756, on the twenty-ninth of July, the body of Marie Sallé, spinster, who died the day before yesterday in this parish, rue Saint Honoré, about forty-nine years old, was buried in this church. Present: François Moylin, bourgeois of Paris, uncle of the deceased, residing in the above-mentioned street and parish, and Denis de La Noue, wine merchant, of the same street and parish, who signed the register. Collated with the original by me, undersigned priest, keeper of the said registers, this 22nd of November, 1757. Lourdes.]

---

[6] See Charlton and Hibbard, *"'My father was a poor Parisian musician'"*, p. 197; Sarah McCleave, *Dance in Handel's London Operas* (Rochester, NY, 2013), pp. 119–20.

[7] Dacier, p. 270.

[8] This statement on her death certificate is the reason why Marie Sallé's birth date was given as 1707 in most biographies until the discovery of her baptismal certificate in 2018 by Jean-Philippe van Aelbrouck.

[9] Dacier, p. 287.

All the registers of the church of Saint-Roch were destroyed during the Revolution and Sallé's death certificate has survived only because a copy, now in the Archives Nationales, was sent to the royal household by Rebecca Wick when she was claiming a payment of arrears from Sallé's pension.

Francisque, Simon, and Marguerite Cochois, along with a paternal uncle named Sallé of whom nothing is known, contested Sallé's will. Thanks to these documents, we also know that in 1757 François Moylin, 'bourgeois de Paris', was living in the rue Saint-Honoré, though only for the duration of this lawsuit, which he was conducting on behalf of the other members of the family. Simon was living in retirement in Toulouse; and Marguerite, now 'la veuve Cochois', was in Nancy.[10] As Dacier has pointed out, nothing further seems to have come of their claims. Francisque's signature on this document is the last known example of his handwriting.

Martin Simon Moylin

Martin Simon, son of Francisque's brother Guillaume, was born in Lille in 1720, and grew up with his uncle's troupe. In the early 1740s he married another company member, Catherine Fompré (sometimes Fonpré/Defonpré etc.). She was probably the daughter of Marie-Antoinette Tourneville, who had been with Francisque's company in London in 1734–5, and who at that time was described in a wedding certificate as the widow Defompré; she acted as godmother when the son of Martin and Catherine, Guillaume-Antoine, was baptised in Lille on 3 June 1744 and died there only ten days later.[11] Martin seems to have had ambitions. The *Mercure* of 14 August 1741 reports a revival at the Comédie-Italienne of *l'Embarras des richesses*, in which 'le Sr. Moylin, comédien de la troupe qui était à Compiègne l'année dernière, débuta pour la première fois sur le théâtre de l'Hôtel de Bourgogne et y joua le rôle d'Arlequin avec applaudissement.'[12] [in which Mr. Moylin, an actor from the troupe which was in Compiègne last year, made his début on the stage of the Hotel de Bourgogne and played the role of Arlequin to applause.] Emile Dacier claimed that this actor was Simon Moylin but in 1741 Simon was much too old to appear (let alone 'débuter') as Arlequin either at the fairs or, even more improbably, at the Comédie-Italienne.[13] It seems far more likely that the actor in question was Martin Simon Moylin, who was 21 years old, an appropriate age for a beginner. Antoine d'Origny's account of his début is far more negative: 'cette tentative fut si malheureuse, qu'il ne tarda point à renoncer au

---

[10] AM Toulouse, GG 344 (St-Étienne).
[11] AM Lille, 1GG/77 (St-Étienne); AM Lille, 1GG/95 (St-Étienne).
[12] *Mercure*, August 1741, p. 1885.
[13] Dacier, p. 289, n.1.

Théâtre, pour lequel il avait moins de dispositions que de goût'[14] [this attempt was so unfortunate that he soon gave up the theatre, for which he had less talent than inclination]. In fact, far from giving up the theatre, Martin Simon continued to tour the provinces. He is next heard of in October 1751, as 'Martin Moylin, danseur, originaire de Lille en Flandres âgé d'environ trente ans' [a dancer, from Lille in Flanders, aged about thirty], in the troupe of Deshayes in Lorient, where Deshayes was authorised to present 'des comédies françaises et italiennes.'[15] 'Deshayes' could well be the actor who had been with Francisque in London and Nancy.[16] In Amsterdam between July 1752 and July 1753 the names of Martin Moylin and François Deshayes appear in press advertisements for a company of French players,[17] showing that they were performing many of the plays which had been in Francisque's repertoire in London. The plays of the Comédie-Italienne had largely disappeared from Francisque's last season in Dijon, but they feature prominently in the Amsterdam repertoire. Although his first wife was still alive, while in Amsterdam, Martin married Marie Fromageot [Fromajot], in the French Catholic chapel.[18] A Benefit for the couple was announced in the *Amsterdamsche Courant* of 10 March 1753. Its programme was *Le Nouveau Monde*, a 'pièce à grand Spectacle' (spectacular play) interspersed with extensive song and dance; Francisque had produced the same piece as a 'Spectacle brilliant', at which Martin may well have been present, two years earlier in Dijon.[19]

The records of the births or baptisms of the couple's children – Julie in Nantes in 1750, Matthieu in Dunkirk in 1753, Marie Anne in Besançon in 1757[20] – make it clear that they were still touring, but not always successfully. In Amiens a legal complaint for non-payment was filed by some innkeepers in 20 April 1755, against 'M. et Mme Moulain comédiens', who are almost certainly Martin and his wife.[21] Two months later, still in Amiens,

---

[14] Antoine d'Origny, *Annales du Théâtre italien depuis son origine jusqu'à ce jour* 3 vols (Paris, 1788), vol. 1, p. 178.

[15] Jean-Louis Debauve, 'Théâtre et Spectacles à Lorient au XVIIIe siècle', *Revue d'Histoire du Théâtre*, 18:1 (1966), 1–166, at pp. 13–15. Debauve speculates, wrongly, that Martin might be a son of Francisque Moylin.

[16] This seems to me further evidence that the Deshayes in London and Nancy was not the de Hesse/Dehesse of the Comédie Italienne (see, above, [n.7, pp. 349–50]).

[17] See Jan Fransen, *Les Comédiens français en Hollande au XVIIe et au XVIIIe siècle* ([Paris, 1925] repr. Geneva, 1978), p. 358.

[18] AM Besançon, GG 161 (Saint Maurice). This document is the source of the information concerning the couple's marriage in Amsterdam.

[19] Rudolf Rasch, *Muzikale advertenties in nederlandse kranten, 1621–1794* (Utrecht, 2018).

[20] AM Besançon, GG 161 (Saint Maurice).

[21] AM Amiens, FF 1302.

the couple suffered the loss of their two-year old son Matthieu.[22] Martin Moylin eventually settled in Marseille, where he died in 1768.[23] (His first wife, bound unlike him by French law, waited until the following year to remarry.) Martin's daughter Marie Anne was married in Marseille in 1776 to the actor, translator and dramatist 'Gilles-Anselme Bruyas, dit Bursay, chevalier de grâce de l'ordre religieux et militaire de Christ et académicien des arcades de Rome'[24] [honorary knight of the religious and military order of Christ and member of the Roman Arcadian Academy]. After the births of two children, the family moved to Brussels. When another daughter was baptised in 1789, the family is described as 'demeurant à la Monnaie sur la Comédie'[25] [living at La Monnaie beside the theatre]. Almost sixty years after Francisque's season at the Théâtre de la Monnaie, his great-niece and her children returned in style.

The Cochois Children

The five children of Marguerite and Michel Cochois – Francis, Barbe (known as Babet), Marianne, Marionette and Gogo – had grown up in Francisque's companies and seem to have remained with him until they were recruited for the court of Frederick the Great. The whole family arrived in Berlin in autumn 1742 and performances began in Frederick's new theatre in December of that year.[26] Thanks to the memoirs of the Chevalier de Mainvillers, we have a colourful account of their offstage intrigues (mostly amorous). The virtuous and watchful Madame Cochois presided so imperiously over her brood that gossips at court called her 'la reine mère' [the queen mother].[27] Husband Michel Cochois, now old and retired, was given a pittance by his wife to drink and gamble with his cronies. His absences allowed the young de Mainvillers to form a passionate attachment to Madame Cochois and he wished that 'l'éternel Cochois' would 'avoir la complaisance de se dépêcher de mourir,

---

[22] AM Amiens, registre 17 (St-Firmin-en-Castillon).

[23] AM Marseille, GG 350 (St-Ferréol).

[24] AM Marseille, GG 229 (St-Martin). Les Arcades de Rome were a distinguished literary society, originally founded by poets in the court of Queen Christina of Sweden, which had branches in France as well as Italy.

[25] Bruxelles, Archives de la Ville, Registres paroissiaux, registre 174 (Ste-Gudule).

[26] For a full account of Frederick's company in Berlin, see Jean-Jacques Olivier, *Les Comédiens Français dans les Cours d'Allemagne au XVIIIe siècle, deuxième série: la cour royale de Prusse* ([Paris, 1901–1905], Geneva, 1971).

[27] Gustave Desnoiresterres, *Voltaire et la société au XVIIIe siècle* 8 vols ([Paris, 1871] Berlin, 2010), vol. 4, p. 24.

pour me céder la main et le lit de sa femme'[28] [be good enough to hurry up and die, and leave me the hand and the bed of his wife]. The Chevalier's passion was however frustrated by her virtue, 'une barrière impenetrable'[29] [an impenetrable barrier].

The three older siblings danced in the court ballets, and Marianne Cochois rivalled the famous La Barbarina as one of Frederick's favourite dancers. Like her sister and her famous cousin, she seems to have had a high sense of decorum. In 1747 she visited Paris in the company of the Marquis d'Argens, who reported approvingly to King Frederick,

> La Muse de la danse est arrivée en fort bonne santé à Paris; je l'ai remise à sa cousine, la Sallé. Je suis fort content de sa conduite; elle a refusé de danser à l'armée, malgré les sollicitations de plusieurs seigneurs qui l'ont vue et reconnue à Liège; il faut qu'elle continue de même à Paris.[30]

> [The Muse of The Dance arrived in very good health in Paris; I entrusted her to her cousin, Sallé. I am very happy with her conduct; she refused to dance for the army, despite the entreaties of several lords who saw her and recognised her at Liège; she must continue thus in Paris.]

The fact that Marianne was apparently staying with Sallé indicates that the family ties were still close. D'Argens' last sentence may reflect his concern that Marianne would be lured back to Paris, and in fact, although she became principal dancer in Berlin after the departure of La Barbarina, she did return to Paris in 1748, married the Parisian ballet master Desplaces, and disappeared from view in the 1750s.

Barbe, known as Babet, was a versatile actress and dancer who, as d'Argens wrote to Frederick the Great, was admired in Paris as 'une fille de beaucoup

---

[28] Henry Lyonnet, *Dictionnaire des comédiens français* ([Paris, 1912]; repr. Geneva, 1969), vol 1, p. 366. This again disproves Dacier's contention (p. 290, note 1) that she was already a widow by 1736.

[29] Chevalier de Mainvillers, *Le Petit-maître philosophe: ou voyage et avantures de Genu Soalhat, Chevalier de Mainvillers, dans les principales cours de l'Europe* (London, 1751), vol. 3, pp. 26–7, and p. 42. There seems little reason to doubt de Mainvillers' account of his stay in Berlin, many aspects of which can be corroborated from other sources. He said that it would have made 'un bel roman' and in fact it inspired a five-act comedy by Alexandre de Longpré, *La famille Cochois, ou Un mariage dans la coulisse*, performed in Paris at the Théâtre de l'Odéon in 1844.

[30] The marquis d'Argens to Frédéric, Paris, 15 August 1747. in Frédéric le Grand, *Œuvres*. https://friedrich.uni-trier.de/fr/oeuvresOctavo/19/18/.

d'esprit' [a very clever woman] and even coveted by the Comédie-Française.[31] As well as acting and dancing, Babet was a gifted linguist, writer and minor 'philosophe'; she married the Marquis d'Argens in January 1749 and eventually retired with her husband to his house near Aix-en-Provence. The family were visited by Casanova, who left a lively account of his cordial reception at the country house of d'Argens' brother, the marquis d'Éguilles.[32] After the death of her husband in 1771, Babet continued to correspond with Voltaire, Mirabeau and members of the Prussian royal family. She died in Aix-en-Provence on 29 February 1792.[33]

In the painting of Babet on stage by Antoine Pesne, now in Berlin's Charlottenburg Palace, the small masked figure peering from the bushes to her left is surely her brother, the Arlequin Francis Cochois. Francis, who had been trained almost from infancy by his uncle Francisque, became a celebrated Arlequin in Berlin. On 5 December 1742 King Frederick wrote to his sister, 'Aujourd'hui nous avons comédie; l'Arlequin est aussi bon qu'on en puisse avoir.' [We have a play today; the Arlequin is as good a one as could be found anywhere]. Francis also danced in the corps de ballet with both his sisters. In 1745, when the famous dancer-choreographer Jean-Barthélemy Lany produced his *Pygmalion et Psyché, ballet pantomime*, the eighteen-year-old Jean-Georges Noverre, Marianne Cochois and Francis Cochois are listed among the dancers.[34] Sarah McCleave suggests that Lany, as 'Sallé's former Opéra-Comique colleague',[35] was influenced by her work in his production of this ballet; more to the point is the fact that the whole Cochois family had almost certainly seen their illustrious Sallé cousin dance as Galatea in London in 1734–5. Her first Pygmalion, Jean-Baptiste Malter, also danced with, and probably continued to instruct the Cochois children in London and Nancy. Thus, the Cochois siblings, along with their parents, were uniquely well-placed to give both Lany and Noverre first-hand details of their cousin's innovations. Sadly, any advice they may have given, especially on the revolutionary simplicity of Marie's costume, seems to have gone unheeded. Jean-Jacques Olivier notes that the lavishly ornamented and bejewelled ballet costumes were worthy of a painting by Lancret.[36]

---

[31] The marquis d'Argens to Frédéric, Paris, 5 September 1747. in Frédéric le Grand, *Œuvres*. https://friedrich.uni-trier.de/fr/oeuvresOctavo/19/25/.

[32] Giacomo Casanova, *Mémoires de J. Casanova de Seingalt, écrits par lui-même* 8 vols (Paris, 1880), vol. 8, chapter 1.

[33] AM Aix-en-Provence, 1792 (Saint-Sauveur). Through the couple's only child, Barbe Boyer d'Argens, the descendants of Francisque's niece Babet can be traced to the present day.

[34] Noverre was in the Berlin corps de ballet from 1744 to 1747.

[35] McCleave, 'Marie Sallé, a Wise Professional Woman of Influence', in Lynn Matluck Brooks, ed., *Women's Work: Making Dance in Europe before 1800* (Madison, 2007), p. 174.

[36] Olivier, *Les Comédiens Français*, p. 66.

Fig. 12   Babet Cochois and her brother Francis (in Arlequin mask), by Antoine Pesne, now in Charlottenburg Palace, Berlin (Alamy).

Both the talents and temperament of Francis Cochois are recalled in the Mainvillers memoirs:

> Pour Cochois fils, excellent Arlequin, et encore meilleur Comique brillant, il était quelquefois aimable, et fort souvent d'une humeur insupportable [....] Généreux au surplus au-delà de toute expression, il portait dans le corps d'un Comédien l'âme d'un Roi [...].[37]
>
> [As for Cochois the son, an excellent Arlequin and an even better comic actor, he was sometimes amiable, and very often in an unbearable mood [...]. Moreover, he was generous to a fault, and he had the soul of a king in the body of an actor.]

A letter from the Baron de Sweerts to Frederick reveals that on one occasion Francis suggested an alternative to the play that the King had requested:

> Couchoy [Cochois] m'a assuré que dans celle qu'ils voudront donner mercredi prochain, il y avait beaucoup plus de jeu que dans *Arlequin Apprenti philosophe* dont les rôles ne peuvent être copiés et appris jusqu'à ce temps-là; cette pièce s'appelle *l'Embarras des Richesses*.[38]
>
> [Couchoy [Cochois] assured me that in the one they want to give next Wednesday there was much more action than in *Arlequin apprenti philosophe*, whose roles cannot be copied and learned by then; the play is called *L'Embarras des richesses* ...]

Francis had of course seen Francisque as Arlequin in this play in London in 1734–5, with his parents taking minor parts.

By the mid-1740s, Frederick was more concerned with war than with court entertainments and his notorious stinginess led many members of the Berlin company to look for more lucrative positions elsewhere. In 1746/7 Francis Cochois was lured to the St Petersburg court of the Francophile Russian Empress Elizabeth. The marquis d'Argens viewed his loss as a serious blow: 'c'était, il est vrai, un fou et un insolent; mais c'était un excellent comédien, aussi au-dessus de tous les comiques de la Comédie-Française de Paris que Hauteville était en folie au-dessus de tous ses camarades.'[39] [it is true he was mad and insolent; but he was an excellent actor, as far above all the comic

---

[37] De Mainvillers, *Petit-maître*, vol. 3, pp. 26–7. Julia Gasper summarises de Mainvillers' amusing account in Chapter 7 of *The Marquis d'Argens: A Philosophical Life* (Plymouth, 2014).

[38] Olivier, *Les Comédiens Français*, pp. 100–1.

[39] The marquis d'Argens to Frederick, Paris, 5 September 1747, in Frédéric le Grand, *Œuvres* https://friedrich.uni-trier.de/fr/oeuvresOctavo/19/25/.

actors of the Comédie-Française in Paris as Hauteville was above all his comrades in madness.]

Francis Cochois and François de Hauteville were among the new recruits from Berlin in St Petersburg, but the company seems not to have prospered, partly because of the rise in the 1750s of a vigorous native Russian language theatre. By 1758 most of the French actors had gone. Dieudonné Thiébault wrote later that Francis Cochois died in Russia 'de mélancolie, dans un âge peu avancé, et sans héritiers'[40] [of melancholy at an early age, and without heirs]. However, an item in a Moscow newspaper in July 1758 indicates that Cochois was planning to return to France,[41] and Julia Gasper in her study of the Marquis d'Argens claims that in 1759 he 'resumed acting at the Comédie-Française.'[42] Francis Cochois, who had never performed at either of the official theatres, could not 'resume' acting there, and the Cochois who made his début at the Comédie-Française on 10 November 1759 cannot be identified with Francis. Scant though the evidence is on both sides, on balance, it seems likely that Francis did indeed die in Russia or on the voyage home.

Most accounts speak only of three Cochois children, but de Mainvillers' memoirs reveal that in Berlin there were in fact two more daughters, Gogo and Marionette. Gogo (surely a pet name) was still a child around 1742–3, but Marionette was old enough to have been courted by Alexandre, Marquis d'Eguilles, brother of the Marquis d'Argens, during his brief visit to Berlin, and later by Claude Darget, the Prussian king's secretary.[43] According to de Mainvillers, Francis Cochois thwarted Darget's courtship in favour of Noverre, who, long before he became 'father of the dance', had hoped to wed Marionette Cochois. Had he done so, he would have become a cousin by marriage to the dancer he admired above all others, Marie Sallé. Sadly, both Marionette and Gogo, who would surely have followed their siblings onto the stage, died of smallpox in Berlin c. 1745–6. De Mainvillers wrote, 'Ces deux jolies filles

---

[40] Dieudonné Thiébault, *Mes Souvenirs de vingt ans de séjour à Berlin* 5 vols (Paris, 1805), vol. 5, p. 352. 'Cochois (mort à Saint Petersbourg en 1758).' A modern researcher seems to support this view: see Robert-Aloys Mooser, *Annales de la Musique et des Musiciens en Russie au 18me siècle* (Geneva, 1948), p. 230.

[41] 'The actor Cochois departs from here for France, and those who have any business with him can find him on the Admiralty Side on Lugovaya street in the house of the Armenian merchant Shiriman.' *Sankt-Peterburgskie Vedomosti*, 54, 7 July 1758 [18 July NS]. The street is now called Bolshaya Morskaya and the house is still standing today. I am grateful to my friend and colleague Ekaterina Chertkovskaya for providing this information.

[42] Gasper, *Marquis*, p. 159.

[43] Marionette must have been born around 1727. She may have been just old enough to be one of 'Cochois' Lilliputians' in London in 1734–5.

moururent entre les bras de leur Mère et entre les miens'[44] [These two pretty girls died in their mother's arms and mine]. In 1747, when the theatre director withdrew Madame Cochois' pension and ordered her to cease interfering in the affairs of her remaining daughters, she abandoned her family and, helped by the adoring de Mainvillers, fled to Lorraine. Unlikely as this sounds, this event is confirmed by a letter of March 1747 from King Frederick's sister, Crown Princess Luise Ulrike of Sweden: 'La fuite de la vieille Cochois devait avoir mis la comédie en désordre. Je n'aurais jamais cru qu'elle eût fait cette incartade.'[45] [The flight of old Madame Cochois must have thrown the theatre into disarray. I never imagined she would commit such a misdemeanor.] Her sudden departure was thought by some to be an elopement, but de Mainvillers, who accompanied her as far as Lunéville, left her there without receiving his hoped-for 'reward'. Madame Cochois was still living in nearby Nancy, capital of Lorraine, in 1756, when, as 'la veuve Cochois', she contested her niece's will. She was eventually reconciled with Babet, marquise d'Argens, and ended her days in her daughter's house in Provence.[46]

Francisque

The evidence of parish registers recently discovered by Jean-Philippe van Aelbrouck makes it possible to reconstruct something of Francisque's later years. He outlived all his siblings, with the possible exception of Marguerite, whose date of death is still unknown. Guillaume Moylin died in Bordeaux in 1748. Simon Moylin died in Toulouse on 5 November 1767, aged seventy. In Nantes, Jean-Baptiste Malter, who had remarried after Catherine Labbé's death, died on 8 April 1758. His children, who had settled in Nantes, seem to have become a family to the Moylins. When Francisque's wife Marie-Catherine died on 17 October 1761, one of those present was Étienne Malter, a son of Jean-Baptiste. Marie-Catherine's death certificate stated her age as ninety, which seems unlikely, given that both she and Francisque were described as 'mineurs' on their marriage certificate in 1710. As for Francisque

---

44 De Mainvillers, *Petit-Maître*, vol. 3, pp. 70–1. De Mainvillers does not give the date for this event; I assume that it must have been 1745–6.

45 Luise Ulrike, *Luise Ulrike, die schwedische Schwester Friedrichs des Großen: Ungedruckte Briefe an Mitglieder des preußischen Königshauses*, ed. Fritz Arnheim 2 vols (Gotha, 1910), vol. 2, p. 19. Another of Madame de Cochois' admirers may have been the playwright Michel Procope-Couteaux, in whose first play the young Marguerite had performed in 1719. At his death in 1753 he left a bequest to 'la femme Cochois'. See Gustave Bord, *La Franc-maçonnerie en France des origines à 1815* (Paris, 1908), p. 306.

46 Elsie Johnston, *Le Marquis d'Argens: sa vie et ses œuvres* (Paris, 1928; repr. Geneva, 1971), p. 135.

himself, 'François Moylin, en son vivant veuf de Catherine Lesuisse, âgé de quatre vingt deux ans' [François Moylin, widower of Catherine Lesuisse, aged eighty-two], was buried in Nantes on 13 January 1770.[47] Again, it is possible that the age given here was only a guess, since no member of the Moylin family was present. The register in Nantes was signed by François Malter, the Malter son who had been baptised in Grenoble in October 1729.

Just three years after the death of Francisque, on 27 January 1773, a company led by a certain Desmarets and a man who claimed to be 'François Moylin, dit Francisque' performed in Angers, probably coming from Nantes. In April 1783 a new twelve-year licence was granted by the comte de Provence, governor of Anjou, to 'le sieur Moylin dit Francisque'.[48] Who might this person have been? There was indeed another François Moylin, the son of Francisque's brother Guillaume. He was born in La Rochelle in 1717 and Francisque was his godfather, but this was not he. The matter is clarified in the parish registers of Nantes. On 26 March 1788, the records of the Church of Saint Nicolas in Nantes record the death at the age of 45 of 'le Sieur François Moilin, fils de Sr. François Moilin dit Francisque'. However, the parish priest, who had found a birth certificate among the papers of the deceased, added a corrective marginal note stating that the man was in reality the illegitimate son of unknown parents.[49] The Comte de Provence, informed of this death three days later, granted the Moylin licence to a new manager.[50] This curious postscript suggests that for almost twenty years after his death, the name 'François Moylin dit Francisque' still had a certain prestige and celebrity in the region of Nantes.

Francisque's Cultural Legacy

In retrospect, it is possible to see that the Moylin-Sallé-Cochois family, over half a century, was quite exceptional in the theatre world, both within and beyond the borders of France. In an age when itinerant players were ranked not far above vagabonds, and 'filles d'opéra' were thought to be little better than prostitutes, they received an unusual degree of respect. Francisque had led the way at the Paris Fairs between 1715 and 1726 with his stubborn refusal to conform to the straitjacket conditions imposed by the official theatres. With

---

[47] AM Nantes (Saint-Similien), 1770, vue 4/96. He was buried in the cemetery of Saint Similien. The death certificate gives his residence as Place de Bretagne, an ancient market place destroyed by bombing in 1943.

[48] See Emile Queruau-Lamerie, *Notice sur le théâtre d'Angers (1755–1825)* (Angers, 1889), pp. 29, 68, 75.

[49] I am grateful to Jean-Philippe van Aelbrouck for giving me a transcript of the parish register.

[50] Queruau-Lamerie, *Notice sur le théâtre d'Angers,* p. 76.

the help of his playwrights, this versatile actor-impresario made his powerful enemies appear ridiculous. In 1722, when all seemed lost, in alliance with Alexis Piron he created the monologue *Arlequin Deucalion*, a *tour de force* of personal and artistic insubordination; and when all speech was banned, he brazenly staged 'by his own authority' a fully spoken prologue and the three-act *Tirésias*, paying for his temerity with the closure of his theatre. In Brussels he refused to lower his subscription prices, performing to a half-empty theatre rather than giving in to the demands of the courtiers and the gentry. Both in Paris and in London, he seems to have attracted an audience of the 'persons of quality' mentioned by Lady Pennyman and by the London press, and the Latin tags that Piron sometimes gave him to speak suggest that he was better educated than many fairground performers.

Marie Sallé, encouraged and emboldened by her family's example, refused time and again to conform to the low production standards of her managers (Lebeuf at the Paris Opéra and John Rich in London) or the lax moral codes of her fellow dancers at the Opéra. Her letter to the Duchess of Richmond, who entrusted Sallé with the teaching of her children, reveals her professionalism and dedication to her art.[51] It seems that Francisque's sister Marguerite Cochois, whose high moral standards were a source of wonder at the Berlin court, also inculcated self-respect into all her children, which, in the case of Francis Cochois, was something more like high-handedness. Babet Cochois became the wife and 'philosophical' correspondent of the marquis d'Argens, at a time when any other actress in Europe might have been content to be his mistress. In an age of patronage and deference, these performers shared a powerful sense of independence, both on and off the stage.

Many historians of eighteenth-century French theatre focus on the second half of the century, a period for which fuller documentary evidence has survived. Yet, as I hope the foregoing chapters have shown, Francisque Moylin and his family had already achieved in the first half of the century many of the things which have been hailed as innovations in the second half. What Lauren Clay has said of a later generation of established provincial theatres – 'the pace of production as well as the sheer variety of the repertory presented by these companies is almost inconceivable' – was already true of Francisque.[52] When, in 1726, Francisque turned his back on the Fairs (and the Fair repertoire), he made Parisian theatrical high culture accessible to provincial audiences who rarely if ever had the opportunity of visiting the capital. By the end of the eighteenth century only three French cities had more than 100,000 inhabitants: Paris, Lyon, and Bordeaux, closely followed by Nantes, Rouen, Lille and

---

[51] Unlike Sallé, who reportedly refused a thousand guineas for her 'favours', her near contemporary, the soprano Mlle Petitpas, was said to have returned from London 'avec 40,000 livres, beaucoup de joie et un petit mylord dans le ventre.' [with 40,000 pounds, a lot of joy and a little milord in her belly]; Dacier, p. 111.

[52] Clay, *Stagestruck*, p. 114.

Toulouse.[53] While travel conditions would improve in the second half of the century, Francisque's troupe regularly visited every one of these major cities at a time when travel from Paris to the borders of France took weeks rather than days and journeys between London and Paris could take even longer. In all, members of the Moylin-Sallé-Cochois clan performed in at least 30 towns and cities across France, the Low Countries, England, Prussia and Russia, not counting the many stopping places for which no records survive. The only really comparable troupe at the time was led by the Hus brothers, members of another dynasty of provincial players, slightly younger than Francisque. Unlike Francisque, they never ventured to cross the Channel.

Always alert to the differing needs of his different audiences, Francisque often reflected local conditions or events in his programme, whether transporting Barbier's comedy from Lyon to the banks of the Thames or staging an allegorical opera-ballet to celebrate the marriage of the duc de Lorraine with Maria Theresa. He treated the Marseille audience to two characters who spoke only in the local dialect of Provençal, while in Dijon the public applauded '*Gustave Vasa*, fort belle tragédie de M. Piron, notre compatriote'. As the years went on, his vast and varied repertoire evolved further away from Arlequin and the Franco-Italian genre to include the latest works from the official theatres and the Opéra-Comique, culminating, in his last recorded season in Dijon, with a performance of Mme de Graffigny's comedy *Cénie*, just months after its première at the Comédie-Française.

An aspect of Francisque's career which has hitherto received little attention is his involvement in the evolution of pantomime and dance. Francisque's wife had been the leading dancer at the theatre in Bordeaux, and his brother Guillaume was described on his marriage certificate as 'maître à danser'. All Francisque's nieces and nephews were dancers from early childhood and all of them took their first steps in their uncle's troupe, where Guillaume and Francisque must have been their first teachers and models. The mimed *commedia* Night Scenes which Francisque took over from the Alards, Sorin and Baxter, contained simple narratives which are acknowledged forerunners of the pantomimes of Weaver and Rich, and thus of the *ballet d'action* (see p. 162, above). The company's proficiency in dance was further enhanced by the arrival of Jean-Baptiste Malter. Lesage's *Les Comédiens corsaires* made it clear that as early as 1726 the official theatres envied the distinctive dance style of Francisque's company; its ballets in that season were far more elaborate than usual, surely due in no small part to Malter's presence. Although Marie Sallé's innovative creations in the London season of 1733–4 have been hailed as landmarks in the history of dance, little attention has been paid to the fact that these were a joint venture with Malter.

---

[53] Maryse Fabriès-Verfaillie, Pierre Stragiotti, Annie Jouve, *La France des villes: le temps des métropoles?* (Rosny, 2000), pp. 43–5.

In London, despite the hostility to French troupes, individual French dancers were appreciated as members of the patented theatre companies. Since several of Francisque's dancers stayed on in London, their dancing must have been of as high a standard as that of the French soloists at Covent Garden and Drury Lane. Many of the company's young children (the 'Lilliputians' of the 1734–5 season) could have been pupils of Marie Sallé during their stay in London.[54] Marie Chateauneuf, who had danced in London in 1734–5 and had been billed to appear on Francisque's opening night in 1738, returned to London in October 1739, and at Drury Lane on 7 November she performed by command of the Prince and Princess of Wales. She remained in London for several years and was judged by Benjamin Victor to have been 'the best French Dancer here at that Time.'[55] Mimi Forcade seems to have returned from Nantes after the death of her husband in 1746 and her daughters danced at Drury Lane in 1749–50 with 'master Maletere', surely one of the Malter children.[56] The Graniers and their children (former Lilliputians) stayed on through the 1730s and 1740s as both dancers and teachers.[57]

Yet Francisque's most important claim to fame may be his introduction of French theatre in the original language to London audiences. He was responsible for the first performances in England of dozens of important plays, including the 'philosophical' comedies of Marivaux, Delisle and d'Alainval. Unfortunately, in 1738, the Haymarket mob destroyed all hope of Anglo-French theatrical exchanges for the rest of the century. So effective was the rout of what Garrick had called 'Harlequin's Invasion' that by the later years of the century all memory of the enormous success of Francisque's 1734–5 London season had been lost. Indeed, in 1776, the Francophile scholar John Andrews, discussing the Paris theatres, confidently described Arlequin and the Comédie-Italienne as things entirely alien and unknown to British audiences.

> [The French] have, however, one species of drama we are yet utter strangers to, and that is what they call the Italian Comedy, though both plays and actors are mostly French. The principal merit of this entirely depends on the person who acts the part of Harlequin. [...] The wit and ingenuity of the Harlequin on this stage is not merely motional as in our Pantomime entertainments. So far is he from a mute that what he says is the very life of the cause. [...].[58]

---

[54] See Philip Highfill, et al., *A Biographical Dictionary of Actors, Actresses, Musicians, Dancers, Managers, and Other Stage Personnel in London, 1660–1800*, 16 vols (Carbondale, 1973–93), vol. 5, pp. 305–9, vol. 10, pp. 63–5.

[55] Benjamin Victor, *A History of the Theatres of London and Dublin*, 2 vols (London, 1761), vol. 1, p. 38.

[56] Highfill et al., *A Biographical Dictionary*, vol. 5, pp. 361–2.

[57] Highfill et al., *A Biographical Dictionary*, vol. 6, pp. 305–9.

[58] John Andrews, *A comparative view of the French and English Nations, in their Manners, Politics, and Literature* (London, 1785), pp. 354–6. Andrews first published

Andrews, who was born in 1736, knew nothing of the great season of 1734–5 or the riot of 1738, but his glowing evaluation of the French 'speaking Harlequin' serves as an ironic comment on what had been lost to the London stage. The mute and merely 'motional' English Harlequin was already in Garrick's lifetime increasingly confined to pantomimes which themselves, by the nineteenth century, had become seasonal Christmas entertainments. Although silent harlequinades clung on in these pantomimes, much diminished in importance, until the dawn of the twentieth century, they eventually disappeared altogether from the British stage.

After the disaster of 1738, de la Barre wrote patronizingly of Francisque that 'il doit compter pour beaucoup le singulier honneur d'avoir intéressé à son sort deux des plus puissants Royaumes de l'Europe, la Grande-Bretagne et la France'[59] [he must count it a singular honour to have had his case taken up by Great Britain and France, two of the most powerful kingdoms of Europe.] However absurd de la Barre may have found it that so much importance should be given to a mere actor, it is now possible to place Francisque in a wider political context. A recent study by Pauline Lemaigre-Gaffier has discussed how the presence of French theatre companies across Europe contributed to a government policy of propagating French power and influence. 'C'est entre les années 1730 et les années 1750 que le théâtre galant, art de cour par excellence, est utilisé de manière volontariste comme instrument de puissance à l'encontre des nations étrangères'[60] [It was between the 1730s and the 1750s that 'le théâtre galant', a courtly art par excellence, was deliberately used as an instrument of power against foreign nations.] At the end of the Seven Years' War, after the defeat of France and the loss of her colonies, Voltaire wrote, 'Aimons le théâtre, c'est la seule gloire qui nous reste …' [Let's love the theatre; it's the only glory that remains to us]. The statesman César de Choiseul-Praslin was also convinced that the presence of travelling companies of French actors across Europe could do more than armies; it constituted 'le moyen de faire goûter aux autres nations notre Théâtre et notre littérature et d'étendre l'usage de la langue française en Europe ce qui est un avantage réel et une espèce de gloire pour notre nation'[61] [the way to give other countries a taste for our theatre and our literature and to extend the use of the French language in Europe, which is a real advantage and a kind of glory for our

---

a shorter version in French as *Essai sur le caractère et les mœurs des François comparés à ceux des Anglais* (London, [1776]). The British Library holds only the French edition.

[59] Antoine de la Barre de Beaumarchais, *Amusemens Littéraires: ou Correspondance Politique, Rhétorique, Philosophique, Critique, et Galante pour l'Année MDCCXXXVIII*, 2 vols (Frankfurt, 1739 and The Hague, 1740), pp. 334–6.

[60] Pauline Lemaigre-Gaffier, *Administrer les menus plaisirs du roi: L'État, la cour et les spectacles dans la France des Lumières* (Champ Vallon, 2016), pp. 318–19.

[61] Lemaigre-Gaffier, *Administrer*, p. 319.

nation]. For Voltaire and the duc de Choiseul-Praslin the theatre was a perfect example of what today is called 'soft power'.[62] However, the gentlemen of Les Menus-Plaisirs who regulated the official theatres felt that the royal companies should be primarily at the service of king and court in Paris and Versailles. Actors from these companies were forbidden to perform in the provinces or abroad without permission, a permission which was often denied. In 1756, the actor Lekain went, without express authorisation, to perform at the court of Bayreuth; on his return he was arrested and incurred the unusual punishment of three weeks' imprisonment. In their Paris, London and Brussels seasons, Francisque and his niece Marie Sallé, and later his Cochois nieces and nephew in the courts of Berlin and Saint-Petersburg, had already played a significant role in realising the aspirations of Voltaire and Choiseul-Praslin.

Although Britain remained stubbornly resistant to French theatrical culture for almost a century after the departure of Francisque, the brief visit to London of the actors Talma and Mlle George in 1817 signalled a softening of attitudes. In the other direction, after a troubled first attempt in 1822, Paris finally welcomed Shakespeare in English in 1827 in the ground-breaking performance of *Hamlet* with Charles Kemble and Harriet Smithson. Thereafter, French plays were tolerated in London at the small Saint James Theatre, with visiting stars such as Mlle Mars in 1828, and Mlle Rachel in 1841. As Barry Duncan explains, these companies could obtain the Lord Chamberlain's licence because they 'were not in competition with the major theatres',[63] but in 1848 the attempt by a visiting company from the Théâtre-Historique to perform Dumas' *Monte Cristo* in French at Drury Lane was greeted with a five-hour riot.[64]

But after one hundred and thirty-three years of resistance and hostility, London made honourable amends when, at last, in May 1871, it welcomed the impoverished Comédie-Française, coming to London from the bleak and beleaguered Paris of the Commune. By an irony which none living could have suspected, their season began with Molière's *Le Tartuffe*, a play which had been given its first London performance in the original by Francisque in 1719. Marivaux's *Le Jeu de l'Amour et du Hasard* also returned in triumph, but without Arlequin. In adopting Marivaux from the Comédie-Italienne, the Comédie-Française had replaced Arlequin with a native French servant, Bourguignon, played in London by the actor Benoît-Constant Coquelin. Not only was this two-month London season an artistic success, but it also

---

[62] See the chapter on 'La Galanterie et la puissance douce', in Rahul Markovits, *Civiliser l'Europe; Politiques du théâtre français au XVIIIe siècle* (Paris, 2014), pp. 57–95.

[63] From 1842, 'it became known as "the French theatre" whilst its notepaper was printed "Théâtre Français, King Street à Londres".' Barry Duncan, *The St James's Theatre; Its Strange & Complete History 1835–1957* (London, 1964), p. 60.

[64] See John Stokes, *The French Actress and Her English Audience* (Cambridge, 2005), pp. 7–8.

rescued the company from financial disaster. Even so, 'a number of articles condemning the Comédie's acting and deploring the "invasion" of the French players in London were also published in conservative newspapers.'[65] Plus ça change....

At the start of this study, I quoted Max Fuchs' call, almost a century ago, for a detailed reconstruction of the history of the Moylin family troupes. I hope that in these pages I have responded to his appeal. From the muddy roads and peasant patois of the French provinces to the refined courts and capitals of Europe; from fairground songs and playlets to the comedies of Molière and Marivaux and the tragedies of Racine and Voltaire; from rudimentary *commedia* Night Scenes to the *ballet-pantomime* and the *ballet d'action*: such was the artistic itinerary of the combined forces of the Moylin-Sallé-Cochois families, led by Francisque for over forty years. As the inspired and inspiring head of a troupe whose influence was felt right across Europe, a versatile actor, a shrewd businessman and a brave ambassador for French culture in the land of Shakespeare, Francisque was beyond simple categorisation. His achievements remain unique in the annals of Franco-British theatre history.

---

[65] Ignacio Ramos Gay, 'The Comédie-Française in London (1879) and the Call for an English National Theatre', *Revue de littérature comparée*, 345:5 (2013), 5–16, at p. 14, n. 35.

Appendix I

Contract for the Théâtre de la Monnaie: Brussels 1733

Ce jourd'huy le 3 août 1733, par-devant nous, notaire soussigné admis par le Conseil Souverain de Brabant résident à Bruxelles et en présence des témoins ci en bas dénommés comparurent personnellement le Sieur Jean-Baptiste Meeus d'une part et le Sieur François Moilin[1] comédien d'autre part lequel premier comparant a déclaré d'avoir loué et donné à titre de bail au dit Sieur second comparant l'usage de son grand Théâtre situé sur la Monnaie pour le terme à commencer le premier octobre prochain finissant au premier jour du Carême prochain pour le prix de quatre mille florins pour le dit terme pour y pouvoir donner toutes sortes des comédies Opéra Comiques et ballets avec la troupe lui appartenant ce tout sous les conditions suivantes.

Primes en cas que le jeu des cartes ou tous autres jeux viennent à être permis le profit qui en pourra revenir et proviendra se partagera entre le premier et second comparant, savoir 1/3 pour le profit du premier comparant et les 2/3 au profit du second comparant.

Que le dit premier comparant se réserve sa loge ordinaire pour lui et ses amis et la petite Lorniette y attenante ainsi que devant au second rang ainsi que celle au second rang quand la suite de S[on] A[ltesse] S[érénissime] l'occupent au jour que sa dite A. S. l'honorera de sa présence.

Se réservant aussi la Boutique des Liqueurs et la seule permission d'en distribuer avec les gens nécessaires tant aux spectacles qu'aux ballets sauf au jour de la fête de St Charles.[2]

Que le dit premier comparant sera tenu de faire mettre le dit théâtre en bon et dû état des réparations nécessaires savoir faire boucher les trous et fentes qui sont au dehors et dans l'intérieur de l'orchestre, faire ôter les planches pourries qui peuvent se trouver sur le théâtre et en faire mettre des neuves afin d'éviter les accidents qui pourraient arriver aux comédiens et danseurs.

Qu'il fera donner à l'acceptant jouissance pleine et entière des trappes, machines, contrepoids, cordages, décorations, monstres, chars et autres choses

---

[1] This is the spelling of the scribe, but Francisque's signature, which I have examined, reads 'Moylin', and has a diaeresis above the letter y.

[2] November, feast of St Charles Borromeo, patron of the Austrian Emperor.

dépendantes et annexes au matériel du dit théâtre appartenant au dit Sieur premier comparant.

Que pareillement le dit acceptant aura la jouissance des plaques, lampions, chandeliers, poêles à feu tant pour les loges des comédiens que pour la salle et le théâtre comme aussi des bancs, tables, chaises et autres choses mobiliaires dépendantes du dit théâtre desquelles se fera inventaire par notaire s'il est besoin afin d'éviter contestation à la fin du dit terme.

Que pareillement le dit premier comparant fera délivrer au second comparant lorsque sa troupe aura besoin des habits des danseurs et compars, hallebardes, casques, cuirasses et autres ustensiles qui se trouvent dans le magasin du dit premier comparant à lui appartenant lesquelles lui seront remises aussitôt pièces jouées si mieux n'aiment pour éviter l'embarras les donner au dit second comparant par inventaire qui s'en dressera pour le rendre de même à la fin du dit terme. Et que le second comparant trouve bon de faire quelque nouvelle décoration rideau de fond, ou autres embellissements audit théâtre il lui sera permis d'en disposer en tous temps comme des choses à lui appartenantes parmi laissant les choses comme il l'aura trouvé à son entrée le tout dans leurs espèces.

Bien entendu que les [a]méliorations que le dit second contractant fera ou aura fait, tant au dit théâtre qu'aux habits du dit magasin et autres machines resteront au dit théâtre sans qu'il puisse pour ce prétendre aucune diminution sur son rendage.

Que ledit Sieur premier comparant laissera jouer la troupe du second comparant durant ledit temps pleinement et entièrement des privilèges portés dans l'octroi par ledit Sieur premier comparant obtenu de S. M. I. et C. pour ce qui regarde l'avantage et les prérogatives du dit grand théâtre.[3]

Que le dit second comparant sera maître tant de la salle du dit théâtre que de toutes ses loges, bien entendu qu'il sera permis au dit second contractant de barrer toutes les portes qui ont communication au dit théâtre et ce pendant les spectacles et bals.

Quant à ce qui regarde le concierge du dit théâtre Laurent Noël à son aide pour regarder au feu il n'y aura point de novation et le tout sera observé comme ci devant touchant la remise des clefs et le droit de ses appointements.

Que le second contractant ne pourra relouer ni céder le présent bail à d'autres ne fût du consentement du dit Sr. Premier comparant.

Que le premier comparant aux jours que la troupe du second comparant n'aimera pas de jouer pourrait trouver à louer son théâtre à quelques compagnies bourgeoises il le pourra faire parmi que le boni qui en pourra provenir se partagera encore moitié par moitié entre les contractants.

---

[3] Sa Majesté Impériale et Catholique, i.e., the Emperor Charles of Austria.

318   APPENDIX I

Et concernant le terme et assurance de paiement les parties sont convenues qu'il se fera savoir de mois en mois **à rate de ladite somme** dont le premier paiement se devra faire le 15 novembre ainsi de mois en mois.

Que le second comparant ne pourra prétendre aucune diminution sur tels et quelconques prétextes qu'ils puissent être.

[…]

[There follows an almost illegible marginal note restating the obligations and penalties of the contracting parties. The document is signed by the contracting parties and their witnesses in the presence of the notary.]

[Signé] J.-B. Meeus; François Moylin dit Francisque; J.-B. Fompré; Pierre Philippe du Moulin; Et me J.-T. Boote not. 1733.'

Translation

Today, the 3rd of August 1733, before the undersigned notary licensed by the Sovereign Council of Brabant resident at Brussels, and in the presence of the witnesses named below, there appeared, in person, Monsieur Jean-Baptiste Meeus for the first party and Monsieur François Moilin, actor, for the second party. The first party has stated that he has rented and contracted with the second party for the use of his grand theatre located on the Monnaie for a term beginning the 1st October next and ending on the first day of Lent following, for the price of four thousand florins for the said term, in order to present all sorts of comedies, opéras-comiques, and ballets, with the troupe belonging to him, under the following conditions:

Should cards or any other gaming be permitted, the profits that may accrue shall be divided between the first and second parties: that is, a third for the first party and two-thirds for the second.

The first party reserves his usual box for himself and his friends and its small anti-chamber as well as the front of the second balcony when the entourage of her Serene Highness occupy it on the day that the said Serene Highness shall honour it with her presence, also reserving to himself the refreshment room and the exclusive right to serve drinks from there with the necessary staff, both at plays and ballets, except on the day of the Feast of St Charles.

The said first party is to put the said theatre into good and fit condition with the necessary repairs: namely, to fill the holes and cracks that are outside and inside the orchestra pit, remove any rotten floorboards on the stage and have new ones laid down in order to avoid accidents to the actors and dancers.

He is to give the recipient full and entire use of the trap doors, machines, counter-weights, ropes, sets, stage monsters, chariots and other items supplementary and auxiliary to the equipment of the said theatre belonging to the said first party.

That likewise the said recipient will have full use of the brackets, lamps, chandeliers, stoves, both for the actors' dressing rooms and for the foyer and the theatre, as also of the benches, tables, chairs, and other furnishings belonging to the said theatre, of which an inventory will be taken by notary if necessary to avoid disputes at the end of the term. That, similarly, the said first party will have delivered to the second party, when his troupe needs them, costumes for dancers and the like, halberds, helmets, breastplates and other items located in the storeroom of the first party and belonging to him, which will be returned to him as soon as the play is ended, unless, to avoid inconvenience, they prefer to lend them, with an inventory, to the second party who will undertake to return them at the end of the said term. And should the second party decide to make any new backdrop or other embellishments to the said theatre, he will be permitted to dispose of them at any time as his own possessions, while leaving other things of all kinds as he will have found them on his arrival.

On the understanding that the improvements that the second party will make or have made, as well to the theatre as to the costumes of the said storeroom and other machinery, will remain at the said theatre without his being able to claim any reduction of his returns on that account.

That the first party shall allow the troupe of the second party to benefit during the said season fully and entirely from the privileges contained in the grant which the said first party has obtained from H.I.C.M. [his Imperial and Catholic Majesty, the Emperor Charles of Austria], as regards the rights and prerogatives of the said Grand Theatre.

That the said second party will be master as well of the foyer of the said theatre as of all its boxes, on the understanding that the second party will be permitted to bar all the doors that communicate with the said theatre, including during performances and balls.

With regard to the concierge of the said theatre, Laurent Noel, and to his assistant the fire-watchman, there will be no change and all will remain as hitherto concerning the custody of keys and his emoluments.

That the second party to this contract may not sublet or yield the present contact to others without the consent of the first party.

If the first party, on days when the troupe of the second party does not choose to perform, is able to rent the theatre to any group of local citizens, he may do so, provided that any receipts shall be divided equally between the signatories of this contact.

With regard to the times and terms of payment, the parties are agreed **as follows: monthly**, the first payment to be made on 15 November, and thereafter month by month.

That the 2nd party cannot claim any reduction in the payment on any grounds whatsoever.

[...]

[There follows an almost illegible marginal note concerning duties and penalties and then a formulaic conclusion. The document is signed by the contracting parties and their witnesses in the presence of the notary.]

[Signed] J.-B. Meeus; François Moylin dit Francisque; J.-B. Fompré; Pierre Philippe du Moulin; Et me J.-T. Boote not. 1733.'
Bruxelles, Archives générales du Royaume, Notariat général de Brabant, registre 1029, notaire Tobie Boote.

Appendix II

The repertoire of the London season 1734 to 1735

Taken from *The London Stage*, Part 3, vol. 1, 1729–1747

1734

Sat. 26 Oct. *L'Embarras des Richesses. Arlequin Hulla.*
Mon. 28 Oct. *Arlequin Sauvage. La Sylphide.*
Wed. 30 Oct. *Timon le Misanthrope. Le Portrait.*
Thur. 31 Oct. *Le Jeu de l'Amour et du Hasard, ou Arlequin maître et valet. Arlequin poli par l'amour.*
Mon. 4 Nov. *La Fille capitaine ou la Fille savante. Arlequin gardien du fleuve d'oubli.* [*Daily Journal* 2 Nov. also gives *De mon cousin l'allure*]
Wed. 6 Nov. *Timon le Misanthrope ou Le Vol Innocent d'Arlequin. Arlequin Hulla.*
Thurs. 7 Nov. *Arlequin Astrologue, Ramoneur, Statue, Enfant et Perroquet.*
Fri. 8 Nov. *Le Divorce ou les Fourberies d'Arlequin. Arlequin Esprit follet*, or *Harlequin the mad sprite.*
Mon. 11 Nov. *La Double Inconstance ou Arlequin à la cour malgré Lui. Les Animaux raisonnables.*
Wed. 13 Nov. *La Foire de St Germain*; *La Baguette de Vulcain.*
Thur. 14 Nov. *Arlequin Astrologue, Ramoneur, Statue, Enfant et Perroquet* with the scene of the Moor. *Les Amours de Nanterre.*
Fri. 15 Nov. *Arlequin cru Colombine et Colombine cru Arlequin, ou l'Heureux Naufrage. Les Animaux raisonnables.*
Mon. 18 Nov. *La Fausse Coquette ou Arlequin Magicien. Arlequin Hulla.*
Wed. 20 Nov. *Le Tartuffe;* . Tartuffe – Francisque; Orgon – Desessars; Valère – Lesage Jr; Damis – Lesage Sr; Cleanthe – de Verneuil; Loyal – Cochois; l'Exempt – Malter; Elmire – Mrs Francisque; Mme Pernelle – Mrs Desessars; Marianne – Mrs Fompré; Dorine – Mrs Verneuil. *Arlequin poli par l'Amour.*
Thurs. 21 Nov. *La Foire de St Germain*: *Les Amours de Nanterre.*
Fri. 22 Nov. *Arlequin Misanthrope. Le Carillon de Maître Gervaise et Dame Alison.*
Mon. 25 Nov. *L'Embarras des Richesses. Le Tombeau de Maître André.*
Wed. 27 Nov. *Le Tartuffe. La Sylphide.*
Thurs. 28 Nov. *Le Médecin malgré lui. Les Deux Arlequins.*
Fri. 29 Nov. *Le Jeu de l'Amour et du Hasard, ou Arlequin maître et valet. Le Français à Londres.*
Mon. 2 Dec. *Samson, Judge of Israel*; Samson – Lesage Jr; Phanor – Verneuil; Acab – Lesage Sr; Emmanuel – Desessars; Azaël – Delisle; Zamec – Dubuisson;

Ascalon – Harlequin; Dalila – Mrs Malter; Armilla – Mrs Francisque. *Le Carillon de Maître Gervaise et Dame Alison.*
Wed. 4 Dec. *Arlequin Tirésias. Le Français à Londres.*
Thur. 5 Dec. *L'Embarras des Richesses. Le Français à Londres.*
Fri. 6 Dec. *Arlequin Astrologue, Ramoneur, Statue, Enfant et Perroquet.* With a new scene of Arlequin Skeleton. *Arlequin Hulla.*
Mon. 9 Dec. *Samson, Judge of Israel. Le Français à Londres.* Le Marquis de Polinville – Lesage Sr; Le Baron de Polinville – Lesage Jr; Lord Craff – Verneuil; Lord Houssay – Young Master Cochois; Roast Beef – Desessars; Eliante – Mrs Mimi; Finette – Mrs Verneuil.
Wed. 11 Dec. *Le Médecin malgré lui* or *The Mock Doctor. Les Deux Arlequins.*
Thur. 12 Dec. *Arlequin Sauvage. L'Étourdi ou Arlequin Fourbe, fourbe et demi;* or *Harlequin a cheat and a half.*
Fri. 13 Dec. *Le Joueur* or *The Gamester.* Valère – Lesage Jr; Le Marquis du Hazard – Lesage Sr; Dorante – Verneuil; Géronte – Dubuisson; Toutabas or Count Cogdie – Cochois; Galonnier – Malter; Hector – Desessars; Angélique – Miss Mimi; La Comtesse – Mrs Verneuil; Nérine – Mrs Lesage; Mme La Ressource – Mrs Desessars; Mme Adam – Mrs Malter. *Arlequin Gardien du fleuve d'oubli.*
Sat. 14 Dec. *Arlequin Astrologue, Ramoneur, Statue, Enfant et Perroquet* with the scene of the skeleton, and by way of prologue *Le Baron de la Crasse* or *My Lord Sloven.* Le Baron – Francisque, unmasked.
Wed. 18 Dec. *Arlequin et sa troupe de Comédiens Esclaves*
Thur. 19 Dec. *Arlequin Sauvage. L'Étourdi ou Arlequin Fourbe, fourbe et Demi,* or *Blunder upon blunder* or *Harlequin a Double Cheat.*
Fri. 20 Dec. *Amphitryon* or *The Two Sosias.* Amphitryon – Lesage Sr; Jupiter – Lesage Jr; Alcmena – Mrs Fompré; Cléanthis – Mrs Lesage Jr; Mercure – Verneuil; Sosia – Desessars. *Isabelle Fille Capitaine et Arlequin sergent ou Colombine Fille savante;* with the scene of the Professor of Love. Professor – Arlequin, unmasked.
Mon. 23 Dec. *Le Malade Imaginaire,* or *The Mother-in-Law.* Argan – Desessars; Cléanthe – Lesage Jr; Beralde – Verneuil; Diafoirus – Dubuisson; Thomas Diafoirus – Lesage Sr; Apothecary – Malter; Beline – Mrs Desessars; Angelique – Mrs Fompré; Antoinette – Mrs Lesage Jr; Louison – Miss Malter. *Arlequin poli par l'Amour.*
Thur. 26 Dec. *L'Embarras des Richesses. Harlequin always Harlequin.*
Fri. 27 Dec. *Arlequin Balourd* or *Harlequin Blunderer.* Harlequin – Francisque; Léandre – Lesage Sr; Doctor – Desessars; Géronte – Verneuil; Pierrot – Malter; Scaramouche – Cochois; News-Crier – Dubuisson; Raree-Showman – De Lisle; Marinette or Countess Leonora – Mrs Malter; Isabelle – Mrs Mimi; Colombine – Mrs Francisque.
Sat. 28 Dec. *Arlequin Balourd. Le Français à Londres.*
Mon. 30 Dec. *Inès de Castro* or *Royal Justice.* Don Pedro – Francisque; Alphonse – Verneuil; Don Rodrigue – Lesage Jr; Don Henrique – Dubuisson; Ambassadeur – Desessars; The Queen – Mrs Verneuil; Constance – Mrs Malter; Inès de Castro – Mrs Fompré. *Isabelle Fille Capitaine et Arlequin son servant* with the scene of le Professeur d'Amour. Woman-captain – Mrs Cochois; Sargeant

APPENDIX II   323

– Harlequin; Colombine – Mrs Francisque; Tortillon – Desessars; L'Arc en ciel – Dubuisson; Octave – Lesage Jr; Scaramouche – Cochois; Pierrot – Malter; Le Professeur – Harlequin, unmasked.

1735

Wed. 1 Jan. *Amphitryon. Les Filles errantes ou Arlequin aubergiste* or *The Wandering Maids or Harlequin an Innkeeper*.
Thur. 2 Jan. *Arlequin Balourd. La Sérénade*.
Fri. 3 Jan. *Belphégor ou Arlequin aux enfers, Le Baron de la Crasse. Arlequin gardien du fleuve de l'Oubli*.
Mon. 6 Jan. *Arlequin Astrologue, Ramoneur, Statue, Enfant et Perroquet* with the scene of the Moor and the skeleton. *Les Filles errantes*.
Wed. 8 Jan. *Le Festin de Pierre ou l'Athée foudroyé* or *Don John or the Libertine destroyed* Don John – Lesage Sr; Don Philip – Lesage Jr; Don Alvarez – Dubuisson; Ghost of Don Pedro – Verneuil; Grand Prevost – Cochois; Le Pèlerin – De Lisle; Don John's servant – Harlequin; Amarille – Mrs Cochois; Shepherdess – Mrs Mimi; Bride and Groom – Malter and Mrs Malter. *Le Français à Londres*.
Thur. 9 Jan. *Zaïre*. Zaïre – Mrs Fompré; Orosmane – Lesage Sr; Chatillon – Desessars; Corasmin – Dubuisson; Melidor – De Lisle; Fatime – Mrs Mimi; Lusignan – Verneuil. *Harlequin always Harlequin*.
Fri. 10 Jan. *Tartuffe, Attendez-moi sous l'Orme* or *The Reformed Officer*. Dorante, the officer – Francisque.
Mon. 13 Jan. *Le Bourgeois Gentilhomme* or *The Citizen turn'd Gentleman*. Jourdain – Desessars; Cléonte – Lesage Jr; Covielle – Verneuil; Dorante – Lesage Sr; Singing master – Dubuisson; Mme Jourdain – Mrs Desessars; Lucille – Mrs Fompré; Nicole – Mrs Lesage Jr; Dorimène – Mrs Mimi.
Wed. 15 Jan. *Le Bourgeois Gentilhomme. Arlequin poli par l'amour*.
Thur. 16 Jan. *La Vie est un Songe ou Arlequin bouffon à la cour de Naples* or *Life is a Dream*. [Arlequin – Francisque]; Segismond – Lesage Sr; King Basil – Verneuil; Duke of Muscovy – Lesage Jr; Clotalde – Desessars; Ulric – Dubuisson; Sophronia – Mrs Malter. *Arlequin Cartouche, Grand Prévost et Juge*.
Fri. 17 Jan. *Agnès de Chaillot*; being a critick and paradox upon *Inès de Castro*. *Arlequin Hulla. Arlequin et Scaramouche déserteurs*.
Mon. 20 Jan. *Les Amants réunis* or *The Lovers' Happy Meeting or Harlequin in love without knowing it. Arlequin Sauvage*.
Tues 21 Jan.. *L'Embarras des Richesses. L'Étourdi*.
Wed. 22 Jan. *Timon le Misanthrope*. With the usual prologue, to which will be prefixed *La Feinte véritable* or *The Tender Return*.
Thur. 23 Jan. *La Double Inconstance or Harlequin a Courtier against his Will. La Sylphide*.
Fri. 24 Jan. *Arlequin Tirésias* or *The Lovers metamorphose* To which will be prefixed in three acts *Les Amants réunis*.
Mon. 27 Jan. *La Femme Jalouse* or *The Jealous Wife; Arlequin Empereur dans la lune*. Not acted these sixteen years.

Wed. 29 Jan. *Arlequin Empereur dans la lune; La Femme Jalouse.*
Fri. 31 Jan. *Arlequin Conjuror, Statue, Enfant* with the scene of the Moor and the skeleton. *Arlequin poli par l'Amour.*
Sat. 1 Feb. *La Surprise de l'Amour* or *Harlequin in love against his will. Arlequin Empereur dans la lune.*
Mon. 3 Feb. *La Double Inconstance* or *Harlequin a courtier against his will. Arlequin Empereur dans la lune.*
Wed. 5 Feb. *Gustave Vasa* or *Gustavus the Great, King of Sweden.* Gustavus – Lesage Jr; Christierne – Verneuil; Frédéric – Lesage Sr; Casimir – Desessars; Rodolphe – Dubuisson; Adélaïde – Mrs Fompré; Léonor – Mrs Verneuil; Sophie – Mrs Lesage Jr. *Arlequin et Scaramouche déserteurs.*
Thur. 6 Feb. *La Fille Capitaine.* The Professor – Francisque, unmasked. *The French Cuckold* to be performed by Mr Cochois' Lilliputians. *Arlequin Sauvage.*
Fri. 7 Feb. *Le Mariage forcé. Le Malade Imaginaire* or *the Mother-in-Law.*
Mon. 10 Feb. *La Double Inconstance. Arlequin Sauvage.*
Wed. 12 Feb. *Samson Judge of Israel. Le Carillon de Maître Gervaise et Dame Alison.* The Part of Dame Alison by Mr. Francisque, unmask'd.
Thur. 13 Feb. *La vie est un Songe. Arlequin Empereur dans la lune. Le Français à Londres.*
Fri 14 Feb. *Arlequin Balourd The French Cuckold*
Mon. 17 Feb. *Le Prince travesti ou l'Illustre Aventurier* or *Harlequin an innocent Traitor. Arlequin esprit follet.*
Tues. 18 Feb. *L'Heureux Naufrage* or *Harlequin supposed Colombine and Colombine supposed Harlequin. Le Mariage forcé.* Dr Pancrace – Francisque.
Thur. 20 Feb. *La Fille capitaine et Arlequin Sergent. Arlequin Sauvage.*
Fri. 21 Feb. *Le Faucon et les Oies de Boccace* or *Harlequin an Anchoret. L'Isle des Esclaves* or *Harlequin in the Island of slaves.*
Mon. 24 Feb. *La Fausse Coquette. Le Français à Londres.* Le Français – a new actor just arrived from Paris who never appeared in England before.
Wed. 26 Feb. *La Double Inconstance. Arlequin Sauvage.*
Thur. 27 Feb. At Lincolns' Inn Fields. *Arlequin Astrologue, Statue, Enfant, Ramoneur, Nègre et Squellette* with two new scenes viz: *The Elbow chair* and *The Dog. Harlequin always Harlequin.*
Fri. 28 Feb. *L'Embarras des Richesses. Arlequin Hulla.*
Mon. 3 Mar. *Le Jeu de l'Amour et du Hasard. The French Cuckold. Les Deux Arlequins.*
Wed.5 Mar. *La Double Inconstance. Arlequin Sauvage.*
Thur. 6 Mar. *La Vie est un Songe. Arlequin Cartouche.*
Fri. 7 Mar. *L'École des Maris. Le Faucon.*
Mon. 10 Mar. *Le Tartuffe.* Tartuffe – Francisque. *Les Précieuses Ridicules.* Le vicomte Jodelet – Francisque. Le marquis Mascarille – Desessars. *Harlequin always Harlequin.*
Wed. 12 Mar. *L'Avare* or *The Miser. Les Intrigues d'Arlequin.*
Thur. 13 Mar. *Les Folies amoureuses. Les Intrigues d'Arlequin.*
Fri. 14 Mar. *Le Joueur. Les Intrigues d'Arlequin.*
Mon. 17 Mar. *Le Festin de Pierre. Le Baron de la Crasse.* Le Baron – Francisque.
Tue. 18 Mar. *L'Embarras des Richesses. La Sylphide.*

Wed. 19 Mar. *La Fausse Coquette*. La Fausse Coquette – Francisque; Le Prince Poloneux – Lesage; Prudent Gouverneur – Desessars. *Arlequin Intriguant*. Francisque; Scaramouche – Cochois; Pierrot – Malter; Angélique – Mrs Malter. *Le Mariage forcé*.
Thur. 20 Mar. *L'École des Femmes*. Agnès – Mrs Fompré. *Harlequin always Harlequin*.
Fri. 21 Mar. *Arlequin Sauvage. Les Deux Arlequins*.
Sat. 22 Mar. *L'Embarras des Richesses*.
Mon. 24 Mar. *Arlequin Astrologue, Ramoneur, Statue, Enfant, Squelette et Nègre. Arlequin Hulla*.
Wed. 26 Mar. *L'Étourdi. Arlequin Sauvage*.
Thur. 27 Mar. *L'Heureux Naufrage. Arlequin esprit follet*.
Fri. 28 Mar. *Arlequin Balourd*.
Sat. 29 Mar. *Le Faucon. Les Filles errantes*.
[Sunday 30 March – Sunday 6 April – Holy Week]
Mon. 7 Apr. *The French Cuckold. The Intrigues of Harlequin. Don Pasquin d'Avalos* by Lilliputians. *Le Carillon comique*.
Thur. 10 Apr. *Inès de Castro*. Don Pedro – Francisque; Inès – Mrs Fompré. *Agnès de Chaillot*. Bailli de Chaillot – Francisque.
Fri. 11 Apr. *Belphégor. Arlequin gardien du fleuve d'oubli*.
Mon. 14 Apr. *Timon le Misanthrope*; prologue *Les Comédiens esclaves*.
Wed. 16 Apr. *Athalie*. Athalia – Mrs Verneuil; Joas – Master Cochois; Joad – Verneuil; Zacharias – Mrs [sic] Cochois; Salomith – Mrs Mimi Fourcade [formerly Verneuil]; Abner – Deshayes; Ismael – Dubuisson; Nathan – Desessars; Nabal – De Lisle; Azarias – Francisque. *Arlequin et Scaramouche déserteurs*.
Fri. 18 Apr. *Arlequin Tirésias. Arlequin Sauvage*.
Mon. 21 Apr. *Tartuffe. Attendez-moi sous l'Orme*.
Wed. 23 Apr. *La Double Inconstance*. Lisette – Mme Villepierre, the first time of her appearing on that stage. *Le Portrait*.
Fri. 25 Apr. *La Fille Capitaine et Arlequin son Sergeant ou La Fille Savante, or the Woman Captain and Harlequin her serjeant, or The Philosophical Lady. Les Deux Arlequins or The Mistake*.
Mon. 28 Apr. *Harlequin Astrologer, Infant, Chimney Sweep, Statue, Parrot and Skeleton, with the scene of the elbow chair. Arlequin Hulla*.
Thur. 1 May *L'Embarras des Richesses. La Sylphide*. by Castiglione.
Fri. 2 May *L'École des Femmes*. Agnès – Mrs Fompré. *Arlequin Hulla*.
Mon. 5 May *Les Folies amoureuses. The French Cuckold*, performed by the Lilliputians. *Arlequin poli par l'Amour*.
Thur. 8 May *Le Jeu de l'Amour et du Hasard, Le Cocu imaginaire*. Never acted before in England.
Fri. 9 May *Georges Dandin* or *The Wanton Wife*. Dandin – Desessars; De Sotenville – Verneuil; Clitandre – Deshayes; Lubin – Malter; Colin – Cochois Lilliputian; Angélique – Mrs Malter; Claudine – Mrs Cochois; Mme De Sotenville – Francisque. *Le Cocu imaginaire*.
Mon. 12 May *L'Embarras des Richesses. Harlequin always Harlequin*.
Thur. 15 May *Arlequin Balourd, Arlequin et Scaramouche déserteurs*.

Mon. 19 May *Le Tartuffe.* [as 10 March] *Arlequin et Scaramouche déserteurs.*
Wed. 21 May *Timon le Misanthrope* [as 6 Nov]. *Arlequin esprit follet.*
Fri. 23 May At Goodman's Fields. *L'Embarras des Richesses. Harlequin a French Gardener.* Arlequin – Francisque; Pamphile – Deshayes; Chrysanthe – Desessars; Plutus – Verneuil; Midas – Dubuisson; Briareus – De Lisle; Pierrot – Malter; Tailor – Cochois; Mlle Midas – Mrs Francisque; Floris – Mrs Cochois; Chloe – Mrs Malter. *Arlequin Hulla.*
Mon. 26 May *Harlequin Astrologer, Statue, Infant, Chimney Sweeper, and Parrot, with the scene of the Negro and the elbow chair.*
Wed. 28 May *Le Faucon. Les Intrigues d'Arlequin.*
Mon. 2 June *Arlequin Sauvage. The French Cuckold.*
Wed. 4 June Final Performance. At Goodman's Fields. *Arlequin Sauvage. The French Cuckold.*

Dances and dancers in Francisque's Haymarket company 1734–5

Dancing was mentioned in the playbills for virtually every performance. But only on the following days was further information given:

26 October. Dancing by the company of French comedians lately arrived.
30 October. *Les Caractères de la Danse* by Mlle Chateauneuf.
31 October. *Les Caractères de la Danse* by Mlle Chateauneuf.
7 November. *The Double Face* by Mlle Chateauneuf. *Wooden Shoe Dance* by Master Francis Cochois.
20 November. *Harlequin Dance* by Miss Chateauneuf.
6 December. *The Caprice* by Miss Chateauneuf.
26 December. *The Frolick* by a Gentleman for his Diversion and Miss Chateauneuf.
27 December. A new *Chaconne* in several Characters: Harlequin Man – Cochois Jr; Harlequin woman – Miss Chateauneuf; Pierrot man – Roland; Pieraite – Mrs Mimi; Punch – Villeneuve; Dame Jigogne – Malter; Scaramouch [*sic*] man – De Lisle; Scaramouche Woman – Mrs Le Sage Jr.
28 December. *Tambourine* by Miss Chateauneuf.
30 December. *Tambourine. La Frolick.*
2 January. *The Frolick. L'Allemande* by Miss Chateauneuf.
5 February. *Shepherd and Shepherdess.* Granier and Miss Chateauneuf.
6 February. A Lilliputian dance called *La Polissonne.* Benefit Cochoy, Mrs Cochoy and their children.
13 February. *Pierrot and Pieraite.* [*sic*] Le Sage Jr and Miss [Mimi] Verneuil. Benefit Le Sage Sr and Jr.
17 February. *Les Caractères de la Danse* by Mlle Chateauneuf.
3 March. A new *Lilliputian Scotch Dance.* Benefit Malter, the Pierrot.
21 March. *The Jealousy between Three Lilliputians. The Harlequin* by Young Mr. Cochoy.
28 March. I. *Les Warriors.* II. *Les Transfigurations.* III. *The Prisoner.* IV. *Comical Pantomime Dance.* V. *Pierot and Pieraite.* [*sic*] *Wooden Shoe Dance. Pantomime after the Venetian Manner.* All by Castiglione. Benefit Castiglione.

11 April. I. *The Country Wedding.* II. *The Ghosts of the Elysian Fields.* III. *A Grand Dance.*

3 April. The last *Lilliputian Scotch dance.* A new Lilliputian *Chaconne of Characters*: Harlequin man and Woman. Pierot and Pieraite. [sic] Punch and Dame Ragondy. Scaramouche.

25 April. *Two Pierrots* by De Lisle and Badouin. *Harlequin* and *Wooden Shoe Dance* by Cochois, the Lilliputian [Master Francis Cochois].

1 May. Dancing by Castiglione. Scotch Dance between Lilliputians.

2 May. The First *Grande Dance* by the Lilliputians, performed here in England. *Pierrot and Pierraite* by De Lisle and Badouin.

5 May. For the benefit of Mlle Grognet. At the desire of several persons of quality ... With Entertainments of Dancing between the Acts by Mademoiselle GROGNET and others. Particularly a Minuet and a New Dance call'd *The Wedding* by Madem. Mimy Verneuil and Madem. Grognet in Man's Clothes.

12 May. Dancing by Lilliputians.

23 May. At Goodman's Fields. Dancing by Castiglione.

26 May. *A Chacone of Characters* by the Lilliputians as *Harlequin Man and Woman, Pierrot and Pierraite, Scaramouche and Scaramouchette, Punch and Dame Jigonde.*

2 June. A Grand dance by the Lilliputians; Scotch dance by the Lilliputians. Grand Ballet by De Lisle, Badouin, Mrs Fompré, Mrs Mimi Fourcade.

4 June. At Goodman's Fields. Dancing as 2 June.

Appendix III

Micault's manuscript list of performances in Dijon, 1739–40 and 1750–1

This has been adapted and amplified from the manuscript calendar of Claude Micault, which gives only dates and titles of plays. I have added authors' names, genre, theatrical origin, and year of first performance.

CF   Comédie Française
ATI   Ancien Théâtre Italien
NTI   Nouveau Théâtre Italien
TF   Théâtre de la Foire

'Troupe de Moylin'

1739

December

20 Sun. *Timon le misanthrope*, Delisle, comedy, 3 acts, prose, NTI. 1722.
29 Tues. *Belphégor*, Legrand, comedy-ballet, 3 acts, prose, NTI. 1722.
Le Français à Londres, Boissy, comedy, 1 act, prose, CF. 1727.

1740

January

3 Sun. *Le Jeu de l'Amour et du Hasard*, Marivaux, comedy, 3 acts, prose, NTI. 1730. *Arlequin Hulla*, Either Lesage/d'Orneval, opéra-comique, 1 act, TF. 1716, or Dominique & Romagnesi, 1-act comedy, NTI. 1728.
6 Wed. *La Belle Esclave*, Claude de l'Estoille, tragi-comedy, 5 acts, verse, 1643, and *Le Je ne sais quoi*, Boissy, comedy, 1 act, verse, NTI. 1731.
17 Sun. *L'Embarras des richesses*, d'Allainval, comedy, 3 acts, prose, NTI. 1725.
24 Sun. *Arlequin misanthrope*, Claude-Ignace Brugière de Barante, comedy, 3 acts, prose, ATI. 1696.

February

7 Sun. *Les Contretemps*, Le Grange, comedy, 3 acts, verse, NTI. 1736.
Le Retour de tendresse, Fuzelier, comedy, 1 act, prose, NTI. 1728.
16 Tues. *La xxxx*, *Comédie Anonyme*, Boissy, 3 acts, verse, NTI. 1737.
17 Wed. *Le Préjugé à la mode*, Nivelle de la Chaussée, comedy, 5 acts, verse, CF. 1735. *L'Op****[indecipherable]. *L'École des mères*, Marivaux, comedy, 1 act, prose, NTI. 1732.

23 Wed. *Arlequin sauvage*, Delisle, comedy, 3 acts, prose, NTI. 1721.
Le Je ne sais quoi, Boissy, comedy, 1 act, verse, NTI. 1731.
25 Thurs. *La Femme jalouse*, Jolly, comedy, 3 acts, verse, NTI. 1726.
Le Galant Coureur, Legrand, comedy, 1 act, prose, CF. 1722.
26 Fri. *La Double Inconstance*, Marivaux, comedy, 3 acts, prose, NTI. 1724.
Le Tombeau de Maître André, Brugière de Barante, comedy, 1 act, prose, ATI. 1695.
29 Mon. *Isabelle fille capitaine [La Fille savante]*, Fatouville, comedy, 3 acts, prose, ATI. 1690. *Cracovie* [? MS indecipherable]

March

7 Mon. *L'Heureux Stratagème*, Marivaux, comedy, 3 acts, prose, NTI. 1733.
Attendez-moi sous l'orme, Regnard comedy, 1 act, prose, CF. 1694.
10 Thurs. *La Fausse Coquette*, Brugière de Barante, comedy, 3 acts, prose and verse, ATI. 1694.
Pantomime [*Pantomime anglaise* as at Compiègne, 1740?]
12 Sun. *La Foire des poètes*, *L'Isle du divorce*, *La Sylphide*, Dominique & Romagnesi, 3 comedies, prose, 1 act each, NTI. 1730.

Dijon calendar 1750–1

1750

December

18 Fri. *Gustave Vasa*, Piron, tragedy, 5 acts, verse, CF. 1733.
L'Époux par Supercherie, Boissy, comedy, 2 acts, prose, CF. 1744.
20 Sun. *Mélanide*, Nivelle de la Chaussée, comedy, 5 acts, verse, CF. 1741.
L'Amant auteur et valet, Cérou, comedy, 1 act, prose, , NTI. 1740.
26 Sat. *Le Bourgeois à la mode*, Dancourt, comedy, 5 acts, prose, CF. 1692.
Le Bal bourgeois, Favart, 1 act, opéra-comique, TF. 1738.
31 Thur. *La Nièce [vengée]*, Fagan & Panard, opéra-comique, 1 act, TF, 1731. *Le Babillard*, Boissy, comedy, 1 act verse, CF. 1725.

1751

January

1 Fri. *Arlequin misanthrope*, Brugière de Barante, 3 acts, prose, ATI. 1696.
3 Sun. *Les Dehors trompeurs*, Boissy, comedy, 5 acts, verse, CF. 1740.
Les Visionnaires, Desmarets, comedy, 5 acts, verse, hôtel de Bourgogne. 1637
12 Tues. *Sémiramis*, Voltaire, tragedy, 5 acts, verse, CF. 1749. *Ballet des Moissoneurs*.
28 Thur. *La Gouvernante*, La Chaussée, comedy, 5 acts, verse, CF. 1747.
Les Grâces, Saint-Foix, comedy, 1 act, prose, CF. 1744.
29 Fri. *Œdipe*, Voltaire, tragedy, 5 acts, verse, CF. 1718. *Œdipe travesti*, com. 1 act verse, Dominique, NTI. 1719.
30 Sat. *Le Jaloux détrompé* [? *Le Jaloux désabusé,* Campistron, comedy, 5 acts, verse, CF. 1709. *L'Amour vainqueur*. [?Marivaux, *Le Triomphe de l'amour*, comedy, 3 acts, prose, NTI. 1732.]
31 Sun. *Le Bourgeois Gentilhomme*, Molière, comedy, 5 acts, prose, CF. 1670

February

4 Thur. *La Force du naturel*, Destouches, comedy, 5 acts, verse, CF. 1750.
L'Œil du Maître, Pontau, ballet-pantomime, 1 act, TF. 1742.
11Thur. *L'Homme à bonne fortune*, Regnard, comedy, 3 acts, prose, ATI. 1690.
La Chercheuse d'esprit, Favart, opéra-comique, 1 act, TF. 1741.
14 Sun. *Turcaret*, Lesage, comedy, 5 acts prose, CF. 1708. *La Nouvelle Actrice*, P. Poisson, comedy, 1 act, verse [See Léris, *Dictionnaire des Théâtres*, 1743, p. 6.]
16 Tues. *Phèdre et Hippolyte*, Racine, tragedy, 5 acts, verse, CF. 1677.
La Rose, Piron, opéra-comique, 1 act, TF [banned]. 1726.
21 Sun. *Les Quatre Spectacles* [from CF, NTI, Opéra, TF]
26 Fri. *Esther*, Racine, tragedy, 3 acts, verse, CF. 1689.
Le Magnifique, La Motte, comedy, 2 acts, prose, CF. 1731.

March

2 Tues. *Le Méchant*, Gresset, 5 acts, verse, CF. 1747.
L'Ami de tout le monde, ou Le Philanthrope, Legrand, comedy, 3 acts, prose, CF. 1723.
4 Thurs. *Andromaque*, Racine, tragedy, 5 acts, verse, CF, 1667. *L'Oracle*, Saint-Foix, 1 act, prose, CF. 1740.
9 Tues. *Venise sauvée*, de la Place, tragedy, 5 acts, verse, CF. 1746.
La Sérénade, Regnard, 1 act, prose, CF. 1694.
12 Fri. *La Mort de ?Protas/Procris* [MS Illegible: ?*Procris ou la Jalousie infortunée*, Alexandre Hardy, tragi-comedy, 5 acts, verse, 1606.]
Le Procureur arbitre, Poisson, comedy, 1 act, verse, CF. 1728.
14 Sun. *Athalie*, Racine, tragedy, 5 acts, verse, CF. 1690. *La bonne amie* [?].
18 Thurs. *Rhadamiste et Zénobie*, Crébillon, tragedy, 5 acts, verse, CF. 1711.
La Rose, Piron, see above.
21 Sun. *Gustave Vasa*, Piron, see above.
Le Retour imprévue, Regnard, 1 act, prose, CF. 1700.
25 Thur. *Le Spectacle brillant* (a candle-lit soirée]
Le Nouveau Monde, Pellegrin, comedy, 3 acts verse, CF. 1722.
Le Magnifique, see above.
28 Sun. *Cénie*, Mme de Graffigny, comedy, 5 acts prose, CF. June 1750.
Les Vendanges de Tempé, Favart, comedy-pantomime, 1 act, verse, with airs, NTI. 1745.

April

2 Thurs. *Nouveau Spectacle brillant*.
Clôture de Pâques [Closing for Easter] 3 April.

BIBLIOGRAPHY

Manuscripts

Archives municipales et départementales (AM/AD):

Aix-en-Provence, AM, année 1792 (paroisse Saint-Sauveur)
Amiens, AM FF 1302; FF 1307; FF 1308
Amiens, AM, registre 15 (BMD St-Firmin-en-Castillon); registre 17 (BMD St-Firmin-en-Castillon)
Avignon, AD 3E9(2)/215, Notaire Mounier; B ROTE 199 and AD 3E9(2)/218, Notaire Mounier; B ROTE 200
Besançon, AM, Paroisse Saint Maurice, GG 161
Bordeaux, AM, GG 151 (paroisse Saint-Christoly)
Bordeaux, AM, GG 573 (paroisse Saint-Pierre)
Bruxelles, Archives de la Ville, registre 174 (Ste-Gudule)
Dijon, AM, réf: 2011 / 287. GR microfilm 555, reproducing ff 2v–3r (troupe de Moylin) and 9v–10r (troupe de Francisque) from Part 2 of the *Mercure dijonnois* (MS 742 bis). Réf: 2011/287.GR
Ghent, AM, registre 142 (St-Nicolas)
Grenoble, AM FF 43; ibid., f. 297; FF 44; registre GG 104 (paroisse Saint-Hugues)
La Rochelle, AM registres GG 354 (Saint-Jean-du-Pérot); GG 590 (Saint-Sauveur)
Lille, AM (BMD St-Étienne 5 Mi 044 R 045)
Lyon, AM, registres 413, 415 (BMD Ste-Croix); registre 620 (BMD St-Pierre St-Saturnin)
Marseille, AM, FF 307; FF 308; FF 309 GG 229, 232 (BMS St-Martin); GG 315, 320, 350 (BMS St-Ferréol); GGL 202
Metz, AM, GG 64 (BMD St-Gorgon)
Nantes, AM, GG 243, 748
Rennes, AM, GGTous77 (paroisse Toussaints)
Rouen, Bibliothèque municipale, registre 640 (BMI St-Vincent)
St-Étienne, AM, 1GG/75 1719 – 1730
Toulouse, AM, GG 313, 325 (BMD St-Étienne)
Tours, AM (Saint-Venant)

332 BIBLIOGRAPHY

Archives Nationales:

Les archives de l'État en Belgique, Registres paroissiaux, Notre-Dame du Finistère, Bruxelles 01/01/1729 – 01/06/1740

Minutes et répertoires du notaire Sylvain BALLOT, 1721, MC/ET/CXVI/214-MC/ET/CXVI/362, MC/RE/CXVI/4-MC/RE/CXVI/5- MC/ET/CXVI/230/B https://francearchives.fr/fr/facomponent/b438853321e125ba3824818d948f1a1810a59a6a

Minutes et répertoires du notaire Nicolas DUPORT, MC/ET/XXVII/70 (C1n23) https://www.siv.archives-nationales.culture.gouv.fr/siv/rechercheconsultation/recherche/ir/rechercheGeneralisteResultat.action?searchText=Michel+Cochois&formCaller=GENERALISTE*Minutes et répertoires du notaire Antoine de LA FOSSE*, MC/ET/X/248-MC/ET/X/418, MC/RE/X/7-MC/RE/X/10-MC/ET/X/353. https://francearchives.fr/es/agent/19111541

https://francearchives.gouv.fr/es/findingaid/74e91b08556eba35b0a8c09e4590774d2258b4be

Minutes et répertoires du notaire Antoine de LA FOSSE http://www.archivesportaleurope.net/ead-display/-/ead/pl/aicode/FRFRAN/type/fa/id/FRAN_IR_041351/dbid/C46915057/search/0/sieur+francisque#sthash.KMNz5Uej.dpuf

Other:

Bibliothèque Historique de la Ville de Paris, ms. 26700

Journal de Lyon, ou Mémoires historiques et politiques de ce qui s'est passé de plus remarquable dans la ville de Lyon et dans la province depuis le commencement du XVIIIe siècle, 7 vol. in folio. Musée Gadagne, Lyon, Inv. N 24811

Minutier central des notaires de Paris, XCVIII, 372bis, 21 mars 1710. Archives nationales

Ms. BnF, f.fr. 25471 (ff° 161–87), and f.fr. 9314 (f° 68–77) [Three unpublished MSS from *Le Théâtre de la Foire*]

Ms. BnF, fr. 25480 Don Juan ou Le Festin de Pierre

Ms. BnF fr 9336 *ff*. 34–5, 209–24, 295–7

Ms. BnF fr 9336 & Musique Rés. Th 8 [Guarantors of Lalauze]

'Nouveaux Mémoires sur les spectacles de la Foire, par un entrepreneur de Lazzis, dédiés à l'acteur forain', ms. Bibliothèque de l'Opéra, Rés. 611

West Sussex County Record Office, Goodwood MS 145

Newspapers and periodicals

Newspapers and periodicals cited are available online in the Burney Collection of the British Library or in the Bibliothèque nationale de France

Primary Sources

Amadis de Gaule, Édition critique, ed. Georges Bourgueil (Albi, 2008)

Andrews, John, *Essai sur le caractère et les mœurs des François comparés à ceux des Anglais* (London, 1776)

———, *A comparative view of the French and English Nations, in their Manners, Politics, and Literature* (London, 1785)
Anon, *Memoirs of the Life and Times of Sir Thomas Deveil, Knight, one of His Majesty's Justices of the Peace* (London, 1748)
Anon. (attributed to Biancolelli, Jean-François), *Les Plaisirs de La Tronche, 1711*, ed. Pierre Monnier and Jean Sgard (Grenoble, 2006)
Annales politiques, littéraires et statistiques de Bordeaux, ed. Pierre Bernadau (Bordeaux, 1803)
Annuaire dramatique pour 1840 (Paris, 1840)
Annuaire Dramatique de Belgique pour 1839 (Paris, 1839)
Annuaire Dramatique de Belgique pour 1840 (Paris, 1840)
Archives historiques du département de la Gironde, vol. 6 (Paris, 1864)
Argenson, René-Louis de Voyer de Paulmy, marquis d'Argenson, *Notices sur les œuvres de théâtre*, ed. Henri Lagrave, Institut et musée Voltaire (Geneva, 1966)
Audibert, Jean-Baptiste, *Le Fortuné Marseillois, comédie, en un acte, en Provençal et en Français* ([Amsterdam, 1736] 2nd edn, Marseille, 1775)
d'Auriac, Eugène, *Théâtre de la Foire, recueil de pièces* (Paris, 1878)
Les Avantures d'Abdalla fils d'Hanif, envoyé par le Sultan des Indes à la découverte de l'ile de Borico, où est la fontaine merveilleuse dont l'eau fait rajeunir (Paris, 1712)
The Aviary: or Magazine of British Melody (London [1745?], repr. 1765)
Barbier, Edmond Jean François, *Chronique de la régence et du règne de Louis XV (1718–1763), ou Journal de Barbier*, fifth series (1731–53) 8 vols (Paris, 1857)
Barbier, Nicolas, *La Fille à la mode* (Lyon, 1708)
———, *L'Heureux Naufrage* (Lyon, 1710)
de la Barre de Beaumarchais, Antoine, *Amusemens Littéraires: ou Correspondance Politique, Rhétorique, Philosophique, Critique, et Galante pour l'Année MDCCXXXVIII*, 2 vols (Frankfurt, 1739, and The Hague, 1740)
Baudrais, Jean, *Petite Bibliothèque des Théatres; contenant un Recueil des meilleures Pièces du Théatre François, Tragique, Comique, Lyrique et Bouffon, depuis l'origine des Spectacles en France, jusqu'à nos jours* (78 vols, Paris, 1783–88)
Bernadeau, Pierre, *Annales Politiques, Littéraires Et Statistiques De Bordeaux* ([1803] repr. Kessenger, 2010)
Biancolelli, Dominique, *Arlequin fille malgré lui*, ed. Soazig Le Floch et Marie Berjon, in Rubellin, ed., *Théâtre de la Foire*
Biancolelli, Pierre-François, *La Fausse Belle-Mère* (Toulouse, 1712)
——— (*dit* Dominique le fils), *La Promenade des Terreaux de Lyon* (1712), ed. G. Couton, M. Pruner, J. Rittaud-Hutinet, Centre d'études et de recherches théâtrales (Lyon, 1977)
[Blanc, *dit* la Goutte, François], *Épître en vers, au langage vulgaire de Grenoble, sur les Réjouissances qu'on y a faites pour la Naissance de Monseigneur le Dauphin* (Grenoble, 1729)
Boileau-Despréaux, Nicolas, *Œuvres*, 2 vols (Paris, 1969)
Bonnault-d'Houët, Baron Xavier de, *Le Camp de Compiègne de 1739, suivi d'un menu royal: extraits des mémoires de Scellier avec introduction et notes par le Baron de Bonnault-d'Houët* (Compiègne, 1897)

Bouhier, Jean, *Correspondance littéraire du président Bouhier*, 14 vols, ed. Henri Duranton, vol. 9 (2): Lettres de Mathieu Marais (Saint-Étienne, 1988)
The British Musical Miscellany, or The Delightful Grove (vols 1–2, London, 1734; vols 3–4, London, 1735)
Casanova, Giacomo, *Mémoires de J. Casanova de Seingalt, écrits par lui-même* 8 vols (Paris, 1880)
Chambers, Robert, *Chambers' Book of Days* (2 vols, Edinburgh, 1864)
Chamfort, Nicolas, ed. Joseph and Sebastien Laporte, *Dictionnaire Dramatique* (Paris, 1776)
Chetwood, W., *A General History of the Stage* (London, 1749)
Choron, A., and F. Fayolle, *Dictionnaire historique des musiciens*, 2 vols (Paris, 1817)
[Cibber, Colley], *An Apology for the Life of Colley Cibber, Comedian*, ed. B. R. S. Fone (Ann Arbor, 1968)
———, *The Dramatic Works of Colley Cibber* ([London, 1777] New York, 1966)
———, *The Non-Juror. A comedy. As it is acted at the Theatre-Royal, by His Majesty's servants.* (London, 1718)
Cleland, John, *Tombo-Chiqui, or The American Savage, A Dramatic entertainment in Three Acts* (London, 1758)
Collé, Charles, *Journal et mémoires de Charles Collé sur les hommes de lettres*, ed. H. Bonhomme (Paris, 1868)
A Collection of Miscellany Poems (London, 1737)
A Complete Collection of Old and New English and Scotch Songs, with their respective tunes prefixed (4 vols, London, 1735)
The Connoisseur, A Satire on the modern Men of Taste (London, 1735)
Cowper, Mary, *Diary of Mary Countess Cowper* (London, 1864)
Defoe, Daniel, *La Vie et les Avantures surprenantes de Robinson Crusoe, Contenant entr'autres événemens, le séjour qu'il a fait pendant vingt & huit ans dans une isle déserte, située sur la côte de l'Amérique, près de l'embouchure de la grande rivière Oroonoque. Le tout écrit par lui-même.* Trans. Justus van Effen and Thémiseul de Saint-Hyacinthe (Amsterdam [Rouen], 1720)
Degauque, Isabelle, ed., *Les Dieux travestis, Le Galant brutal* and *Le Sault de Leucade*, available at http://cethefi.org/memoire_master.htm
The Delights of the Muses (London, 1738)
Delisle de La Drevetière, Louis-François, *Arlequin sauvage: Timon le misanthrope* (Paris, 2000)
———, *Arlequin sauvage, Le Faucon et les oies de Boccace*, ed. David Trott (Montpellier, 2004)
Desboulmiers, J.-A. [Jean-August-Julien, *dit* Desboulmiers], *Histoire anecdotique et raisonnée du Théâtre Italien depuis son rétablissement en France, jusqu'à l'année 1769*, 7 vols (Paris, n.d. repr. Geneva, 1968)
———, *Histoire du Théâtre de l'Opéra Comique* (2 vols, Paris, 1769)
Desroches de Parthenay, J.-B. et al., *Mémoires historiques, pour le siècle courant* (Amsterdam, 1738)
Deveil, Thomas, see Anon.
d'Hannetaire, Jean Nicolas Servandoni, *Observations sur l'art du comédien* (Paris, 1775)

Dictionnaire des sciences médicales ed. Chales-Louis-Fleury Panckoucke, 58 vols (Paris, 1812)

Dictionnaire Historique de la Ville de Paris et de ses environs, ed. Pierre T. N. Hurtaut (Paris, 1779)

Dubos, Jean-Baptiste, *Réflexions critiques sur la poésie et sur la peinture: Nouvelle édition revue, corrigée et considérablement augmentée* (Paris, 1733)

Dufresny, Rivière, *Œuvres de Monsieur Rivière Dufresny* (Paris, 1731)

Dumont, Gabriel, *Parallèle de plans des plus belles salles de spectacle d'Italie et de France* ([s.n., 1770], New York, 1968)

Egmont, First Earl of, *see* Perceval, John, First Earl of Egmont

Elizabeth-Charlotte, duchesse d'Orléans, *Correspondance complète de Madame duchesse d'Orléans*, trans. M. G. Brunet, vol. I (Paris, 1857)

Encyclopédie méthodique, ou, par ordre de matières (Paris, 1804)

Fontenelle [Bernard le Bovier de Fontenelle], *Œuvres de Fontenelle* (Paris, 1818)

Frédéric le Grand [Frederick the Great], *Œuvres* (édition électronique), http://friedrich.uni-trier.de/de/oeuvres/

Furetière, Antoine, *Dictionnaire universel* (The Hague, 1690); http://xn–furetire-60a.eu/index.php/home

[Garrick, David], *The Plays of David Garrick: Garrick's own plays, 1740–1766*, eds Harry Pedicord and Frederick Bergmann (Carbondale, 1980)

Gastelier, Jacques-Elie, *Lettres sur les Affaires du Temps: 1738–1741*, ed. Henri Duranton (Paris-Geneva, 1993)

Gherardi, Evariste, *Le Théâtre italien ou le recueil général de toutes les comédies et scènes françaises jouées par les comédiens italiens du roi* (Paris, 1741, repr, 1969)

[Gildon, Charles], *A Comparison Between the Two Stages: A Late Restoration Book of the Theatre*, ed. Staring B. Wells (New York, 1971)

Gillier, Jean Claude, *Recueil d'airs Français, Sérieux & à Boire. A une, deux, & trois Parties. Composé en Angleterre* (London, 1723)

———, *Airs de Monsieur Gillier pour la Comédie de la Foire S. Germain, représentée sur le théâtre des Comédiens Italiens* (Paris, 1696)

Godard de Beauchamps, Pierre-François, *Recherches sur les Théâtres de France* (Paris, 1735)

Goethe, Johann Wolfgang, 'Alexis Piron', *Goethes Werke* (Stuttgart, Tübingen, 1830), vol. 36, pp. 190–3

de Gouvenain, Louis, *Inventaire-sommaire des archives communales antérieures à 1790, ville de Dijon*, 3 vols (Dijon and Paris, 1867–92)

de Graffigny, Françoise, *Correspondance de Mme de Graffigny,* ed. English Showalter, Peter Allan, J. Alan Dainard, Oxford University Studies in the Enlightenment (SVEC) (15 vols, Oxford, 1985–2016)

Gras, Louis Pierre, *Dictionnaire du patois forézien* (Lyon, 1863)

The Happy Courtezan: Or, the Prude demolish'd. AN EPISTLE from the Celebrated Mrs. C-P. to the Angelick Signior Far-n-li (London,1735)

Hervey, John, *Lord Hervey and his Friends 1726–38*, ed. Earl of Ilchester (London, 1950)

Histoire des Maires de Bordeaux (Bordeaux, 2008)

The Historical Register for the Year 1738, vol. 23, no. 92 (London, 1739)

Inventaire sommaire des Archives communales antérieures à 1790, ville de Nantes (Nantes, 1899)

Journal de la Cour et de Paris depuis le 28 novembre 1732 jusques au 30 novembre 1733, ed. Henri Duranton (Saint-Étienne, 1981)

Journal de Lyon, ou Mémoires historiques et politiques de ce qui s'est passé de plus remarquable dans la ville de Lyon et dans la province depuis le commencement du XVIIIe siècle, 7 vols in folio. Musée Gadagne, Lyon

Kelly, John, *The Plot. As it is Performed by His Majesty's Company of Comedians at the Theatre-Royal in Drury-Lane, with the Musick prefix'd to each Song* (London, 1735)

de La Harpe, Jean-François, *Lycée ou cours de littérature* (Paris, 1801)

Lahontan, Louis Armand de Lom d'Arce, baron de, *Dialogues curieux entre l'auteur et un sauvage de bon sens qui a voyagé* (The Hague, 1703)

——, *Mémoires de l'Amérique Septentrionale ou la suite des voyages de Mr. le baron de Lahontan*, ed. Réal Ouellet (Montreal, 2003)

Lapaume, Jean, *Anthologie nouvelle, autrement Recueil complet des poésies patoises des bords de l'Isère* (Grenoble, 1866)

Laurenti, Jean-Noël, *Valeurs morales et religieuses sur la scène de l'Académie royale de musique* (Geneva, 2012)

Legrand, Marc-Antoine, *Le Roi de Cocagne* (Paris, 1718)

Lenoble, Eustache, *The two Harlequins* (London, 1718)

de Léris, A., *Dictionnaire portatif historique et littéraire des Théâtres* (Paris, 1763)

Lesage, Alain-René, and Jacques Philippe d'Orneval, *Le Théâtre de la Foire ou l'opéra-comique*, 10 vols ([Paris, 1721–37], Slatkine reprint, 2 vols, Geneva, 1968)

Letters to a young gentleman, on his setting out for France (London, 1784)

[Luisa Ulrike, Queen of Prussia], *Luise Ulrike, die schwedische Schwester Friedrichs des Großen: Ungedruckte Briefe an Mitglieder des preußischen Königshauses*, 2 vols, ed. Fritz Heinrich Arnheim (Gotha, 1910)

Luynes, [Charles Philipe Albert, duc de Luynes], *Mémoires du duc de Luynes sur la cour de Louis XV* (Paris, 1860)

Mainvilliers, Genu Soalhat, Chevalier de, *Le Petit-maître philosophe: ou voyage et avantures de Genu Soalhat, Chevalier de Mainvillers, dans les principales cours de l'Europe* (London, 1751)

Marivaux, Pierre, *Le Prince Travesti* (1724)

[——], *Le Paysan Parvenu: or, the Fortunate Peasant. Being memoirs of the life of Mr. —Translated from the French of M. de Marivaux* (London, 1735)

[——], *Seven Comedies by Marivaux*, trans. O. and A. Mandel (Ithaca, 1968)

[——] *Théâtre complet*, ed. Bernard Dort, préface de Jacques Scherer (Paris, 1982, 1964)

Marlborough, [Sarah, Duchess of Marlborough] *Letters of a Grandmother 1732–1735.*, ed. Gladys Scott Thompson (London, 1943)

Mémoires de la Commission des antiquités du département de la Côte-d'Or (Dijon,1885) (for *Le Mercure dijonnois*)

The Merry Man's Companion and evening's agreeable entertainer (London, 1750)

Miller, James, *Art and Nature, a comedy* (London, 1738)

——, *The Man of Taste* (London, 1735)

——, *A Seasonable Reproof* (London, 1735)

Monnet, Jean, *Supplément au Roman comique, ou Mémoires pour servir à la vie de Jean Monnet* (London, 1772)
Montfleury [Antoine Jacob], *Les Bestes Raisonnables* (Paris, 1661)
de Morand, Pierre, *Théâtre et œuvres diverses de M. de Morand*, 3 vols (Paris, 1751)
Le Nouveau Théâtre Italien ou recueil général des comédies (Paris, 1733)
Nouveaux Mémoires sur la Foire. See Websites: Ourcel
'L'Ombre de la Foire', in Rubellin, ed., *Théâtre de la Foire*
D'Origny, Antoine J. B. A., *Annales du Théâtre Italien depuis son origine jusqu'à ce jour* (3 vols, Paris, 1788)
Ozell, John, trans., *L'Embaras [sic] des Richesses. The Plague of Riches, a Comedy in French and English*, [by Léonor Jean Christine Soulas d'Allainval] in the English Translation by Mr. Ozell (London, 1735)
[———], *The Fair of St. Germain. As it is acted at the Theatre in Little Lincoln's-Inn-Fields, by the French Company of Comedians, lately arriv'd from the Theatre-Royal at Paris. All in the characters of the Italian Theatre. Done into English by Mr. Ozell* (London, 1718)
Parfaict, Claude, and François Parfaict, *Mémoires pour servir à l'histoire des spectacles de la foire* (2 vols, Paris, 1743)
———, ———, and Quentin Godin d'Abguerbe, *Dictionnaire des théâtres de Paris* (7 vols, Paris, 1767; repr., 1967)
Pellassy de l'Ousle, Jean, *Histoire du Palais de Compiègne* (Paris, l'an 2 [1793–4])
Pennyman, Margaret, *Miscellanies in Prose and Verse by the Honourable Lady Margaret Pennyman, containing her late Journey to Paris* (London, 1740)
Pensées Nouvelles & Philosophiques (Amsterdam, 1777)
Perceval, John, First Earl of Egmont, Manuscripts of the Earl of Egmont, *The Diary of the First Earl of Egmont*, Historical Manuscripts Commission (London, 1923)
Pétis de la Croix, François, *Histoire de la sultane de Perse et des vizirs; Les Mille et un jours, contes persans; Les Aventures d'Abdalla*, ed. Pierre Brunel with Christelle Bahier-Porte and Frédéric Mancier, Bibliothèque des Génies et des Fées, vol. 8 (Paris, 2006)
[Philathes], *Majesty Misled: Or, the Overthrow of Evil Ministers, as intended to be Acted at one of the Theatres, but was refused for certain reasons* (London, 1734)
[Piron, Alexis], *Piron: complément de ses œuvres inédites*, ed. H. Bonhomme (Paris, 1866)
———, *Gustave-Wasa*, ed. Derek Connon, Critical Texts, 57 (Cambridge, 2016)
———, *L'Antre de Trophonius et La robe de dissention, ou le faux-prodige*, ed. Derek Connon (Cambridge, 2011)
———, *Œuvres choisies de Piron*, ed. Jules Troubat, Introduction by C. A. Sainte-Beuve (Paris, 1866)
———, *Œuvres complètes*, ed. Jean-Antoine Rigoley de Juvigny (7 vols, Paris, 1776)
———, *Œuvres inédites, prose et vers, accompagnées de lettres adressées à Piron*, ed. H. Bonhomme (Paris, 1859)
Poetical Miscellanies, consisting of original poems and translations by the best hands. Publish'd by Mr. Steele (London, 1714)
Powell, S. (publisher), *Recueil de Pièces de Théâtre*. vol. 1: Marivaux, *La Double Inconstance, Le Jeu de l'amour et du hasard, L'Isle des esclaves*; Delisle, *Arlequin sauvage, Timon le misanthrope*; Boissy, *L'Homme du jour*; Nivelle de La Chaussée, *Mélanide, L'Ecole des amis* (Dublin, 1749–50)

Prévost d'Exile, Antoine-François [L'Abbé Prévost], *Le Pour et contre: ouvrage périodique d'un goût nouveau* (Paris, 1734–5)
―――, *Le Pour et contre* (pirated edition) (The Hague, 1735)
Procope-Couteaux, Michel, *Arlequin balourd* (London, 1719)
Queruau-Lamerie, Emile, *Notice sur le théâtre d'Angers (1755–1825)* (Angers, 1889)
Raunié, Emile, ed., *Chansonnier Historique du XVIIIe siècle*, 10 vols (Paris, 1880)
Ravaisson, François, *Archives de la Bastille* (Paris, 1881)
Registers of the Catholic Chapel Royal and of the Portuguese Embassy Chapel, 1662–1829, Catholic Record Society Publications (Leeds, 1941)
Regnard, Jean-François, *Comédies du Théâtre Italien*, ed. A. Calame, Textes Littéraires Français (Geneva, 1981)
―――, and Rivière Dufresny, *Les Chinois* (1692), http://www.theatre-classique.fr/pages/programmes/edition.php?t=../documents/DUFRESNYREGNARD_CHINOIS.xml
Relation des réjouissances faites à Grenoble au sujet de la naissance de Monseigneur le Dauphin (Grenoble, 1729)
Rex, Walter, *The Attraction of the Contrary: Essays on the Literature of the French Enlightenment* (Cambridge, 1987)
Riccoboni, L., *Sansone* in *Le Nouveau Théâtre Italien*, vol. 1 (Paris, 1733)
Romagnesi, J.-A., *Samson* (Paris, 1730) https://books.google.be/books?vid=GENT900000016007&printsec=frontcover#v=onepage&q&f=false
―――― et al., *Le Nouveau Théâtre Italien ou recueil général des comédies*, 10 vols (Paris, 1733)
Rousseau, Jean-Jacques, *Correspondance complète de Jean Jacques Rousseau*, ed. Ralph. A. Leigh, 52 vols (Geneva,1965)
―――, *Œuvres complètes*, 5 vols (Paris 1959–95)
The Royal Dictionary, ed. Abel Boyer (London, 1699)
Rubellin, Françoise, ed., *Théâtre de la foire, Anthologie de pièces inédites 1712–1736* (Paris, 2005)
Rundle, Thomas, *Letters of the late Thomas Rundle, LL. D. Lord Bishop of Derry in Ireland, to Mrs. Barbara Sandys, of Miserden, Gloucestershire* (Dublin, 1789)
Saint-Simon, duc de, *Mémoires sur le siècle de Louis XIV et la Régence* (Paris, 1858)
Sauval, Henri, *Histoire et recherches des antiquités de la ville de Paris* (Paris, 1724)
Seymour, Robert [John Mottley], *A Survey of the Cities of London and Westminster, Borough of Southwark, and parts adjacent* (2 vols, London, 1734–5)
Steele, Richard, *The Epistolary Correspondence of Richard Steele*, ed. John Nichols, 2 vols (London, 1787)
―――, *The Theatre*, ed. J. Loftis (Oxford, 1962)
Swift, Jonathan, *Poems on Several Occasions* (Dublin, 1735)
Thiébault, Dieudonné, *Mes Souvenirs de vingt ans de séjour à Berlin* 5 vols (Paris, 1805)
Vézian, Antoine, *Ode au roi sur son avènement à la couronne* (London, 1727)
Victor, Benjamin, *A History of the Theatres of London and Dublin* 2 vols (London, 1761)
Voltaire, [François-Marie Arouet], *Dictionnaire Philosophique*, ed. Christiane Mervaud (Oxford, 1994)

———, *Œuvres Complètes de Voltaire*, 205 vols (Oxford, 1968–2010)
Walpole, Horace, *The Yale Edition of Horace Walpole's Correspondence*, 48 vols (New Haven, 1937–83)
Weaver, John, *The Loves of Mars and Venus; a dramatic entertainment of dancing* (London, 1717)

Secondary Sources

van Aelbrouck, Jean-Philippe, *Les comédiens itinerants á Bruxelles au xviii siècle* (Brussels, 2022)
———, *Dictionnaire des danseurs à Bruxelles de 1600 à 1830* (Liège, 1994)
Arbellot, Guy, 'La grande mutation des routes de France au XVIIIe siècle', *Annales*, 28:3 (1973), 765–91
Aspden, Suzanne, 'Ariadne's Clew: Politics, Allegory, and Opera in London (1734)', *The Musical Quarterly*, 85:4 (2001), 735–70
Attinger, Gustave, *L'Esprit de la Commedia dell'arte dans le Théâtre Français* (Neuchâtel, 1950)
Avery, Emmett L., 'Dancing and Pantomime on the English Stage, 1700–1737', *Studies in Philology*, 31 (1934), 417–52
———, 'Two French Children on the English Stage, 1716–1719', *Philological Quarterly*, 13 (1934), 78.
———, 'Foreign Performers in the London Theaters in the Early Eighteenth Century', *Philological Quarterly*, 16 (April 1937), 105–23
———, 'The Shakespeare Ladies Club', *Shakespeare Quarterly*, 7:2 (1956), 153–8
———, et al., eds, *The London Stage, 1660–1800*, 11 vols (Carbondale, 1960–68)
de Baecque, Antoine, 'Les éclats du rire. Le Régiment de la calotte, ou les stratégies aristocratiques de la gaieté française (1702–1752)', *Annales, Histoire, Sciences Sociales*, 52:3 (1997), 477–511
Bahier-Laporte, Christelle, *La Poétique d'Alain-René Lesage* (Paris, 2006)
Baldensperger, Fernand, 'Un Incident théâtral franco-anglais au XVIIIe siècle', *Revue de littérature comparée* (1929), 573–8
Baldwin, Olive, and Thelma Wilson, '"250 Years of Roast Beef", *The Musical Times* 126 (1706) (April 1985), 203–7
Barberet, Victor, *Lesage et le Théâtre de la Foire* (Nancy, 1887; reprint, Geneva, 1970)
Barlow, Jeremy, and Moira Goff, 'Dancing in Early Productions of "The Beggar's Opera"', *Dance Research: The Journal of the Society for Dance Research* 33:2, Dance and Opera Essays to Honour the Memory of Andrew Porter (1928–2015) (2015), 143–58
Barnes, Clifford, 'Vocal Music at the Théâtres de la Foire (1697–1762); Part 1: Vaudeville', *Recherches sur la musique française classique* 8 (1968), pp. 141–60
Barthélemy, Maurice, 'L'opéra-comique des origines à la Querelle des Bouffons' in Vendrix, *L'Opéra-comique en France au XVIIIème siècle*
Beaucé, Pauline et Françoise Rubellin, 'Vos pièces sont farcies de Gascons: enjeux d'une figure comique sur les scènes parisiennes du XVIIIe siècle', *Littératures classiques* 87:2 (2015), 301–15
Berthiaume, Pierre, 'Lesage et le spectacle forain', *Études françaises* 15: 1–2 (1979), 125–41.

Bleys, Rudi, *The Geography of Perversion: Male to Male Sexual Perversion outside the West and the Ethnographic Imagination, 1750–1918* (New York, 1995)
Bord, Gustave, *La Franc-maçonnerie en France des origines à 1815* (Paris,1908)
Bouissou, Sylvie, *Jean-Philippe Rameau* (Paris, 2014)
Bourqui, C., *Les Sources de Molière* (Paris, 1999)
Brady, Valentini Papadopoulou, *Love in the Theatre of Marivaux* (Geneva, 1970)
Brenner, Clarence D., *The Théâtre Italien, its repertory 1716–1793* (Berkeley, 1961)
Brown, Gregory Stephen, *A Field of Honor: Writers, Court Culture, and Public Theater in Literary Life from Racine to the Revolution* (New York, 2005)
Brunot, Ferdinand, *Histoire de la langue française* (Paris, 1967)
Bulletin de la Société des historiens, vol. 7 (Paris, 1936), p. 120
Burnet, Mary Scott, *Marc-Antoine Legrand* (Paris, 1938)
Burrows, Donald, *Handel* (Oxford, 1994)
——— and Rosemary Dunhill, *Music and Theatre in Handel's World: The Family Papers of James Harris, 1732–1780* (Oxford, 2002)
Calder, Andrew, *Molière: The Theory and Practice of Comedy* (London, 1993)
Campardon, Émile, *Les Spectacles de la Foire* ([Paris,1877] (reprint, Geneva, 1970)
———, *Les Comédiens du roi de la troupe italienne pendant les deux derniers siècles* ([Paris, 1880]; reprint, Geneva, 1970)
Castillo, Susan P., *Colonial encounters in New World writing, 1500–1786: performing America* (London, 2005)
Chahine, Loïc, *Louis Fuzelier, le théâtre et la pratique du vaudeville: établissement et jalons d'analyse d'un corpus* (3 vols, doctoral thesis, University of Nantes, 2014) http://archive.bu.univ-nantes.fr/pollux/show.action?id=98d824f0-0c66-4eb3-beb8-d58a8a9fb96b
Chancerel, Léon, *Les Animaux au Théâtre* (Paris, 1950)
Chaponnière, Paul, 'Les comédies de mœurs du théâtre de la Foire', *Revue d'Histoire littéraire de la France* 4 (1913), 828–44
———, *Piron: sa vie et son œuvre* (Paris, 1910)
Charlton, David, and Sarah Hibberd, '"My Father Was a Poor Parisian Musician": A Memoir (1756) concerning Rameau, Handel's Library and Sallé', *Journal of the Royal Musical Association* 128:2 (2003), 161–99
Cheilan-Cambolin, Jeanne, 'Notes sur les trois premières salles d'Opera et de Comédie de Marseille', *Provence Historique* vol. 40, Fascicule 160 (April-May-June 1990), 147–55
Chinard, Gilbert, *L'Amérique et le rêve exotique dans la littérature française au XVIIe et XVIIIe siècle* (Paris, 1913)
Chrissochoidis, Ilias, 'Handel at a Crossroads. His 1737–1738 and 1738–1739 Seasons Re-examined', *Music and Letters* 90:4 (November 2009), 599–635
Clay, Lauren R., *Stagestruck: The Business of Theatre in Eighteenth-Century France and Its Colonies* (Ithaca, 2013)
Coley, William B., ed., *Henry Fielding: Contributions to The Champion, and Related Writings* (Oxford, 2003)
Colley, Linda, *Britons: Forging the Nation 1707–1837* (New Haven and London, 1992)
Conisbee, Philip and Aaron Wile, "Antoine Watteau/The Italian Comedians/probably 1720," French Paintings of the Fifteenth through Eighteenth Centuries,

NGA Online Editions, https://purl.org/nga/collection/artobject/32687 (accessed October 10, 2024).

Connon, Derek F., *Identity and transformation in the plays of Alexis Piron* (London, 2007)

———, 'Piron's Arlequin-Deucalion: Fair play or Anti-fair Play?', in *Essays on French Comic Drama from the 1640s to the 1780s*, ed. Derek Connon and George Evans (Berne, 2000)

Cook, William, *Elements of Dramatic Criticism* (London, 1775)

Cordier, Jean-François, 'Le Polype au Cœur de Jean-Jacques Rousseau', *Bulletin de l'Académie Nationale Médicale* 202: 1-2-3 (2017), 485–93.

de Courville, Xavier, *Un Apôtre de l'art du théâtre au XVIIIe siècle, Luigi Riccoboni dit Lélio* (Paris, 1945)

Coward, David A., 'Attitudes to Homosexuality in Eighteenth-Century France', *Journal of European Studies* 10:4 (1980) pp. 231–55

Cruickshanks, Eveline, and Howard Erskine-Hill, *The Atterbury Plot* (Basingstoke, 2004)

Cunningham, Hugh, 'The Language of Patriotism', in *Patriotism: The Making and Unmaking of British National Identity* (London, 1989)

Dacier, Émile, *Une Danseuse de l'Opéra sous Louis XV, Mlle Sallé (1707–1756)* (Paris, 1909)

Davis, C. A. C., 'John Rich as Lun', *Notes and Queries* (May 31, 1947), 222–4

Debauve, Jean-Louis, 'Théâtre et Spectacles à Lorient au XVIIIe siècle', *Revue d'Histoire du Théâtre* 18:1 (1966), 1–166

Dégranges, M. E., 'Mémoire à consulter sur l'état général des théâtres en province, et sur celui de Bordeaux en particulier', *Recueil des actes de l'Académie Royale des sciences, belles-lettres et Arts de Bordeaux, neuvième année* (Bordeaux, 1847), pp. 469–524

Desnoiresterres, Gustave, *La Comédie satirique au XVIIIe siècle* (Geneva, 1970)

———, *Voltaire et la société au XVIIIe siècle* (8 vols [Paris, 1871]; vol. 4, reprint, Berlin, 2010)

Destranges, Étienne [Étienne Louis Augustin Rouillé], *Le théâtre à Nantes depuis ses origines jusqu'à nos jours, 1430?-1893* (Paris, 1893)

Detcheverry, Arnaud, *Histoire des Théâtres de Bordeaux* (Bordeaux, 1860)

Deutsch, Otto, *Handel: A Documentary Biography* (London, 1955)

Dhondt, Frederik, *Balance of Power and Norm Hierarchy: Franco-British Diplomacy after the Peace of Utrecht* (Leyden, 2015)

Dickason, Olive Patricia, 'The Concept of l'homme sauvage and early French colonialism in the Americas', *Revue française d'histoire d'outre-mer* 64: 234 (1977), 5–32

Drack, Maurice, *Le Théâtre de la Foire, La Comédie Italienne et L'Opéra-Comique* ([Paris, 1889] repr., Geneva, 1970)

Duchartre, Pierre Louis, *La Comédie Italienne* (Paris, 1925)

Dugasseau, Charles, *Notice des tableaux composant le musée du Mans: précédée d'une notice historique* (Le Mans, 1870)

Ehrman, Esther, 'Huguenot participation in the French theatre in London, 1700–1750', *Proceedings of the Huguenot Society* 24:6 (1988), 480–92

Erenstein, R. L., 'De invloed van de commedia dell'arte in Nederland tot 1800', *Scenarium* 5 (1981), 91–106

Ewald, Alexander Charles, *The Life and Times of Prince Charles Stuart, Count of Albany* (London, 1875)

Faber, Frédéric, *Histoire du Théâtre Français en Belgique*, 5 vols (Paris and Brussels, 1877–82)

Fabre, Carole, *La Problématique du jeu et son architecture dans le théâtre de Lesage* (Ph.D. dissertation, City University of New York, 2007)

Fabriès-Verfaillie, Maryse, Pierre Stragiotti and Annie Jouve, *La France des villes: le temps des métropoles?* (Rosny, 2000)

Fétis, Édouard, *Les Musiciens belges* (Brussels, 1850)

Fletcher, Ifan Kyrle, 'Ballet in England, 1660–1740', in Fletcher, Selma Jeanne Cohen, and Roger H. Lonsdale, *Famed for Dance, Essays on the Theory and Practice of Theatrical Dancing in England, 1660–1740* (New York, 1959)

Font, Auguste, *Favart, L'Opéra-comique et la Comédies-Vaudeville aux XVIIe et XVIIIe siècles* ([Paris, 1894] repr. Geneva, 1970)

Foreman, Carolyn Thomas, *Indians Abroad, 1493–1938* (Norman, OK, 1943)

Fortin, Christine Annie, *Théâtre Forain, Culture Française* (University of Maryland, 1997)

Fransen, Jan, *Les Comédiens français en Hollande au XVIIe et au XVIIIe siècle* ([Paris, 1925] repr. Geneva, 1978)

Fuchs, Max, *La Vie théâtrale en province au XVIIIe siècle et Lexique des troupes de comédiens* ([Paris, 1944] repr. Geneva, 1976)

———, *La Vie théâtrale en province au XVIIIe siècle II*, ed. Henri Lagrave (Paris, 1986)

——— and P. Fuchs, 'Comédiens Français à Londres (1738–55)', *Revue de Littérature Comparée* 13, Paris (1933), 43–72

Gaiffe, Félix, *Le Rire et la scène française* (Paris, 1931)

Gasper, Julia, *The Marquis d'Argens: A Philosophical Life* (Plymouth, 2014)

Gay, Ignacio Ramos, 'The Comédie-Française in London (1879) and the Call for an English National Theatre', *Revue de littérature comparée* 1:345 (2013), 5–16

Gelléri, Gábor, *Philosophies du Voyage, visiter l'Angleterre aux 17e-18e siècles* (Oxford, 2016)

Gerrard, Christine, *Aaron Hill: The Muses' Projector, 1685–1750* (Oxford, 2003)

———, *The Patriot Opposition to Walpole: Politics, Poetry, and National Myth, 1725–1742* (Oxford, 1994)

Gidal, Eric, 'Civic Melancholy: English Gloom and French Enlightenment', *Eighteenth-Century Studies* 37:1 (2003), 23–45

Girdlestone, Cuthbert, 'Rameau's Self-Borrowings', *Music and Letters* 39:1 (January 1958), 52–6

Goff, Moira, 'The "London" Dupré', *Historical Dance* 3:6) (1999), 23–6

———, *The Incomparable Hester Santlow: A Dancer-Actress on the Georgian Stage* (Aldershot, 2007)

———, 'The Adroit and Elegant Monsieur Nivelon', in Segal, ed., *Dancing Master*, pp. 69–78

———, 'John Rich, French Dancing and English Pantomime', in Joncus and Barlow, *'The Stage's Glory'*

Gorrie, Richard, *Gentle riots? theatre riots in London 1730–1780* (Ph.D. thesis, University of Guelph, 2000)
Gouhier, Henri, *Rousseau et Voltaire: portraits dans deux miroirs* (Paris, 1983)
Goulbourne, Russell, 'The Comedy of National Character: Images of the English in Early Eighteenth-Century French Comedy', *Journal for Eighteenth-Century Studies* 33:3 (2010), 335–55
de Gouvenain, Louis, *Le théâtre à Dijon, 1422–1790* (1888)
Grundy, Isobel, *Lady Mary Wortley Montagu* (Oxford, 1999)
Guichemerre, Roger, '*La Princesse de Carizme* de Lesage; L'adaptation d'un conte persan au Théâtre de la Foire' in Yvonne Bellenger et al., eds, *L'Art du Théâtre; Mélanges en Hommage à Robert Garapon* (Paris, 1992), pp. 371–9
Hallays-Dabot, Victor, *Histoire de la censure théâtrale en France* (Paris, 1862)
Halsband, Robert, '"Condemned to Petticoats," Lady Mary Wortley Montagu as Feminist and Writer', in Robert B. White, Jr., ed., *The Dress of Words: Essays on Restoration and Eighteenth Century Literature in honour of Richmond P. Bond* (Lawrence, Kansas, 1978)
———, 'The First English Version of Marivaux's "Le Jeu de l'amour et du hasard,"' *Modern Philology* 79:1 (August 1981), 16–23
Hanson, Craig, 'Dr. Richard Mead and Watteau's "Comédiens Italiens"', *Burlington Magazine* 145 (April 2003), 265–72
Harris-Warrick, Rebecca, *Dance and Drama in French Baroque Opera: A History* (Cambridge, 2016)
Haydon, Colin, *Anti-Catholicism in Eighteenth-century England, c. 1714–80: A political and social study* (Manchester, 1993)
Hayley, Rodney L., 'Cibber, Collier, and *The Non-Juror*', *Huntington Library Quarterly* 43:1 (1979), 61–75
Herlaut, A.-P., 'Les enlèvements d'enfants à Paris en 1720 et 1750', *Revue historique* 139 (1922), 43–61
Heulhard, Arthur, *La Foire Saint-Laurent, son histoire et ses spectacles* (Paris, 1878)
d'Heylli, Georges, *La Comédie-Française à Londres (1871–1879)* (Paris, 1880)
Higgins, Ian, *Swift's Politics: A Study in Disaffection* (Cambridge, 1994)
Highfill, Philip H., Jr., Edward A. Langhans and Kalman Burnim, eds, *A Biographical Dictionary of Actors, Actresses, Musicians, Dancers, Managers, and Other Stage Personnel in London, 1660–1800*, 16 Vols (Carbondale, 1973–93)
Hillhouse, James T., *The Grub-Street Journal* (Durham, N.C., 1928)
Hostiou, Jeanne-Marie, Introduction and notes to *L'Ombre de la Foire*, in Rubellin, ed., *Théâtre de la Foire*, pp. 221–7
———, and Isabelle Degauque, eds, *Olivette Juge des Enfers*, in Rubellin, ed., *Théâtre de la Foire*, pp. 291–305
———, 'De la scène judiciaire à la scène théâtrale: le cas de l'année 1718 dans la querelle des théâtres', in J.-M. Hostiou et A. Viala, eds, *Littératures classiques*, 'Le Temps des querelles', 2013/2:82, 107–18
———, *Les miroirs de Thalie: le théâtre sur le théâtre et la Comédie-Française (1680–1762)* (Paris, 2019)

Hume, Robert D., 'Handel and Opera Management in London in the 1730s', *Music and Letters* 67:4 (October 1986), 347–62
———, *Henry Fielding and the London theatre, 1728–1737* (Oxford, 1988)
———, 'Henry Fielding and Politics at the Little Haymarket 1728–1737', in J. M. Wallace, ed., *The Golden and the Brazen World: Papers in Literature and History 1650–1800* (Berkeley and Los Angeles, 1985), pp. 79–124
The International Encyclopedia of Dance, ed. Selma Jeanne Cohen and Dance Perspectives Foundation (Oxford, 1998)
Isherwood, Robert M., *Farce and Fantasy: Popular Entertainment in Eighteenth-Century Paris* (Oxford, 1986)
Isnard, E., 'Notes sur la vie théâtrale à Marseille au XVIIIe siècle', *Bulletin de la société des historiens du théâtre*, 3 (1935), 5–13 and 37–49
Jacquot, Albert, *Notes pour servir à l'histoire du Théâtre en Lorraine*, Réunion des Sociétés des Beaux-Arts (Paris, 1892)
Johnston, Elsie, *Le Marquis d'Argens: sa vie et ses œuvres* ([Paris, 1928]; repr. Geneva, 1971)
Joncus, Berta and Jeremy Barlow, eds, *The Stage's Glory: John Rich, 1692–1761* (Newark, DE, 2011)
Kelly, Debra and Martyn Cornick, eds, *A History of the French in London: Liberty, Equality, Opportunity* (London, 2013)
Kelly, Deirdre, *Ballerina: Sex, Scandal, and Suffering Behind the Symbol of Perfection* (Vancouver, 2012)
Kenny, Robert V. 'The Théâtre Italien in France', in *Italian culture in northern Europe in the eighteenth century*, ed. Shearer West (Cambridge, 1999), pp. 172–86
———, 'The Edifying Spectacle: Images of *Le Sauvage* and *La Nouvelle-France* in the Theatre World of Early Eighteenth-Century France', in *Focus on Québec 2: Further Essays on Québécois Society & Culture,* ed. Ines Christine Molinaro and Christopher Rolfe (Edinburgh, 2000), pp. 15–29
———, 'A French Première on the London Stage: *Arlequin Balourd*, 1719', Society for Theatre Research Occasional Essays series (Feb. 2024) https://www.str.org.uk/publications/theatre-notebook/occasional-essays/arlequin-balourd-a-premiere-in-london-1719/
———, 'Dr Johnson, Francophobia and the Haymarket Theatre Riot of October 1738', forthcoming in *The New Rambler* (2025)
———, 'Mademoiselle Sallé and her Discontents', in Sarah McCleave's Dance Biography blog at Queen's University, Belfast (Jan. 2024): https://blogs.qub.ac.uk/dancebiographies/tag/robert-v-kenny/
Kern, Jean B., *Dramatic satire in the age of Walpole, 1720–1750* (Ames, IA, 1976)
Kinservik, Matthew J., *Disciplining Satire: The Censorship of Comedy on the Eighteenth-Century London Stage* (Lewisburg and London, 2002)
Kirkus Reviews, https://www.kirkusreviews.com/book-reviews/john-walters/the-royal-griffin-frederick-prince-of-wales-170/
Koon, Helene, *Colley Cibber: A Biography* (Lexington, KY, 1986)
Lagrave, Henri, *La Vie théâtrale à Bordeaux, des origines à nos jours*, vol. I, *Des origines à 1799* (Paris, 1985)
———, *Le Théâtre et le public à Paris de 1715 à 1750* (Paris, 1972)

Lang, Andrew, *A History of Scotland from the Roman Occupation* (Edinburgh, 1907)
Langford, Paul, *A Polite and Commercial People: England, 1727–1783* (Oxford, 1989)
La Porte, Joseph and J. M. B. Clément, *Anecdotes dramatiques*, vol. 1 (Paris, 1775)
Larthomas, Pierre Henri, *Le Théâtre en France au XVIIIe siècle* (Paris, 1980)
Laurenti, Jean-Noël, *Valeurs morales et religieuses sur la scène de l'Académie royale de Musique (1669–1737)* (Geneva, 2002)
Lemaigre-Gaffier, Pauline, *Administrer les menus plaisirs du roi: L'Etat, la cour et les spectacles dans la France des Lumières* (Champ Vallon, 2016)
Lepore, Ilaria, *Le théâtre polémique ou comment faire l'histoire sur la scène La concurrence entre Comédie Française, Comédie Italienne et Théâtres de la Foire et ses effets sur la vie théâtrale pendant la première moitié du XVIIIe siècle* (doctoral thesis, Sorbonne, 2017) https://hal.sorbonne-universite.fr/tel-04007506v1
Levenson, Erica Pauline, *Traveling Tunes: French Comic Opera and Theater in London, 1714–1745* (Ph.D. dissertation, Cornell University, 2017) https://ecommons.cornell.edu/items/c5703427-5b01-4921-bf3f-9fd40ba8088a.
Liebrecht, Henri, *Histoire du Théâtre Français à Bruxelles au XVIIe et au XVIIIe siècle* (Paris, 1923)
Lockwood, Thomas, 'Cross-Channel Dramatics in the Little Haymarket Theatre Riot of 1738', S*tudies in Eighteenth-Century Culture* 25 (1996), 63–74
Loftis, John, 'The London Theaters in Early Eighteenth-Century Politics', *Huntington Library Quarterly* 18:4 (August 1955), 365–93
———, 'Richard Steele and the Drury Lane Management', *Modern Language Notes* 66:1 (January 1951), 7–11
Long, Lynne, 'Lady Mary Translates Marivaux: A Female Perspective?', *Palimpsestes* 22 (2009), 129–47
de Luca, Emanuele, *Il Repertorio della Comédie-Italienne di Parigi (1716–1762)* (Paris, 2011)
———, *'Un uomo di qualche talent.' François Antoine Valentin Riccoboni (1707–1772): vita, attività teatrale, poetica di un attore-autore nell'Europa dei Lumi* (Pisa-Roma, 2015)
Lurcel, Dominique, ed., *Le Théâtre de le Foire au XVIIIe siècle*, Collection 10/18 (Paris, 1983)
Lyonnet, Henry, *Dictionnaire des Comédiens Français* ([Paris, 1912]; repr. Geneva, 1969)
Mackey, A., and H. L. Haywood, *Encyclopedia of Freemasonry*, 3 vols ([Chicago, 1912]; repr. Kessinger, vol. 1, 2003, vols 2 & 3, 2010)
Marcetteau-Paul, Agnès, 'Les Théâtres des Foires Saint-Germain et Saint-Laurent dans la première moitié du XVIIIe siècle (1697–1762)' Unpublished thesis, École des Chartes (1983)
Markovits, R., *Civiliser l'Europe; Politiques du théâtre français au XVIIIe siècle* (Paris, 2014)
Marshall, Louise, *National Myth and Imperial Fantasy: Representations of British Identity on the Early Eighteenth-Century Stage* (London, 2008)
Martin, Isabelle, *L'Animal sur les planches au XVIIIe siècle* (Paris, 2007)

——, *Le Théâtre de la Foire : des tréteaux aux boulevards* (Oxford, 2002)

——, 'Usage et esthétique du miroir dans une pièce orientale : "La Statue merveilleuse" de Lesage', *L'Esprit Créateur* 39:3 (Fall 1999), 47–55

Mattauch, Hans, 'Inès, Agnès, *Inesilla*: Parodies françaises et espagnoles d'Inès de Castro', in Sylvain Menant, and Dominique Quéro, eds, *Séries parodiques au siècle des Lumières* (Paris, 2005), pp. 29–40

Mazouer, Charles, *Le Théâtre d'Arlequin : comédies et comédiens italiens en Belgique au XVIIe siècle* (Paris, 2002)

McCleave, Sarah., *Dance in Handel's London Operas* (Rochester, NY, 2013)

——, 'Dancing at the English Opera, Marie Sallé's Letter to the Duchess of Richmond', *Dance Research* 17:1 (Summer 1999), 22–46

——, 'Marie Sallé and the development of the ballet en action', *Journal of the Society for Musicology in Ireland* 3(2007–8), 1–23

——, 'Marie Sallé, a Wise Professional Woman of Influence', in Lynn Matluck Brooks, ed., *Women's Work: Making Dance in Europe before 1800* (Madison, 2007)

McEachern J.-A. and D. Smith, 'The First Edition of Mme de Graffigny's Cénie', in David Garrioch, Harold Love, Brian McMullin, Ian Morrison and Meredith Sherlock, eds, *The Culture of the Book. Essays from Two Hemispheres in Honour of Wallace Kirsop* (Melbourne, 1999), pp. 201–17

McGeary, Thomas, 'Farinelli and the English: "One God" or the Devil?', *Revue LISA/LISA e-journal* 2:3 (2004), paras. 19–28

——, 'Farinelli's Progress to Albion: The Recruitment and Reception of Opera's 'Blazing Star"', *Journal for Eighteenth-Century Studies* 28:3 (December 2000), 339–60

——, *The Politics of Opera in Handel's Britain* (Cambridge, 2013)

——, 'Verse Epistles on Italian Opera Singers, 1724–1736', *Royal Musical Association Research Chronicle* 33 (2000), 29–88

McPherson, Heather, 'Theatrical Riots and Cultural Politics in Eighteenth-Century London', *The Eighteenth Century: Theory and Interpretation* 43:3 (Fall 2002), 236–52

Menant, Sylvain, and Dominique Quéro, eds, *Séries parodiques au siècle des Lumières* (Paris, 2005)

Michel, Artur, 'The Ballet d'Action before Noverre', *Dance Index* 6:3 (April 1947), 64–6

Migel, Parmenia, *The Ballerinas, from the Court of Louis XIV to Pavlova* (London,1972)

Miles, Dudley, 'A Forgotten Hit: *The Nonjuror*', *Studies in Philology* 16:1 (January 1919), 67–77

Milhous, Judith, 'Opera Finances in London, 1674–1738', *Journal of the American Musicological Society* 37:3 (1984), 567–92

——, 'The Capacity of Vanbrugh's Theatre in the Haymarket', *Theatre History Studies* 4 (1984), 38–46

——, 'The Economics of Theatrical Dance in Eighteenth-Century London', *Theatre Journal* 55:3 (October 2003), 481–508

Milhous, Judith and Robert D. Hume, 'Construing and Misconstruing Farinelli in London', *British Journal for Eighteenth-Century Studies* 28:3 (December 2005), 361–85

―――, 'Handel's London: the Theatres' in Donald Burrows, ed., *The Cambridge Companion to Handel* (Cambridge, 1997)
―――, 'Handel's Opera Finances in 1732-3', *The Musical Times* 125 (1692), February 1984, 86-9
Mitchell, Louis D., 'Command Performances During the Reign of George II', *CLA Journal* 31:2 (December 1987), 223-39
Monod, Jacques, *Jacobitism and the English people, 1688-1788* (Cambridge, 1989)
Mooser, Robert-Aloys, *Annales de la Musique et des Musiciens en Russie au 18ème siècle* (Geneva, 1948)
de Morembert, Henri Tribout, *Le Théâtre à Metz*, vol 1: *Du moyen age à la revolution* (Metz. 1952)
Morris, Thelma, *L'abbé Desfontaines et son rôle dans la littérature de son temps, Institut et musée Voltaire* (Oxford, 1961)
Nevile, Jennifer, *Dance, spectacle, and the body politick, 1250-1750* (Bloomington, 2008)
Nicolas, Jean-François, *Journal de ce qui s'est passé à Nancy*; see Pfister
Nicoll, Allardyce, *A History of Early Eighteenth Century Drama: 1700-1750* (Cambridge, 1925)
―――, *History of English Drama* (Cambridge, 1959)
―――, *The World of Harlequin, A Critical Study of the Commedia dell'Arte* (Cambridge, 1963)
Nye, Edward, 'L'Allégorie dans le ballet d'action: Marie Sallé à travers l'écho des parodies', *Revue d'Histoire littéraire de la France* 108:2 (2008), pp. 289-309
O'Brien, John, *Harlequin Britain: Pantomime and Entertainment, 1690-1760* (Baltimore and London, 2004)
Offredi, Frédérique, *Monologues en France du Moyen Age à Raymond Devos* (Ph.D. thesis, Queen's University, Kingston, Ontario, Canada, 2010): https://qspace.library.queensu.ca/items/3a4b6a35-e1f9-49ef-a212-e8410a6641be/full
Olivier, Jean-Jacques, *Les Comédiens Français dans les Cours d'Allemagne au XVIIIe siècle, deuxième série: la cour royale de Prusse* (Paris, 1901-5)
O'Reilly, Patrice-Jean, *Histoire complète de Bordeaux*, 7 vols (Bordeaux, 1860)
Orsino, Margherita, 'Les Errances d'Arlequin, Pierre-François Biancolelli aux Théâtres de la Foire entre 1708 et 1717', in Irène Mamczarz, ed., *La Commedia dell'Arte, le Théâtre Forain et les spectacles de plein air en Europe: XVIe-XVIIIe siècles* (Paris, 1998)
Ouellet, R. 'Adario: le Sauvage philosophe de Lahontan', *Québec français* 142 (2006), 57-60
Papetti, Viola, *Arlecchino a Londra: la pantomima inglese, 1700-1728 (studi e testi)* (Naples, 1977)
Paul, Agnès, 'Les auteurs du théâtre de la foire à Paris au XVIIIe siècle', *Bibliothèque de l'école des chartes* 141:2 (1983), 307-35
Pelkey, Stanley, 'Political discourse and the Representation of Authority in the music of Handel', *Newsletter of the American Handel Society* (1998) 13(3): 5. https://www.americanhandelsociety.org/static/newsletters/Winter_1998.c6ddb7046f63.pdf
Pfister, Christian, ed., 'Journal de Jean-François Nicolas', *Mémoires de la Société d'archéologie lorraine et du Musée historique lorrain* 49 (1899), 216-386
―――, 'Le Théâtre à Nancy au XVIII siècle', *Le Pays Lorrain* 7 (1900), 98

———, *Histoire de Nancy* (Paris, 1908)
Poisot, Charles, *Histoire de la musique en Belgique* (Paris, 1860)
Pougin, Arthur, *Un ténor de l'Opéra au XVIIIe siècle: Pierre Jélyotte* (Paris, 1905)
von Proschwitz, Gunnar, ed., *Influences: relations culturelles entre la Belgique et la Suède* (Gothenburg, 1988)
Prou, Fanny, *Pour une nouvelle historiographie foraine. Constitution, analyse et édition d'un répertoire (1717–1727)* (doctoral thesis, 3 vols, University of Nantes, 2019)
Quesnay, François, *Œuvres économiques complètes et autres textes* (Paris, 2005)
Rex, Walter, *The Attraction of the Contrary: Essays on the Literature of the French Enlightenment* (Cambridge, 1987)
Richardot, Anne, 'Cythère redécouverte: la nouvelle géographie érotique des Lumières', *CLIO: Histoire, femmes et sociétés* 22 (2005), 3–4 & 12
Richards, K. and L. Richards, *The Commedia dell'Arte, a Documentary History* (Oxford, 1990)
Richtman, Jack, *Adrienne Lecouvreur: The Actress and the Age* (Englewood Cliffs, NJ, 1971)
Ritchie, Fiona, *Women and Shakespeare in the Eighteenth Century* (Cambridge, 2014)
Rizzoni, Nathalie, 'Le Geste éloquent: la pantomime en Belgique au XVIIIe siècle', in Jacqueline Waeber, ed., *Musique et Geste en Belgique de Lully à la Révolution: études sur la musique, le théâtre et la danse* (Berne, 2009)
Robarts, Leslie Michael Martin, *A bibliographical and textual study of the wordbooks for James Miller's Joseph and his Brethren and Thomas Broughton's Hercules, oratorio librettos set to music by George Frederic Handel, 1743–44* (Ph.D. thesis, University of Birmingham, 2008) https://core.ac.uk/reader/77530
Roberts, Edgar V., 'Henry Fielding and Richard Leveridge: Authorship of "The Roast Beef of Old England"', *Huntington Library Quarterly* 27:2 (February 1964), 175–81
Rogers, Nicholas, 'Popular Protest in Early Hanoverian London', *Past & Present* 79:1 (1978), 70–100
Rogers, Vanessa L., 'John Gay, Ballad Opera and the Théâtres de la Foire', *Eighteenth-Century Music* 11:2 (2014), 173–213
Rooke, Deborah W., *Handel's Israelite Oratorio Libretti: Sacred Drama and Biblical Exegesis* (Oxford, 2012)
Rose, Gilbert, Metz et la musique au XVIIIe siècle (Metz, 1992)
Rosenfeld, Sybil, *Foreign Theatrical Companies in Great Britain in the 17th and 18th Centuries*, The Society for Theatre Research Pamphlet Series, no. 4 (London, 1954–5)
Ross, Mary Ellen, 'Amazones et Sauvagesses: rôles féminins et sociétés exotiques dans le théâtre de la foire', in Haydn Mason, ed., *Miscellany/Mélanges,* Studies in Voltaire and the Eighteenth Century 319 (Oxford, 1994), pp. 29–53
Rothbard, Murray N., *Economic Thought before Adam Smith* (Aldershot, 1995)
de Rougemont, Martine, *La Vie théâtrale en France au XVIIIe siècle* (Paris, 2001)
Rubellin, Françoise, 'Marie Sallé : du nouveau sur sa naissance (1709) et sur ses premiers rôles à la Foire', *Annales de l'Association pour un Centre de recherche sur les Arts du Spectacle aux XVIIe et XVIIIe siècles* 3 (June 2008), 21–5
———, ed., *Théâtre de la Foire: anthologie de pièces inédites, 1712–1736* (Montpellier, 2005)

Sadler, Graham, 'Rameau, Piron and the Parisian Fair Theatres', *Soundings* 4 (1974), 13–29
Sakhnovskaia-Pankeeva, Anastasia, 'Chronique d'une petite guerre. Autour d'une parodie inédite de Lesage: *La Reine des Péris*.' In Sylvain Menant and Dominique Quéro, eds, *Séries parodiques au siècle des Lumières* (Paris, 2005)
———, *La Naissance des Théâtres de la Foire: influence des Italiens et constitution d'un répertoire* (doctoral thesis, 2 vols, University of Nantes, 2013) http://cethefi.org/doc/SAKHNOVSKAIA%20THESE%20VOLUME%20I.pdf
Sarcey, Francisque, *Quarante Ans de Théâtre* (Paris, 1900)
Schuchard, Marsha Keith, *Emanuel Swedenborg, Secret Agent on Earth and in Heaven* (Leiden, 2012)
Scott, Virginia P., *The Commedia dell'Arte in Paris, 1644–97* (Charlottesville, 1990)
———, 'The Infancy of English Pantomime: 1716–1723', *Educational Theatre Journal* 24:2 (May 1972), 125–34
Sée, Henri, *La France économique et sociale au XVIIIe siècle* (Paris, 1925)
Segal, Barbara, ed., *Dancing Master or Hop Merchant: The role of the Dance Teacher through the Ages* (London, 2008)
Sells, Arthur, *Les Sources Françaises de Goldsmith* ([Paris, 1924]; repr. Geneva, 1977)
Sgard, Jean, *Le 'Pour et contre' de Prévost* (Paris, 1969), introduction, tables et index
———, *Dictionnaire des Journalistes (1600—1789)* 2 vols (Oxford, 1999).
Smith, Ruth, *Handel's Oratorios and Eighteenth-century Thought* (Cambridge, 1995)
Spaziani, Marcello, *Il Teatro della Foire* (Rome, 1965)
Stokes, John, T*he French Actress and Her English Audience* (Cambridge, 2005)
Storey, Robert F., *Pierrot: A Critical History of a Mask* (Princeton, 1978)
Striker, Ardelle, 'A Curious form of Protest Theatre: The *Pièce À Écriteaux*', *Theatre Survey* 14:1 (May 1973), 55–71
Sund, Judy, 'Why So Sad? Watteau's Pierrots', *The Art Bulletin* 98:3 (2016), 321–47
Sweet, Julie Anne, *Negotiating for Georgia: British-Creek Relations in the Trustee Era, 1733–1752* (Athens, Georgia, 2005)
Thompson, E. P., *Whigs and Hunters. The Origin of the Black Act* (London, 1975)
Thorp, Jennifer, 'From Scaramouche to Harlequin: dances 'in grotesque characters' on the London stage', in Kathryn Lowerre, ed., *The Lively Arts of the London Stage, 1675–1725* (Farnham and Burlington, 2014), pp. 113–27
———, 'Pierrot strikes back: François Nivelon at Lincoln's Inn Fields and Covent Garden, 1723–1738', in Joncus and Barlow, eds, *The Stage's Glory: John Rich, 1692–1761 (2011)* pp. 138–43
Tinant, Julie, 'Introduction to *Magotin*' (Master's thesis, University of Nantes, 2014)
Todd, Helen, *Tomochichi, Indian friend of the Georgia Colony* (Marietta, GA, 2005)
Trott, David, 'Pour une histoire des spectacles non-officiels : Louis Fuzelier et le théâtre à Paris en 1725–6', *Revue de la Société d'Histoire du Théâtre* 3 (1985), 255–75
Trousson, Raymond, *Le Thème de Prométhée dans la littérature européenne* (Geneva, 2001)

Vaughan, Alden T., *Transatlantic Encounters: American Indians in Britain, 1500–1776* (Cambridge, 2006)
Vendrix, Philippe, ed., *L'Opéra-comique en France au XVIIIème siècle* (Liège, 1992)
Verèb, Pascale, *Alexis Piron, poète (1689–1773): la difficile condition d'auteur sous Louis XV* (Oxford, 1993)
Vince, Stanley, 'Marie Sallé, 1707–56', *Theatre Notebook* 2:1 (1957), 7–14
Vinti, Claudio, *Jean-Antoine Romagnesi al 'Théâtre Italien'* (Naples, 1988)
Walsh, Paul, 'Henry Brooke's *Gustavus Vasa*: The ancient constitution and the example of Sweden', *Studia Neophilologica* 64:1 (1992), 67–79
Walters, John, *The Royal Griffin, Frederick Prince of Wales 1707–51* (New York, 1972)
Wells, Mitchell P., 'Some Notes on the Early Eighteenth-Century Pantomime', *Studies in Philology* 32:4 (1935), 598–607
Wolff, Larry, *The Singing Turk: Ottoman Power and Operatic Emotions on the European Stage* (Stanford, 2016)
Woodfine, Philip, *Britannia's Glories: The Walpole Ministry and the 1739 War with Spain* (Woodbridge and Rochester, NY, 1998)
Zazzo, Lawrence, *'Not Local Beauties': Handel's Bilingual Oratorio Performances, 1732–1744* (Ph.D. thesis, Queen's University, Belfast, 2015) https://pureadmin.qub.ac.uk/ws/portalfiles/portal/339474120/Not_local_beauties_Doctoral_Thesis_Lawrence_Zazzo_Queens_2015.pdf

Websites

https://www.siv.archives-nationales.culture.gouv.fr/siv/rechercheconsultation/recherche/ir/rechercheGeneralisteResultat.action?searchText=Moylin&formCaller=GENERALISTE
Buffon, [Georges-Louis Leclerc, comte de Bouffon], *Correspondance de Buffon*, édition électronique, http://www.buffon.cnrs.fr/
CÉSAR (Calendrier électronique des spectacles sous l'ancien regime et sous la révolution) https://cesar.huma-num.fr/cesar2/
CETHEFI (Centre d'Etudes des Théâtres de la Foire et de la Comédie Italienne) http://cethefi.org/memoire_master.htm.
CIDRE (Centre Interdépartemental de Documentation et de Recherche, University of Nantes)
Conisbee, Philip, Aaron Wile, 'The Italian Comedians', *French Paintings of the Fifteenth through Eighteenth Centuries*, National Gallery of Art Online Editions. https://purl.org/nga/collection/artobject/32687
Cummings, Graham, 'Handel's Organ Concertos (HWV 290–93) and Operatic Rivalry', *The GFH Journal*, 1 (2007), p 6. https://core.ac.uk/download/pdf/60395.pdf
Dorneval or d'Orneval, Jacques Philippe, *L'Isle du Gougou*; http://www.theatre-classique.fr/pages/programmes/edition.php?t=../documents/LESAGEDORNEVAL_ILEGOUGOU.xml
Goff, Moira, *Dance in History*, 'The Love of Mars and Venus in context', https://danceinhistory.com/?s=love+of+mars+and+venus
———, 'Season of Dancing: 1716–1717': https://danceinhistory.com/2021/06/19/season-of-dancing-1716-1717/

Handel at Boughton, http://www.boughtonhouse.co.uk/wp-content/uploads/2017/04/Handel-A0-All-Panels_lower-res.pdf

Hostiou, Jeanne-Marie Fiche, *Querelle des théâtres en 1718*, https://obvil.huma-num.fr/agon/querelles/querelle-des-theatres-en-1718

Kenny, Robert V., 'Mademoiselle Sallé and Her Discontents', https://blogs.qub.ac.uk/dancebiographies/tag/marie-salle/

'Un Lazzo italien: la scene de nuit', *Théâtre à la Source,* https://alexandrin.org/focus/scenesdenuit/

Lesage, Alain-René, Jacques-Philippe d'Orneval, *Magotin*, http://jtsbook.blogspot.co.uk/2016/06/presentation-dune-piece-magotin-de.html

McCleave, Sarah Y., 'Dance Biographies' blog; https://blogs.qub.ac.uk/dancebiographies

———., 'Italian dancers in eighteenth-century London',;https://www.academia.edu/4681376/Italian_dancers_in_eighteenth-century_London

Merle, René, (digital blog) 'Théâtre en provençal, 18e siècle, notices biblio-bibliographiques', http://archivoc.canalblog.com/archives/2014/10/17/30740314.html

Ourcel, Bertrand, ed., *Edition critique de trois manuscrits* (Fuzelier, *État des pièces*; Fuzelier, *Opéra Comique*; Anonyme, *Nouveaux Mémoires sur la Foire*), 2009 http://cethefi.org/memoire_master.htm

Poèmes satiriques du XVIIIème siècle; https://satires18.univ-st-etienne.fr/texte/b%C3%A9quille-barnaba-revue-de-d%C3%A9tail-mme-de-mailly-cardinal-de-fleury-%C3%A9v%C3%AAques-du-mans-de-vienne-ml

Prescott, Andrew, *Farewell lecture to the Centre for Research into Freemasonry*, 20 February, 2006: http://www.freemasons-freemasonry.com/prescott16.html

Rasch, Rudolf, *Muzikale advertenties in nederlandse kranten, 1621–1794*. See p. 58 of https://muziekinderepubliek.sites.uu.nl/wp-content/uploads/sites/413/2018/12/Muzikale-advertenties-1751-1755.pdf

Anne Richardot, 'Cythère redécouverte: la nouvelle géographie érotique des Lumières', *CLIO: Histoire, femmes et sociétés* 22 (2005), pp. 3–4 & 12.https://journals.openedition.org/clio/1747

Rizzoni, Nathalie, 'Féerire à la foire', *Féeries*, 5 (2008); http://feeries.revues.org/691

Romagnesi, J.-A., *Samson*, 1734 edition https://www.google.co.uk/books/edition/Samson/3QUUAAAAQAAJ?hl=en&gbpv=1&dq=Samson+Bruxelles+1734&pg=PA1&printsec=frontcover

Rubellin, Françoise, 'Images of Theatrical Rivalry: Form and Function of the Fair Theater's Engraved Frontispieces', *Proceedings of the CESAR/Clark Symposium*, Williamstown, Mass., USA, September 2008; http://www.cesar.org.uk/cesar2/conferences/conference_2008/rubellin_08.html

Tinant, Julie, ed., Introduction to *Magotin* (from unpublished master's thesis edition, University of Nantes, 2014); http://jtsbook.blogspot.co.uk/2016/06/presentation-dune-piece-magotin-de.html

Wick, Rebecca, biographical information: https://francearchives.fr/en/search?q=WICK+Rebecca

INDEX

Page numbers in bold refer to illustrations and their captions.

'à la muette' 163, 289
Abbot, William 80
Académie Française 151
acrobats 13–14, 51–2, 74
acting profession
   actors vs. fairground entertainers 64
   and Catholic church 7, 117
Addison, Joseph 76
   Cato 237
Aelbrouck, Jean-Philippe van
   discovery of parish registers viii, 6, 308
   Hus letter 247 n.30
   Malter(s) and the Opéra 179 n.28, 241 n.8, 290
   Marie Châteauneuf 180 n.30
   Marie Sallé's birth date 8, 299 n.8
Agapit Chicagou, Chief 212
Agincourt, battle of (1415) 200, 252
Alard, Marguerite (née Lalauze) 105
Alard family
   Alard père
      Foire Saint-Germain (1678) 9–10
      Les Forces de l'amour et de la magie 9–10
      ghost figure in *L'Ombre d'Alard* 93
      Night Scene at Drury Lane 15
   brothers Charles and Pierre
      Foire Saint-Laurent (1711) 8–9
      Francisque's entertainment in imitation of 51
      Harlequin dances 19
      'mimick scenes' 79
      Night Scenes 14, 15, 15 n.48, 20, 311
   Charles
      death after onstage fall (1711) 9, 93
      ghost figure in *L'Ombre d'Alard* 93
   Pierre
      Foire Saint-Laurent (1721) 94
      married to Lalauze's sister Marguerite 105
      retirement from stage and dentistry 105
Alembert, Jean Le Rond d' 156
Allainval, Léonor-Jean-Christine Soulas d'
   Arlequin sauvage wrongly attributed to 214
   Comédie-Italienne author 195
   in Dijon season programme (1739–40) 287
   L'Embarras des richesses 188 n.1
      1733–4 Brussels season 171
      1734–5 London season 191, 196, 197, 210
      1738 London season (discontinued) 254, 263
      1739 Compiègne season 278
      Benefit for Francis Sallé's widow 203
      a favourite of Francisque's 171
      frontispiece of 1735 London edition **172**
      revived by Francis Cochois 306
      revived by Martin Simon Moylin 300–1
   Francisque's introduction of his plays to England 312
   roles played by Thomassin and Francisque 208
ambigu-comique 152, 288
Amelia, Princess 191
Amiens
   Francisque's company (1733) 168
   Francisque's company (1738) 248

Michel Cochois's performance
(1714)   6 n.11
Simon Moylin and J.-B. Lesage's
troupe (1741)   289–90
Amusemens Littéraires   256, 273
Anderson, Misty G.   258 n.28
Andrews, John   312–13
Anglicus (*nom de plume*)   255–6
Anglophilia   163
Anglophobia   289
see also Francophobia; xenophobia
Anne, Princess Royal and Princess of
Orange   191, 196, 198, 211, 223
Annuaire Dramatique de Belgique (pour 1840)   174 n.9
application concept   220, 221
Archives Générales du Royaume,
Brussels   170
Argens, Barbe Boyer d'   304 n.33
Argens, Jean-Baptiste de Boyer, marquis
d'Argens   247 n.28, 303–4, 306–7,
310
Argenson, René-Louis de Voyer de
Paulmy, marquis d'Argenson   82,
123–4, 213, 228, 230, 278–9
Aristophanes, *The Wasps*   229
Arlequin (Harlequin)
Arlequin and Harlequin as used in
book   x
'Arlequin philosophe'   195, 208, 210,
213
'Arlequin sauvage'   212, 213
'Chaconne pour Arlequin' (notated by
Le Roussau)   78, **79**
'the dog Harlequin'   217, 218, 235
English and French Harlequins in *The
Two Dogs* (poem)   235–6
Garrick
and Harlequin as Shakespeare's
demonic Other   270
Harlequin's Invasion   270, 312
silent Harlequin   183, 199, 219, 313
speaking Arlequin   20, 65, 199, 207,
213, 312–13
see also under Francisque (François
Moylin, known as Francisque)
Arlequin à la Foire (1986 student
production)   viii
Arles
Simon Moylin's troupe (1743), *La
Vengeance trompée* (Pierre de
Morand)   291

Arne, Richard   181, 182, 185
Arne, Susanna   181, 182, 185
Arne, Thomas   181, 183
Dido and Aeneas   182, 185
Attenborough Theatre Workshop   viii
Atterbury, Francis, Bishop of
Rochester   215, 218
Atterbury Plot (1722)   215, 218, 225
Attinger, Gustave   10, 11
Aubert, Jacques   124, 148
Audibert, Jean-Baptiste, *Le Fortuné
Marseillais*   244
Autreau, Jacques, *Le Naufrage au
Port-à-l'Anglais ou les Nouvelles
Débarqués*   36
Avery, Emmett L.   50 n.22, 193 n.15, 197
see also *The London Stage* (Emmett L.
Avery et al., eds)
Avesnes, N. Bertin, *Arlequin Apprenti
philosophe*   306
Avignon
Francisque's company (1736)   244
Francisque's company (1737)   247
Simon Moylin's troupe (1733)   168

Bahier-Porte, Christelle   26 n.13
ballet d'action   162, 289, 311, 315
ballet-pantomime   162–3, 295, 315
La Guinguette anglaise   162
La Noce anglaise   162, 163
Ballon (or Balon), Claude (often
incorrectly named Jean)   15, 16,
18, 180
Banks, John, *The Albion Queens, or
the Death of Mary, Queen of
Scotland*   182
Bar, Mlle de (Marie-Thérèse Quenaudon
known as Mlle de Bar)   107, 122,
125, 127
La Barbarina (Barbara Campanini, known
as La Barbarina)   303
Barberet, Victor   99
Barbier, Edmond Jean François   277, 290
Barbier, Nicolas   311
*Arlequin cru Colombine et Colombine
cru Arlequin; ou, l'Heureux
Naufrage*   88, 121 n.47
La Fille à la mode   54–7, 58, 86
Barlow, Jeremy   161 n.42, 191–2
*The Stage's Glory: John Rich
(1692–1761)*   2
Barnard, John, Sir   239

INDEX

Baron, Michel 64
Baudoin 191
Baune, Catherine de (née Vonderbeck) 9, 13, 22, 24
Baxter, Richard
  Drury Lane performances 20, 21
  English Arlequin 9, 15, 20–1, 85, 105
  Foire Saint-Germain (1712) 9
  Foire Saint-Germain (1716) 15
  Foire Saint-Laurent (1715) 11
  Foire Saint-Laurent (1716) 15
  Foire Saint-Laurent (1721) 94
  Harlequin dances 19
  Lun identity mystery 20–1
  'mimick scenes' 79
  Night Scenes 14, 15, 20, 311
  revival of Alard brothers' act 51
  withdrew to hermitage 105
Behn, Aphra
  Agnes de Castro, or the Force of Generous Love 227
  Harlequin Emperor of the Moon 20, 49
belle danse 19, 94, 183
Belloni (Italian banker) 217–18
Belloni, Antoine 8
Benefits
  concept 203
  expected profits 43
  for Farinelli (March 1735) 204, 206
  for Francis Sallé's widow (March 1735) 203
  for Francisque (1719) 46
  for Francisque (1720) 76
  for Francisque (February 1735) 204, 205–10, 236
  for Jean-Baptiste Malter (1735) 192 n.14
  for Marie Sallé (1734, March) 184–5, 204
  for Marie Sallé (1735, April) 204–5
  organised by Rich (1719) 46
'La Béquille du Père Barnaba' (song) 277–8
Berlin, Frederick the Great's court 2, 293, 298, 302–4, 306–7, 310, 314
Bertin de la Doué, Toussaint, *Ajax* 148
Berwick, James FitzJames Stuart, 2nd Duke of Berwick 233
Besançon 7, 167, 292, 301
Biancolelli, Domenico (Dominique) 7, 78 n. 35, 207

Biancolelli, Jeanne-Jacquette (née Tortoriti) 7
Biancolelli, Louis
  Arlequin misanthrope (with Dufresny/ Brugière de Barante) 49 n.18
  Les Pasquinades Italiennes ou Arlequin médecin des mœurs (with Dufresny/Brugière de Barante) 49 n.18
Biancolelli, Pierre-François see Dominique (Pierre-François Biancolelli, a.k.a. Dominique)
Bibiena, Francesco 241
biblical drama, ban on in English theatre 231
Bienfait, Nicolas 143 n.44
Bill for the Regulation of the Stage (1735) 239, 250
Blanc, François, known as Blanc la Goutte, *Épître en vers, au langage vulgaire de Grenoble* 163–4
Boileau (Nicolas Boileau-Despréaux) 119
Boinard, Jean 135 n.16
Boisfranc, N. de, *Les Bains de la Porte Saint Bernard* 49
Boissy, Louis Michel de
  L'Epoux par Supercherie 293–4
  Le Français à Londres 195, 197, 200, 203, 273, 287
  La Vie est un songe 195, 197, 230–1, 278
  La xxxx, Comédie anonyme 287
Boizard de Ponteau, Claude-Florimond, *L'Œil du maître* 295
'*bon sauvage*' see sauvages (savages)
Bonhomme, Honoré 127 n.60, 141
Boniolo (or Bognolo) 140
Bonnault d'Houët, Xavier de, baron 277
Booth, Barton, *The Death of Dido* 182
Bordeaux
  fires
    Hôtel de Ville (1862) 285, 286, 290 n.58
    theatre (1731) 166–7
    theatre (1755) 284 n.32
  first purpose-built theatre 284
  Francisque's and siblings' strong links with 5, 284
  Francisque's company (1730–1) 165–7
  theatre fire during Dorimond's *Le Festin de Pierre* 166–7
  Francisque's company (1731–2) 167

INDEX

Francisque's company (1739)
   Le Chevalier à la mode
      (Dancourt) 286
   Francisque's letter to the
      jurats 284–6
   Francisque's wedding 6
   Jean-Baptiste Malter's marriage
      certificate 140
   Marie-Catherine Moylin leading
      dancer at Bordeaux theatre 311
   Michel Cochois' troupe (1717) 6 n.11
   Moylin-Lesage troupe (1741) 283–4, 290–1
   Les Salinières ou La Promenade des Fossés (Dominique) 55 n.42
   Simon Moylin's wedding 6–7, 161
Boucher, Paul 50 n.23
Boudet, Jacques 162
Bouhier, Jean 151
Bourbon, Louis Charles de *see* Eu, Louis Charles de Bourbon, comte d'Eu
Bourbon, Louis Henri, duc de Bourbon 124
Bourgeois, Thomas-Louis 156
Brémont 284, 285
British country and ethnic dance 19
Brooke, Henry
   Gustavus Vasa or the Deliverer of his Country 226–7
   Universal Beauty 226
Broschi, Carlo *see* Farinelli (Carlo Broschi known as Farinelli)
Browne, Willim, Sir, 'The Pill Plot' 217, 219
Bruey, David-Augustin de, *Le Grondeur* 31
Brugière de Barante, Claude-Ignace
   Arlequin misanthrope 49 n.18, 287, 294
   La Fausse Coquette 49 n.18
   Les Pasquinades Italiennes ou Arlequin médecin des mœurs 49 n.18
Brussels
   capital of Austrian Netherlands 170
   de Grimberghs' activities in 74, 89
   Francisque's company heading for (1720) 73
   Francisque's company's performance of Romagnesi's *Samson* (1739) 178
   Francisque's lazzi in drag 58
   Francisque's season (1733) 3
   Louis XIV's bombardment of (1695) 170
   Malter children's birth location 141 n.34
   Marie Sallé's possible trip to (1733) 180–1
   Moylin family's connection with 5
   see also Brussels season (Théâtre de la Monnaie, 1733–4)
Brussels season (Théâtre de la Monnaie, 1733–4)
   background
      Francisque's contract with theatre 170, 173, 174, 187, 316–20
      including dancing 174
      incompleteness of records 170, 173–4
      Marie-Elisabeth of Austria's presence 170, 171, 173
      Simon Moylin's possible contribution 174
      ticket price war and financial success 174, 310
   performances
      Andromaque (Racine) 171
      Arlequin maître et valet (*Le Jeu de l'Amour et du Hasard*) 171
      Athalie (Racine) 170–1, 233
      Les Deux Arlequins (Le Noble) 173, 174
      La Double Inconstance (Marivaux) 171
      L'Embarras des richesses (d'Allainval) 171, **172**
      Polyeucte martyr (Corneille) 171
      Le Prince travesti (Marivaux) 171
      Rhadamiste et Zénobie (Crébillon) 171
      Samson (Romagnesi) 171, 174–8, 295
      Zaïre (Voltaire) 171
Bruyas, Gilles-Anselme *see* Bursay, Gilles-Anselme Bruyas, known as Bursay
Bruyas, Marie Anne (née Moylin) 301, 302
Buffon, Georges-Louis Leclerc, comte de 165–6, 284
Bullock, Christopher 46
   The Perjuror 63

Burney, Charles 205
Burrows, Donald 232
Bursay, Gilles-Anselme Bruyas, known as Bursay 302

Calder, Andrew 222 n.25
Calderón de la Barca, Pedro, *La Vida es Sueño* 195, 208, 230
Camargo, Marie-Anne de Cupis de 162
Cambis, Louis Dominique de, comte 248, 249, 250, 257, 258, 260–1, 264
Campardon, Émile 1, 52, 95n19, 105, 123, 140 n.33, 141
Campbell, Graham viii
Campistron, Jean Galbert de 90
  Le Jaloux désabusé 294
Cantrell, Mrs 203 n.41
Carestini, Giovanni 233
Carey, Henry 213 n.69
Le Carillon du ménage entre Maître Gervais le savetier et Dame Alison la ravaudeuse (comic ballad) 53–4
Carlin (Carlo Antonio Bertinazzi, known as Carlin) 288 n.49
Carolet, Denis 94, 98, 121
Caroline, Princess 191, 196, 223
Caroline of Ansbach, Queen consort of Great Britain and Ireland
  accession celebrated in Vézian's ode 58 n.50
  attending Francisque's 1735 Benefit 206
  attending Francisque's performances (1734–5) 191
  death of and closure of theatres 248, 249
  Egmont, confidant of 197
  Handel, King and Queen's favourite 189
  low opinion of son Frederick 222–3, 231
  not attending Marie Sallé's 1734 Benefit 185
Carton, Florent *see* Dancourt (Florent Carton, known as Dancourt)
Casanova, Giacomo 304
'*Castigat ridendo mores*' phrase 215
Castiglione 191
Castillo, Susan P. 213
castrati 233

Catholic Church
  and acting profession 7, 117
  castrati identified with Catholic priests 233
  hostility to Freemasonry 225
  Piron's criticism of clergy 110, 112–14, 116, 128
  as Whore of Babylon 231
  see also Catholics; Les Nouvelles Catholiques (religious society); Popery
Catholics 64, 215–16, 223, 225, 230, 232, 234
  anti-Catholicism 64, 216, 223
  see also Catholic Church; Popery
Cauchois *see* Cochois
Cazeneuve, François *see* Desgranges (François Cazeneuve known as Desgranges)
CÉSAR (Calendrier électronique des Spectacles sous l'Ancien Régime et sous la Révolution) viii
Chabot, Marie-Louise *see* Verneuil, Marie-Louise de (née Chabot)
'Chaconne pour Arlequin' (notated by Le Rousseau) 78, **79**
Chahine, Loïc 131, 132, 146 n.1
Chambéry, Les Charmettes 245
Champlain, Samuel, *Des sauvages ou Voyage fait en la France Nouvelle* 68
Chancerel, Léon 131
Chantilly, Fêtes de 124
Chaponnière, Paul 108, 120
Chapuis 290
Charke, Charlotte 219 n.16
Charles Edward Stuart, Prince 233–4, 235
Charles II, King of England, Scotland and Ireland 42, 263
Charles XII, King of Sweden 224
Les Charmettes (near Chambéry) 245
Charpentier, Marc-Antoine, *Intermède* 78
Châteauneuf (owner of Marseille *jeu de paume*) 168, 244
Châteauneuf, Étienne 173, 173 n.5, 180
Châteauneuf, Marie 173, 180–1, 191, 205, 254, 312
  Les Caractères de la danse (Rebel) 180
Chetwood, William 180 n.30

Cheyne, George 59
child kidnappings (Paris, 1720) 70
Chinese Festival riots (1755) 270
Choiseul-Praslin, César de *see* Praslin, César Gabriel de Choiseul, duc de Praslin
Choron, A. 242 n.9
Christian II, King of Denmark, Norway and Sweden 226
Church of England 62–3
Cibber, Colley 17, 65, 219 n.16
  The Non-Juror 62–3, 221
Cibber, Theophilus 181–2, 183, 185, 202, 213, 265
Cicognini, Giacinto Andrea 230
Clay, Lauren R. 310
Cleland, John, *Tombo-Chiqui, or The American Savage* 214
Clive, Kitty 194, 202
Cochois, Barbe or 'Babet' (daughter of Francisque's sister Marguerite)
  date of birth and baptism 124, 129, 132 n.11
  daughter of Marguerite and Michel Cochois 2, 6
  death 304
  in *L'Hymen vainqueur* (as a child) 241–2
  Marguerite spending her last years with 308
  marriage to marquis d'Argens 247 n.28, 304, 310
  minor philosopher 304
  Pesne's painting of 304, **305**
  starred at Frederick the Great's court 2, 302
  trained by Marie Sallé 180
  versatile talents 303–4
Cochois, Francis (son of Francisque's sister Marguerite)
  child of Marguerite and Michel Cochois 2, 6
  death in Russia (probably) 307
  London season (1734–5) with Francisque 191
  personality traits 306–7, 310
  Pesne's painting 304, **305**
  recruited for Elizabeth of Russia's court 2, 306–7
  recruited for Frederick the Great's court. 302, 304

roles
  celebrated Arlequin in Berlin 304, 306
  in *L'Hymen vainqueur* (as a child) 241–2
  in *Pygmalion et Psyché, ballet pantomime* 304
  in *Racine's Athalie* 171, 234
Cochois, Gogo (daughter of Francisque's sister Marguerite) 302, 307–8
Cochois, Marguerite (née Moylin, Francisque's sister)
  children 2, 6, 124, 129, 242, 302
  date of birth 5
  date of death 308
  Foire Saint-Laurent (1718) 42 n.5
  Francisque's London season (1734–35) 191
  godmother to Martin Simon Moylin 73
  godmother to Pierre Malter 244
  high moral standards 302–3, 310
  Marie Sallé's will contested by 300, 308
  marriage to Michel Cochois 8, 9 n.24
  reconciliation with daughter Babet 308
  recruited with children for Frederick the Great's court 293, 302–3, 308
  retirement in Provence 308
  roles
    Angélique in *La Foire de Saint-Germain* 48 n.15
    Dorine in Molière's *Le Tartuffe* 62 n.55
Cochois, Marianne (daughter of Francisque's sister Marguerite) 2, 6, 83, 180, 241–2, 302, 303, 304
Cochois, Marionette (daughter of Francisque's sister Marguerite) 302, 307–8
Cochois, Michel (husband of Francisque's sister Marguerite)
  children 2, 6, 132 n.11, 243, 302
  Francisque's London season (1734–35) 191
  at Frederick the Great's court 302–3
  Lilliputians (child dancers/actors) 191, 227 n.39, 242, 307 n.43, 312

marriage to Marguerite Moylin 6, 8, 9 n.24
roles
La Fausse Foire (in drag) 96
Loyal in Molière's *Le Tartuffe* 62 n.55
Scaramouche 48 n.15, 192
Saint-Germain fair (1710) 8
Saint-Germain fair (1712) 9
Saint-Laurent fair (1718) 42 n.5
Saint-Laurent fair (1721) 96, 133
Saint-Laurent fair (1724) 131, 132
Simon Moylin's wedding 7 n.13, 161
summer season in Lille (1712) 9 n.24
Collé, Charles 207
Collier, J. Payne 255
Comédie-Française
ban on/complaints against fairground players 10–13, 22, 30, 31
increased tolerance 69, 81
closure because of intense heat (1718) 25
Comédie-Italienne, rivalry with 66, 95, 98
Comédie-Italienne's approach different from 177
Dancourt's work for 23, 24, 34
Dartenay's unsuccessful debut 12
Dufresny's work for 24, 34
financial difficulties 38
Fontainebleau performances (1739) 274
Francisque's staging of its plays at 1718–19 London season 61–5
Francisque's staging of its plays at 1739 Compiègne season 278
Francisque's staging of its plays at 1750–1 Dijon season 294–5
Francisque's troupe at 1721 Saint-Laurent fair, support for 95, 98
Gillier's compositions for 24
London season (1871) 314–15
Luigi Riccoboni's troupe, rivalry with 13
Michel Procope-Couteaux's work for 155
as portrayed by La Foire in
Arlequin Deucalion (Piron) 109
Les Comédiens corsaires (Lesage, d'Orneval, Fuzelier) 152, 154–5
La Désolation des deux Comédies (Dominique and Riccoboni) 37
Les Funérailles de la Foire (Lesage, d'Orneval, Fuzelier) 35
Le Monde renversé (Lesage, d'Orneval, Fuzelier) 33
Le Procès des Théâtres (Dominique and Riccoboni) 37–8
La Querelle des Théâtres (Lesage and La Font) 30–1
Le Rappel de la Foire à la Vie (Lesage, d'Orneval, Fuzelier) 102–3
Le Retour de la Chasse du cerf 158–9
repertoire
L'Assemblée des Comédiens (Procope-Couteaux) 58 n.48, 138 n.25
Athalie (Racine) 195
Cénie (Graffigny) 295, 311
La Chasse du cerf (Legrand) 158–9
Le Cocu imaginaire (Molière) 83
L'Ecole des amis (La Chaussée) 278
Électre (Crébillon) 184
La Femme juge et parti (Montfleury) 83
Les Folies amoureuses (Regnard) 278
Le Français à Londres (Boissy) 195, 287
La Française Italienne 152, 154
Le Glorieux (Destouches) 278
Gustave Vasa (Piron) 195, 224
L'Héritier ridicule (Scarron) 278–9
Inès de Castro (La Motte) 195
Le Jeu de l'Amour et du Hasard (Marivaux) 314
Les Ménechmes (Regnard) 278
Œdipe (Voltaire) 39
Le Préjugé à la mode (La Chaussée) 278, 287
La Princesse d'Élide (Molière and Lully) 280
La Pupille (Fagan) 287
La Réunion des amours (Marivaux) 196
Le Roi de Cocagne (Legrand) 38

INDEX

Le Tartuffe (Molière) 314
Turcaret (Lesage) 10, 30
Zaïre (Voltaire) 195
seat prices 276, 282
Simon Moylin's staging of its plays at 1739–40 Dijon season 287
village plays 34
Comédie-Italienne
  Ancient and New Théâtre Italien
    Ancien (pre-1697) 7, 10, 32 n.25, 42–3, 193, 207, 278, 287, 294
    Nouveau (post-1716) 13, 193, 210, 287, 294
  Arlequin-Thomassin 88, 159 n.33, 206–7, 208, 275
  Comédie-Française, rivalry with 66, 95, 98
  Foire Saint-Laurent seasons
  1721 season 94–5, 103, 105, 133–4, 136, 137
  three not very successful seasons (1721–23) 130
  Fontainebleau performances (1739) 273–4
  Francisque's direct contact with its traditions 7–8, 12, 141
  Francisque's staging of its plays at Compiègne (1739) 278
  Jean-Antoine Watteau's paintings inspired by 78
  Jean-Baptiste Foulquier in orchestra 192, 288 n.49
  Michel Procope-Couteaux's work for 155
  Mitchigamea's performance with Rameau's music 212
  mixture of genres 177
  as portrayed by La Foire in
    Arlequin Deucalion (Piron) 109
    Les Comédiens corsaires (Lesage, d'Orneval, Fuzelier) 152, 154
    La Désolation des deux Comédies (Dominique and Riccoboni) 36–7, 39
    La Foire renaissante 39–40
    Les Funérailles de la Foire (Lesage, d'Orneval, Fuzelier) 35
    Le Procès des Théâtres (Dominique and Riccoboni) 37–8, 39
    La Querelle des Théâtres (Lesage and La Font) 29–32

Le Rappel de la Foire à la Vie (Lesage, d'Orneval, Fuzelier) 103
Le Régiment de la Calotte (Lesage, d'Orneval, Fuzelier) 104–6
repertoire
  Agnès de Chaillot (Dominique and Legrand) 130 n.1, 228
  Arcagambis (Dominique and Romagnesi) 278 n.18, 281
  Arlequin, enfant, statue et perroquet 278
  Arlequin Astrologue 207
  Arlequin Hulla (Dominique, Riccoboni, Romagnesi) 193 n.18, 278 n.18
  Arlequin poli par l'amour (Marivaux) 254, 278 n. 18
  Arlequin sauvage (Delisle) 93, 113, 213
  Arlequin toujours Arlequin (Dominique, Romagnesi, Riccoboni) 208
  Les Comédiens esclaves (Dominique, Romagnesi, Riccoboni) 152, 154, 193 n.17, 288
  Danaé (Saint-Yon) 136, 137
  Les Deux Arlequins (Le Noble) 278
  Diane et Endymion ou l'Amour vengé 91
  La Double Inconstance (Marivaux) 278 n.18
  L'Embarras des richesses (d'Allainval) 171, 300–1
  La Fille savante ou Isabelle fille capitaine (Fatouville) 278
  La Foire des poètes (Dominique and Romagnesi) 287
  L'Heureux stratagème (Marivaux) 278 n.18
  Les Intrigues d'Arlequin 278
  L'Isle du divorce (Dominique and Romagnesi) 287
  L'Italienne Française 152
  Le Jeu de l'amour et du hasard (Marivaux) 177
  Le Naufrage au Port-à-l'Anglais ou les Nouvelles Débarqués (Autreau) 36
  Philomèle (Piron) 143 n.42

Pirame et Thisbé (Dominique, Riccoboni, Romagnesi) 159
Polyphème (Legrand and Riccoboni) 121–2
Le Prince travesti (Marivaux) 278 n.18
Samson (Romagnesi) 174, 175, 177, 195, 230
La Surprise de l'amour (Marivaux) 156, 164
La Sylphide (Dominique and Romagnesi) 287
Les Terres australes (Dominique and Legrand) 105
La Vie est un songe (Boissy) 195, 230
La vita è un sogno (Luigi Riccoboni) 230
La xxxx, Comédie anonyme (Boissy) 287
'Comédiens du Roi' title 2, 279–80, 282
comedy, *Castigat ridendo mores* 215
commedia all'improvviso 9, 50
commedia dell'arte 17, 19, 45, 51
see also Night Scenes
Common Sense (journal) 263, 265, 266, 267
Commune de Paris (1870–1) 314
A Comparison between the Two Stages (Charles Gildon?) 14
Compiègne (1739 season)
  background
    Compiègne summer military camp 273, 276, 277
    Francisque in charge of theatre troupe 275
    Francisque invited and paid by Louis XV 273–4
    Francisque's purpose-built theatre 274–5
    Louis XV making Francisque's company 'Comédiens du Roi' 279–80, 282
    Louis XV's hunting expeditions 276, 277
    Louis XV's mistresses and satiric songs 277–8
    Louis XV's theatre attendance 276, 279
    magnificent international gathering 276–7
    number of Francisque's performers 275–6
    performances for courtiers and townsfolk 276
    quality and originality of the troupe 281–3
    seat prices 276, 282
    theatre balls 280, 281, 286
  repertoire
    Les Animaux raisonnables (Lesage, d'Orneval, Fuzelier) 278, 279
    Arcagambis (Dominique and Romagnesi) 278 n.18, 281
    Arlequin, enfant, statue et perroquet 278
    Arlequin Hulla (Dominique, Riccoboni, Romagnesi) 278 n.18, 281
    Arlequin poli par l'amour (Marivaux) 278, 281
    Arlequin sauvage (Delisle, as in London 1734–5) 278
    Les Deux Arlequins (Le Noble) 278
    La Double Inconstance (Marivaux) 278 n.18
    L'Ecole des amis (La Chaussée) 278
    L'Embarras des richesses (d'Allainval) 278
    Le Faucon et les oies de Boccace (Delisle, as in London 1734–5) 278
    Les Fées (Romagnesi and Procope-Couteaux) 278
    La Fille savante ou Isabelle fille capitaine (Fatouville) 278
    Les Folies amoureuses (Regnard) 278
    Le Glorieux (Destouches) 278
    L'Héritier ridicule (Scarron) 278–9
    L'Heureux stratagème (Marivaux) 278, 278 n.18
    Les Intrigues d'Arlequin 278, 279, 281
    Les Ménechmes (Regnard) 278
    Le Préjugé à la mode (La Chaussée) 278, 287
    Le Prince travesti (Marivaux) 278 n.18
    La Princesse d'Élide (Molière and Lully) 278
    Samson (Romagnesi) 178, 278

INDEX

La Statue merveilleuse or *Le Miroir sans fard* (Lesage) 278
Timon le misanthrope (Delisle, as in London 1734–5) 278
La Vie est un songe (Boissy) 278
Compiègne (1940 season)
  background
    with Francisque and Simon Moylin 288
    last Compiègne season 289–90
    Louis XV's attendance 289
    performances for courtiers and townsfolk 289
    plays from all official Paris theatres 288–9
  repertoire
    Arcagambis (Dominique and Romagnesi) 288
    Arlequin toujours Arlequin (Dominique, Romagnesi, Riccoboni) 288
    Arlequin valet étourdi 289
    Les Comédiens esclaves (Dominique, Romagnesi, Riccoboni) 288
    L'Occasion 288
    La Statue merveilleuse or *Le Miroir sans fard* (Lesage) 289
Connon, Derek F. 109, 128
Cook, William, *Elements of Dramatic Criticism* 20, 21
Coquelin, Benoît-Constant 314
Cornbury Plot (1733) 215
Corneille, Pierre 90, 209
  Le Cid 64, 116, 155, 229
  Polyeucte martyr 171
Covent Garden theatre
  background
    John Rich's new theatre 178
    Licensing Act impact 248, 253
    maximum capacity 205
    number of dancers 192
    Handel's 1734–5 season *see under* Handel, George Frideric
    Marie Sallé's 1733–4 season *see under* Sallé, Marie (Francisque's niece)
    performance interrupted by Haymarket rioters 261
  performances
    Apollo and Daphne 185
    The Burgomaster Trick'd 185
    Henry V (Shakespeare) 253
    Nivelon's comic dance 182
    Richard Leveridge's songs 203
Cowper, Mary, Countess 77
The Craftsman 199 n.34, 217 n.10, 218, 221–2, 259, 261, 262, 263
Crébillon, Prosper Jolyot de 90
  Électre 184
  Rhadamiste et Zenobie 110, 171, 294
Crécy, battle of (1346) 200, 252
Cromwell, Oliver 232
Cruickshanks, Eveline 215 n.2
Cumberland, Duke of *see* William, Prince, Duke of Cumberland
Cummings, Graham 205 n.48, 236
Cuzzoni, Francesca 269

Dacier, Émile
  biographer of Marie Sallé 1
  on Francisque
    'pérégrinations' (1734) 186
    role as a bear 124
    and Sallé children's whereabouts (1723) 129
  on Marie Sallé
    companion Rebecca Wick 240, 241 n.6
    Covent Garden season 183–4
    possible return to England 298
    unpredictable behaviour 299
    will contested by family members 300
  on others
    Marguerite Moylin's widowhood 242 n.11, 303 n.28
    Mlle Petitpas 310 n.51
    Simon (i.e. Martin Simon) Moylin 300
The Daily Advertiser 189, 204, 255
The Daily Courant
  announcements of publication of '*Tartuffe*, or *The French Puritan*' (1718) 63
  Francisque's troupe
    'Arlequin will Tumble' advertisement (1719) 51–2
    King's Theatre performance of *Arlequin empereur dans la lune* (1719) 49 n.20
    Lincoln's Inn Fields performance (1718) 37
    Little Theatre in the Haymarket season (1721) 86, 87–8, 89

362 INDEX

performance of Piron's *Gustave
  Vasa* (1734–5 season) 224
French 'Pantomims' 79, 163
letter denouncing Joshua Ward as
  Papist 217, 218
Sallé children's London
  performances 17, 18
Sorin and Baxter's Night Scene 14
The Daily Gazetteer 248, 253, 263
The Daily Journal 89, 182, 182 n.34, 182
  n.36, 183, 211 n.62
The Daily Post 73, 88
d'Alembert *see* Alembert, Jean Le Rond d'
dance
  ballet d'action 162, 289, 311, 315
  ballet-pantomime 162–3, 295, 315
  belle danse of the Opéra 19, 94, 183
  British country and ethnic dance 19
  commedia dell'arte-based 17, 19
  cross-fertilisation between dancing
    traditions 19
  emergence as independent narrative
    art 17–18
  in English theatre, importance
    of 191–2
  in Francisque's company's
    performances 52–4, 65
  Francisque's contribution to evolution
    of 311
  French dancing techniques 52
  London-Paris cross-cultural
    influences 13–14, 161–3, 312
  mimic dancing 17
  opéra-comique sophisticated
    dancing 150
  peasant dancing 19
Danchet, Antoine 143 n.44
Dancourt (Florent Carton, known as
  Dancourt) 23, 24, 34
  Le Chevalier à la mode 286
Dancourt, Louis 149
Dangeville, Jean-Baptiste 74 n.21, 75, 76
Darget, Claude 307
Dartenay, François 12
Dauphin *see* Louis, Dauphin of France
Davis, C. A. C. 19, 20
Debauve, Jean-Louis 301 n.15
Defoe, Daniel, *Robinson Crusoe* 81, 93
Defompré *see* Fompré
Degauque, Isabelle 150
Dégranges, M. E. 290, 292
Delagarde (or de la Garde), Charles 53

Delanoe (publisher) 177
Delaplace, Antoine
  Foire Saint-Germain (1707) 8
  Foire Saint-Germain (1712) 9
  Foire Saint-Germain (1722), *Pierrot
    Romulus, ou Le Ravisseur poli*
    (marionettes) 107
  Foire Saint-Germain (1723) 124
  Foire Saint-Laurent (1724)
    Les Captifs d'Alger (prologue by
      Lesage and d'Orneval) 130,
      138
    hired by Maurice Honoré 130
    L'Oracle muet (Lesage and
      d'Orneval) 130, 138–9
    La Toison d'or (Lesage and
      d'Orneval) 130
  work with Francisque and siblings 8,
    9
Delisle (actor) 178, 191
Delisle, Mlle *see* Lisle, Mademoiselle de
Delisle de La Drevetière, Louis-François
  Arlequins of in Francisque's
    repertoire 208
  Dijon season (1739–40) 287
  Francisque's introduction of his plays
    to England 312
  works
    Arlequin sauvage 93, 113, 195,
      196, 197 n.30, 210, 211–14,
      215
    *Le Faucon et les oies de
      Boccace* 195
    Timon le misanthrope 195, 197
      n.30, 219 n.17
Des Essars *see* Desessars or Des Essars
  (Barthélemy Durocher, known as
  Desessars)
Desboulmiers (Jean Auguste Julien,
  known as Desboulmiers) 88, 96
  n.24, 99, 100, 105
Deseschaliers (or Deschaliers) de
  Vaurenville, Louise 74 n.21, 75
  n.26, 86
Desessars, Mrs (wife of Barthélemy
  Desessars) 191
Desessars or Des Essars (Barthélemy
  Durocher, known as
  Desessars) 160–1, 165 n.56, 171,
  178, 191, 249
Desfontaines, Pierre-François
  Guyot 113–14

Desgranges (François Cazeneuve known as Desgranges) 8
Deshayes, François 191, 241, 242, 301
   see also Hesse, Jean-Baptiste (sometimes known as Deshayes)
Desmarets (manager of theatre company) 309
Desmarets, Jean, *Les Visionnaires* 294
Desplaces (husband of Marianne Cochois) 303
Destouches, Philippe Néricault (known as Destouches) 218–20
   La Force du naturel 295
   Le Glorieux 278
   Issé 109
   Le Philosophe marié 219 n.17
   Télémaque parody with Pellegrin 12 n.33
Detcheverry, Arnaud 284, 285, 286 n.40, 292 n.70
Deutsch, Otto 15, 16, 19, 19 n.59
Devaux, François-Antoine 273–4, 275
Deveil (or de Veil), Thomas 254, 255, 257, 258, 260, 263, 264–5
D'Hannetaire (Jean-Nicolas Servandoni known as D'Hannetaire) 173 n.6, 286
Dickason, Olive Patricia 213
Dictionary of Actors see Highfill, Philip
Dictionnaire des Danseurs see Aelbrouck, Jean-Philippe van
Dictionnaire des Théâtres de Paris 125, 150
Dictionnaire Historique de la Ville de Paris et de ses environs 174 n.10
diglossia 244
Dijon
   Francisque's last known visit 151
   Francisque's troupe (1720s) 166
   Piron's native town 107, 151
   Sallé's troupe (1708) 8
   Simon Moylin's troupe (1731) 167
   see also Dijon season (1739–40); Dijon season (1750–1)
Dijon season (1739–40)
   background
      Micault's manuscript list of performances 328–9
      Simon Moylin's troupe 286, 293
   repertoire
      Arlequin Misanthrope 287
      La Belle Esclave (L'Estoile) 287

      La Fille savante ou Isabelle fille capitaine (Fatouville) 287
      La Foire des poètes (Dominique and Romagnesi) 287
      Le Français à Londres (Boissy) 287
      L'Isle du divorce (Dominique and Romagnesi) 287
      Le Préjugé à la mode (La Chaussée) 287
      La Pupille (Fagan) 287
      Samson (Romagnesi) 178
      La Sylphide (Dominique and Romagnesi) 287
      works of Delisle, d'Allainval, Boissy and Marivaux 287
      La xxxx, Comédie anonyme (Boissy) 287
Dijon season (1750–1)
   background
      Francisque in charge 293
      Micault's manuscript list of performances 329–30
      mostly Comédie-Française plays 294, 295
      new generation of actors 293
      probably his last provincial tour 296
   repertoire
      Andromaque (Racine) 294
      Arlequin misanthrope (Brugière de Barante) 294
      Athalie (Racine) 294
      Le Bourgeois Gentilhomme (Molière) 294
      Cénie (Graffigny) 295, 296, 311
      L'Epoux par Supercherie (Boissy) 293–4
      Esther (Racine) 294
      Favart pieces 295–6
      La Force du naturel (Destouches) 295
      Gustave Vasa (Piron) 293–4, 311
      Le Jaloux désabusé (Campistron) 294
      Le Magnifique (La Motte) 296
      Le Nouveau Monde (Pellegrin) 294, 296
      Œdipe and Sémiramis (Voltaire) 294
      L'Œil du maître (Boizard de Ponteau) 295

Phèdre et Hippolyte (Racine) 294
Rhadamiste et Zenobie (Crébillon) 294
La Rose, ou le Pucelage (Piron) 295
Le Spectacle brillant 296, 301
Turcaret (Lesage) 294
Venise sauvée (La Place) 294, 295
Les Visionnaires (Desmarets) 294
Dolet, Charles
   Carolet's parody of *Tirésias* for Dolet's marionettes 121
   Foire Saint-Germain (1707) 8
   Foire Saint-Germain (1712) 9
   Foire Saint-Germain (1722), *Pierrot Romulus, ou Le Ravisseur poli* (marionettes) 107
   Foire Saint-Germain (1723) 124–5, 129
   Foire Saint-Laurent (1724) 137
     Les Captifs d'Alger (prologue by Lesage and d'Orneval) 130, 138
     hired by Maurice Honoré 130
     L'Oracle muet (Lesage and d'Orneval) 130, 138–9
     La Toison d'or (Lesage and d'Orneval) 130
   seasoned fair player 22
   work with Francisque and siblings 8, 9
Dominique (Pierre-François Biancolelli, a.k.a. Dominique)
   chef de troupe, writing and touring 7
   Foire Saint-Germain (1710) 8
   Foire Saint-Germain (1712) 9
   Foire Saint-Laurent (1714) 88
   Foire Saint-Laurent (1715) 11
   Foire Saint-Laurent (1716) 12–13
   Foire Saint-Laurent (1717) 13
   Foire Saint-Laurent (1721) 94–5
   Francisque's association with 9, 12, 13, 50
   joined 'legitimate' theatre company 13
   marriage to Pascariel's daughter 7
   Nicolas Barbier, links with 54–5, 88
   performances
     Arlequin peintre et la Fille muette 12–13
     Danaé (Saint-Yon) with Riccoboni 94–5
     La Précaution inutile, ou Arlequin gazetier de Hollande 12
     La Surprise de l'Amour (Marivaux) 156
   works
     Les Deux Pierrots 88
     La Promenade des Terreaux de Lyon 55 n.40
     Les Salinières ou La Promenade des Fossés 55 n.42
   works with Fuzelier, *Arlequin larron, juge et grand prévôt* 50
   works with Legrand
     Agnès de Chaillot 130 n.1, 228–9
     Les Terres australes 105
   works with Riccoboni
     La Désolation des deux Comédies 36–7, 39 n.43
     Le Procès des Théâtres 37–8
   works with Romagnesi
     Arcagambis 193, 278 n.18, 281, 288
     La Foire des poètes 287
     L'Isle du divorce 287
     La Sylphide 196, 287
   works with Romagnesi and Riccoboni
     Arlequin Hulla 191, 193 n.18, 196, 278 n.18, 281
     Arlequin toujours Arlequin 208, 288
     Les Comédiens esclaves 152, 154, 193 n.17, 288
     Pirame et Thisbé 159 n.33
Dorimond (Nicolas Drouin, known as Dorimond) 160 n.38
   Le Festin de Pierre ou l'Athée foudroyé 166, 195, 222–3
D'Orneval *see* Orneval, Jacques-Philippe d'
Drouin, Nicolas *see* Dorimond (Nicolas Drouin, known as Dorimond)
Drury Lane Theatre
   Baxter's and Sorin's performances 14, 15, 20–1
   dancers
     Anthony Francis Roger 74–5
     Catherine Roland 205
     Fourcade and Malter children 312
     Louis Dupré 53
     Manon Grognet 183
     Marie Châteauneuf 312
     Miss Robinson 162

number of dancers 192
French comedians' influence 52, 65
Licensing Act, unaffected by 248
Night Scenes 14–15
  'The Whimsical Death of Harlequin' 15
night's takings compared to Francisque's 65
pantomime 185
reputation as bastion of Protestant Whigs 64
Riot Act, use of (1737) 258
riots (1755) 270
riots (1848) 314
seat prices 191
Shakespeare plays 77, 80
Theophilus Cibber's quarrel with 181–2, 185
works performed at
  Art and Nature (Miller) 213–14
  The Burgomaster Trick'd (Nivelon) 185 n.53, 218–19
  Dame Ragundy and her Family 17
  Dido and Aeneas (Arne) 182
  The Dumb Farce (after *Macbeth*) 51 n.26
  The Loves of Mars and Venus (Weaver) 17, 18–19
  The Man of Taste (Miller) 202–3
  The Non-Juror (Colley Cibber) 62, 221
  The Plot or Pill and Drop (Kelly) 201–2, 218–20
  Timon in Love or the Innocent Theft (Kelly) 195, 219 n.17
Dubos, Jean-Baptiste 74 n.22
Dubroc (or Dubrocq), Pierre 74 n.21
Dubuisson 171, 178, 191
Duchemin 284, 285
Dufresny, Charles
  at Comédie-Française
    'genre villageois' 34
    plays with Gillier's music 24
  works
    Arlequin misanthrope 49 n.18
    La Baguette 49 n.18
    Les Chinois 76
    La Foire de Saint-Germain 43, **44**, 45–6, 48–9, 64 n.62
    La Foire de Saint-Germain, scène des deux carosses 49
    Les Momies d'Egypte 158
    L'Opéra de campagne 49
    Les Pasquinades Italiennes ou Arlequin médecin des mœurs 49 n.18
Dulondel 74 n.21
Dumas, Alexandre (père), *Le Comte de Monte-Cristo* 314
Dumény, Antoine 54
Dumoulin, David 162
Duncan, Barry 314
Duplong (or de Plon), Françoise *see* Moylin, Françoise (née de Plon or Duplong, Francisque's mother)
Dupré, Louis (a.k.a. 'London Dupré') 17, 53
Dusuisse, Elizabeth (sister of Francisque's wife) 140
Dusuisse, Marie-Catherine see Moylin, Marie-Catherine (née Dusuisse or le Suisse, Francisque's wife)
Dusuisse/Dussoye, Catherine *see* Malter, Catherine (née Dussoye/Dusuisse, known as Catherine Labbé, Francisque's niece)
Duvivier (du Vivier) de Saint Bon, *Arlequin jouet de la fortune* 50

écriteaux (scrolls) 11–12, 91, 130, 163
Edward II, King of England 221, 252, 263
Egmont, John Percival, 1st Earl of Egmont 197, 211, 213
Éguilles, Alexandre Jean-Baptiste de Boyer, marquis d'Éguilles 304, 307
Élisabeth-Charlotte, duchesse d'Orléans 25 n.10, 35, 105, 140, 241
Elizabeth, Empress of Russia 306
Elizabeth, I, Queen of England 267
English celebrations
  5th November 215
  17 November 267
English theatre
  ban on biblical drama 231
  vs. Franco-Italian theatre 81
  vs. French theatre 76–7
  tricks and feats 51
Erskine-Hill, Howard 215 n.2
Essex, John 162, 181
Eu, Louis Charles de Bourbon, comte d'Eu 277, 281, 283, 285, 286, 290

The Evening Post 253

Fabre, Carole 96, 98–9
Fagan, Barthélemy-Christophe, *La Pupille* 287
fairs (foires) *see* Foire Saint-Germain entries; Foire Saint-Laurent entries; Théâtre de la Foire
Falstaffe, Sir John (pseudonym), *The Anti-Theatre* 57 n.45, 77
farce
   assumption of Francisque as mere 'farceur' 3, 164, 193, 197
   'Farce and Harlequin shall be no more' (Garrick's *Harlequin Student*) 269
   misleading use of the word 50, 197
   negative perception of French farce 47–8, 77
   ribaldry and fairground farces 120
   traditional French farce at fairs 10
Farinelli (Carlo Broschi known as Farinelli)
   coupled with Francisque in hostile criticism 191, 198, 202, 237, 269
   criticism of his wealth at expense of English performers 237–8
   London 1734–5 season
      Artaserse (Hasse) 189, 204
      celebrity status 208, 269
      hired by Porpora for Haymarket 188, 189, 236
      hysteria *morbus farinellicus* 191
      London 1735 Benefit 204, 205, 206, 216
      Miller's criticism of 213 n.69
   papal chapel member 269 n.53
   targeted as foreigner unaffected by Licensing Act 251
   Te Deum at Portuguese Embassy Chapel 216
Fatouville, Anne Mauduit de
   Arlequin empereur dans la lune 49
      Aphra Behn's English adaptation 20
   Arlequin Grapignan ou La Matrone d'Ephèse 49
   Colombine avocat pour et contre 49
   Colombine fille savante ou La Fille [Isabelle] capitaine 49

La Fille savante ou Isabelle fille capitaine 195, 278, 287
La Précaution inutile, ou Arlequin gazetier de Hollande 12, 49, 54
Favart, Charles Simon 27, 295–6
   L'Ambigu de la folie ou Le Ballet des dindons 297–8
Fayolle, F. 242 n.9
Fêtes de Chantilly 124
Fielding, Henry
   eviction from Little Haymarket 254–5
   theatrical career ended by Licensing Act 250, 251 n.6n 254
   works
      Don Quixote in England 203
      The Grub Street Opera 203
      The Historical Register for the Year 1736 (play) 254
      The Roast Beef of Old England (song)' 203, 257, 258
Finch, Moira viii
fires
   Bordeaux Hôtel de Ville (1862) 285, 286, 290 n.58
   Bordeaux theatre (1731) 166–7
   Bordeaux theatre (1755) 284 n.32
   Lyon theatre (1722) 117–18, 119
Fletcher, Ifan Kyrle 75 n.23
Foire Saint-Germain
   dates and location 8
   Holy Week dispensation 115
   role in Francisque's career as actor-manager 3
   see also Foires Saint-Germain by date
Foire Saint-Germain (1678), *Les Forces de l'amour et de la magie* (Alard père) 9–10
Foire Saint-Germain (1709) 8
Foire Saint-Germain (1710) 8
Foire Saint-Germain (1712) 9
Foire Saint-Germain (1713) 50
Foire Saint-Germain (1714) 50
Foire Saint-Germain (1715) 11–12
Foire Saint-Germain (1716) 15
Foire Saint-Germain (1717) 19
Foire Saint-Germain (1718) 21, 22
Foire Saint-Germain (1719) 38, 39, 46, 102
Foire Saint-Germain (1720)

INDEX

animosity between Francisque and
  Lalauze 66
ban on singing and dancing 66
bleakness and polemical genre 72–3
Francisque's company
  L'Âne du Daggial (Lesage and
    d'Orneval) 71–2
  Arlequin roi des ogres (Lesage and
    Fuzelier) 69, 70–1
  Le Diable d'argent (Lesage,
    d'Orneval, Fuzelier) 69, 73
  L'Isle du Gougou (Lesage and
    d'Orneval) 68–9, 126
  L'Ombre de la Foire (Lesage and
    d'Orneval) 66–8, 73, 108,
    139
  La Queue de vérité (Lesage,
    d'Orneval and Fuzelier) 69,
    71, 73
  tumbling shows with Guillaume
    Moylin 52
Lalauze company, *Le Camp des
  amours* (Lalauze) 26 n.12
Foire Saint-Germain (1721)
  background
    aristocratic patronage 90–1
    Francisque's troupe under brother
      Simon's direction 90, 94
    Francisque's troupe's new
      programme 90
    freedom yet unlicensed by
      Opéra 90
    lacklustre fair 94
    Lalauze's reliance on old
      repertoire 90
  music and dance
    Antoni de Sceaux's theatre 94
    Francis and Marie Sallé's
      dancing 94
    Opéra's complaint against
      Sceaux 94
  opéras-comiques (Lesage and
    d'Orneval)
    Arlequin Endymion 91–2
    La Forêt de Dodone 92
    L'Ombre d'Alard 93
    Magotin 93
    Robinson or *L'Isle de
      Robinson* 93
  prologues
    Lesage's prologue 91
    two prologues 90

Foire Saint-Germain (1722)
  background
    ban on dialogue and songs 107
    Francisque deserted by Lesage and
      colleagues 107–8, 116
    Francisque's plea to Piron 107–8
    permission to perform with single
      speaking actor 107, 108
  Francisque's opening performances
    Les Fourberies d'Arlequin 107
    Ourson et Valentin 107
  marionettes (Lesage, Fuzelier,
    d'Orneval)
    to avoid ban on dialogue and
      songs 107
    *Pierrot Romulus, ou Le Ravisseur
      poli* 107
  Piron's plays
    Arlequin Deucalion 108–15, 119,
      310
    L'Antre de Trophonius 115–17
Foire Saint-Germain (1723)
  background
    Dolet and Delaplace in Francisque's
      troupe 124–5
    Francisque's presence at the
      fair 124 n.57
    no licence from Opéra 124–5
    Piron writing for all three
      companies 124
  performances
    Colombine-Nitétis 143 n.42, 143
      n.44
    L'Endriague (commissioned by
      Opéra) 125–9, 148
    Les Trois Commères (with Lesage
      and Fuselier) 143 n.44, 150
Foire Saint-Germain (1724)
  Le Claperman (Piron) 129, 143 n.42
  La Conquête de la Toison d'or (Lesage
    and d'Orneval) 129
Foire Saint-Germain (1725), *L'Audience
  du Temps* 132
Foire Saint-Germain (1726) 149
Foire Saint-Germain (1740) 289
Foire Saint-Germain (1744) 151
  La Rose, ou le Pucelage (Piron) 295
Foire Saint-Laurent
  dates and location 8
  role in Francisque's career as
    actor-manager 3
  see also Foires Saint-Laurent by date

Foire Saint-Laurent (1711) 8–9
Foire Saint-Laurent (1714) 88
Foire Saint-Laurent (1715) 11
Foire Saint-Laurent (1716) 12, 15
   Arlequin Hulla (Lesage and
     d'Orneval) 193 n.18
Foire Saint-Laurent (1717) 13
Foire Saint-Laurent (1718)
   background
     coming together of Moylin-Sallé-
      Cochois tribe 24, 42
     decree banning theatrical activity at
      fairs 35
     granting of licence to single
      company 24, 103
     hot weather and large
      audiences 25
     Lesage and d'Orneval's new
      opéras-comiques 24
   programme
     Les Amours de Nanterre (Lesage
      and d'Orneval) 34–5
     Les Funérailles de la Foire
      (Lesage, d'Orneval,
      Fuzelier) 35–6
     L'Isle des Amazones (Lesage
      and d'Orneval, not
      performed) 35, 81
     Le Jugement de Paris
      (prologue) 25–6
     Le Monde renversé (Lesage,
      d'Orneval, Fuzelier) 32–4
     La Princesse de Carizme (Lesage
      and La Font) 25, 26, **27**,
      28–9
     La Querelle des Théâtres (Lesage
      and La Font) 29–34, 35
   see also Querelle des Théâtres (Foire
     Saint-Laurent 1718)
Foire Saint-Laurent (1720)
   ban on singing and dancing 81, 83,
    85
   Francisque's meeting with Lady
     Pennyman 83–5
   La Statue merveilleuse (Lesage) 82–3
   L'Isle des Amazones (Lesage and
     d'Orneval) 81–2
Foire Saint-Laurent (1721)
   background
     granting (and withdrawal) of
      nine-year licence to
      Francisque 101–2, 105–6,
      138
     granting (and withdrawal) of
      nine-year licence to
      Lalauze 94, 95, 101–2, 133,
      138
     Lalauze's formal complaint against
      unlicensed Francisque's
      troupe 95, 96, 99–100
     Lalauze's reliance on old
      repertoire .94
     Lalauze's virtual bankruptcy 105
     new opéras-comiques for
      Francisque's troupe 95
     royal support for Francisque 105
     support of Comédie-Française for
      Francisque's troupe 95, 98
   Comédie-Italienne 94–5, 103, 104,
    133
   Danaé (Saint-Yon) 136, 137
   Les Terres australes (Dominique
     and Legrand) 105
   Francisque's company
     La Boîte de Pandore
      (Lesage, d'Orneval,
      Fuzelier) 99–101, 132, 136
      n.19, 137 n.20
     La Fausse Foire (Lesage, d'Orneval
      and Fuzelier) 95–9
     Les Funérailles de la Foire
      (Lesage, d'Orneval,
      Fuzelier) 102, 138
     *Le Rappel de la Foire à la
      Vie* (Lesage, d'Orneval,
      Fuzelier) 102–3, 138
     Le Régiment de la Calotte (Lesage,
      d'Orneval, Fuzelier) 103–5,
      137 n.23
     La Tête noire (Lesage, d'Orneval,
      Fuzelier) 101–2
   Lalauze's company
     Carolet's play, poorly received 94,
      98
     *La Décadence de l'Opéra-comique
      l'Aîné* 105
     *Le Jugement de Pan et d'Apollon
      par Midas* 105
     *La Réforme du Régiment de la
      Calotte* 105
Foire Saint-Laurent (1722)
   fire at Lyon theatre

INDEX

Francisque's company's
    involvement 117–18
Piron's prologue to *Tirésias* on
    fire 118–19, 3190
Piron's play
    Arlequin Tirésias 119–22, 128, 310
    Francisque's arrest on grounds of
        obscenity 121–2
    Francisque's letter to authorities
        (written by Piron) 121–2,
        123–4
Piron's play with marionettes
    ban on speaking after obscenity
        charges 122
    *Le Mariage de Momus ou La
        Gigantomachie* 120, 122–3,
        128
    permission to perform with live
        actors 123
    troubled season and closure of
        theatre 123–4
Foire Saint-Laurent (1723)
    Comédie-Italienne, *Agnès de Chaillot*
        (Dominique and Legrand) 228
    presence of Sallé children 129
Foire Saint-Laurent (1724)
    background
        claims of Francisque's troupe's
            presence 131–2
        Francisque's ghostlike presence in
            repertoire 130, 134–5, 137,
            138–9
        Maurice Honoré's company 130,
            137
        Opéra's granting of licence 106,
            130
        permission to speak granted and
            withdrawn to Dolet and
            Delaplace 130
        permission to use 'écriteaux'
            granted to Dolet and
            Delaplace 130
        Piron and Fuzelier hired by
            Honoré 130
    Dolet and Delaplace's troupe
        Les Captifs d'Alger (prologue by
            Lesage and d'Orneval) 130,
            138
        L'Oracle muet (Lesage and
            d'Orneval) 130, 138–9
        La Toison d'or (Lesage and
            d'Orneval) 129, 130

Fuzelier's works
    L'Assemblée des Comédiens 138
    *Le Déménagement du Théâtre
        ci-devant occupé par les
        Comédiens Italiens* 130
    Les Dieux à la Foire (cast) 131–2
    Les Dieux à la Foire
        (prologue) 133–7, 138, 139,
        146
Piron's plays
    L'Âne d'or 131, 138 n.24
    *Le Mariage du Caprice et de la
        Folie* 115, 138, 143 n.42, 149
Foire Saint-Laurent (1725)
    background
        Honoré's and Hamoche's revivals
            of plays 139–40
        royal presence 140
    plays
        Les Animaux raisonnables (Lesage,
            d'Orneval, Fuzelier) 139
        Les Funérailles de la Foire
            (Lesage, d'Orneval,
            Fuzelier) 138, 139
        Le Monde renversé (Lesage,
            d'Orneval, Fuzelier) 139
        *Le Rappel de la Foire à la
            Vie* (Lesage, d'Orneval,
            Fuzelier) 138
Foire Saint-Laurent (1726)
    background
        Francisque-Honoré
            partnership 140, 146
        Francisque's last fair 160
        plays from all four major fair
            authors 146
    d'Orneval, *Les Arrêts de l'Amour* 148
    Fuzelier
        Les Amours déguisés 156–8
        Le Bois de Boulogne 158
        Les Dieux travestis
            (prologue) 146–7
        Le Galant brutal 147–8
        Le Saut de Leucade 147, 148
    La Font, *Le Retour de la Chasse du
        Cerf* 158–9
    Lesage, Fuzelier and d'Orneval
        Les Comédiens Corsaires 152,
            153, 154–5, 159, 288, 311
        L'Obstacle Favorable 155–6
        Les Pèlerins de la Mecque 146,
            148–9

370 INDEX

Lesage and Fuzelier, *L'École des Amans* 148
Piron
   Olivette juge des enfers 150
   La Robe de dissention ou le faux prodige 149–50
   La Rose, ou le Pucelage 150–1
   post-fair Palais-Royal performances 159
   'un Compliment prononcé par Francisque 159–60
   see also Querelle des Théâtres (Foire Saint-Laurent 1726)
Foire Saint-Laurent (1728) 161
Foire Saint-Laurent (1729) 161, 163
Foire Saint-Laurent (1730) 162
Foire Saint-Laurent (1731) 162, 295
Foire Saint-Laurent (1733) 169
Foire Saint-Laurent (1737) 255 n.21
Foire Saint-Laurent (1740) 289
Foire Saint-Laurent (1743), *L'Ambigu de la folie ou Le Ballet des dindons* (Favart) 297–8
Fompré, Catherine *see* Moylin, Catherine (née Fompré, 1st wife of Martin Simon Moylin)
Fompré, de (unidentified) 167
Fompré, Marie-Antoinette *see* Foulquier, Marie-Antoinette (née Tourneville and widow of Fompré)
Fompré, Marie-Catherine 273 n.3
Font, Auguste 114 n.24
Fontanieu, Gaspard de, High Steward of the Dauphiné 163, 165
Foreman, Carolyn Thomas 211 n.60
Foulquier, Jean-Baptiste 192, 273, 288
Foulquier, Marie-Antoinette (née Tourneville and widow of Fompré) 191, 192, 216 n.9, 273, 288, 300
Foulquier, Marie-Catherine 273
Foulquier, Suzanne-Antoinette 288
Fourcade, Léonard 216, 293, 312
Fourcade, Mimi (née Marie-Josèphe de Pré or Despré de Verneuil) 173, 180, 191, 216, 293, 312
Francine, Jean 102, 125
Francisque (François Moylin, known as Francisque)
   biographical details
      brief biography 2
      childless 7, 297
      date of birth 6
      date of death 309
      exuberant/ebullient personality 3, 83–4
      family background and siblings 5–7
      handwriting and signature 2, 141, 300
      marriage 6, 308
      name, spelling of x
      no known portrait of 2
      outlived wife and (possibly) all siblings 308–9
      private life and beliefs, unknown 3
      retirement in Nantes 293, 296, 297
   brief overview of study 1–4
   cultural legacy
      artistic insubordination 309–10
      from Franco-Italian genre to official theatres' repertoire 311
      French theatre in original language in London 312
      innovative pantomime and dance 311–12
      local conditions/events reflected in programmes 311
      speaking Arlequin introduced to London audiences 312–13
      theatre as soft power abroad 313–14
      theatrical high culture brought to French provinces 310–11
      touring abroad 311
      unique achievements 315
   life as actor-impresario
      actor-dancer, graceful and versatile 16, 315
      better educated than many fairground players 310
      business acumen 186–7, 315
      celebrity status 208
      Comédiens du Roi title 2, 279–80, 282
      commedia all'improvviso skills 9, 50, 51
      English, knowledge of 84
      financial ruin after Haymarket riot (1738) 272
      financial success 40, 174, 293, 296

international *entrepreneur*, seeing
    himself as   60
Italian and Latin, knowledge
    of   32 n.25
mysterious François Moylin after
    his death   309
patronage from royals and
    gentry   46 n.11, 84, 85,
    86–7, 90–1, 105, 225
possible handing over of
    company to brother Simon
    (1741–50)   291
publications associating his name
    with plays/playwrights   177,
    241
ticket price war   174, 310
training in the provinces   43
role as Arlequin
    advertising himself as 'most perfect
        English Harlequin in the
        World'   84, 85, 163
    Arlequin-Francisque first mentioned
        in 1715 procès-verbal   11–12
    comparison with Arlequin-
        Thomassin   88, 207, 208,
        275
    leading Arlequin of the fairs   85
    Le Mercure's glowing
        review   281–2
    playing Arlequin using 'normal'
        speaking voice   107
    playing Arlequin with
        humour   208
    as referred to in *The Two Dogs*
        (poem)   235–6
    speaking Arlequin   20, 65, 199,
        207, 213, 312–13
    in works of Delisle, d'Allainval and
        Marivaux   208
role as Arlequin in
    *Les Adieux d'Arlequin, Pierrot et
        Colombine*   76
    Arlequin Astrologue   206–7
    Arlequin balourd (Procope-
        Couteaux)   58–61, 89, 195
    *Arlequin cru Colombine et
        Colombine cru Arlequin*
        (Barbier)   88, 121 n.47
    *Arlequin Dame Alison ou Le
        Carillon*   86
    Arlequin Deucalion
        (Piron)   108–15

Arlequin Hulla (Dominique,
    Riccoboni, Romagnesi)   191,
    196
*Arlequin Lustucru, grand Turc et
    Télémaque* (Fuzelier)   12
Arlequin sauvage (Delisle)   212,
    214
Arlequin toujours Arlequin
    (Dominique, Romagnesi,
    Riccoboni)   206, 208
The Burgomaster Trick'd as a silent
    Harlequin   183
Colombine fille savante
    (Fatouville)   49
Les Deux Arlequins (Le Noble)   75
L'Embarras des richesses
    (d'Allainval)   191, 196, 254
L'Endriague (Piron)   126–7, 148
L'Etourdi (*Les Fourberies
    d'Arlequin*)   75
*La Fille savante ou Isabelle fille
    capitaine* (Fatouville)   195
La Foire de Saint-Germain
    (Dufresny and Regnard)   48
    n.15
L'Ombre de la Foire (Lesage and
    d'Orneval)   67–8
La Princesse de Carizme (Lesage
    and La Font)   **27**, 29
'Prologue to the Town (Ozell)   43,
    45–6
Les Quatre Arlequins   88
*Le Retour de la Chasse du
    cerf*   159
*La Robe de dissention ou le faux
    prodige* (Piron)   149–50
Le Saut de Leucade (Fuzelier)   147
roles as other characters
    Ajax in *Le Galant brutal*
        (Fuzelier)   148
    Ascalon in *Samson*
        (Romagnesi)   178, 208, 231
    Azarias in *Athalie* (Racine)   233,
        234
    bailiff in *Agnès de Chaillot*
        (Dominique and
        Legrand)   229
    Baron in *Le Baron de la Crasse*
        (Poisson)   61, 75, 195
    a bear at Fêtes de Chantilly   124
    Briguelle in *Le Festin de Pierre*
        (Dorimond)   166

Crispin in *Le Pharaon*
    (Fuzelier) 23
Don Pedro in *Inès de Castro* (La
    Motte) 227, 229
Dorante in *Attendez-moi sous
    l'orme* (Regnard) 75
Duenna and maidservant in
    L'Obstacle Favorable 155
female character in *La Fausse
    Coquette* (Brugière de
    Barante) 49 n.18
female pilgrim in *Les Pèlerins de la
    Mecque* (Lesage, D'Orneval,
    Fuzelier) 149
grotesque dame in *Le Carillon de
    Maître Gervaise et Dame
    Alison* 193
himself in Piron's prologue on
    Lyon fire 118–19
irate female member of the
    public 58, 173, 209
in *Le Malade imaginaire*
    (Molière) 77–8
Mercure in *La Boîte de
    Pandore* 132, 136 n.19, 137
    n.20
Mme de Sotenville in *George
    Dandin* (Molière) 61
L'Opéra in *La Querelle des
    Théâtres* (Lesage and La
    Font) 32
L'Opéra in *Le Rappel de la Foire
    à la Vie* (Lesage, d'Orneval,
    Fuzelier) 102–3
L'Opéra in *Les Funérailles de la
    Foire* (Lesage, d'Orneval,
    Fuzelier) 35, 102
Paris in *Le Jugement de
    Paris* 25–6
Tartuffe in *Le Tartuffe*
    (Molière) 62, 86, 87
Tirésias/Tirésie in *Arlequin Tirésias*
    (Piron) 120
young lovers 12
Francisque, Jean (not related to
    Francisque Moylin) 66 n.2
François Étienne, duc de Lorraine, later
    Holy Roman Emperor
Francophobia 252, 253, 263
    see also Anglophobia; xenophobia
Fransen, Jan 66
Frederick, Prince of Wales
    Francisque patronised by 191
    Francisque's 1735 Benefit 196
    Hanoverian and disliked by
        Jacobites 234
    Marie Sallé's 1734 Benefit 184–5
    Marie Sallé's 1735 Benefit 204
    Masonic ideals 226
    mother Caroline's low opinion
        of 222–3, 231
    Porpora's Opera of the Nobility
        patronised by 189
    strained relations with father
        George 227, 228, 231
Frederick I, King of Denmark and
    Norway 226
Frederick the Great, King of Prussia 2,
    293, 302–3, 304, 306
Freemasons 225, 226
French farce *see* farce
French theatre
    negative image of 47–8, 50, 76–7
    permanent theatre buildings 297
    as soft power 313–14
French Theatre, London *see* Little Theatre
    in the Haymarket (also known
    as French Theatre); Saint James
    Theatre (also known as the French
    theatre)
French tragedy 90
Fromageot (Fromajot), Marie *see* Moylin,
    Marie (née Fromageot/Fromajot,
    2nd wife of Martin Simon Moylin)
Fuchs, Max
    call for detailed history of Francisque's
        troupe 1, 2, 315
    regarding
        Chinese Festival riots (1755) 270
        Dijon season (1739–40) 287 n.46
        Francisque as businessman 186–7
        Francisque's *Le Spectacle
            brillant* 296
        French comedians in London 65
        Giuseppe Tortoriti's troupe 7
        Guillaume Moylin's identity 6 n.9
        Hébrard's shady dealings 292
        Marguerite Moylin's
            widowhood 242 n.11
        'several Francisques'
            speculation x
Fuzelier, Louis
    author of distinction writing for
        fairs 10

editor of *Le Mercure de France* 10, 116–17
on Italian style of singing 23
on marionettes in Piron's *Le Mariage de Momus* 122
Piron's pun on Fuzelier name 110
plays in Lalauze's 1720 Saint-Germain fair programme 66
works
  L'Amour et Bacchus à la Foire 146 n.3
  Les Amours déguisés 154, 156–8, 159
  Arlequin Lustucru, grand Turc et Télémaque 12
  L'Assemblée des Comédiens 138
  Le Bois de Boulogne 158
  Le Déménagement du Théâtre ci-devant occupé par les Comédiens Italiens 130
  Les Dieux à la Foire (prologue) 131–7, 138, 139, 146
  Les Dieux travestis (prologue) 146
  Le Galant brutal 147–8
  Les Indes galantes libretto (for Rameau) 149, 289, 297–8
  Le Pharaon 22, 23
  La Revue des Amours 25 n.12
  Le Saut de Leucade 147, 148
  Les Songes 155
works with Dominique, *Arlequin larron, juge et grand prévôt* 50
works with Lesage and d'Ornival *see under* Lesage, Alain-René

Gaeta, siege of (1734) 233
Gage, Benedicta (née Hall), Lady 257
Gage, Thomas, 1st Viscount Gage 257
Gaiffe, Félix 178
Gaillardet, Jeanne *see* Moylin, Jeanne (née Gaillardet, wife of Francisque's brother Guillaume)
Galland, Antoine, *Les Mille et une nuits* 26, 82
Galliard, Johann Ernst 182
Garrick, David
  Harlequin as Shakespeare's demonic Other 270
  Harlequin Student 269
  Harlequin's Invasion, or A Christmas Gambol 270, 312–13

Marivaux's *L'Ile des esclaves*, production of 194
not in London for Francisque's 1734–5 season 251
prologue to Arthur Murphy's *The Apprentice* 270 n.55
Gascon (comic figure) 146–7
Gasper, Julia 306 n.37, 307
Gastelier, Jacques-Élie 280
Gay, Ignacio Ramos 315 n.65
Gay, John, *The Beggar's Opera* 161, 179 n.25, 180 n.30, 182
Gazette d'Amsterdam 262
Geneva
  ban on public theatrical performances 246
  Francisque's and J-B Gherardi's short-term licences 246 n.25
genre polémique *see* polemical genre
The Gentleman's Magazine 216, 223, 250 n.1, 251–2
George I, King of Great Britain and Ireland
  attending Francisque's troupe's performances 2, 46, 76
  Charles XII of Sweden, enemy of 224–5
  conflictual relations with son George 227
  death of 90
  ignorant of the English language 41–2
  imprisonment of wife Sophia Dorothea 227–8
  invitation to Riccoboni's troupe 42, 43
  neither French nor Catholic 234
  non-jurors controversy 62, 63, 221
  in Vézian's epilogue (1718) 59–60
  in Vézian's prologue (1718) 61
George II, King of Great Britain and Ireland (Prince of Wales)
  accession celebrated in Vézian's ode 58 n.50
  assent for Francisque's 1738 season 249, 250–1, 264–5, 266, 280
  attending Francisque's 1735 Benefit 206
  attending Francisque's troupe's performances 2, 43, 46, 51, 61, 75, 76, 191, 196, 205 n.48

attending Hasse's *Artaserse* with
Farinelli 189
distress over mother's imprisonment
by father 228
Egmont, confidant of 197
Handel, favourite of 189, 205, 205
n.48
many affairs 227
Marie Sallé's 1734 Benefit, not
attended by 185
neither French nor Catholic 234
strained relations with father George
I 227, 228
strained relations with son
Frederick 227, 228, 231
Yamacraws, received by 211
Georges, Marguerite 314
Georgia Trustees 211, 213
Gesvres, duc de 175, 279, 280
Ghent
Simon Moylin and J.-B. Lesage troupe
(1738–9) 272–3
Simon Moylin and J.-B. Lesage troupe
(1740–1) 289
Gherardi, Evariste
editor of *Le Théâtre Italien* 141
member of old Italian troupe 141
Prince Ali role in *La Princesse de
Carizme* **27**
Le Retour de la Foire de Bezons 49
Le Théâtre Italien
Arlequin engraving 49
Arlequin toujours Arlequin
songs 208
Ozell's familiarity with 45
plays in 1718–19 London
season 49 n.18, 49–50
Regnard and Dufresny's *Les
Momies d'Egypte* 158
repertoire of pre-1697 Italian
company 42–3
singing and dancing 52
speaking Arlequin 65
undervalued by some critics 51
Gherardi, Jean-Baptiste Constantin 140,
141, 148, 165, 167, 243–4, 246 n.25
Gigantomachie story 122
Gillier (or Gilliers), Jean-Claude
compositions
for Comédie-Française and
Foires 24

for Procope-Couteaux's *Arlequin
balourd* 60
compositions for 1718 Foire Saint-
Laurent 25, 52
Les Amours de Nanterre (Lesage
and d'Orneval) 34
Les Funérailles de la Foire
(Lesage, d'Orneval,
Fuzelier) 35
Le Monde renversé (Lesage,
d'Orneval, Fuzelier) 33
contribution to opéra-comique
genre 24
regular visitor to London 54, 60
Vézian's interest in 58 n.50
Gillot, Claude, *scène des deux
carosses* 49
Glorious Revolution (1688) 215
Gluck, Christoph Willibald 34n29
*La Rencontre imprévue, ou Les
Pèlerins de la Mecque* 149
Godard de Beauchamps,
Pierre-François 195
Goethe, Johann Wolfgang 128
Goff, Moira 18, 18 n.57, 20, 22, 52, 161
n.42, 191–2
Goodman's Fields Theatre 191, 210 n.58,
253, 269
Gordon Riots (1780) 64
Gouhier, Henri 247
Goulbourne, Russell 60, 201
Graffigny, Françoise de 273–4, 275
Cénie 295, 296, 311
Grafton, Charles FitzRoy, 2nd Duke of
Grafton 250, 255, 262, 263
Granier (family of dancers) 191, 312
Gremont, Mlle de 74 n.21
Grenoble
baptism of François Malter 165
Dominique's wedding 7
Francisque's company (1729) 163–5,
167, 245
*Le Carillon de Maître Gervaise et
Dame Alison* 164
La Surprise de l'amour
(Marivaux) 164, 167
Francisque's company (1736)
possibly 245
Francisque's company (1737),
Voltaire's *Alzire* and Rousseau's
response 245–7

Malter children's birth location 141 n.34
Simon Moylin's presence (1744) 292
Simon Moylin's troupe (1733) 168
Grimberghs, Jean-Baptiste de
  Francisque's 1720 King's Theatre season 74, 76, 78, 79
  Francisque's 1721 London season 86, 87, 88, 89
Grognet, Manon 183, 191, 205, 240 n.2
The Grub-Street Journal 198, 209, 219, 235, 238, 248
Guichemerre, Roger 29
Gunpowder Plot (1605) 215, 217
Gustavus Adolphus the Great, King of Sweden 225
Gustavus Vasa (also known as Gustav I), King of Sweden 224
Gyllenborg, Carl 225

Hamoche, Jean-Baptiste
  famous for playing Pierrot 9, 24, 30
  Foire Saint-Laurent (1712) 9
  Foire Saint-Laurent (1718) 24
    as La Foire in *La Querelle des Théâtres* (Lesage and La Font) 30
  Foire Saint-Laurent (1721) 95, 132
    granting of nine-year licence 102
    Pierrot in *La Boîte de Pandore* 99
    Pierrot in *La Fausse Foire* (Lesage, d'Orneval, Fuzelier) 97, 98
  Foire Saint-Laurent (1724), Pierrot in *Les Dieux à la Foire* (Fuzelier) 132, 133, 137
  Foire Saint-Laurent (1725), Honoré's and Hamoche's revivals of plays 139–40
  Foire Saint-Laurent (1726)
    difficult relationship with Piron 149
    Pierrot in Fuzelier's *Les Amours déguisés* 157
    Pierrot in La Font's *Pierrot fée* 148
    Pierrot in Piron's *La Robe de dissention* 150
    Pierrot in Piron's *Olivette juge des enfers* 150
    singer in Fuzelier's *Les Dieux travestis* 147

Little Theatre in the Haymarket (1721–22) 89–90
  French tragedies (in French) and comedies 89–90
  Le Tartuffe (Molière) 90
  not included in Francisque's 1734–5 London season 192
  Palais-Royal performances (1721) 105
Handel, George Frideric
  Covent Garden (1734–5)
    competition from Porpora and Farinelli at King's 189, 205
    composition of troupe 188
    hiring of Marie-Sallé 189, 205, 298
    not a financial success 236, 298
    royal support 189, 205
    theatre shared with Rich's company 189
  Covent Garden performances
    Alcina 189, 204
    Ariodante 189, 205
    Athalia 221, 231, 232–3, 234, 235
    Deborah 221, 232
    Esther 221, 223, 232, 233
    opera seria, *Il Pastor Fido* 189
    Rinaldo 18, 42, 269 n.52
    Terpsicore 189
    words of English oratorios given to audience 182 n.36
Hanoverian 232
King's Theatre in the Haymarket
  expected number of subscribers 187
  Marie Sallé in *Rinaldo* (1717) 18, 42
  unsuccessful management 41, 59
handkerchief (mouchoir) issue 229 n.42
Hanoverians
  and Atterbury Plot 215
  and Boissy's *La Vie est un songe* 230–1
  and Handel's *Athalia* 232–3, 234, 235
  and Handel's oratorio revivals 221
  and Molière's *Le Tartuffe* 62–3
  and Piron's *Gustavus Vasa* 224–6
  and Romagnesi's *Samson* 231
  ruling Hanoverians 196, 224–5, 227, 230
  and theatres/actors 63–4
  Vézian 58
Hanson, Craig 78

Harlequin *see* Arlequin (Harlequin)
Harris-Warrick, Rebecca 52–3, 78 n.35
Hasse, Johann Adolph, *Artaserse* 189, 204
Hatchett, William, *The Fall of Mortimer* 221
Haughton (Houghton), G. 161, 162, 181
Hauteville, François de 306–7
Haydn, Joseph, *L'Incontro improvviso* 149
Haydon, Colin 215
Haymarket *see* King's Theatre in the Haymarket; Little Theatre in the Haymarket
Haymarket riot (9 Oct. 1738) *see* London season (1738, discontinued)
Haywood, H. L. 225 n.35
Hébrard, François 292
Heidegger, Johann Jacob 41, 42, 58, 59, 73, 189, 236
Henry V, King of England 200, 252, 263
Hervey, John, 2nd Baron Hervey 222–3, 236
Hesse, Jean-Baptiste (sometimes known as Deshayes) 242 n.10, 301 n.16
Higgins, Ian 224, 226
Highfill, Philip H., *A Biographical Dictionary of Actors* 241 n.8, 290 n.59
Hill, Aaron
  Francisque's 1734–5 London season
    hostile criticism 198–200, 206
    Roast Beef Affair 200, 201, 203
    taken to task by True Briton 210
  Francisque's performance of Voltaire's *Zaïre*, silence on 223
  French comedians referred to as 'French vermin' 253
  London and Paris stages compared 238–9
  Miller's *Art and Nature*, cabal against 213
  praise for Arlequin-Thomassin 208
  works
    Henry V 200, 253
    'Tale of Henry's Victories' (Francophobic) 253
    Zara (translation of Voltaire's *Zaïre*) 223
Hillhouse, James T. 210
The Historical Register for the Year 1738 (vol. 23) 261 n.39, 267–8

Hogarth, William
  'The Gate at Calais, or, the Roast Beef of Old England' 258, **259**
  Huguenots in 'Night' and 'Noon' paintings 254 n.15
Holland
  Francisque's troupe's season (1719, The Hague) 66, 73
  Francisque's troupe's tour (summer 1721) 94
Homer, *The Iliad* 235
homosexuality 113
Honoré, Maurice
  Foire Saint-Laurent (1724) 130–1, 132, 133, 137–8, 141
  Foire Saint-Laurent (1725) 139–40, 149
  Foire Saint-Laurent (1726) 140, 146, 149
Hostiou, Jeanne-Marie 36, 68, 85
Howard, Edward *see* Norfolk, Edward Howard, 9th Duke of Norfolk
Howard, Thomas *see* Norfolk, Thomas Howard, 8th Duke of Norfolk
Huguenots 254 n.15
Hume, Robert D. 187, 204, 205, 220, 221, 254–5
Hus, François and Barthélemy 247–8, 311
Hyacinthe (or Jacinte), Antoine 102, 117, 131, 132, 133

Islam 223
island-castaway/shipwreck genre 68, 70, 81, 93
Italian Night Scenes *see* Night Scenes

Jacint(h)e, Antoine *see* Hyacinthe (or Jacinte), Antoine
Jacobites
  Atterbury Plot (1722) 215, 225
  Catholic Jacobites 216, 230
  Charles Edward Stuart preferred over Frederick 234
  Charles Molloy (of *Common Sense*) 263
  Charles XII of Sweden, Protestant hero of 224–5
  Cornbury Plot (1733) 215
  and Freemasonry, spread of 225
  and Handel's *Athalia* 232, 233, 234, 235

Jacobite rebellion (1715)   62, 224, 225
  and *La Vie est un songe* (Boissy)   230–1
  and Molière's *Le Tartuffe*   62–3, 221–2
  and Piron's *Gustavus Vasa*   224–6
  and pre-1697 Italian repertoire   43
  and Romagnesi's *Samson*   231
  and theatres/actors   63–4
James Francis Edward Stuart, Prince of Wales   222, 233
James II, King of England   232, 233
Jassinte, Antoine *see* Hyacinthe (or Jacinte), Antoine
Johnson, Samuel
  Francophobe   263
  London: A Poem in Imitation of the Third Satire of Juvenal   251–3
Jolly, François-Antoine   195
  La Femme Jalouse   278
Joncus, Berta   213 n.69
  The Stage's Glory: John Rich (1692–1761)   2
Journal de la Cour & de Paris   169, 179
Journal Encyclopédique   298
Juvenal   251, 252, 252 n.7
Juvigny *see* Rigoley de Juvigny, Jean-Antoine

Keefe, Rosanna   viii
Keefe, Simon   viii
Kelly, Deirdre   240 n.2
Kelly, John
  English version of Destouches' *Le Philosophe marié*   219 n.17
  The Plot or Pill and Drop   201–2, 218–20, 236–7
  Timon in Love or the Innocent Theft   195, 219 n.17
Kemble, Charles   314
Kern, Jean B.   218
Killing no Murder (pamphlet)   232
King's Theatre in the Haymarket
  background
    façade   **47**
    maximum capacity   205–6
  Francisque's 1718–19 season *see* London season (1718–19)
  Francisque's 1720 season *see* London season (1720, March-June)
  opera (Heidegger and Handel)
    financial difficulties   41, 59
    hiring of Francisque's company (1718)   42
    number of subscriptions expected   187
  opera (Heidegger and Porpora)
    Nicola Porpora's company (1734–5)   188, 189, 204, 205
    not a financial success   236
    see also Farinelli (Carlo Broschi known as Farinelli)
König, Johann Ulrich von, *Die verkehrte Welt*   34n29
Königsmark, Philip Christoph von, Count   228

La Barre (or Labarre) de Beaumarchais, Antoine de   256, 259–60, 261, 262, 267, 272, 273, 313
La Chaussée, Pierre-Claude Nivelle de
  L'Ecole des amis   278
  Le Préjugé à la mode   278, 287
La Coste (or Lacoste), Louis de   24, 25, 28
La Font (or Lafont), Joseph de
  Pierrot fée   148
  La Princesse de Carizme (with Lesage)   25, 26, **27**, 28–9
  La Querelle des Théâtres (with Lesage)   29–34, 35
  Le Retour de la Chasse du Cerf   159 n.35
La Harpe, Jean François de, *Cours de Littérature* (1760)   114
La Motte, Antoine Houdar (or Houdart) de
  Rousseau on in 'Le Verger de Madame de Warens'   245
  works
    Inès de Castro   130 n.1, 192, 195, 227–8, 245
    Le Magnifique   296
    Romulus   107
La Place, Pierre-Antoine de, *Venise sauvée*   294, 295
La Rose, Claude de *see* Rosimond (Claude de La Rose, known as Rosimond)
La Tour d'Auvergne, Henri-Oswald de   113
Labarre de Beaumarchais *see* La Barre (or Labarre) de Beaumarchais, Antoine de

L'Abbé, Anthony   17, 117, 148, 158
Labbé, Catherine *see* Malter, Catherine (née Dussoye/Dusuisse, known as Catherine Labbé, Francisque's niece)
Lafitau, Jean-François   113
Lagrave, Henri
   Compiègne (1739 season)   282–3
   Compiègne theatre post Francisque   290 n.57
   ecclesiastical dispensation at Foire Saint-Germain   115 n.29
   Francisque's company in Bordeaux   284
   'Le Théâtre à la Cour'   275, 276
   Le Théâtre et le Public à Paris   29–32, 39, 72
   La Vie théâtrale à Bordeaux, des origines à nos jours   167
Laguerre, John   185, 219 n.16
Lahontan, Louis Armand de Lom d'Arce, baron de   70, 113, 212
Lalauze, Agathe de (née de Sceaux)   100 n.28, 105
Lalauze, Marc-Antoine de
   animosity towards Francisque over Arlequin role   29, 66
   death of wife Agathe   105
   Foire Saint-Germain (1720)   25 n.12, 66
   Foire Saint-Germain (1721)   90
   Foire Saint-Laurent (1718)   24
   Foire Saint-Laurent (1720)   81
   Foire Saint-Laurent (1721) *see* Foire Saint-Laurent (1721)
   no patronage of people in high places   85
   virtually bankrupt and leaving Paris forever   105
Lalauze, Marguerite *see* Alard, Marguerite (née Lalauze)
Lally, Michael   192 n. 13
Lancret, Nicolas   304
   Marie Sallé painting   **190**
Lang, Andrew   225 n.34
Langford, Paul   234
Langue d'oc   244
Lany, Jean-Barhélémy
   L'Ambigu de la folie ou Le Ballet des dindons (Favart)   297–8
   Pygmalion et Psyché, ballet pantomime   304
Larthomas, Pierre Henri   154–5

Laux, Frédéric   284
Law, John   69, 80, 83
lazzi   33, 50–1, 58, 72, 116, 163, 173
Le Bicheur (or Lebicheur), Pierre   131, 132
Le Noble (or Lenoble), Eustache, *Les Deux Arlequins*   50, 52, 64, 75, 173, 174, 278
Le Roussau, François   78, **79**
Le Suisse, Marie-Catherine *see* Moylin, Marie-Catherine (née Dusuisse or le Suisse, Francisque's wife)
Le Tellier (or Letellier), Jean-François   129, 132 n.11
Le Tellier (or Letellier), Nicholas   12, 42 n.5, 48 n.15, 62 n.55, 129 n.65, 167
Lebeuf   310
Lebrun   185 n.53, 218–19
Lecouvreur, Adrienne   117 n.34, 184, 247 n.28
Lefèvre (or Le Fèvre), Madame   254, 281–2
Lefèvre (or Le Fèvre), Mlles   281, 282
Lefèvre (or Le Fèvre), Monsieur   254, 281–2
Legrand, Charlotte   152, 154
Legrand, Marc-Antoine
   as portrayed in *Le Retour de la Chasse du cerf* (La Font)   159
   as portrayed in *Les Comédiens corsaires* (Lesage, d'Orneval, Fuzelier)   152, 154, 159
   works
      Agnès de Chaillot (with Dominique)   130 n.1, 228–9
      La Chasse du cerf   158–9
      La Foire de Saint-Laurent   135 n.16
      Polyphème (with Riccoboni)   121–2
      Le Roi de Cocagne   38
      Les Terres australes (with Dominique)   105
Lejeune, Philippe   138
Lekain (Henri Louis Cain known as Lekain)   314
Lemaigre-Gaffier, Pauline   313
Leopold I, Holy Roman Emperor   241
Lesage, Alain-René
   background
      author of distinction writing for fairs   10
      on Italian style of singing   23

pun on his name in Piron's
  Arlequin Deucalion 111
 satirical vein (Lesage, Fuzelier and
  d'Orneval) 295–6
 surpassed by Piron (Lesage,
  Fuzelier and d'Orneval) 128
Foire Saint-Germain (1721), writing for
 Francisque with d'Orneval and
 Fuzelier 90–1
Foire Saint-Germain (1722), Lesage,
 d'Orneval and Fuzelier's refusal
 to write for Francisque 107,
 108
Foire Saint-Laurent (1718), new opéras-
 comiques for Francisque with
 d'Orneval 24
Foire Saint-Laurent (1721)
 agreement to provide plays for
  fairs 102
 on Comédie-Française's support for
  Francisque 95, 98
 new opéras-comiques for
  Francisque with d'Orneval
  and Fuzelier 95
 refusal to write for Lalauze 94
Foire Saint-Laurent (1724), Lesage and
 d'Orneval agree to write for
 Dolet and Delaplace 130
Foire Saint-Laurent (1725), revival of
 four plays by Lesage, Fuzelier
 and d'Orneval 139
Foire Saint-Laurent (1726), all four
 major fair authors (Lesage,
 Fuzelier, d'Orneval and Piron)
 writing for Francisque 146
works
 La Ceinture de Venus 23 n.5
 Le Château des Lutins 22
 Gil Blas de Santillane 156 n.23
 prologue for 1721 Foire
  Saint-Germain 90–1
 *Le Retour de la Foire à la
  Vie* 38–9
 Le Roi des Ogres 109
 La Statue merveilleuse or *Le Miroir
  sans fard* 38 n.42, 82–3,
  278, 289
 Turcaret 10, 30, 91, 294
works with d'Orneval
 Les Amours de Nanterre 34–5,
  193
 L'Âne du Daggial 71–2
 Arlequin Endymion 91–2, 93

Arlequin Hulla 193 n.18
Arlequin roi des ogres 69, 70, 212
 n.64
Les Arrêts de l'Amour 148
Les Captifs d'Alger 130, 138
*La Conquête de la Toison
 d'or* 129, 130
Le Diable d'argent 69
La Grand-Mère amoureuse 54
 n.37
L'Isle des Amazones 35, 81–2
L'Isle du Gougou 68–9, 126
Magotin 93
L'Ombre d'Alard 93
L'Ombre de la Foire 67–8, 73,
 108, 139
L'Oracle muet 130, 138–9
La Queue de vérité 69
Robinson or *L'Isle de
 Robinson* 93
works with d'Orneval and Fuzelier
 Les Animaux raisonnables 22, 76,
  88, 139, 193, 278, 279
 La Boîte de Pandore 99–101, 132,
  136 n.19, 137 n.20
 Les Comédiens Corsaires 152,
  153, 154–5, 159, 288, 311
 La Fausse Foire 95–9
 La Forêt de Dodone 92
 Les Funérailles de la Foire 35–6,
  102, 105 n.44, 138, 139
 Le Jeune Vieillard 118–19
 Le Monde renversé 23 n.5, 32–4,
  139
 L'Obstacle Favorable 154, 155–6
 Les Pèlerins de la Mecque 146,
  148–9, 159
 *Pierrot Romulus, ou Le Ravisseur
  poli* 107
 *Le Rappel de la Foire à la
  Vie* 102–3, 105 n.44, 138,
  139
 Le Régiment de la Calotte 103–5,
  105 n.44, 137 n.23
 Le Temple de l'ennui 23 n.5
 La Tête noire 101–2
works with d'Orneval and Piron, *Les
 Trois Commères* 150
works with Fuzelier, *L'École des
 Amans* 148
works with La Font
 La Princesse de Carizme 25, 26,
  27, 28–9

La Querelle des Théâtres 29–34, 35
  see also Le Théâtre de la Foire ou l'opéra comique (Lesage and d'Orneval)
Lesage, Charles (a.k.a. Senior) 66, 173, 178, 191, 192, 216 n.9, 243, 281
Lesage, François-Antoine (Alain-René Lesage's son, known as Pittenec) 82, 171, 173 n.4
Lesage, Jean-Baptiste (a.k.a. Junior)
  fine actor 173
  Francisque's 1734–5 London season 191, 192
  Francisque's 1738 London season 265–6
  Francisque's 1739 Compiègne season (possibly) 275
  Francisque's 1741 Bordeaux season 283–4
  management role 173, 248, 250
  not the son of playwright Alain-René Lesage 173 n.4
  Samson role (Brussels, 1734) 178
  Simon Moylin's 1738–9 Ghent season 272–3
  Simon Moylin's 1740–1 Ghent season 289
  Simon Moylin's 1741 Bordeaux season 283–4, 290–1
Lesage, Marianne (née Petit or Pettite, Charles Lesage's wife) 216 n.9, 243
Lesage, Mrs, Jr. (Jean-Baptiste Lesage's wife) 191
L'Estoile, Claude de, *La Belle Esclave* 287
Levenson, Erica Pauline 2, 64 n.62, 163
Leveridge, Richard, 'The Roast Beef of Old England' (song) 203, 257, 258, 267
Licensing Act (1737) 226, 239, 248, 250–1, 253– 4, 258, 262– 3
Lille
  baptism of Jean-Louis Malter 181 n.31
  Francisque's company (1738) 248
  Francisque's troupe heading to (1720) 73
  Francisque's troupe's summer season (1712) 9
  Malter children's birth location 141 n.34

Lilliputians (child dancers/actors) 191, 227 n.39, 242, 307 n.43, 312
Lincoln's Inn Fields Theatre *see* Theatre at Lincoln's Inn Fields
Lisle, de (actor) *see* Delisle (actor)
Lisle, Mademoiselle de
  Foire Saint-Germain (1725), in *L'Audience du Temps* 132
  Foire Saint-Laurent (1718) 25
  Foire Saint-Laurent (1721) 95, 98, 99, 133, 135–6
  Foire Saint-Laurent (1724) 131, 132
  Foire Saint-Laurent (1726)
    in La Font's *Le Retour de la Chasse du cerf* 159
    in Piron's *Olivette juge des enfers* 150
  King's Theatre (March-June 1720) 74, 75, 76
  Little Theatre in the Haymarket (1721) 87, 88
    not included in Francisque's 1734–5 London season 192
  Palais-Royal performances (1721) 105
Little Theatre in the Haymarket (also known as French Theatre)
  background
    façade **87**
    John Potter's newly-built theatre 86
    maximum capacity 205, 206
  Cibber's breakaway company from Drury Lane 181–2
  Fielding
    Don Quixote in England 203
    eviction from 254–5
  Francisque's 1720–1 season *see* London season (1720–1)
  Francisque's 1734 season *see* London season (1734)
  Hamoche's 1721–2 season 89–90
  Haymarket riot *see* London season (1738, discontinued)
Livrey, Mlle de 74 n.21
Lockwood, Thomas 256 n.22
Loeillet, Jean-Baptiste 54
  The Submission 18
Loftis, John 15, 63
Loinville, Antoine de 244, 288, 292
London, North American tribes' visits 211
The London Daily Post

advertisements for Francisque's 1734–5
    season   222, 223, 224, 231
advertisements for Francisque's 1735
    Benefit   205 n.47, 206 n.52
Haymarket riot affair (1738)   254,
    255–6, 263, 266
    'The Case of the French
        Comedians'   265–6
report of actor sent to prison
    (Licensing Act)   250
The London Evening Post
    advertisement for 1734–5 theatre
        season   188
    Haymarket riot affair (1738)   253, 258
        n.30, 260, 263, 264, 266, 267
    Prince Charles at siege of Gaeta
        (1734)   233
London Journal   86, 89
The London Magazine
    *On the French Players' coming to
        England* (verses)   268–9
    Victor's account of Haymarket
        riot   271
London season (1718–19)
    background
        Francisque's first London
            season   41
        King's Theatre in the
            Haymarket   41, 42, **47**
        Lincoln's Inn Fields Theatre   37,
            42, 58–9
        royal presence   46
        successful incl. financially   65
        wide-ranging repertoire   65
        xenophobia   41–2
    Franco-Italian comedy
        Franco-Italian repertoire and
            politics   63–4
        Franco-Italian repertoire vs.
            Foires   42–3, 64
        French theatre, negative image
            of   47–8, 50
        tricks and feats vs.
            pantomime   50–1
        Vaulting and Tumbling   51–2
        verbal extravagance and outlandish
            plots   65
    King's Theatre in the Haymarket
        Arlequin/Colombine new
            prologue   46, 50, 54, 73
        Fatouville's *Arlequin empereur
            dans la lune*   49

Fatouville's *La Précaution
    inutile*   49, 54
Vézian's prologue to *Arlequin
    balourd*   58–9, 89
Lincoln's Inn Fields Theatre
    dancing shared with resident
        dancers   53
Les Deux Arlequins (Le
    Noble)   50, 52, 64
The Devil's Tabernacle or *School of
    Vanity*   48
La Foire de Saint-Germain
    (Dufresny and Regnard)   43,
    44, 45–6, 48–9, 64 n.62
*La Foire de Saint-Germain, scène
    des deux carosses*   49
Francisque's opening night
    prologue   50
prologue to *Arlequin
    balourd*   58–9, 173
reputation as Catholic and
    Jacobite   63–4
'London plays'
    Barbier's *La Fille à la
        mode*   54–7, 58
    Procope-Couteaux's *Arlequin
        balourd*   57–61, 208
music and dance
    comic and serious dance   52–3, 65
    French dancing techniques   52
    music-singing-dancing show
        Carillon   53–4
    music/songs by Gillier   52, 54
    troupe's and London-based
        musicians   54
plays from Comédie-Française
    repertoire
    genuine actors vs. fairground
        entertainers   64
    Molière's *George Dandin*   61, 64,
        65
    Molière's *Le Tartuffe*   62–3, 64,
        65, 221, 314
    Poisson's *Le Baron de la
        Crasse*   61, 64
    Regnard's *Les Folies
        amoureuses*   62, 64, 65
London season (1720, March-June)
    background
        Francisque's reliance on
            Grimberghs   74

Grimberghs' poor
    management 74, 76
Heidegger and King's Theatre in
    the Haymarket 73–4
from King's to Lincoln's Inn Fields
    for two performances 76
pantomime (*ballets
    d'actions*) 79–80
press reaction 76–7
royal presence 75, 76
Watteau's 'Les Comédiens
    Italiens' 78–81, **80**
repertoire
    *Les Adieux d'Arlequin, Pierrot et
        Colombine* 76
    Les Animaux raisonnables (Lesage,
        d'Orneval, Fuzelier) 75–6
    *Arlequin Grand Provost et
        Juge* 74–5
    Le Baron de la Crasse
        (Poisson) 75
    Le Bourgeois Gentilhomme
        (Molière) 75
    Les Chinois (Regnard and
        Dufresny) 76
    Les Deux Arlequins (Le Noble) 75
    L'Etourdi (ou *Les Fourberies
        d'Arlequin*) 75
    Harlequin a Blunderer
        (*Arlequin balourd*,
        Procope-Couteaux) 75
    Le Malade imaginaire
        (Molière) 77–8
London season (1720–1)
background
    Francisque's troupe first to
        appear at Little Haymarket
        Theatre 86
    Grimberghs' management 86, 87,
        88, 89
    no royal presence 86–7
    problems and
        mismanagement 87–9
    Roger's and Francisque's
        benefits 88
repertoire
    Les Animaux raisonnables (Lesage,
        d'Orneval, Fuzelier) 88
    *Arlequin cru Colombine et
        Colombine cru Arlequin*
        (Barbier) 88

*Arlequin Dame Alison ou Le
    Carillon* 86
*Arlequin Empereur dans la
    lune* 89
Arlequin limonadier 88
Arlequin Major Ridicule
    (cancelled) 87–8
Arlequin Perroquet 88
L'Avare (Molière) 86
comedies by Molière (nine) 89
comedies by Regnard (two) 89
Les Deux Pierrots
    (Dominique) 88
Les Disgraces d'Arlequin 88
*La Fille à la mode, ou le badaud
    de Paris* (Barbier) 86
La Foire de Saint-Germain
    (Regnard) 86
*Les Fourberies d'Arlequin ou
    l'Étourdi* 87
Les Quatre Arlequins 88
Le Tartuffe (Molière) 86, 87
Le Tombeau de Maître André 86
London season (1734)
    Cibber's breakaway company from
        Drury Lane 181–2
    Francisque joining Cibber at Little
        Haymarket 181, 182, 202, 265
performances
    *The Albion Queens, or the Death
        of Mary, Queen of Scotland*
        (Banks) 182
    The Burgomaster Trick'd
        (Nivelon) 182–3, 184, 185,
        289
    Dido and Aeneas (Thomas
        Arne) 182, 185
    *The Mother-in-Law or The Doctor
        the Disease* (Miller) 185
    *Les Ombres des amants
        fidèles* 183
London season (1734–5)
    background on Francisque's contract
        with Duke of Richmond for Little
        Haymarket 181, 188–9, 206,
        248
    extracts from contract 185–7
    background on season
        breadth of repertoire 193–5
        cast list 191–2
        dancing, importance of 191–2

INDEX 383

financial success resented by
    English critics 236–9, 252
great success with audiences 239
memory of success lost after 1738
    Haymarket riot 312–13
not seen by Samuel Johnson or
    Garrick 251
patronage from nobility/
    gentry 196–7, 200, 215
patronage from royal family 191,
    195, 196, 198, 206, 207, 208
professional critics' negative
    reception 197–200
Roast Beef affair 200–3
seat prices 191
Francisque's application plays
  application and personation
    concepts 220–1
  Athalie (Racine) 231–5
  Le Festin de Pierre
    (Dorimond) 222–3
  Gustave Vasa (Piron) 224–7
  Inès de Castro (La Motte) 227–8
  parody of La Motte's tragedy
    (*Agnès de Chaillot*) 228–9
  Samson (Romagnesi) 230, 231,
    233
  Le Tartuffe (Molière) 221–2
  La Vie est un songe
    (Boissy) 230–1
  Zaïre (Voltaire) 223
Francisque's Benefit 204, 205–10,
    236
  Arlequin Astrologue 206, 207
  Arlequin toujours Arlequin 206,
    208
Francisque's French Arlequin
  rivalry with Rich's English
    Harlequin 235
  The Two Dogs (poem) 235–6
plots and the press
  anti-Popery propaganda 215–16
  Francisque and the 'Pill
    Plot' 217–20
repertoire as printed in *The London
    Stage* 321–7
repertoire as referred to in the book
  Agnès de Chaillot (Dominique and
    Legrand) 228–9
  L'Allure 193
  Les Amants réunis 197 n.30
  Les Amours de Nanterre 193

Les Animaux raisonnables (Lesage,
    d'Orneval, Fuzelier) 193
Arcagambis (Dominique and
    Romagnesi) 193
Arlequin Astrologue (*Harlequin
    Astrologer*) 196, 197, 206,
    207
Arlequin balourd (Procope-
    Couteaux) 195, 201
Arlequin Cartouche 197 n.30
Arlequin Esprit Follet 197 n.30
*Arlequin et sa troupe de comédiens
    esclaves* 193
Arlequin Hulla (Dominique,
    Riccoboni, Romagnesi) 191,
    196
Arlequin sauvage (Delisle) 195,
    196, 197 n.30, 210, 211–14,
    215
Arlequin Tirésias (Piron) 121 n.49,
    193
Arlequin toujours Arlequin
    (or *Harlequin always
    Harlequin*) 193, 206, 208
Athalie (Racine) 195, 231–5, 242
    n.10
L'Avare (Molière) 196, 198
Le Baron de la Crasse
    (Poisson) 195
Les Caractères de la danse
    (Rebel) 180, 192
*Le Carillon de Maître Gervaise et
    Dame Alison* 193
Don Pasquin d'Avalos
    (Montfleury) 195
La Double Inconstance
    (Marivaux) 210
L'École des Maris (Molière) 193
L'Embarras des richesses
    (d'Allainval) 191, 196, 197,
    203, 210
L'Étourdi ou les Contretemps
    (Molière) 197 n.30
Le Faucon et les oies de Boccace
    (Delisle) 195
La Fausse coquette 197 n.30
*Le Festin de pierre ou l'athée
    foudroyé* (Dorimond) 195,
    222–3
*La Fille savante ou Isabelle fille
    capitaine* (Fatouville) 195
Les Filles errantes 197 n.30

Le Français à Londres
  (Boissy)   195, 197, 200, 203
Gustave Vasa (Piron)   195, 224–7
L'Ile des esclaves (Marivaux)   194
Inès de Castro (La Motte)   192, 195, 227–8
Le Jeu de l'amour et du hasard
  (Marivaux)   194
Marivaux, seven comedies by   194
Molière, twelve comedies by   193
Regnard, eight comedies by   193
La Réunion des amours
  (Marivaux)   196, 198, 242 n.12
Samson (Romagnesi)   174, 195, 230, 231, 233
La Sylphide (Dominique and Romagnesi)   196
Le Tartuffe (Molière)   192, 220, 221–2
Timon le misanthrope
  (Delisle)   195, 197 n.30
La Vie est un songe (Boissy)   195, 197, 230–1
Zaïre (Voltaire)   192, 195, 223
London season (1737–8)
  effects of Licensing Act (1737)   248
  Francisque's decision not to come   248
London season (1738, discontinued)
  background
    Francisque's licence agreed by George II   249, 250–1, 280
    intercession of Duke of Richmond   248–9
    intercession of French ambassador   248–9, 250
    Licensing Act restrictions on English companies   250–1, 253
  hostility against foreign acting companies
    campaign in written press   251, 253
    Hill's 'Tale of Henry's Victories'   253
    Samuel Johnson's poem *London*   251–3
  Little Haymarket Theatre
    advertisement for Francisque's company   254
    Fielding's eviction from the theatre   254–5
    inflammatory comments from press   255–6
  Little Haymarket Theatre riot
    accounts, diversity of   256–7
    description of riot   257–61, 282
    Francisque's reaction on stage   259–60
  Little Haymarket unperformed repertoire
    Arlequin poli par L'amour (Marivaux)   254
    L'Embarras des richesses (d'Allainval)   254, 263
  post-riot events
    French ambassador's response   262, 264
    limited support from court and nobility   264–5
    press controversies   263–4, 265
    Protestant festivities and French company's departure   267
    rejection of Francisque's appeal in the press   265–6
  religious and political ramifications
    cultural nationalism   267–8
    foreshadowing resumption of warfare between France and England   269–71
    no Anglo-French theatrical exchanges for rest of century   312, 314
  repercussions for Francisque
    company financially ruined   272
    division of company in two   272
    season in Ghent (under brother Simon)   272–3
    season in Toulouse (under Francisque)   272–3
    success of 1734–5 season forgotten   312–13
London season (1739), Francisque's performance of Romagnesi's *Samson*   178
The London Stage (Emmett L. Avery et al., eds)   14, 61 n.61, 197 n.30, 203, 236 n.56, 251 n.4
  repertoire of the 1734–5 London season   321–7
Long, Lynne   194

Lord Chamberlain *see* Grafton, Charles FitzRoy, 2nd Duke of Grafton
Lorraine, Duchy of   241, 243
Louis, Dauphin of France   163–4, 167, 245
Louis Henri, Duke of Bourbon *see* Bourbon, Louis Henri, duc de Bourbon
Louis XIV, King of France
  Alard père given permission to perform by   9–10
  bombardment of Brussels by (1695)   170
  Coudun military camp   273 n.4
  death of   13
  Francisque's father in army of   5
  growing puritanism at end of his reign   7
  Le Régiment de la Calotte   103
  Louis XIV's Arlequin (Domenico Biancolelli)   207
  Lully's music   54
  playing knight Roger in *La Princesse d'Élide*   280
  watching Scarron's *L'Héritier ridicule* twice   278–9
Louis XV, King of France
  'Comédiens du Roi' title to Francisque's company   2, 187, 279–80
  Compiègne military camp and festivities   273–8, 279
  Compiègne theatre visit   289
  coronation and Fêtes de Chantilly   124
  edict about army surgeons (1716)   5 n.3
  father-in-law   243
  mistresses   277–8
  Mitchigamea delegation   212
  Scarron's *L'Héritier ridicule*, bored by   278–9
Louisa, Princess   191
Louise-Élisabeth, Princess   284
The Ludlow Postman or The Weekly Journal   80
Luise Ulrike of Prussia, Queen consort of Sweden   308
Lully, Jean-Baptiste   54, 65, 75
  Acis et Galatée   48
  Alceste   35, 39
  Amadis   92, 95–6, 97, 115

La Princesse d'Élide (with Molière)   280
'Lun' identity issue
  Francisque and 'Lun'   19–21
  Henry Woodward as 'Lun junior'   210 n.58
  John Rich as Lun   19–20, 183, 185, 208, 210
Lund, Judy   78
Lurcel, Dominique   viii
Luynes, Charles-Philippe d'Albert, 4th duc de Luynes   288, 289
Lyon
  baptism of Jeanne Malter (1722)   7 n.14, 117, 140
  Barbier's plays   54–5, 88
  Francisque's company's presence (1715)   9, 12, 21
  Francisque's company's tour (March 1722)
  Hôtel du Gouvernement theatre fire   117–18
  Piron's prologue on fire   118–19
  Guillaume Moylin's wedding (1715)   6, 12, 129 n.65
  Simon Moylin's presence (1745 and 1746)   292

Mackey, A.   225 n.35
Macklin, Charles   255 n.19
Madame (Regent's mother) *see* Élisabeth-Charlotte, duchesse d'Orléans
magic   93, 149–150
Mailly, Madame de (Louise Julie de Mailly-Nesle, comtesse de Mailly)   277–8
Mailly-Nesle sisters *see* Mailly, Madame de (Louise Julie de Mailly-Nesle, comtesse de Mailly); Nesle, Mademoiselle de (Pauline Félicité de Mailly-Nesle)
Mainvilliers (or Mainvillers), Genu Soalhat, Chevalier de,   302–3, 306, 307–8
Malter, Catherine (née Dussoye/Dusuisse, known as Catherine Labbé, Francisque's niece)
  Dalila in Romagnesi's *Samson*   178
  death   293, 308
  Francisque's 1734–5 London season   191

marriage and children *see under*
    Malter, Jean-Baptiste
relationship with Marie Sallé   184
settling in Nantes   293
Malter, Charlotte   161
Malter, Étienne   308
Malter, Étienne-Joseph   173 n.5, 180
Malter, François   165, 309
Malter, Jean-Baptiste
  actor and dancer   192
  biographical details
    Catherine, marriage to   140, 149, 154, 244
    date of death   308
    Gherardi, friendship with   141
    marriage of brother Jean-François   117 n.33
    Moylin family, close relationship with   117
    native of Bordeaux   284
    remarriage   293, 308
    retirement in Nantes   293
  children
    births and deaths, locations of   140–1
    daughters   160, 161, 167, 286
    sons   165, 173 n.5, 180, 181 n.31, 244, 293
  dancing career
    dancing innovative style   311
    letter to Bordeaux magistrates (1741)   290
    with Marie Sallé at Covent Garden (1733–4)   179–80, 181, 183–5, 192, 304
    with Marie Sallé in Brussels   180, 181, 183
    never danced at Opéra   241 n.8, 290
  performances
    Les Amours déguisés (Fuzelier)   158
    Benefit for Francis Sallé's widow   203 n.41
    Francisque's 1734–5 London season   191, 192
    L'Hymen vainqueur   241
    playing Pierrot   192
    La Princesse d'Élide (Molière and Lully) at Compiègne   280
    Pygmalion   183–5

La Robe de dissention ou le faux prodige (Piron)   149
Malter, Jean-François   117, 140
Malter, Jean-Louis   181 n.31, 293
Malter, Jeanne   7 n.14, 117, 160
Malter, Marie-Antoinette   286
Malter, Pierre   244
Malter l'Anglais (not Jean-Baptiste Malter)   290
Mandel, Oscar   194 n.20
Mann, Miss   183, 183 n.39
Marais, Mathieu   151, 183
Maria Theresa, wife of François Étienne (duc de Lorraine), later Holy Roman Empress   241, 242–3, 311
Marie-Elisabeth of Austria, Archduchess   170, 171, 173
marionettes
  Foire Saint-Germain (1722), *Pierrot Romulus, ou Le Ravisseur poli*   107
  Foire Saint-Laurent (1722), *Le Mariage de Momus, ou La Gigantomachie* (Piron)   120, 122, 128
Marivaux (né Pierre Carlet)
  Arlequins of in Francisque's repertoire   208
  d'Alembert on   156–7
  Dijon season under Simon Moylin (1739–40)   287
  Francisque's introduction of his plays to London   194–5, 312, 315
  no Marivaux in Francisque's 1750–51 Dijon season   295
  'School of Marivaux'   195, 215
  Thomassin in Arlequin roles   207, 275
  works
    Arlequin poli par L'amour   254, 278 n.18, 281
    La Double Inconstance   171, 210, 278 n.18
    L'Heureux stratagème   278, 278 n.18
    L'Ile des esclaves   194
    Le Jeu de l'amour et du hasard   177, 194, 314
    La Réunion des amours   196, 198, 242 n.12
    La Mort d'Annibal   110
    Le Paysan parvenu   194

Le Prince travesti   171, 241, 278 n.18
La Surprise de l'amour   156, 164, 167
Mars, Mlle (Anne Boutet Salvetat known as Mlle Mars)   314
Marseille
   Dominique's troupe (1705)   7
   Francisque not making use of old theatre (1737)   247–8
   Francisque's company at *jeu de paume* (1725)   140
   Francisque's company at new theatre (1736), *Le Fortuné Marseillais* (Audibert)   244
   grand family wedding (1725)   140–1, 154
   Simon Moylin's troupe at *jeu de paume* (1733)   168
Marshall, Louise   253
Martin, Isabelle   131 n.7, 159 n.35
Mary, Princess   191
Mary Tudor   267
McCleave, Sarah   181, 184, 205 n.46, 297 n.2, 299, 304
McGeary, Thomas   204 n.42, 206, 220–1
Mead, Richard, Dr   78
Meeus, Jean-Baptiste   170
Mémoires see Parfaict, Claude et François
Mémoires d'un Musicien (anonymous article)   298
Menant, Sylvain   138
Les Menus-Plaisirs   314
Le Mercure de France
   Fuzelier, editor of   10, 116–17
   printing of
      La Tête noire musical score   101
      'un Compliment prononcé par Francisque'   159–60
   regarding
      Agnès de Chaillot (Dominique and Legrand)   229
      ban on Sceaux's Drunkard's dance at 1721 Foire Saint-Laurent   100
      closure of Francisque's theatre after 1721 Foire Saint-Laurent   105–6
      Danaé set by Comédie-Italienne   136
      fairground performers at Fêtes de Chantilly   124

      Foire Saint-Laurent (1721), only Lalauze licence granted   95
      Foire Saint-Laurent (1726)   146
      Francisque's company in Compiègne (1939)   274, 275–6, 278, 279, 281–2, 286
      Francisque's company in Compiègne (1940)   288–9, 290
      Francisque's company in Grenoble (1729)   164, 165
      Fuzelier's *Les Songes*   155
      La Désolation des deux Comédies   37
      Martin Simon Moylin in *l'Embarras des richesses*   300
      Mitchigamea's song and dance   212
      Mlle de Lisle in *L'Audience du temps*   132
      physicians-surgeons quarrel   155
      Piron's *Arlequin Tirésias*   120
      Piron's *Le Mariage de Momus*   122
      Romagnesi's *Samson*   176, 177
Mercure Historique et Politique   256, 261
Metz
   Francisque's company (1723)   129, 132 n.11, 168
   Francisque's company (1723) without Francisque   124, 132 n.11
   Francisque's company (1732)   167–8
Micault, Claude   166, 178, 287, 293–4, 295 n.83, 296
   manuscript list of performances in Dijon (1739–40 and 1750–1)   328–30
Michel, Artur   16
Michon, Léonard, *Journal de Lyon*   118
Milhous, Judith   14–15, 187, 204
militia, use of to keep order in theatres   258, 260
Les Mille et un jours (Pétis de la Croix)   26, 82, 148
Les Mille et une nuits (Antoine Galland)   26, 82
Miller, James
   Art and Nature   213–14
   Harlequin-Horace   231
   The Man of Taste   202–3, 213, 236
   The Mother-in-Law or The Doctor the Disease   185

A Seasonable Reproof (poem)   213 n.69
Milton, John, *Samson Agonistes*   231
Mimeure, Charlotte-Madeleine de   107, 114
Minden, battle of (1759)   271
Mirabeau, Honoré Gabriel Riqueti, comte de Mirabeau   304
Mirrour   48
Misogallicus (*nom de plume*)   263
misogyny   110, 119
Mist, Nathaniel   41
Mitchigamea   212
Molière (Jean-Baptiste Poquelin known as Molière)
  petit-maître character   200
  portrayal of doctors   115, 219 n.15
  portrayal of idle aristocracy   91
  portrayal of lawyers   115
  prominent place in Francisque's repertoire   315
    nine comedies at Little Haymarket Theatre (1721)   89
    twelve comedies during 1734–5 London season   193, 209 n.57
  Voltaire's Regnard-Molière comparison   49
  works
    Amphitryon   192
    L'Avare   31, 86, 196
    Le Bourgeois Gentilhomme   75, 78 n.35, 294
    Le Cocu imaginaire   83
    Dom Juan   222 n.26
    L'École des maris   193
    Les Femmes savantes   31
    George Dandin   29, 61, 64, 65, 99
    Le Malade imaginaire   77–8, 78 n.35, 104, 185
    Monsieur de Pourceaugnac   23, 55, 229
    Les Précieuses Ridicules   202
    La Princesse d'Élide (with Lully)   280
    Le Tartuffe   31, 48 n.15, 62–3, 86–7, 90, 173, 192, 220, 221–2, 314
Molloy, Charles   263, 265, 266
Monnet, Jean   151, 270, 295
Monnier, Pierre   164–5

Montagu, Mary Wortley, Lady,
  Simplicity   194
Montauban   141 n.34, 167
Montesquieu   32
Montfleury (Antoine Jacob known as Montfleury)
  Don Pasquin d'Avalos   195
  Femme juge et parti   83
Montpellier
  Malter children's birth location   141 n.34, 161
  Simon Moylin's presence (1746)   292
Morand, Pierre de, *La Vengeance trompée*   291
mouchoir (handkerchief) issue   229 n.42
Mouret, Jean-Joseph   36, 37, 95, 119, 158, 208, 229
Moylin (spelling of name)   x
Moylin, Catherine (née Fompré, 1st wife of Martin Simon Moylin)   300
Moylin, Christophe (Francisque's father)   5
Moylin, François *see* Francisque (François Moylin, known as Francisque)
Moylin, François (illegitimate son of unknown parents)   309
Moylin, François (son of Francisque's brother Guillaume)   21, 309
Moylin, Françoise (daughter of Francisque's brother Guillaume)   165, 167
Moylin, Françoise (née de Plon or Duplong, Francisque's mother)   5
Moylin, Fréderic (son of Francisque's brother Simon)   167
Moylin, Guillaume (Francisque's brother)
  baptism of Charles Lesage's daughter   243
  baptism of Jeanne Malter   160 n.38
  baptism of Marie Sallé   9
  children   6, 21, 73, 165, 167, 309
  date of birth   5
  date of death   308
  Foire Saint-Germain (1709)   8
  Foire Saint-Laurent (1716)   12
  Foire Saint-Laurent (1718)   42 n.5
  known mainly as tumbler   22, 52
  maître à danser   7, 311
  marriage to Jeanne Gaillardet   6, 12, 129 n.65
  not included in Francisque's 1734–5 London season   192

INDEX 389

retirement 244
roles
   Octave in *La Foire de Saint-Germain* 48 n.15
   Pierrot role 13
   Valère in Molière's *Le Tartuffe* 62 n.55
Moylin, Guillaume-Antoine (son of Francisque's nephew Martin Simon) 300
Moylin, Jean-Baptiste Constantin (son of Francisque's brother Guillaume) 165
Moylin, Jeanne (née Gaillardet, wife of Francisque's brother Guillaume)
   children 6, 21, 73, 165
   Foire Saint-Laurent (1718) 42 n.5
   godmother to Charles Lesage's daughter 243
   godmother to Jeanne Malter 117, 160
   marriage to Guillaume Moylin 6, 12, 129 n.65
   retirement 244
   roles
      in Lesage's *La Statue merveilleuse* 83
      Mariane in Molière's *Le Tartuffe* 62 n.55
Moylin, Jeanne-Marie (née Villeneuve, wife of Francisque's brother Simon) 6–7, 293
Moylin, Joseph-Henry (son of Francisque's brother Simon) 292–3
Moylin, Marguerite (Francisque's sister) *see* Cochois, Marguerite (née Moylin, Francisque's sister)
Moylin, Marie Anne (daughter of Francisque's nephew Martin Simon) *see* Bruyas, Marie Anne (née Moylin)
Moylin, Marie (née Fromageot/Fromajot, 2nd wife of Martin Simon Moylin) 301–2
Moylin, Marie-Alberte *see* Sallé, Marie-Alberte (née Moylin, Francisque's sister)
Moylin, Marie-Catherine (née Dusuisse or le Suisse, Francisque's wife)
   childless 7
   death 308
   Elizabeth Dusuisse's sister 140

Foire Saint-Germain (1712) 9
Foire Saint-Laurent (1712) 9
Foire Saint-Laurent (1718) 42 n.5
Foire Saint-Laurent (1722) 123
Francisque's 1734–5 London season 191
leading dancer at Bordeaux theatre 311
letter to Bordeaux magistrates (1741) 290
marriage to Francisque 6, 308
native of Bordeaux 284
retirement in Nantes with Francisque 293
roles
   Armilla in Romagnesi's *Samson* 178
   Columbine 45–6, 48 n.15, 192
   Deucalion's wife Pyrrha 109
   Elmire in Molière's *Le Tartuffe* 62 n.55
Moylin, Martin Simon (son of Francisque's brother Guillaume)
   baptism 73, 300
   children 300, 301–2
   Guillaume's only actor son 6
   marriage to Catherine Fompré 300, 301, 302
   marriage to Marie Fromageot 301
   retirement and death 302
   theatre work
      Arlequin in *L'Embarras des richesses* (d'Allainval) 300–1
      in Francisque's company 243, 244, 300
      in Francois Deshayes troupe (1751–3) 242 n.10, 301
      touring 301–2
Moylin, Nicolas-Jean-Baptiste-Simon (son of Francisque's brother Simon) 289–90
Moylin, Nicole (daughter of Francisque's brother Simon) 286
Moylin, Simon (Francisque's brother)
   biographical details
      children 6–7, 167, 286, 289–90, 292–3
      date of birth 5
      date of death 308
      Marie Sallé's will contested by 300

marriage to Jeanne-Marie
  Villeneuve 6–7, 161
 settling in Toulouse 293, 300
Comédiens du Roi title 282
Francisque's company
 managerial role in 3, 161, 282
 possibly in charge of
  (1741–50) 291
Maréchal de Richelieu's disapproval of
  his company 291–2
not included in Francisque's 1734–5
  London season 192
plays and roles
 Arlequin 3, 91, 93, 161
 Damis in Molière's *Le Tartuffe* 62
  n.55
 Mezzetin 13, 48 n.15
 Robinson Crusoe 93
 La Vengeance trompée (Morand),
  production of 291
separate company 167, 168
theatrical seasons
 Arles (1743) 291
 Bordeaux with J.-B. Lesage
  (1741) 283–4, 290–1
 Brussels (1733–4) 174
 Compiègne (1739, possibly) 275
 Compiègne (1940) 288
 Dijon (1739–40) 286
 Foire Saint-Germain (1721) 90,
  94, 161
 Foire Saint-Laurent (1718) 42 n.5
 Ghent with J.-B. Lesage
  (1738–9) 272–3
 Ghent with J.-B. Lesage
  (1740–1) 289
 London season with Francisque
  (1738) 248 n.32
 travelling destinations
  (1744–8) 292–3
Mozart, Wolfgang Amadeus, *Die
 Entführung aus dem Serail* 149
muette see 'à la muette'
Murdoch, Tessa 50 n.23
Murphy, Arthur, *The Apprentice* 270
  n.55
music
 composers of opéras-comiques 24, 25
 in Francisque's company's
  performances 52, 53–4

Nancy
 Francisque's company (1736)
  L'Hymen vainqueur (Francisque or
   Verneuil) 241–3
  Le Prince travesti (Marivaux) 241
 Francisque's or Simon Moylin's
  company (1732–3) 168
Nantes
 Francisque, Malters and Fourcades
  settling in 293
 Francisque's company
  (1740–41) 287–8, 291
National Gallery of Art, Washington,
 D.C., 'Les Comédiens Italiens'
 (Jean-Antoine Watteau) 78–81, **80**
Néricault, Philippe *see* Destouches,
 Philippe Néricault (known as
 Destouches)
Nesle, Mademoiselle de (Pauline Félicité
 de Mailly-Nesle) 277
Nevile, Jennifer 18
Nicolas, Jean-François 168, 241
Nicolini (Nicolò Francesco Leonardo
 Grimaldi, known as Nicolini) 269
Nicoll, Allardyce 20, 193, 218
Night Scenes
 commedia dell'arte routine 15
 in pantomimes 14, 15
 performances
  by Alard brothers 14, 15, 20, 51,
   311
  by Baxter and Sorin 14, 15, 20, 311
  in *The Cheats or The Tavern
   Bilkers* 20
  by Francis and Marie Sallé as
   children 19
  in Francisque's 'Tumbling'
   entertainments 51, 315
  in Le Noble's *Les Deux
   Arlequins* 50
  in Lesage and d'Orneval's *Arlequin
   Endymion* 91–2
'noble savage' *see* sauvages (savages)
noms de plume 209
non-jurors 62–3, 221, 222, 232, 234
Norfolk, Edward Howard, 9th Duke of
 Norfolk 225
Norfolk, Maria Howard (née Shireburn),
 Duchess of Norfolk 225
Norfolk, Thomas Howard, 8th Duke of
 Norfolk 225

North American tribes 211–12
Nouveau Mercure galant 11
'Nouveaux Mémoires sur les spectacles de la Foire' 1, 6, 8, 9, 12, 129, 293
Les Nouvelles Catholiques (religious society) 240
Noverre, Jean-Georges 270, 304, 307

O'Brien, John, *Harlequin Britain* 270
obscenity charges 121–2
Oglethorpe, James 211, 211 n.62
Old Pretender *see* James Francis Edward Stuart, Prince of Wales
Oldham, John 252 n.7
Olivier, Jean-Jacques 304
onanism 71
Opéra
  bans on fairground players 10, 66, 81, 83, 85, 90
    see also opéra-comique (licence or *privilège*)
  belle danse 19, 94, 183
  competition from opéra-comique 11, 91
  complaint against Antoni de Sceaux 94
  complaint against Comédie-Française's *La Française Italienne* 152
  dancers
    Ballon and Prévost 15, 16, 180
    Dumoulin and Camargo 162
    Malter family 140
    Malter l'Anglais (not Jean-Baptiste Malter) 290
    Marie and Francis Sallé's training 15, 53, 129, 180, 183
    Marie Sallé's career 161, 179, 241, 297, 310
    reputation for moral laxity 71, 310
  Hébrard's debt to 292
  Lacoste, chorus master and leader of orchestra 24
  late-night balls 104, 280, 286
  performances
    Antoni de Sceaux' 'Danse de l'ivrogne' 53
    Le Jugement de Paris 25
    La Princesse d'Élide (Molière and Lully) 280

Piron's *L'Endriague*, commissioning of 125
  as portrayed by La Foire in *Arlequin Deucalion* (Piron) 109
  La Désolation des deux Comédies (Dominique and Riccoboni) 37
  La Foire renaissante 39
  Les Funérailles de la Foire (Lesage, d'Orneval, Fuzelier) 35
  Le Procès des Théâtres (Dominique and Riccoboni) 38
  La Querelle des Théâtres (Lesage and La Font) 30, 31–2
  Le Rappel de la Foire à la Vie (Lesage, d'Orneval, Fuzelier) 102–3
  stage accident 135 n.15
opéra-comique (genre)
  definition 10
  development of genre 10–11, 23, 24, 26, 29
  and *écriteaux* practice 12
  'genre villageois' (village stories) 34
  movement from satire to pastoral 295–6
  performed by marionettes 107
  political powers' ambiguous attitude towards 36
  retirement of veterans of genre 105
  sophisticated dancing 150
opéra-comique (licence or *privilège*)
  granted by Opéra to fairground players 10
  granted to
    Catherine de Baune (1717) 13, 22
    Francisque (1718) 24, 103, 106
    Francisque (1721) 101–2, 106, 138
    Francisque (1933) 169
    Lalauze (1721) 94, 95, 96, 101, 133
    Maurice Honoré (1724) 130
  satirical criticism of 31, 35
O'Quinn, Daniel 258 n.28
O'Reilly, Patrice-Jean 286, 290–1
orientalism 26, 93
  see also Turquerie
Original Weekly Journal 46
Origny, Antoine d' 300–1
Orneval, Jacques-Philippe d'

392　INDEX

playwright of distinction writing for fairs　10
works
　Arlequin traitant　10
　see also under Lesage, Alain-René
Otway, Thomas
　The Orphan　210
　Venice Preserved　294
Ozell, John　43, 45, 51 n.25
　The Fair of St. Germain　2 n.4, 52

Pacorel (Pagnorel in English press, dancer)　254, 281–2
Paghetti, Pietro　8, 12, 13, 50
Palais-Royal see Théâtre du Palais-Royal
Panard, Charles-François　26
Pandora myth　100
pantomime
　Anglo-French manner　183, 289
　ballets pantomimes　162–3
　English pantomime dancers at Foires (after 1729)　163
　Francisque's contribution to evolution of　311
　vs. Franco-Italian comedies　50–1
　link with silent *commedia* scenes　51
　as mere Christmas entertainments　313
　mute English Harlequin confined to pantomimes　313
　'pantomime anglaise' term　289
　Pantomims (*ballets d'actions*)　79–80
　Rich's contribution to the genre　14–15, 50–1, 79, 185, 311
　Weaver's contribution to the genre　15, 17, 18–19, 51, 65, 79–80, 311
　see also Night Scenes
Papetti, Viola　15 n.48, 61 n.54, 65, 76
Parfaict, Claude et François
　Mémoires and *Dictionnaire*　1
　regarding
　　L'Âne du Daggial　72
　　Antoni de Sceaux's dancing　53 n.34
　　La Boîte de Pandore　100
　　Le Camp des amours　25 n.12
　　Danaé set by Comédie-Italienne　136
　　'danseurs pantomimes anglais'　162
　　Dartenay's unsuccessful Comédie-Française debut　12

Étienne Sallé's lack of stage talent　16
Foire Saint-Germain (1726)　149
Foire Saint-Laurent (1718)　24
Foire Saint-Laurent (1720)　81
Foire Saint-Laurent (1724)　139
Foire Saint-Laurent (1726)　146
Foire Saint-Laurent (1729)　163
Foire Saint-Laurent (1937), English performers at　255 n.21
Francisque's company at Foire Saint-Laurent (1718)　42
Francisque's company's first visit to Paris　8
Francisque's official fair licence　102
Les Funérailles de la Foire (Lesage, d'Orneval, Fuzelier)　35–6
Fuzelier's *Le Bois de Boulogne*　158
Fuzelier's *Les Amours déguisés*　156
Guillaume Moylin as tumbler　52
Lalauze's parodies at 1721 Foire Saint-Laurent　105
Lalauze's rivalry with Francisque over Arlequin role　29
Lesage's *La Statue merveilleuse*　83
Marie and Francis Sallé in *La Princesse de Carizme*　28
Maurice Honoré's company　130, 131, 132
Nicolas Barbier　54 n.39
Les Pèlerins de La Mecque (Lesage, Fuzelier, d'Orneval)　149
Piron's *Arlequin Tirésias*　120, 121
Piron's *Le Caprice* and *L'Âne d'or*　138 n.24
Robinson or *L'Isle de Robinson* (Lesage and d'Orneval)　93
Romagnesi's *Samson*　176
Saint-Yon's *Danaé* at 1721 Foire Saint-Laurent　95 n.16
Simon Moylin playing Arlequin　93
Parfaict, François, association with Lalauze　94 n.14
Paris

Chief Agapit Chicagou's visit
    (1725)   212
child kidnappings (1720)   70
Paris fairs *see* Foire Saint-Germain
    entries; Foire Saint-Laurent entries;
    Théâtre de la Foire
Pascariel (Giuseppe Tortoriti known as
    Pascariel)   7, 9, 43
Patriophilus (*nom de plume*)   197–8, 209
Paul, Agnès   2 n.3, 9 n.24
Pelkey, Stanley   232
Pellegrin, abbé (Simon-Joseph)
    Le Nouveau Monde   294, 296, 301
    Télémaque parody with
        Destouches   12 n.33
Pellegrin, Jacques   11, 12, 94
Pennyman, Margaret, Lady   83–5, 90,
    163, 196, 310
Pepusch, Johann   182
Percival, John *see* Egmont, John Percival,
    1st Earl of Egmont
personation concept   220–1, 234
Pesne, Antoine, 'Babet Cochois and her
    brother Francis'   304, **305**
Pétis de la Croix, François, *Les Mille et
    un jours*   26, 82, 148
Petit (or Petitte), Marianne *see* Lesage,
    Marianne (née Petit or Petitte,
    Charles Lesage's wife)
Petit, Pierre, *Traité historique sur les
    Amazones*   81
Petitpas, Mlle   125, 126, 310 n.51
Pfister, Christian   243
Philates, *Majesty Misled, or the
    Overthrow of Evil Ministers*   221
Philippe II, duc d'Orléans, Regent of
    France   13, 36, 42, 113
Phillips, Ambrose
    *The Distres't Mother
        (Andromaque)*   90
    lines to Francesca Cuzzoni   269
Phillips, Constantia, *The Happy
    Courtezan: Or, the Prude
    demolish'd*   237
physicians-surgeons quarrel   155
pièce à tiroirs   26, 69
Pierrot, in Watteau's 'Les Comédiens
    Italiens'   79, **80**
'Pill Plot'
    Joshua Ward, plot scare over   217–18
    Kelly's *Plot or Pill and Drop*   218–20
piracy   152 n.19

Piron, Alexis
    background
        biographical details   107
        Francisque's cry for help   107–8
        friendship with Francisque   141
        working with Honoré and
            Hamoche   149
    Foire Saint-Germain (1722)
        L'Antre de Trophonius   115–17
        Arlequin Deucalion   108–15, 119,
            310
        note on Sallé children   110
    Foire Saint-Germain (1723)
        Colombine-Nitétis   143 n.42, 143
            n.44
        L'Endriague   125–9, 148
        invited to write for all three
            companies   124
        Les Trois Commères (with Lesage
            and Fuselier)   143 n.44, 150
    Foire Saint-Germain (1724), *Le
        Claperman*   129, 141, 143 n.42
    Foire Saint-Laurent (1722)
        Arlequin Tirésias   118, 119–22, 128,
            310
        letter to Lieutenant de Police for
            Francisque   121–2, 123–4
        *Le Mariage de Momus, ou La
            Gigantomachie*   120, 122–3,
            128, 135 n.15
        prologue to *Tirésias*   118–19
    Foire Saint-Laurent (1724)
        hired by Maurice Honoré   130, 141
        *Le Mariage du Caprice et de la
            Folie*   115, 138, 141, 143
            n.42, 149
    Foire Saint-Laurent (1726)   146
        Olivette juge des enfers   150
        *La Robe de dissention ou le faux
            prodige*   149–50
        La Rose, ou le Pucelage   150–1
    Francisque's Dijon season (1750),
        Gustave Vasa   293–4, 311
    Francisque's London season (1734–5),
        Gustave Vasa   195, 224–7
    other works
        Callisthène   151
        Les Enfants de la Joie   112
        Epître à Francisque   141–5, 175
        Philomèle   143 n.42
        La Rose, ou le Pucelage   295

Samson (unfinished)   141–2, 145, 175, 176, 177, 178
  views and quotes
    anti-clericalism   110, 112–13, 116, 128
    'irregularity of the Fair Theatre'   116 n.30
    loathing of Desfontaines   113–14
    mock-epitaph for himself   151
    short life of fairground plays   139–40, 144 n.46
Pittenec *see* Lesage, François-Antoine (Alain-René Lesage's son, known as Pittenec)
Plon, de (or Duplong), Françoise *see* Moylin, Françoise (née de Plon or Duplong, Francisque's mother)
Poisot, Charles   24
Poisson, Raymond, *Le Baron de la Crasse*   61, 64, 75, 195
polemical genre   29–30, 35, 39, 42, 67, 72–3
  La Fausse Foire (1721 Foire Saint-Laurent)   95–9, 103
  see also Querelle des Théâtres (Foire Saint-Laurent 1718); Querelle des Théâtres (Foire Saint-Laurent 1726)
The Political State of Great Britain   204 n.45
politics, and Franco-Italian repertoire   63–4
Pope, Alexander   226
Popery   267
  anti-Popery propaganda   215–18
  see also Catholic Church; Catholics
Popish Plot (1679)   64
Porpora, Nicola   189, 205, 236
Portuguese Embassy Chapel   216
Potter, John   86, 255
Pougin, Arthur   179 n.28
Powell, S.   194 n.20
Praslin, César Gabriel de Choiseul, duc de Praslin   313–314
Prévost, Antoine-François, Abbé   174, 185, 188–9, 191, 205, 208, 236
Prévost, Françoise   15, 18, 94, 180
Prince of Wales *see* Frederick, Prince of Wales; George II, King of Great Britain and Ireland (Prince of Wales); James Francis Edward Stuart, Prince of Wales

privilège
  for Romagnesi's *Samson*   177
  royal *privilège*   7, 285
  see also opéra-comique (licence or *privilège*)
Procope-Couteaux, Alexandre   156
Procope-Couteaux, François   156
Procope-Couteaux, Michel
  association with Francisque
    Arlequin balourd written specifically for Francisque   57–8
    Procope on Francisque   57
  comique portrait of in
    Le Docteur Fagotin   156 n.23
    Gil Blas de Santillane (Lesage)   156 n.23
    L'Obstacle Favorable (Lesage, Fuzelier, d'Orneval)   155–6
  reference to in, *Les Funérailles de la Foire* (Lesage, d'Orneval, Fuzelier)   35 n.32
  Vézian's praise of his qualities   61
  works
    Arlequin balourd   57–61, 75, 89, 173, 195, 196, 201
    L'Assemblée des Comédiens   58 n.48, 138 n.25
    Les Fées (with Romagnesi)   278
prologue, French vs. English tradition   10
The Prompter (theatrical journal)   198, 203, 216, 223, 238 n.63
Protestant succession   62, 215, 226, 234
Protestants   62–3, 64, 216, 232, 267
Provençal language   244, 311

Quenaudon, Marie-Thérèse *see* Bar, Mlle de (Marie-Thérèse Quenaudon known as Mlle de Bar)
Querelle des Théâtres (Foire Saint-Laurent 1718)
  fairground plays targeted at official theatres
    Les Funérailles de la Foire (Lesage, d'Orneval, Fuzelier)   35–6, 102
    La Querelle des Théâtres (Lesage and La Font)   29–32
    Le Rappel de la Foire à la Vie (Lesage, d'Orneval, Fuzelier)   102–3

Le Régiment de la Calotte (Lesage, d'Orneval, Fuzelier)   103–5
response from Comédie-Française, Legrand's *Le Roi de Cocagne*   38–9
response from *Comédie-Italienne*
  La Foire renaissante   39–40
  La Désolation des deux Comédies (Dominique and Riccoboni)   36–7, 39
  Le Procès des Théâtres (Dominique and Riccoboni)   37–8, 39
Querelle des Théâtres (Foire Saint-Laurent 1726)
  fairground plays targeted at official theatres
    Les Comédiens Corsaires (Lesage, d'Orneval, Fuzelier)   152, **153**, 154–5, 159
    Le Retour de la Chasse du Cerf (La Font)   158–9
Quesnay, François   156
Quiberon Bay, battle of (1759)   271

Rabelais, François   125
Rabon, Mlle   161, 162
Rachel, Mlle (Elisabeth Félix known as Mlle Rachel)   314
Racine, Jean
  Francisque's staging of his tragedies   209, 315
  Hamoche's 1722 London season   90
  parody of Racinian tragedy   48
  works
    Andromaque   18, 31–2, 67, 152, 171, 294
    Athalie   170–1, 195, 231–5, 242 n.10, 294
    Esther   294
    Mithridate   152
    Phèdre (or *Phèdre et Hippolyte*)   30, 35, 177, 294
    Les Plaideurs   229
Raguenet, Jean-Baptiste   12
Rainton (or Rinton or Renton)   161, 162
Rameau, Jean-Philippe   125, 126, 127, 149
  Les Indes galantes   149, 289, 297–8
  Les Sauvages   212 n.63
Read's Weekly Journal   260 n.35
Rebel, Jean-Féry, *Les Caractères de la danse*   94, 180, 192
Regent *see* Philippe II, duc d'Orléans, Regent of France
Le Régiment de la Calotte (under Louis XIV)   103–4
Regnard, Jean-François
  captured by pirates   152 n.19
  Francisque staging
    eight comedies in 1734–5 London season   193
    two comedies in 1721 Little Haymarket season   89
  Gillier's songs and dances for his plays   24
  Voltaire on   49
  works
    Arlequin, Homme à bonne fortune   49 n.18
    Attendez-moi sous l'orme   75
    La Baguette   49 n.18
    Les Chinois   76
    Le Divorce   49 n.18
    La Foire de Saint-Germain   43, **44**, 45–6, 48–9, 64 n.62, 86
    La Foire de Saint-Germain, scène des deux carosses   49
    Les Folies amoureuses   62, 64, 65, 278
    L'Homme à bonne fortune   294 n.78
    Les Ménechmes   278
    Les Momies d'Egypte   158
Relations véritables (Brussels journal)   171
Rex, Walter   34, 108 n.6, 112, 114
ribaldry   120–1
Riccoboni, François
  'grand spectacle' with Dominique, *Danaé* (Saint-Yon)   94–5
  work with Legrand, *Polyphème*   121–2
  work with Romagnesi, *Les Sauvages*   242 n.10
  works with Dominique
    La Désolation des deux Comédies   36–7, 39 n.43
    Le Procès des Théâtres   37–8
  works with Dominique and Romagnesi
    Arlequin Hulla   191, 193 n.18, 196, 278 n.18, 281
    Arlequin toujours Arlequin   208, 288
    Les Comédiens esclaves   152, 154, 193 n.17, 288

Pirame et Thisbé 159 n.33
Riccoboni, Luigi 13, 39, 42, 43
   Sansone 174–7
   La vita è un sogno 230
Rich, Christopher 20
Rich, John
   dancers, hiring of
      Francis Sallé 161, 162
      French dancers 52, 163
      Marie Sallé 161
      Nivelon 161, 162, 182, 183 n.40
      Sallé children 15, 17, 42, 53
   dancers, relationships with
      disliked by Marie Sallé 178–9, 184, 310
      sued by Nivelon for non-payment of salary 182
   Francisque, relationship with
      1718–19 season deal 42, 58–9, 65
      mutual animosity 206, 235
      not supporting him after Haymarket riot 266
   Harlequin role
      epitome of English Harlequin x, 2
      Harlequin-Faustus performance interrupted by Haymarket rioters 261
      as Lun 19–20, 183, 185, 208, 210
      reference to in Kelly's *The Plot or Pill and Drop* 218–19
      reference to in Ozell's prologue 45–6
      referred to in *The Two Dogs* (poem) 235–6
      the silent Harlequin 199, 219
   Hill's attack on 199
   mimics and pantomime 14–15, 50–1, 79, 185, 311
   The Stage's Glory: John Rich (1692–1761) 2
   see also Covent Garden theatre; Theatre at Lincoln's Inn Fields
Richardot, Anne 82
Richelieu, Louis-François-Armand de Vignerot du Plessis de 291–2
Richmond, Charles Lennox, 1st Duke of Richmond 46
Richmond, Charles Lennox, 2nd Duke of Richmond 46 n.11, 181, 185–7, 225, 248–9, 264
Richmond, Sarah Lennox, Duchess of Richmond 178, 181, 310

Rigoley de Juvigny, Jean-Antoine
   Francisque's first meeting with Piron 107–8
   Francisque's letter to d'Argenson 124
   Francisque's Lyon theatre fire 118 n.37
   Mlle de Bar's knowledge of medieval French 127
   Piron's *Arlequin Deucalion* 108–9, 110 n.9, 114
   Piron's *Arlequin Tirésias* 118, 121, 122
   Piron's *Le Caprice* and *L'Âne d'or* 138 n.24
   Piron's letter to Fuzelier 122
Riot Act (1714) 258
riots
   anti-Catholic riots 64
   Chinese Festival riots (1755) 270
   Drury Lane riots (1755) 270
   Drury Lane riots (1848) 314
   Gordon Riots (1780) 64
   Haymarket riot (9 Oct. 1738) see London season (1738, discontinued)
   theatrical riots 270
Ritchie, Fiona 253
Rizzoni, Nathalie 71, 162–3
Roast Beef affair 200–3
The Roast Beef of Old England (song) 203, 257, 258
Robard, Guillaume 167–8
Robarts, Leslie Michael Martin 231–2
Robinson, Miss (later Mrs Campbell Price) 162, 181, 183
Roger, Anthony Francis 74–5, 76, 79, 86, 88, 161, 162
Rogers, Nicholas 41–2
Rogers, Vanessa L. 54
Roland, Catherine 191, 205
Romagnesi, Jean-Antoine
   Samson
      Brussels edition (1734) 177
      Brussels season (1733–4) 171, 174–8, 295
      Compiègne season (1739) 178, 278
      London season (1734–5) 195, 208, 230, 231, 233
      popularity and numerous editions 178
   work with Procope-Couteaux, *Les Fées* 278

work with Riccoboni, *Les Sauvages* 242 n.10
works with Dominique
  Arcagambis 193, 278 n.18, 281, 288
  La Foire des poètes 287
  L'Isle du divorce 287
  La Sylphide 196, 287
works with Dominique and Riccoboni
  Arlequin Hulla 191, 193 n.18, 196, 278 n.18, 281
  Arlequin toujours Arlequin 208, 288
  Les Comédiens esclaves 152, 154, 193 n.17, 288
  Pirame et Thisbé 159 n.33
Rooke, Deborah W. 232
Rosenfeld, Sybil
  brief account of Francisque's London seasons 1–2
  emphasis on 'tricks and feats' in Francisque's entertainments 50 n.22
  Francisque's 1718 Palais-Royal performance 37
  Francisque's aborted 1738 London season 248 n.32, 250
  Grub-Street Journal's account of Francisque's 1734–5 season 198 n.31
  no royal patronage at Francisque's 1721 London season 86–7
  use of word 'pantomime' 79
Rosidor, Pierre 160 n.38, 167
Rosimond (Claude de La Rose, known as Rosimond), *Le Nouveau Festin de Pierre* 222
Ross, Mary Ellen 81–2
Rouen
  birth of Moylin children 165, 167
  Francisque's company (1730 and 1731) 167
  Malter children's birth location 141 n.34
  performance of Piron's *La Rose, ou le Pucelage* 151
Rougemont, Martine de 2
Rousseau, Jean-Jacques
  bon sauvage theory 213
  on Francisque's *Alzire* in Grenoble 245–7

referred to in relation to *La Boîte de Pandore* 100–1
works
  La Découverte du Nouveau Monde (lost) 247
  'Le Verger de Madame de Warens' 245
Rowe, Nicholas 62
Roy, Pierre-Charles 143 n.43
royal permission *see privilège*
Rualt (or Ruault) 241–2
Rubellin, Françoise 127, 150
Rundle, Thomas 77
Russell, Barry viii
Rusty Bacon (*nom de plume*) 251

Saint James Theatre (also known as the French theatre) 314
Sainte-Beuve, Charles-Augustin 114, 151
Saint-Edme, Louis and Marie Gauthier de 9, 24
  Saint-Edme troupe 12, 13, 22
Saint-Évremond, Charles de 59
Saint-Germain fair *see* Foire Saint-Germain
Saint-Laurent fair *see* Foire Saint-Laurent
Saint-Petersburg, Elizabeth of Russia's court 306–7, 314
Saint-Simon, Louis de Rouvroy, duc de 113, 273 n.4
Saint-Yon, *Danaé* 94–5, 136, 137
Sakhnovskaia-Pankeeva, Anastasia 2, 9, 9 n.24, 130–1, 139, 158
Sallé (Marie Sallé's paternal uncle) 300
Sallé, Étienne (Francisque's brother-in-law)
  with Francisque in Lyon (1722) 117
  in Francisque's company (1718) 42 n.5
  manager of his children Marie and Francis 161
  marriage to Francisque's sister Marie-Alberte 6
  no stage talent 16
  at Rich's theatre 20
  roles
    in *La Foire de Saint-Germain* (Dufresny and Regnard) 48 n.15
    in *Le Tartuffe* (Molière) 62 n.55
Sallé, Francis (Francisque's nephew)
  background

dancer from very early age 6
death of at twenty-seven 179, 180, 181
English pantomime, link with 90
marriage to English actress 161, 179 n.25
Opéra training 53, 129
pupil of Françoise Prévost and Claude (Jean) Ballon 15, 18
Benefit for his widow (1735) 203
Foire Saint-Germain (1720), in *L'Isle du Gougou* (d'Orneval and Lesage) 69
Foire Saint-Germain (1721) 94
in *La Forêt de Dodone* (Lesage and d'Orneval) 92
Foire Saint-Germain (1722), in *Arlequin Deucalion* (Piron) 110, 114
Foire Saint-Germain (1723), in *L'Endriague* (Piron) 127
Foire Saint-Germain (1724)
in *Le Claperman* (Piron) 129
in *La Conquête de la Toison d'or* (Lesage and d'Orneval) 129
Foire Saint-Laurent (1718) 42 n.5, 110 n.9
in *Le Jugement de Paris* 26
in *La Princesse de Carizme* (Lesage and La Font) 28
Foire Saint-Laurent (1723) 129
Foire Saint-Laurent (1726), in *La Robe de dissention* (Piron) 150
Foire Saint-Laurent (1728 and 1729) 161
Foire Saint-Laurent (1730 and 1731) 162
London (1716–17)
child dancer at Lincoln's Inn Fields 3, 16–20, 21, 42
in Racine's *Andromaque* 18
in *Rinaldo* (Handel) 18
in *The Submission* (Tomlinson) 18
in *Two Punchinellos, two Harlequins and a Dame Ragonde* 17
London (1718–19)
child dancers' popularity 53, 65
in *Les Deux Arlequins* (Le Noble) 52
London (1725–)

in *The Burgomaster Trick'd* (1725–6) 183
Rich's leading dancer at Lincoln's Inn Fields 161
Sallé, Marie (Francisque's niece)
background
ballet d'action pioneer 289
baptism 8, 299 n.8
celebrity status 208
Dacier's biography 1
dancer and choreographer 4
dancer from very early age 6
death in obscurity 298, 299–300
Duchess of Richmond, letters to 178, 181, 310
Duke of Richmond, patronage of 46 n.11, 225, 248
English pantomime, link with 90
from fairgrounds to *belle danse* 2, 94, 184
Francisque, close relationship with 140, 181
Francisque's presence at her burial 299–300
François Malter's baptism 165
high artistic and moral standards 310
high sense of decorum 303
illness 178, 179, 240, 299
John Rich, dislike of 178–9, 184, 310
Nicolas Lancret's painting **190**
Noverre's admiration for 307
Opéra training 53, 129
pupil of Françoise Prévost and Claude (Jean) Balon 15, 18, 94, 180
quiet and modest life in Paris 299
Rebecca Wick as her companion 240–1, 299, 300
speculation on her return to London 298–9
theatre as soft power abroad 314
training of cousins and Marie Châteauneuf 180
training of Lilliputians 312
training of young dancers at fairs 297
will 298, 300, 308
Benefit for Francisque (1735) 206
Benefit for Francis's widow (1735) 203

INDEX 399

Benefit for herself (1734)   184–5, 204
Benefit for herself (1735)   204–5
Foire Saint-Germain (1720), in *L'Isle du Gougou* (d'Orneval and Lesage)   69
Foire Saint-Germain (1721)   94
   in *La Forêt de Dodone* (Lesage and d'Orneval)   92
Foire Saint-Germain (1722),
   in *Arlequin Deucalion* (Piron)   110, 114
Foire Saint-Germain (1723), *in L'Endriague* (Piron)   127
Foire Saint-Germain (1724)
   in *Le Claperman* (Piron)   129
   in La Conquête de la Toison d'or (Lesage and d'Orneval)   129
Foire Saint-Laurent (1718)   42 n.5, 110 n.9
   in *Le Jugement de Paris*   26
   in *La Princesse de Carizme* (Lesage and de La Font)   28
Foire Saint-Laurent (1720), in *La Statue merveilleuse* (Lesage)   82
Foire Saint-Laurent (1723)   129
Foire Saint-Laurent (1726), in *La Robe de dissention* (Piron)   150
Foire Saint-Laurent (1743), contribution to Favart's *L'Ambigu de la folie ou Le Ballet des dindons*   297–8
London (1716–17)
   child dancer at Lincoln's Inn Fields   3, 16–20, 21, 42
   in Racine's *Andromaque*   18
   in *Rinaldo* (Handel)   18
   in *The Submission* (Tomlinson)   18
   in *Two Punchinellos, two Harlequins and a Dame Ragonde*   17
London (1718–19)
   child dancers' popularity   53, 65
   in *Les Deux Arlequins* (Le Noble)   52
   in *Le Tartuffe* (Molière)   62 n.55
London (1725 and 1730), leading dancer at Lincoln's Inn Fields   161
London (1725–6), in *The Burgomaster Trick'd*   183
London (1733–4)

   Covent Garden season   178, 179–81
   dancing at Benefit for brother Francis's widow   203 n.41
   delayed departure to London   178–9
   innovative creations   311
   partnering with Jean-Baptiste Malter   179–80, 181, 183–4, 192, 304
   possible detour to Brussels   180–1, 183, 240
   Pygmalion   183–5, 304
   royal presence   184–5
London (1734–5)
   Covent Garden season with Handel   188, 189, 298
   financial success   189, 205
   Handel's *Alcina*   189, 204
   Handel's *Ariodante*   189, 205
   Handel's *Terpsicore*   189
   partnering with Michael Lally   192 n. 13
   royal presence   189
   triumph and unhappy end of season   189, 191, 240, 299
Opéra
   1727–32 contracts   161, 179
   1735 performances   241
   'Acte des Fleurs' in Rameau's *Les Indes galantes* (1735)   289, 297–8
   choreography of several roles   297
   retirement and special royal pension   297
   Sallé's dislike of low production and moral standards   310
Palais-Royal (1721), in *Les Caractères de la Danse* (Rebel)   94
performances after Opéra retirement, Fontainebleau (1752)   299
Sallé, Marie-Alberte (née Moylin, Francisque's sister)   6, 8
Salway, Thomas   219
Santeul, Jean-Baptiste, *Castigat ridendo mores*   215
Santlow, Hester   18
Sarcey, Francisque   295
sauvages (savages)
   bon sauvage   70, 93, 213
   'noble savage'   212, 213 n.66
   savages' sexual mores   113

Yamacraws no longer considered
      'savages'   211
Scarron, Paul
   L'Héritier ridicule   125, 278–9
   Typhon ou la Gigantomachie   122
Sceaux, Agathe de *see* Lalauze, Agathe de
      (née de Sceaux)
Sceaux, Antoni de
   Foire Saint-Germain (1721)   94
   Foire Saint-Laurent (1718)   42 n.5
   Foire Saint-Laurent (1720)   81
   Foire Saint-Laurent (1721)   100
   Francisque's London season
         (1718–19)   46, 65
   performances and roles
      'Danse de l'ivrogne'   53, 100
      Mme Pernelle in Molière's *Le
            Tartuffe*   62 n.55
      Pierrot   45, 48 n.15
      Vaulting and Tumbling scenes   51
Scellier, Gabriel, *Le Camp de Compiègne
      de 1739* (journal)   274–5, 276–7,
      278, 279, 280, 282
Scherer, Jacques   207
Schmeling, Manfred   29
Scott, Virginia P.   20, 49 n.19
Scouten, Arthur   250–1
scrolls (*écriteaux*)   11–12, 91, 130, 163
Senauki, Queen   211
Senelick, Laurence   20
Senesino (Francesco Bernardi known as
      Senesino)   188, 198, 251 n.6
Seven Years' War (1756–63)   313
Seymour, Robert   196–7
Sgard, Jean   164–5, 188 n.3, 247 n.28
Shadwell, Thomas   222
Shakespeare, William
   Drury Lane in competition with French
         comedians   77
   Garrick and Harlequin as
         Shakespeare's demonic
         Other   270
   performances in original language in
         Paris   80, 314
   unveiling of statue in Westminster
         Abbey   269
   works
      1 Henry IV   51 n.26
      Hamlet   51, 314
      Henry V   253, 258
      King Lear   51
      Macbeth   51 n.26

Othello   229 n.42
Shakespeare Ladies' Club   253
Shireburn, Maria *see* Norfolk, Maria
      Howard (née Shireburn), Duchess
      of Norfolk
sifflet-pratique (swazzle)   111
silent performances *see* 'à la muette';
      écriteaux (scrolls)
silver tickets   187, 206
Simons, Robin   78 n. 38
Slaughter's Coffee House (St Martin's
      Lane, London)   79
Smith, Ruth   223, 226–7, 232–3
Smithson, Harriet   314
sodomy   113–14
'Song Occasion'd by the FOREIGNERS
      meeting with so much
      Encouragement here'   238 n.61
Sophia Dorothea of Celle   227–8
Sorin, Joseph
   Drury Lane performances   20, 21
   Foire Saint-Germain (1712)   9
   Foire Saint-Germain (1718)   22
   Foire Saint-Laurent (1721)   94
   Harlequin dances   19
   Lincoln's Inn Fields contract
         (1696)   13–14
   'mimick scenes'   79
   Night Scenes   14, 15, 20, 311
   retirement from stage   105
   revival of Alard brothers' act   51
Spaziani, Marcello   26, 28, 96
Spiller, James   20
Stair, John Dalrymple, 2nd Earl of
      Stair   15
Stanisław I Leszczyński, King of Poland
      and Duke of Lorraine   243
Staunch Old Briton (*nom de plume*)   238
St-Bon, *Les Deux Arlequins*   50
Steele, Richard, Sir   15, 42
   The Conscious Lovers   77, 233 n.52
   The Tender Husband   64
   The Theatre article   76–7
   verses calling for Nicolini's
         departure   269
Storey, Robert F.   51 n.25
Straub, Kristina   258 n.28
Stuarts   232, 233, 234
Sund, Judy   74 n.22, 79
surgeons-physicians quarrel   155
swazzle (*sifflet-pratique*)   111
Swift, Jonathan   32

'Upon the horrid plot' 218, 235

tableaux changeants 135
Talma, François Joseph 314
The Hague, Francisque's troupe's season (1719) 66, 73
Theatre at Lincoln's Inn Fields
  background
    John Rich's theatre **16**
    Licensing Act impact 253
    maximum capacity 205
    reputation as Catholic and Jacobite 63–4
    theatre's financial difficulties (1717) 42
  Francisque's 1718–19 season *see* London season (1718–19)
  Francisque's 1720 performances (two only) 76
  Francisque's 1735 Benefit 206, 209
  Joseph Sorin's contract 13–14
  Marie and Francis Sallé
    as child performers 16–20, 21, 42
    leading dancers as adults 161
  performances
    1 Henry IV followed by 'epilogue by Spiller riding on an ass' 51 n.26
    The Burgomaster Trick'd (Theobald) 182–3
    The Cheats or The Tavern Bilkers 19
    Harlequin Emperor of the Moon (Behn) 20, 49
    The Perjuror (Bullock) 63
    de Sceaux' 'Danse de l'ivrogne' 53
    Sorin and Baxter's Night Scene 14
    for Tomochichi and Senauki. 211
Théâtre de la Foire
  academic resources
    CÉSAR website viii
    historical sources and studies 1–3
    Lesage and d'Orneval collection viii, x, 10
  actors vs. fairground entertainers 64
  audience diversity and participation 12, 29, 32, 84–5
  fairground rivalries 13, 99, 130–1, 138, 139
  see also Foire Saint-Germain; Foire Saint-Laurent; opéra-comique (genre); opéra-comique (licence or *privilège*); polemical genre; Querelle des Théâtres (Foire Saint-Laurent 1718); Querelle des Théâtres (Foire Saint-Laurent 1726)
Le Théâtre de la Foire ou l'opéra comique (Lesage and d'Orneval)
  background
    brief selection and Slatkine Reprints viii
    evolution of new genre 10
    freely available online x
    publication of first volume 42, 108
  references
    1718 Foire Saint-Laurent repertory 25
    1721 Foire Saint-Germain missing plays 93
    Les Arrêts de l'Amour (d'Orneval) 148
    Les Comédiens Corsaires, frontispiece **153**
    Les Comédiens Corsaires (Lesage, d'Orneval, Fuzelier) 152
    L'École des Amans (Lesage and Fuzelier) 148
    Lesage's *Preface* on verbal grossness at fairs 35
    Les Pèlerins de La Mecque (Lesage, Fuzelier, and d'Orneval) 146
    Le Pharaon (Fuzelier) 23
    La Princesse de Carizme, frontispiece **27**
    La Statue merveilleuse (Lesage) 38 n.42
Théâtre de la Monnaie (Brussels)
  de Grimberghs' management 74
  see also Brussels season (Théâtre de la Monnaie, 1733–4)
Théâtre du Palais-Royal
  Francisque's troupe (1718) 36, 37, 140
  Les Funérailles de la Foire (Lesage, d'Orneval, Fuzelier) 35, 138
  Francisque's troupe (1721) 140
  Les Funérailles de la Foire (Lesage, d'Orneval, Fuzelier) 105, 138
  Le Rappel de la Foire à la

Vie (Lesage, d'Orneval, Fuzelier) 105
Le Régiment de la Calotte (Lesage, d'Orneval, Fuzelier) 105
Francisque's troupe (1726)
   Les Amours déguisés (Fuzelier) 159
   Les Comédiens corsaires (Lesage, d'Orneval, Fuzelier) 159
   L'Obstacle favorable (Lesage, d'Orneval, Fuzelier) 159
   Les Pèlerins de la Mecque (Lesage, d'Orneval, Fuzelier) 159
   Le Retour de la Chasse du cerf 159
   'un Compliment prononcé par Francisque' 159–60
Marie Sallé, in 'Les Caractères de la Danse' (1721) 94
Théâtre Italien
   Ancien Théâtre Italien (pre-1697) 7, 10, 32 n.25, 42–3, 193, 207, 278, 287, 294
   Nouveau Théâtre Italien (post-1716) 13, 193, 210, 287, 294
   see also Comédie-Italienne
Le Théâtre Italien (Evariste Gherardi) *see* Gherardi, Evariste
theatre tickets *see* tickets
Théâtre-Historique 314
Theatre-Royal *see* Théâtre du Palais-Royal
theatrical benefits *see* Benefits
theatrical exchanges (between France and England)
   none after Haymarket riot (1738) 312, 314
   softening of attitudes (from 1817) 314–15
Theobald, Lewis, *The Burgomaster Trick'd* 182–3, 185
Thieriot, Nicolas-Claude 240
Thomassin, Simon 88, 177, 206–7, 208, 275, 288 n.49
Thorp, Jennifer 78, 185 n.51
Thousand and One Nights and Thousand and One Days 26
tickets
   Francisque's London season (1734–5) 191
   Francisque's ticket price war (Brussels, 1733–4) 174
   silver tickets 187, 206
Tinant, Julie 93 n.10

Tomlinson, Kellom
   The Art of Dancing Explain'd by Reading and Figures 18
   The Submission 18
Tomochichi, Chief 211, 212, 214
Tonson, Jacob 43
Tories 224
Tortoriti, Giuseppe *see* Pascariel (Giuseppe Tortoriti known as Pascariel)
Tortoriti, Jeanne-Jacquette *see* Biancolelli, Jeanne-Jacquette (née Tortoriti)
Toulouse
   death of Malters' five-year-old daughter Catherine 167
   Francisque's and siblings' strong links with 5
   Francisque's company (1736) 165, 243
   Francisque's company (1738–9) 272–3
   Francisque's company (1739–40) 284, 286, 287
   Malter children's birth location 141 n.34
   marriage certificate of Catherine Labbé/Malter 140
   Pascariel's troupe 7
   Simon Moylin settling in 293, 300
Tourneville, Marie Antoinette *see* Foulquier, Marie-Antoinette (née Tourneville and widow of Fompré)
Tours
   baptism of Jeanne Malter 160
   Malter children's birth location 141 n.34
Tourteville, Louis 160 n.38
travesti roles 62 n.55
Tribout de Morembert, Henri 129
Trott, David 23
Trotter, Catherine, *The Revolution of Sweden* 224
Trousson, Raymond 100–1
True Briton (*nom de plume*) 209–10
Tumbling *see* Vaulting and Tumbling
Turquerie 149
   see also orientalism
The Two Dogs (poem) 235–6

University of Leicester, French department, *Arlequin à la Foire* (1986 student production) viii

Vanbrugh, John 46, 196–7
Vaulting and Tumbling 51–2, 75, 84
Verèb, Pascale 120, 141, 151 n.16
Verelst, William 211
Verneuil, Louis-Joseph Despré de 66, 73, 173, 178, 191, 192
   'Compliment' to announce *L'Hymen vainqueur* performance 241, 242–3
Verneuil, Marie-Josèphe (Mimi) de Pré or Despré de see Fourcade, Mimi (née Marie-Josèphe de Pré or Despré de Verneuil)
Verneuil, Marie-Louise de (née Chabot) 66, 73, 173, 191, 192, 221 n.22
Versailles
   Louis XIV's 'Les Plaisirs de l'île enchantée' week 280
   royal court at 276
Vertot, René-Aubert, Abbé, *History of the Revolutions in Sweden* 224, 226
Vézian, Anthony (or Antoine) 58–61
Victor, Benjamin 257, 261, 271, 312
Villandon, Mlle de, *L'Amazone française* 81
Villeneuve (dancer) 191
Villeneuve, Jeanne-Marie see Moylin, Jeanne-Marie (née Villeneuve, wife of Francisque's brother Simon)
Villepierre, Mlle 191
Villeroy, François Paul de Neufville de 117 n.34
Vince, Stanley 297 n.2
Violanta, Madame 74 n.21, 76
Virgil, *Aeneid* 118, 119, 122
Voltaire
   Babet Cochois, correspondence with 304
   Desfontaines, loathing of 113–14
   Piron, exchanges with 107, 114–15, 128
   Rousseau on in 'Le Verger de Madame de Warens' 245
   tragedies of, performed by Francisque's company 315
   tragedies of, performed in French in London 90
   views and quotes
      'Aimons le théâtre, c'est la seule gloire qui nous reste' 313, 314
      liberty of expression in London vs. Paris 63
      Louis XV and Scarron's *L'Héritier ridicule* 278–9
      Marie Sallé's loss of beauty 240
      marquis d'Argens's actress mistress 247 n.28
      Regnard's talent 49
      use of word 'spleen' in French 57 n.47
      'world turned upside down' topos 32
   works
      Alzire 242 n.10, 245–7
      Artémire 110
      Histoire de Charles XII 224
      Œdipe 39
      Œdipe and Sémiramis 294
      Zaïre 171, 173, 192, 195, 223, 227, 245
Vonderbeck, Catherine see Baune, Catherine de (née Vonderbeck)

Walpole, Horace 280–1, 283
Walpole, Robert, Sir
   campaign against 221–2, 223, 231, 233, 251
   French players favoured by the King and some of Walpole's party 196
   interception of ambassadors' dispatches 257
   Licensing Act (1737) 254
   machinations against Fielding 255
War of the Austrian Succession (1740–48) 269
War of the Spanish Succession (1701–14) 269
Ward, Joshua 217–18, 219
Ward's downfal: or, the plot detected. A poem 235
Warens, Madame (Françoise-Louise) de 245–7
Watteau, Jean-Antoine 276
   'Les Comédiens Italiens' 78–9, **80**, 81
Weaver, John
   dancing
      contribution of French colleagues 163
      'Dramatick entertainment of Dancing' 21
      mimic dancing 17

pantomime
  birth of English pantomime   15, 51, 311
  History of the Mimes and Pantomimes   15
  influence of French comedians   65, 79–80
  The Loves of Mars and Venus   17, 18–19
The Weekly Amusement, or The Universal Magazine   203, 237 n.60
The Weekly Journal or British Gazetteer   46 n.10, 47
The Weekly Journal or Saturday's Post   41
The Weekly Miscellany   216
Wells, Mitchell P.   50–1
Whigs   64
Wick, Rebecca   240–1, 299, 300
Wilkinson, Tate   20, 21
William, Prince, Duke of Cumberland   191, 208, 223, 228
William III, King of England, Scotland and Ireland (or William of Orange)   14, 62, 215
women
  comic misogyny   110, 119
  'fickle women' stereotype in Lesage's *La Statue merveilleuse*   82
  machismo denounced in Piron's *La Robe de dissention*   149
  practice of female roles played by men   221 n.22
Woodfine, Philip   257
Woodward, Henry   210 n.38

xenophobia   41–2
  see also Anglophobia; Francophobia

Yamacraws   211
York-Buildings
  Epilogue spoken after Addison's *Cato*   237–8
  Licensing Act impact on actors   250

Zazzo, Lawrence   221, 233

Printed in the United States
by Baker & Taylor Publisher Services